A COMING STORM
"The Return"

By William Casselman

A COMING STORM

By William Casselman

Scripture for A Coming Storm is from The Holy Bible-New International Version, 1978 Copyright, by Zondervan Bible Publishers of Grand Rapids, Michigan

Published by:
Alaska Dreams Publishing
www.alaskadp.com

First Printing December 2013
Revised 5/29/2014

ISBN numbers:
ISBN-13: 978-0-9903454-0-4
ISBN-10: 0-9903454-0-8

E-Book versions available.
Visit www.alaskadp.com for links.

CONTENTS

DEDICATION

To Mona Sue, my wife, best friend and very special companion of 33 years and counting. A courageous Alaskan woman who has faced both human and animal predators in our 20 years of police work and multiple battles against the enemy.

She said my first manuscript was written like a police report and it was only upward from there. I've bounced many a story idea off of her and made a lot of changes from her ideas.

I thank the Lord for her every day, for she has given me an incredible strength to weather the difficult times and a hope for the future, as we travel together toward an eternity in Heaven.

ACKNOWLEDGEMENTS

Like any other writer, I have a lot of people to thank for assisting me in finishing this story. But I know I need to first thank the Lord God and the 32 years He has allowed me to walk with Him, or the many times He has carried me over those rougher spots. I've often wondered how our lives would be different if we made a right turn at an intersection in life, down a different hallway or through another doorway then we planned. The many choices we have made every single day that could have changed our future by the free will the Lord blessed us with. Through my experiences in Vietnam, my 10 years in the military and two decades as a police officer, the Lord has saved me so many times over from an early death. I've witnessed so many miracles in the lives of my wife, our children and grandchildren. But the Lord has continued to bless us and I thank Him for being there to forgive me when I fall, to stand me back up on my feet and to listen with a kind ear to my various complaints. For without the Lord, this story would not exist. He provided me with the ideas through some very special means, which included a series of dreams showing the coming comet I used in this story, the attack on Alaska by an enemy army, collapse of the United Nations and U.S. Economy, and downsizing of the U.S. Armed Forces. Of the great quakes, towering tsunamis and mighty storms, plagues and wars that destroys most of the world as the Book of Revelations foretells.

I want to thank Karen Simon and John Holloway, my editors, who kept this lengthy story flowing and with their skills removed all of the writing errors I so often make in the first half-dozen drafts. Though the Lord blessed me as a story teller, it was a struggle to learn how to be a writer. The use of the English language has always been a difficult chore for me to handle, especially in written form.

I want to say a special thanks to my many children and 13 grand children for their patience in my long years of learning what it means to become a writer. They have endured many long drives and repetitious nights of listening to my story ideas. They rarely complained, but the dull look to their eyes displayed a weariness to the sound of my voice and yet, they were patient with the old man. However, they liked this story and family and friends looked forward to reading this one in its completed form.

I also greatly appreciate Robert Jacobson and Alaska Dream Publishing for giving me this opportunity to present you with this apocalyptic tale.

Thank you to that special someone who mysteriously and extremely quietly, left a brand new boxed-up computer and monitor on our front porch in the middle of a summer day, which enabled me to continue writing. I was right in the middle of a story when my some-what ancient computer went gunny-bags and foresaw a long wait until we could purchase a new one.

The Alaska Defense Force, identified in this tale is a mixture of active military units based in Alaska, Alaska State National Guard forces and a state militia, is actually a recognized Alaska militia force and I wish to acknowledge the services of the men and women who volunteer for this unit. I want to also recognize the members of the US Military who stand ready to defend the United States and the many chaplains who serve with them from numerous religious backgrounds.

PRELUDE

Chronological listing of particular events in the years leading up to World War III and beyond.

FROM THE BLACKNESS OF DEEP SPACE - JULY 1

Coming on as an unstoppable juggernaut, a previously unidentified comet enters the Solar System and catches NASA observers unaware, as first reports of the new comet come in from two amateur astronomers. Excited NASA scientists begin to follow the newly named "Tariq-Leroy" Comet, named for the two backyard astronomers, with the powerful Hubble Space Telescope, as the space rock continues along its mysterious and soon to be discovered, ominous journey.

Working tirelessly for hours, NASA's learned men and women finally believe the comet, which strange behavior and slow travel is unprecedented will end its fateful passage with a tremendous explosion of frightening magnitude upon collision with Earth. Impact is believed capable of releasing a burst of destructive energy equal to that of over 500 thermonuclear bombs and could possibly push the planet Earth out of its orbit, killing every living thing on the planet in the process.

Public announcement of the comet's sighting and its collision course with earth is withheld by order of the President and other world leaders, in an attempt to prevent panic on a global-wide scale. But the secret becomes known before too long and the panic, the government had feared, begins to occur around the planet.

PARIS, FRANCE - JULY 15th,

While news of the comet rapidly circulates through the scientific community, a German news agency releases a minor third-page story concerning the creation of a Neo-Nazi church in Berlin. Known as the Unified World Church Alliance (UWCA) - a one world church organization, reporters show it is supported and funded by a growing number of skinhead hate-groups and other Anti-Semitic organizations.

A COMING STORM

The UWCA immediately sets into motion a worldwide propaganda campaign, through television, radio and internet, which spreads Anti-Semitism lies and vile accusations of non-white ethnic groups, identifying them as being the root of all the world's problems. Behind the scene, UWCA members begin their first steps in a reign of terror in Germany, France and Spain, with the burning of Muslim mosques and Jewish synagogues. Their henchmen quickly turn to kidnapping and eventually the killing of various religious leaders. Rumors quickly spread of UWCA members publically assaulting non-white Christian missionaries, but heavily funded, the UWCA propaganda machine seems to have control of the various news agencies in Europe and these reports never hit the major European papers or prime time news television and radio shows.

Within days, critical editorials appear in newspapers, spreading accusations that Europe's financial problems come not from capitalist America, but Middle Eastern and Asian money markets, supported primarily by their vast oil industry.

SOUTH AFRICA-USA-ENGLAND - JANUARY 12TH

With growing civil unrest spreading across South Africa and reports of voter fraud and tribal warfare, large scale race riots break out in Johannesburg, in response to the opening of several UWCA churches under construction there. A new heavily armed uniformed security force appears on the scene, protecting UWCA members and using strong arm tactics to drive non-whites out of Johannesburg's wealthier neighborhoods. Such tactics include fire bombing and drive-by shootings. Meanwhile, overwhelmed South African police and military forces are sent elsewhere to handle a new breakout in violent tribal warfare reminiscent of the 1960-1970's.

In London, a major religious riot pitting skinheads against Muslims causes the death of 158 citizens and 504 injured. Neo-Nazi members of the UWCA and Muslims clash in a religious street parade. In minutes the festive and tourist lined streets of London escalate into a war zone. British troops are called in to bring the riot to an end with the use of armored personnel carriers armed with tear gas cannons and water hoses.

In one of the hottest summers on record, racial disturbances explode along the southern borders of the United States. With local, state and federal law enforcement stretched far too thin and with the growing number of illegal immigrants from Mexico, South America and Cuba, they're unable to handle the growing number of rioters. Southern governors order National Guardsmen out to suppress the violence. Martial Law is declared in Georgia, Alabama and Mississippi, Arizona and New Mexico, imposing a 6 p.m. curfew and seizure of all civilian firearms.

Once thought dead, the KKK rises into the limelight in the American south, staging a One Million Man march on Washington D.C. Though the KKK numbers are far from the expected response, African-Americans stage their own massive rally in D.C., bringing over a hundred thousand people into the streets of the Nation's Capital with plans to close down all roads in an attempt to block the KKK rally.

Angry Neo-Nazi and KKK members and African-Americans meet in a violent clash; filling area-wide hospitals and morgues with 107 injured and 34 dead. A total of 31 city and federal police officers are also killed or injured while attempting to separate the two warring factions.

UNITED NATIONS, NEW YORK - MARCH 13TH

Unable to keep the Tariq-Leroy Comet a secret any longer, UN and NASA science officers make a public address over TV and radio stations, and internet sites to warn the world of impending danger from the oncoming menace. The public address repeats every hour that day and is followed by a dinner-hour address by the US President over all networks in an attempt to keep the American people calm. The President declares Martial Law throughout the United States; all prices and wages are frozen; hoarding of food and water is classified as a federal felony offense and then orders the surrendering of all privately owned firearms.

Such declarations cause numerous state militias to rise up in anger and publically refuse the order to turn over their firearms, bringing about several encounters between militia forces and federal authorities.

In the weeks to follow, other governments around the world take similar action as civil unrest spreads throughout the population.

NEW YORK, NEW YORK - JUNE 5th

The New York Stock Exchange stuns the public when it suspends all business following a month of extreme financial upheaval created by the comet scare. The world economy exists in a state of havoc with fear, mass population shifts, martial law, and the virtual destruction of most manufacturing and transportation facilities whether by war or natural disaster. People stop paying bills; banks and other financial institutions fail quicker than experts ever thought possible. Credit card debt reaches an all-time high, food riots begin at neighborhood stores and unemployment skyrockets above 30%. US Federal Assistance Programs begin to fail and Social Security and Medicare are declared bankrupt before the summer is over. Before the end of the year money in the free world becomes worth less than 10 cents on the dollar.

The US falls into the worst depression in its history and out of basic survival, the age-old tradition of bartering and trade returns to the streets of

America. As factories close items of value soon become scarce. Sugar, flour, various spices, fuel oil and canned and dehydrated foods, become the most valuable commodities, leading to the formation of black markets. Ammo, illegal weapons and drugs become items for secret trade fairs; locations carried by word of mouth and guarded by heavily armed private security.

JERUSALEM - NOVEMBER 22

Already being carried by news services throughout the Middle East, U.S. news services begin to report the sudden appearance of two omniscient beings at the Holy Wall. Crowds numbering in the thousands surround the men, who are strangely attired in radiant garments of royal blue and surrounded by a sparkling field of luminescent silver light. To the stunned amazement of crowds, their words are heard in all languages and even the deaf hear them, as these two heralds prophecy the coming of the Lord.

Authorities attempt to remove them, but they cannot breach the silver veil and as word of their appearance spreads, Christians around the world believe these beings to be the Two Witnesses foretold in the Book of Revelation.

Christian churches throughout the US fill to standing room only with lines of un-saved people waiting to hear the Word of God. Christians believe these two men to be a fulfillment of the Word of God and acknowledge that their days are numbered, while the unsaved surrender themselves to the Lord and ask for His promised salvation.

NEW YORK CITY - JANUARY 12th

NASA and European scientists announce over worldwide television, internet and radio that the Tariq-Leroy Comet will impact near the Cambodia-Thailand border. Estimated time of impact is expected to be late April or very early May of next year. This shocking proclamation initiates a mass exodus from Southeast Asia; by boat, plane and on foot. Millions of people rush to leave the expected point of impact, blocking all roadways, airports and harbors with panicking people.

China surprises the world as it opens its' borders to all refugees, setting up massive camps and providing ground transportation for all those fleeing their homelands.

The catastrophic announcement causes strained political relations between countries to disintegrate even further. Border wars break out among smaller nations, leading to a brief, but deadly nuclear exchange between Pakistan and India. There is a repeat of the Iraq-Iran war, pitting Muslims against one another over ancient tribal feuds from centuries of bloody warfare.

Anti-Semitism spreads like wildfire with the UWCA continuing to spread its hate filled messages to frightened people; men and women who now look for someone to blame for their misfortune with knowledge their world is soon coming to an end. As soon as hatred controls fear, UWCA leadership adds certain Christian leaders to their hate list. They begin a reign of terror, with a mixture of blaming Jews and the followers of Christ, for the world's woes.

With waves of violence erupting throughout the cities, Christians begin to ask, "Just who do the members of this UWCA worship?"

Taking advantage of the situation and knowing a politically induced downsized U.S. military is not up to the task of supporting its allies; China launches a Blitzkrieg invasion across the border of Vietnam. China desperately needs to secure the deep-water ports and rice belts of Vietnam before the comet's impact and informs the United Nations this invasion is needed to feed the refugees coming in from Southeast Asia. But the world is in such a mess, the delegates of the UN Security Council hardly have time to listen to Vietnam's complaints of the many atrocities committed by Chinese troops against the people of Vietnam.

UNITED NATIONS, NEW YORK - MAY 8th

Ignoring threats by various UN officials hoping to pass a resolution against the seizure of Vietnam, the Chinese ambassador to the UN boldly interrupts normal scheduled business in the General Assembly to announce the signing of an alliance pact between China and the countries of Thailand, Cambodia and Laos, Burma and a Unified Korea, Japan and now Vietnam.

News services immediately begin calling this alliance the Oriental Alliance Pact (OAP). One British reporter is heard to have said, "The dragon stirs and now we must fear its awakening".

Moments after this announcement, the Chinese ambassador to the UN asks other Asian countries to join this alliance in the creation of a new Oriental empire. Immediately afterward, OAP delegates walk out of the UN: the first of many who will withdraw from a collapsing United Nations over the next three weeks.

Surprising no one, Russia, holding to its return to a communist platform and the appointment of a new party leader, forms a shaky alliance with the OAP. Within 24 hours of receiving OAP support, Russia begins large scale live-fire training exercises along its Western European border. This action brings NATO air-and-ground forces to a higher state of alert, but with the United States withdrawing its troops from England and Europe to deal with growing domestic problems and thousands of border incursions from Mexico, South America and Cuba, NATO finds itself greatly outnumbered by Russian's armor and air power.

MEXICO CITY, MEXICO - JUNE 11

The World Health Organization announces the outbreak of a new Class Four disease found in the festering slums of Mexico City. First thought to be a highly virulent form of Super flu, WHO later confirms a far more contagious virus and informally classify the virus as the Mexican Plague; simple sounding, but extremely deadly. With no cure in sight, the disease rapidly spreads across Central America and down into the Southern Continent.

Stricter border enforcement between Mexico and the United States is imposed, but with so many people fleeing to escape the flu's deadly path, the disease is carried by ship, raft, foot and plane to the US and other continents. Within three months of the outbreak in Mexico City, the first cases show up in America's Pacific Southwest and in numerous European ports. During the first six months, the plague leaves millions dead with a sustained kill rate of nearly 99%. By the end of the year, nearly one third of the world's population has perished in the virus's lethal wake. When possible, the dead are buried in mass graves, otherwise, bodies are left to rot in homes and abandoned hospital wards.

THE WORLD AT LARGE - NOVEMBER

In fear of the comet and what may happen in a post-strike Earth, civilization crumbles as throngs of frightened people riot all over the world. Race riots in massive proportions cripple the Southern US, while local, state and federal law enforcement agencies, supported by National Guardsmen, can do little to stop the destruction or protect the population. The US President orders active duty US Army and Marine personnel into the streets, while Navy forces protect the southern ports from possible infected illegal aliens arriving on boats and rafts. The order is given to sink all craft and let not a single person reach shore, but not all the servicemen can obey such an order when children are involved and infected people make it into American cities.

Civil War breaks out in Canada, with Quebec Freedom Fighters, supported by treasonous federal troops, revolting against Canada's oppressive authority and it's near non-existent economy. Street fighting breaks out across Eastern Canada, fires are started in Montreal and Toronto business districts. The US/Canadian border is closed and, Civil War splits Canada in half with Ontario Province a major battlefield for the two warring fronts and the death toll numbers in the hundreds of thousands.

THE UNITED STATES OF AMERICA - DECEMBER 25 (Christmas Morning)

Borrowing an idea from a James Bond movie, The OAP uses specially equipped Saudi Arabian flagged super tankers to secretly ferry OAP nuclear submarines across the Pacific Ocean and into the Gulf of Mexico. The appearance of being headed for American oil refineries raises no alarm and clever concealment prevents US satellites from observing the release of missile subs, which take up positions in the deepest waters of the Gulf of Mexico.

At 7:00 a.m., Eastern Standard Time, the OAP sub crews launch a lethal missile attack against the continental United States. Flight time for the missiles is less than three minutes for most targets, catching the American military completely by surprise. The US military, waking up to celebrate Christmas, is caught completely unprepared. With dwindling numbers and abandonment of the Star Wars Program due to budget cuts, the US military can do little to prevent annihilation of the United States. Thermonuclear, chemical and biological weapons rain down on most of the major military installations and numerous large cities. For the people of the United States, World War III lasted less than 10 minutes.

Washington D.C. is taken out completely with two direct thermonuclear missile strikes, NORAD, reported to be defensible against such devastating weapons from the skies, was struck from within by chemical weapons released by deep cover suicidal operatives. With the exception of Alaska and Hawaii, for all intents and purposes, the United States ceased to exist as a nation before 8 a.m. Eastern Standard Time, on Christmas Day.

US WEST COAST - DECEMBER 25-26

The Earth cannot withstand the severe shock it has sustained from so many nuclear missile impacts and gradually, the geological plates begin to shift. The result is great quakes of 9.5 or higher magnitude, bringing separation along major fault lines throughout the planet.

The western shores of Central and Southern California, and parts of Northern Baja California, simply disappear under a series of towering tsunami waves rolling across heavily populated areas. San Francisco slides into the bay and within moments, Los Angeles and San Diego are also swept under water. Several aircraft divert to Alaska from continental U.S. destinations. Some of these aircraft crews flying across the Pacific warn Hawaii and Alaska Emergency Warning Centers of massive ocean swells, but notifications come far too late for most of the people living in the coastal communities along the Gulf of Alaska and Southeast Alaska, to have time to evacuate to higher ground. With 60 to 80 and even 200 foot waves slamming the shores with the force of an 18-wheeler truck and trailer plowing over a tot's tricycle, most of the citizens are lost under the towering waves.

CHINA/RUSSIAN BORDER- JANUARY 14

OAP forces abruptly break off their alliance treaty with Russia and invade Eastern Russia. They begin with a massive aerial bombardment of non-nuclear weapons, dropping tens of thousands of pounds of high explosive down upon fleeing Russian troops. This is soon followed by a land force invasion of 18 OAP Combat & Armor Divisions and though the Russians put up a courageous stand, OAP warlords capture Siberia within only two weeks.

Western Russia military leaders, fearing the possibility of dwindling food supplies after the impact of the Tariq-Leroy Comet, abandon Eastern Russia to the OAP and launch their own invasion of Western Europe to secure fuels, military equipment and desperately needed food supplies.

The battle with an overwhelmed NATO force begins with a massive artillery bombardment, followed by wave after wave of heavy Russian tanks moving on Germany. It isn't long before television, Internet and radio news ceases.

Meanwhile, from the ashes of a French battlefield, an unknown French Lt. Colonel emerges from the devastated NATO ranks to lead a brilliant counter attack north of Paris. Under his dazzling leadership, NATO forces miraculously turn the tide and against all possible hope, push the Russians back. Though rumored to be a church officer in the Unified World Church Alliance, this officer distinguishes himself repeatedly on the battlefield with great acts of heroism. He rises up through the dwindling ranks to assume supreme command of all French forces and leads the French Army to one victory after another. Given command of all NATO forces, his clever strategy drives the retreating Russians back across their border and a new NATO front line forms on Russian territory.

Recognized for his brilliant military strategy, vast knowledge of European politics and ability to speak a minimum of 12 languages, this charismatic young officer with reportedly strong ties to French nobility, brings about the formation of the New European Empire (NEE). The NEE consists of ten NATO countries and continues war against Russia. In a surprising move, NEE military forces prepare a naval force for a second offensive toward the Middle East in an attempt to secure the massive oil reserves of Saudi Arabia.

The hero of France, supported overwhelmingly by a growing UWCA membership, no longer denies rumors connecting him to the organization and accepts coronation as the First NEE Emperor. Hours after the ceremony the UWCA opens secret reserves and begins providing food, clean water and needed medical supplies to scores of homeless starving war victims. Within a short time, this new Emperor has become more popular than the Pope, who is now missing. The UWCA propaganda machine spreads rumors that the Pope is being held prisoner by Jewish forces in Israel, stirring up anger amongst the Catholic NEE troops. Within a week, the new Emperor issues an order directing all Christian and Jewish church leadership to register with local NEE police agencies or face imprisonment. All Christians are required to display a white cross on outer garments and once again, the Jewish people are required to wear the Star of David. The proclamation brings back sad bitter memories of Adolph Hitler's reign of terror between 1933 and 1945. Citizens who have sworn allegiance to the NEE Emperor turn a blind eye to the persecution as long as UWCA workers continue to hand out food parcels on time.

A new proclamation orders all citizens of the NEE to demonstrate loyalty by having a small tattoo of the UWCA coat of arms on their wrist; a ram's head with a medieval knight's double sided sword blade pointed upward on either side. The swords clearly resemble upside down crosses and knowledgeable Christians see this as a signature of Satan. The tattoo is to be used for identity when NEE citizens receive goods and use NEE services. Not too surprisingly, hungry and injured people tend to ignore the comparison of the loyalty tattoo to the Mark of the Beast foretold in the Book of Revelation. Upon hearing of this proof of loyalty, believers soon realize the Beast has truly reared his ugly head and the time of the Lord's return is near.

FAIRBANKS, ALASKA - FEBRUARY 2

In the aftermath of the great quakes, dormant volcanoes around the Pacific Rim of Fire erupt with violent force. Massive clouds of volcanic ash descend across the northern hemisphere; nuclear winter grips on the world; disease contamination is rampant. The sun, moon and stars are blocked from view, leaving only a few people with the ability to follow Tariq-Leroy's menacing approach.

Civilized America no longer exists. The massive factories of the United States are reduced to fiery rubble, medical services and civilian law enforcement are nearly non-existent and the US military has all but disappeared. Only a few pockets of democratic society still exist and those remain besieged by growing gangs and spreading starvation. Clouds of volcanic ash and radiation have reduced the availability and supply of clean water. The United States has turned an ugly gray and only the strong survive.

A COMING STORM

In areas of Alaska untouched by tsunami and volcanic eruptions, remaining US military forces have combined services with Alaska National Guardsmen and State Militia to become the newly named Alaska Defense Force. With the federal government in the lower 48 non-existent, survivors of the Alaska legislature assume control over all federal land, powers of law and all civilian personnel in Alaska and then grants the Governor of Alaska the powers of Commander in Chief over all military units in Alaska. Martial Law remains in force implementing a strict food-rationing program. Alaska Defense Forces, working with former US Customs and Immigration officers set up a line of defense along the Alaska/Canadian border. Surviving US Coast Guard vessels, work with various fishing fleets, patrolling the western shorelines of Alaska for any sign of the OAP's advance. Fishing boats search for uncontaminated catches, because Alaska has a lot of hungry mouths to feed and no more trucks or planes are arriving from the Lower 48 with food and supplies.

Facing impending invasion by OAP forces, the Alaska Defense Force first organizes and then sends its undermanned 1st Division to the City of Wales in preparation for the OAP's expected drive across the Bering Strait ice bridge. Natural resources are few and Alaska knows the OAP's attack of Alaska is about to begin.

In Fairbanks, local police are about to prepare the evacuation of Alaska's 2nd largest city, while facing record breaking crimes, OAP spies, food rationing and the total darkness of a nuclear winter and clouds of volcanic ash.

But there is a wave of hope coming from the ashes of Phoenix, Arizona, where a church pastor responds to the Word of God and prepares his flock for a strange odyssey through the rubble of America and the eventual destination of Fort Greeley, Alaska.

This is the Last Days.

It begins –

1 – THE BLUE KNIGHTS

Blessed is the one who reads the words of this prophecy, and blessed are those who hear it and take heart what is written, because the time is near.

Revelation 1.3 NIV

Now the deeds of the flesh are evident, which are immorality, impurity, sensuality, idolatry, sorcery, enmities, strife, jealousy, outbursts of anger, disputes, dissensions, factions, envying, carousing, and things like these of which I forewarned you that those who practice such things shall not inherit the kingdom of God.

Galatians 5:10-21 New American Standard

SOUTH CUSHMAN STREET, FAIRBANKS, ALASKA, OUTSIDE KCVF RADIO STATION - MARCH 12 - 11:37 HOURS

Through two feet of crusty snow and heavy splashes of gray volcanic ash, a feeble old man in tattered clothing slowly stumbled down a darkened street. He wore a ragged navy blue watch cap, which covered all but a few strands of scraggly gray hair and the reddened tips of frostbitten ears and a pair of mismatched threadbare wool mitts on bony, arthritic hands; one blue and the other a filthy gray. He cradled a filthy dark brown bottle of homemade squeeze against his chest, as if it was a treasure he needed to protect. Known on the street in this area of town as simply "Geeze", he'd been down this street a thousand times and knew every foot by heart. He always followed a well-traveled foot path, staying just a foot off the deep snow ruts made by military traffic and avoiding the dozens of darkened doorways and alleys. His old drinking buddy's place was nearly five blocks from his current flop; an abandoned storefront off South Cushman Street and 15th Avenue where he was able to stay warm by burning scrounged pallet wood from area loading docks and deserted warehouses. He had survived many long months of bitter cold by out-maneuvering the neighborhood's bottom-feeder predators and knew all too well how dangerous the streets of Fairbanks had become. As was his custom, Geeze cautiously made his way through thick ice fog stopping every few steps to listen for possible danger. Tonight, his foul breath was filtered through a recently acquired stained white wool scarf, to prevent the extreme cold from freezing his lungs. He stopped to cough and lean against a power pole, wishing he had taken his friend's advice and stayed the night. But he didn't want to share his brew, knowing this recent batch would have to last him for another couple of days.

Sensing danger, he moved to the middle of the street to give this next set of buildings a wide berth. Ice fog closed in around him and he hoped to remain invisible for the next block or so. Twice in the past month he was attacked on this same block by street thugs and had barely escaped with his life, but had been forced to give up his precious cargo of either firewood or homebrew. He carried nothing more valuable, simply because he didn't own anything- except for the clothes on his back, a rusty sheath knife inside his coat which he used to cut up the wood and a fire starter kit he'd traded some homebrew for. Still, it was today's thick ice fog that kept him from noticing the shadowy figure stalking him.

From behind a tall stack of 16 inch rusty steel pipe encrusted in thick ice, the attacker; a man who had survived by stealing from others and occasionally killing his prey, prepared to make his move on Geeze. Known on the street as Weasel, he had trouble controlling body shivers caused by severe cold and the rattling of what was left of his blackened teeth; pale white cheeks and ears were evidence of frostbite. He was clothed in only a stretched-out black wool cardigan sweater buttoned over a soiled blue Seattle Seahawks windbreaker. Winter gloves, taken from the frozen body of one of his first victims, kept his hands from severe frostbite, but they were still icy cold and he hoped to find a better pair or wool inserts before he lost all use of his hands. A pair of torn gray parka pants shoved into dirty scuffed white rubber bunny boots, blackened by ash, completed his winter apparel. Weasel had a shaggy brown beard and long moustache; bloodshot dark brown eyes, ringed in black soot were covered by goggles with yellow lenses. His rather large nose had given him his street name, along with his thin build and filthy habits. A chunk of lead pipe in hand, he silently closed in behind the old man stepping into his foot prints to avoiding crushing snow, which might alert old Geeze. Sure that they were alone and as the old man stepped out into the roadway, Weasel rushed forward, grabbed the old man from behind and threw him to the ground. Then with a handful of stocking cap, hair and jacket collar, he dragged his frightened prey back toward a darkened alleyway some 12 feet away.

The pint and a half of brew, so prized before, now lay all but forgotten in the street by the old alcoholic, who gave way to sudden panic and began thrashing about. When Geeze saw the weapon Weasel held above his head, he stopped struggling, went limp and began to whimper. In a darkened spot in a side alley, Weasel tossed Geeze into the snow and stood over him, enjoying the thrill of having his victim cower at his feet. He looked both ways, wanting to insure he was alone before he completed his act. He felt safe for the moment, a dangerous thing to do in the street, and glared down at his quarry, studying the prize before him. Then, without warning, he suddenly struck the old Geeze with a violent blow to the side of the head with the pipe. Dark red blood splattered over the snow and the old street bum collapsed to the ground semi-conscious. An incoherent mumble escaped his near-frozen lips, causing Weasel to wonder if it was a moan of pain or cry for help. Not that it mattered. Weasel, his face scarred from too many lost battles, reached down and jerked the old guy's fatigue jacket off. His score today was the cost of one old man's survival - a soiled camouflage jacket that carried the faded shoulder patch of the US Army 101st Airborne - the Screaming Eagles. Trembling from cold, Weasel quickly pulled the coat on and whispered a complaint under his breath because of the tight fit. He then glared at his wounded prey and briefly debated with himself on how best to finish the Geeze off. Most muggers would have left at this point, wanting to escape before anyone happened by. Not this low-life, Weasel wanted to finish off the old man simply for the pure thrill of the kill. With the wild bloodshot eyes of a crazed animal, he lifted the pipe over his shoulder for a fatal blow. A microsecond before his swing, he stopped abruptly, when a man's voice from behind caused a rush of fear to surge through him.

"You were kind of rough on the old codger, weren't you, Weasel?" A sincere, but contemptuous voice said.

Poised like a cat, vile smelling breath visible in the extreme cold and pipe still gripped tightly in hand, Weasel visibly trembled as he slowly turned to face this interloper. "I'd mind mah own bus..." His words froze in mid-sentence, as his frightened eyes grew wide. Quickly, he dropped the pipe to the ground and assumed a surrendering stance with both hands halfway-raised and his face turned to the side and cowering. This was his reaction to facing a large caliber revolver aimed in his face from only a few feet away. The predator had suddenly become the prey and was now fearful for his life. Voice hesitant with fear, the Weasel made a final boisterous attempt of mock bravado and tried to reason with the Good Samaritan, "You're no cop! You got no uniform or badge. So, why don't yuh jus' butt out an' let me go?" Then with an evil glint in his eyes and a partially raised eyebrow, he added in a hopeful tone, "We'll split what's left on him...fifty-fifty?"

The man, speaking through a soiled doctor's face mask to keep the ash from entering his lungs and his parka's furred hood up to protect his ears, held a Smith & Wesson Model 29 .44 caliber revolver with a six inch barrel slowly moved his head from side-to-side to say, "No". He never took his eyes off Weasel, "You're exactly right, buddy. I'm no cop. But that doesn't mean I like seeing street-scum like you mistreat our senior citizens this way.

You were gonna finish Geeze off, weren't you? Steal the dude's coat an' then kill him...for a coat! My god, man, have you sunk that low?"

With contempt in his eyes, he gave Weasel a thorough look, while his trigger finger began to apply a small amount of pressure. He backed off on the trigger and silently studied the low-life for a moment, while he made a decision, "I'm not sure if I'm doing anyone a favor by letting you live, Weasel...but, I'm no executioner and we'll freeze to death if we stand here any longer and wait for some police patrol to come driving by." As if mad at himself for making his decision, he shouted, "Now, get out of here before I change my mind."

Streetwise, he kept the revolver aimed at Weasel's head and watched as the character slowly brought his hands down, took off the old man's coat and cautiously lowered it to the ground beside the old man. Then without uttering a word of thanks, he slithered into the fog and quickly vanished down the alley.

In this severe cold, Ron Larson knew he didn't have time to administer first aid to Geeze's head wound and noting that the old man was still breathing regularly by the frost pumping out of his lungs, Ron slid his revolver into his parka pocket and began dragging him towards the front door of the radio station. He remained watchful for Weasel, in the event the man tried to return bringing others. He had known the street people down here for quite a while, even before the bad days and he couldn't stand by and let the Weasel get away with killing the Geeze.

Ron shuddered when he picked up the odor emanating off Geeze; a mixture of soiled clothes, poor hygiene and homebrew. He was extremely grateful for good luck when he heard a vehicle coming and looked up to see a white/green camouflage Army MP Truck approaching. Ron waved and the vehicle jerked to a stop. This time it was Ron's turn to stare down the barrels of two lethally aimed M-16's. Luckily, one of the uniformed MPs recognized Ron and didn't have him assume the spread-eagled position over the hood of the truck. Ron still had to show his weapon permit because the butt of his revolver was poking out of a coat pocket and it was making the other MP a wee bit nervous. After explanations, the MPs agreed to take the old Geeze to the hospital and didn't bother Ron for a tape recorded witness statement. This wasn't the first time they had dealt with the old man and attacks of this kind were increasing. As bad as the Weasel was, the truth was, no one had time to chase down a street mugger. Not with the Chinese threatening to invade at any moment and a chunk of space rock on its way to smack into the world.

In fact, Ron was wondering how so many of the citizens of Fairbanks were continuing to hold together at all. He knew for a fact that the trading of homebrew was on the rise and backyard manufacturers were having a hard time keeping up with the demand. Although he had hope that it was simply the strength of will that Alaskans displayed every winter under such severe conditions, he was beginning to believe it had a lot to do with the amount of military personnel present in the city and the courageous people in charge of the new government. In the old man's case, it was extremely fortunate that Ron had been on his way to work, since the rest of the street's businesses were now deserted. Most street people were apt to look the other way when something like a robbery or assault went down or they simply disappeared- a case of survival instinct in a dying world. With the economy now nearly non-existent, the stores in town all nearly closed and warehouses abandoned, only the lost souls wandered into this forgotten area in search of firewood or a flop. Except for Ron, who as the only disc jockey, acting manager and sole employee of KCVF Radio-Fairbanks, had just arrived to open for the scheduled noon broadcast.

With this little bit of excitement now behind him, Ron let out a deep sigh thinking of the town's loss of humanity and with hands trembling from severe cold, he pulled out a small set of keys attached to a metal key ring with a five inch crescent wrench attached. He opened two heavy padlocks hanging from a reinforced steel grate, which covered the front door. Extra security was provided by an industrial strength deadbolt lock strong enough to keep most people from making illegal entry into the station's lobby. The windows were covered by reinforced steel bars and boarded up from the inside with thick slabs of spruce wood. Ron often thought he was entering a bank instead of a radio station with all the locks and him carrying a small cannon. Sliding his face mask down to his chin, he used a nine volt flashlight to illuminate the way as he entered the station, locked the deadbolt lock behind him, slid a 2" by 4"chunk of wood into place between steel brackets to reinforce his door and then walked down the dark hall to the generator room. It always took a few moments to get the old Sears generator started. This often required a bit of incentive before running smoothly and that meant giving it a swift kick and a violent shake. Once started, a soft purring rumble vibrated the room's walls and he was able to turn on a single overhead 40 watt light bulb. The medium-sized generator handled all the station lights and radio equipment, including a small electric heater Ron kept in the DJ booth to keep warm during his twice-a-day broadcasts.

Ron walked across the room to a coal furnace, made sure it was keeping the station a very cool 35°; barely enough to protect the machinery from freezing and then shoveled a double load of coal into the boiler. Closing the heavy steel door, he made sure to lock it down tight. The new coal allowed the station temperature to raise 10° for the brief time he was inside. Any warmer than 45° and Ron would find himself in violation of the new

Emergency Use of Energy Act for semi-use private businesses. Such a violation could force him out of his job and he didn't want to lose this part-time work. Without work, he'd be in uniform and probably on his way to Wales to join the 1st Division. Either that or he'd be working labor details as the government prepared the city of Fairbanks for war. Neither of these jobs thrilled him all that much, so he did his best to keep the station within the required limits of operation.

Ron listened to the furnace for a moment and decided 45° would feel downright snuggly compared to the outside temperature of a chilly minus 42°. After making sure that the outside systems were activated, he entered the sound booth and smiled when he saw the beautiful glow of his electric heater. The heater was actually a violation, but since it was a gift from the local police he didn't think he was going to receive a violation notice for it.

He pulled off his black gloves, pushed his hood back, took off his face mask and the dark brown scarf from about his neck and, placing them on a small table beside the console, began rubbing his hands together to get the circulation going. Only then did he remove his heavy parka. He wore a one-piece black snowsuit which he kept zipped up until the sound booth was warmer. After releasing the buckles that held it in place, he removed his shoulder holster and set it on top of the scarf on the table, close just in case he needed it. Then he unzipped his snowsuit down to his stomach, exposing a threadbare black Grateful Dead t-shirt: rock & roll memorabilia from his old man's favorite band. He always smiled when he recalled that his dad, the accountant and Baptist deacon, was a former dead head. Ron tied the arms of the snowsuit around his waist and plopped down into his dark brown, high-backed wheeled leather chair to inspect the console. The chair had once belonged to the station manager, Mr. Rosenberg, but Ron didn't think he was missing it. Rosenberg was drafted by the Alaska Defense Force and was now somewhere helping the cause with his executive skills and Ron hoped his old boss was keeping warm. It was Rosenberg who submitted Ron's name for this solo gig and he greatly appreciated it.

He glanced down at his revolver and frowned as he remembered the last time someone had tried to break into the station during a broadcast. Two young men had used an eight foot long 6"x 6" chunk of wood to break the door open, which at the time did not have a heavy deadbolt lock or the added 2 x 4. They caught Ron by surprise, but the revolver was in his hands instantly and the armed thugs went out the front door in black body bags. His quick actions had gained the respect of the local police and he became a minor legend among most of the street people. Military authorities had allowed him a weapon permit, which was a job perk he didn't want to lose. Gang warfare was increasing and people behaving strangely; he felt a lot safer being armed on those long walks between his quarters on Fort

Wainwright and the radio station. It was slightly more than four miles and there were many dangerous spots along the way where he kept the revolver in his hand, but always re-holstered before reaching Fort Wainwright.

Relaxed somewhat in his comfortable chair, Ron flipped the red "ON THE AIR" switch to the 'on' position activating the red light bulb over the broadcast booth door and on the vacant sound tech's consul. He really didn't need it, but turning it on gave a sense of normalcy and reminded him of when the station was full of busy people; coffee pots always full and hot. Little Suzy O'Bannon had his favorite donut waiting when he arrived; Mr. Rosenberg always on his case for arriving late and not giving himself enough time to study news notes before going on the air. Now, when he could use it most, there was no hot coffee or donut and sadly, no Suzy. She was somewhere up north running communications for the Alaska Defense Force's 1st Division.

From a large manila envelope inside his parka, Ron pulled out his notes from this morning's briefing with the Office of Information on Fort Wainwright. He reviewed his notes again waiting for the equipment to warm up; whistling a tune that he seemed to recall as a childhood favorite of his older brother which they could never remember the name of, but knowing his dad, Ron was sure it had to have been a Grateful Dead melody played by leader, Jerry Garcia.

The Office of Information, a 12 clerk department on Fort Wainwright was supervised by a female Alaska Defense Force major who kindly allowed Ron 20-minutes to make his two daily broadcasts; one at noon and the other at 8 p.m. Electricity and coal was strictly rationed and it took a lot of pull from the Fairbanks City Council to pressure the military into allowing these broadcasts to keep up the citizen's morale. In exchange for his twice-a-day broadcasts and maintaining the station's equipment, Ron received a single meal once a day and had to share crowded quarters in military barracks with five other guys, whose job it was to maintain ADF Blackhawk helicopters.

From a green plastic G.I. canteen, left from last night, Ron took a sip of icy cold water and glanced up at the big battery-operated wall clock mounted on the wall in front of him. 10-seconds away from exactly 12 o'clock, Ron flipped a black toggle switch to the 'on' position and slowly turned the console's large gray volume dial to the right, as he counted off the power-strength numbers in his head. Turning away from the microphone to clear his throat, Ron assumed his announcer's voice using a much lower tone in hopes of reassuring the citizens of Fairbanks how calm he was. He had come to love the people of the north and sure wished he had better news to give them then these boring government announcements and frightening news bits.

A COMING STORM

"Hello Fairbanks! Its' 12 noon an' you're listening to Ron Larson, comin' at you live from KCVF-Fairbanks…That's 98.5 on your AM dial. So, keep your feet warm, your coffee hot an' listen up for the most up ta date news."

29 year old, Ron Larson was a one-man show and glad to have the job. Most men his age were on active duty with the Alaska Defense Force. Some were on the front lines lugging around a rifle and others were busy filling thousands of canvas sandbags with gray snow. Not mechanically minded like his brother, who could dismantle an aircraft carrier and put it back together again, Ron prayed daily for the station's radio equipment to hold up. Otherwise the ADF would have no need for a disc jockey and he'd probably end up lugging that rifle he feared with 120,000 other guys. It would also mean he would have to cut off his long red ponytail; five years in the making which many a young beauty had said went so well with his striking green eyes. Not that he was a vain man, he simply thought of himself as one of the last hippies and a holdout from the 60's era. Although the fact he'd been born in the early nineties had no bearing on the matter, he proudly displayed his large silver-plated peace sign on a braided leather necklace; another leftover from his dad's more delinquent days.

Twice a day, Ron broadcast from the only civilian radio station north of Anchorage. The U.S. military issued the news after a thorough censorship. Covert operatives working in Canada provided the international news to them through short-wave radio by way of Whitehorse, Yukon Territory, and then bounced through towers in Tok, Alaska. Almost all of the satellites were rendered useless by Day 2 of World War III and in the rest of the Northern Hemisphere stations stopped receiving due to war, fallout and volcanic ash. Teenagers who had lived on the devices, found cell phones rendered useless. Suddenly the world found itself back in a time of short-wave radio; line-of-sight microwave transmitters and military walkie-talkies. Some old fashioned landlines were even usable. Radio Calgary, a major communications installation for the Western Royal Canadian Army, was the closest hub of information for Alaska and received some info from underground sources in Quebec. It was rumored that Calgary was receiving some info from landlines running through the American Midwest and thankfully, the ancient telephone undersea cable was still working which allowed Quebec to maintain contact with allies in England and Europe.

"Our current temperature is holding at a very brisk -42 °and by latest reports, Radio Calgary is still up and running. This allows our gracious Office of Information to provide you with the following information for your listening pleasure. Item one on our daily hit parade- the space rock is still heading our way, unfortunately. This was verified when a group of scientists in London, who reportedly caught a break in the sky, got one last reading on it and now say impact will certainly be in the Udon-Tani region of Northern Thailand."

Ron pulled back from the microphone, cleared his throat and gazed out into the empty station. As a kid he had often wondered what a squashed bug felt like and now it appeared the people in Thailand were about to find out. Remembering he was on and that dead air was unprofessional, Ron continued, "Weather note from the local police department: Extreme cold and ice fog to continue throughout the week, probably the month, so they're asking all drivers to keep it slow. And I might add, if you see me hoofing it, please take mercy and give me a ride. I'll be the one frantically waving for assistance.

Okay, item number three; seems the Royal Canadian Western forces have reached a stalemate with Quebec French freedom fighters on the eastern border of Ontario Province. Royal Canadian Command in Calgary has requested a 24-hour temporary cease- fire to evacuate the wounded by train. Canada's civil war has left most of that country in ruin, hospitals are full on both sides and it seems there is no end in sight as all attempts for scheduling of peace talks have been shunned by Quebec.

Next item, umm... the Plague... man, I don't know about you but this plague junk really rattles me. First off, sources now reveal it was actually a bio-weapon created in South Africa, accidently released in Mexico City by a courier...Hope he got it first! It's lethal and there's still no known cure." Ron stopped to take another sip of water before continuing. With each newscast he felt his so-called DJ professionalism fading as the news grew worse and his listeners were strangely becoming like family to him.

"Sorry 'bout that, I needed to clear my throat... The Office of Information requests I keep these newscasts as impersonal as possible, that, and as I've reported to you before, they won't allow me to play any music either. So, don't complain to me. File all that hate mail with the Office of Information...if you can find a stamp or an open post office.

"The plague continues to spread across radiation free zones through the South Central United States. Supposedly, they're getting this information from a few scattered shortwave operators in the Midwest. We know our Canadian brothers have issued a 'shoot first and ask questions later policy' for any Americans attempting to cross into Canada. Now that's gotta hurt tourism," Ron said as he placed the first page of notes to the side and began reading from the next page.

"Some news on the Lower 48: at last report the Acting U.S. Senate, continuing to operate out of St. Paul, Minnesota, has declared the following states prohibited zones due to either radiation, volcanic ash or the plague...California, Oregon, Washington, Utah, North an' South Dakota, Nevada, Colorado and the entire eastern seaboard. Today, they've added

Texas, Arkansas and Missouri to the list. Winds continue to spread radioactive fallout throughout those states. Civil unrest reportedly remains rampant throughout the few states still untouched by the grim reaper. Food and clean water supplies are nearly non-existent and hospitals are now turning people away."

"Makes me glad I'm up here, folks. But it also sounds like a few big guys with guns have proclaimed themselves the big cheese on the block. Several big-wigs are setting up their own personal governments in contamination free zones, supported by what few military troops are left scattered about. I guess so many of those old sci-fi flicks had it right, survival of the fittest. I'm probably gonna hear about that remark, the big boys on post really dislike it when I start sounding off...well, too bad - I got a right to have an opinion." Ron remembered the threat of shouldering a rifle for the ADF and silenced his personal opinion.

"No further word on the war in Europe or what might be happening in the Middle East. As to the growing clouds of volcanic ash, scientists say it's continuing to enlarge in size and spreading across the Northern Hemisphere. We have reports the thickening grayish ash clouds are now crossing Southern Canada's border and covering parts of Northern USA. These same ADF scientists say they do not expect these clouds to cover the entire US and actually believe the radiation from the missile strikes may keep the ash from spreading south. Now I'm not sure how that would work, I'm no scientist. I do have confirmation that Alaska's Mt. Spur and Mt. Redoubt continue to erupt, along with several minor volcanoes along the Aleutian chain. As to the volcanoes in the Lower 48, we have no official word and I'm under strict orders not to speculate.

"We now turn to local news; OAP forces continue to mass in Siberia and I sincerely hope they're freezing their butts off! On the western side of the state, Canadian authorities continue to hold the Alaska-Canadian border closed. But I've already covered that so it would seem we're in this last little ball game all by ourselves," He stopped to clear his voice again before continuing and beginning to wonder if he was catching a cold. His throat was scratchy, but now wasn't the time to come down with a cold. Wouldn't wonder, with all those long walks through freezing temperatures, trudging through deep snow and forced to sleep in a drafty room...*Ah, quit complaining, dope, and admit it! You're luckier than most, now get on with the broadcast.*

For the next five minutes, Ron issued pertinent information on what people should do in the event of air attack, the government's water purification methods and food storage. He reminded his listeners of times and locations for this weekend's Trade & Barter Fairs.

"That's about it for this afternoon, Fairbanks. In closing, let me remind you that I'll be back on the air at 8 p.m. sharp with more news. In the meantime, stay warm and continue praying for our troops. Our brave men and women have some tough days ahead. This is Ron Larson leaving you and wishing you a nice day from KCVF Radio-Fairbanks." Ron turned the volume meter to the left and flipped both power switches off at once.

Tossing his notes into a gray metal trashcan, he screwed the top back on his canteen and stood to pull up his snowsuit. Looking around the station through three walls of thick glass, he felt a wave of loneliness pass over him as he thought of the chaotic days of the past. Rosenberg yelling, people running about like their butts were on fire and looking for the nearest fire extinguisher...*I sure miss it*. It happened every time he finished a broadcast, and thought the people he used to work with or what the future held. Pretty depressing with a million Chinese less than 700 miles away and a hunk of rock hurtling toward earth.

After strapping his shoulder holster into place and pulling his parka on, Ron turned the heater off and checked the small thermometer hanging inside the booth, "All of 56 degrees...man, this place is hard to warm up."

He remembered to shovel one more load of coal into the furnace and languished in the heat coming through the open furnace door. He had learned from experience that the station would be about 45° when he came back for the evening broadcast. He removed the two by four and opened the door, glancing outside before he stepped out and closed the heavy door quickly behind him. Ron always double-checked all three locks before grudgingly making his way to Fort Wainwright. He stopped suddenly, looked all around and mentally kicked himself for not checking first to make sure the mugger hadn't returned with friends. *You get yourself killed that way, idiot. Gotta check each and every time!*

He sucked in a lung full of icy air through his face mask and reminded himself of all those times he complained about public transportation and its drain on the taxpayer. *I'd give just about anything to ride a commuter bus, a Yellow Cab...maybe even a dog sled... anything, just as long as it kept my tootsies from freezing'*. A couple of yards from the station, he disappeared into the thick ice fog and hunkered forward as he trudged through the crusty gray snow. *Wonder if that MP truck is in the area...I'd really, really like a ride.*

SAWYER RESIDENCE - GOVERNMENT HOUSING UNIT 19, APT # 5, FAIRBANKS - MARCH 12

Unable to put it off any longer, a weary-eyed Brad Sawyer released the deep mournful sigh of an older man and in frustration, flung his squashed-up pillow across the bed to hit his dresser. He rolled over to his right side and slowly stood to his feet as he slid off the bed feeling and listening to his spine un-kink and his knees crackle from arthritis. Slowly, he straightened his back, carefully threw back his shoulders and pulled up his drooping blue and green plaid flannel boxers before they could drop to his knees. All of his clothes were getting too big for him, including his underwear it seemed.

Brad reached up and rubbed his unshaven chin with his right hand and ran the other large callused hand through his bushy gray-black hair and scratched the back of his head. He rotated his head several times and cringed as he listened to the crackle, and felt again, his aged neck complain. Then, as part of his normal wake-up routine, he knelt down on one knee and looked under the bed for his tried-and-true brown leather slippers. He dragged them out, unsure why he always seemed to kick them halfway under the bed and slid them on his size 14 4E feet.

He stepped away from the bed to do a few half-windmills to get some of the creaks out and muscles stretched. Having completed his daily, but somewhat strenuous routine, Brad headed for the bathroom to relieve his bladder. He was in bad need of a shower; hot shower, even a short one to conserve electricity, was nearly the highlight of his day; the other hugging his family. After the quick but steamy shower, he stood before the bathroom mirror with a heavy white bath towel wrapped around his waist and used a dry wash cloth to wipe the fog from the mirror. For a brief moment, he studied his aging face and his after-shower wet-head expression of utter delight turned into a deep-lined frown of stark reality. Each day he went through this same routine, wondering who that old man in the mirror was and then spotted yet another new wrinkle around his tired bloodshot brown eyes and drooping bloodhound under eye pouches.

"I'm beginning to look like Walter Matthau, just before they buried him!" From his dad, Brad had inherited a set of rebellious eyebrow hairs, some bushy nose hairs and those ever pesky ear hairs his wife always threatened to braid; which only added to his over-the-hill look. Worst of all, the ear hairs continually tickled driving him crazy and he was always trying to drive his thick stubby index fingers halfway through his brain to stop the tickling. A big man, Brad stood a broad shouldered 6'6", wore a size 56 XL coat, and weighed 243 lbs. Before the world began falling apart, he weighed 284 lbs. No expensive gym costs, no exercise tapes or food programs, he simply didn't eat and with government rationing he had no choice in the matter. Brad liked to think he sort of resembled a middle-aged John Wayne; his favorite old-time movie star. Not that anyone else made the comparison-most people thought he looked like his dad- which really worried him.

Dried, he pulled on a fresh set of plaid under-shorts and a well-worn Notre Dame T-shirt with the sleeves torn off. Brad stepped back into the bedroom and glanced at the mirror on his dresser top. He decided that for a middle-aged man with hairy ears and his own teeth, minus a few, he didn't look all that bad. He sighed and finished dressing, which was much like being on a personal assembly line; first, a set of long white lightweight cotton underwear pants, followed by a long-sleeved extra-warm shirt. Then a Kevlar bulletproof vest held together by six-Velcro elastic straps. After the vest was shifted into a comfortable place and straps retightened, he stepped into a fresh set of insulated, dark-blue police coveralls. Zipping up his coveralls, he felt a twinge of pain in his lower back and groaned a bit as he took a moment to stretch it out. *Gotta face it, Kid, you're 42 years old and starting to look an' sound like dad. Now even my neck is taking on that same Sawyer saggy-look. Geez! Maybe I shouldn't have given up racket-ball.* A 3 inch U.S. flag patch was sewed on the left shoulder of his coveralls and on the opposite shoulder, the dark blue and gold embroidered police patch of the Fairbanks City Police Department. Under the patches were three gold stripes of a police sergeant, of which he was extremely proud. Brad picked up a shiny gold sergeant's badge from a wooden tray on top of his dresser, buffed it off with a sleeve and pinned Badge #77 through the provided eyelets over his left breast pocket. Most of the officers on the department had gone over to the cloth badges, but not Brad. He'd worn this badge for nearly nine years and long before him it had belonged to his dad and he wasn't about to replace it now.

With everything zipped up and in place, he quickly brushed back his short hair with a horsehair wooden brush, a birthday gift from his son two years ago. He picked up his 26 pound black basket-weave leather police belt before going downstairs. His belt equipment consisted of two sets of Smith & Wesson Handcuffs passed down from his father, when the old man retired after 27 years with the Fairbanks Police Department; four extra .40 caliber 12 round loaded magazines and an 8 inch Buck sheath knife. He also carried a new telescoping stun baton powered by two rechargeable 12 volt batteries with the ability to drop the largest of men through the thickness of a heavy parka. He had carried a Taser weapon, but now preferred the stun baton and its dual purpose as an old fashioned police nightstick. There was an unloaded sawed off 12-guage shotgun upstairs; the .00 rounds hidden on his closet's top shelf, but he kept his service weapon locked in the gun safe in the downstairs hallway closet with an assortment of other weapons. He unlocked the safe, removed his duty weapon from the top shelf and took a moment to admire his new pistol; a Model 93 Smith & Wesson laser guided .40 caliber automatic with attached high beam flashlight. He inserted a loaded magazine, pulled the slide back and seated a round before placing the weapon into its leather basket weave breakfront holster. Manufactured only last year, which ended up being the final year for Smith & Wesson Manufacturers, the pistol held six Teflon armor piercing rounds, alternating with six semi-jacketed wide-mouthed hollow point Hydro-shocker bullets. At first Brad disliked giving up his old Glock, but had grown to like this new pistol, and now everyone in the department carried the same ammo and could interchange magazines if need be.

Checking his appearance one last time in a five foot long door mirror, he found himself semi-satisfied, if somewhat dismayed by how tired he looked. He paused and glanced at the framed photograph on top a living room shelf. There were other photographs on shelves, mostly his kids and two of his wife's parents; who were now deceased. But his wife kept one photograph separate from the others, knowing how much it meant to her husband. This was the only photograph they had of his dad in police uniform. Brad stood to his dad's left, at the time nearly three inches shorter than the old man. Ed, his kid brother, knelt down at their father's right side with a new football in his hands. Their mom had died when Brad was 13 and with his father's long hours, Brad had pretty much raised Ed. They had many good times together; the old man loved to watch his sons play high school football and rarely missed a game.

Brad touched his father's image, remembering the day he came home from work, a brand new corporal, to find his old man lying on the kitchen floor, dead from a massive coronary and by all the signs it had been quick. Ed had flown home from Arizona for the funeral, where he was attending Arizona State University on a football scholarship. That was the last time the two brothers had seen each other. They stayed in contact with the occasional phone call, some letters and of course the many Christmas cards and gifts for Brad's kids. Ed never forgot his nephew and niece's birthdays; their walls were covered with ASU junk and assorted Apache Indian artifacts. But everything stopped when the missiles rained down on the US. All mail had ceased and Brad didn't know if his kid brother was still alive. Ed, unmarried, was serving as a patrol lieutenant with the Arizona State Police when the war broke out and Brad grieved for the loss of his brother over the weeks to follow. He had spent many a long hour at his father's gravesite talking to the frozen ground and sharing the pride his dad would've had of Ed's progress in law enforcement. Brad looked at Ed's innocent young face in the photograph and wondered, as he did every day, whether or not his kid brother was somehow still alive? He could only hazard a guess at what life in the Lower 48 must be like for the survivors and sometimes, depending on his mood, hoped Ed had joined the hereafter with their dad, instead of trying to survive the sheer hell he suspected would follow a nuclear war. He'd watched enough sci-fi movies and read a lot of books to wonder what kind of life the survivors must be facing and didn't want to wish that on his brother, or anyone else.

He pushed thoughts of Ed away and went in search of Kathy; his 39 year old wife of 21 years. A green-eyed brunette, Kathy stood more than a head shorter than her bull of a husband and was less than half his weight.

Like so many other wives and mothers in this world's current state of affairs, she bore a weathered look on her face out of concern for her family, too little sleep from worry and a near starvation diet. Yet, Kathy only displayed a few extra wrinkles about her tired eyes and a couple more red lines to her blood shot eyes from being a cop's wife. Mostly, she had aged more recently from having to watch Brad go out every day to face a more barbaric world and wonder when the food would run out or if the Chinese would attack first.

The people of Alaska knew it was only a matter of time before the food rations would discontinue, the space rock would strike and the OAP armies would march on Alaska. Their future was bleak, but still the Sawyer family prayed often and loved each other even more dearly with each passing day. Such was the way in the Sawyer household and Kathy wouldn't want it to change.

By the level of noise coming from upstairs, Kathy knew her heavy-footed husband was up and stumbling about. He made enough noise for two-men and on those mornings he had the chance to wrestle with his son, he surely wondered why the ceiling hadn't given away to collapse down upon her kitchen. In the old days, she might have felt playful and run the hot water in the kitchen sink when he was in the shower, then listened to him scream and shout as he pounded the shower wall. He sometimes did it to her, both knowing it was done in fun. Being playful seemed to have passed as the planet was going up in flames and both heat and water were not to be wasted.

She put her kitchen chores aside, tossed her dishtowel on the counter and met him at the kitchen doorway for one of his bear hug embraces. As always lately, he dampened the romantic moment with, "Need some clean socks, babe."

"Lover to the core...Babe," Kathy stepped back, pushed him away and led him into the kitchen.

"Hey, I'm still a lover..." Brad said as he looked about the kitchen counters, "...but, where's my lunch? Kathy nodded her head in mock-frustration, a leering raised eyebrow over her left eye and a mischievous grin on her face as she crossed her arms and waited. "What?" Brad asked and then recovered somewhat with, "Where's my lunch you beautiful and desirable woman?"

"Better." She knew her husband loved her, but with strict food rationing, his one meal a day was also a high priority in his life. She pointed to his navy blue duty bag sitting on the kitchen floor by the outside door, "All packed and ready, Lover."

Almost to the point of overheating, he plopped down on a metal folding chair by the door that squawked loudly in protest. Bundled in thick outdoor clothing he grunted with exertion as he pulled on clean woolen socks and then slipped his size 14 feet into insulated black winter boots. Brad preferred bunny boots in these extreme sub-zero temperatures but they were definitely not made for driving. Often referred to as Bozo the Clown shoes, rubber Bunny Boots were huge in comparison to other winter boots. It was impossible to put pressure on only one pedal at a time and stepping on the gas and brake pedals simultaneously caused many frightening moments during Code 3 runs. Several times he ended up in a lengthy slide across icy streets and on one occasion sideswiped an ADF heavy equipment truck. Thankfully, outside of some ribbing by his fellow officers, there were no injuries, but now his bunny boots were left in his locker at work.

"What did the Militia want with you this time?" Kathy asked, as she put wet clothes into the dryer. They were allowed only two wash/dry cycles a day and with two kids, she had to devote one to just them. No longer were things separated by color, items were simply tossed in together. Except for Brad's uniforms, which were washed by hand in the tub and hung up downstairs to dry by the steam pipes. He didn't want to show up for work with an assortment of faded colors on his navy blue jumpsuits. With the change in weather, the old uniforms were packed away and now he was down to three sets of coveralls.

"Militia?" Brad asked.

Outside of the Alaska Defense Force, the Alaska civilian Militia remained intact because the state constitution prevented it from being swept up by federal troops. These "good old boy" forces trained separately, stayed in groups made up of friends and relatives and until recently, had been under the command of civilian leaders elected by militia forces. Currently, the new Alaska legislature was trying to change the law to allow the militia to be governed by ADF commanders and senior officers, but for now they remained under civilian leadership and made their own assignments. Large scale deployment of Militia forces had to be approved by the governor. There were no Militia forces in Wales, but they were divided up elsewhere around the state. Another problem lay in the officer's program; Militia officers did not need college diplomas, but ADF officers did.

"You got home late, remember?" Kathy reminded him. "You said Militia Headquarters wanted to talk with you."

"Just another tedious meeting like last time," Brad said. "They spent the better part of an hour asking me questions about my job, my ideals and beliefs. Guess it was some kind of loyalty interview they wanted since I'm the number two man in the department now." Brad stood up and wandered into the living room. He had hoped to get outside before his body was coated in sweat. Once outside the sweat quickly froze and he would have the chills before he got to the police department.

"Where are the kids, honey?"

On cue, Bob, an energetic 12 year old with short brown hair and freckled cheeks, wrapped his arms around his dad's waist, only a micro-second before Becky, a precocious 9 year old with a mouthful of braces and long straight blonde hair, grabbed a hold of her father's right leg. Bob backed off for a brief moment and then launched forward to hit Brad at the waist with an NFL caliber body tackle, making it hard for Brad to maintain his feet. Becky was forced to let go of her father's leg and shouted out, "Morning, Daddy!"

"More like afternoon, Princess," Brad hugged her tightly while Bob, now glaring down at his little sister, added in his share of the hug. "Whatever happened to those two sweet, quiet children who lived here?" Brad asked.

"Those were my kids, these two monsters take after your side of the family," Kathy replied.

After a moment with the children, Brad turned to Kathy and looked deeply into her eyes. Bob, knowing that silly look on his father's face, hustled Becky upstairs so mom and dad could have a quiet moment together. "C'mon, squirt," Bob said. "We're not needed here and they're gonna get all kissy."

"Kissy? I like that," Brad said and switched back to his stomach needs. "Hope you got something good tonight. I'm having trouble keeping my pants up with all the weight I've lost. I nearly lost my boxers when I rolled out of bed."

"Good, you keep losing weight an' I'll tuck in your boxers." She gave him a classy Mae West vixen eye, accompanied by a hand on hip and in a thick slurry voice, "Honey, you haven't looked this good since you came back from the police academy."

Brad's left eyebrow shot up, "I've noticed you're getting that hour glass figure back too, my dear. Maybe I could take a couple hours off tonight an'…"

He stopped when she pointed that accusing finger at him and said, "Hush, the kids will hear you."

"They've heard a whole lot worse from their friends. Bob's 12 an' I remember how much I knew when I was that age."

"You have a dirty mind, old man," Kathy said in jest.

Working 12-15 hour shifts seven days a week made for little family time. Especially after the government declared a State of Emergency followed by a Declaration of Martial Law and now nearly all his home time was devoted to a few pitiful hours of sleep. Still, Brad considered he was one of the lucky ones and couldn't complain too much. Not only was he blessed with a fantastic family and a great job, he was provided with private housing.

With the exception of certain military units, including military police and senior officers, all military personnel in the Fairbanks region were required to reside on Fort Wainwright or Eielson Air Force Base. Both installations were bursting at the seams and had become crowded beehives of activity as Alaska prepared for war. Civilian personnel shared crowded quarters, sometimes four to five families sharing a three or four bedroom house. Conditions were only getting worse as outlying villages were evacuated and people moved into town for safety sake.

Apartment buildings had been taken over by the government and a quick engineering job had all off base units heated by underground pipes routed from Fort Wainwright's enormous steam plant. Off post electricity was provided by the city power plant's massive generators fueled by gigantic coal burning furnaces. Power and water were strictly rationed.

Brad joked that meter readers had the most dangerous job in town now because people viewed them the same way they used to view IRS agents. He knew it had grown worse in the last couple of weeks and now meter readers were escorted by a squad of ADF soldiers. One meter reader was nearly trampled to death by a roving band of troublemakers, men who refused duty and lived wildly off the work and pain of others. Meters were occasionally found damaged, which brought police to investigate. People found abusing utilities were fired, moved and provided housing in less desired living conditions; usually multi-bed arrangements in large storefront buildings where privacy was extremely limited and soldier work in their future.

Coal was transported by rail north from the Healy coal mines where work was non-stop as the black gold was dug from the ground. Heating oil and various fuels needed by the Alaska Defense Force came from the North Pole Oil Refinery, receiving crude oil directly from the North Slope's Prudhoe Bay oil fields. Alaska had taken over the oil fields and the black crude was now funneled directly into the refinery through the trans-Alaska pipeline. Privately owned companies like British Petroleum and Shell Oil no longer existed. Everything was operated by the Alaska government to handle the emergency and impending war. No one was paid; everyone shared in duty to the people, to Alaska and for one meal a day. Socialism and Capitalism had been slammed together in a compromise of existence, but only a few people complained. Anarchists or supporters of the OAP were rounded up, tried and sent to Healy where they were issued a shovel and ordered to dig coal or starve.

The military enforced strict food rationing with each citizen being provided one balanced meal a day and its make-up was juggled daily by various dieticians. After the last food riots in Anchorage and Fairbanks, the Governor ordered military authorities to seize all food from every store and restaurant. In the weeks that followed, and under order of Martial Law, house to house searches were made and stockpiles of food seized and stored in well-guarded aircraft hangers on Fort Wainwright. In Anchorage, supplies were held on Fort Richardson and Elmendorf Air Force Base. Smaller cities and towns were handled by local militia, but with factories in the Lower 48 destroyed and trucking stopped, everyone knew that whatever food was at hand was the last to be had. There would be no more crops, farmlands to the south were contaminated with radiation and most, if not all, the people who worked the land were dead.

Once a week, a well-guarded convoy delivered seven days of rations to block leaders in Fairbanks. Heavily guarded leaders then handed out provisions every other day to each family based on size. Strict accounting was followed to maintain an accurate supply record, which helped the Office of Emergency Management track the number of people being fed and housed. Violators or hoarders were quickly arrested and sent to the Healy Coal Mines, which had become the new prison colony. Those with boat experience were sent to Bristol Bay to help the new Alaska fishing fleet. A brief trial was held where evidence was presented before a military judge. Trials lasted less than half a day; there was no jury, no bail and no appeal. The current civilized world no longer had time for such things, survival mattered and individual rights took a step down to the rights of the whole body to live. Fairbanks school buses were converted into prison buses with windows covered by cage wire and every evening one left Fairbanks in an armed convoy for the 95 mile journey to Healy. Thick ice fog and icy roads made driving hazardous so three snow plows and a sand truck led the convoy; a slow mournful trip for the prisoners. Cargo aircraft left Anchorage or Fairbanks twice a week with prisoners bound for Bristol Bay. The post nuclear world was not always a fair one, but so far the system worked and the shadow of doom from three fronts hung heavily over the population.

Non ADF single people 18 years and older in the Fairbanks region were housed on Fort Wainwright with one daily meal provided at Army dining halls between the hours of 6 a.m. and 6 p.m. Individual meals, prepared by ADF dieticians, came with a sealed package containing three cigarettes quickly making them a major barter item between non-smokers and nicotine addicts. Meal time became a social event of sorts. Musicians were on hand to play, time was allowed for conversation and even board games were provided for the one hour meal breaks. After a 12 hour work day, rest and relaxation was needed and people enjoyed themselves for those often festive

60 minutes. Then it was back to work. During off duty time, most people slept, but work was continual 24/7 as Alaskans prepared for the final days.

There was always hope that some would survive the disasters and that miraculous events would unfold to save Alaska. Churches conducted daily prayer services and probably for the first time in man's history, the various sects worked hand in hand to help one another. Christians and Muslims, Hindu and Buddhist worked side by side for the greater good. Individual prayer time or worship service was held separate as each person came to realize it was religious bigotry that had helped destroy the world and bridges needed to be built to bring humanity back together.

In Alaska, Christianity was the main religion and the Sawyer family had always attended Lighthouse Community Church, a non-denominational charismatic fellowship under the leadership of Pastor John Knight. This meant among other things, they held a time of family prayer before Brad left for duty. Today, after prayer, Kathy had blessed him with an affectionate kiss and whispered into his ear, "God keep you safe, my darling". He always nodded in response, gave her a final hug and picked up a dark blue duty bag with F.P.D. embroidered on the side in gold. The bag contained his meal, another set of non-insulated coveralls for working on his patrol car inside the city garage, a set of clean long underwear, a couple of handkerchiefs, two pair of wool socks and a black wool balaclava to keep his face warm for those lengthy periods of time he spent outside. Because he didn't like them, he left his face mask and goggles in his patrol car, wearing them only when he had to work outside or made traffic stops. There were extra flashlight batteries, his stun wand and a small first aid kit.

With temperatures of - 40° outside Brad and Kathy didn't stand at the door making small talk. When the door opened, a blast of frigid air and a cloud of frost gave Kathy a cold shiver. He hustled through the doorway and she quickly closed the door behind him and double-locked it. When the family moved into this apartment, Brad had spent most of a day making it safe for when he wasn't around. The front door was reinforced with an extra deadbolt lock and a steel rod to prevent the door from opening. He placed steel bars on the windows to keep intruders out and Kathy knew where the shotgun and ammo were kept in the event she needed it. Brad had also brought home three extra fire extinguishers and placed them about the apartment, making sure to go over fire escape plan with the kids.

Kathy placed the steel rod across the door and then looked through a side window to watch Brad disappear into a grayish wall of thick ice fog. Once more, she asked God to protect her man. She sighed deeply, turned around and said in a loud voice, "Time for school." In the living room she found the kids going through a pile of Bob's old comic books and got the response she expected from her children.

"Aw mom, why?" Bob asked in a pitiful tone, as he dropped an old Archie Comic to the floor. Doing his best impersonation, he grasped his hands together and pled for leniency from a cold-hearted judge.

She did not buy it and smiled sweetly, "School gives you something to stay busy with, to widen your horizons, but we'll begin with our Bible reading first if you wish."

"Aw, mom...." Bob stood up and shuffled off for the dining room table.

"You should 'a shut-up, Bobby," Becky said. "Now mom's gonna make us read the Psalms again. Psalms is boring."

"Drop dead, twerp," Bob lashed out and shoved her forward.

"Mom, Bobby told me ta drop dead again."

Kathy looked at both of her children and shook her head in frustration, "Just once I'd like to be the one going out on patrol and leave Brad home with you two." Kathy prodded her daughter toward the table and placed the family Bible down in front of her son. "Today, you get to read Psalms 119."

"That's the one that goes on forever," Bob complained.

"Not forever, but maybe you'll be too winded afterward to abuse your little sister."

*****

Taking in icy air in short gasps, trying to ignore the burning in his lungs, Brad was delighted to see his patrol car running. He smiled in appreciation to see that his partner was out first today and had started the cold beast then shook his head in amusement when he saw the sour expression on his partner's face.

Brad gave Officer Scott Radley a quick wave and waited for him to open the trunk from inside the car. He tossed his duty bag inside the darkened cavity, which was already packed with duty equipment then closed the lid down with a loud slam. The trunk mechanism was giving them trouble lately, like the rest of the vehicle and a slam was necessary to keep it closed. Normally, Brad drove but this morning, because Scott had come in early and started the cold car, he opened the front passenger door, slid his immense bulk inside and situated his legs around the 12 gauge shotgun mounted to the floor and dash. Brad gave Scott a friendly pat on the arm and said in his worst Irish accent, "An' a good afternoon to you too, Officer Radley."

Scott glared back at Brad with cold narrowing eyes and slowly shook his head in disgust. Not for Brad, but for the rotten weather. Only after putting the transmission into reverse did he speak, "Sounds like you got too much sleep, O' Sergeant...Sir."

"Well, my man, can I help it if I'm just a cheerful man in a gloomy world?"

"C'mon, Sarge, what makes you so darn cheery on a day like this? We got us at least 12 hours ta work in this freezer, the sky is falling an' at least a million Chinamen wantin' ta make sushi out of us."

"Actually, I don't think the Chinese eat sushi, but they probably got enough Japanese in their ranks or whoever else to turn us into fish food. As to your question regarding my outlook on life, I live a good life, have a great family an' as much as you hate to hear me say it, I believe in Jesus Christ as my Lord and Savior."

"Oh no, please don't get started on that again. It's way too early for Father Brad's Evangelist Show, okay?"

"No problem, I'll give you a couple hours of slack time before condemning you for your sinful life." Brad smiled widely as Scott pulled out of the parking spot and headed down the road at a cautious speed.

"Looks like you remembered to pull out the plug this time." Brad was referring to the last time Scott drove and forgot to unplug the electrical cord running from a stationary power outlet to an electrical heater mounted on the vehicle's engine block. They ended up nearly dragging a 25 foot power cord all the way to the station garage and taking a bad ribbing from their fellow officers. In extreme cold, plugging in was the only way to keep vehicles from freezing and the oil turning to sludge. Each vehicle was equipped with a battery blanket, block heater and an oil pan heater. More than once, kids had pulled the plug, forcing Brad and Scott to get a ride to work while their vehicle was towed to the garage to warm-up, which made for a very bad day on patrol.

Officer Radley was 24, Afro-American and nearly as tall as Brad, but not as heavy. Once a trim 230 lbs., he had dropped rapidly to his current 197 lbs. He kept his hair short, but maintained a semi-bushy moustache that went below the corner of his mouth. Scott, a former MP stationed at Fort Wainwright, left the military to pursue a career in civilian law enforcement and had been on the force for three years. He had spent the last four months teamed up with Brad in a two-man radio car and now didn't think he had much time for a career left. Though single, Scott was provided with a one bedroom apartment in Brad's building complex. The building supervisor, an older gentleman who had retired from the Army 14 years earlier, had the key to Scott's apartment and was responsible for placing Scott's food rations inside while Scott was at work. Scott often found something extra in his ration box and knew it had come from his manager, who had cancer and was eating less and less. Scott wished he could do something for the old guy, but he didn't know what. So, he accepted the extra gifts and always remembered to say thank you when he saw the man ambling about the complex on his rounds.

Though Scott dealt with the war and the loss of parents and siblings, he often had trouble sleeping because of nightmares from his time in the military. When the nightmares came, he awoke, sat in his living room and thought about such trivial things as the loss of cable television which had ended with the first missile impacts. With all the death and destruction, it surprised him how much he missed the National Football League and professional golf. As an alternative to the daily violence he dealt with on the job, he had turned his attention to DVD movies, but this ended when all television sets, DVD players and stereo components were confiscated by the military to provide back-ups for needed electrical parts. He then became addicted to military and action based fiction novels; W.E.B. Griffin and Clive Cussler being his favorite authors. He often traded novels with Brad and others in the department.

"You're kind of quiet today, something on your mind?" Brad asked as the patrol car plowed through the snowy streets and fishtailed around a slippery corner, as Scott fought to maintain control.

"Naw, jus' thinkin' 'bout pretty girls walkin on a sandy beach an' a hot summer sun beatin down on their tanned...."

"Hold it, buddy. Remember I'm a married man. My heart can only stand so much imagination and take it easy on the turns."

"You asked." Scott weaved to avoid hitting a pedestrian in the middle of the street. In thick ice fog, a pedestrian could suddenly pop up in front of them, so Scott drove 25 mph on most city streets and sometimes as slow as 15 mph.

"So, mister married man, what do you do when you see a pretty girl?"

Brad grinned, "I'll withhold my answer based upon my 5th Amendment rights."

Scott laughed, "That's what I figured." He gestured with his left hand in a wide wave over the steering wheel, "Come on, Kathy don't care if you look at the merchandise, does she? You ain't buying any."

"You're not going to get me into this conversation, my lad." Brad waved to a heavily insulated man standing on the corner, unsure if he recognized him or not and if in fact it was a him? With the extra padding it was hard to tell anymore. "I can't tell if that was a woman or a man. No merchandise to worry about."

Scott shook his head in response, grinned again and turned off Cushman Street to pull into the police department's parking garage.

Advising the dispatcher by radio they were outside, an automatic door slowly creaked open to allow them entry. Cold air struck the warm room, creating a thick plume of icy mist as Scott pulled into an empty parking spot.

FAIRBANKS POLICE DEPARTMENT

The new police department building was constructed in the late 1990's and attached to the aging Fairbanks K-12 school building, built in the early part of the 20th century. The old school had been abandoned after weathering nearly a century of arctic winters, then the City resurrected the three story facility and transformed it into Fairbanks City Hall. A section of the lower level had been used for the Fairbanks Boys & Girls Club until the current emergency and was now being used for the storage of emergency goods. The street level floor of the police department, connected to the City Hall by a length of heavily carpeted hallway, was made up of a visitor's gallery, a large meeting room for officer's shift briefings and a smaller room with desks, computers and file cabinets for officers to complete their reports. Here they also conducted basic interviews with victims and witnesses. There were three separate interrogation rooms for in- depth chats with suspects down the hallway, which led to a loading dock and the department's vehicle garage. The department also provided a shower/locker room for the officers with a small weight room for all personnel to use and secured rooms for evidence and records keeping, just beside the large well-equipped dispatch area. On the upper level were offices for sergeants, lieutenants and captains, a larger office for the department detectives to share and a well-decorated office for the Chief of Police.

The former Police Chief had spent a good share of the department's budget to redecorate his office in rich deep rosewood paneling, thick dark brown carpeting, and decorative floor rugs. His desk was nearly nine feet long, weighed 600 lbs. and had a heavily stained oak top. Facing the desk were three brown upholstered chairs; behind it stood the flags of the USA and Alaska. Along one wall was a cushy and quite comfortable gold and brown couch; opposite that were four 5 drawer dark wood file cabinets.

The current chief disliked the office, knowing the amount of money spent, not that it mattered now but saw no reason to redo it. In fact, due to his medical problems, Chief Osborne actually felt rested in the darkened office and often retreated to it when the stress level reached the intolerable range - like now. Having come from yet another lengthy meeting with His Honor the Mayor, Chief Bob Osborne was in a foul mood and had high hopes he could avoid everyone on the way to his office. A veteran of 19 years, all with FPD, Chief Osborne received his current appointment when a military court convicted his predecessor on a charge of hoarding over 4,000 lbs. of food in his mother-in-law's basement. A second charge of bartering these same illegal foods for personal needs garnered him an additional five year sentence at Healy. Though there was no proof his wife was involved, his mother-in-law was found guilty of the same charges, but due to advanced age she was sentenced to four years general laborer at Fairbanks Memorial Hospital. Sadly, she left the courtroom ranting and raving, threatening the judge and behaving very much unladylike.

Since martial law had been declared, military authorities had taken over the court system. Local judges were granted Reserve ADF Commissions as majors or above, while civilian and military police continued to work together. State prosecutors and defense attorneys were drafted into military service as captains. A number of defense lawyers and two prosecutors fought it, but all soon found themselves in uniform taking orders. Those who flatly refused to serve were given a shovel and quickly assigned to a labor force. No one had time to deal with pampering left wing liberals and if they refused to shovel, they didn't eat- simple as that.

Having just attended a senior law enforcement officer's convention on the east side of Tacoma, Washington, then police Captain Bob Osborne's Christmas morning breakfast was cut short when Seattle took a direct hit from a Chinese ICBM. Only 27 miles from ground zero, the blast caught him sitting next to a window over-looking a parking lot and he was temporarily blinded by the intense blast. It was only due to the actions of a dear friend, a senior counsel member in the Washington Governor's Office, along with Captain Osborne's position with the FPD and his Alaska Army National Guard rank of Lt. Colonel that allowed him quick transportation home on the last Alaska Air Command's cargo flight to leave Washington State. Had he waited another four hours, clouds of radioactivity from a second and third impact carried over the state causing all flights to be canceled? When doctors in Anchorage removed the bandages, they diagnosed Bob as a victim of White Eye; a newly diagnosed condition resulting from close proximity to nuclear blast where all color pigment is burned from the eye by gamma radiation. It left him extremely sensitive to bright lights confined to living in a black and white world. His eyes still wrapped, Osborne overheard the aircrew speaking to one another in surprise that the OAP had left Alaska seemingly untouched while striking the west coast with more than a dozen confirmed nuclear blasts. The pilots feared their flying days were over with radiation and volcanic ash spreading across the skies. At that point, Captain Osborne wished he had died with so many others. He was dying slowly from radiation, which was attacking his brain and nervous system.

In the following days, seismic movement caused by nuclear blasts led to a series of eruptions. The remaining summit of Mount St. Helens, followed by majestic Mt. Hood and beautiful Mount Rainier erupted, sending ash and debris nearly 20,000 feet into the air adding thick billowing clouds of volcanic ash to the darkening skies. California's Mt. Shasta soon followed, covering the famous lake and ski resort in volcanic ash and fiery lava. Thousands perished in the initial eruptions, later those numbers grew into millions. If the missiles didn't get you, radiation or earthquakes and tsunami, plus smothering ash did.

Depressed from his chewing out by the mayor, Chief Bob Osborne stopped in the hallway to rub his temples in an attempt to drive back yet another surge of painful headaches. They tended to strike like an ice pick to the right side of his skull. He opened his eyes in time to see Brad and Scott approach and quickly adjusted his protective mirrored sunglasses that looked more like ski goggles than glasses, and made a futile attempt to conceal his physical discomfort by going on the offensive. "You two sure look like crap, do either one of you own an iron?"

Chief Osborne was dressed in non-insulated uniform coveralls, with various patches in place and four gold stars of a Police Chief on each collar point. He wore a brown leather shoulder holster with department issued pistol. Due to growing back problems he didn't wear the normal police belt, but under his coveralls wore a wide black canvas back brace. Like Brad, the brass shield of a Police Chief was positioned over his left breast pocket and he was proud of it. His hair was short so no one would notice how much gray hair he was losing and there was no facial hair on his narrow pale face. His chin was long and pointed, with a single dimple at the end; a single scar 2 inches long arced over his left eyebrow- a gift from a female suspect with a knife 5 years earlier. He stood 5'11", with slightly drooping shoulders and was now down to 148 lbs. His hands, once quite strong were now pale with long fingers which were starting to curl from arthritis and he struggled to write his signature. He disliked shaking hands and offered up various reasons for same, but those who knew him well understood what was happening to him and one of those was Sgt. Brad Sawyer.

"And a very good afternoon to you too, Chief," Brad said cheerfully, as he stopped before his boss. "I was just stopping by to see if you have anything you want me to add to roll call?" Brad noted Osborne's pain; the sheer tension in his friend's face radiated with it and he knew better than to say anything in front of Scott. Even with three years under his belt, the Chief still saw Scott as a rookie and rookies didn't need to know the inner workings of the department and that meant the lives of the senior officers.

"Yeah, tell your hoodlums to be more polite with John Q Citizen," Osborne ordered in a stern voice. "I'm still getting complaints from the mayor about police harassment in the clubs. Mr. Good Politics says you got one clown, his label, not mine, doing some name calling down on South

Cushman. No name yet, but this guy's apparently got a pretty foul mouth for the ladies and he's making us all look bad."

Brad understood the problem, "Working these long shifts without break is wearing my guys down, Chief. Add in our new mandatory diet plan and you got some guys walking the edge." Brad patted his stomach to illustrate the point, "If someone were to offer me a New York cut as a bribe I just might take him up on it."

"Listen Sergeant Sawyer, I give you an order right here and now, with this officer as witness, if someone offers you a good cut of beef for a bribe, you send him my way. Rank still has its privileges in this man's outfit," Chief Osborne said and followed it with a brisk goodbye as he opened his office door.

Brad and Scott shook their heads in bewilderment and continued on to Roll Call.

Closing the door behind him, Osborne stopped the pretense and stumbled over to his massive desk. Placing both hands on the desk top for support, he slowly lowered himself into a high-backed black leather chair. Under great physical strain, he opened his center top desk drawer and pulled out a large half-filled vial of white capsules, opened his bottom drawer and grabbed a nearly full quart of confiscated homebrew moonshine. He washed down two pills with a brew chaser and spent the next few minutes fighting down the urge to vomit. It wasn't the taste of the brew, though it burned all the way down his throat, but the radiation sickness that was clearly taking its toll on Chief Osborne. For now though, only his doctors knew the seriousness of his illness and he wanted to keep it that way for as long as possible. Thankfully, the office came with its own restroom, so no one knew when he was having stomach or bowl problems. He knew he only had a couple weeks to continue working and hoped Brad was ready to take over the department when that time came.

ROLL CALL - 2 P.M. (1400 HOURS)

Eight officers were spread out among 20 chairs, some ready to take notes; others fighting to stay awake. The seven day a week shift was beginning to show on the best of them and even their old union couldn't help once Martial Law was declared. They were all dressed and armed like Brad, but not all uniforms looked duty ready and Brad made a mental note of it. "Okay, you lunkheads… the Chief received another complaint on some blue suiter givin' some poor civvies a hard time. Now I don't care who it is, or why, but try to remember you're still police officers. Our job's to protect those people, not hassle 'em. And while we're at it, keep your hands off those ladies workin' the lounges and clean up your mouths. They've already got enough trouble with the soldiers an' militia dudes pawing at them. They sure don't need some love hungry cop pushin' himself on 'em. Like that old movie said- we're the last of the knights...the Blue Knights. So get that through your thick skulls an' start acting like it. Wear that badge with pride, don't tarnish it... or you'll be facing me and my tolerance level has reached an all-time low."

The military seized control of and converted three Fairbanks strip clubs into recreation halls for soldiers and militia. The girls working were told to put on some clothes or find another job. Lounges were set up inside the clubs, providing privacy for young off duty singles to meet, dance and socialize amidst the noise of a few rowdy games of ping pong, darts and billiards. One club was devoted to country music, another to a mixture of rock & roll, karaoke and rocking country tunes, and the third smaller club to disco. For the disabled or those too young or too old for military service, two car dealership display rooms were divided – one side to show movies, the other set up to play bingo and card games.

The library was open 24/7 with an area set aside where professional counselors came to help people deal with the current situation and as the days passed the number of clients continued to grow. The hospital was packed with people who suffered severe mental issues; the more violent were moved to a section of the Fairbanks Correctional Center where doctors could better serve their needs.

With fighting about to break out at any moment, the military considered dropping enlistment age to 16. A large number of high school kids were eager to join, but an equally large number of parents wanted them to wait until it was unavoidable and the wolf was at the door.

Looking over his men, Brad could identify with the weariness reflected on faces and more than a few bloodshot eyes. Under high stress, short of manpower and growing crime; hours of sleep continued to decline and he was down to five hours at best. He spotted two men who had failed to shave before reporting in and this upset him, but decided to cover it at inspection before releasing them for duty.

"Okay, last item, keep your speeds down. The roads are a mess and the city crews can't keep up with snow removal. Gas rationing is only going to get tighter, so keep it down to 25 mph or less. You wreck a patrol vehicle and you will be walking patrol. Those old Dodges and Fords can only take so much and there will be no replacements."

Brad and Scott drove a white 2010 Ford Expedition, with "Fairbanks Police Department" written across each side that was covered in dents and scratches and badly in need of a paint job. There was a low profile light bar on top and three flood lights mounted on the front bumper capable of turning night into day for at least 75 feet. Both bumpers had nasty dents; the rear left passenger window was badly cracked and a crack was crawling across the windshield and there was nothing they could do about it. The city shop had run out of parts and Brad had been denied permission to strip parts off civilian vehicles as all vehicles would be needed in the event of evacuation.

Closing his notebook, Brad ordered the men to line up for inspection and ignored the deep sighs and moans, "Now let's see how bad you all look today." He watched as they lined up in a loose, ragged formation in front of the first row of chairs. "From the way some of you smell, I'd say it's time to wash your socks an' underwear... and c'mon, take a shower! If your patrol partner doesn't throw you out of the car, one of the bad guys is sure to smell you coming and get the drop on you." The response was loud sighs and one loud burp. "Nice, real nice, there's always a clown in the bunch."

First in line was Corporal Whitehead, not one of Brad's favorites, who had lately become a real problem child. Under normal circumstances, he would've stripped the corporal stripes off Whitehead's sleeves, but it didn't matter anymore and Whitehead was still good when large fights broke out in recreation halls. "Zip up your coveralls, Corporal, and shave before you leave the station. You look like a slob." Brad matched glare for glare before Whitehead dropped his hard gaze and reluctantly nodded in compliance.

Brad couldn't help but smell the heavy dousing of cologne emanating from the next officer. "Use a bit less cologne, Thomas. Believe me it doesn't cover up the stench of brew." Brad moved in closer, "This is also your last warning. Next time you come in here reekin' of brew I'll hand you over to the MPs for a 72 hour detox. Afterward, they'll ship your butt off to some militia camp for permanent KP duty. You'll be peelin' potatoes for months... You get the picture?"

"Yes, Sarge...I got it."

Brad stepped back to address the whole squad, "Look, I don't mind if you down a brew or two after shift to calm nerves. I know we're out there doing a near impossible job and all the good booze is gone...But be careful with what you're drinking- lots of poison out there. And be sober when you show up for work. No more warnings... you show up for my roll call with brew on your breath and you'd better be ready to pay for it with your hide." After making sure everyone understood him, he dismissed the shift with his usual, "Stay alert, stay safe an' stay warm."

After Martial Law was declared, all liquor stores were closed and on hand supplies confiscated for hospital use. Personal liquor was limited and there would be no more arriving. A bottle of good whiskey was worth quite a bit in trading stock, even a six-pack of beer could go for a high barter. Within days, home breweries were in operation. First potatoes and then just about everything was used to make brew, which eventually led to illness and occasionally death by poisoning.

Signing off on the duty roster, he made a few notes regarding the inspection and warnings, then found Scott waiting for him at the head of the stairs. Before heading out on patrol, Brad wanted to have a few words with the Chief. "Scott, grab another cup of coffee an' tell Susie some of your lies."

"Lies?" Scott attempted to look hurt, but gave it up and wandered into dispatch as Brad walked down the hall to Chief Osborne's office.

Susie Andrews was sitting behind the radio console when Scott appeared in the doorway. A former 300 lb. semi-professional female cage fighter she had short red hair and soft green eyes. She wore the same dark blue coverall as the chief and kept a loaded department pistol at her side. As required by policy, an old nightstick was kept under her desk, held in place by two clips beside a leather holster, which held a department Taser. All precautions in the event of troublemakers, but it had only happened twice and she had dealt with the problem with her own fists and responding officers found the suspects unconscious.

"Coffee hot?" Scott asked as he pointed to the coffee pot with both index fingers.

"Always is, honey...if you can call it coffee." Susie keyed the microphone in response to a radio check as the oncoming shift prepared to leave the station.

Grabbing a heavily stained mug off the shelf, Scott wiped it out with a napkin before pouring himself a cup of extremely watery coffee from a 50 cup chrome plated urn. With his first sip he let out a depressing moan. "You might call this stuff hot, but, Susie, calling it coffee is a gross exaggeration by anyone's standards. Hard to remember what real coffee tasted like," he added as he took another sip, grimaced and then asked, "How many times you used these grounds, girl?"

"You don't have ta drink it, honey," Susie said and flashed Scott a quick wink.

"Well, it's sure better than antifreeze. So, what's new?" Scott asked as he sat down in a chair across from the radio console and admired Susie's arm muscles, which were nearly the size of Scott's thighs. He wished now that he had seen her fight but was glad he had never been on the punishing side of her huge fists; those mittens of hers looked like 15 lb. sledge hammers, even with red fingernails.

Brad knocked once on the Chief's door and opened it without waiting for an invitation. The two of them went back a long way and together they had climbed up through the ranks. Chief Osborne had been a pallbearer for Brad's father and most importantly, his dad had trusted him. So it was Corporal Osborne who was assigned to break Brad in as a rookie, just as Sergeant Sawyer had broken Osborne in 9 years earlier.

When Brad had come aboard, the FPD had a roster that included 78 officers, 6 detective investigators and a support staff of 16. The detectives were gone now and there were 18 officers left, not including the chief. Osborne's civilian staff of clerks, custodians and dispatchers had been reduced to an overburdened support staff of 3 dispatchers who worked 8 hour shifts around the clock. FPD had lost most of their officers to the Alaska Defense Force because they needed experienced men to guard prisoners at the Healy Coal Mines and to work convoy guard for the bi-monthly food convoys coming north from Anchorage.

Brad knew of at least three fellow officers who had been busted by Military Police for black marketing and were now shoveling coal in Healy beside their former police chief. Except for mental patients, prisons and jails had been closed at the outbreak of war and after failed legal challenges to stop such closures all convicted criminals were required to work hard labor or not eat. The Healy Coal Mine was possibly the last penal colony in the United States and for those working there it had become Devils Island. Outside of sending people to Bristol Bay for the fishing fleet, lesser criminals worked inside the various steam plants, shoveling coal into the big furnaces or unloading coal cars as they came in on the railroad. Hard labor had taken on a whole new meaning in Alaska.

"Okay, Bob, what's going on?" Brad asked. "You look like you're about to shoot someone." Brad didn't wait to be asked before he plopped his massive self into the chair in front of Bob's desk, then waited silently for his old friend's response.

Following a brief hesitation, Bob shook his head in mock-frustration and answered in a whisper of a voice, "This is between you and me, Brad. No one else can know and I do mean no one. An' that includes your partner… your church pastor and even your wife…at least for now anyway. Agreed?" Osborne waited until Brad nodded his head in agreement, confused by his friend's unusual behavior. "Close the door, Brad." Bob took out his bottle and poured one ounce of squeeze into a half-filled coffee mug. "I know you don't drink, so I won't offer. It's either this vile stuff or more pills an' I'm getting real tired of those pills. Side effects make me dizzy at times." Bob stopped long enough to gulp down his brew and wipe his lips with an unfolded faded gray handkerchief. "Don't judge me, Brad, I try to keep it down while I'm on duty. But lately I'm always on duty." Bob took off his mirrored glasses and briefly glared at Brad with those near hypnotizing white eyes of his.

Those bizarre eyes reminded Brad of an old horror-flick he'd seen when he was a kid, where all the children had strange powers and white eyes. It frustrated him until he recalled the movie title, oh yeah, *Village of the Damned*"- scary movie. "I'm not judging you, Bob," Brad said as he

51

closed the door and sat back down. "I don't know the level of pain you're in, but I do know the strain you're under would cause a lesser man to swallow his gun."

"Right you are!" Bob exclaimed. He gave Brad a half-smile and put his sunglasses back on. The overhead lights were bright enough to cause him pain and he wasn't exactly sure why he'd taken them off in the first place or why he wanted to make his best friend uncomfortable. *I'm losing it, but I got to hold on- I can't let it beat me... not yet.* "Well, you wanted to hear this, so I'll tell you. I guess you should know anyway, since you're my second in command." Bob glanced at Brad's collar and asked, "By the way, why won't you wear those captain bars I gave you?"

"Been a sergeant for a long time, Chief and I earned these stripes. Only reason I'm your number two-man now is because of seniority and the city isn't hiring anymore," He said.

He pointed to his stripes, "I'm proud of these, just like my dad was."

"Yeah, he was a good man...could use him here now...Well, you're down on the organizational chart as a captain, not that it really matters."

"Well, we covered that so now go on with what's got you all stressed out."

Chief Osborne glanced around the room, unsure how to begin and then looked back at his friend, "General Saunders held a briefing today with the mayor and I was present, along with a couple of others. The inner counsel you might say... Anyway, we were informed that any offer to surrender to the OAP means certain death for every man, woman and child in Alaska. Simply, it comes down to a matter of food. They can't feed us and their own soldiers, too, during an occupation. Saunders feels their offer of a peaceful surrender was a ploy to take us without a fight in order to protect what food reserves we may have. That and the oil; they need fuel and our processing capabilities to fuel their drive across Canada."

Brad smiled, "They're a greedy bunch, but it's a moot point, Chief, General Saunders knows we'd never surrender. Alaskans are just too hardheaded ta give into someone threatening us. Harder they push, the harder we'll fight. General knows that and so do you, so what's the real reason you got me in here behind a closed door?"

It didn't seem to surprise Bob how well Brad could read him. They had been friends too long. He stood up and limped over to an office window that looked out over a deserted roadway deep in gray snow. He shook his right leg to get the kink out of it and said, "Brad, I need your promise of silence before I can go on."

"I thought I just gave it to you."

Bob hesitated, but he had to tell someone he could trust and it spilled out of him, "Our food supply in Fairbanks will be non-existent in approximately 90 days. Our only hope of prolonging this situation is to get a shipment of frozen fish up from Anchorage and hopefully several tons of shrimp from Prince William Sound."

Brad stared at him, "We don't have 90 days, Chief. The comet will hit us way before then. If we survive that, then I guess we can eat seafood when all our canned goods give out."

"Always the eternal optimist," Bob said and then shrugged his shoulders and slowly sat down behind his desk, trying to hide the pain in his body. "One piece of good news though, they stumbled across several underground warehouses in Whittier well stocked with Vietnam era C-rations. Health officials have cleared the canned goods and a hundred pallets should be heading north within the week - if they can keep the tracks cleared. If for some reason we don't get those supplies…then sometime in late June, barring the space rock, people are going to be starving. When that happens, there's going to be a lot of gun play as everyone will be looking out for number one. Bob pointed to an Alaska map on his wall, "Even with the shipment, Alaska has less than five months to survive. Nothings coming in from Canada, our fishing fleets keep throwing out nets of contaminated fish…if and when they can weather the storms out there… they've lost a dozen boats and most of the crews on them…gutsy guys…women too! You'd never get me on one of those boats! I'd turn green and be sick for a week." Bob pointed to Wales on the Seward Peninsula where the 1st Division was positioned. "Plus, we still have the OAP to deal with when they make their move."

Brad had trouble thinking about the OAP, he could only visualize Kathy and kids starving - it left a bad taste in his mouth. "Starving kids…war, why should we even bother worrying about crime?" Brad asked, his voice growing louder before he shot up from the chair to begin pacing the room.

Bob remained silent as Brad walked in a tight circle in front of his desk. Stopping after a moment, he looked back at the Chief, "So, how many people know this uplifting bit of news about the food supplies?"

"26 including you and in 10 days it will become evident to people working in the Office of Emergency Management and of course those working in the warehouses," Bob said, as he looked at Brad with a strange expression on his face. "Times like this I wish I was a believer like you," he said in a low voice.

His admission startled Brad, to the point of switching from his concern for the family to focusing on his friend's salvation, "It's not too late, Bob. No matter how bad it gets, I know the Lord is still here. You just now reminded me of that fact."

"A lot of bad things happening out there right now, buddy. What's your Good Book say about all this?"

"The Bible has a whole lot to say about the End Times, more than I can understand. But my pastor truly believes our Lord's return is drawing near, all the puzzle pieces from Biblical prophecy are coming together."

"If you say so, but what about all that rapture stuff I heard so much about? Don't most of you believe you'll escape the tough times by some flight into space to meet your God? I sure don't see any wings on you, partner and...and what about that comet? Your Bible say anything about it?"

Brad couldn't help but smile, it was rare when his friend wanted to discuss Biblical prophecy, "First, rapture is a tough one to chew on. Even highly educated Christians debate that subject and how it will be played out. Some see it only as western civilization escapism." Brad began to pull out his pocket Bible, "Here, let me read you a verse or two."

"Not now, Brad...maybe later." He gestured to the door, "You'd better get on the streets, but remember to be safe out there tonight. Who knows, maybe you'll grow those wings yet and you can carry me up with you. Hey, maybe that God of yours can just swat that big old comet out of the sky." Bob was growing weak again and he didn't want Brad to see him throwing up.

"I know you're not mocking me, Bob. Fear is understandable and truly not un-Christian to feel. It's how we stand up when we're afraid that counts, and you're a courageous man."

"If I didn't know better, I'd think you were hitting me up for a raise." Bob smiled as he pointed at the door again, "Get out 'a here, you big lug." Knowing their meeting was over; Brad nodded and headed for the door. He stopped and turned when Bob spoke again, "Remember, Brad, when it was all black and white? We took the lowlifes off the street so our liberal courts could set 'em free. It was a game we played and now...now we're facing total annihilation. Seems so unreal, almost like we're living some weird sci-fi movie and there's no happy ending in sight." Bob sat back in his chair and stared at the Alaska map as Brad closed the door behind him in silence. Alone again, Chief Bob Osborne took his sunglasses off to rub his eyes in hopes of getting the pain to back off. The doctors had given him the word two days ago, "Your form of cancer is one hundred percent fatal, Chief. Soon, you'll be totally blind and for a few short weeks, maybe a month of agonizing pain... you'll be bedridden until death ends the pain. With limited drug supplies we will not be able to offer you much in the way of pain meds. I'm very sorry."

He was startled when his intercom came to life; "Chief, you're being summoned to the mayor's office again. He wants you there in ten minutes."

"Thanks, Susie." Bob pulled a couple of breath mints out of his top drawer, popped them into his mouth and stood up. A wave of dizziness struck him and he was forced to grab the desk to keep from falling down and dropped back into his chair. A moment later, the dizziness passed and he walked out of his office headed for City Hall. Between buildings he began mumbling to himself, "Who knows, maybe Brad's right with all this Jesus stuff he preaches. Maybe this bearded guy will ride across the sky on a flying horse and He'll sweep the OAP away with the wave of a mighty sword. Hey, He'll probably jus' kick that big old comet right back out into the sky like Jack Hicksford booted that winning field goal to win the last Super Bowl" ...*Right! And moose can fly.*

A COMING STORM

2- THE FIGHTING FIRST

"Then the seven angels who had the seven trumpets prepared to sound them."
Revelations 8.6 NIV

1st LIGHT INFANTRY DIVISON, ALASKA DEFENSE FORCE, CITY OF WALES, ALASKA - JUNE 12

In the frozen northlands of Western Alaska, only a 28 mile ice covered span of Arctic Ocean separated the village of Wales from the US owned island of Little Diomede. Less than two and a half miles further west was the island of Big Diomede, once owned by Russia but currently in the possession of OAP warlords. 23 miles separates Big Diomede from Russia's Chukotsk Peninsula. Both of these small islands were part of the Bering Strait land bridge that once connected North America and Siberia. Ice begins to form in the northern regions of the Bearing Sea in November and moves south to create a seemingly endless white ocean of pack ice which, in most places, is four to six feet thick. Beneath this ocean of ice is dark blue-green icy water where surprisingly the depth is often only a shallow 40 feet.

Built upon a rocky coastline covered by the thickening ice of winter, the village of Wales'had aged little in the last 120 years. This Eskimo community of unknown age is where the first humans probably wandered across the ice bridge from the Asian continent in search of food. The town consisted mainly of modern weather beaten wood frame homes, some with new metal roofs and a few late 1970's style modular units brought in by barge during summer months. There was a modern K through 12 school in the center of town which also served as the town's civic center on weekends and bingo hall on Wednesday and Friday nights. It was also where local dancers and drummers practiced for the annual gatherings held in either Anchorage or Fairbanks.

Unlike modern Alaskan cities, Wales was laid out without consideration for roadways. There were no standard city blocks, no sidewalks or parks and the few street lights were privately owned. Homes were planted to and fro, but mostly close to the water's edge and hard packed dirt roads meandered throughout for the few trucks and numerous 4 wheelers with trailers behind for pulling smaller boats. Larger boats, old fashioned skin type to newer aluminum, were left on the beach, but checked often or not in the event a sudden shift of ice crested the bank and endangered them. There was a definite lack of trees of any kind, but absolutely no shortage of dogs which were abundant in every size, shape, color, and breed.

Normally, Wales had a population of 150 to 200 Inupiak Eskimos - native people, who spent their lives in obscurity, living a traditional subsistence life style of hunting, whale and walrus and some trapping. Artists had an ample supply of walrus ivory and whale baleen for carving and scrimshaw. A few people still ran dog teams. But everything changed when Alaska learned of OAP's plan to invade North America and that Wales would be the point of entry.

In six months Wales had become a heavily populated military installation with more than 20,000 soldiers and civilians. Most of the soldiers were crowded into heavy canvas 12 man tents, barely heated by foul smelling oil stoves. Former U.S. Air Force KC-135 Tankers, once used to refuel aircraft, were now busy shuttling fuel oil from Eielson Air Base to Wales to keep troops warm and vehicles running.

MSgt. Sam Iukapah, First Sergeant for Charlie Company, 3rd Battalion, 1st Regiment of the1st Light Infantry Division, was responsible for both the general welfare and discipline for his ill trained troops. It was his job to keep his people from dwelling on an unpromising future facing the enemy's overwhelming strength awaiting across the ice. A hard task, since most of the younger troops felt they were here on a sure fire suicide mission. Originally from the Yupik village of Savoonga on the eastern shores of St. Lawrence Island approximately 150 miles southwest of Wales, MSgt. Iukapah was one of several hundred natives assigned to the 1st Division. Most of the native troops had come from the villages of Nome, Kotzebue, Point Barrow and Bethel. When the call went out, Inupiat People joined the army by the hundreds to fight off this new invader.

Many native people had family connections in eastern Russia and were concerned about them after the OAP moved in. They tried to keep hope, but the little intelligence circulated through camp concerning OAP tactics and prisoner policies left little room for hope. Trained since childhood to hunt, trap and survive off the land in harsh winter conditions, the Inupiat made up the tough backbone of the 1st Light Infantry Division. Considered by most U.S. Army survival instructors as equally qualified in the frozen north as any Army Special Forces unit, the young Inupiat continually struggled with the military's strange way of doing things. They often had to be reined in when they felt it was time to walk away from training sessions to do something more interesting. These actions brought them to the attention of MSgt. Iukapah and other Division NCOs who worked constantly to keep the troops focused on the job at hand. For the most part, it was going well enough, except at the moment- Iukapah was none too happy with one of his squads. Standing outside a recently completed snow-bag bunker, which resembled a large turtle shell, MSgt. Sam Iukapah pulled the hood of his parka back and looked overhead. He looked up wishing to see the stars but the sky above was blanketed in clouds of thick volcanic ash.

A light mixture of ash and snow was falling, coating the ground in dismal gray and it made him sad he couldn't see the northern lights dancing across the sky. He recalled how the multi-colored lights actually seemed to snap at times when the temperatures dropped suddenly to -40 and -50. His favorite was the bluish light, or when a starburst formed directly above him and shot out in all directions. Now, the air was filled with a foul pungent odor from volcanic activity; a smell he couldn't get used to. He hated having to wear a face mask to protect his lungs, but some of the men who had refused to wear the mask were now in the hospital with breathing problems and he needed to set an example. Lowering his gaze, Sam lifted the night goggles from his eyes and checked the luminous dial on his watch once again. 3rd squad was running late again, 16 minutes overdue on a short compass course over a well-plotted area of ice. For the last three hours they'd been running night maneuvers and Sam knew the men were growing weary of them, but with an attack eminent, the games could quickly become a case of plain survival and he wanted his troops ready. Not one was going to die because he hadn't trained them well enough.

Sam was a small man, even by Inupiat standards, and his wrinkled and leathered brown face made him appear much older than his 59 years. His Eskimo heritage left him with thick calloused stubby hands, short muscular arms and short bowed legs. Before he had proved himself, some of the white officers had referred to him as "fireplug", but he didn't really mind it. Back then he thought most white officers were ignorant and over arrogant savages.

Leaving Savoonga after his wife of 31 years died of heart failure, Sam and his only son joined family members in Anchorage where his son could finish high school and, hopefully, the memories less painful for both of them. Sam, desiring to better himself and live in the modern world enrolled in the University of Alaska and graduated with a Master's Degree in Anthropology. Invited to stay on as member of the staff, Sam taught a two year class on Arctic Living Conditions; Understanding the Eskimo People.

Then his son had died - a victim of cocaine's deadly curse. After the funeral, Sam left Anchorage and returned home to Savoonga, to mourn and escape the city life that killed his boy. He spent many long hours walking the beaches or hunting walrus; he disliked whale hunting, simply because it involved too many people. He had learned about reindeer herding as Savoonga's new herd grew with each season. Savoring these few quiet moments, Sam thought about better times and remembered his last walrus hunt and the long, but pleasant trip back home; and the deep green waters of the Bering Strait around him. He had encountered other hunters, but he was in no mood to say more than hello, before motoring off. With no family on the island, he was happy just to contribute most of the meat to the community - especially when an old toothless grandmother of some age came up and hugged him. His memories and peace were abruptly interrupted when 3rd squad finally showed up with a load of excuses for their tardiness. Not buying into the lies and knowing by the looks on their faces they'd been goofing off, Sam sent them on an additional 2 mile hike. Adding that they were to bring back a note from 2nd Battalion's CP, located out on the ice pack to show they had indeed made it there. Ignoring boisterous complaints, he watched them disappear into the darkness and then returned to the warmth of Charlie Company's CP. He'd put his time in on the ice, now it was time for the young ones to learn the true harshness of navigating the ice pack without stars to guide them.

Captain Myers, C Company's Commander sat at his desk, which had been acquired from a school classroom, reviewing personnel files. He looked up when Sam entered the tent. "Have all the squads returned, Sam?" Myers asked.

"Yes, sir, but I sent 3rd squad out two miles for bein' last. Next time they move faster."

"It's pretty cold out there, Sam. Those boys aren't as tough as you."

"They keep walkin', won't freeze. They have lights and ears. Use other camp lights to guide on and come back same way, not too hard," Sam said briskly. He warmed his hands over one of the three tent stoves used to keep the CP almost livable, but he disliked the stench of the burning oil.

Captain Myers shook his head and smiled, he knew Sam's pretense of a limited vocabulary would often crop up when he was upset about something, or when his act of playing the ignorant Eskimo helped him escape extra duties when some new white officer was assigned to the unit. In actuality, Sam's language skills in the proper use of the English language were quite extraordinary and he could speak in four separate Eskimo and Indian dialects. Myers knew that Sam was studying the Russian language when the Alaska Defense Force called upon his services. "Just the same, send one of the corporals out looking for them if they don't show up within 45 minutes. I don't want them freezing to death out there or scrounging off another unit."

"Yes, Captain." Sam often thought Myers pampered the troops too much, but he liked the young man and respected his authority. *Must have been pretty confusing for him, a white army officer from Idaho, to come up here and find himself placed in charge of a bunch of unruly Eskimos.* Sam had read in the history of the USA how the army had often placed white officers in charge of other racial forces; Japanese-Americans and Afro-Americans in World War II and both units had served with distinction. The Japanese-American had been the most decorated battalion in World War II, while the Afro-Americans became well known for the construction of the Alaska-Canada Highway, which joined Alaska to the Lower 48. With patience on the part of the white officers, Sam hoped the 1st Division would join the ranks of distinguished units. He would do his best to make it so - even if that meant leading a few ivy-league 2nd lieutenants by the hand when the shooting started.

"Is there any new word from our men on Little Diomede," Myers asked his communications man.

"No, sir...you want me to check with the Command Center?"

"Naw, I was just wondering." Myers laid the paperwork aside, sipped from a Styrofoam cup and then promptly spat the liquid out onto the plywood floor, "Can't someone please make a decent pot of coffee around here?" He poured the rest of the coffee out in disgust and stood up to zip up his parka, "C'mon, Sam, let's go out and check the line."

"You said it was cold out there, Captain, sir," Sam said as he pulled his fur mittens back on.

"I keep hearing how tough you Eskimos are and yet, I keep seeing you guys standing around the stoves."

"We're tough, not stupid...sir," Sam said with a sheepish grin.

Charlie Company's area of responsibility consisted of a quarter mile of shoreline positioned between Bravo and Delta Company. Charlie Company was living in tents protected by stacked up snow filled canvas bags while their heavy weapons platoon manned eight small bunkers built of two feet thick ice blocks. It took the engineers several days to build these structures; ice was cut from the off-shore icepack, hauled back to Wales and cut to form before being arranged and stacked to form the bunkers. But this would protect the 81mm mortars and heavier 30mm Gatling Guns from flying shrapnel when the enemy's expected artillery barrage began. Winds, which sometimes gusted to 80 mph or better, blew in off the ice pack encasing the snow bag bunkers in a fine sheet of ice and camouflaging them until they faded into the surrounding landscape.

Outside of the heavy weapons platoon, the large company bunkers were armed with single ASP 20mm Cannons, supported by two of the old reliable Browning .50 caliber machineguns. Smaller bunkers were armed with Vietnam era Saco M-60 machineguns and Saco MK-40mm automatic grenade launchers. A lot of the older weapons had come from US Army storage warehouses, but they were serviced by men and women who knew what they were doing and they had plenty of ammo.

Foul smelling oil stoves kept those inside the bunkers from freezing to death, but it certainly was not warm and the smoke could give their bunker position away to heat source imagery devices. Still, this allowed the men and women to survive the rotating 8 hour shifts, as they waited for the enemy to attack. The weather people had shown the actual temperatures at -45° but wind chill factor plunged it to -64° or lower. Exposed flesh could freeze quickly at those temperatures so troops had to keep a constant awareness of survival.

Behind the front line positions was a second series of mortar batteries, with both 60mm and 81mm tubes. Further back in town, camouflaged from aerial surveillance, M-119/105 mm artillery units stood ready to repel the invader's armored vehicles. It had taken nearly two hundred flights by cargo aircraft and helicopter to fly all the needed equipment out to Wales, and that was only after the engineers had installed lighting, lengthened the airstrip to handle the planes and cleared a large helipad. They had lost one Blackhawk helicopter and the nine men and women aboard. Two C-130 cargo aircraft had broken down, but were up and flying within hours. Despite the hurried activity, the evac hospital reported only 22 cases of 2nd and 3rd degree frostbite and 14 other injuries related to the quick movement of equipment and construction of fortifications.

A painful gust of icy wind struck a line of shivering soldiers outside a large tent adjacent to the school gym forcing them to huddle together for warmth while they waited for the chow line to move. Extra tarps were hung to offer some protection, but the wind blew through openings and penetrated the thick parkas the troops wore. The chow line was moving slower than normal and after leaving Captain Myers at C Company's Headquarters, Sam went to find the cause. He bypassed the line, ignoring complaints by troops who didn't recognize him and thought he was taking cuts and walked inside the chow hall – a tent of giant proportions; 70 feet long, 16 wide and nearly 24 feet high in the center. Since rations were served only once a day, no one complained about the quality of chow, but they did object to the quantity and occasionally a fight broke out between combat troops and cooks.

"Hey, Sarge, any chance we can get a couple days leave in Anchorage?" Pvt. Asghook asked with a hopeful gleam in his youthful eyes when he saw it was Sam passing. Everyone knew the answer to that one, but joking about it seemed to help. Leaves were canceled months ago and short weekend passes were only issued on an emergency basis.

Before Sam could reply, a heavyset corporal from another squad butted in, "Only way you're gettin' to Anchorage is in a body bag, troop. No leaves, no passes, no…" The corporal stopped when he saw the icy glare in Sam's eyes.

Sam turned away to face Asghook, "Why would you want to leave here? You got good chow, good friends to share your misfortunes with and even a warm bed. All provided by the Alaska Defense Force…What more could you want, private?"

Before Asghook could reply, another young soldier piped up, "But, Sarge, Asghook's got no friends and he lost his bunk in last night's poker game." Laughter broke out among those close enough to hear the exchange. Pvt. Asghook, who had joined the laughter, stopped when he realized the joke was on him and glared at the corporal.

Sam got the line moving again after having a brief, but stern word with the head cook about speeding things up. As he turned to leave, he spotted an unshaved PFC standing over a stew pot with a smoldering cigarette dangling from his lower lip. Walking up to the man, Sam surprised him by slapping the butt from his mouth, "I don't like ashes in my food, cookee, and these men don't either. You smoke outside with the rest of the troops…or don't smoke at all. It's a disgusting habit!"

"Yes, sir…I mean, yuh got that right, Sarge."

Sam looked to the man's supervisor, "This clown needs a shave and probably a bath, Sergeant. Food might taste better coming from a squared away troop."

"I read you five-by-five, First Sergeant. Consider it done."

1ST DIVISIONAL HEADQUARTERS

A large white bed sheet hung from the ceiling and was tacked to the side of the Command tent wall. On it was hung the organization chart for the 1st Division and under the 1st Division were three black lines going downward to identify the 1st, 2nd and 3rd Regiments. Each regiment was commanded by either a major or lieutenant colonel and underneath the regiments were similar black painted lines going to each regiment's 1st, 2nd and 3rd Battalions. These units were commanded by majors and under each of these battalions were listed Alpha, Bravo, Charlie and Delta Companies, which were commanded by captains. Each company was made up of thee platoons and a heavy weapons platoon, and these platoons were commanded by either 1st or 2nd lieutenants. Below that, but not shown on the chart, were the individual rifle squads, all commanded by corporals or sergeants.

Colonel Freeman was well past the normal age for military retirement and, at 71, he was a bit of a grizzly old fellow, whose bite was far worse than his bark. What was left of his white hair was cut extremely short and he wore a pair of silver rimmed reading glasses perched atop his nose. He was dressed in Army leaf pattern camouflage, a bit faded from years of wear in active military days and his arctic boots were bloused 4 inches above his ankles. He wore a left side shoulder holster, which held a very old Colt .45, 1911 model pistol with aged ivory grips on which one of his Eskimo artists had scrimshawed "1st Div." with the eagle symbol of his current rank beneath. There were some who thought the colonel resembled former President Dwight D. Eisenhower, but the colonel had never made the comparison. Privately, he liked to think he was more like General George Patton, especially after George C. Scott had played the title role in "Patton". With one hand on his hip, holding a paper, he stood behind a large plywood map table, held up by three sets of saw horses. The map showed the placement of his command around the Wales area. He was reviewing a newly arrived radio message from ADF Command-Fairbanks.

From his commander's sour expression, Major Jeb Stewart, newly assigned as the Division Intelligence Officer, knew his Division Commander was none too happy with the contents of the message.

Crumbling up the message and tossing it into a special burn bag, Colonel Freeman lifted his eyes and addressed Stewart in a stern voice, "That's it! Command says they've sent us all the supplies they can. We are officially on our own from this moment on."

"Sir, no disrespect to Command, but someone on the General's staff has a screw loose. They must realize we're standing out here like the proverbial sacrificial lamb. Command can't expect us to stop an invasion with only one division against a whole army of hardened combat veterans, supported by heavy armor and air cover. The OAP has just come off an invasion of Russia… it will be like stopping a massive wave of army ants…Who do they think we are, idiots or superheroes?"

Colonel Freeman stifled a laugh as he looked at Major Stewart and replied in a softer tone, "Probably a little of both, Jeb. But our task is a simple one. Hold the line while our other forces can prepare an adequate defense in the interior." He walked over to a large map of Alaska, pinned to a section of canvas tent wall and pointed to Wales with his left index finger; a finger missing the outer joint and fingernail - victim of frostbite from an act of sheer stupidity during a long ago caribou hunting venture. "General Saunders knows there's no way we can hold the OAP here, but we can slow them down some and in the process, reduce their strength as they cross the ice. They have no cover out there and remember- we have the high ground."

Jeb could only shake his head in respectful awe for his commander, but he couldn't help but state the obvious, "Sir, I might point out this high ground you speak of is only a large mound of dirt dug up when they built the school and it only sticks up 12 feet ."

"Measured it, did you?" Freeman asked as he stepped away from the map.

"Might I also point out a similar situation in our nation's history- we called it the Alamo and you know how that one ended?"

Colonel Freeman tossed the radio message onto his desk and plopped his old body down to rest his arthritic legs, "Strange you bring that particular battle up, Jeb. Helps me make a point you're missing. Sure, those Texas heroes knew it was suicide to stay and fight against the overwhelming strength of General Santa Ana's army. They could have left or surrendered, but they made a choice to stand tall. They did their duty and from inside that old mission, they inflicted heavy losses upon the Mexican Army. By the time Santa Ana faced General Houston's army at San Jacinto, his numbers had been depleted and they lost the war. Texas was born and it was those few courageous men in the Alamo who helped win that freedom." Colonel Freeman gazed at a miniature globe sitting on the corner of his desk, "This planet of ours is about to die, Jeb and we're probably going the way of the dinosaur unless God can stop it from happening. We've got freak storms, volcanoes, earthquakes, flood and plague... mankind has finally accomplished what sci-fi writers have foretold for decades. We've actually blown ourselves out of existence and some alien race will visit this little burned out rock and wonder what happened here?"

"You believe in little green men, Sir?" Jeb asked.

Colonel Freeman smirked in response to the question and then remembered a line heard long ago, "A learned man once answered that question with, 'It would be a shame, that with all that's out there we'd be all alone.'"

"Maybe so, Colonel," Jeb replied as he glanced down at the Colonel's globe and for a brief moment focused on the eastern coastlines of the U.S. His thoughts drifted to his parents. He knew they were dead. From the best intelligence he could gather, several OAP missiles impacted the Washington DC area and his parent's home was only 14 miles from the nation's capital.

"Jeb, I've got an assignment for you."

"Sir?" Jeb's mournful thoughts slowly broke away from home. He'd been thinking of Christmas morning; his mother probably making a lavish breakfast for his dad, making coffee and rolling out those huge cinnamon sweet rolls Jeb loved...eggs and bacon, sliced ham and mounds of hash browns...her routine Christmas breakfast. *And Dad...he'd still be in the shower...and I hope to dear God they never felt a thing. In a microsecond she and Dad, maybe some of the family, perished along with several million other souls. Damn those people...I hope we kill them all!*

"Major, if I can have your full attention...I'm sending a platoon out to relieve some of the men on Little Diomede and you're going out there with them."

"Little Diomede?" Jeb sounded confused, he wasn't a combat soldier.

"Catch up with me, Major. We're about to go to war!"

"Sorry, sir. I was just thinking about...never mind. What are my orders, Colonel?"

"I need new intelligence, Jeb and a prisoner or two could make that possible. Command needs to know when the OAP is planning to make their move. So, get your gear and report back here in one-hour for a mission briefing." Colonel Freeman returned Jeb's salute, eased back in his canvas camp chair and began to rub his eyes. Between the fumes from the oil stoves and tension of command, he had one nasty headache brewing up. It was only concern for his beloved Alaska that he returned to uniform, but at this moment he wished he was back at his cabin, sitting in front of his woodstove with a good book in his lap. Now he doubted he'd ever see the old homestead again. He reached into his soft canvas briefcase and pulled out a clear unlabeled container of Aspirin. He washed three of them down with a swig of canteen water and stood up to return to the map board. When he did, several other staff officers moved up to join him with note pads ready.

As he left the Command tent, Jeb was struck in the face by a wall of icy air that nearly froze him in his tracks. A strong pungent odor accompanied the falling ash that had taken time to grow accustomed to. Many of the troops were still dealing with upset stomachs and breathing problems. Disliking the issued face masks, he preferred to pull a green wool scarf up to cover his mouth and nose from falling ash. But it was still freezing cold and he shivered as he walked through the darkness. Halfway to his tent he stopped suddenly as he remembered Colonel Freeman's new orders... *did he say prisoners? That means...Oh, God...I'm not a combat troop! I work intelligence, sit at a desk and review documents. I'm trained to interrogate prisoners; I don't go out to enemy lines to kidnap some wayward Chinaman. People can get killed doing that!*

Inside his command tent, Colonel Freeman half-listened to one of his staff give a briefing on logistics, while he fingered one of the silver eagles pinned to his collar and thought of his concern for the readiness of his command. His aged eyes were surrounded by deep worry lines and his cheeks, pale from weathering the constant cold, were lined with deep canal-like wrinkles. The ravages of age nearly hid a two-inch long scar earned in Desert Storm, when he commanded an elite Special Forces team against Saddam's finest. Well respected by the men and women of his command, Freeman's Division maintained the lowest desertion rate in the Alaskan Command and the least amount of court-martials or Article 15 administrative actions for lesser offenses. He was proud of his troops and was always the first to point out to Command how these statistics were mostly due to the integrity of his Eskimos and Interior Athabascan Indian troops. The Eskimo people and interior Indians had rarely gotten along and many centuries of battles were fought over hunting grounds and blood feuds, but now they had a common enemy and they had put aside their own problems to join forces and face the OAP. Rubbing his chin and feeling the coarse two day growth, Freeman decided he was in need of a shave. Though he had issued a directive to allow the men to grow beards to help protect their faces from the severe weather, he preferred to keep his face shaven and wasn't surprised to see that most of his troops had followed suit with their commander. Putting all the reports aside, Freeman dismissed his staff and stood up. He opened the top drawer of a file cabinet beside his desk retrieved his leather shaving kit, an old Christmas gift from his wife; donned his parka, notified his Exec where he would be, and headed for the latrine tent.

"Need to clean up, Doug...I'll be back in a minute or two."

"Yes, sir. We'll keep the coffee hot."

LITTLE DIOMEDE ISLAND, ALPHA COMPANY- 2112 HOURS

Major Jeb Stewart, wearing a heavy military parka with attached white camouflage snow shell, nervously accompanied an undermanned platoon of 27 Eskimo Scouts out to Little Diomede Island. He was bundled up in a thick goose down sleeping bag for the cold, riding in one of five MT-850 ATV dual-track vehicles. First manufactured for recreation, these hardy little transports were soon part of the military fleet because of their capability of holding (8) combat personnel with personal equipment or a ton of field equipment. Early 800 models were gas fed, but the newer 850 models were powered by a low-geared 6.2 diesel engine. Making the 28 mile drive out to Little Diomede in less than four hours, Jeb looked out the front windshield, partially frosted over from the severe cold, and gripped his rifle tightly when he spotted a lone figure standing beside a large ice-covered fortification.

"It's okay, Major...He's one of ours," Lt. Jerry Johnson said.

Jeb nodded his head and then lifted his infrared night vision goggles from his eyes when the vehicle came to a halt. Jeb dismounted, still warily holding a .45 caliber pistol ready at his side as the heavily garbed man approached. He didn't notice any of the Eskimos getting excited, but he wanted to be cautious. He'd never been this close to the front before and didn't want to be stupid on his first trip.

Lt. Jerry Johnson, a full blooded Inupiat Eskimo, unfolded himself from the cramped ATV, tossed his field pack to the ground. Shouldering his rifle, he walked up to Lt. Upulak, who approached Johnson and slapped him on the shoulder with friendly enthusiasm, "Jerry, I heard those buggies of yours almost fifteen minutes ago. They're making too much noise on the ice.

Some OAP patrol probably heard you too. You should've parked further out and hiked in the last couple of miles."

Johnson ignored the kindly rebuke and replied, "I'll remember that the next time I come out to relieve you."

"Relief?" Upulak asked in surprise. "Thought you was comin' out to reinforce us."

"Brought one platoon out here with me an'..." Lt. Johnson stopped when he suddenly remembered he had a superior officer standing there in the cold. "I'm sorry, sir." He then quickly gestured to Lt. Upulak, introduced the two officers and then asked, "Where's the CO?"

Since salutes were not required on the front lines, Lt. Upulak offered his gloved hand and welcomed Jeb to the front. "Welcome to our island resort, Major." Upulak pointed to the west, "Our beach may be off limits at the moment, but I can guarantee you'll find a beautiful island girl behind every palm tree." This was an old Arctic joke, being that there were no palm trees, nor any other type of tree on Little Diomede or throughout most of the Arctic Region.

"Real cute, lieutenant, now how about you taking me to your CO?"

"Yes, Sir... you'll find him in the dungeon."

"Dungeon?" Jeb asked, and then added, "What are you talking about?"

Upulak shook his head once before he pulled his parka hood up and then replied further with a loud, "Follow me, Major and please watch your footing- slippery ice."

Jeb holstered his pistol, shouldered his rifle and followed Upulak down a snowy path leading to the front door of an old concrete building. With no visible lights and their observation post far too close to the enemy to show even as much as a flashlight, the men and women on Little Diomede relied on infrared and touch to make their way. Soon, Jeb, again wearing infrared goggles to keep from running into a wall of sheer ice over grumbling granite, found himself walking down a stairwell coated in thick, but slippery ice. Surprisingly, Jeb, who, like everyone else, was wearing chains on his boots for traction, noticed that the farther down they went, the colder the air seemed to get.

Knowing what the major was probably thinking, Lt. Upulak said, "Place is like a freezer, even colder down here than outside."

"How's that possible?" Jeb asked.

"I'm not a scientist, Major, but we think it's the icy walls combined with a touch of humidity from our presence that makes it feel colder," Upulak explained as he led Jeb down the last set of stairs. Inside, a rope handrail helped them find their way down and offered a sense of support on the icy stairs. When they reached what Jeb thought to be the lower level, Lt. Upulak made a sweeping gesture, "This is home, Major; you'll find Captain Blackstone in the next alcove."

"Thank you, lieutenant," Jeb said. A blind spot in his goggles indicated a light showing in the distance. Removing his goggles and the scarf that protected his mouth, he headed toward the light and found it was produced by a small kerosene lantern surrounded by several troops, who were using the illumination to play cards or read an old letter. One of them sat on a rolled sleeping bag writing a letter using a pencil that had been chewed down to the wood; most of the pens had frozen. Rounding another bend, Jeb found Captain Blackstone sitting on his rolled sleeping bag changing wool socks. Flickering flames from two candles gave the large room an eerie appearance; casting strangely shaped shadows that danced on the icy walls as Captain Blackstone and the men moved about. "I gather you must be Captain Blackstone," Jeb startled Blackstone and stood back as the officer jumped to his feet with only one boot on.

"Sorry, sir," Blackstone said. "But, I wasn't advised of your arrival."

"Put your boot on, Captain," Jeb ordered. "I'm Major Stewart, the new Intel Officer from Colonel Freeman's senior staff."

Blackstone pulled the remaining black bunny boot on and shook hands with Jeb, "What brings you all the way out here, Major?"

"Brought out a relief platoon and some mail," Jeb replied. "Colonel Freeman wants to rotate the men out here every 48 hours. Send the men and women back for some hot chow, a hot shower and a couple warm nights of sleep before the proverbial balloon goes up."

"They'll appreciate that. Hold on, sir," Blackstone said and then shouted, "Lieutenant Upulak, get your men ready to move out and the mail handed out." The order echoed through the concrete cavern and hurt Jeb's ears.

Upulak popped out from a darkened corridor, "Mail's already in progress, sir and my troops are ready to go."

"Pretty sure of yourself aren't you?" Blackstone asked in a sarcastic tone.

"We've been out here the longest, sir. Beat the other two platoons by at least a good three minutes and its only right we go in first...Captain, Sir."

Blackstone shook his head, smiled and pointed toward the entrance, "Get 'em moving an' bring me back some more coffee grounds...maybe something sweet if you can find it. My sweet tooth is complaining something awful."

"Can do, Sir... if I can find any and don't have to kill anyone for it."

Blackstone ignored Upulak's response and turned back to Jeb, "Upulak is a good officer, Major. His men know this place pretty well. In fact, most of 'em hunted this area before the war. Some of the older ones even know the first names of the Russian Border Guards who worked on the big island."

Blackstone led Jeb over to a nearby propane cooking stove and offered him a cup of coffee from a blackened and badly dented coffee pot.

"It's weak," Blackstone apologized, "Our supplies are getting low and we need more propane."

"Won't the enemy detect the heat source or see your lights from a flyover?"

"You climbed the stairs, sir. We're too deep for our lights to be detected from overhead and there's nothing we can do about thermal imagery. Our own bodies produce enough heat to be detected if the OAP get close enough."

Jeb glanced around the concrete structure, "What is this place, Captain?"

Blackstone was a bit surprised by Jeb's question, having thought the division's Intel Officer would know all about Little Diomede Island. "US military built it back in the early days of the cold war to eavesdrop on the Russians. Now the only thing left is the ruins. All the radar equipment was carted off or stolen long ago. I had hoped to find some wood to burn, but I learned the hunters had burned it up long ago and now propane is our only source of heat."

Captain Blackstone sipped from his canteen coffee cup and watched as Jeb looked around the room, "What else is on your mind, Major?"

Without looking at Blackstone or answering right away, he continued to inspect some of the ancient graffiti scrawled on the wall, most still visible under the layers of ice. He replied, "Command wants to know when the OAP will attack so Colonel Freeman wants prisoners and I'm out here to lead a patrol over to Big Diomede to grab a couple."

Blackstone stared into the bottom of his cup and shook his head, "Sounds more like a suicide mission if you ask me, sir. The enemy holds Big Diomede. I doubt we can even reach one of their listening posts before they send a drone or one of their helicopters out." Blackstone stared at Jeb over the lip of his tin cup, his dark brown eyes bloodshot from too many sleepless nights and the constant cold.

A sergeant sitting nearby cleaning his rifle couldn't help but notice the physical resemblance between the two officers. *Almost look like brothers; Major mus' have Indian blood in him to have such high cheekbones and narrowing nose.* Both officers were 5'8", each had thick black hair, large dark brown eyes, thick bushy eyebrows and strong block shaped chins. The major difference was Blackstone's flat nose that came from Eskimo lineage and Jeb's sharp, previously broken nose produced by Irish-Scot heritage and one too many fights in high school.

"You know that old saying, Captain, 'ours is not to reason why, but to do an'..." Jeb lowered his coffee cup and looked about the room, "I need a squad of fearless lunatics, led by a tough lion tamer of a sergeant to make sure I survive this insane assignment."

"No problem, Major, but are you sure you want to tag along? Sounds like a job for some glory seeking 2nd lieutenant."

"My job," Jeb answered, without bravado, as he stretched his back out.

"Major, you surprise me. Here I was thinking all you Intel boys were a bunch of paper pushers and now I find a true warrior in their midst."

"Captain, I'm much more afraid of disappointing Colonel Freeman then facing the OAP," Jeb said. "Besides, I'll keep your sergeant out in front of me to stop all the bullets."

Blackstone broke out in a big smile and then hollered, "Sergeant Upasauk!" A moment later, a grim-looking soldier of miniature proportions appeared from out of the darkness. Jeb couldn't help but grin, the man wasn't big enough to block much more than a small breeze, much less a bullet coming above Jeb's hips. He estimated the man at less than 5 feet in height and probably 10 years older than Colonel Freeman.

"Major, this is Sergeant Upasauk. Don't let his size disturb you... he's one of my best men and a former Alaska National Guard Army Scout." Blackstone advised Upasauk to relax, speaking in their Eskimo dialect. "I apologize for being rude, Major, the sergeant's English isn't the best, but he knows the area better than anyone else in the regiment and you can take my word for it, he's one tough little Eskimo. He's hunted whale and walrus all through this region... he'll bring you back...alive."

Taking a brief moment to study the man, Jeb's initial opinion began to change. He liked what he saw in the sergeant's eyes, *He's got the eyes of a hunter and there's a lot of experience in those wrinkles.* It didn't escape Jeb's notice that Upasauk apparently viewed him with a not-to-subtle look of contempt for a white-faced staff officer and it caused a slight smile of appreciation to appear on Jeb's face.

Technically, Jeb was leading the patrol, but in actuality it was Sgt. Upasauk who was in charge of the 8 man squad. Jeb would walk in line behind Upasauk, with PFC Mayo pulling point man and staying at least 50 yards out in front of the patrol. Wearing white camouflage shells over parkas and covered in spotty volcanic ash, they wore black leather and fur lined caps and fur lined black leather mittens. Only the trigger finger on their shooting hand was separate, allowing them to fire if the need arose. They used infrared goggles to see and steel crampons with one inch spikes to bite into the ice as they cautiously worked their way towards Big Diomede. Their packs contained basic equipment for survival, extra ammo and a pick axe for ice work. One man carried a radio for line-of-sight contact with Blackstone.

Leaving the shores of Little Diomede they soon bypassed huge walls and towers of ice jutting up 6' to even 10' created by impact as the ice pack grew in size. They walked hunkered down, forcing each step forward, while fighting the icy wind blowing against them. Their faces were completely covered by the heavy wool black balaclava and the infrared goggles they wore over it. Visibility was still poor, but improved slightly the further they moved from Little Diomede and the winds slackened some.

Jeb initially hoped they could come across an OAP listening post, but they made no contact of any kind. This surprised him and he wondered why the enemy wasn't taking better precaution with the Alaskans so near. Then they came up to a large pile of pack ice and once having traversed it, had no problem seeing the bigger island. Bright red, yellow and orange flames from thousands of bonfires burned across the width of the island. With such brightness, members of the patrol were forced to keep adjusting their night goggles as they worked forward. Finally, Jeb exchanged his infrared goggles for his normal snow glasses.

Estimating they had traveled nearly seven miles, Jeb advised Upasuak to halt the patrol for a rest period. After placing the squad into a night defensive perimeter ring, Jeb had Upasuak lead him out to where PFC Mayo was waiting up ahead. Using high-tech 9 volt battery powered Motorola head mikes, which provided a maximum range of one mile and operated on a scrambled frequency, the squad was able to stay in contact without worry of being overheard by the enemy's sound detection equipment.

The fires appeared to be one continuous wall of flame, adding strength to the rumor Jeb heard through Command Intelligence that the OAP had torn up all the railroad ties from the Russian Railroad in Siberia. They were apparently burning the wood to keep troops warm. *So much for the Siberian Railroad…it's not going to be running again for a long-long time.*

Reaching PFC Mayo, Jeb and Upasuak knelt down beside the man and stared in silence at the size of the enemy's spearhead. Judging by the number of fires and the perimeter of the encampment, Jeb estimated the spearhead could easily be more than 100,000 soldiers. And that was only the forward element. Command Intel reported OAP troop carriers, heavy tanks and support equipment backed up all across Siberia's wilderness. *Why wasn't the United States better prepared for this? Why were we stripping our military? China was buying up everything they could get their hands on and we twiddled our thumbs.*

"Must be ten thousand fires...never seen so many people." PFC Mayo whispered over his radio, to be heard over the sound of the harsh winter wind. "I can't make out if they have any heavy armor, just too much glare. On most nights we can see the glow from Wales, bouncing off the ash clouds. But I didn't expect this."

Using a pair of binoculars, Jeb scanned the horizon and slowly shook his head in awe. "I had hoped to get closer, but it's much too risky. I won't endanger the patrol this way. I had wanted to find an LP or some patrol we could ambush, but the OAP appear to be overly confident with their force and have failed to put out an advanced guard."

"Light's to their backs, we could sneak up and grab one or two." PFC Mayo suggested.

"No. We're going to need every man and woman we've got when the attack comes. No sense foolishly wasting a patrol out here now." Jeb gave the enemy encampment one more look through the binoculars and then snapped several photos with his mini-camera, "I've seen enough, let's head back."

Sgt. Upasuak replied with two words, "Back now" and then tapped Mayo on the shoulder. "Wait, you count 90 beats then you follow."

"Yes, Sergeant," Mayo replied. He turned to watch the enemy front and slowly shook his head in awe.

Following Upasauk, Jeb figured 90 beats meant heartbeats. *I guess it makes more since checking your pulse than having to stare at your watch and screwing with your night vision.* Jeb rounded an 8 foot tall chunk of ice, which had shot up when the ice pack formed, lost his footing and barely caught himself before nearly falling flat on his face. The wind was picking up and he used his rifle to help boost him to his feet. Only then did the reality of his location hit him, *I'm walking on the Arctic Ocean...six feet below is...is the ocean...what if it cracks...I could fall right through.* From that moment, Jeb stepped a bit more cautiously worried about falling through a crack at any moment. He remembered walking out on to a pier with his dad when he was young, frightened he might fall through the narrow cracks between the boards and drown in the surf below. *Stupid, childish fears! I gotta shake them.* Jeb's uneasiness was heightened when he suddenly heard a strange growling noise in the wind to his left and stopped mid-stride. *What the...*He didn't finish his thought because a truck sized shape slammed violently into him, drove him against a massive wall of standing ice and knocked the air out of him. A great creature of nightmarish qualities lay upon him and ripped his night vision goggles off his head, before rendering him unconscious with a painful blow to his head. His last conscious thought was of a fuzzy white teddy bear, like the one he gave his girlfriend in high school.

"Major...wake up, Sir!" Upasauk held Jeb's bandaged head in his lap as he attempted to revive him.

With a not-too gentle shaking, Jeb finally opened his eyes ever so slightly and asked the proverbial, "What happened?" Sitting up with Upasauk's assistance, Jeb winced when a piercing pain stabbed him through his right shoulder; his head felt like someone had been using it for a wild game of kickball. The rest of his upper body throbbed in rhythm with his heartbeat and a bad case of nausea was along for the ride. "What hit me?" Jeb asked and then jerked to his left as he vomited.

Upasauk waited and then replied, "A bear, Sir." He pointed to Jeb's right, where a large and very dead polar bear lay.

"Polar bear? I was attacked by a polar bear!?" The trembling began as he recalled the frightening sound of the bear's teeth scraping across his helmet and the pain of his claws digging into his shoulder. If not for the helmet and Kevlar vest, Major Jeb Stewart knew he would have most likely joined the ranks of bear victims.

"600...maybe 650 pounds... thought they all dead," Upasauk said. He turned away from Jeb to admire the great beast and in a mournful voice, said, "He hunted us, stayed downwind until make attack."

"How...how'd you kill it?" Jeb noticed the rest of the squad had moved up and set up another defense perimeter around him and the bear.

"With this." Upasauk held up his rifle with a bloody bayonet attached to it. "Too close to enemy, no shoot."

"You took on a Polar Bear with a bayonet?" Jeb asked in astonishment.

"Mayo use his too...bear was busy with you. Had back to us. Make quick kill."

Jeb was stunned, but he remembered to say thanks a few dozen times while the squad skinned the bear.

"You need to stand up, Major. Ice kill if you down too long." Upasauk helped Jeb to his feet as two of the older men used sharp skinning knives to remove the bear's thick white coat and cut the meat up into small portions for easier transport. Upasauk recovered the bear's skull, wrapped it in a grayish poncho cover and placed it, along with the bear's claws, into his field pack. When they had finished, the patrol returned to Little Diomede with a bloody bear hide stretcher carrying their injured officer. Once dismissed, they rushed to share news of the great bear that had nearly killed Major Stewart. To Jeb's surprise, most of the men were more interested in the bear story than hearing about the size of the enemy force on Big

Diomede. Except for Captain Blackstone, who wanted to know every detail Jeb could provide about the enemy. Stretched out on a sleeping cot while a medic worked on him, Jeb asked Blackstone how many troops could concealed out here?

"Major, I'd rather have a single squad out here with me. That's all I need to issue an alert when the OAP make their move. They'll sweep right over this place, even with a full company of shooters. So, unless you can dig up a couple more divisions, it's better to lose a single squad."

"You'd like me to pass that along to Colonel Freeman?"

"Yes, sir… Have him remove most of my company except for a squad-sized force of unmarried volunteers. That's all I need to handle the watch an' work the radio."

Jeb, tired of being messed with, pushed the medic away and attempted to rise, "Okay, I'll make your request." Jeb gritted his teeth as a jolt of intense pain shot through his shoulder and caused his world to spin. Medical Specialist Norman Iverson grabbed a hold and gently lowered him back down on to the cot.

"Major, I think your shoulder is dislocated. I might be able to reset it here, but I'd prefer to stabilize it and let the hospital take care of it. I've also sewn your head up; you'll have some impressive scars to show the women folk. But I'm sure the hospital will do a better job on your shoulder and back wounds with staples, so I have them all taped up."

"You are one lucky man, sir," Iverson said. "Not many men would have survived such an attack."

Captain Blackstone spoke to the medic, "Get him loaded up on whatever dope you've got left, Norm. He's got a rough ride ahead." Blackstone stood up and went in search of Sgt. Upasauk.

Iverson opened his medic bag and retrieved a second small ampule of morphine. He was getting low on the drug and hoped to get more soon. Two men had broken bones from falls on the ice and had pretty much used up his limited supply.

A moment later, Jeb was again floating off into la-la land and didn't let out as much as a squeak as four men loaded him into a track vehicle and cushioned him with sleeping bags. On the trip back he entertained the men with strange tales of his boyhood and a yellow dragonfly he called Dudley.

1ST DIVISIONAL CP - 1322 HOURS

"Yes, sir, that's the way I see it, too. Blackstone requires only one squad to serve as a listening post. He'll know when the OAP starts to move an' they'll probably be dead 60 minutes later." Jeb, bleary eyed from a lack of sleep and holding his injured shoulder and arm in a sling, sat on a stool beside Colonel Freeman, as the two men looked over a large map of the area.

"Colonel, we could use the rest of Blackstone's company back here to man the line," a staff member added.

"How do you feel, Jeb?" Freeman asked in a friendly concerned voice.

"Like some kid's old rag doll, sir. But thanks to Sergeant Upasauk and PFC Mayo, I'll live. I owe my life to them."

Colonel Freeman agreed and said, "Captain Blackstone has recommended them for citations and I'll send along my signature of acknowledgment and support."

"They deserve it, sir." Jeb slowly pulled his arm out of the sling and cautiously began to rotate it. "Another couple days an' I'll be as good as new, except maybe my face. Last time I looked in the mirror I nearly frightened myself." His face was lined with four distinct claw marks, each swollen and dark bluish in color. The stitches Iverson had used were removed and the wounds were stapled closed by a surgeon. Thankfully, Jeb was under anesthesia for the procedure.

"You'll heal up just fine," Colonel Freeman said. "But you'll have some nasty scars, my boy. Either you'll look like a dashing rogue or a patchwork dummy, depending on how much plastic surgery you'll need. But at least you're alive. Very few people survive a Polar Bear...Yes, you are one lucky man."

"Do you want me to send a message out to Captain Blackstone and have him select his volunteers?"

"No Jeb. For a message like this I'll deliver it in person. I want to look those men in the eye when I order them to their deaths. I'm going out there tonight." Colonel Freeman sent Jeb back to bed and returned to his desk; he needed to send a flash- message to Command about his decision to reduce the force on Little Diomede.

1ST DIVISIONAL CP, 0210 HOURS-

Opening the tent flap wide with his good arm, Jeb entered the CP and was surprised to find Colonel Freeman sitting on the floor beside one of several diesel heaters used to keep the CP livable. Freeman had his boots off and was trying to warm them and his feet, the ride to Little Diomede and back had been a cold one.

"You wanted to see me, Colonel?"

"Give me your hand an' help an old man up off the floor," Freeman said to a nearby sergeant. He held his right hand up and the man clasped it to bring the commander to his feet. Seated behind his desk, Freeman grunted as he pulled on his boots.

Jeb again asked, "You sent for me, Sir?"

"I picked something up for you on Little Diomede, a gift from Sergeant Upasauk." Freeman dug into his green canvas map case and pulled out a dog-tag chain with (12) polar bear claws, each one drilled through at the base and attached by leather bonds.

Awestruck by the gift, Jeb didn't know what to say. After a brief hesitation, he took the necklace from Freeman's hand and pulled it over his head. "Well?"

"Looks great, Jeb, that's a real fine gift and I'm a might jealous."

"Thank you, sir. Did Sergeant Upasauk come back with the rest of the company?"

"That old man was the first to volunteer… in fact the whole company volunteered. It was tough, but Blackstone selected his squad and Upasauk was his first choice. The rest of the company remained absolutely silent on the drive back an' that's what I call real loyalty." Freeman turned sideways in his chair and stood to his feet.

He gave Jeb a thorough look before speaking, "How do you really feel, Major?"

Jeb was surprised by his formal tone and knew Colonel Freeman wanted an honest answer. "Sir, I'm a bit sore, but I'm ready for duty."

"That's what I wanted to hear." Freeman reached down and pulled out a thin file from his top drawer. "Jeb, I've got a request here for an Intelligence Officer with field experience. You're a good G-2, but what happens from now on out here doesn't require talents of your caliber." He tossed the file to the middle of his desk top, "I want you on the next plane scheduled for Fort Wainwright."

"But…but, Colonel, I want to be here and I don't really have any field experience."

"This decision is final, Major. You earned your field experience out there on the ice. You were smart enough not to risk your men against such overwhelming odds and that decision will always come first with me. Another officer might have risked his command to bring back a prisoner and in the process gotten his men killed or taken prisoner for no other reason than to obey that order. You weighed that order based on your situation at the time and knew that to carry that order out would assuredly kill troops. Enough said about that." Freeman's voice had taken on that stern formal tone that came with a long period of command. "Any questions?"

"Sir, do you have any idea what the assignment is?" Jeb asked then added "Who do I report to at Fort Wainwright?"

"It's in your orders, which you'll pick-up before you leave for the air field. You're traveling with a Priority AAAA travel rating. That means you leave on the next available transport. Understand, Major."

"I'll be ready, Sir," Jeb said. His tone expressed his disappointment in leaving.

Colonel Freeman respected Major Stewart for his response and knew he had made the right decision by getting him out of here. "Good luck, Jeb. It's been a pleasure serving with you."

"Thank you, sir." Leaving headquarters, Jeb walked out and looked in the direction of Little Diomede. His gut churning, Jeb struggled with a mixture of his nightmarish thoughts over the bear attack and the sad feeling he was deserting his comrades. "Probably be some desk job, interrogating suspected OAP spies or chasing down NEE sympathizers." Kicking a chunk of ice away, he marched off to pack his gear.

2ND & 3RD LIGHT INFANTRY DIVISIONS- COMMAND- FAIRBANKS - FORT WAINWRIGHT, 1450 HOURS

Buffeting strong head winds, the white and gray C-130 was forced to stay below the clouds of black ash, flying through valleys and barely missing a peak or two before it began its approach to Fort Wainwright. They couldn't fly through the clouds; the pilot knew all too well that ash sucked into the engines and the electrical energy caused by the volcanic eruptions would create havoc with the C-130's controls causing them to crash into some mountain. During those sporadic times when the ash began to fall, usually mixed with dirty snow, all the aircraft stayed on the ground. When it occurred during flight time, the pilot hugged the ground in the event he was forced down. The crew knew this was going to be a rough landing; dense ice fog was requiring the pilot to land solely based on his avionics. Staying beneath the ash and above the fog until the last moment, the C-130 groaned like the old beast it was, and shook wildly, as if the bolts and rivets were popping out causing great alarm to the aircraft's sole passenger. Jeb was sharing cargo space with several tons of damaged helicopter parts and a groggy loadmaster. He was beginning to understand what bronco riding might be like when he heard the loadmaster bellow their arrival over the aircraft's P.A. Struggling to keep from upchucking again, Jeb kept one hand clutched to the rim of a plastic bucket and the other, arm still in a sling, grasped tightly to a tie down strap. In the last hour he'd emptied the contents of his stomach into the bucket provided by the loadmaster, who kept reassuring him, "That's okay, Major. I've seen worse. Most army guys can't handle real flying." Adding to his discomfort was the smirk on the loadmaster's face. *He's really enjoyin' this…I think I'll kill him when we land…if I can stand up that is.* He stopped his thoughts of fantasy when the aircraft shook with the first bump of what pilots laughingly refer to as a three-point Alaskan landing; no crash-no burn-no law suit. Moments later inching through the ice fog, staying closely behind a "follow me" pick-up; close enough the pilot could reach out and tickle the driver's ears, the plane slowly taxied to the terminal to off-load the human cargo and pick up additional freight bound for Elmendorf Air Force Base. Once all four engines stopped, the loadmaster opened the aircraft's side door and tossed Jeb's baggage out. The aircraft quickly filled with an icy mist as the extreme cold air from outside met with the somewhat warmer air inside the plane. Thinking someone was on the tarmac catching bags, Jeb was enraged to see his lying on their sides with no one around. If it wasn't for how bad he felt, he'd have a harsh word or two with that loadmaster or someone on the ground crew. He pulled his parka hood and scarf up to protect his ears and to keep his lungs from freezing. He recalled that the Interior was colder than most parts of Alaska and always wondered why. Carrying his luggage, with some painful exertion, he had started toward the lighted terminal when a green camouflaged HUMMVV pulled up beside him. Leaving the engine running, the driver stepped out and presented a crisp salute. The man was attired in full ADF parka gear, including a golden colored cold-weather beaver fur hat reserved for officers.

"Major Stewart, sir?"

"I'm Stewart." Jeb dropped a bag and responded with a quick return salute and cringed from the pain it caused.

"Sir, I'm Captain Roberts. I've been sent here to pick you up."

"Fine. Would you help me with my bags and let's find someplace warm." Jeb picked up two smaller bags while Roberts grabbed the heavy duffle bag.

In the vehicle, where the temperature picked up to a sweltering -15°, Jeb asked Roberts for his Army Officer's I.D. card and was not in a good mood when Roberts replied with, "I'll show you mine, Major, if you show me yours." Exchanging I.D. cards and Intel I.D., both men began to relax a bit, neither of them admitting to the other that they had kept one hand close to a pistol if needed. There were so many spies and fanatics about, it paid to be careful and Intelligence officers tended to be a cautious lot when dealing with strangers, especially, when they appeared suddenly out of a curtain of thick fog with no one else around. Captain Wayne Roberts was the first to break the silence as they proceeded down a dark road, "Sir, in reviewing your file, I see that your uncle was a Medal of Honor recipient."

Jeb was surprised, "My uncle's medal was awarded posthumously, Captain. His name is ...was on the Wall." It saddened Jeb to think that a Chinese ICBM had destroyed all the great monuments of a proud nation.

"Sorry, sir, I didn't mean to bring up sad memories." Captain Roberts turned right at the next corner and nearly sideswiped another vehicle entering the intersection from the left.

"That was close!" Jeb exclaimed.

"Still a miss, Major," Captain Roberts replied.

The near accident sent a painful jolt through Jeb's shoulder and he grunted, "Still a stupid way to end one's life, Captain."

"When the ice fog is so thick, Major Stewart, which it is most of the time now, you get used to near misses, and a few fender-benders."

"I'd like to arrive safe and sound, Captain, if you don't mind."

"Not a problem, Major," Captain Roberts said, as he slowed to 25 mph.

After a moment of silence, Jeb finally asked, "What's happening around here that needs another Intel officer so badly?"

"Sorry, sir, this vehicle may have ears. You'll be briefed when we reach Command."

"Well, nice weather you have here. It's like driving through an ice cold cotton swab. What's the current temperature?"

"- 43° and dropping. Weather predicts -50° within eight hours and even lower tomorrow. Did you bring your sun block, sir?"

"Old joke, Captain, one very old joke indeed." Jeb was relieved that his stomach was beginning to relax. It helped that Captain Roberts was driving a bit slower. Seeing nothing beyond the windshield, except the headlights reflection against the thick wall of ice crystals, Jeb asked, "How do you drive in this? I'm having trouble seeing past the hood."

"I know the roads; where the stop signs are. Usually headlights cut through the fog when you drive slow enough. You look to the side now and then to see the sides of the road to make sure you're still on them." A few minutes later they stopped in front of a large building, but all Jeb could see was a wide set of concrete stairs. Anything above the stairs was concealed behind a barrier of sparkling ice crystals in a gray cloud.

"Just leave your bags in the vehicle, Major. We'll only be here briefly and then I'll take you to your room." Leading Jeb into the building, through one hallway and down another, Roberts stopped in front of a large set of double doors guarded by two very large MPs. Both of them scowled as they studied the two officers in front of them. After checking both Officer and Intel I.D. one of the MPs opened one of the double doors to allow them entry. In the next small office, a female sergeant in a crisp two piece dress uniform again checked I.D. cards before opening the next door. Such strict security surprised Jeb and even more so when he entered the next office to find General Glenn Saunders sitting behind a large ornate wooden desk.

Commanding General for all military forces in Alaska, General Saunders, 68, wore the four stars of a regular U.S. Army general. He was a native born Alaskan from a little community called Salcha. Raised mostly in the state's interior, he had risen up through the ranks, then retired here to fulfill his dreams of owning a remote hunting and fishing lodge on the Nenana River; a dream that was shattered with the outbreak of war. Called back to active duty by the Governor, he devoted 100% of his time to the military and the building up of Alaska's defense. An impressive set of black cloth qualification badges hung over his left shirt pocket; Airborne Jump Wings with three stars, each representing a combat jump; Army Master Aviation Wings and a Combat Infantry Badge with two stars. Over his right shirt pocket were qualification badges signifying Korean Jump Wings, Thailand Jump Wings and a British SAS award. A heavyset man with a rising hairline of mostly gray and a pair of gold-rimmed glasses perched upon his nose, Saunders stood 5"9" and had trimmed down to 164 lbs. In freshly starched gray camouflage with shirt sleeves rolled up past the elbow, the general gave little indication that he put in long hours since the loss of his wife of 38 years. He had a long hawkish face filled with character lines. Pained and bloodshot eyes clearly spoke of a man who had experienced one too many battles and sleepless nights. Yet it was his mouth that caught Jeb's attention, it was a bit too wide for his face and an old scar marked the right side from chin to the upper jaw.

Standing briefly with a stunned look, Jeb suddenly caught himself and jumped to attention as Gen. Saunders began to speak, "Major Stewart, your reputation precedes you. Please have a seat and I'll have the sergeant bring you some hot coffee. Captain?"

"Yes, Sir, I'd love some hot coffee," Roberts replied. He ushered a very nervous major toward a cushy brown soft leather chair, one of three situated in front of the general's desk.

"Sir, I apologize for my idiotic reaction. I wasn't expecting to be appearing before my Commanding General." Jeb turned to give Roberts a dirty look.

"Don't concern yourself. We're a pretty tight group around here. You'll get used to seeing me stumbling around the hallways." Gen. Saunders keyed an intercom and ordered the sergeant to bring in coffee for three then turned his attention back to Jeb.

"Colonel Freeman briefed me. I liked what I heard. You kept your head out there on Little Diomede. Some of the reports you've filed with my staff were quite well written and informative. You tend to be more thorough than some of my other officers, I like that."

Jeb was nervous and hoped the coffee would arrive soon. *He's setting me up for something…but what? Majors don't usually appear before the Commanding General to make small talk and receive compliments on their report writing. I've gotten myself into something.*

General Saunders waited for the coffee to be served and after the sergeant left, asked Roberts to provide Jeb with a brief rundown of the current situation.

"Major Stewart, the OAP has offered us unconditional surrender. This will be refused of course, but mainly because we've learned through reliable sources that the OAP plans to slaughter every man, woman and child after they seize control. There will be no state of occupation or labor camps as they promised because there simply is not enough food to feed everyone. Right now the OAP forces are going hungry. They have no known supply line with China since hostilities ended with the Russians. They've depleted nearly all the supplies they recovered from captured stockpiles in Siberia. Basically, the OAP army to our west is much too large for the supplies they allotted for this invasion and they're beginning to starve."

"We've received reports of cannibalism within the OAP ranks, using Russian and Native prisoners to fill their stew pots." General Saunders added.

That single statement caused Jeb's stomach to sour. The thought of human beings turning to cannibalism, he wasn't sure he could believe it. "Cannibalism?" Jeb's throat tightened up.

"Basic survival, Major," General Saunders said abruptly then advised Roberts to continue with a wave of his hand.

"They've marched through every town, hamlet, village and city, destroying everything in their path and committing every atrocity you can imagine. They've made the Rape of Nanking look like a college prank and even ripped up the Great Russian Siberian Railroad to burn the ties for heat and cut off any possible line of supply by train."

"Yes, I've seen that…the fires I mean…So, how can we stop them?" Jeb asked.

"We can't, Major Stewart," General Saunders replied. "I'm afraid there's simply too many of them to stop. Oh, they might starve to death or perish from the cold and we're really counting on that, but it's not within our power to defeat them. And that's why you've been brought here, Jeb." General Saunders stood up from behind his desk and took a seat in an unoccupied chair next to Jeb. He looked at Captain Roberts, "Wayne, why don't you fill Jeb in on our little plan."

Jeb? Boy, I'm really being set up now. First names usually mean suicidal operations like the last one I went on. I should have listened to them when they offered me that cushy supply office position in California…No, I'd still be stone cold dead there too-probably glowing in the dark or under tons of water.

Captain Wayne Roberts stood up and approached an old-fashioned school slide projector, picked up a remote control and lowered the lighting in the room then used the remote to lower a screen from the ceiling. The first slide displayed a map of Alaska, and the Canadian provinces of Yukon, Northwest Territories, British Columbia and Alberta. "As you are aware, major, the OAP are massing on the Chukotsk Peninsula and have a spearhead force spreading out on Big Diomede. We believe they will commence their attack on Wales somewhere around July 1st, within 24 hours of the time limit provided in their request of our surrender. Once their spearhead breaks through our defenses…" Roberts stopped himself, momentarily having forgotten that Jeb had just left a lot of friends behind in Wales. "My apologies, Major Stewart…Please understand, I in no way wish to confer that these men and women do not matter to me. I tend to conduct intelligence briefings in a matter-of-fact way. I know you've left behind friends and comrades."

"You may continue, Captain." Jeb said in a flat tone and gave the captain a hard glare.

"Thank you, sir. As I was saying we expect the spearhead to cross the Seward Peninsula in approximately two weeks. Once they reach the Dalton Highway, they have access to hard surfaced road for a direct approach on Fairbanks and control of the pipeline. At that point we presume they will send a sizeable force north toward Prudhoe Bay. If we have their plans down correctly, that spearhead will launch its attack on Fairbanks and Fort Wainwright in approximately 18 to 21 days. Eielson Air Base will probably be in their hands two days after that. Lack of roads will slow them down some until they reach the Dalton, but with the tundra and rivers frozen over, there won't be much to stop them. Once they secure Fairbanks, Fort Wainwright and Eielson, we expect the main OAP force to move south for Anchorage. They may or may not send a small force toward Fort Greely, depending on what their spies tell them or if the weather changes greatly and their planes can fly."

"What is our current strength here?" Jeb asked.

"At this moment we have the 2nd and 3rd Divisions posted here, a mixture of regulars and former National Guard, plus the North Air Wing at Eielson…roughly 44,000 troops and an estimated 10,000 militia." Roberts replied.

General Saunders added, "4th Battalion of the 3rd Division is spread out along the Alaska-Canadian border to keep the locals from making a mad dash across the border, upsetting our neighbors and getting themselves killed in the process. 4th and 5th Divisions are stationed in Anchorage and the 7th Battalion of the 4th is spread thinly between Seward, Valdez and Whittier, along the Prince William Sound." General Saunders coughed to clear his throat and continued, "Jeb, our plan is to position our main fighting force at Fort Greeley. All units will pull back from city centers prior to the enemy's approach, abandoning towns to the OAP - except we'll leave them empty of supplies and heavily booby-trapped. We'll make our last stand together at Greeley, fighting as Alaskans and Americans."

"Why Fort Greeley, General?" Jeb asked struggling to process all this in one gulp.

"There's a lot of open ground at Greeley - good for taking on tanks with shoulder mounted anti-tank weapons." General Saunders pointed to an AT-4 tank weapon in the corner of his office. Jeb wondered why the Commanding General would have such a weapon inside his office, but didn't ask and Saunders continued. "We know the OAP will be bringing a lot of heavy tanks against us. I've read the report on the defeat of the Russians; those tanks of theirs are steel juggernauts of destruction. Each one is twice as large as our Abrams and runs on less fuel than a HUMMVV. They carry multiple weapon systems and with three inch armor plating, those babies are nearly indestructible. I saw a photo of one; carried something like a cattle prod on the front. Word is they use it to mow obstructions down and that includes ice…or people. They'll mow a road across the peninsula and come plowing down the Dalton like a bunch of flaming banshees."

"Why have I been brought here, General?" Jeb asked, almost afraid to hear the answer. He sincerely hoped the general couldn't see the slight trembling in his sweaty hands.

"Jeb, you and Captain Roberts here are going on a trip…into Canada to be exact."

"Sir?" Jeb's jaw dropped and his mouth hung open for a brief moment. Not a typical officer's response, but this had all come as a shock and he was still healing up from his confrontation with the polar bear.

"You two will be carrying a special message to General Howard-Wright, Commanding General of all Royal Canadian Army forces in Western Canada, and an old friend of mine. Your mission is classified Top Secret Alpha and only General Howard-Wright is to know the contents of your message. I'll provide you with some bits of personal information to prove to Wright you've truly come from my staff."

Jeb was silent for a moment as he sorted this all out. Saunders took a sip of coffee. Wayne turned the lights on and the projector off. Jeb nervously took a gulp of coffee, cleared his throat and broke the awkward silence with the obvious question, "I gather then we're asking the Canadians to step in and give us a hand."

"Why not? Once the OAP controls Alaska, they'll march on Canada. Wright knows that, but that civil war with the French in Quebec has him pretty busy. He's probably waiting to see how much of a fight we can put up and what kind of numbers the OAP is bringing across. The papers you'll carry will provide that information and our plan for Greeley's all or nothing last stand defense."

"Is Fort Greeley the best location for a stand, Sir? I'd think Fairbanks…" Jeb stopped when he saw that General Saunders was about to interrupt him.

"With heavy armor leading the way, they'd blow Fairbanks into rubble and us with it. By placing our first line of defense in Delta Junction, eight miles from Greeley, the OAP will have to bring heavy tanks down a single lane highway across a major river and a bridge. We'll have them in a bottleneck and its good fighting ground. And like I said before, Greeley is good ground if you have to take tanks on."

"Why do you believe the OAP will stay on the roadway and not spread out?" Jeb asked. "The flats around there will still allow the OAP units to spread out."

"Based on the tactics they used in Russia, they prefer to keep the tanks on solid roadways or railroad beds whenever possible. They apparently left a lot of tanks bogged down in the early days of the Russian campaign and we're hoping they lose a lot more of those beasts on the trek across the Seward Peninsula. Now let's allow Captain Roberts to continue."

Wayne stood before the two officers, "Thank you, General… With the Canadian forces in support of our own, we may be able to defeat the OAP, or at least drive them back across the ice pack. We have possibly 400,000 civilians to call upon, a number of which are already enlisting to fight. Our navy, mostly former US Coast Guard vessels and three State Trooper boats are presently defending our fishing fleet. At last report, now several days old, our Intel has the OAP's great fleet approaching the southern tip of South America headed for the Strait of Magellan. By now, they've crossed into the Atlantic and though they face some horrific storms out there, we suspect their larger ships may be headed for the Mediterranean Sea and the Suez Canal. There's some pretty heavily contaminated zones out there, but again, Intel reports those new superships have been built to deal with that. Reports indicate that they plan to engage Israel, Libya and Egypt – the only three coastal countries still strong enough to oppose them. After that, with the exception of the European Empire, Canada and us, pretty much the remainder of the world will bow to the OAP Empire. They'll have the great oil fields of Saudi Arabia and North Africa, plus the massive farmlands of

South America and Africa to feed the survivors of the Tariq-Leroy Comet… if there are any. Doesn't make sense – something missing???"

"Jeb, your journey through Canada must be with great stealth and cunning. Nothing can stop you," General Saunders pointed to Wayne, "Captain Roberts is one of my best men from Special Forces and it's his job to keep you alive. We can't risk making radio contact with Calgary because General Howard-Wright has his own French spies to contend with and he might never get the message."

Both Wayne and Jeb were quiet. General Saunders seemed to know what they were thinking, "Yes, it is possible you two may be shot as spies, but you must reach him within seven days and how you do it is up to you. Beg, borrow or steal whatever vehicle you need, but try not to kill anyone unless you have no other choice. The important thing is to get those documents to him in person, he'll probably have a lot of questions and Jeb, be honest with the man."

Captain Roberts spoke up, "Our biggest concern will be Quebec sympathizers and Canadian deserters. Once across the border, we'll be in Canadian Army Officer's uniforms; that's why the general said we could be shot as spies."

Jeb shrugged and nodded, "Sounds like a lot of fun. I'll have to thank Colonel Freeman for volunteering me for this choice assignment." Jeb gave Roberts a strained smile, "Captain; how do we get across the border without getting our butts shot off?"

"We can't risk encountering military authorities until we reach Calgary. Hopefully forged documents will allow us to hitch a ride down the Al-Can Highway. A helicopter will drop us off close to the border and we'll simply cut across on foot, stay in the backwoods, parallel with the highway until we judge it's safe to hit the road and hitch a ride."

"And if we encounter patrols in those backwoods?" Jeb asked.

"I've planned for us to be dropped off approximately five miles south of the highway. We know the Canadians have no patrols that far off the roads. Their main concern is vehicle traffic, some crazed idiot trying to break through their barricades."

"Last time that happened, we nearly went to war with Canada. 23 dead Canadians and 35 dead Alaskans after a 14 hour fire fight. Not counting dozens of wounded." General Saunders said as he studied Jeb, wondering if the man was physically up for this journey. He switched channels and directed his question to Roberts, "What was the name of that jerk who led that convoy of fanatics?"

"He was a self-appointed Alaska Independent Party Militia colonel by the name of Weeks…Jason Weeks. Promised his people they could find safety in Wyoming and it cost him his life and the end of the Alaska Independent Party Militia." Jeb replied.

"Thankfully, cooler heads prevailed and war didn't break out. General Howard-Wright kept that from happening when other senior officers were crying for blood," General Saunders said.

"We've received word Quebec forces have entered an alliance with the New European Empire whose new emperor is a certified whacko," Roberts said " He sounds like another Adolph Hitler, calling himself a prophet from Heaven to save the white race. He got the job after becoming a big hero driving the Russians back and saving Paris from destruction."

"But this is good news for us because General Howard-Wright, who is also a Christian, believes this man to be the Antichrist foretold in the Book of Revelations." General Saunders hesitated when he saw the confused expression on Jeb's face. "Antichrist...it's from the Bible. In the Book of Revelations it's foretold that an Antichrist will come forth in the End Times."

"Sorry, sir, I'm not much of a church goer." Jeb cringed as he said it, remembering that General Saunders was known to be a strong believer in the Bible.

"Well your time is rapidly running out, Jeb. Time for you to make a stand against..." General Saunders stopped. "I apologize, Major, now isn't the time for this. As to Canada; this civil war with Quebec, and now their allegiance to a demonized emperor may very well be the catalyst to gain Howard-Wright's support. He doesn't need two enemies and prior to the outbreak of hostilities Alaska and Canada were on good terms."

"What if we don't make it through, General?" Jeb asked.

"We have back up plans, but in the event of capture, the less you know the better."

"When do we leave?" Jeb asked, hoping for a few hours of sleep before undertaking another life or death mission.

"About four hours from now, at 2000 hours. I'll see you off myself."

"Great, I'd better get some shuteye." Jeb stood up and presented a salute; General Saunders stood and returned it as the men left his office.

Studying the map before him, General Saunders sat down at his desk and whispered a brief prayer of safety for the two men then turned to the next item on his agenda, dealing with food shortages and deserters.

SOUTH OF NORTHWAY, ALASKA BORDER

A darkened Black Hawk helicopter touched down in a small clearing, the pilot using night vision goggles to see. Staying only long enough to drop off his two passengers, the crew chief flashed a thumbs-up gesture to Jeb and Wayne before the bird lifted off and vanished into the night.

Wearing heavy parkas with white snow shell, elbow length winter mittens and thick insulated boots, Jeb and Wayne crouched in the snow to check their equipment after the rotor blast lessened. Each carried an M-19, 9 mm Dutch assault rifle; a Beretta 10mm pistol; 8 inch sheath knife; two-piece hatchet and shovel tool. A field pack contained Canadian officer's uniform; Jeb's, that of a captain and Wayne's a First Lieutenant, five days rations and two full canteens of water, a flashlight with extra batteries, a shelter half and sleeping bag, first aid kit and a packet of waterproof matches. They both carried a good supply of warming pads; broken open from their plastic bags the warmers heated upon contact with air. They slid them into each glove to keep their hands warm. Wayne also carried two discs for the Canadian General. Each held copies of documents provided by General Saunders. In the event one was lost, the second disc was a back-up.

"You ready for this?" Wayne asked in a low whisper.

"A little late to ask that now, isn't it?" Jeb said with a definite note of sarcasm in his voice. "You lead and I will surely follow." Jeb slipped his night vision goggles on and fitted his feet into a pair of aluminum snowshoes.

"How long do you think it will take us to reach Calgary?" Jeb asked, now speaking into his Motorola headset.

"On foot...'bout three months. So, we gotta find some wheels as soon as we get across the border.

"Strange isn't it, we were made officers and gentlemen by an act of congress and now I'm trespassing into another country and about to steal a car," Jeb said.

"Before this mission is over, Major, I imagine you'll be committing far worse than stealing a car."

"Here, put one of these discs in a safe place on your person, not in your pack. This way if I get hurt or killed, you can continue on." Wayne handed the plastic case to Jeb.

"How nice, I always wanted to be a spy and now I'll probably be a felon too." Jeb took the disc and placed it inside a pouch he carried around his neck, which also contained his ADF and Intel I.D. Cards. He then snapped the snowshoes into place and lifted his right foot to trudge forth through the heavy snow. With only two hours of sleep, he knew this was starting off to be quite a trip. Another 4 to 5 miles of snowshoeing through the pristine arctic wilderness, *I'm either going to break my neck usin' these Bozo booties or I'll end standing before a firing squad to be shot as a spy. Thank you, Colonel Freeman!*

3 - THE BELIEVERS

"These are the words of him who has the sharp, double-edged sword; I know where you live - where Satan has his throne. Yet you remain true to my name. You did not renounce your faith in me, even in the days of Antipas, my faithful witness, who was put to death in your city- where Satan lives.

Revelations 2.12-13 NIV

HIGHWAY 17, NORTH OF PHOENIX, ARIZONA - MARCH 12

For three long unbearable months, frightened citizens in Phoenix, Arizona lived in a world gone mad. Anarchy became the order of the day as blood crazed mobs, spurred on by waves of insanity and sheer gut wrenching desperation, looted and burned the business districts. The thirst for violence still unquenched, attention turned to private residences. Drug crazed arsonists ran amok, torching abandoned vehicles and any burnable structure in their path. Homes and garages were set ablaze by the thousands, expensive buildings and years of landscaping lost as one neighborhood after another fell victim to a fiery death. Day and night blended into one continual reign of terror; the screams of injured and dying blended with the taunting shrieks of both marauding youth and adult gangs. Human life was of little value here and there were no police left to protect and defend them from brutal barbaric attacks. Firemen and other emergency crews fled, having lost too many men and women to street gangs armed with automatic weapons. Some of these same civil servants who had once sworn an oath to serve and protect, joined the rank and file of those bent on destruction, if for no other reason than to protect themselves from the mob's wrath. Every city, county, state and federal officer in uniform, from crossing guard to dogcatcher, had become a target. Mr. Citizen was fed up with politician's empty promises and a system that had come crumbling down around them. They needed someone to turn their aggression against, to focus their fears and anger on and the first targets of opportunity became those who wore any symbol of authority. Mailmen were mugged before the mail service came to an abrupt halt with all the Phoenix area post offices vandalized or burned to the ground. Any deliveryman still employed and in uniform, Federal Express or UPS, quickly became a victim in the first days of the riots. Company vehicles were overturned, set afire and a few used as battering rams for looting department stores. Anything connected to the military, either Air Force blue or Army green, was hit with Molotov cocktails. When Army National Guard was deployed, they were overwhelmed by sheer numbers and seized weapons used against other military units, until the National Guard ceased to exist as a unit and the armories were stripped bare.

A state of lawlessness now held this once proud metropolis captive. Towering buildings and massive shopping malls had become shells of blackened rubble. Nothing could stop the fire from engulfing the entire city. Armed men and women gunned down frightened citizens, either those fleeing or the few who had mistakenly hoped to surrender. Some, unable to accept what had happened to their civilized world, stood on street corners arguing with one another about whose fault it was. Others simply cried out in dire hope someone might stop to listen to their tale of woe and offer some degree of help. Confused, some dropped to their knees, whimpering and begging for mercy as a stranger with maddened eyes stepped forward with a blood stained axe, knife or gun. There was no one to help, no one to respond to pleas for mercy. Only the sound of yet another shriek followed by shotgun blast and yet another body lay before the oncoming flames. Here lay a city where debauchery, hate and violence were allowed to run rampant and go unchallenged. Here, where the courts, whether conservative or liberal, handed out one too many suspended sentences to violent felons and District Attorneys made plea deals with pedophiles, drug dealers and repeat violent offenders, and failed to come to grips with the skyrocketing crime rate, illegal immigration of fanatical terrorists and a lifeline of illegal drugs coming across the country's borders.

Here too, where a nightmarish creature with a thousand faces destroyed a once beloved home of a young lady of 16 years. Where night after terrifying night and all those dreadful days in between, she was too afraid to speak or make a sound, while her father and mother alternated guard duty in a darkened living room. Armed with an old double barreled shotgun, they watched as their neighborhood burned down around them. In her youthful innocence, she hoped and prayed for some hero to come forth, to find and rescue her from the demons who now stalked the very streets and sidewalks she had grown up on. But no one came and she had only the flames to hold the darkness back. Those horrendous moments in her young life had now awakened to a new nightmarish reality as a soft moan of pain escaped her lips and she whispered, "My head hurts, Dad." Slowly and with excruciating effort, she opened her eyes, first one and then the other, but everything remained a blur. Clarity soon came, along with a strange pungent smell of something very hot. "Daddy…Mom?" Suddenly, her eyes popped wide open as she remembered hearing her mother's scream. A flash of memory caused her to tremble as if in a dream she recalled a vehicle swerving across the centerline on a bend in the road, coming straight at them. "Oh, god..." An attempt to lift her head resulted in a sharp stabbing pain at the base of her neck, joined by a piercing clamp like headache that made her think her head was about to explode. She tried to bring her right hand up, but the effort was too great and resulted in a tingling sensation along her right shoulder and down her arm. "Daddy, Mom...I'm hurt. Don't you see? I'm hurt!" She cried out, but only a strange eerie silence enveloped her. "Daddy!" Her cry grows more intense, matching her level of fear, but her father couldn't answer and he never would again.

On an all but deserted stretch of highway that twists through the low foothills of a lonely desert plain north of Phoenix, two vehicles traveling in opposite directions had collided head on. The driver of the pickup was intoxicated and paid for it with his life and in the process had killed this young lady's parents. Her father, a man pressed to the breaking point of sanity and who never wore a seatbelt, had been thrown out of the vehicle and now lay face down on the pavement, his dark brown lifeless eyes open; his head lying at an unnatural angle. A broken neck and massive head injuries had killed him almost instantly when he was thrown through the windshield, onto the hood of the truck and landed in a mangled mess some 11 feet away from the smoldering wreckage.

Gritting her teeth against the pain, the girl forced herself up enough to peer out through the space where the windshield had once been. Shards of glass protruded from the edges of the frame and her mother's broken body was draped over the dash and hood of their car. Thankfully, her mother's mutilated face was turned away. Panic set in and she fought to escape, but a jammed seat belt prevented her from doing so. She used every ounce of strength to struggle, gritting her teeth to bite back the pain in her shoulder and pulled hard against the belt. Then collapsed as the effort left her sobbing and exhausted. She slumped down in her seat in an attempt to avoid seeing her parents and tried to gather up strength for yet another attempt to pry open the seat belt mechanism. Her attention was suddenly drawn away when a blast of steam burst from a vehicle's radiator. Her imagination jumped into high gear and she shouted, "Fire!" *Our car's on fire, I gotta get out 'a here...* "Help!" she yelled. "Someone, please help me!" Tugging and jerking frantically against the belt, she abruptly stopped again when she heard a flapping sound outside the car. A large ugly black bird had descended to land on her father's back and as she watched, the bird, with dark unblinking eyes, began to peck at her dad's body; a horrifying sight to witness. Unable to speak, yell or scream, she watched the bird in shock until a shriek burst from deep within her lungs. With her expended effort, darkness followed and she slipped into unconsciousness as other desert vultures soon joined the unfazed bird.

FRANK AND JOEY

"Ah'm tellin' yuh, Frank, ah did hear a chick screamin' back down there. One of those chicks is still 'live, probably thu one in thu car," Joey said. He looked to his big brother, trying to get his attention, "We oughta go back an' check, Frank."

"You're an idiot, Joey. No one's alive back there," Frank replied and then lightly slapped his younger brother across the face, the closest he ever came to showing any affection for his dimwitted sibling.

"But Frank, Ah think its dat girl...thu pretty one in duh backseat. Mabee she's jus' hurt...Mabee we cun have some fun wit' her." Joey's leering smile only made him appear more stupid than he was, but it did cause Frank to stop walking and consider going back for a look see.

Joey was too slow to remember it was Frank's idea to flee Phoenix without a car, without water and little food. He simply enjoyed being out with his big brother. For three days they had hiked this mostly deserted roadway in search of a ride to Flagstaff; where Frank's old girlfriend, Cindy Ellen, lived. Frank had thought they could hitchhike, but there was hardly any traffic on the highway and no was going to pick these two street thugs up anyway. They were a walking advertisement for Lowlife Anonymous. When they had reached the crash site, they joked about how the driver of the car had such a venomous and judgmental expression on his face as he had sped by them earlier. Now two hours later, they found Old Mister, "I ain't gonna give you two lowlife a ride anywhere", and his family dead in a fatal car crash.

A day earlier, Frank had hotwired an abandoned car, but they only traveled ten miles before the engine ran out of gas and before finding the accident scene, the brothers had become heavily dehydrated from their long hike and were in sorry need of water. The accident scene revealed many riches for this starving and thirsty twosome. In the truck, they discovered several full water bottles, 2 bags of assorted canned goods and a bag of shelled walnuts. In the car, they found various foodstuffs, some additional water and best of all, a loaded shotgun, which Frank made Joey carry.

Passing his 21st birthday in the Maricopa County Jail, Frank was serving a 2 year sentence for Attempted Rape; his third felony conviction in 3 years of adulthood. The victim's older brother happened to come home early and nearly killed Frank before the police arrived on the scene. The responding officers nearly arrested the wrong man before things got all worked out and the victim was able to explain what had happened. Frank had followed the girl home from the movies, knocked on the door when he saw she was alone and forced his way in. Frank spent 4 days in the hospital as a result of injuries received in the beating. Before his arraignment and seeing his condition, a liberal judge took mercy on him, even though he had other felonies on his record and was on probation for drug possession with intent to sell. But that was prior to the war. During the third month of rioting, mobs stormed the county jail to break out friends. A battle between the mob and guards lasted more than 10 hours, but then the defensive positions collapsed and guards fled to escape harm.

After he escaped, he murdered an elderly couple and looted their house for food then made his way home to gather some additional supplies for the trip north. He hadn't counted on finding anyone home, but wasn't all that surprised to find Joey hiding in the basement. Joey said he was still waiting for their mother to come home, after leaving 2days earlier with an alcoholic biker boyfriend. Knowing that two could survive better than one in a hostile climate, Frank dragged Joey out of the basement and together they fled a less than savory neighborhood with torch bearing fire-freaks close behind.

Rather than carry all the goods they'd taken from the two crashed vehicles back with them, Frank told Joey to hide what them behind a large boulder. "We'll put it out of eyesight from passing motorists," Except they hadn't seen another car since leaving the accident scene. "We'll walk back and check, but you'd better be right! I don't like the looks of that sky," Frank pointed to the north, "Gettin' darker all the time. Storm's comin' an' I'd like to find some cover before it hits."

"Jus' some rain, Frank… C'mon, let's go look." Joey was excited and it grew with every step closer to the scene. He was out of breath when he ran up to the station wagon and collapsed over the hood, dropping the shotgun to the ground. For the last two hundred yards, he had raced to beat Frank to the pretty girl. All the noise he made rushing up to the vehicles scared most of the birds and they began circling overhead. Joey cringed as he went by the man; the birds had done a thorough job, but then he glanced into the station wagon and saw evidence of life; the girl continued to breathe. He shouted over his shoulder, "She's sure enough alive, Frank. Jus' like I told yuh she was…Like I told yuh. I was right, ain't I?"

Frank picked up the shotgun and slammed it into Joey's chest, "Shut up and get out of my way!" Frank pushed him away from the vehicle's door. Seeing she was alive, a lustful sneer broke across his face. He'd been locked up far too long, "Christmas time, Little Brother and look what Santa done brought us."

Unable to to open any of the doors jammed in the collision, they tried to yank the girl out of the car forcefully. But she wouldn't come out and Joey was afraid they might bust her and he began to pound his fist on Frank's back.

With a burst of profanities, Frank grabbed his little brother by the back of his neck and jerked him away from the vehicle. "Stop it! Another stupid stunt like that an' I'll leave you here like him." Frank pointed to the dead father. By now more than a dozen black birds were flying overhead in a loose circular pattern. Frank grabbed the shotgun from his brother and fired off one of the barrels, killing one of the birds. This scared off most of the others, but a few maintained their vigilance from above. "Here, hold this and this time don't lie it down!" He shoved the shotgun at Joey again.

"Reload it... an empty barrel won't do us any good if trouble comes," Frank ordered then unfolded a large Buck knife which he had stolen from the old couple in town and sliced through the seat belt that held the girl in place. Then none-to-gently, he grabbed her by the hair and yanked her bodily out of the car headfirst. Severe pain jarred her awake and she screamed as Frank dropped her hard to the ground.

Her eyes wide open now, she was startled to find a filthy, sweaty man with greased back black hair bent over her. She looked into his cold eyes and what she saw terrified her. She'd seen that same vile look in a lot of the ghoulish men and women who wandered the streets in front of her home. She had known this was one of the reasons her parents sought to escape the neighborhood she had known all her life, to get out before these people learned of their existence and broke into the house.

Seeing her fully awake, Frank dropped down to straddle her as he began ripping the shoulder straps of her dress with the blade of his knife. This caused painful jolts to her injured shoulder and another scream burst from her lips. But this time Frank clamped down hard on her mouth with a sweaty hand palm tasting of grime and salt. She tried to wrestle free, but Frank was too strong and held her head firmly in place.

From behind the one man, she heard a strange squeaky laugh and knew there were at least two of them. When Joey came into view, she saw him holding a shotgun much like her father's and glaring at her with the dark brown eyes of a weasel. Hopelessness and despair filled her and she prayed to the Lord for help.

"Pretty thing, you can jus' scream all yuh want too. It's only you, my addle-brained brother Joey an' me out here," Frank said.

"Yeah," Joey added in a mocking voice, "Poor momma and daddy are both dead, they ain't gonna help you no more."

Frank's teeth were black and his face smeared with dirt and grime from hiding in buildings, fishing food out of trash dumpsters and sleeping in alleyways to escape the city gangs. Joey looked much worse. With a hard glare of sheer deviltry, Frank looked much like a cat ready to devour its prize mouse, while Joey talked and waited his turn. But Frank began to wish

Joey would go somewhere else for a while. He didn't like an audience when he performed, preferring to be alone with his victim.

"Joey, shut up!" Frank ordered. "You got the gun, go guard something and give me a moment with this little lady...then she's yours to play with." Droplets of Frank's sweat bounced off her reddish cheeks; she thrashed about in a vain attempt to avoid them. She yelled at him, trying to strike or kick him, but Frank held her secure. Increased levels of pain softened the short surges of anger and gave way to fear; threats became pleas for mercy, which only caused the animal to laugh. Adding to his amusement, she began crying out to the Lord, pleading with Him to save her.

"Stupid girl, there ain't no God no more," Frank said mockingly. "But you can pray to me, beg me...I'll be your God." Frank ripped away the rest of her dress top, which had been a Christmas gift from her parents. Then he stopped and sat back, deciding he was in too much of a hurry. He had plenty of time to enjoy this one, no fear of being caught like last time; the pavement was too rough on his knees and the back of the station wagon would be a lot cozier and a bit more private. Frank stood up and dragged her to her feet, ignored her shrieks of pain and pulled her toward the back of the station wagon. "C'mon, we'll use your car." He turned to Joey, "You keep watch, don't be lookin' at me an' her or I'll get angry an' you won't get your turn."

Of course, that was exactly what Joey had in mind. He wanted to watch, so when Frank slammed the girl down into the back of the car, Joey hustled over to the side window and stared as his brother commenced to rip the rest of the dress off the hysterical girl. Joey gave up all pretense of keeping watch as his mind filled with lustful ideas for when his turn came.

Using his knife, Frank cut her underwear away, leaving several lacerations on her abdomen and legs. Then he stopped abruptly, his knife poised an inch over her left thigh as droplets of blood dripped down onto her stomach. *Music!?* He was hearing music and wondered where it was coming from? It was getting louder; the unmistakable sound of drums and electric guitars filling the air with a pulsating rhythm. Frank glanced up and saw Joey's eyes wide with fear and locked on someone or something out of Frank's view. Then a loud threatening voice boomed from behind him and Frank knew they were in some serious trouble.

THE CONVOY

"Stop what you're doing! Let me see your hands! Both of you; do it now...raise them real slow like... or die!" A voice with authority ordered.

Frank froze; hesitated, contemplating options out of this mess. His hand tightened around the knife, *'the girl could be used as a shield or maybe a hostage.'* He could just see his kid brother, visibly trembling; shotgun already held high in surrender.

"You're not listening, buckaroo. Raise those hands like you're praying to God Almighty Himself." The voice took on a more ominous tone, "Do it now, or die…your choice."

Because he could not see the threat, Frank hesitated. He considered sacrificing his brother to gain some advantage, pushing Joey toward the threat while he dragged the girl behind the other side of the car. He heard the sound of others and the all too unmistakable threatening sound of a pump action shotgun slammed into play.

"You're making us tired all over, Mister. You're friend here is being smart, why don't you take his lead and give it up. Fun time is over, you've been busted," a second voice said.

Frank started to raise the knife, so the intruders could see how close he had it to the girl.

"Hey, stupid, we've had to dig three graves already, won't tire me out anymore to make it four or five," a third voice said in a casual manner.

Frank's single ounce of bravado caved in. "Okay, don't shoot. I'm backin' away." Frank kept the knife in plain sight as he climbed off the girl and dismounted the vehicle's tailgate. When he saw what they were up against, he realized how close he had come to death. More than a dozen men surrounded the accident scene and all weapons were aimed by people who looked as if they knew what they were doing

Semi-conscious, the girl rolled out of the station wagon and cried out as she hit the hard pavement on her left side. The last thing she remembered was a tall man in a blue denim jacket holding a lethal looking rifle in his hands and a look of true concern in his eyes. Then she was unconscious again.

A middle aged Black man ordered Frank and his brother to lay face down on the roadway – a position both Frank and Joey knew all too well. The man expertly patted them down for weapons, while two others kept rifles leveled until they were cuffed and lifted to their knees. There they remained under guard by a man the size of an Alaskan Brown Bear, and a look on his face twice as scary.

Former Arizona State Trooper Lieutenant Ed Sawyer, younger brother of Brad Sawyer in Fairbanks, walked up to Frank and slowly shook his head in disgust. 6'4" and broad shouldered, with short brown hair and in dire need of a good shave, Ed bore a small scar over his left eye from high school football and a second, larger scar on his chin from a bar fight in Flagstaff. He was an imposing sight, especially with an M-16 in his hands and an icy-cold look in his eyes as he glared down at the two prisoners.

"Now I just have to figure out what I'm going to do with the two of you?" Ed shook his head in disgust and turned away to walk back towards a line of vehicles.

Around a gradual bend in the road 50 yards south of the accident scene waited a rather odd looking convoy of trucks and automobiles with engines turned off to conserve fuel. Stretched out for nearly 350 yards in a loose single file convoy was an assortment of 4 wheel drive utility vehicles in all shapes, sizes and colors. At the front of the line was a World War II vintage Dodge Ambulance in original green paint, recently touched up for the trip and with a huge red cross painted on both sides. Behind it, a two ton flatbed with side rails was stacked with supplies tied down under a large blue tarp and then a newer model three ton flatbed with a matching blue canvas tarp. Both trucks were pulling 500 gallon water trailers. Further down the line was a light blue and white Maricopa County Sheriff's patrol car with several bullet holes in the windshield and across the body of the car. Beyond that was a yellow Maricopa County school bus loaded with noisy children of various colors and ages. A retired silver colored Brinks armored car was followed by a 15 ton Kenworth Tractor pulling a blue 40 foot container van that had seen better days. Another diesel of similar size was hooked to a pair of massive fuel tanks; one marked for diesel fuel and the other gasoline. Following that was a white commercial 5 ton wrecker with all-wheel drive. Behind the trucks was a scattering of Blazers, Broncos and Expeditions of various colors and age. There was a blue City of Phoenix police car with flashing blue and red lights rotating, which was leading several mid-sized pick-ups and three Jeep Wagoneers.

Every vehicle in line was packed to the gills with survival and camping equipment, dozens of bicycles of different manufacture and an assortment of canoes, and strangest of all, was a flatbed truck hauling a large blue and white circus tent; the groups portable meeting house. Four loud speakers and three separate radio antenna were mounted on top of the ambulance and it was from here the music of Amy Grant's House of Love could be heard rocking out across the desert.

Ed used the PA system in the ambulance to advise every one of the situation and told them to be ready to move out in 30 minutes. This gave the women in the school bus time to escort the kids out into the desert to take care of physical needs before heading north.

It was little over an hour later before the young lady awakened in the ambulance. Surprised to find she was lying on a narrow gurney with an IV line in her left arm, she attempted to rise, but two firm but gentle hands stopped her.

"Not so fast, young lady. I've got a good line running and Doc says you need some time flat on your back. You were pretty dehydrated when we found you and this IV will help. But don't you worry; it's only a sugar water solution."

She looked to the tube taped to her arm and then at the woman treating her, "Who are you?"

"Nurse Nancy Sanders at your service and from the ID we found in your purse, you must be Kira Woods."

Kira moaned as she tried to shift her injured shoulder, "What's wrong with my arm?"

"Actually, your arm is fine, but you did dislocate your shoulder and Doc set it back into place while you were unconscious. You'll be fine."

"You're a nurse?" Kira asked.

"You betcha, a real board certified emergency room RN from Phoenix General Hospital. I worked there for 12 years, before I started driving this ol' crate for Doc." As she talked, Nancy checked Kira's pulse and used a narrow beam pocket flashlight to observe Kira's pupil dilation. "Was that your parents in the car?"

Kira hesitated before answering, she didn't want to remember all those birds and how they were... "Yeah." Tears began to flow and she accepted a tissue from Nancy's hand.

"We buried them on the hillside, along with the other accident victim. Graves are marked in case you ever want to find them again. Pastor spoke over them and I think you would have..." Nancy stopped, now wasn't the time to discuss funeral services.

Kira wiped her tears away, "I'll be all right, besides I've been told time heals all things."

"Well, I'm not too sure about that, but it's a pretty grown up way of thinking about things for a 16 year old." Nancy checked the IV line and tucked the edge of blanket around Kira's legs.

"What about those two...men?" Kira asked.

"Those weren't men, darling. No, they were pure hated-filled animals." Nancy tossed a glance over her shoulder toward the back of the ambulance, "Some of the men gave them a ride back down the road a ways. With the way the country is, we'd probably never run across any civil or military authorities to turn them over to, and we sure don't want to feed the likes of them. At least that's what I think. Pastor had to keep some of our men from staking them out over an anthill."

"Did they do anything...I mean was I...Did they rape me?"

"Doc examined you and except for losing your dress and underwear, you're just fine. Oh, we had to put a stitch in here and there from a few cuts, but you'll heal up fine."

A sob expressed her relief and Nancy reached over and cautiously hugged her, not wanting to hurt the injured shoulder. Kira wept for several moments, filling up a small plastic trashcan with used tissues as quick as Nancy handed them to her. Dry-eyed, Kira leaned back and asked, "Who are you people?"

"Us?" Nancy asked and then quickly answered, "We're only people heading north to escape the madness in the city and in search of sanctuary."

"Sanctuary?" The word confused Kira.

"Sorry, that did sound a bit melodramatic didn't it? Actually, there's about 200 of us in this rag-tag outfit and we're heading north to Alaska."

"Alaska? That's like…like 10,000 miles away."

"More like 4,000, but I'm sure it will feel like 10,000 before this trip is over."

"Why Alaska?" Kira asked. "Can you escape the comet up there? An' what about the nuclear winter my dad told me about?" Thinking of her dad and mom produced more tears.

Nancy handed her another tissue, "Our leader, Pastor James R. Woodway from Camel Mountain Faith Fellowship, is leading us to the new Promised Land."

"Alaska's the promised land? I thought it was just snow and ice."

"Alaska is the New Canaan for us," Nancy said as she broke into a smile. That look of confusion on Kira's face matched her own when she first heard the plans for this bizarre journey. "Are you a Christian, Kira?" Nancy asked as she looked into Kira's eyes.

"Methodist, but we didn't attend church all that often, especially during football season. Dad was a big Cardinals fan."

"I was a Cardinal fan myself, even caught a few games last year." Nancy lightly brushed aside some of Kira's hair. "Anyway, Pastor Woodway had a vision, well more like a series of visions last summer in which the Lord directed him to take his flock to Alaska." Nancy stopped, seeing the doubt register in Kira's eyes. "No, we are not religious nuts; we only sound like it at times. But you got some real top hand characters in this bunch who take Pastor Woodway's vision very seriously."

"I remember a tall man with a blue jean jacket, who's he?"

"I think you mean Ed Sawyer, big guy who zeroed in on the thugs. He was a lieutenant with the Arizona State Police, grew up in Alaska. We've taken to calling him our Wagon Master. He handles logistics, strategy and manpower. Most of the people here are members of Camel Faith Fellowship, but we have a few who aren't. Ordinary people like us fleeing the city, who decided to tag along for the ride."

"My dad was trying to reach Flagstaff, hoping to meet others heading east for Texas." Kira took a couple of sips from a canteen Nancy offered her and looked up into those middle-aged eyes. She felt a sense of trust and then committed a social blunder by asking Nancy her age.

After a brief hesitation and a serious look at Kira with a raised eyebrow, Nancy grinned and decided to tell her, "Can you keep a secret?"

"Sure."

"Well, I tell everyone I'm 49, but it jus' ain't so, and most of them probably don't believe it no how. I'm really 59, about two months shy of the big 6-0."

"You don't look that old," Kira replied.

Nancy smiled and said a polite, "Thank you."

Nancy had light brown hair in combed back into a tight bun and covered by a faded desert camouflage boonie-hat; a gift from her dad, who wore it in Vietnam. She was dressed in well-worn camouflage green leaf US Army fatigue shirt and pants with lots of pockets that she stashed all kinds of supplies and medical instruments in. An assortment of Tootsie Roll Pops was tucked in her upper left pocket for times she needed to treat the kids. The skin around her blue green eyes was lined by dozens of small wrinkles that she liked to think of as battle scars from far too many long hours in the emergency room; especially these last few months. Nightmares of the carnage she had witnessed and worked on left her sleepless many nights.

"Do you really believe in this vision stuff?" Kira asked, hoping she wasn't offending her new friend.

"Must admit I had my doubts at first, like you, but then I witnessed what only God could have done in Phoenix." Nancy's eyes grew wide as she remembered the miracles. "Yes, the Lord surely had his hand on our Pastor, using him in a mighty way in a city filling with so many foul acts of bloodshed; so many people killing for the sheer thrill of doing it and all those who looked the other way. Yup, Pastor wouldn't make a move without talking to the Big Man upstairs."

"So, what happened?" Kira wanted to hear more.

"Like I said, it began last summer… Pastor was having these strange visions about what was coming. It was a pretty heavy time for our church, a lot of dissension and there was talk of a church split. Well, Pastor's vision didn't help any and clearly added some fuel to the furnace for those opposing him. Old Satan was having some fun with our little congregation and a lot of people fell away. Marriages broke apart, runaway kids joined street gangs and a couple cases of adultery among the leadership. Strange though, Pastor seemed to know it was all coming. He told us later it was God allowing Satan room to cull the crop, because only those strong in faith would survive this journey. More than half of the church survived though and we were asked to fast and pray over several months. There were some, the stronger ones, who fasted for 40 days while they prayed for this journey we are undertaking. Then the shoe dropped, missiles flew over us and Phoenix became a living Hell."

"How'd you all make it out of Phoenix? We were only one car and almost didn't make it out. Gangs had roadblocks up everywhere, shootings and…worse." Kira fought the images back, not wanting to remember those last couple of days as her father hid them in garages of unoccupied houses, camouflaging their car with trash piles in alleyways and driving like a maniac across yards and through hedges because the streets were crowded with abandoned vehicles. Twice he had run down armed thugs to escape the crazies and sideswiped one leather clad outlaw biker in order for them to escape.

"Pastor ordered us to stockpile our food, medical supplies and everything from tents to tools and even auto parts. We stored it all on the church property, filling the buildings and then stacking it out in the open. We looked like we were staging a final End-of-the-World sale." Nancy stopped when she felt movement at the back of the ambulance and saw Doc climbing inside.

"Ah, I see our patient is awake," Doc said. He was an elderly Afro-American in his late 70's and he gave Kira a big smile before moving to a small metal sink to wash his hands with bottled sterilized water. Drying his hands with a paper towel, he traded places with Nancy and reviewed Kira's chart. "You had us a mite concerned, thought you might have sustained a concussion and possible spinal injuries. But you look fine." Doc turned to Nancy, "I don't see a recent set of vitals on her chart."

"Don't you get huffy with me, Doc," Nancy said. "We got chatting and I hadn't recorded them yet." Nancy pulled the chart out of Doc's hands and wrote down Kira's current blood pressure, pulse rate and temperature; all within normal range.

"Well, looks like you can advise his royal chieftain we can start moving again," Doc said in a whimsical tone, which caused Kira to smile.

"Gotcha." Nancy popped Doc a crisp salute and moved forward to straddle over the driver's seat and pounded the horn three times to get Ed Sawyer's attention. A moment later, Ed appeared at the driver's door, where Nancy advised him they could get the convoy moving again.

"It's about time!" Ed complained as he looked at his watch. "Fire 'em up; let's get this train rolling," he ordered as he moved from the door and pumped his right arm three times. Satisfied that the signal to move had been seen, Ed walked around the front of the ambulance to climb into the passenger seat. Kira saw him climb in and for the first time really took notice of his great size, handsome features and the weapon he placed into a carrier beside his seat. She'd seen photographs of the rifle and remembered that it was an army rifle.

Nancy had a microphone in her hand, connected to the vehicle's PA system, "Start your engines! It's time to roll," She announced. In response, the air was split with the sound of several vehicle horns and a few blasts from truck air horns. "Like children on parade, men love to have their toys," Nancy said. She hung the microphone up and ignored Ed's disapproving glare.

Startled by the order to move, Kira looked at Doc and asked, "Are you taking me with you?"

"Unless you want to be dropped off on the side of the road, I guess so," Doc placed a reassuring hand on top of Kira's uninjured arm. "You'll be safe with us."

"No...No I want to come with you. I've...I haven't got anyone else." New tears began to well up and she reached up to wipe them away with a clean tissue.

"Nothing wrong with tears, young lady. They wash away the sadness in our lives or show our joy pouring out." Doc offered Kira another tissue.

Nancy looked over her right shoulder, "Seems like you've joined our band of wandering gypsies."

Doc grinned at Nancy and then turned to his patient, "Kira, I'm Doc Majors, you already know Nancy and that ornery old cuss up front is Mr. Edward Sawyer."

Ed studying an AAA Road Map spread partially out over his lap remained silent. He didn't have time for teenage girls, the responsibility of taking this group to Alaska rested heavily on his shoulders and the weight was getting mighty uncomfortable.

"He's a rude man at times, spent too many years as a police officer, where they drag their knuckles, choke stale doughnuts down and spend hours learning how to misspell tax payer," Doc said hoping to bait Ed into a conversation, but the big guy wouldn't bite.

"Nancy, what should we call it?" Doc asked, giving Kira a wink.

"Call what?"

"Our trek to the frozen north, of course," he said. "Maybe we could call it our quest to find the fabled Camelot, a search for the Holy Grail, or a journey to the mythical Xanadu, or reaching for the Lost Horizon?"

Nancy had no verbal response at first, only shaking her head at each idea Doc offered. But then she replied, "You've read too many books, Doc."

"Exodus," Ed said, his eyes glued on the map. "Call it our Exodus, like the Biblical Israelites escaping Egypt. Like them, we've fled the burning funeral pyres of an ancient bird." He turned to look over his shoulder at Kira, "Can you cook or do laundry, maybe handle some kids?"

"Why?" Kira asked in surprise. She was actually expecting something more like, 'Hello, I'm really glad you weren't hurt too badly'.

"Miss..."

"Her name is Kira Woods, Ed," Nancy reminded him.

Ed ignored her, "Miss Woods, everyone on this...Exodus," Ed frowned at Doc, "...has a job to do. In return, they share in the safety and protection of this convoy, and a portion of the food and water. You'll have to find a job or go hungry." He returned to his road map.

"C'mon, Ed. Give her some time to mourn the loss of her family. She needs to heal. Quit playing the..." Nancy stopped. She saw that hard look of 'Butt out! This is my job' in his eyes and knew she was treading on thin ice.

Ed turned his glare on Nancy and looked back at Kira, "Better for you to stay busy, not dwell on your problems. Besides, you look healthy enough to help out in the kitchen for an hour or so at least."

Kira was about to explode; ready to cut loose with a reply that would sear Mr. Ed Sawyer's eyebrows off. But right then a pack of hard looking men on chopped motorcycles raced by and the sight and sound of them brought back terrifying memories of the night an outlaw motorcycle gang roared down their street, gunning down neighbors in yards and looting several homes. One of her friends was carried off, thrashing and kicking and she could still remember her frightened screams.

Doc saw Kira tense up and the fear in her eyes. "It's okay, Honey. Those overweight hooligans are our guys, born-again bikers. We call that big dude up front Point Man and the others like to call themselves His Misfits; five of the biggest bikers you'll ever run across and yet, real gentle fellows."

"Doc, Point Man might object to being called a gentle fellow," Nancy added.

"True." Doc nodded as he looked back at Kira, "They're the eyes and ears, and advance scouts for this...Exodus of ours." Doc shot a sneer Ed's way.

Kira looked at Ed, "Is he a Christian too?" She hadn't known of too many Christian cops and at the moment, Ed wasn't behaving like any Christian she knew.

Doc grinned and then sent the question forward, "Ed, the young lady here wants to know if you're a Christian?"

This finally brought a smile out to his prickly unshaven face, and he turned to face Kira, "Born again, through and through. I was saved at a Promise Keepers Rally. Some 10,000 men gave their lives to the Lord that weekend, a real sight to behold." Ed folded up his map and reached for the microphone to make contact with Point Man over the CB radio.

Seeing the look on Kira's face, Doc suspected his young patient was beginning to form a case of hero worship and he wondered how Ed would deal with it. Shaking his head in amusement, he began securing medical supplies for the long bumpy road ahead. Each and every item was valuable, possibly irreplaceable and he didn't want to take a chance on losing even a bottle of sterilized water to a pothole. Doc was quite a character, with short curly white hair; a pair of rimless reading glasses hung from his neck by a knotted string; a safeguard to ensure he didn't misplace them again. He wore a long sleeved white button down shirt with a dark blue bow tie, a pair of faded black suspenders kept his sagging pants from falling off. Doc's wife had fallen victim to cancer two years back and both of his sons, serving at England Air Force Base in Louisiana, were presumed dead after the first wave of missiles. Not always a physician, he had retired early and sat on the Board of Deacons at his neighborhood church in South Phoenix until he lost his sons. He became angry with the Lord and displayed it through the inhospitality he dealt out when Pastor Woodway called and responded to Doc's anger with, "The Lord has sent me here, Doctor Majors. You are needed now for a great task and your time of grieving is to end - now."

It wasn't immediate, but the barriers soon came down and before he knew what was happening, Doc found he'd been shanghaied by God for this bizarre journey and though Pastor always said Doc had volunteered, Old Doc in his cantankerous way, continued to call it kidnapping to whoever would listen. Evenly matched, Doc and Pastor Woodway had spent many a long hour over a chessboard, while Pastor kept him up to date on what lay ahead and what kind of medical emergencies he foresaw through mysterious visions and dreams.

The convoy continued traveling north on Highway 17, holding speed to 45 mph to conserve fuel. There was no other traffic on the road but Point Man radioed back about various abandoned vehicles they had passed. Men were assigned to stop to check each vehicle for supplies, gasoline or diesel and needed auto parts. There wasn't time to bury the dead simply because there were just too many. Driving down a major desert highway devoid of traffic gave them all an unsettling feeling, but few spoke of it. Highway businesses were closed down, some boarded up and those that were not gave mute testimony of looting with broken glass and debris strewn about.

Point Man and His Misfits located a wide patch of hard packed desert sand and selected it for night camp. The vehicles were drawn into a tight circle with camp set up inside. Six armed men were positioned outside the circle of vehicles and additional guards were assigned to the water trailers and food truck. The large big top circus tent, which had once been rented out for various political, religious and entertainment and circus events was located exactly in the center of the circle and the kitchen was set up on one side of it. It took 30 hardworking people 22 minutes to set up the big tent and even less time to bring it down. The first time had taken more than four hours. Setting up was only one of the many chores they practiced in the weeks prior to leaving. Folding chairs and tables carried on one of the flatbeds did double duty; providing seating for dining and then for nightly meetings.

Dinner was served GI style; half a dozen women serving a slow moving chow line of survivors who received what the women put on their plates without complaint. Tonight's menu consisted of canned beef stew cooked over open pit fires, hot biscuits with real butter, hot coffee or tea, and cherry Kool-Aid for the kids. Seasoning consisted of ketchup, salt & pepper and small personal sized packets of barbecue sauce. Desert was a choice of hard candy and butter cookies. One of the men had found a pallet loaded with large tins of German butter cookies and Doc, the group's dietician, thought they'd probably stay fresh until all were consumed. Pastor had popcorn for the late evening song service and the cooks popped it over the open fire in large handmade metal baskets. They knew the butter wouldn't last long, but they'd enjoy what they had for as long as it did.

Parked beside the kitchen area, a 40 foot container van held the group's food supply; every item was catalogued on a 62 page clipboard, which Ed kept with him in the ambulance. A copy of the list was also kept inside the trailer for the head cook. Both head cook and wagon master met after dinner to compare lists regarding daily consumption and Ed added to the supply list, any items picked up along the line. Pastor had briefed Ed on the importance of keeping strict record of food supplies on hand and what was served for each meal giving them a firm idea of how long the food would last. Their schedule was to make this trip north in 14 to 17 days and Ed had foodstuffs for a 22 day journey, giving him a 5 to 8 day safety buffer based on current needs.

Water had to be rationed, allowing each member a quart of water every day for drinking. An additional five gallons was set aside for washing pots after evening meal. There were showers or baths unless they came across an uncontaminated water source, to be checked by Doc before use. Plates, cups and dinnerware were paper or plastic, and were burned after dinner. Each campsite was sterilized by a crew of 6 men and 3 women after the convoy departed in the morning. All trash was burned and ashes buried to keep the size of the group unknown to any scavengers and bandits driving the roads in search of plunder.

Though nursing a sore shoulder, Kira helped in the kitchen stirring stew with a huge wooden ladle over one of the open fires. She hoped Ed might see her, but he was busy somewhere else and one of the men took his meal to him.

Following the evening meal, Pastor Woodway led the group in a spirited Bible study, unlike anything Kira had ever attended before. Right from the beginning, his teaching style captivated her. His words and gestures brought the Word of God to life for her; she'd never seen a church leader speak with such enthusiasm about scripture. Worship began with a heavy beat backed up by instrumental CD's played over the PA system. It reminded her of old Rock & Roll, yet the words spoke of God's love. In closing, the music was much quieter, now supported by half a dozen people playing guitars and one violin. Kira could sense a spirituality she'd heard about from other Christian friends at high school. She really liked it.

After meeting with other teenagers after service, each one hoping to cheer her up, Kira took a moment to herself. Walking behind the school bus with a small flashlight, she studied the desert floor for scorpions and rattlesnakes. She soon spotted Pastor Woodway walking alone out into the desert without a flashlight and was about to follow him, when she was startled by someone tapping her on the shoulder.

Frightened, she jerked around with her good arm up in a defensive posture, "Don't..." She stopped when she realized it was Ed Sawyer standing before her.

"I didn't mean to scare you Ms. Woods, but I saw you watching Pastor and thought you might be planning to interrupt his evening prayer time."

"Oh, I thought he was out for a walk and might want company." She relaxed, feeling safe in Ed's presence. "And yeah, I did have a few questions for him."

"He does it every night. It's his time to commune with God and we pretty much leave him alone. He started it back in Phoenix, him talking to the Almighty and breaking into song now and then. Some people thought it weird, but then some strange things began occurring and no one thought it was weird anymore."

"Like what?" Kira wanted to hear about those strange occurrences. Nancy had started to tell her, but Doc interrupted them.

"Remember how all the mobs began to loot and murder, no one could stop them. Not even the police; we were outnumbered 1,000 to 1 by this point and no one would listen to us."

"Yeah, I saw it." Kira looked out over her shoulder, trying to see the Pastor, but he'd vanished into the darkness.

"We had vehicles, supplies and weapons stockpiled on church property, food for a small army and most of it in plain view. Not one item was touched. The mobs never stepped onto our land; it appeared they never even looked in our direction as we loaded the trucks." Ed thought back over those last three nights, he'd gone without sleep for nearly 72 hours and not one item was taken off the trucks nor was a member of the church injured. He had never seen anything like it, as if an invisible wall surrounded them and kept them from harm. "Not even the arsonists bothered us and when it came time to leave, Pastor had two of our men blow a couple of ram's horns; they're called shofars, for over five minutes. Those guys were red faced and tired by the time they were done. Then we prayed and left." Ed gestured toward the vehicles with a wave of his arm. "For over ten miles we drove through... we'll, I'd call it Hell; fires everywhere, people killing and people dying. Reminded me of one of those paintings...Dante' Inferno, that's it. A boat being rowed through the fiery lakes of Hell...Anyway, it was strange how this corridor opened up for us as Pastor instructed Nancy which roads to take until we reached the highway. We covered the bus windows so the kids couldn't see..." Ed looked into the desert. It was so hard for him, a police officer, to ignore what was taking place, but Pastor had advised him earlier regarding who and what he was responsible for now. They were not to stop for any reason, not even to assist the injured.

"So, how'd you do that...get away I mean?"

"God..." Ed said with respectful awe. "Simple as that, God provided the way and protected us as we drove across the city."

"Sound pretty hocus pocus. Like the Holier than Thou stuff I used to hear on TV."

"I thought you believed in the Lord, Kira?"

She felt anger building in her, "Where was He when my mom and dad died? None of that Bible stuff saved them, did it?" Kira turned away. Even standing here in the darkness of night she was concerned Ed might see her tears. Then she turned her anger on Ed, "You were a cop, what happened to the police - those men and women who were supposed to protect us?"

"Right, everyone likes to blame the police. Back in 2001, when the World Trade Center towers went down, everyone loved the police and firefighters. People waved as we drove by, but that sure didn't last very long. Within a year we were back to be calling pigs again.

"After 9-11 the government got heavy handed with people's rights and Mr. and Mrs. John Q Citizen objected. First, peace demonstrations over the war with Iraq: the second war and then Afghanistan. In 2014, someone got the idea to bring home some of our battle hardened troops and combine them with UN blue helmets to put down the demonstrations over talk of reinstituting the military draft. It was Kent State all over again."

"Kent State?"

"Sorry, you're too young to remember and actually, so am I. But it happened over the Vietnam War when some young inexperienced Army National Guardsmen fired on college students at Kent State; killing some of them."

"How horrible!" Kira recalled hearing about the turbulent 1960's and 70's, but this was the first time she'd heard of the Kent State incident.

"Yeah," Ed agreed. "With that comet coming our way and the United World Church Alliance preaching their 'Whites Only' propaganda, it wasn't long before race riots broke out across the country. That was followed by food and anti-government riots and some elected officials expected us to fire on women and kids. Trouble was, most of the police officers agreed with what the people were saying; the government had lost control and taxes were too high for the average middle class worker to handle - much less those in poverty. That old saying of 'Big Brother is Watching You' became reality and everyone became suspicious of everyone else. Militia from a dozen states organized and marched on state capitals and then battled it out with National Guardsmen for control of the cities. After that, prices skyrocketed until money became worthless. The police couldn't do anything, even with Martial Law in effect throughout the country. It was easy for the Chinese to sneak in and blow up the US. Nobody was watching because everyone was worried about within. Phoenix was lucky at first, for some reason the Chinese ignored Luke Air Force Base. Not that it mattered a whole lot. The fighter wing was downsized to only an alert strip and the airplane bone yard outside Tucson was no threat." Ed bent down and picked up a rock and then tossed it out into the darkness. "Within a few days angry people started shooting up the town, looting the downtown business districts and malls, and police cars became targets. They saw us as a symbol of what went bad, of a government that failed them." Ed didn't say it, but he remembered all too well the night he drove into an ambush, losing his windshield to a shotgun blast and driving out of the neighborhood with three flat tires and a car riddled with bullet holes. "I saw once dedicated police officers rip off their badges, even their shirts, to join the mobs. They set fire to City Hall, destroyed police department substations and after that, the city was lost to anarchy. I almost made it to the church by car, but my engine blew about a mile away. Funny thing, when I finally got there, Pastor was waiting for me as if he knew I was on the way. He handed me some new clothes because my uniform was a mess and told me to take charge."

Kira was stunned speechless for a moment, "Dad...Dad told mom and me a little of what was going on, but I only remember the schools closing in early December, earlier than usual for Christmas break...and...and I wasn't allowed out of the house unless I was with him or Mom. Then we couldn't leave the house at all, praying the people would think the house was deserted and leave us alone."

"It's old news now." Ed adjusted the M-16 he carried over his right shoulder. "Hey, I have to check on my guards, make sure they stay alert. But I wanted to apologize for how hard I sounded earlier...I know you've been through a really tough time and I saw you helping in the kitchen and..."

"Thanks, it did help me to take my mind off my troubles," Kira said.

"Good. Then I'll say good night." Ed walked off, using a bright flashlight to guide him as he checked the vehicles. Every night he inspected tire treads; the last thing he needed was a blow out; they only had so many spare tires for the bigger rigs.

Sensing, rather than hearing someone behind him, Ed turned to the desert with rifle ready in one hand and illuminated Pastor Woodway. "For a man of God, Pastor, you really know how to sneak up on a man." Not having any reason too, Ed had never checked into Pastor's background, not that he would have found much.

Pastor Woodway had been a member of a combined US Army/Navy Seals Special Forces Black Op group and his personnel file was sealed. Pastor never spoke about his service days to anyone or explained how he got his limp, or even how he came to become a church pastor. The military part of his life was buried long ago, it had died the night Pastor became a Christian in the hills of Eastern China and a new life was laid out before him.

Ed turned the light off, slid the flashlight into his coat pocket and then re-shouldered his rifle.

"At least you're on the ball, Ed," Pastor said and then in a reproof, added, "Three of your guards are busier watching inside the camp than outside and another was standing out in the open between vehicles, silhouetted by camp lights. That makes for an easy target."

"I'll have a word with them, Pastor...a very stern word."

"I've already embarrassed them enough by surprising them. They should perform their duties as assigned for the rest of the night at least, but you might want to schedule a little briefing for those you have assigned to guard duty and express the true danger we're in by taking this journey across a hostile land." Pastor knelt down, reached out and grasped a handful of sand that slowly filtered out through his fingers. He then looked up at Ed,

"My friend, the next few days will be very hard on our people, we must stay vigilant to the enemy's schemes…and be extremely wary of strangers."

"I really dislike it when you get so ominous sounding… like those Old Testament prophets you talk about."

"Sorry, it happens every time I study the Book of Revelations in the King James Version. Gloom and doom, before the happy ending."

"I prefer the Message. The Bible's easier to read like a novel," Ed said and as he escorted Pastor toward the next guard position, Pastor suddenly brought the subject of Kira up.

"I noticed you were talking to that young lady we' picked up today. She's gone through quite a lot, much too much for a young woman to endure."

"She's a tough one for her age, but it makes me wonder how many others like her we're liable to pick up along the way, or what we might be forced into with other types we come across," Ed said.

"Doc told me you brought up the name Exodus for our trip, I find it very fitting. Now, I'm certainly not a Moses and I'm not asking you to fill the Joshua role, but we do have the Lord's covering for a long journey through the desert. I'm sure we'll have our surprises, I only hope we don't have to wait 40 years before we reach our Canaan." Pastor slapped Ed on the shoulder and walked between two vehicles to join the others who were sitting around a large communal fire.

Ed thought of those 40 years Pastor had spoken of and the idea of spending over a month on the road gave him an unsettled feeling in his stomach. Not enough food, too many unknowns and no tornado of flame to lead us… and I still don't know what manna is and if I'd even like eating it?

Seeing Ed approach, Joey Roberts stepped away from the desert side of the rear fuel tanker and whispered sarcastically, "Halt and be recognized, Bub."

"You watched far too much TV, and if you ask for a password I'll shoot you myself." Ed walked up to his friend and patted him on the shoulder, "At least you're alert. Some of our guys failed the Pastor Woodway inspection.

"Ouch!"

"Right you are. He gave me a subtle reprimand to get them ship shape before something bad happens. So, tomorrow, we'll all have a little talk about proper procedures for guard duty… or they can miss a meal or two to remind them."

"I repeat myself, ouch!"

Joey Roberts was a pencil-thin, darker than average Afro-American of 37 years. He had long arms and long fingers perfect for playing basketball. A long knife scar marred the left side of his narrow face from ear to chin; a reminder of his gang days in South Phoenix but he hated the thought of plastic surgery. A 12 year veteran of the Phoenix Police Department, he had been assigned as sniper to their highly trained SWAT Team. Extremely efficient with firearms, he would often fire off over a thousand rounds on the range every week to stay proficient. He drove the blue and white police cruiser in the convoy and was accompanied by his wife and two very noisy kids, "Are we there yet?", "I got to go to the bathroom!" A large supply of weapons and ammo traveled with them in the car's trunk.

Joey had met his wife while working drugs, having arrested her - the former Cindy Windsor - for possession of marijuana and cocaine. He had felt drawn to her and helped her beat the drugs and gang life; several months later they were both saved during a street crusade. A surprise to herself, Cindy displayed a spiritual gift of Intercession and eventually became Pastor's lead intercessor and worship leader. She tried over and over to get Joey to join the worship team, but the man wouldn't give in. "I sound like an old frog with a busted honker and I will always sound like an old frog. If I want to sing to the Lord, I'll do it in the shower."

Ed and Joey talked for a few minutes, each scanning the desert for any sign of an intruder. But the desert night remained still, no headlights on the highway and none glowing from the desert horizon.

"So dark out here; clouds from the north moving in keeping the stars and moon hidden. Makes me kind of jumpy," Joey said. He held one of his five rifles; he preferred an M-16 for guard duty, like the one Ed carried, but his was loaded with a 30 round banana clip.

"Getting cold," Ed said. "I'll have someone bring you some hot coffee."

"I really would appreciate that sentiment, Mr. Wagon Master - Sir."

"You fall asleep and I'll tie your shoelaces together." Ed wandered off headed toward the school bus. It was one of the nosier vehicles in camp as several ladies struggled valiantly to bed down 14 orphans: six boys and eight girls - all under the age of 11. Larry O' Brian, a four year All-Pro Tackle for the Arizona Cardinals, finally succeeded in quieting them with the promise of a bedtime story and was turning the first page of a book when Ed climbed on board to say good night. Ed couldn't help but smile when he saw Larry cuddling three of the little ones in his massive arms. He was their Knight in Shining Armor; protector against all that was evil. Larry had lost his wife during the Christmas attack. She had gone to stay with her mother in San Diego, California, grieving over Larry's refusal to commit to their marriage and end his fooling around with NFL groupies. She had requested he attend marriage counseling with Pastor Woodway, but he refused and didn't even bother to see her off at the airport. Everything changed in Larry's life with her death. Overwhelmed with grief, he found himself on the Pastor's doorstep and by the end of the afternoon had given his life to Jesus Christ to become a changed man. Now much more passive, Larry welcomed the chance to serve as the convoy bus driver. An orphan himself, he could relate with these little ones. It was he who had found the bus in a school district's garage and procured it for their needs. Pastor Woodway counseled Larry on the misappropriation of county property, but when they tried to return it, they discovered the bus barn burned to the ground and over 20 buses torched. Circumstances allowed Larry to keep the bus, but Pastor kept a close eye on Larry's scrounging activities after that.

Ed felt a sense of security knowing he had such good men backing him up; men like Joey, Larry and the leather clad band of bikers - Point Man and His Misfits. Standing 6'7" and weighing 340 pounds, Point Man looked like Sasquatch atop a kid's bicycle when he roared down the roadway on his Harley-Davidson – a 1500cc dark blue and highly polished chromed out chopper. Faded tattoos covered most of his upper body as well as his 21 inch biceps. His light brown hair; gray at the temples, hung down his back in a long ponytail and most often he wore a faded black t-shirt, aged black leather vest with an assortment of silver ornaments, torn threadbare Levis and scuffed black leather biker boots. When it turned cold, he donned a waist length black leather bomber, which at one time had borne the colors of an outlaw motorcycle club. The black leather saddlebags on his bike held a wide assortment of weaponry and equipment. A sawed off 12gauge shotgun was mounted within easy reach. His Misfits wore matching clothing and were of similar size, except that all sported long beards. With the collapse of civilian law, Point Man and His Misfits had tossed aside their riding helmets to feel the wind in their hair once again. Being on bikes was a freedom they were willing to fight and die for and for once, they were completely at peace being on the right side.

The five were best friends – ex-marines who had served together in Afghanistan where they forged a bond during the horrible days of desert fighting. After their return home to the states, they had ridden with various outlaw motorcycle clubs including the notorious Devil's Disciple Motorcycle Club out of Tucson. Point Man was the first to come to the Lord during the annual Sturgis, South Dakota bike rally. Excited by what he'd heard, he literally dragged his best friends to a meeting and nearly had to sit on a couple of them to keep them from leaving. It didn't happen as fast for them, but Point Man was persistent and eventually, all four gave their lives to the Lord and became His Misfits. There were arrest warrants out on them for everything from Grand Theft Auto, Forgery and Weapons Misconduct to Creating a Riot so they kept their real names private and only

Pastor knew them. Some barriers had to be broken down, especially with Ed and Joey, who thought all bikers should be, "...staked to the ground, covered with honey and call in the bears". But the Lord prevailed and a respect developed that eventually turned into sincere friendship between cops and bikers before the convoy left Phoenix.

FLAGSTAFF

The concerned citizens of Flagstaff had formed a militia which kicked a troublesome outlaw biker group out of town, sending several of them to a mass grave outside city limits. Afterward, the militia erected roadblocks to prevent people from entering town from the southern and eastern roadways. Old cars and trucks were piled up as a barricade against any vehicle approaching town and a well-armed militia held the gate to turn outsiders away and patrol the city. The Arizona highway system allowed traffic to bypass Flagstaff and head for Holbrook, and all points east. That is exactly where Point Man and crew headed at a fast clip when several people behind the barricade opened up on them with rifle and shotgun fire.

Outside of Flagstaff, Point Man radioed Ed over the CB and briefed him on the encounter. Ed mounted a large white flag on the ambulance radio antenna to show they meant no harm as they bypassed the city. It worked. No shots were fired as the people at the roadblock watched the convoy pass and wondered where this strange band of people might be headed. 19 miles east of town Point Man was waiting on a wide stretch of open land for a scheduled refueling stop. As he looked north in the direction they were heading, he noticed an ominous dark sky. Black and gray clouds appeared to form a barrier; a seemingly impenetrable wall of volcanic ash, snow and ice which reportedly covered all of North America. George C. Washington, a short, heavyset Afro-American, wore a faded black LA Dodgers baseball cap on top of his bald head and a pair of greasy blue fuel stained coveralls with the name George Sr. stitched in white thread over the zippered left breast pocket. He drove the 98 foot long double fuel tanker; one tank of gasoline; the other diesel. It was his job to refuel the vehicles and keep an accurate log of fuel consumption.

Charlie White Ear, an elderly Apache Indian, rode with George to assist with fueling. Ed Sawyer had found Charlie sitting alongside the road with his thumb out on the day he had sped through town in a bullet ridden patrol car. Not sure why at the time, Ed braked hard, brought the vehicle into a 40 foot skid, jumped out and pulled Charlie intro the back seat. Doc looked him over and told Ed that Charlie, who reeked of alcohol and displayed the tell-tale signs of long term alcohol use, was the victim of a brutal assault. Despite the evidence that Charlie needed some time to sober up, the next day, Pastor Woodway spent a couple of hours with him and learned that the old Indian had been Sachem of his tribe but lost the position due to alcoholism and stealing a man's wife. Pastor insisted Charlie be allowed to travel along and George, a recovered alcoholic and long standing member of Alcoholics Anonymous, agreed to see him through the DT's. Doc provided medicine to help, but George spent several nights with little sleep as Charlie washed the poison out of his system. Even now, Old Charlie was shaky, but a deep friendship had formed between George and the elderly Indian.

THE DEATH OF WINSLOW

When they reached the outskirts of Winslow, Point Man radioed Ed that the city was mostly destroyed by fire. "Smoke everywhere, Boss, and the streets are littered with bodies. Man, I'm tellin' you it looks like the war zone we left behind - Over."

"Okay, continue on. We've got a few hours of light left - Over," Ed replied.

"10-4, Good Buddy-I'm out." Point Man waved to his crew and they roared off, leaving behind a burned out town that was once a major Arizona tourist destination. When the convoy began passing, Ed was overwhelmed by a sudden urge to flee. This place was giving him the heebie-jeebies. Black smoke hung like a pall over the town and there was a foul pungent odor in the air.

Struggling with inner warnings and a need for supplies, Ed contemplated taking a crew in to search for supplies, but Pastor vetoed the idea. "Ed, I sense a strange evil there. We'll stay out."

"You are the man." Ed didn't even think about arguing, he wanted to put distance between them and Winslow. Several other members of the convoy felt the same sense of unease that Ed and the Pastor experienced. It was well they heeded it – the plague had swept through Winslow after arriving with a family of infected border runners and decimated the entire population within days. Fires were set in a failed attempt to stop it leaving Winslow a silent ghost town.

MAKING CAMP

Kira was using her good arm to unload a small box of supplies from the van when Ed appeared and took the box from her. "I'll carry it for you, where's it going?"

"To the kitchen, where else would it go?"

"How much longer are you going to be using that sling?" Ed asked as he set the box down on a tabletop.

"Afraid I'm not doing enough?" Kira's dander was up, but she stifled a nasty remark when she saw the smile on Ed's face.

"Cool down, little girl. I know how hard you're working. Keep the mind and body busy and don't think about your loss." Ed unloaded the box of paper plates and napkins.

"Have you ever lost anyone, I mean close?"

Ed shook his head, he didn't want to have this conversation and especially with a dumb kid. He couldn't understand why he was over here in the first place; he had enough of his own work to do.

"Did you lose a wife?" She asked and from the look on his face thought she had struck a nerve. "I'm sorry, that's none of my business. Forget I asked and I'll go knock my nosy self against the side of the van a few dozen times."

Ed was surprised when the words popped out of his mouth, "No, not a wife, but someone I loved once." He wanted to stop, but something inside was compelling him to answer, "I was living with a lady who worked for the state...a probation officer. We had this little condo off Indian School Road, a real nice place. We'd been together about 16 months when I got saved...That night I came home ready to share everything and complete the night by asking her to marry me. Funny, we'd never talked about God before; she didn't want to hear it. She laughed and made jokes about it. A pretty bad scene all told. Anyway she packed her stuff and left before midnight with all the neighbors witnessing our little heated exchange. They'd have called the police, except they knew I was a state trooper." Ed looked away; the memory still cut deep.

"Did you ever see her again, try to work it out?"

"No, a few months later she was murdered by one of her parolees."

Kira felt as if she'd been struck in the chest with a large rock. She remained silent as both of them stood caught in the awkward moment.

"I'm sorry, Ed. I can see how much you loved her."

"Long time ago, maybe a whole different life time. Now I've got this bunch to ride herd over." Ed caught the shine off Kira's cheeks from the fire and saw her tears.

"Don't cry, Kira. You and I have shed enough tears to last us a long time." He provided his handkerchief, thankfully a fresh one and watched as she wiped her cheeks.

"Thanks." She started to hand it back, but stopped. "I'll wash it if you want?"

"No." He took it from her hand and tucked it back into his pants pocket. "Look, I got rounds to make so I need to move along. You'll be okay?"

"Sure...thank you for sharing that with me."

"Good night." Ed walked over to where Pastor was standing with Joey and Cindy.

"I see you have an admirer," Cindy said noting the frown of disapproval from her husband.

"Aw, she thinks I'm her hero. She'll grow out of it in no time."

Cindy ignored her husband's - 'can't you mind your own business look' - and continued on, "I doubt it, Ed. That girl's in for the long haul."

"Cindy!" Joey exclaimed.

"Cindy, I'm twice her age...and I don't have time for this." Ed was flustered and Pastor didn't help when he added his words to the matter.

"Most of the world sees girls her age as fully grown, and she's been forced to grow up in these last few days."

"Pastor, I sent men to jail for even thinking what you're suggesting I think about. I can't even believe we're having this conversation. C'mon, Joey help me out here."

"Well, Pastor has a point. Married women in the Bible were quite a bit younger than Kira. She is of child bearing age and would probably make a great young wife." Joey was fighting to keep from smiling. He was actually feeling sorry for taking advantage of Ed's good nature.

"All right!" Ed exclaimed in a raised voice and then added, "That's enough, Joey." He started to walk off, but turned and pointed a finger at his friend, "I'm gonna make sure you get extra guard duty and... Cindy, that's two extra nights in the kitchen. As for you, Pastor... I give up. I wonder how you ever talked me into this trip in the first place." Flustered, Ed stomped off, while behind him, his three friends were quietly laughing.

That night the snow came, over a foot had fallen before morning and more than one tent collapsed under the heavy load. It made a mess of things getting the convoy back on the road. Vehicles had to be dug out; a labor intense exercise with only hand shovels. Five people received minor injuries and Ed had his hands full keeping the snowball fights to a minimum.

For Point Man and crew, the snow meant the end of riding until they returned to drivable pavement. It also gave five rather large men an excuse to set off the first snowball fight, clobbering Ed in the chest with a huge mushy one. If not for their size, those five might have been shot on the spot for the ugly mood their boss was in.

It was nearing noon by the time the vehicles were lined up with chains on - a laborious task. They continued east and seeing the foul mood Ed was in, Nancy remained silent and Doc decided it was a good time to inventory medical supplies. Driving an older model Dodge 6 passenger 4x4 pickup, Point Man and crew left a half hour earlier and with great joy reported dry roads 31 miles east of Holbrook. After a quick stop to remove chains and unload the choppers, the Misfits were once more on the road.

4 - IS IT COURAGE OR FAITH?

He who has an ear, let him hear what the Spirit says to the churches. He who overcomes will not be hurt at all by the second death.

Revelations 2.11 NIV

With the Tariq-Leroy Comet visible to the human eye, its bright tail following behind for miles, the terrified people of Southeast Asia began fleeing their homelands by the millions. Some escaped overland toward the northern provinces of India and China, overwhelming Chinese border camps and the not too happy Indian forces, who were in place to prevent such an event from happening. Others choose to escape by way of the sea, swarming over ships and smaller watercraft in hopes of reaching Australia before impact and evade the great tsunami waves that world scientists said would follow throughout the Indian and Pacific Oceans.

In Christian refugee camps hidden in the hills outside Burma, throughout Thailand and on several Islands of the Philippines, missionaries and flocks of believers took this frightening time to pray, to help one another overcome fears.

For the citizens of the world the next four weeks would truly become a time of faith testing. Some would stand, knowing that whatever the outcome, they would soon be rejoicing at the Lord's Table; others cast their lot with false gods and sought salvation from the Dark One - Satan.

LIGHTHOUSE COMMUNITY CHURCH- FAIRBANKS, ALASKA - MARCH 14

Every Christian church in Fairbanks was filled with new believers who come in search of peace in a world gone completely insane. Lighthouse Community Church was compelled to keep its doors open 24 hours a day to handle the growing crowds. Be it Bible study, a lengthy four hour message by team teaching dual speakers, or a floor stomping worship service, the multitudes gathered day and night to hear God's Word.

Outside in the freezing cold, there were still those who stood shivering to mock those in attendance with profanities and accusations for faith in a false God who was now the source of all woes. Only when they resorted to violence were the police brought in to chase them off, but as soon as the police left, they quickly returned to resume demonstrations with even more vigor.

Located on Third Avenue in downtown Fairbanks, Lighthouse Church normally held 308 metal folding chairs, set up in half moon curved rows in front of a tall wooden pulpit, and was usually less than two thirds full. Now all of the chairs were in use around the clock, and still people packed the space standing backs to wall and sitting on the floor. It had become a point of refuge; a place of safety in a time of utter turmoil where no one was turned away. Even the demonstrators were invited in to get out of the cold and share a cup of coffee or hot tea, but an invisible barrier seemed to keep them away.

A tall slender lady with blond hair sat at an electric keyboard; the drummer, a sweaty acne faced older teenager whose long hair was pulled back into a ponytail and three men on electric guitars made up the worship team. There was a heavy older gentleman playing congas, his long gray hair braided and weary eyes bloodshot from too many sleepless nights. The small choir- -made up of all sizes and races did not sing in harmony. What they lacked in harmony, they more than made up for with enthusiasm and the crowds loved the music.

This was Lighthouse Church; a modern Pentecostal church - one of 12 remaining churches in the city. Pastor John Knight, eyes closed and head bowed, stood in front of the congregation and swayed side-to-side with the rhythm of the music. After a few more moments of song, he gestured for the worship leader to tone it down and then approached the pulpit. His voice was amplified through the church as he spoke.

"Time's running out people and there's still a lot of sheep out there in the wilderness who need to be gathered in. Each one...I repeat...each one of you has a responsibility to reach out and spread the Lord's Word to the lost." Pastor Knight looked out over the crowd attempting to look into everyone's face to make a connection. That one man or woman you pass by and fail to witness to may very well be on a downward spiral to Hell. Do you want to live with that? Shake off your pride, cast your fears aside and reach out to these lost souls." He looked to the front row and pointing a finger, swung his arm from side to side, "How many of you would be here today if someone hadn't taken the time to tell you about the Lord's love?" Pastor Knight watched heads nod, heard dozens shout out "Amen", before he continued. "So, what are you going to do about it?" He asked loudly. "I say let's get out there and spread the Lord's Word throughout this beautiful city of ours. Our King is coming soon, the clock is ticking and I don't want to lose a single soul to the enemy." He stepped back from the pulpit and signaled for the worship leader to start up again.

Pastor Knight felt a wave of weariness pass over him, his legs crying out for rest as his knees wobbled a wee bit. He'd gone without break for three hours, using the chairs normally set aside for the disabled and elderly. Thankfully, this was the last song and he had a long break before the next service, which involved a baptism for twenty two new believers. Pastor of Lighthouse for the last 11 years, John, half white and half Athabascan Indian, had grown up in two diverse cultures and after graduating from Bible Temple in Oregon, returned to Fairbanks with a deep desire to bring these two groups together. Surprising no one, he married Cindy Williams, his high school sweetheart. A year later, on a beautiful Saturday morning, their son Richard was born and today stood tall - a young vibrant man of 16.

Lighthouse Church had conducted services downtown since leaving behind the burned ruins of their church on Farmers Loop Road two years before. It had been firebombed by suspected UWCA members and Pastor Knight had found his youth pastor, Lucas Longman, lying on the ground in front of the church shot in the back six times with what police later said was .357 magnum.

Following the firebombing of four other churches and the murder of three church leaders, authorities finally caught up with the suspects outside the 1st Assembly of God Church on Airport Way armed and carrying unlit Molotov cocktails. Lab tests confirmed the .357 Smith and Wesson Model 66 Pistol taken from the leader was the weapon used to execute the four pastors. Interrogation of the suspects confirmed the men to be members of the Unified World Church Alliance, but beyond that they refused to say anything more. Convicted of murder and arson, both capital offenses, the defendants were executed without appeal by an ADF firing squad.

For over a year there were no further anti-Christian or anti-Semitic incidents, but recently another hate group had shown its ugly face, slinking through the shadows like a venomous snake and Pastor John Knight suspected it might be the UWCA again. He had attended a pastor's meeting last Saturday afternoon with 11 other nervous pastors, where he learned that some of the men had already received death threats. Pastor Underwood of the 1st Baptist Church discovered the words, "You're dead meat, Christ lover!" painted in large black letters on his apartment door. Others told how church members were being harassed at work, especially after someone began rumors blaming Christians for the Plague. Pamphlets were being handed out, saying it was a Christian doctor who developed the virus as a bio-weapon to be used against homosexuals.

"I've heard that one myself," Bishop Reedly said.

"What are we going to do?" Reverend Walters asked, adding, "I mean, of course, besides praying."

Pastor John Knight replied, "Sergeant Brad Sawyer of the Fairbanks Police Department is a member of my congregation; I'll have a word with him. I'm sure he can offer up some advice and hopefully provide some added patrols around our churches."

"Prayer is of course good, but I also feel a few armed guards around our churches would go a long way to dissuade these... animals." Bishop Reedly's statement received a few nods of agreement.

John didn't agree and voiced his concern, "Brothers, I would rather have the police deal with this matter before I have some of my church members risking their lives in a shootout to protect a simple building. No, I'll not have another man killed for four walls and some chairs."

Remembering the depressing mood of the pastor's meeting, John decided to leave the services early to make contact with Brad. It was a long cold walk to the Sawyer's apartment, and he never suspected someone was following him. There were two threatening looking men lurking in the fog and shadowing his every step.

THE KNIGHT APARTMENT

Home alone and anxiously waiting for her husband to return for dinner, and some much needed rest, Cindy Knight was in the kitchen preparing their meal of one 24 ounce can of chicken stew, one package of Saltine crackers, a 4 ounce tin of military issue generic cheese spread, three small packets of salt, one 2 ounce package of instant coffee and one package of presweetened Kool-Aid. For a normal luncheon it didn't look too bad, but this was their only meal for the day. Another 24 hours would pass before the next meal, leaving Cindy to wonder how much longer they could continue on this manner.

Cindy, at 40, could easily pass for being in her mid to late twenties. Losing 17 pounds from rationing didn't hurt the hips any and wearing her dark brown hair in a single long braid down the middle of her back only enhanced her youthful looks. A strong intercessor, Cindy had experienced a series of dreams over the last few weeks; the kind that woke her in a breathless state and left her body trembling and covered in sweat. In her dreams she saw Fairbanks in flames, mangled and burned bodies scattered about the city streets as huge metal monsters devoured buildings with great bellows of fire. The monsters reminded her of fairy tale dragons, only these were made of metal.

Stirring the stew, she used a pinch or two of her highly coveted salt and some pepper her son had scrounged to add some value of taste. "Not too bad," she muttered. She was startled by a loud thump at the front door. Secured by a deadbolt lock, John had warned her against opening the door unless she knew for sure who was on the other side. For extra security, John and Richard had devised a knock similar to the old "shave and haircut two bits" knock. Simple, but it worked. Again, there was another hard thump as if someone was kicking it. There was a loud double knock, followed by a terror filled moment of silence.

"Who is it?" she asked, in a frightened voice. She knew this wasn't Richard pulling a joke. The boy would not be able to sit down for a week with the tanning she would give him if it was. There was no response, only an eerie silence from the other side of the door. She was about to ask again when someone violently kicked the bottom of the door. Startled, Cindy jumped back in alarm and yelled out in a trembling voice, "Go away!"

A deep threatening voice shouted back, "You tell that sanctimonious preacher we'll be back. An' next time, we won't let this door stop us!"

Slowly she backed away from the door, tripped over a table and knocked an old ceramic lamp to the floor, breaking it. Continuing backwards, she landed on the couch and froze, staring at the front door with terror written across her face. She grabbed a couch pillow for security, grasped it tightly in front of her and fought to get her fear under control, praying her husband and son would return soon.

Young Richard Knight had left Fort Wainwright after a couple of hours of participating in the fort's daily swap meet. It was held at the enlisted recreation club and usually drew quite a crowd. People brought in gold, silver and precious gems from old jewelry, items that no longer had such high value. It struck him funny to think gold and silver were now all but worthless. Now the hot items were sugar, salt, chocolate, flashlight batteries and hard candy, books and animal traps, ammunition and hunting, or skinning knives. Survival was the name of the game and bartering was the common system of exchange. There wasn't much of an economy, but time was limited and waste meant a stack of gold coins, an ounce of silver or a bag of diamonds.

His hands were full of treasures when Richard kicked the bottom of the front door with the standard code to get his mother's attention. Cindy had returned to her stew when she heard the knocking and nearly dropped a full ladle of stew on the floor as her heart skipped a beat. Not knowing what else to do, she picked up a large black handled carving knife and cautiously approached the front door. "Who is it?" She asked in a loud voice.

"It's me, mom. Come on, open up! My hands are full."

Relieved to the point of tears, Cindy quickly opened the door with her free hand and stepped back as Richard entered. The front room filled with a cold fog, which quickly disappeared after Cindy slammed the door shut and made sure the dead bolt was secured.

"Hey, take it easy," Richard said as the door nearly struck him in the shoulder. Only then did he see the knife in her hand. "What's going on?" Without answering, she took one of the bags from him and walked straight toward the kitchen. "Mom... hey, what's wrong?" Richard asked as he followed her into the kitchen and set his bag down on the counter. "Come on, I'm sixteen...Is it Dad?" Richard was worried and seeing his mother's watery eyes only made things worse. "Has somethin' happened to Dad?" He waited for her to answer as he jerked off mittens, heavy parka, wool scarf encased in ice from his freezing breath, and a heavy sweater. He piled them on the floor and wrapped his arms around his trembling mother as she stared at the front door with the knife still clutched tightly in her hands. She welcomed the hug and rested her head against his shoulders. After a moment, she backed away, put the knife down and looked into his caring eyes, "We had a visitor... maybe visitors...I don't know." She shook her head. "There's people out there who want to harm us, son." She stopped wishing John was present to explain it better. Frustrated, she turned the stew off and walked over to the kitchen table where she sat down and gestured for Richard to join her.

"Why...why do people want to harm us? We got nothin' ta steal," Richard said as he turned a chair around and sat down across from his mother.

"These people hate us because of who we are...Christians."

"Because we're Christians?" Richard was confused and his scrunched expression showed it. She'd seen it many times, first in his father and now in their son; an upper lip curled to the side and left eyebrow raised when they were confused or racking their memory for the answer to something.

"There's a faction out there, son, a movement that's spreading across the planet. Here we call them the Unified World Church Alliance; I think that's who visited me today. They preach fear to the frightened and call out for the persecution of Jews and Christians alike." She stopped long enough to retrieve a glass of water from the counter and take a sip. "Remember, the Book of Revelations foretold of such happenings. Christians will be persecuted for their beliefs, much the same way the Jewish people were persecuted before and during World War II. For years it happened to Christians in Malaysia, Indonesia and all over Africa. We just never thought it would come here, not in America. But it did. Now it's happening right here. In Europe, that new Emperor demands all Christians and Jewish leaders to register with the government. Once they've all registered, we'll see a second Holocaust. Whole communities will be searched without warrant and people will vanish in the night. You watch. The ones who don't kowtow to this Emperor will be executed first. I've heard him called the Anti-Christ and he very well may be." With a sigh, she reached over and clutched her son's hand. "Your Dad speaks of this in his sermons and you've read the scripture...of how the Anti-Christ will rise up in the End of Days." She took another sip of water, sighed, glanced up at the ceiling and then looked into her son's young eyes, "I'm rambling on, but don't worry...we'll be all right." Her tone was not very convincing.

Richard looked to the front door and then to his mother, "I'm worried about Dad, he's late." Usually John beat Richard home, but not today.

"I think today he planned to see Brad Sawyer...Still, times like this I really miss having a phone." All civilian telephone service had been discontinued; wire and instruments confiscated or turned in for ADF purposes. Wanting to change the subject, Cindy looked at the dark green trash bags on the counter and asked, "Why don't you tell me how well you scored today?"

Richard nodded, smiled and stood up. "The cold kept a lot of people home, but I made a couple pretty good deals." Richard slid his chair back in and walked over to the kitchen counter. Opening the first bag, he pulled out two large multi-colored homemade candles; one 3 inch vanilla scented and the other a 5 inch apple scented. There was a well-used goose down sleeping bag with working zipper in the bottom of the bag. From the second bag he removed a red wool scarf and a pair of matching homemade mittens which he handed to his mother and for which he received a big smile and a hug. "I've got two bars of homemade soap and a new wooden hair brush... a package of dry milk," he pulled each item out and handed them to his mother then pulled out a dozen packages of instant tomato soup and broke into a grin when he reached in to the bottom of the bag and pulled out two Louie L'amour paperbacks for his dad. "...and I don't think he's read these two, do you?"

"No, I think you might have scored big here." After hugging Richard, she asked how his trading stock was holding up. Included in each meal ration was a sealed baggie, one for each occupant of the domicile which contained mixed brands of cigarettes and other tobacco products. Since these items were no longer being produced they were hot trading items with those who hadn't kicked the nicotine habit; men and women who were going down kicking and screaming till the last butt was smoked. They were trading off just about anything and everything for one last puff. With no smokers in the Knight household, Richard stockpiled his cigarettes and was truly shrewd for someone his age. For his mother, he searched the barter tables for chocolate. He wanted to surprise her with some for her birthday, but so far he hadn't scored any. Most chocolate and other candies vanished from the shelves and stock rooms during the first food riots. The military had discovered a good-sized quantity of Hershey candy in container vans sitting in the Anchorage Port, having been shipped up from Seattle before the missiles flew. The supply was held by the ADF and used in the children's wards of area hospitals.

At trade fair, a Hershey's chocolate bar, if one was available, was worth 200 cigarettes. A one cup bag of white or brown sugar was going at 150 cigarettes and corn syrup was worth 150 cigarettes a measured cup. There was no honey to be found; bees had disappeared; their demise being blamed on volcanic ash contamination .Handgun ammunition was always a hot trade and handled under the table, even for the black powder shooters. As with everything else, gunpowder was no longer manufactured, all rifle ammo was confiscated by the ADF with the onset of Martial Law and only a few pistols or revolvers were allowed in private hands; by permit only. Detergents, soaps and clothing items became hard to find items once everyone realized the Lower 48 was no longer capable of shipping anything north to Alaska. Ingenuity stepped in and a lot of people started up cottage industries to make up for the goods lost with the onset of war. Caribou and moose hides, Musk Ox hair and pelts from smaller animals were used for mittens, hats and coats. Goat milk was used for soap and mixed with on hand chemicals to make detergents.

The one single thing that affected people most was learning how little the major stores had kept on hand in Alaska stores. . Early Emergency Preparedness studies of the 1990's showed that most major chain stores in Anchorage and Fairbanks only stocked enough foodstuffs to last approximately 30 days. They counted on continual supplies from the Lower 48, arriving by barge, container van or truck - a supply line that was cut off for a very long time to come. If it hadn't been for the military seizing supplies from stores and restaurants, and taking custody of the newly arriving container vans, Alaska would probably have begun starving within 45 days of the OAP missile attack.

Propane was in short supply for civilian use, so stoves were used only once a day for cooking the single meal. For those who had wood stoves all the nearby supply of wood had been exhausted and people either went without or formed work parties that trekked in an ever widening area in search of suitable fuel. Without trucks, they were forced to pull huge sleds through deep snow to reach the next standing line of trees and green wood was hard to burn. Some of the standing black spruce was burnable, but it was used up fast and with this 6 month cold spell, a winter like none had experienced before, all of the nearby woods had been cut down for several miles and the wood parties had ended. The dire need that so many people had warned about and urged the development of; was alternative energy sources. Now they were surviving on only coal and oil, and the supply of both was rapidly dwindling.

KNIGHT APARTMENT

Freezing from a brisk cold walk through -40° weather, Pastor John Knight finally reached his front door and proceeded to tap out the family knock. Although the doorknob locks worked, the government never was able to find keys to all of the apartments and there were too few locksmiths, and too many jobs for them to have gotten around to Knight's apartment building. The trick was not locking yourself out, especially when the mercury was down in the basement and your breath froze solid before crashing to the ground

Swinging the door open, Cindy waited for John to dash in and quickly closed the door behind him. She surprised him by wrapping her arms around his neck and presenting him with a deep and emotional kiss. Though he greatly appreciated the unusual welcome, John was troubled when he looked down at his wife and saw the nervousness in her eyes and knew she had been crying. "Okay, what's up?"

Silent at first, she took his coat, scarf, gloves and hat and hung them on wall hooks then led him into the living room and after sitting him down knelt at his feet to help remove his heavy winter boots. Then maintaining a calming voice and while carrying the boots to the front door, she began to tell him of her earlier experience. As she did, she witnessed the anger grow within him and surprisingly, it made her appreciate her husband even more.

He remained silent for a long moment while he digested the information and then startled her when he launched himself from the couch like a NASA rocket. He growled out in anger and began to pace the floor in silence, his arms behind him as he seemed to be studying the floor. From long experience she waited quietly, knowing he would speak when he was ready. Finally, he stopped, looked at her and began to talk, while she listened in silence, "I stopped by to see Brad, but he was asleep. Kathy said she'd tell him I was by and why." He brought his right arm around and clasped her hand in his, "We'll be all right."

Hearing his dad, Richard came out of his bedroom, relieved to see his father safe.

Cindy was impressed with his ability to let the rage in him slowly subside, turning it over to God. With a grateful smile she looked into his eyes and replied, "I know." With a look over her shoulder to her son, Cindy told Richard to show his father his surprise. Richard nodded, walked back into the bedroom and returned with the two books he had traded for. John was delighted. He enjoyed reading westerns above everything else; except for the Bible of course.

After the stew was warmed up again, they had a quiet dinner. Later, John was sitting on the couch reading one of his new books when there was a light knock at the door. John immediately glanced to his wife, "Relax Hon, it could be one of our neighbors or someone from church." Standing, he walked over to the door, but before opening he asked, "Who's there?"

"Two Police Popsicles...Open up!" Brad Sawyer shouted. Recognizing the booming voice, John opened the door to let Brad and Scott Radley inside. "Come in, come in." He quickly closed and re-bolted the door, "Here, let me have your coats...Honey, can we offer these gentlemen something hot to drink?"

"We're okay, Pastor," Brad replied, but by the frost on his eyebrows and Scott's mustache, John knew they'd welcome a warm up.

"At least some hot tea?"

Brad nodded in agreement. Normally he would have gladly accepted refreshment, but with rationing he knew the Knights would be dipping into their limited supplies to play host.

"Kathy told me why you stopped by, but why don't you give us a replay," Brad said. He settled onto the couch, adjusting his police belt to prevent it from squeezing off the blood flow to his legs or ripping the couch material.

While Cindy was in the kitchen, John shared the statements of the clergy and the various threats and harassment received by members of the different congregations. He finished off with the experience Cindy had gone through earlier in the day. Brad and Scott glanced up at her as she brought in a pot of unsweetened hot tea and decorative ceramic mugs on a metal tray. "You'll have to accept it oriental style - no sweetener."

"Hot is jus' fine with me, Ma'am." Scott replied.

"I was hoping it wouldn't start up again," Brad said. He spoke in almost a whisper.

"What?" Cindy asked.

Brad shook his head, but then said, "You'd think with that rock hanging over all of us that maybe we'd all join together. But no, that...." Brad stopped, remembering Cindy and Richard were in the room. "It seems the UWCA has reared its ugly head again." He pulled a small spiral notebook out and handed it to Pastor Knight, "Why don't you give me the home addresses for all the pastors. We'll increase the patrols around the churches and drive by their homes on a regular basis, when possible."

"I'm sure that will help, Brad," John said.

Cindy poured tea for all of them, "Please, help yourself."

"Are there any firearms in the house, Pastor?" Scott asked.

"I've never felt the need for them. I'm not a hunter anymore, the one rifle I had I gave up to the ADF in January."

"We'll be right back." Standing up, Brad grabbed his parka and turned to his partner, "Let's take a look around outside. See if we can spot anyone nosin' around." He turned to Pastor Knight. "You go ahead and write down those addresses, we'll be back in a minute or two.

"Here I go again, ever the volunteer," Scott said in a tone of sarcasm. He took his coat from Brad's hand. "Please keep the tea hot, it sure tastes mighty good."

"Do you really think someone's watching us?" Cindy asked, with a note of fear to her voice.

"I don't know, Cindy. Let's see what we turn up before we jump to conclusions," Brad said. A short time later, Brad and Scott were back inside the apartment, thawing out. Scott had used his handkerchief to wipe the melting ice crystals off his moustache, which brought a smile to Richard's young face. Brad carried a black canvas bag into the apartment that he had retrieved from the trunk of the patrol car, while Scott did a bit of scouting around. Back on the couch with some hot liquid in him, Brad directed his conversation to Pastor Knight, "John, times are changing too fast for civilized people to keep up." He reached into the canvas bag and pulled out a brown leather shoulder holster with an old Smith & Wesson Model 27 .357 Magnum Revolver and two loaded speed loaders. Laying the outfit on the floor, he reached back in again and pulled out a Smith & Wesson Lady Elite .357 caliber 5 shot Revolver in a black canvas holster. The Elite was built with a special light frame for a woman's use. He also provided a box of Winchester .357 hollow point ammo for both revolvers.

"Feels like Christmas, do I get anything?" Richard asked hopefully, knowing the Elite was for mom and the heavier Model 27 for Dad.

Brad had to chuckle, "Not this time, buster. I'm not about to arm a 16 year old with a firearm. Besides, I've seen that hunting knife you carry."

"Where'd you get these?" John asked. "How will I pay you...trade for 'em?"

"You can't, these are on loan only; you don't have time to apply for a permit and wait on the ADF to approve it. I keep extra weapons in my car – just in case." Brad let the weapons thaw out, wiped them down and then opened them to show that both revolvers were unloaded. "Now, I think today was harassment, but next time might be the real deal. You have to be ready and a .357 will do the job nicely. Even the noise will frighten most people off, but if you have to hit someone, you aim for center mass. An inexperienced shooter who tries to wound will usually miss and then...you're dead." Over the next few moments, Brad and Scott gave a short class on firearm safety and shooting techniques which ended when a radio call came in from dispatch - they were needed elsewhere.

"Thank you," John said. He held the heavy revolver in his hands and liked the feel of the well-balanced weapon. "Wonder why I never bought one of these?"

"Pastor, jus' you make sure that if you have to use it, you shoot ta kill," Scott said. "Otherwise, you'll be the one dead, like Brad said. Don't threaten anyone, while you're busy talkin' the other guy is gonna be busy killing you." Scott then turned to Cindy, "Keep that somewhere you can get to it fast an' practice running to it so it becomes natural. If you don't practice, you'll forget you have it when the emergency hits.

"Someone comes knockin' at the door, grab the revolver right away. If it's not Richard or Pastor, tell 'em ta come back later." Scott looked at the front door, "You got yourself a good thick door there and a strong lock, but don't rely on it. We didn't find anyone out there, but ah think your fears are justified. People are gettin' mighty weird an' we should know." Scott stopped as he pulled his heavy coat on.

"Thank you so much," Cindy said as he flashed a grateful smile and then added, "You're both welcome here, anytime."

"Scott, you're always welcome in the House of God too," Pastor said. He patted Scott affectionately on the right shoulder before he could escape out the door.

"Umm...thanks." Scott tossed a fast wave to Richard and hustled outside while Brad made a few closing comments. Back in the car, Scott noticed the smile on Brad's face and in a frustrated tone he remarked, "Double teamin' me ain't gonna help none."

"I didn't say anything," Brad said.

"You didn't have too, I recognized that look on your face."

Brad grinned, "That wall you put up to protect yourself has some crack forming, my young friend."

"There you go again!" Scott exclaimed. "I ain't got no wall and it's got no cracks in it. Come on, let's see what's got Dispatch all fired up."

AIRPORT WAY, FAIRBANKS 9:07 P.M.

A fiery explosion erupted from the 1st Assembly of God building, breaking out all the windows of the main sanctuary and those of several nearby homes. Flames shot upward over two hundred feet and debris showered the parking lot. By the time the fire department arrived, the church was totally engulfed in red and yellow flames. The intense heat drove firefighters back and one firefighter was later heard to have said, "Like walking out of a freezer and into a raging furnace."

The bitter cold transformed ground water leaking from tanker fire hoses into sheets of slick ice. Heavy fog from the water spray mixed with the black clouds bellowing out from the fire. Bystanders stared hypnotically, unable to take their eyes off the fire or grasp the seriousness of the destruction.

The church tower, a bronze colored pinnacle, slowly toppled to the ground and no one uttered a word until the 8 foot metal cross disappeared into the flames, bringing a deep mournful cry from onlookers. Courageous firefighters continued to fight a no win situation. Again and again they charged forward with two inch hoses gushing water only to be forced backward by the intensity of the heat. As they advanced and retreated, their yellow turnouts were covered first in a layer of ice and then with running water. All too rapidly, survival clothing was darkened to black from ash and soot

"Hey, George, you got any ideas how it started?" Brad Sawyer asked the Battalion Captain, George Sandy.

"A guy who lives over the fence said he was outside with his dog and remembered hearing some noises behind the church before the fire began.

"The old girl went up fast and I'm thinking too fast for anything but arson. Love ta get my hands..." George looked at Brad, "You thinking what I'm thinking... it's starting again? Isn't it?"

"Yeah, the UWCA is apparently back in town. I'm almost positive this is their work. Remember, this was where we caught them last time." Brad looked to the fire, "Guess they came back to finish the job."

Brad scanned the crowd of bystanders, wondering if any one of them might be a member of the UWCA.

"Stop 'em, Brad!" Sandy ordered. "Stop 'em now, before they kill someone." Sandy's eyes widened when he saw the Senior Pastor of the Assembly of God arrive; two of his elders were comforting him as they prayed for protection over the firefighters.

"Find them, Brad," Sandy said. His tone was almost a plea as he walked away to have a word with the pastor.

Brad watched the firefighters for a moment; then decided it was time to put on his investigator hat and get to work. "Scott, let's interview witnesses and ask questions before everyone takes off. Have one of the guys take some photographs of the crowd. Someone's face may stick out later on."

"You got it," Scott replied. He was back in a moment, "Do we still have any photos of the old gang?"

"The ones we caught were executed, but someone in the department might recognize someone; I'll send copies over to ADF Intelligence." Brad was freezing and knew he still had at least 10 to 15 minutes out here, maybe more. He took two instant warmer packets out of his coat pocket, opened them and inserted the packets inside his gloves. At least his hands would be warm for a while, now he just needed to worry about the rest of his body.

FAIRBANKS POLICE DEPARTMENT

Chief Bob Osborne was upset after leaving yet another heated session with the Mayor. When he returned to his office, he was not all happy to find Brad waiting. "Whatever you got, you can keep it. I need my chair and some liquid pain relief." Without another word, Bob carefully lowered himself into his chair wincing from severe back pain, he sighed deeply and sat back to put his feet on top of a lower open drawer, before leaning back in his chair. His eyes closed behind mirrored sunglasses, Bob hoped Brad had taken the hint and left him in peace. But that wasn't to be. When Bob propped open one eye, Brad was still standing with that fierce all too familiar Rottweiler sizing up his quarry expression on his face.

"Okay, I give up," Bob said in surrender. He pulled his feet down, leaned forward, rested his elbows on the desktop and cupped his chin in his hands.

"I want to talk with you about the church bombing."

"Great. No rest for the weary." As Bob stood up, pain surged through him and he cringed as he walked around the desk, "I'll have you know I've been the better part of an hour in the Mayor's office discussing that very subject." Bob gestured to his backside with his right index finger, "Check it out. See if I have any rear left to chew on." Bob walked over and slammed his door shut, sending echoes down the hall and throughout the nearly vacant building, then swung angrily back to face Brad. "That damn...pardon my French, his Honor the Mayor gave me my marching orders. Hunt those UWCA animals down or I'll find myself back on patrol. Can you believe it, that man actually said, 'Chief, read 'em their rights with hot lead.' That man watched one too many cop shows."

"Only one witness and he couldn't see anything through the ice fog." Brad pulled his notebook out, turning to the page filled with addresses for the various pastors. "I've learned that several church leaders have been threatened with hand written notes or their doors painted with witty slogans and sayings." He pulled a Polaroid print from his breast pocket, "This morning, my pastor, John Knight, got hit." He handed the photo to Bob. It showed an apartment front door with a large Nazi symbol painted in black over a red Christian cross. The paint was running down the door, so Brad suspected the job was accomplished with spray paint.

"Yeah, that looks like UWCA work…the rise of the Fourth Reich." Bob handed the photo back. "Work with the ADF Intel people, but get me some results. I really don't want to be riding patrol, Brad." Bob returned to his chair. "You do understand what I'm saying here, right?"

"Pull out all stops, step on some toes and kick some doors in. I gotcha."

"Good. Now get out of my office!" Bob ordered and then added a sincere, "Brad, be careful out there. This isn't normal police work anymore…We've got spies, deserters, collaborators, hate groups and loonies, and they come in all shapes, colors and ages. I can't afford to lose you."

"My, I didn't know you cared," Brad said as Bob hustled him out the door.

"I don't really," Bob yelled. "But who'd run my nightshift?"

ADF PROVOST MARSHALL'S OFFICE, FORT WAINWRIGHT

Leaning over Captain Susan Riley's desk, Brad showed her the photo of Knight's apartment door and said, "Scary how a simple symbol can be."

A former Anchorage Police Department lieutenant, Susan Riley had seen a lot in her 11 years police experience. Called into the ADF with her USAF reserve status as a 2nd lieutenant in the Office of Special Investigation (OSI), she was soon promoted and posted to her current position as Provost Intelligence Officer. Good friends, Brad and she had worked together numerous times in joint operations over the last three months.

"I've seen similar propaganda on post, Brad. We've got several MP investigators working on it. We also have someone spreading anti-Christian and anti-Jewish literature through the ranks, and we're attempting to locate the source. Unfortunately, with all the troops we have processing in, we've apparently picked up some Neo-Nazi's in the bunch."

"We think it's the UWCA again," Brad said.

"I agree." Susan walked Brad out of her office, offering him some hot coffee and then noticing that Brad's partner, Scott, was already at the coffee pot making small talk with a couple of MP's.

"Thanks, Susan, but I'll take a rain check. Too much coffee; can't seem to get a decent sleep anymore- not that I have much time for it anyway."

"Yeah, I know what you mean." She walked him to the door. "I'll keep you appraised from my side and we'll talk soon."

Brad looked over at Scott, "C'mon, partner, let's go."

By 0300 hours, Brad and Scott were parked near the police department; both about to call it a night. Twelve hour shifts had quickly become 14 to16 hour shifts as they searched for any sign of the UWCA, following up any lead and talking to dozens of informants. "I either slug some coffee down, or I'll pass out at the wheel. How about you… you want some java?" Brad asked his partner.

"We got any left?"

"Yeah, I refilled the thermos at the Rec Center while you were shootin' the breeze with those good looking ladies."

"Who, I might add were all married, thank you so very much," Scott complained.

"Their old men are pulling duty up north at Prudhoe, so they get together in mass to protect one another from all us single guys. It also keeps 'em in line, leaning on one another when the walls start to close in. But I sure do enjoy talking to 'em; they feel safe with me…Must be the uniform."

"Well, it sure ain't those wolf pup eyes of yours." Brad pulled the thermos out and poured two hot cups of heavily diluted coffee into two well used Styrofoam cups that Scott held steady. Screwing the lid back on the thermos, he took his cup and let the warmth filter its way through his hands. Taking a sip, he wished he could remember the taste of fresh cream and a double helping of sugar in his coffee.

"We don't talk about it much, Scott…and in fact you get downright perturbed when I do bring the subject up." Brad didn't get very far before Scott interrupted him.

"Aw… c'mon, Brad, leave it alone will yuh? Ah'm too tired for a lecture on Jesus an' what he could do for me." Scott looked hard into Brad's eyes, then softened his gaze, "Listen, I am really fond of your family an' I guess you're my best friend. But I jus' don't buy into this Christian voodoo. I got a rock hanging over mah head, a million Chinese wantin' my skin an' you wanna see mah soul saved. Its mah soul, man- can't you leave it alone?"

"Sure, but it hurts me to picture you in the flames of Hell because I let up on you. That I didn't use every moment we have left to…." Brad was cut off again.

"Brad, I know all about Christianity. I've heard it all before, in triplicate and it didn't take then either." Scott's eyes began to water, something unusual for Brad to see in his partner who kept his emotions buried pretty deep.

"When was this?" Brad pursued him; he felt he was on to something here.

Scott remained quiet for a moment, then spoke with a slight tremor in his voice, "Okay, ah'll tell you…if yuh promise ta leave it alone for the rest of the night.

Okay?"

"For the rest of tonight, you got it," Brad agreed.

"Okay. I met a girl...a woman. She was the kindest, mos' beautiful woman in the world. Was back in mah Army days. She was a colonel's daughter and for some reason took a fancy to me. Like you, she was a Bible thumper...boy, she done tried ever which way to get me ta church. She always carried that Bible with her...loved singing the Psalms and she had this beautiful voice...like Diana Ross. Her daddy, he was a Christian too an' saw right through me. He knew what I wanted, knew who I was and had a shotgun on the wall all loaded up for me if I ever got out of hand." Scott went quiet for a moment and Brad waited as he sipped his coffee, leaned forward to adjust the heater fan and listened to the police radio.

"I broke it off because I couldn't stand it. All this fine woman in my arms and she wanted marriage first before we did the bed dance. Ah told her to make a choice, either her God or me...I lost." Scott looked to his right at his reflection in the window glass and sipped his coffee. He remembered her all too clearly and the heart pain welled up inside of him.

"What happened to her?" Brad asked.

"I got orders for Alaska and never saw her again. I could tell I broke her heart, but that girl stood by her convictions. She loved me, Brad. I knew it, but I wanted more. Hey, I'm a man. I need that physical stuff when my blood boils and she wanted the whole ring bit. "

"So why didn't you marry her?" Brad asked the question, but he already knew the answer.

Scott's eyes grew hard again he looked away, gazing outside as he gave Brad an honest answer, "I asked her once, but she wouldn't marry me unless I became a Christian. Something about this unequally yoked business...don't recall now. All I do remember are the tears she shed for me, the pain I caused her. Never felt the same about a woman since...But don't make that public, okay?"

"No problem, did you ever hear from her again?"

"She wrote me a couple times, wanting to know how I liked it up here. By then I was seeing a couple other girls, mah pride took over an'...I never wrote her back."

"Do you think she made it...Maybe she survived?"

Scott shook his head, "No. Her father got orders about the same time I did. He went to the Pentagon."

"Oh." The Pentagon, in Washington D.C. and most of the East coast, was lost in the first volley of missiles. That part of the United States now glowed from intense radiation. Those who didn't die from the first impacts, perished soon afterward from radiation sickness.

"You're getting a second chance here, Scott."

"What?" Scott looked up from staring into his coffee cup and glanced over at Brad. "Thought we had an agreement?"

Brad nodded and reached into his inside coat pocket to pull out a small copy of the New Testament; a gift from his father a long time ago. The pages were well worn. "I agreed and I'll not bug you the rest of the shift. I want to give you this. My Dad carried this on patrol and I've carried it ever since. I think he'd agree that it was time to pass it on now. This is the New Testament, NIV version and easy to read." Brad attempted to hand it to Scott, who put his hand up in refusal.

"Ah don't need your Bible an' that was your dad's."

"I'm not preaching to you, simply offering you a gift." Brad put it in his partner's objecting hand. "Take it. You don't wanna read it, don't. But I find it real unfriendly not to receive a gift from a partner."

"Okay, ah'll take the book if it'll make you happy. But don't expect no book report." Scott shoved the Bible inside his own inside pocket and hoped the matter would be dropped. To his surprise, Brad didn't bring the subject up again for the rest of the shift.

SCOTT'S APARTMENT

Unable to sleep and too wired to read one of his novels, Scott ambled about his apartment in hopes of finding something, anything, that might slow his mind down. Glancing at his parka hanging on a brass hook beside the front door, Scott suddenly remembered Brad's Bible. *As boring as that thing mus' be, It's bound ta put me ta sleep.* Retrieving the Bible, Scott flopped down on his couch and opened to the first page of Matthew remembering this was a favorite book of hers. Then with a smirk on his face, fed by ego, he began to read the scripture.

Reaching the first verse from the Book of John, Scott glanced at his watch and the time startled him, *Can't be! Ah've been readin' for nearly four hours...Ah'm not even sleepy.* He took a moment to reflect over the words before him. It wasn't hard to visualize her face, recalling those moments when she talked of her God's love. He never admitted it, but he remembered the radiance about her as she shared with him and now, here he was, reading the Bible for the first time. This time it was his own tears beginning to flow as emotion began to melt his hard shell. He wouldn't tell anyone, not even Brad, but for a moment, he almost felt as if she was sitting there beside him and it warmed him. Then his loss came into full reality and Scott released a roar of deep rage that burst from within him and vanished through the ceiling. He could hear her words, all those long ago moments of her sharing about this Jesus character he was now reading about.

Memories gave realism to what he was taking in, knowing how she felt and the stand she made for this Lord of hers.

Scott had questions, hundreds of them that needed to be answered right this moment and wasn't sure where he should go to ask. Of course Brad came to his mind first, but by now, Brad would be in a deep sleep and there was only a few hours to go before next shift. Thinking about it further, he remembered Pastor John Knight's invitation and knew this was the answer. Quickly he pulled on his uniform coveralls and taking the patrol car, headed for the Knight apartment.

By divine coincidence, Pastor John happened to be home. He was dressed in old clothes and laying on the kitchen floor with his head stuck under the sink working on a leaking pipe when Scott knocked at the door. Welcomed in, Scott spent the next couple of hours sitting on the sofa with John, discussing the Word of God. A large Bible lay open between them as Scott asked away with his questions. Not new to this, John responded to nearly every question by referring to the Word of God for the answer, showing Scott the scripture and asking Scott to read it out loud. This was followed by discussion as John put the meaning of the Word into simple and often, modern terms. While the two men were in the living room talking, Cindy was in the bedroom praying for Scott.

Again tears flowed as Scott spoke about his life and then suddenly, catching John off guard, he dropped off the couch and knelt before John with his head bowed. "Please, Pastor, show me what I need ta do." John slid off the couch and knelt beside Scott, placing his arm around the big man's shoulders and guided him through the sinner's prayer. Right there in John's living room, Scott asked the Lord Jesus Christ into his life, repenting for his sinful life and receiving the Lord's forgiveness.

Before Scott left, John and Cindy hugged him warmly and once more, tears were in abundance. Except this time it was tears of joy. As he headed out to the parking lot, Scott was grinning from ear to ear under his wool scarf and imagined the surprised look on Brad's face when Scott told him all about what had happened.

Putting the patrol car into gear, making sure he remembered to unplug it first, he didn't give much thought to the fact he'd gone the whole day without sleep. He felt energized and ready for another 12 hour shift. Later, in the early morning hours, a smiling but bleary eyed patrolman was relieved to know a full thermos of hot coffee was nestled in the seat beside him.

A COMING STORM

5 - ABOVE AND BEYOND THE CALL OF DUTY

"They said to you, 'In the last times there will be scoffers who will follow their own godly desires.' These are the men who divide you, who follow their natural instincts and do not have Spirit." – Jude 1.18 NIV

OFFICE OF THE GOVERNOR, ANCHORAGE, ALASKA - MARCH 19TH

When towering tsunami waves swept up the Inland Passage in the wake of the great quakes, the surging waters wiped out Juneau and most other Southeast Alaskan coastal communities. On Baranof Island, the once extinct volcano, Mt. Edgecombe, erupted, destroying Sitka with massive quakes and covered the island's snow under several feet of ash. More than 8500 people perished on the island, along with thousands of others who were swept away by the massive tsunami waves carried up the Inland Passage.

Anchorage was hit with a 7.4 earthquake, causing major damage and aftershocks in the 4.0 range were still rattling windows. The eruptions of Mt. Spur and Mt. Redoubt were of great concern. A series of violent eruptions sent ash and debris more than a mile into the air and heavy lava flows into river beds and over one large oil tank farm

With these nearby eruptions, massive clouds of dark ash had covered South Central Alaska. All flights were canceled, airports shut down and the elderly were trapped inside homes because the air had turned foul. . By the middle of the second week only sporadic clouds of ash hampered city operations and the airport was open again for limited flights.

While Anchorage was measuring ash at 10 inches, the Kenai Peninsula was covered in nearly a foot of black ash and it was still falling mixed with heavy snow. Every piece of emergency equipment was out, struggling to keep the main roadways open and deal with buildings affected by the initial quake. People were trapped inside homes, but thankfully the holidays had kept the office buildings mostly empty. Several of these larger buildings had suffered extensive damage and one 8 story building had collapsed and landed on its parking garage.

Breathing gear or at least face masks were now required for anyone outside and within hours, the outside temperatures began to drop and by nightfall the temperature was hitting 0 degrees and growing colder. When temperatures hit - 30 °, heat exhaust from the city's steam and electrical plants, combined with that from local businesses and vehicle exhaust created ice fog. Unlike normal fog, this unusual phenomenon is made up of ice crystals and much denser than any London fog. Headlights seem to bounce off the fog and often interfere with the driver's vision, slowing traffic to a near crawl.

Believed by some to be an act of divine providence, Governor Dave Andrews was visiting family in Anchorage for Christmas when Juneau vanished beneath the catastrophic waters. A lifelong Alaskan, Governor Andrews was greatly concerned about mass civil disobedience when the general public learned of the Lower 48's fate at the hands of the OAP.

Unfortunately, the Lieutenant Governor and most of the regulatory branch of the state government were all presumed dead: having not been able to escape the onslaught of an estimated 200 foot wave. Governor Andrews moved the state's seat of power from Juneau to the State Court House in Fairbanks and crammed his surviving cabinet members, state employees and volunteers into other state buildings and empty office space throughout the city and at the University of Alaska Fairbanks campus. His new political appointees were chosen to satisfy the urgent need for oversight with World War III breaking out across the globe and Alaska fearful of a missile attack. It took nearly a week before the new government was considered to be operational. While the courthouse was being hurriedly prepared for Governor Andrews and his staff, he spent the first 7 days working out of the 2nd floor of the Carlson Sports and Entertainment Center. Being used as a temporary Emergency Operations Center for the Alaska Army National Guard/Alaska Department of Public Safety/Red Cross and Salvation Army/ State and City Disaster Preparedness Ops, the massive structure had only sustained minimal damage in the statewide great quake and the aftershocks that followed. Power had been knocked out to most of the interior during the massive quake, but the Alaskan Interior did not suffer the extent of damage the coastal areas of Alaska did and power was restored to almost all areas within 48 hours. However, food was another problem.

In the belief that all that remained of the United States was a smoldering pyre, Governor Andrews was temporarily appointed by the new standing legislature to the Office of President for the United States' last stronghold. He now stood simply as an aged man, his shoulders slumped, his body weary from too many sleepless hours and his faced ridged with tension and stress from the near overwhelming weight of his office. Weariness lay heavily over Governor Andrews' long narrow face. His pointed chin, which ended in a single dimple, and high cheek bones, were bristly because he hadn't taken time to shave the last two mornings. His hair was cut short and at 68 years, what wasn't gray had turned a snowy white. Dave Andrews stood a lean bodied, wide-shouldered 6'1", with long arms. A faded tattoo of a 1932 Ford coupe on his left shoulder was a reminder of freedom on his 21st birthday. The fabric of his dress slacks could not completely conceal the taut muscles of legs developed from many days of hunting and fishing across his beloved Alaska. Reading glasses sat on his desk and this morning's navy blue tie was draped over the back of his office chair. The sleeves of his light blue dress shirt were rolled up to the elbows, a habit from his earlier days as a teacher and his navy tweed suit coat lay over the arm of a black leather couch.

He closed his eyes tightly and began to ask God for some sign, some evidence, that he had made the right decisions for the hundreds of thousands of people he was responsible for. In his hands he held the Articles of Surrender provided by an Oriental Alliance Pact courier and as he finished his prayer, he knew what he must do.

In the Presidential outer office sat an extremely nervous OAP courier who was closely guarded by two very stern faced uniformed members of the Alaska State Troopers. The courier was waiting to return Andrews' response to Siberia by plane, which was waiting for him at the Fairbanks International Airport.

Andrews tossed the document aside with disgust and dropped into a heavily cushioned brown suede easy chair for a brief moment of peace and a chance to wish that all this was a only a nightmare and he would wake up to find himself back in Juneau, arguing over budget woes with his staff and political foes.

Reality returned and he whispered, "Surrender?" This was a vile word and he could taste the foul sensation as it rolled off his tongue. "No, Alaskans are too independent for surrender...too bull headed," he whispered. He often talked to himself, a habit he had picked up while hunting or fishing alone. Dave turned to pick up the first page of the 12 page document. It sickened him to handle such treachery, knowing the offer of peace was only a farce. He'd delayed in sending the courier back for over a week, hoping every moment would help his military prepare for attack. Now, the time was up and the OAP was demanding his decision immediately.

With a deep animal-like growl, he ripped the Articles of Surrender into pieces, before throwing them to the floor then summoned Jason Webbing, his private secretary. When Webbing appeared, Andrews picked up a few pieces of the shredded papers and handed them to him, "Give these back to that courier out there. I'm sure they'll get the message." Andrews began to turn away, then added, "Make sure he makes it to the airport safely, I want my reply delivered."

"Yes, Governor, he'll have an escort to his aircraft and we've got two fighters on the tarmac to provide escort for the plane to the limits of our airspace."

"Thank you, Jason."

President Andrews received daily intelligence briefings regarding OAP's plans for the people of Alaska. One of his locked top secret file cabinets held reports on the heinous acts committed by the OAP personnel in their takeover of Asia and Eastern Russia. There were papers listing the atrocities accomplished by OAP warlords in order to keep their people in submission during their long march across Siberia. In some areas, mass murder was ordered, as whole native communities were forcefully shoved into open pits and buried alive to save ammo. The one report that sickened him above all others was the one which described increased acts of prisoners being butchered to feed starving soldiers on the long march.

We'll never surrender to a people like that. Better to die fighting for our land than be butchered like cattle. Andrews reached into his desk drawer and pulled out two antacid tablets for his sour stomach. *On top it all, I'm getting an ulcer!* Looking out the window again, President Andrews whispered a quiet prayer for the Lord's speedy return. "…It's all on you, Lord. I don't know how else to stop their war machine."

Unusual for a major league politician, where the ability to get a job done often interfered with one's integrity, President Andrews had strongly believed in the Lord Jesus Christ since the age of five. To the amazement of his staff he continued to spend several hours each week on his knees in prayer and reading his ever present worn Bible; which had once belonged to his father, who had carried it through the Korean War and an early tour in Vietnam.

Even as a history teacher at North Pole High School, President Andrews had suspected that China would one day march on Alaska. Because of this, he began beefing up Alaska's National Guard when he was elected to office. He warned others to be prepared, but few had listened and scoffed at him for spending millions on equipping and arming his Alaskan troops.

He had watched the news every morning and observed the signs as first China and then the OAP prepared itself for war. China was buying up all the armament it could and building its army to unheard of numbers. These preparations made Dave recall an old saying, "For let the dragon (China) sleep, for when she awakens the world will tremble." He believed Winston Churchill had quoted it, but wasn't sure.

Dave was right on the mark when he advised his staff to watch China's military activity around Vietnam, "You watch. Vietnam will be the key to

China's intentions." He believed Vietnam needed to be taken first in order to give China access to Vietnam's deep water ports and its abundant rice crops to supply the invasion force for the seizure of Western Russia. And that's exactly what happened.

The intercom buzzed quietly and Dave reached over to press a little black button on the desk's telephone/intercom, then waited for Webbing's raspy voice to announce the cause of the intrusion. *It's going to be one of those days, constant interruptions by people expecting me to have all the answers. I should have stayed in teaching. I could've been retired by now...maybe own a small auto parts store?*

"Mr. President, General Saunders is here, sir," Webbings said.

"Send him in please," Dave replied in a strong voice which clearly demonstrated his enthusiasm for seeing an old friend. He stood up to greet him and when Saunders walked in, the General immediately presented a crisp salute before offering his hand.

"Thank you for seeing me, Mr. President."

"Can we please dispense with formalities, Glenn? You and I were hunting partners long before I entered politics and you put on that first star." He shook his friend's hand with a good strong grip. Having met through mutual friends, Dave and then Lt. Colonel Glenn Saunders became close friends and enjoyed many moose seasons together before General Saunders pinned on his first star and was reassigned to a regimental commander's position at Fort Bragg, Kentucky.

Walking over to the large windows that overlooked the Chena River, Saunders glanced back toward President Andrews with a thoughtful expression. "Intel says we can expect heavy bombing of military targets, but no nukes. OAP forces plan to wage a polite little conventional war. Simply stating, they plan to mow us over with strength in numbers and those armored beasts of theirs."

"What else, my friend?"

"Surviving Russian troops are in full retreat to the west, abandoning their armor and leaving wounded to the mercy of the enemy."

"Mercy?" Dave asked as he shook his head in wonder. "I know what that means for the wounded and so do you."

Glenn nodded in agreement, "The OAP now owns Siberia. They've taken possession of the Great Russian Railroad and the vast Siberian oil fields. On a more favorable note though, they've torn up the railroad for fuel and the oil fields are currently buried under 20 feet or more of snow." Glenn came away from the window and carefully lowered himself into the brown easy chair. His back was bothering him again; one too many parachute jumps with the 82nd Airborne while he trying to prove to those young troops he still had it in him and was now paying for it.

"I recall that you told me those pompous Russian generals thought they could easily handle China," David said. He returned to his desk and sat down in his black leather high backed chair. "So, how do we look?"

Glenn grinned, "Like two old men who spent too much time hiking through the woods, making too much noise with balmy songs, drinking too much beer and eating far too much junk food. But as to the army, we'll be ready in a few more days."

"Troop morale?" David asked with one eyebrow raised. He wasn't in a mood to talk about old times, so he didn't respond to the General's mostly mistaken account of their early days. *I never sang balmy songs!*

"Better than you or I could expect. We have some great troops out there, Mr. President," Glenn said, reverting back to his friend's title. He leaned forward "Still, I wish you'd let me pull the 1st Division out of Wales. I don't expect...."Glenn was interrupted, something that rarely happened to a four-star general.

"Glenn, we've been over this and as I recall, you were the one to recommend putting the 1st Division into Wales in the first place. 'Perfect spot to make our initial stand'- your exact words if I remember. Also added with a bit of, 'We'll hit 'em hard, pull back an' make 'em bleed for every inch of ground.' A real Audie Murphy speech! "

Glenn frowned in response, "You have a good memory for such an old geezer." Then added in a grumpy voice, "Yeah, I said that, but now I've had time to realize how many good men and women are going to die for that ground." Glenn sat back in his chair and adjusted his position to take some of the strain off his lower back.

"We can't stop the OAP, Glenn and we might not be able to stop them at Greeley. Our only chance is if the Canadians come in with us, but even that's a long shot. General Howard-Wright has his own civil war to deal with and the strength of his army is limited."

"Mr. President, he knows what will happen if we fall. The OAP will be on his doorstep and he'll have no ally to call upon." Glenn glanced out the window, the lights and afterburner glow of two F-15 Eagles taking off from Fort Wainwright had caught his attention and he watched as they rose and soared across the sky. The ceiling elevation for jet aircraft was 1500 feet unless a sortie required a risk of shooting up through the clouds of volcanic ash and falling snow. Then a pilot would have to listen to his crew chiefs' rant and rave as they struggled to clean the ash out of the engines. "Mr. President, you've seen the same reports I have. Like the men and women under me, I'd rather go down fighting then be buried alive in some ditch or worse; barbecued on some spit."

"Me too!" Dave replied. He studied his old friend for a moment, imagining the stress his commanding officer must be under and then broke the awkward silence by slapping the top of his desk, "All right then, what else is on your mind today?"

Glenn pulled a blue folder from his briefcase and Dave could see it was marked, "Top Secret-Eyes Only for the Commanding General or those designated by same". A small list attached to the folder showed the "Eyes Only" meant five people: the President, General Saunders and three ADF senior Intel Officers. Before handing the folder to the President, Glenn glanced around the room and admired the furniture. "The judges sure loved their offices. Makes me wonder who paid the bill for all this finery?" Glenn looked back at Dave, "Politics, what a strange game you people play."

"Glenn, you're sidestepping something. What is it?"

Hesitating, he reluctantly handed the folder across to the President, "Operation Cactus Tree, I need your permission to implement it immediately."

"Brief me again on what this plan entails," Dave said.

"The strategy people in War Plans, those little men and women who stayed locked up under ground for weeks at a time; came up with 'Cactus Tree' when OAP forces first captured Vietnam. The operational part of the plan calls for the total destruction of all communities on the Seward Peninsula, to include those townships along the Yukon River. The object: to prevent OAP forces from finding shelter or needed supplies along their course of travel. It was felt by the Intel gnomes that an unmerciful Alaskan winter would further deplete OAP ranks and resources, a benefit to the ADF and hopefully bring the OAP to a standstill. Extreme winter conditions stopped Napoleon and Hitler from conquering Russia- the Intel gnomes thought maybe it would do the same against the OAP."

Dave studied the blue folder in his hands. He had reviewed the operational plan before and as it did then, it left a bitter taste in his mouth. He dropped the folder to the top of his desk, cleared his throat and asked, "Now, Glenn? We have to move on this now? They haven't even attacked yet."

"Mr. President, we won't have a lot of time once the OAP spearhead begins to move across the ice. This operation will take at least 7 days, maybe more, to complete in its entirety."

"Glenn, when I took this office I never thought I'd be ordering the destruction of hundreds of homes and people's businesses...My God, whole communities belonging to the very people who voted me into this job."

"Once the balloon goes up, Mr. President, the 1st Division will be too busy to carry out this operation. Our one big weapon against the OAP is our winter. We know Siberia hurt them bad. Now we need to slow them down and starve them. We let the land cripple them, let the blizzards kill them and as for the communities, we can rebuild those later... if we survive the comet."

Dave stood quietly for a long moment, while his general waited just as quietly. Both men knew how hard a decision this was to make and it was with a strained voice when President Andrews finally agreed, "All right. Get it done and I'll go down in history as the most hated man in Alaska."

"Mr. President, I'll be the one carrying out those orders. People remember General Sherman's march in the Civil War, not that President Lincoln ordered him there. We fight the battles we can fight, others we have to leave to God." Glenn felt very old at this moment. He would like nothing better than to toss his hands in the air and let someone else carry out these major operations.

Dave slowly stood to his feet "Strange, I suddenly know how Abraham Lincoln must have felt when he ordered the destruction of the South. No wonder he grew a beard, it was to hide his grief."

"I forgot you were a history teacher," Glenn said, a half-smile on his face.

Dave nodded, buzzed his secretary and asked that he and Captain Campbell, the duty security officer, come in. With both of them present, Dave requested the office tape recorder be turned on and then faced Glenn to make a statement of record, "General Saunders, I've reviewed this document entitled Operation Cactus Tree and having done so, I, as President of Alaska and the surviving United States, am ordering you to implement this operation immediately." He turned to his secretary and security officer and asked that they give their names, the date and time for the recording.

"You didn't have to do that," Glenn said to his friend after the two gentlemen left the room.

"Yes, I did. Who knows what will survive when this is all over. I don't want the survivors blaming you."

"May God go with us, my good friend," Glenn said as he placed the operational plans back inside his briefcase.

"These last few years have really put my faith to the test. I've called out to the Lord so often, only to hear silence and yet, I still know in my heart He's in charge. I know these events must transpire for prophesy to be fulfilled. But this faith stuff can be tiring, old buddy. So many times I've wanted to walk out of this office, fling up my arms and shout, 'I quit!'"

"You're too good a man, Mr. President. The Lord chose you for this job; you're the right man at the right time." General Glenn Saunders assumed the position of attention and rendered another crisp salute. "Permission to leave, Mr. President?"

"Permission granted, General." President Dave Andrews returned his salute, not as crisp as the general's, but the affection was noticeable. The two men shared a look of deep respect for one another and then General Saunders did an about face move and walked out of the office with his shoulders locked back and his chin out. In the outer room, he was met by his MP escort. One of them handed him a shoulder holster, which contained a well-used Model 1911 Colt .45 semi-auto pistol with reindeer horn handgrips. Even old friends gave up their weapons when visiting the President; a couple of very large and well-armed uniformed Alaska State Troopers assigned to the President ensured this practice.

1ST DIVISION HEADQUARTERS, CITY OF WALES - MARCH 19TH

Colonel Freeman, undaunted by a - 42° temperature and wearing 32pounds of arctic gear with an M-16 hanging upside down over his right shoulder, was outside shooting the breeze with some of his enlisted sentries when a captain from headquarters appeared at his side, "Colonel, you have a priority call."

"All right, Captain." Freeman addressed his men, "Stay alert and keep warm when you can. The shooting war will be starting soon." Reaching his office, Freeman leaned his M-16 on the right side of his desk and picked up a black radiophone. Connected by 33 feet of thick black cable to a portable Microwave Base Station and using line-of-sight relay to Fort Wainwright through a large assortment of recently installed microwave towers, Freeman was able to speak with ADF Headquarters with less than a second delay time. "This is Colonel Freeman - Over."

"Stand-by, Sir," a female radio officer said. She asked if the scrambler system was on.

"Scrambler activated - Over," Freeman replied.

"Freeman, this is Saunders. Prepare to authenticate - Over."

"Stand by one, Sir." Reaching into his left shirt pocket, Freeman pulled out a small green notepad and turned to the page which contained current ADF codes which were changed daily at 0001 hrs. The codes were supplied by an escorted Intel courier at the end of the month, to commence on the first day of the new month. Under normal situations, the code book would be secured in a wall or floor safe, but being out here in Wales and living in a tent, Freeman thought it safer to carry the codes with him. Had anything happened to him, either by death or kidnapping, the code would be considered compromised and new codes would be issued.

"Go ahead, Sir - Over," Freeman said.

"7-9-3-4-4-4-0-Bravo - Over," General Saunders said into the radiophone from his end. They were reasonably sure the enemy could not pick up the ground based microwave signals, but there was only so much they could do without satellites and couriers could take too long.

"I copy 7-9-3-4-4-4-0-Bravo and reply with Zebra-1-9-0-3 Foxtrot - Over."

"I concur," General Saunders said. "Jake, I have a tough one for you and I know you are the right man to carry it off." He hesitated for a moment and then ordered, "You are to implement Op Plan 41A-Bravo India immediately - Over."

"Stand by, Sir."

General Saunders stared at the wall, avoiding everyone in the Command Post as he gave Freeman a moment to pull out the op plans book from his locked safe. Freeman was stunned when he discovered that 41A-Bravo India was Operation Cactus Tree. He'd gone over all the operational plans, but could never remember which code numbers went with which plan. He often blamed this memory problem on his age.

"Yes, Sir...Over," Freeman said. He knew his voice sounded a bit hesitant.

"Do you understand your orders, Colonel? Over," General Saunders asked. Surprisingly, his voice was extremely calm and this seemed to irritate Colonel Freeman.

"Affirmative, Sir. We will get it done - Over." There was no hesitation in his voice, but General Saunders wasn't able to see the slight trembling of Colonel Freeman's hands as he held his orders and looked at the men and women around him.

"Questions? Over," General Saunders asked.

"Negative, Sir. - Over." Freeman heard General Saunders sign off with a quick, "Alpha-Charlie-One, now signing off."

Freeman dropped the handset into its cradle, opened the file in his hands and began reviewing the outlines for Cactus Tree. Nearly an hour later, he walked into the main section of headquarters and cleared his throat to get everyone's attention, "Attention please. Officer's call in exactly one hour in the high school gym and I want every officer including E-7 and above, who can be released from duties. I want a ring of tight security around the entire building while this meeting is in progress." Freeman looked to his staff members, "Get it done, now."

Papers flew as runners grabbed coats and headed for various commands. Clerks manning field phones notified outlying groups, while a senior staff member arranged for MP security. True to form, Colonel Freeman walked into the base gym 60 minutes later while dozens of officers and non-commissioned officers were still arriving. Shouts of "Attention!" echoed through the huge gym, bringing more than 600 men and women to their feet. Making his way to a stage usually used for school assemblies and plays, Colonel Freeman broke habit and refrained from pleasantries with anyone along his way. A microphone was set up and a pitcher of water and a single plastic cup were placed on a small wooden side table. He stepped up to the microphone, looked out over the mass of men and women, young and old pressed tightly together in a room that normally held a maximum 400 people. He was extremely proud of these people and did not look forward to the upcoming events. This wasn't going to be fun; *I'll be lucky if they don't lynch me.*

Colonel Freeman waited until his Operations Officer signaled that everyone who could be was present. Only those required to stay at duty posts to maintain command structure were absent. "First, let me express to you General Saunders' and President Andrews' complete faith in our abilities to carry out the task set before us. He has replied to the enemy," Colonel Freeman waited for the suspense to build and then shouted out, "Alaska will not surrender! Alaskans will fight to the last man, woman and child." The gym shook as applause, shouts, foot stomps and whistles burst forth from the gathered assembly. *Well, that one item went down pleasantly, now for the bitter pill.* Colonel Freeman gestured with his hands for silence and almost immediately, the crowd quieted. "Now, what I am about to say is going to have a profound..." Colonel Freeman hesitated then stepped back from the microphone. He thought he was prepared for this and now he wasn't sure. Exactly how could he order these people, most of them from the Seward Peninsula, to destroy their very own communities some of which were hundreds of years old, the older homes passed down for generations and history recorded in the framework of the tribal halls.

The assembled members of the 1st Division felt uneasy with Colonel Freeman's hesitation and tension began to build inside the gym. Returning to the microphone and taking a single gulp of water to clear his throat, he continued. "The 1st Division has drawn a rough one, even tougher than waiting here for the invasion we know will come." He gazed around the room, seeing the faces of men and women he knew, knowing which towns and villages they called home. "These orders are unlike any you've ever been told to carry out." Freeman took a deep breath and exhaled slowly as over 600 sets of eyes focused on him. "At exactly 1800 hours today, elements of this division will initiate Operation Cactus Tree." He watched as signs of comprehension passed through the ranks of senior staff officers. Flashes of anger added apprehension to those who had no idea what this operation entailed. "Normally, I would have briefed Regimental and Battalion Commanders alone, allowing orders to trickle down through the chain of command. Not this time. You deserve to get these orders directly from me. However, due to simple logistics, I leave you to brief the enlisted personnel under you. You will have the toughest job. This operation is going to be a rough one, but the order has been given and we...the men and women of the 1st Division, will carry it out to the best of our abilities." Freeman looked down, "When the OAP begins to move, we won't have time to complete this operation, so it's vital that it be carried out to the full extent of the order. As our friends down south used to say, 'we'll be up to our backsides in alligators'; the only way we can stop the OAP is to starve them out and let our Alaskan winter freeze them to death. No shelter, no food and no chance to rest. From our forward observers, we know the OAP is burning up most, if not all, of their remaining wood supplies - ties from the Siberian Railroad. We cannot afford to leave them anything that will aid their crossing of Alaska. We will attack them at every opportunity, ambush them at every pass and make them bleed as they cross our beloved home. In order to do this, we cannot allow them the use of any resources -buildings, homes, food, fuel or any other supplies we have stockpiled in our communities." Freeman looked over the mass of confused faces and took another drink of water before he continued. "They will come across our land like a wave of locusts, but will find nothing to feed upon. We will bleed their flanks as they move across the north and meet them in force at a spot designated by our general staff. We will show them the folly of their actions and send them packing back across the ice like scurrying rats." Freeman glanced back over his shoulder to his senior staff; each and every one nodded in support. " Now, to make this completely clear, this operation means that every township in the Seward Peninsula and along the Yukon River must be burned to the ground and nothing...and I mean nothing, left for the enemy to use."

The gym was absolutely silent as the order sank in. Then suddenly, from Colonel Freeman's side, Major Whitely, Operations Officer, normally a quiet and humble man, moved up and shouted, "Can we do it?"

First a couple of shouts came up from the stunned audience, immediately followed by dozens more and before long the whole room shook with voices raised in support. A chant began that grew in volume, "Alaska, Alaska, Alaska..." Freeman let it continue for a moment before bringing it back under control.

"Orders will be delivered to the units involved in Cactus Tree and I expect every officer, non-com and soldier in my command to carry out these orders. Units remaining here will continue to prepare for action. God Bless us all. You are dismissed!" Colonel Freeman shook hands with his Ops

Officer and whispered, "Thank you." then walked outside into the bitter cold.

Fighting back a wave of nausea, he made his way back to his tent and collapsed onto his cot. For the first time in his military career, Freeman had wrestled with thoughts of resigning, but after watching those men and women inside the gym, knew he couldn't. *With troops like those, we may actually pull this off.*

1st Battalion, 2nd Regiment was airlifted by Black Hawk helicopter to Nome in a massive airlift, with more flights to Kotzebue. Incendiary devices were put into place once a complicated and not well appreciated evacuation was carried out by hurried troops. Evacuees were flown out by C-130 cargo aircraft and delivered to Fort Wainwright and Fairbanks International Airport. From these locations, they were taken by bus convoy to Fort Greeley to be housed in once abandoned military barracks restored after the Missile Defense System was placed at Fort Greeley. Additional barracks, long deserted, were hurriedly cleaned up and prepared to house families as they arrived. Beyond that, 15 and 30 man Arctic canvas tents with wood and oil stoves, many brought to Greeley from other military installations and Alaska Army National Guard supply stockpiles, were going up by the dozens. Some, seized by the authorities for the emergency, came from commercial outlets. In the past, Fort Greeley was the US Army's Arctic Training Grounds and Survival School and took up a large amount of acreage for the main base; housing, schools, offices, chow halls and personnel offices, headquarters, hospital, Military Police and fire department, armory and barracks. Fort Greeley also had a massive military reservation of flatlands; with the Richardson Highway and a dribble of river to the west, Delta Junction 8 miles north; great grasslands, backed by forests to the south and small rolling hills to the east, which were covered in a mixture of green and black spruce, white birch and cottonwood.

Immediately after evacuee departure from each community, Explosive Ordinance Disposal troops ignited the incendiary devices and stood by to ensure the townships were burned to the ground and nothing was left for the enemy. Families were only allowed to take one pet with them. The ADF wanted to ensure the remaining animals, mostly sled dogs, could not be used to feed the enemy and the sad duty of destroying them fell upon the shoulders of a dozen or more mournful soldiers. Sled dogs had always been valued in the frozen north and most of these troops had owned such dogs in the. Young and old ADF troops stood around blackened smoldering ruins, tears in their eyes as they threw the bodies into the funeral fires with debris, some from their own houses. Hatred for the OAP grew with a burning intensity to match that of the flames before them.

Company Alpha and Bravo, 1st Battalion, 2nd Regiment, were airlifted by 28 helicopters, both Black Hawk and once retired UH-1 Hueys, to the Yukon River communities of Nulato, Grayling, Anvik and Stuyahok, Russian Mission and Pilot Point, St. Mary's and the township of Mountain Village. Once these villages were evacuated, and it took some doing because a lot of the people wanted to stay and fight for their homes against the enemy's advance, the homes and businesses were burned to the ground. At St. Mary's a young captain had to set fire to several homes, including that of his own family before he could get the townspeople to leave as endured the harsh glares of his family members. At each of the communities the ADF seized privately owned aircraft to prevent the OAP access. Those that were flyable were flown by the owners to Fairbanks, where they became part of the Northern Air Wing and used for recon or courier duties.

Finished with assigned communities the two companies moved eastward by helicopter along the Yukon River, destroying homes, hunting lodges or cabins along the way. Eventually, they joined the remainder of 1st Battalion, which had flown south from Kotzebue to assist in the evacuation and destruction of Kokrines, Ruby, Tanana, Rampart and Stevens Village.

In Tanana and Stevens Village, ADF troops came up against stiff resistance and several times force had to be used to evacuate the villages. Shots were fired and three ADF troops were killed by angry citizens. After that, the ADF swept in with rifle squads and drove the reluctant citizens out of town and onto waiting helicopters.

Eskimo and Athabascan Public Information Officers, supported by ADF military Police, were on hand to explain in full detail why the action had to be taken, but still there were those who wanted to stay and defend their communities. There were even a few who were sympathetic to the OAP, seeing them as cousins and much preferred to the American government. These few families were taken into custody and transported to Eielson Air Force Base for imprisonment. There was scattered talk among angry troops to simply leave these treasonous folks for the OAP, but the officers had their orders.

Hundreds of villagers joined the ranks of the ADF and were flown to ADF Command-Fairbanks for last minute training and equipping. Unfortunately, with so little time, training consisted primarily in teaching them the ADF rank structure, the necessity of obeying orders, weapons qualification and a brief class in first aid: mostly in the handling of severe trauma.

1ST DIVISION HEADQUARTERS:

Colonel Freeman held an unsheathed bayonet in his right hand and used it as a pointer while he conducted a briefing with his three regimental and nine battalion commanders, "Nothing, I mean nothing will be left here for the enemy. I want this entire city booby trapped, as well as every sandbagged bunker and foxhole.... Just ensure everything is safe for our troops. When the enemy enters Wales to go souvenir hunting, I want them to be surprised by the gifts we left behind." Colonel Freeman paused briefly to catch his breath. "Prepare all artillery pieces ready for hook up to track vehicles for the order to move. We're going to bug out quick when the word is given and I don't want anyone or anything of value left behind." Freeman studied the faces of his senior officers. *Good men, I'm proud to be leading them. I only hope most of them come through this.* A seasoned commander, he knew the numbers of killed and wounded were going to be extremely high. He deeply hoped he wouldn't have to leave any wounded behind, not even his dead if at all possible.

"Make sure the troops completely understand, we will not leave our wounded behind and if possible, we will also take our dead with us. I do not want to leave them for the enemy to abuse... or end up in some stew pot." That thought sickened him and as he looked around the circle of soldiers, he could see the soured stomachs in their faces. He knew each of his commanders knew what he was talking about. Everyone in the senior staff had seen the intelligence reports on the OAP and the word *cannibalism* had stood out like a red flag.

"I think that's about it, you all have your orders, most likely in triplicate, and you know what I expect from each of you." He stopped to wipe sweat from his brow with a white handkerchief. *40 something below outside and I'm sweating?* Freeman laid the bayonet atop his desk, "That's all for now. We got limited time, so stay busy and continue to keep your people's spirits up. This isn't a good time for anyone, so we need to stick together to complete our task."

The officers nodded in agreement, closed their pocket sized notebooks and tossed their Styrofoam coffee cups into a trash bag supplied by a female PFC clerk. As they began to file out, Colonel Freeman remembered something else and called out to one of his battalion commanders, "Major Harbours, I have need of your Captain Myers... as soon as you can locate him."

"Yes, Sir," Major Harbours replied. He was a short heavyset man with a leathered face, graying black hair, highly alert eyes and a rather flat nose.

"Have him report with his company's 1st Sergeant, it'll save time."

"Yes, Sir," Harbours said. He left the tent in search of Myers, trying to remember the quickest route to Myers' position on the perimeter. By the sounds of things, he suspected he was about to lose his newest company commander and possibly the entire company. It would thin out the line some, but he'd have time to stretch out his battalion to take up the gap, if and when he lost Captain Myers.

34 minutes later, an out of breath Captain Myers and a rugged looking MSgt. Iukapah were standing at attention before a sleepy Colonel Freeman. The newest company commander in the division, Captain Myers looked a bit nervous to be called before the Old Man.

"Sir, Captain Myers and MSgt. Iukapah reporting as ordered."

"Stand at rest, gentlemen," Colonel Freeman said.

Myers and Iukapah automatically assumed the position of parade rest, not quite what Freeman had in mind and he repeated himself, "I said at rest. If you want to sit, you may and if you want coffee?"

"No, Sir," Myers answered for the both of them. The thought of sitting before the colonel was really making Myers nervous and a bead of sweat broke out on his brow. *Whatever this is about, it's not good!*

"Captain Myers, I'm sorry we haven't had time to get to know one another. I usually make it a policy to have a chat with all of my company commanders, but there wasn't time."

"Yes, sir...I understand," Myers said. He was confused more than ever as to why he and MSgt. Iukapah were before their commander. Skeptical, he waited for the other shoe to drop and sincerely hoped he wasn't being assigned to the detail at Little Diomede. He'd heard the main force was recalled from there, but he knew the military often reversed itself and he hoped this wasn't one of those times.

"Captain, Sergeant, I have an important mission for your company to undertake. But right now, all you will need to know is the following; you are to prepare your troops for a long range foot patrol, taking all the extra ammo and food you can carry on snow sleds. You will not have the use of vehicles or sled dogs, so make sure you have your strongest men on those sleds, as I expect them to be quite heavy. You'll report to the division armory and secure extra heavy weapons, to include Stinger missiles, heavy machineguns and 81mm mortars. A list of what you are to carry with you has already been sent to the armory. You will be driven only so far by trak vehicle, so do not load your sleds. They'll be attached to the top of the traks until you reach your jumping off location. Departure time is 2200 hours tonight, report back to me here at 2100 hours for final briefing. Understand?"

"Yessir, umm...should I bring my platoon commanders, Sir?"

"No, the two of you will be fine. That's all, you're dismissed." Both men snapped to attention and he returned their salutes then watched as they departed; his thoughts already on other matters. A very confused captain and his 1st sergeant made their way through the maze of desks to exit the overly warm tent. Outside the command tent, Myers pulled his parka hood up, sighed and shook his head in bewilderment, "Long range foot patrol in this weather? Sergeant, I'm beginning to feel like an Idaho mushroom."

"Mushroom, Captain?" Iukapah asked as he fought to keep step with the taller officer. His face mask was back in place along with his pair of old snow machine goggles.

"You know… mushrooms. They're kept in the dark and fed...never mind. Let's get cracking, lot's to do between now an' 2100 hours."

During the next hour, Freeman again called for his regimental commanders. They stood around one of three large map tables, while Colonel Freemen briefed them, "We'll be taking our troops through valleys most of us have never seen before. This will be a very long haul; over 500 miles overland to reach the Dalton Highway and then another 150 miles or more south to Fairbanks. We can expect heavy bombardment from enemy aircraft and attack by advancing enemy troops. Whenever possible we will engage the enemy, in force or in small units. We will use anything and everything to slow the OAP and give our main forces in the Interior time to prepare."

"Is there any good news, Jake?" Lt. Colonel Sam White, 3rd Regimental Commander, asked.

"Not this time, Sam. No air cover to speak of and the terrain...." Freeman shook his head.

"Is it too late to resign my commission?" Lt. Colonel George Umiat, 2nd Regimental Commander, asked in mock seriousness.

"Sure, George, but then I'll draft you as a private and assign you to Immigration Control. You can stay here to check the enemy's passports."

"Never mind, Jake," Umiat said laughing. "Besides, my wife likes to tell her family how much of a big shot I am. She keeps telling my mother-in-law I'll make general someday, but the old woman always tells her there's too many other good men who should make it before I do...I've never been good enough for her daughter," A couple of senior officers provided the expected polite chuckles as he leaned over the maps to note some ground coordinates in his pocket notebook.

"All through our history, the American Army has provided the services of valiant men and women to be sacrificed as blocking and rear guard forces. This time, the duty has fallen to the Fighting First and I'm proud to say I know our men and women will serve gallantly."

1ST DIVISION HEADQUARTERS, 2100 HOURS

A cup of sugarless hot coffee in hand, Colonel Freeman glanced up as Captain Myers and 1st Sergeant Iukapah made their way through the large smoky tent. He imagined they must have stood around outside, probably waiting for the exact time specified before they reported in. As they walked up to his desk, Freeman looked about the room and realized his headquarters probably appeared as if someone had yelled, "Fire!" and no one knew where the exit was. I guess this fits under the description of 'organized chaos'.

Files were secured and loaded onto waiting trak vehicles and other papers placed in burn bags. Unused furniture was hauled to the school to be used as kindling when the school building was set afire. The tent would eventually be loaded onto a trak vehicle for the long treacherous journey southeast. Other than a company of scouts, no one else and no other vehicles were being sent out, at least not until word was given to fall back. Each man and woman in the command tent was given a task breaking headquarters down - load it or throw it into burn piles. A large pit had been dug into the snow and a fire was to be set for the purpose of burning documents as soon as the small force at Little Diomede issued warning of the enemy's approach.

Captain Myers noted that the map displayed the northwestern side of Alaska and the Bering Sea.

"Gentleman, I'm sure you recognize Wales and the Seward Peninsula before you. In approximately 60 minutes your company is about to leave on one of this division's strangest and possibly most treacherous journeys," Freeman's tone was ominous as he looked into their faces to ensure they knew the gravity of this assignment. "Once dropped off by traks, you're in for a very long walk - mainly because I can't spare the helicopters. They're all committed elsewhere and I do not want the enemy knowing where you're headed. But, to save time I will have you transported by trak to the Village of Sinuk. From there, you're on your own and I mean exactly that."

"Sir, you haven't mentioned where we're headed and why?" Myers finally located Sinuk, a small townships south of Nome.

Freeman glanced from Myers to Iukapah, not surprised to find the sergeant's face remained impassive. "Captain, you're taking your company across the ice, from Sinuk to Savoonga on St. Lawrence Island. Approximately 140 to 170 miles across the deadliest terrain imaginable and we expect you to reach Savoonga within seven days."

"Sir?" Myers was stunned... St. Lawrence Island?

"We expect the ice to be 6 to 8 feet thick, so that's not a problem. You can't take the traks, enemy aircraft would pick you up immediately and make short work of you. It will have to be done on foot, wearing snowshells and large white tarps over your sleds to conceal you. But the treacherous part I spoke about is the ice itself. You'll come across sharpened ridges, spirals sticking up 10 to 15 feet and in some places I imagine you'll have to divert your course to get around walls of ice... I'm not sure how high. But this is pack ice and it's been jamming up against itself all fall and winter, you're bound to come up against the impassible and impossible and will have to divert your course to get around it. I don't expect it, not with this severe cold, but you might even come across large sections of open water, so do not take any chances...but you must reach your goal within the time limit. Now, I've selected your company for this because most of your troops, including 1st Sergeant Iukapah, are from Savoonga. They know the land and how to survive on the island."

"Aah...Sir, shouldn't I ask for volunteers for a mission such as this?" *I mean, hey, I didn't volunteer for this kind of...* Myers thoughts were interrupted.

"No time, Captain. You'll carry two of our new line of sight radios; there's nothing between St. Lawrence and here to block the feed. At 2400 hours, March 26 you will make contact with ADF Command-Fairbanks. Because of the curvature of the earth, various relay points will have to pass you through to the interior and if there is human relay, authentication will be required. Without satellites, we've had to place relay sites on every mountain range in the state to maintain radio contact; several of these sites have radio teams, and you'll be carrying the codes. I expect you to destroy those codes if it appears you might be taken prisoner, Captain."

"Why the 26th, sir?" Iukapah asked. It was the first time he had spoken and his question impressed Freeman. But Freeman had been impressed with his Native Alaskans since the very first day he assumed command.

"We expect the OAP forces to hit us on the evening of the 26th. After initial contact, our division will be in full retreat, most likely running for our lives, but we'll be striking at the enemy at any and every opportunity." Colonel Freeman walked away from the map table, leaving Myers and Iukapah time alone to record all the coordinates they would need. A few moments later, they were back in front of Freeman's desk.

"I have the traks standing by. My comm officer will give you the call signs, codes and frequencies you'll need on your way out."

"Colonel, you still haven't told us the purpose behind our mission. What are we to accomplish in Savoonga?" Myers asked.

"I apologize, Captain. I've conducted so many briefings over the last few days I forget who, when, what and why." Freeman picked up a sealed envelope, "These are your orders. But in a nutshell, you're to reach Savoonga and provide information about enemy movements, aircraft and land forces moving across the ice in your region. Until relieved or ordered elsewhere, you are to avoid any enemy contact if at all possible. If the OAP finds out you're there, they'll attack in force. No heroics, you'll be no good to the ADF or Alaska if you're dead." Freeman took a sip from his coffee cup. "You'll make contact on the hour at 1200 and 2400 hours....it's in the orders. If we don't hear from you after 24 hours have passed, you'll be considered lost." Freeman tossed his cup into a plastic trash bag and leaned forward, "This mission is classified Top Secret-Alpha, meaning only a very few people outside of this room know about your assignment." He watched as they both nodded and then asked, "Any other questions?"

"Colonel, with the distance between the island and the mainland, an army could move by us and we'd never know it. What does Command really think we can accomplish out there, Sir?" Myers glanced to Iukapah, who kept his eyes locked on the colonel.

"Captain, our air force is out manned by better than 40 to1 odds. A reconnaissance aircraft wouldn't last five minutes up there. I need good men on the ground, watching the enemy's southern flank in the event they make a move south for Bethel. Some of the Intel people think the enemy has another front planned, possibly a move toward Bethel and the mouth of the Yukon River. They could use that frozen river as a highway into the interior. Now do you understand?"

"Yes, Sir. My company will be ready to move out at 2200 hours."

"Good, here's a folder for you...it contains some things you'll need to know about enemy aircraft identification. You should be able to position a listening post several miles east of the island, which should help you hear or even see a large invasion force moving toward Bethel. It's pretty flat out there on the ice, you'll be able to see for miles and if the OAP does go that way they'll have heavy air cover." Freeman handed a thin folder to Myers and then said to Iukapah, "Our last flight over Savoonga showed a mid-sized herd of reindeer nearby. They might help with your platoon's food supply."

"Colonel, it will be good to be back home. Thank you for this opportunity, Sir," Iukapah said as he clasped Freeman's offered hand.

Myers was about to leave when Freeman added, "Captain, remember one thing above all others, the OAP does not treat their prisoners very well. If it were I, Captain Myers, I'd rather die fighting then be taken prisoner... even if that meant taking my own life and that of my wounded. Take care of yourself and good luck."

"Thank you, Colonel." Myers almost forgot to salute before turning to leave, his mind packed with thoughts and worries. He glanced over at Iukapah and wondered about the man's calm composure, *He looks as if we just got ordered to participate in a 4th of July parade. Tough people, these Eskimos.*

Following a rough 12 hour ride by MT-850 Trak Vehicles, Captain Myers and his 96 soldiers; 82 men and 14 women, arrived at Sinuk. Most of the troops were complaining of bruised elbows and knees suffered in the ride, bumped from one side to another, as the vehicles traversed the uneven terrain. The odor of diesel fumes seeped into the cab and sickened some, but silence fell when they dismounted the vehicles and saw the deserted village. The only sound was that of the wind as it blew mournfully through the deserted town. Without the sound of a barking dog or the laughter, shouts and cries of children, the looming silence was both ominous and eerie and it gave the men and women an unsettled feeling as they formed up to unload the Trak vehicles. As soon as they were unloaded, the MT-850s left for the return trip to Division. It didn't take long to unpack and load the heavy unassembled wood and fiberglass sleds. Putting them together reminded several men of the last time they tried to assemble a child's Christmas bicycle - it took longer than they thought. Tempers flared and a few profanities were heard, but soon the Sleds were assembled, loaded and ready to go. The troops were then ordered to set the village ablaze. It took the better part of the afternoon to reduce the village to ash.

When there was nothing left for the enemy to salvage, Myers and his three platoons of edgy soldiers stepped out onto the ice. The distant horizon was obscured by ice fog and particles of black ash which also hastened the darkness of nightfall. Captain Myers felt as if he was walking off the edge of the world as they began their long trek westward to Savoonga. He assigned six soldiers to each of the seven long sleds, each one carrying food, equipment, weapons and ammo. Company staff included extra communications personnel for the special radio equipment and two extra medics from Division, remaining squad members were sent out to point, flank and rear security positions. The last man to leave the shoreline of Sinuk was PFC Mary Osolik. Staring at the smoldering remains of her mother's village, she wept openly. She had set fire to her grandfather's home and Osolik imagined she could see his mournful face in the flames. She wiped her eyes with a mittened hand, sniffled, turned her back on Sinuk and walked out on to the ice to follow her command.

YUKON TERRITORY, MARCH 23RD

Cold and weary, Major Jeb Stewart reluctantly followed Captain Wayne Roberts across Canada's wilderness territory. Temperatures were nearing -50 when they stole two snow machines from a loosely guarded military motor pool. They traveled 63 miles before the first one ran out of gas, the second died a mile and half further on. On foot again, and over 100 miles inside Canada, Wayne opted to try hitchhiking along the Alaska-Canadian Highway. Almost an hour later, when the bitter cold had them near the point of hypothermia an Army supply truck appeared and stopped to pick them up and they found themselves in the company of a foul smelling camp cook. The man was an uncouth slob, who released a continuous stream of gas snorting and belching as the truck bounced down the icy road. Still, it was a ride and they were warm, if not a bit overwhelmed by the man's flatulence. Seven weary long hours later, they arrived in Whitehorse. A roadblock was posted at the intersection of the North Klondike Highway and military traffic increased until they reached the intersection that led downhill into town where they waved a fond and grateful farewell to their robust odorous chauffer.

With forged papers, the two cautiously wandered the streets of the city in search of transportation, stopping only long enough to consume a cup of soup. Resuming their walk, they came upon an unattended Army one ton panel truck idling unattended outside a small recreation center. As if it was theirs, they walked up to the truck, climbed in and made a fast getaway. At the top of the hill they turned east headed toward Watson Lake and the next known check point.

Four hours later they stopped abruptly when Wayne spotted a roadblock about a mile ahead. The truck slid across 30 feet of icy road before he pulled over to the side while Jeb slept through it all. Large lights, powered by diesel generators, gave off a glow that could be seen from quite a ways. Two armored personnel carriers, each with a mounted .50 caliber machinegun, were positioned across the road and Wayne suspected they were supported by at least an infantry platoon. A quick check of the vehicle revealed no travel documents for points outside Whitehorse, which forced them to abandon the vehicle in a pull off. Since there were several farms in the area, the truck wouldn't raise any undue attention; at least until they were a safe distance away.

On foot again they were forced to snowshoe through deep snow as they gave the roadblock a wide berth. Later, out of breath from exertion, they returned to the highway and caught a ride with a military fuel tanker. Because they wore officer uniforms the driver, an enlisted man, maintained a solemn respectful silence, speaking only when spoken to. He dropped them off at the intersection of the Al-Can and the Cassiar Highway and they were sorry to lose him.

Shortly after midnight, ready to drop from exhaustion, they were again picked up - this time by a civilian hauling supplies from Whitehorse to his small community and he appreciated the company on the dark night. If not for their uniforms, he would have passed them; for a brief moment, he suspected they might be deserters. Wayne entertained him with humorous stories of military life convincing him that they were home on a short leave and returning back to their command. When they came upon a small military encampment pitched beside the road, Wayne asked the driver to drop them off.

"We've got friends here who can take us the rest of the way."

"You two take good care of yourselves," The driver replied as he pulled over. They shook hands and after the two officers climbed out with their packs, he slowly pulled away leaving them standing in the dark.

After they checked the camp, Wayne and Jeb sought out the chow tent and filled up on coffee, canned tuna and crackers. An hour later, Wayne rendered a motor pool perimeter guard unconscious with a sleeper hold. Sure that no alarm would be raised soon, they located a suitable vehicle, hotwired it and were back on the road.

Half a day passed while they alternated between driving and napping before the lights of Prince George appeared ahead. From earlier reports they knew the city was enclosed behind a ring of heavy security. Every vehicle going in and out was closely inspected and every person was examined for signs of infection and checked to make sure they were not deserters or AWOL soldiers. Outside the city was a large tent city, completely encircled by barbed wire and watchtowers. This was the designated isolation area where guards wore biological suits and only doctors and body collectors were allowed access. Bodies sealed in plastic and wrapped in white sheets were transported to a large trench nearby and burned, the ashes buried by bulldozers.

Jeb, who had been bounced around in vehicles, forced to hike through deep snow in icy weather, and without any real sound sleep for over 24 hours, decided to focus his displeasure on Wayne, and in sarcastic wit asked, " Well, Captain, what's next on our agenda? Do we lie, steal or simply kill to obtain travel documents for this area. And why exactly, I must ask, didn't anyone think about that?" He stifled a yawn.

Holding his temper, as any good captain would when dealing with a superior officer, Wayne attempted to explain it - again, "As I've already explained, Major, each area has its own travel document, signed by the local military authority and updated weekly. In answer to your question, we simply didn't have time." Wayne's nerves were on edge and Jeb's uppity attitude was beginning to wear thin on him.

"I know! We can steal a tank and blow our way through! Or…maybe we can just turn ourselves over to the next Mountie we see…" Jeb didn't get a chance to finish, Wayne had his right hand pressed against Jeb's throat, shutting off his air flow with a martial art move intended to disable an adversary.

"You'll have to forgive this violation of military courtesy, Major, but what in the hell is wrong with you?" Wayne pressed in for a moment longer before releasing him.

Jeb fought to breathe, his eyes bulging as he shot daggers at the officer who had dared to assault him. The two of them sat in the idling vehicle, Wayne staring out the windshield, his gloved hands grasped tightly to the steering wheel while Jeb struggled to regain his composure.

"I apologize for that, Major. You may report me when and if we get back. But I'm not sure what you expect out of me or this mission."

Jeb glanced around, rubbing his neck and then turned to face Wayne. He couldn't even remember seeing Wayne move and Jeb knew for a certainty, Wayne could have killed him just as fast had he wanted too. He remained silent for a moment, thinking about what he wanted to say and then cleared his throat, "Captain, I see no reason to report an incident that never happened. You are quite right. I've been behaving like a spoiled child. I've been mad at you because I couldn't stay and die with my division in Wales. In the books they refer to it as survivor's guilt. You won't hear me complain again." Jeb wiped tears from his eyes, "One more thing, you'll have to teach me that move sometime."

Relieved, Wayne grinned as he considered their next option and decided the first thing to do was get some sleep. "We need some sleep. We're both stretched pretty tight and the few winks we got on the road haven't given us any true rest. Let's find a place to get some shut eye; then we'll decide what our options are."

On an access road, they spotted a dilapidated multi-colored billboard advertising an R.V. park and a mile later, came upon several abandoned trailers. One was a 14' x 70' single wide with the rear master bedroom caved in from an old fire. Searching it, weapons ready for any surprise, they found two soiled single mattresses undamaged by the fire in one bedroom. After pulling them into the living room, they pulled down a set of old drapes to use for bedding then took a chance and built a small fire in the blackened shell of a small red barbecue that no longer had support legs. They stayed in their arctic gear to keep from freezing to death while the fire melted a crust of ice off fragile pieces of wall paneling. When the paneling dried, they broke it into smaller pieces and soon had a steady warm fire going, with smoke bellowing out through an open hole in the roof. Having been cold for so long, the warmth of the fire was over powering and neither man could stay awake. If not for their thick padded arctic wear, both men would have frozen to death after the fire went out. As it was, they were both quite chilled when they finally did wake up and got another fire going.

1ST DIVISION, LITTLE DIOMEDE ISLAND, MARCH 23RD

Captain Blackstone stood up like an old man with arthritis of the spine and cringed as he stretched the kinks out of his back, legs and arms. The cold penetrated his bones, making every day a little more difficult to limber up without the benefit of a hot shower. Finished with his exercises, he walked over to the radio where Sgt. Upasauk sat on a rolled sleeping bag reading a well-worn Zane Grey paperback, "When's the last time you checked the guard, cowboy?"

Upasauk smiled, "Captain, I'm on radio watch. You're supposed to check the guard…sir," Upasauk answered. He liked his captain, but he couldn't very well maintain radio duty while tromping around outside to see if one of his buddies had nodded off.

"Yeah, you're right…This time!" Blackstone exclaimed good heartedly slapping Upasauk on the shoulder, "Guess the cold is gettin' to me." He turned around, grabbed his rifle and proceeded down the darkened icy corridor taking small steps to maintain balance on the slippery floor despite using crampons. He was about to emerge into the night, when the sound of gunfire stopped him. Automatic weapons fire was coming from a short distance away and he could identify at least one M-16 exchanging fire with possibly several AK-50s.

"Notify Division to standby, we've got company!" Blackstone yelled back down the hallway loud enough for Upasauk to hear. His rifle ready and clicked over to full auto fire, Blackstone waited at the mouth of the tunnel until Upasauk and six men joined him. "Sir, Division notified. They will assume invasion has begun if we fail to make contact in 20 minutes."

"Then let's not waste time." Blackstone pulled night goggles over his eyes and signaled for the men to separate three to the right and four to the left. Another spurt of automatic fire from an M-16 told Blackstone that at least one of his men was still alive. He began to step forward, but Sgt. Upasauk grabbed his arm, "We'll check it out, sir. Better you stay here, make contact with Division if needed and give them a sit-rep."

Blackstone didn't like it, but he knew Upasauk was right. If this was the invasion, it would be up to him to report strike force strength, vehicles and other pertinent info. *You could do the same thing. You'd just rather go out there and do some hunting and let the officer stay back here safe and sound.* "Okay, you handle it, but stay alive and get back here pronto." They had ringed the area with old reliable Claymore mines wired to a single detonator; the charge handle was only inches from his hand. The charges were set to turn several tons of ice into deadly projectiles to welcome the OAP visitors to Little Diomede. Another burst of gunfire came from the north, followed by several M-16 single shots followed by a long moment of silence broken by several AK-50s going off and then again, silence. Out here on Little Diomede Island, where there were no trees to absorb it, every sound carried, even the crunching of ice as one man attempted to sneak up on another and weapons fire carried for several miles. Blackstone didn't like it; he checked his watch every few seconds, scanned the icy landscape before him and grew more nervous as he waited impatiently for Upasauk's return. It had started to snow again, a mixture of black ash and white snow. Time seemed to stand still and what seemed like an hour was only ten minutes. Suddenly, Upasauk popped up beside him followed by three men dragging a body in ADF uniform.

"What happened?" Blackstone hurriedly asked as the body of Corporal Nanpuik was carefully pulled past him and carried down to the bottom level.

"Small patrol; nine men an' they not very good. Make too much noise. Nanpuik had no choice, took down four of 'em before he got it. We got other five, used their own weapons to confuse them. Guards back in place, we only lose Nanpuik." Upasauk handed Nanpuik's dog tags to Blackstone. "Chinese may be good in Russia, but no Eskimo."

"Okay, take care of Corporal Nanpuik, while I contact Division." Blackstone pulled off his goggles and went back down to the bunker, passing Nanpuik's body as his friends removed personal items. He wanted to stop and say something, but his first priority was making contact with Command. He could only imagine the chaos in Wales as they waited to hear the word - "Invasion!"

Freeman talked with Blackstone directly; it didn't take him long to make the decision to pull Blackstone and his men out. "They know you're there now, no sense sacrificing you and your men. Set your charges around the complex, use enough explosives for us to see it from here - Over."

"Affirmative, sir. I've got enough C-4 to make Little Diomede look like a volcano eruption - Over."

*Don't know why we didn't do this in the first place...*Colonel Freeman keyed his radio phone, "Report to me when you make it back - Over."

"Affirmative," Blackstone replied. "We'll be leaving here within the hour - Over an' out." He looked up to see Upasauk enter, "Prepare all the explosives, then assemble our troops for departure." They only had one trak vehicle and he hoped it wouldn't give them any trouble for the ride back. *Gonna be a long walk if it does.*

Upasauk gazed down at Nanpuik's body and saluted his fallen comrade, "We will make the price high for taking one such as you." Upasauk thought about how he would break the news to this man's wife who was a sniper scout with another company. *She is strong, but she will need quiet time. I wonder if she will have that time and how many Chinese she'll kill to even the debt now owed her?* His heart saddened by the loss of Nanpuik, Upasauk looked down through the ice corridor and wondered what kind of soldiers they were facing? He knew there were other oriental races with the

Chinese and he sincerely hoped he would not have to kill some of his Russian Eskimo cousins in the fight ahead.

1ST DIVISION HEADQUARTERS

His eyes watery and bloodshot from the trak's diesel fumes and his sore shoulders bent over from a long bumpy ride back to Wales, Captain Blackstone reported in to an equally weary Colonel Freeman, "Your orders, Sir?"

Freeman returned his salute and put him at rest, "You look like you're about to fall down, Captain. How many hours have you gone without sleep?"

"I've dozed off and on, Colonel, but feel ready to go." Blackstone hoped this wouldn't take long. He wanted to make sure Corporal Nanpuik's body was taken care of and his effects turned over to his wife. Afterward, he hoped for some dearly needed hours in a warm cot.

Colonel Freeman looked hard into Blackstone's eyes, "Captain, I need you in Galena tonight, to assist in Cactus Tree." Freeman led Blackstone over to a small map table. "You'll be Assistant Brigade Commander, a new force made up of six companies drawn from our strength here. Lt. Col. Welch is your superior, a good man, but he has some difficulty in understanding the Eskimo and Athabascan people. The brigade has nearly every Black Hawk in the Division, but I'll send you and your best men down with three Hueys. The two separate units will rendezvous with you in Galena once they finish their assigned tasks. You're to destroy Galena; most importantly, render that runway useless to the enemy." Freeman looked into Blackstone's eyes, seeing the extreme fatigue and knowing he still had to go a bit longer before he could rest.

"Sir, I'm only a captain...."

"Negative. Effective this date you are promoted to the rank of major. Upasauk is promoted to the rank of 2nd Lieutenant and assigned to you."

"Wow, field grade status...an' my dad thought I'd never amount to anything. Thank you, Colonel."

Colonel Freeman shook his head, "If you still have some humor, you've got a few more miles left in you. But you've earned it. Now your last job under me is a tough one, a poor reward for a job well done." Freeman pointed to the map, "This is the Yukon River an' this is the bridge on the Dalton Highway. You are to take your force to that bridge, send half on to Fairbanks and half to hold that bridge at all costs."

"We're to hold the bridge?" Blackstone was confused, partly from fatigue.

"Stay with me, Major, you're to hold the bridge in the event some of 1st Division survives long enough to make it that far. In any event, even if our troops are within a mile of the bridge, you will destroy that bridge completely if you see any enemy troops. Do you understand me, Major?"

"Affirmative, Sir, but what about our men?" Blackstone wasn't sure he liked these orders.

"Listen carefully to my orders, Major and listen well." Freeman waited until he was sure that he had Blackstone's complete attention, "Under no condition will you allow that bridge to fall into enemy hands. We have to slow them down, even if that means sacrificing some of our troops."

"I understand, sir." Blackstone studied the map, "What about proper demolitions? Colonel, that's one big bridge constructed of heavy gauge steel."

"A demolition team from Fort Wainwright should already be on site setting everything up for you. Only reason we're holding off on blowing it up is to save what troops and equipment we can. But I must stress, that bridge cannot be taken intact."

"Yes, sir." Blackstone's eyes began to droop.

"Stay awake a bit longer, Major. You'll get some sleep in a moment."

"It's this warm tent, Colonel…makes me kind of groggy."

"Okay, as soon as you blow the bridge, you are to proceed south to Fairbanks and join up with the forces there."

"One request, Colonel."

"One? If I was you I'd have my Christmas wish list out. But go ahead."

"I'd like a proper military burial for Corporal Nanpuik."

"He'll get it, my promise. We'll blow a hole out with C-4 if need be. I've notified ADF Command-Fairbanks that I am awarding him the Bronze Star for his actions on Little Diomede."

"I'm sure his family will appreciate it, Colonel."

Colonel Freeman placed his right hand affectionately on Blackstone's shoulder, "It's not much consolation, but we'll always remember the brave young men and women of the Fighting First Division and the ultimate price they paid." He removed his hand and pointed to the tent's entrance, "Now go get some sleep, I'll have them find you when it's time to depart."

"Thank you, Sir." Blackstone presented a somewhat less than crisp salute before leaving headquarters with hopes of finding his cot before falling flat on his face.

CITY OF FAIRBANKS, RADIO STATION KCVF

"It's time once again for the evening news with Ron Larsen reporting for KCVF Radio Fairbanks. I won't be saying a lot tonight, reserving some of my minutes for evacuation notifications when the time comes. It's a chilly one outside, -29 ° and falling fast with a possible low of 45 below - so much for today's heat wave." Ron stopped to take a sip of hot tea; his hot plate was working again and he'd discovered a small stash of British Breakfast tea bags in the manager's office. *Sure hope they don't call this hoarding, I'd hate to spend my last days shoveling coal.*

"On the local front, the ADF wants me to remind all of you to be prepared for the city wide evacuation scheduled for the 25th of this month. That's only two days for those folks who used their calendars for kindling. According to my wall clock, that's a bit over 45 hours from now, so everyone be ready. If you happen to miss evacuation, plan on being part of the OAP welcome wagon." Ron sipped more tea, briefly savoring the aroma and remembering a much better time.

"Story number two: Military Police were involved in a shootout with three looters last night, all pronounced dead at the scene after attempting to break into a food storage garage. A futile gesture on their part, the garage was empty and they paid for it with their lives.

"Now we go to story number three: Fairbanks Police are remaining quiet about the recent church bombing, but the rumor mill is saying this was the work of the Unified World Church Alliance; the new master race spreading more hate an' violence for anyone not meeting their standards or believing as they do. Sound familiar? If not, check out World War Two history under Joseph Stalin and Adolph Hitler. Between them, they killed more than 20 million people. C'mon, whatever happened to love thy neighbor an' freedom of religion?" *Better tone it down boy, either the ADF or the UWCA is gonna pull your plug for sure.*

"Right now for a quick recap of the world news; Radio Calgary reports the civil war between Eastern and Western Canada continues to escalate with word of England providing troops and equipment in support of Quebec's new Freedom Brigade. Calgary further reports a large scale communications blackout with all sources in the Middle East and Europe. At last report the war between Pakistan and India has created a massive cloud of radiation spreading over most of Saudi Arabia, Afghanistan, Iraq and Iran. It appears that conflict has possibly signaled the end of Islam in the Middle East."

"Now to wrap the news up, the flight path of the Tariq-Leroy Comet and expected point of impact remains unchanged." Ron tossed his notes into a trashcan, took another sip of tea and reported a long list of evacuation points throughout the city after which, he prepared to sign off, "This is Ron Larson advising you to stay warm, stay safe and good night."

6 - THERE ARE WOLVES AMONGST US

"Surely the day is coming; it will burn like a furnace. All the arrogant and every evildoer will be stubble, and that day that is coming will set them on fire,' says the Lord Almighty. 'Not a root or branch will be left of them, but for you who revere my name, the sun of righteousness will rise with healing in its wings. And you will go out and leap like calves released from the stall. Then you will trample down the wicked; they will be ashes under the soles of your feet on the day when I do these things,' says the Lord Almighty.

Malachi 4.1-3 NIV

EAST OF HOLBROOK, ARIZONA- HIGHWAY I-40 - MARCH 20TH

With a thunderous roar reminiscent of an F-15 Eagle fighter cooking off on afterburners echoing across the desert flatlands, an unruly and trashy band of outlaw-bikers raced out of Holbrook in a long continuous line. Known for their extremely violent behavior, bloodthirsty games and senseless slaughter of the innocent, these vermin behaved much like a wild pack of predators from Hell.

Long straight chrome exhaust pipes curled up beside three foot high decorative sissy bars, satanic symbols were embossed on stickers and clothing and proudly displayed as jewelry. The pack mounted multi-colored Harley Davidson choppers; the cycles exploded growling and howling like banshees as they terrified victims and ran them to ground like animals.

In Arizona and New Mexico they were known as the Devil's Disciples, the foul scum of the outlaw biker world; men and their women, true lowlifes of humanity reigning like royalty in a lawless world, they stole and killed at every given opportunity. They had left a few of their number in Flagstaff when locals started shooting back and drove the Disciples off.

Warned by the convoy's rear guard over CB radio, Ed Sawyer quickly began issuing orders, "Stay in line, no doubling up and no passing. We do this just like we practiced. Keep cool an' shoot straight if fired upon."

From behind the convoy came the terrifying sound of automatic weapons fire; the bikers were pressing their attack on the rear vehicle. Dozens of bullets riddled a 1999 Ford Explorer, until the mortally wounded driver lost control and collided with a stretch of metal guardrail. Grinding steel sent sparks flying as friction burned the sides of the car away. A tire blew and the Ford flipped over on its side to skid down the pavement for several hundred feet. A passenger in the front seat was thrown clear, only to fall victim to the Disciples heavy concentration of fire. Suddenly a fiery explosion lifted the Explorer into the air and it landed burning on its collapsed roof. Two men, brothers who had lost their parents to the riots and had volunteered to pull rear guard, suffered a violent death as the vehicle burned. But no one could stop. To stop meant to die so the convoy surged ahead with the Devil's Disciples nipping at its heels.

A running battle ensued over the next eight miles with vicious bikers moving up the length of the convoy, some shouting threats and waving weapons in the air, while others took random potshots at the vehicles in hopes of getting the convoy to stop.

Much to the Disciples' surprise however, convoy members began to shoot back with deadly accuracy. Four Disciples are quickly knocked off their bikes before the outlaws realized they'd taken on a curly dog with a nasty bite.

Ed emptied nearly half a magazine from his M-16 to take down a dark complexioned biker with a fancy painted sidecar. At the same time, an extremely excited Nancy struggled to keep the ancient ambulance on its wheels as they sped down the road at breakneck speed. She had the gas pedal glued to the floor and the old World War II relic moaned and rattled as the speedometer climbed and for this antique, anything over 50 mph was near lethal.

In the back, Doc was hanging on for dear life, tossed from side to side as he fought to keep his medical supplies from flying about. It was difficult keeping an eye out the back window to see if one of the bikers was trying to move up on Nancy's blind spot.

Hanging partially out the right passenger window, Ed looked to the rear and spotted a new target moving up. He sighted and squeezed off a quick three round burst. With no expression of satisfaction, Ed watched as another biker; a long haired blonde fellow with snazzy mirrored sunglasses and clad in black leather, found a painful ending to his sinful life. Falling off his bike as it tumbled end over end, both biker and bike rolled off the highway and bounced over a low metal guardrail. A large plume of sand and black smoke rose into the air as the bike began a long slide across the desert floor for nearly 40 feet.

With the sound of heavy gunfire all around them and Ed shooting from only a couple feet away, Nancy couldn't make out the chatter coming over the CB radio. Not that it mattered, the convoy's frequency and the emergency channel were jammed with people either pleading for assistance or shouting as the Disciples continued to move in, looking for openings to disable vehicles and stop the convoy.

"Jimmy, yuh got a biker comin' up on your right side."

"I need help! I'm runnin' low on ammo..."

"They shot Becky...They shot Becky... Oh God, they shot Becky...Help us!"

"He's on your right, Jimmy... No Idiot... your other right!"

"Swerve to your left, Carlos...yeah, you got him!"

The battle raged on and there was nothing Ed could do except keep the convoy moving forward. Speed and staying together was their only chance to survive until Point Man could find an open piece of ground to circle the wagons. That was all part of the plan and he only hoped it worked out as well as it did when they practiced it on the classroom chalkboard.

Nancy, a Glock Model 17, 9 mm pistol with extended 30 round magazine held tightly in her left hand, spotted a filthy looking character coming up on her left. She noticed the greasy blue bandana wrapped around his forehead first and then the devious smile on his bearded face and missing upper front teeth. He was wearing a black leather vest and a long sleeved blue and white flannel shirt with the sleeves partially rolled up to reveal several undistinguishable tattoos on his forearms. His filthy blue jeans were tucked inside the top of heavily scuffed black leather boots and around his neck was a long beaded necklace with a large silver pentagram. He was waving a sawed off single-barrel 12 gauge shotgun in his left hand, while his other gloved hand gripped the bike's throttle. Keeping one eye on him in the side mirror and one eye on the roadway, she continued to struggle with the thrashing motions of the beast she drove. But the crazed outlaw was now close enough to see Nancy's face in the ambulance mirror and he sneered at her. In return, she simply swerved the ambulance to the left and nearly swatted him off the highway. But braking saved his life. He was mad now, no more games; he let out an animal growl and accelerated to close up the distance.

The ambulance speedometer registered 68 mph, the best the old beast could offer and the temperature gauge was slowly climbing. She glanced into the mirror again and recognized the look of determination on the biker's face, *He's moving in for a kill shot an' that shotgun's gonna have a wide pattern. Not enough penetration to blow these old heavy tires, so he's after a kill shot on me. So, no more time for playing games. I've got to act fast or suffer the consequences - big time.*

Coming up fast, he lifted his shotgun for a quick shot, gave Nancy a sly wink and began to apply pressure on the trigger. At the same moment, Nancy switched the Glock to her right hand and brought up the weapon, turned partially to the left, and fired off three 9mm rounds in quick succession over her left shoulder. An expert shot from hours of practice on the range, two of the rounds entered the chest of a very shocked biker and the third round penetrated the Harley-Davidson's pearl colored tear drop shaped gas tank.

A dead man, his lifeless fingers still grasping the throttle, his dearly loved Harley swerved across the road and collided with the guardrail. The motorcycle smashed into the metal barrier and sent the body flying out onto the desert floor. A much relieved Nancy never looked back. The Glock back in her lap, Nancy turned to see Ed's look of admiration, "Someone should of told that clown it was against the law to chase ambulances."

"Nice shooting, lady," Ed said and returning to the business at hand, took aim on another biker, fired off another three round burst, blowing the front tire of the bike and sending the Disciple off the road into a fiery crash.

George Washington Sr. didn't have time to return fire. It took all his driving skill to swerve his double-tanker from right to left and back again like the whipping tail of a diamondback rattlesnake, in an attempt to keep more of the bikers from passing him. A few of the braver ones, or maybe the more foolish, were able to get by. Washington knocked two more off the road and one was run over by following vehicles.

One Disciple, Crazy Sam, gestured to get the attention of Blue Billy, who was hauling a partner in a sleeked down sidecar. Crazy Sam, known to take any dare for a profit, pointed to the tanker's ladder and moved the fingers on his left hand to indicate that the rider jump off the bike and climb to the top of the tanker. Catching on, Billy smiled and steered his old Harley-Knucklehead close enough for his rider to grab the ladder on the front tanker. After the rider caught the ladder and began climbing, the swerving rear tanker nailed Blue Billy's bike and sent him crashing into the guardrail. Shaken at seeing his bud fly to his death, Little Jim Fremont of San Diego lost his footing on the ladder and George Washington never noticed the bump.

Ed had trained the convoy drivers himself, spending hours on chalkboard displays and when possible, practicing out in the desert for an event such as this. According to plan, the big diesel wrecker and the Kenworth Tractor pulling the 40 foot food van, moved up alongside the school bus to protect the women and children. He knew it looked good in practice, but he also realized that sooner or later these guys were going to start shooting at the tires to cause a wreck. He was surprised they hadn't already done so.

Point Man tried to contact Ed on the CB, but couldn't get through all the radio traffic. He and His Misfits had found a suitable location for the convoy to pull off and form a defensive circle. He also realized that unless

Ed spotted him in time, they'd drive right by and then he and His Misfits would end up having to catch up. Meaning, they'd have to drive right up through some of their old biker buddies and in the heat of battle, they'd risk getting shot at by both enemy and friend alike.

Ed did spot Point Man about a mile ahead and grinned, seeing his massive point element jumping up and down like kids at a soccer game, frantically waving their arms to get his attention. "Nancy, start pulling toward the right a little an' slow this old beast down. Aim right at Point Man, I think he's trying to get our attention."

"Gotcha," Nancy shouted to be heard over the wine of the old 6 cylinder engine.

"Time to circle the wagons and I hope everyone remembers the drill," Ed said. He glanced at the speedometer and promptly reminded Nancy she was still going too fast.

"I know…I know…Let me do the driving, okay, or we can trade places and I'll do the shooting!"

"You two can fight later!" Doc snarled. "Get this thing stopped before I lose anymore saline solution or I'll be using plain trailer water to irrigate you all with." In the back, Doc was behaving like a four armed short order cook, switching between catching anything fragile that was flying about and struggling to push other items back behind the metal racks before they could topple out.

Nancy looked into her rearview mirror and shouted to Doc, "You wanna drive this thing, old man? I know what I'm doin'!"

Doc couldn't help but see the fire in Nancy's eyes and he shut up, just in time to catch a full bottle of aspirin from launching off a shelf.

Passing Point Man at over 40 mph, she drove off the highway through a flat sandy stretch, where there was no guardrail and onto the hard packed desert floor. His Misfits were kneeling behind their bikes, taking shots at the bikers with sawed off M-4 automatic rifles and praying they weren't about to get run over by the oncoming vehicles.

Point Man reached into his saddlebag and calmly pulled out a broken M-79 grenade launcher. Long experience with the weapon, gave him the speed to assemble the stock and load it with a single round of (H-E) high explosive.

"Bring it around tighter, "Ed yelled at Nancy, who growled back at him in response.

"Tighter!" Ed shouted again, as sand and dust began to come in through the windows and floorboards.

A COMING STORM

The single file maneuver of circling the vehicles in the same manner as wagon trains of old caught the bikers completely by surprise. Clouds of sand reduced visibility to near zero limiting each driver's view only to only the vehicle directly in front and so on down the line. Unable to see in the billowing clouds of dust, five outlaws crashed into slowing vehicles and died under the wheels of those following.

The driver of a rebuilt 1985 Chevy Blazer couldn't see at all, his eyes stinging from sand grit coming up through the ancient floorboards. Jerry O'Connor of Mesa, Arizona, swerved out of line, frightening his terrified wife even more and instantly became lost in the swirling clouds of sand. He cranked the steering wheel hard right, fighting to tune a deaf ear to his wife, Mary. But he turned too tight, lost control and rolled the Blazer several times making them easy prey for the enraged Disciples who obliterated the vehicle with automatic fire and a single shotgun blast that ended the O'Connor's lives.

The sound of screeching brakes filled the air as the convoy circled into place. Men, women and children leapt from vehicles and took to up fighting positions behind them for the impending attack. They knelt behind wheels for protection from bullets coming under the cars and ricocheting off the desert floor.

The school bus moved to the center of the circle and stopped. Larry O' Brian made sure all women and children were on the floor before he stepped out to guard the entrance with an eight shot police 12-guage riot gun. A woman, who had been an avid bird hunter, took up position at the rear emergency door armed with her own shotgun.

As the dust began to settle, Point Man spotted a dozen or more bikers sitting on a small knoll on the far side of the roadway waiting for the dust to clear enough for them to sweep down upon their victims. The convoy had too many things the bikers needed: fuel, food, equipment and women. Point Man understood these men and their actions. He'd ridden with them and knew they wouldn't give up unless they made it too costly for them.

Oh, I recognize you Big John, been a few years an' you is jus' as ugly lookin' as ever. Point Man had spent many a day riding with Big John, looting and shooting as they terrorized rural Arizona and New Mexico. The Devil's Disciples had replaced the Hell's Angels as the main outlaw biker band in the Southwest, a fact Point Man was no longer proud of. *We covered a lot of miles together, Johnny Boy, but you ain't changed an' you're sure not gettin' your hands on this group. No sireee...* Setting his open field sights, Point Man took aim with his M-79 and fired off his first round. Three seconds later, the 40mm grenade round exploded 30 feet in front of the bikers.

"You're short!" One of the Misfits exclaimed.

"Hurt 'em some though," Point Man answered as he watched two bikers topple off their machines from flying shrapnel. He reloaded and fired again, coming closer to the mark; the explosion sent a lethal wave of shrapnel through four more bikers. "That got their attention!"

Big John shook his head as he watched his Disciples fall and considered his options, some of his best were either dead or wounded and his strength was cut to less than half of what he began with. He recognized Point Man with the grenade launcher and remembered how effective his old buddy could be with it. Decision made, Big John signaled the others to head west and stopped only long enough to shout at Point Man, using his real name with a few profanities and added a profane gesture for good measure. The battle was over and the Devils Disciples were abandoning the attack.

"How many did we lose, Boss?" Point Man asked Ed as he rode up and shut off his bike.

Ed shook his head from side to side, grief heavy upon his face, "We've lost nine men, two women an' three vehicles. Another seven are wounded and under Doc's care," he replied in a low voice and then added, "Could have been worse... much worse. Good shooting with that launcher, I forgot you carried one."

"Worked pretty well for me in Somalia, picked one up when I got home."

Ed grinned. He was never surprised the bad guys could always get their hands on illegal weapons, while congress was always trying to limit the good guys from owning anything above a single shot .22 caliber rifle. He remembered how the police were always outgunned, but at least this time his side had the fire power.

"I gotta check on the vehicles. Why don't you go see if Doc needs anything...maybe you can hold his stethoscope or something?"

"Okay, Boss," Point Man said. He knew the deaths had shaken Ed and he needed a few moments alone. Leaving Ed to finish counting bullet holes in the sides of his ambulance, he walked away. Doc had his field hospital set up under a large canvas canopy attached to the top of the ambulance and staked to the desert floor by lengths of rope. As soon as the men put the circus tent up, he'd move into it. But in the meantime, while Doc was busy with more serious cases, minor wounds were tended by Emergency Medical Techs; EMT 1's he'd trained in the final weeks prior to leaving Phoenix. Nancy roved about, checking each, running an IV here and there as needed, but was often called away to assist Doc with a major case. A smaller 10 man canvas wall tent was set up under the shade of the rising circus tent and here, Doc conducted surgery assisted by either Nancy or one of the EMTs.

He noted how rapidly the supply of oxygen, morphine and other pain medication was being used up.

Inspection of the vehicles revealed that all but two had bullet holes in them, the school bus and a passenger van. Surprisingly, no engines or tires were hit in and this made Ed wonder why, if the Lord was protecting them, had so many died?

All of the dead were gathered, graves dug and Pastor conducted graveside services which at first angered those who thought the bikers should be left to rot. Pastor explained that Jesus had sacrificed himself for all humanity and it was left to God to make final judgment. This quieted down the disgruntled and later in the day, a memorial service was held for the deceased congregation members. The convoy had been hurt badly; physically, emotionally and spiritually. When the memorial service ended, several people began to speak out in anger towards God, blaming Him for the long journey, the danger and their loss. Murmurs of discontent carried through the gathering and a few even suggested they turn back before more died.

"Enough!" Pastor Woodway shouted, walking away from a wounded teenager and glared at those who had spoken, "You vile sinners, have you forgotten so early what you left behind in Phoenix? Do you not remember how the Angels of the Lord protected us as we gathered for departure? You are not so unlike the Israelites who escaped Egypt and complained when frightened like small children; even as great miracles occur around you...Where is your golden calf?" Pastor challenged. "Who among you dares to speak out against God? I say to you, your tongue will bring a mighty curse down upon you." Pastor spoke in a strong booming voice heard by all. Waving his Bible in the air, he exclaimed, "Be watchful of your words, be a guardian of your tongue before you perish like the serpent! Those of you with evil in your heart, you will not finish this trip. No! Repent now or face these final days alone, separated from the Lord as Satan in his pit of Hell." Pastor looked around at the stunned expressions on their faces, turned his back to them and in silence walked away to be alone with the Lord. This moment had surprised him. He didn't normally speak out in old King James English and knew it could only have come through him from the Lord. Still, it left him weak and he needed a quiet moment alone in the desert.

There was no service that night and no music in the camp; next morning, a very subdued convoy moved out and traveled deep into the afternoon. Ed noticed the lack of traffic coming from the opposite direction and it unsettled him. In the days past, they'd seen one or two vehicles traveling west, but not today. He had been hoping to pick up a few survivors to help with camp defense, especially after losing several in the battle with the Disciples.

Late in the day the convoy came upon a rough looking twosome walking along the highway. Steve Agar was an experienced hitchhiker who had toured the Pacific Southwest on his thumb begging or stealing when he could find no other way to procure what he needed to survive. He was accompanied by a tall muscular woman named Kathy Looney. Neither of the castaways carried baggage, other than a canteen of water; Ed thought it strange to be crossing the desert without food or belongings. She carried a 10 inch Buck sheath knife which Point Man confiscated and handed to Ed. Steve wasn't carrying any weapon, which Ed found unusual and since Steve's close resemblance to a desert ground squirrel made Ed uneasy, he decided that all weapons were to be kept away from him.

He considered leaving them with a supply of water and food, but seeing how desperate they looked alone on foot in the middle of the desert, he was moved to offer them mercy. He told Pastor that if they worked out, Steve and Kathy could come with them to Alaska, if not, they would be dropped off at the nearest town. Pastor looked them over and smiled at Kathy, who didn't drop her gaze but rather returned a hard glare. Strangely enough, she felt as if this quiet man could see into her very soul and this unnerved her some. Despite her sense of unease she immediately sensed him to be quite different from other men. Pastor Woodway nodded, turned to Steve and shook his head and disgust. Ed knew right then that Steve's time with the convoy was limited, but they were still quite a few miles from civilization and they'd keep Steve with them for a while.

Steve weighed only 138 lbs. and stood 5'6", slumped over at the shoulders with his neck bent to the right from a boyhood injury. His greasy dark brown hair hung over his shoulders by a good three inches. A long thin face ended in a pointed chin giving him an almost wizardly cartoonish look. A week old scraggly beard and moustache that accentuated his dark circled bloodshot hazel eyes only added to the overall effect. On his left shoulder was a colored tattoo of a skimpy bikini clad dancing woman which he liked to show off to the teenage men until Ed stopped it with a stern warning. Steve was wearing a torn filthy black t-shirt on the front of which was a faded golden dragon grasping a large sword in its talons and a black leather vest three sizes too large held together in front by three tarnished silver chains. A 4" by4" patch was sewed on one thigh of threadbare black jeans torn at the knees and his greasy white Nike tennis shoes looked as if they were two or three sizes too large. It was evident that their newest guest had most likely scrounged nearly all of his clothes. Ed wondered where and who he had taken them from and, thinking of Winslow, he grew concerned. He more closely resembled some kind of desert ground squirrel and decided that all weapons were to be kept away from him.

Ed saw someone far different in Kathy. For a woman she was of tower height, almost an Amazon; 6'4" and Ed estimated she probably tipped the scales at 170 to 180 lbs., and most of that was lean and mean. Dark blonde hair hung in a single braid down the length of her back, tied by a thin strip of black leather. In a face that showed the marks of stress and tension, her eyes were a remarkably clear radiant dark blue, almost cobalt. Ed, who preferred women to be natural, thought Kathy was wearing far too much make-up, but he'd let the other women deal with that. He liked the strength he saw in her broad shoulders, but thought the tattoos on her arms were somewhat strange. A large snake curled around her right arm from shoulder to wrist and on her left arm was the face and upper body of a beautiful Geisha holding a large extended Japanese fan covered in symbols that Ed didn't understand. Kathy was wearing a dark blue tank top with an oil stain on the front, extremely form-fitting black jeans and a pair of high heeled mid-calf black leather boots with silver decorations.

Ed soon discovered that Steve was a lazy individual, who never volunteered for any of the work, and whenever possible would sneak away and find someplace to doze off. It also turned out he was a thief, who would steal food and whatever else he thought was valuable. Unfortunately for Steve, there was someone in the convoy who was watching him and keeping a mental list of his foul deeds. Someone who had his own ideas and believed Steve might be the very man he needed when the time came.

Kathy was quite different. She pitched in right away helping with chores and was found to be as strong as any man in the group. She remained almost mute that first day al through meal preparation.

Steve stood beside an armed night guard while they waited for the call to chow. He joshed about all this God stuff and Pastor's "holier than thou rap" from yesterday. The guard, disgusted with the little man, glared at Steve, "You don't believe in God?"

"Nope... Sure don't. Ah'd heard all that rap 'bout the Big Man upstairs, but as ah see it, he's jus' some crutch for all the weaklings to hang on to."

The guard shook his head in distaste, "You don't mind if I move along, I'd really hate to be standing close when the lightening hits." He looked back over his shoulder at Steve and walked off to make his rounds. He'd eat later.

Watching the man walk away, Steve laughed. "Lightening...right!" He looked to the heavens and shouted, "Okay, Big Guy, bring it on...do your worst!" Silence was his only answer and Steve shrugged in response, "Yeah, like I thought." He had lived a tough life, putting himself before all others, never looking back at the ripples he had caused. Not even the criminal element liked him knowing that for the right money or deal with a District Attorney's office, Steve would squeal on anyone. He was known to rob from friends and the few foster parents he'd had. He made his own way in life, no matter what harm it brought to others. Abandoned by his mother at age two, Steve lived in one state foster home after another and was constantly returned for poor attitude and refusal to obey house rules. Foster homes led to juvenile detention centers and then to the city jail and eventually prison. His numerous crimes consisted of narcotic possession and sale, shoplifting, burglary, forgery and auto theft. The only crimes he shied away from were ones involving violence, for Steve suffered from cowardice.

Out of fear, Steve had never made a pass at Kathy Looney; she scared the wits out of him. Kathy had somehow escaped from the Devil's Disciples just a few hours before they laughingly abandoned Steve in the desert to die of thirst. Walking along the highway, she came upon him sitting on the side of the road and thought he might be of some help in reaching civilization. He wasn't, but she stayed anyway.

When the dinner bell rang, Steve ran to the front of the line pushing and shoving; a teenage girl fell to the ground. This act of rudeness didn't go unobserved. Larry O' Brian, normally passive, except when his children were endangered, decided it was time to teach Mr. Attitude some manners. While others watched in amusement, Larry picked Steve up off the ground by his vest, carried him outside the circus tent and threw him bodily through the air for nearly 10 feet. "When you can act like a man, you can come back here an' be treated like one. You understanding what I'm saying here, mister or do you need another lesson?"

Embarrassed, frightened and a bit battered, Steve slowly stood up and behaved like a spoiled toddler, pout and all. "You leave me alone! You...you...I'll get you for this. No one does that to me... No one!" Steve brushed himself off, wiped the sand off his cheeks and limped away to sulk.

A strange heaviness hung over the camp, social interaction was at a low, people left a few food crumbs on plates. Ed and most of the combat veterans had seen it before. Remorse: weary after effects from prolonged adrenalin rush; initial stages of Post-Traumatic Stress Disorder (PTSD). It came down to individual experience. Forced to take a life, watch a friend or family member die, high speed chase involving a gun battle; stressful events very few of them had ever encountered and it had caught up with them.

Pastor could see and feel the depression which hovered over his people and he sent the word out, "Time to gather for worship." This wasn't a time for foot stomping praise. No, this involved a single acoustic guitar and the voice of Cindy Roberts singing a soft song of love to the Lord. Before the evening was over, a refreshing breath of the Holy Spirit had blown through the camp.

Kathy Looney was disturbed by this event. She didn't understand any of it. Watching these people worship together puzzled her. *Friends, family members dead or wounded an' here they are singing? Don't make no sense, who are these people?* Yet as the night wore on, memories of a better time in her life drifted back - *Ten years...ten long years since I talked ta God. Wonder if the man even bothered ta listen?*

A high school dropout in sophomore year, an early pregnancy followed by a painful abortion at a so called family clinic, Kathy, at 18, went to work as a topless dancer in one sleazy joint after another. A large and extremely good looking woman, she was always a main draw at any of the clubs she worked. They had wanted her to go totally nude, but even back then she had drawn the line at topless only with absolutely no porn or hooker work. Drifting from town to town, she used her skills to raise money to support her and her kid brother. Both parents were long dead and the only men who drifted into her life seemed to have other things on their mind besides a loving relationship. All too frequently she attracted a lot of lookers who tried to exploit her. Eventually, the money got better and she was able to put her brother through the first two years of electrician's trade school in Phoenix. While he sat at home studying wire diagrams, wattage and voltage, she spent six out of seven evenings dancing from 9 p.m. to 2 a.m., entertaining drunks, vile perverts and disgustingly lonely men.

During those sad years, Kathy bounced between boyfriends. Never taking a relationship seriously, she went through a lawyer hooked on cocaine, played second fiddle to a biker's hog and an ex-con on the run for probation violations who finally owned up to having a wife in Kansas. These were samples of the kind of men who hung out at girly bars and dated strippers; looked upon as losers by the men they entertained.

Thinking about her brother brought back memories of the night he was killed. She found him outside the apartment lying face down in a puddle of blood, the victim of a drive by shooting when the riots first broke out. For the next five days, Kathy hid in her apartment until forced out when the building caught fire. She ran and hid for the next four days, barely escaping rape by using a form of street fighting she had learned from a bar bouncer and the large hunting knife she carried. To escape the carnage of Phoenix, she began hitchhiking north, refusing several rides when she recognized the lust in the eyes of the men who stopped to check her out. Finally, against her better judgment, she accepted a ride with a man with a kind face. It was a mistake. Her knife saved her from possible death at the hands of Mr. Kind Eyes, leaving him with a nasty cut on his arm to remember her by. Once more she found herself on foot. Then the Disciples came and she had no choice, there was far too many of them to escape.

Now I'm standin' here listenin' ta hymns, who'd believe it? Wonder what these holy rollers would do if they found out what kind of sinner they got here? Kathy's thoughts were interrupted when someone gently touched her arm, startling her. Survival instinct took over as she assumed a defensive stance and reached for the knife that was no longer there.

"Pardon me, Miss, I'm Pastor Woodway…we met earlier. I thought we might chat. Is everything alright?" Pastor seemed to ignore Kathy's martial art stance.

Kathy relaxed, "Uh-h, sure… Everythin' jus' fine." She glanced around to ensure that no one was walking up from behind. As she looked at Pastor, she was surprised by the strange feeling of safety she now felt in his presence.

"Name's Looney… Kathy Looney. Thanks for thu meals an' umm, thu ride." Kathy was nervous, still somewhat confused by the vibes this man was sending out - vibes she wasn't used to anymore.

"Who taught you martial arts skills?" Pastor asked.

"Old boyfriend... a Marine... He worked as a bouncer where I…" She stopped, fearful that these Christians might feel less kindly about her if they knew she'd been an exotic dancer.

"I recognize that stance, but you need to relax a bit more…too rigid." Pastor held his Bible at his side and looked out across the dark desert as a few flakes of either ash or dirty snow fell upon them. "I used to use a similar skill, but now I make war with this." He lifted up his Bible for her to see.

"A Holy Roller…Uh, sorry," Kathy replied.

"I've been called a lot of things, Kathy and Holy Roller isn't by far the worst."

Pastor smiled gently and then added, "I understand you spent some time with those bikers before we picked you up." He sensed her unease.

"Those sons of...Sorry...again...Those boys got a bit rough with me before I escaped, they picked me up north of Phoenix."

"Do you want to talk about it? Sometimes it helps… maybe you could speak with one of the women if you prefer?"

"No big thing. They'd party down, kidnap some broads...they do like to play rough. That's 'bout it." There was a lot more, but Kathy's defensive wall sprang up and she was done talking about it.

"Can you tell me anything about your friend?"

"We're not friends! He was with the Disciples...until they got tired of him. They didn't want to waste a bullet and thought it more amusing to let the desert take care of him. I thought maybe two of us could be better than one...Well I couldn't leave him out there to die. He is one worthless piece of ... Sorry... again. Steve's a real weasel."

Pastor had to stifle off a laugh, "Then I'll say good night with letting you know we are happy to have you along." He smiled and then walked off into the darkness.

Strange cat, but nice in a weird way. Kathy lit her last cigarette, taking a moment to enjoy the peace that surrounded her. Then, hearing a noise behind her, she tensed, dropped the cigarette and whipped around in defense stance, hands clenched into fists. But instead of an aggressor, she found a teenage girl with big eyes standing in front of her.

"Hi, I didn't mean to startle you."

"Who are you?" Kathy asked as she relaxed. *Pastor fellow was right, I'm too tensed up and my stance stinks.*

"Kira."

Kathy reached down and picked up the cigarette, "What'cha want, kid?" There was annoyance in her voice.

"Nothing. I thought you might like some company, that's all."

"You thought wrong, kid. Now beat it before your momma gets worried."

"My mom an' dad are dead," Dejected, Kira lowered her head and hoped the tears wouldn't come as the memory of the crash flooded over her.

"Sorry, kid," Kathy said. "Things are rough all over." She began to turn away, but something inside cut deep and drew her back - the brat resembled her kid brother.

"Why are you looking at me like that?" Kira asked.

"Not to worry, you jus' looked a bit like someone I knew once...a long time ago." Kathy took a deep puff on her cigarette and blew out a smoke ring, "What's your name again?"

"Kira...an' I'm almost 17, so quit calling me a kid." Kira wiped her eyes with the cuff of her long sleeved red and black flannel shirt - a loan from Nancy.

"Okay, don't get your dander up...So, Kira how long you been with this outfit?"

"A few days... Ed, he's the wagon master, and the others rescued me from two guys...They attacked me on the road. I was unconscious...a car wreck... it killed my mom an' dad. So now I'm with them an' we're headin' north to Alaska."

"North to Alaska, ain't that the title of some stupid song. They always play it in the bars and I hate it...Alaska, you gotta be joshin' me...Like...that must be 4,000 miles."

Kira explained to Kathy what Nancy had shared concerning Pastor's vision, "And if Ed says we can make it...Well, I believe him."

"Sounds like to me like you got a bad case of hero worship goin', girl."

Kira frowned in response to Kathy's remark, but then her eyes smiled, "Can you keep a secret?" She asked.

"Only if it suits me," Kathy replied harshly taking a final puff on the cigarette. She dropped the butt to the ground, stepped on it and ground it into the sand.

"Oh well, I'll take a chance on you," Kira said looking around to make sure they were alone and then burst out with, "I plan to marry Mr. Ed Sawyer."

"Marry? Ain't you kinda young for that?"

"Nope... all those old rules are out an' the old, old rules are back in. I'm old enough to have babies, so as I see it, I'm old enough to fall in love an' get married. Next year was to be my senior year. Lots of girls my age get married if their parents' consent to it."

Kathy realized this young lady had a real head on her shoulders. She fought back memories of her pregnancy and the stupid decision to get that abortion, all because the dude didn't want to get married or father a kid. She couldn't help but see that Kira was in fact older than she was when she had gotten pregnant, which made her wonder if this Ed dude knew what kind of female tempest was about to hit him from all sides, "What does this Ed think about the idea?"

Kira grinned, "Oh, he doesn't know about it yet, but he will soon enough."

"Well, you go girl!" Kathy said with a twinkle to her eyes. She liked this kid.

From the kitchen came a loud shout, "Kira! You're needed over here."

"I'm comin'!" Kira yelled back and turned to Kathy, "Gotta go, hope we can talk later."

"Sure. See yuh later, kid...Kira." Kathy watched as Kira ran towards the kitchen, *Cute kid, this poor Ed guy's about to be hunted down an'*...Kathy noticed someone else coming her way, *I'm sure mighty popular tonight, didn't even have ta take my clothes off and dance.*

Larry O' Brian shuffled his feet through the desert sand as he slowly approached Kathy. She recognized him as the man who had given Steve the heave ho at dinner. *Not that the twerp didn't deserve it.*

"Hello, I'm Larry O'Brian... school bus driver and mechanic extraordinaire." He offered her his catcher-mitt sized paw.

"Hello, yourself, Larry O'Brian. My name is Kathy Looney an' yes, I've heard all the loony tune jokes I want to hear...okay?" Kathy shook Larry's hand and was surprised how gentle he was. *Most creeps like to shake my arm off to show how strong they are, intimidated by my size.*

"Seems like I've seen your face before...I know...you're that football player! Right? Arizona Cardinals?"

"Good memory," Larry replied. "For six years, but that's all gone now."

"And you're a Christian too?" Kathy asked in disbelief as she looked Larry over in the limited light. She wasn't used to seeing such a good looking man who could go eye to eye with her in height...and a Bible thumper too. In the past, she'd been verbally assaulted by offensive and judgmental Christians and all they done in the process was to turn her off toward God.

"Eleven months. My...uh, my wife talked me into going to church with her. I liked what Pastor had ta say and later, I kept coming back until I got the Word."

"Which one's your wife, Larry?" *Married. Too bad.* "Isn't she going to be upset with you out here in the dark talking to a strange woman?

"She's not here, Kathy," Larry said mournfully. He missed his wife so much and looked forward to the day he could join her in heaven. "My Debbie was killed last year while I was off doing my thing. I was an idiot...didn't realize what a treasure...and then the war took her from me. I had Pastor Woodway...He...well, he spent a lot of time with me and helped me through my grief. I gave my life to the Lord and that's when things started making sense to me."

"I'm sorry about your wife." *So he is single...umm.* "So, why don't you blame God for taking your wife...lots of people blame Him for what's wrong and what's happened to Phoenix."

Larry shook his head, "People always like to blame God, but it was a man who pushed buttons to launch all those missiles. It was man who rioted in the cities and it was man who turned his back on God long ago." Larry looked down at his feet and shuffled the sand around. "No, I don't blame God and now I know He's forgiven me for my adultery and lack of care for my wife."

Kathy was stunned. She wasn't used to such a manly guy talking about God this way. This bunch amazed her; first a handsome guy wielding an M-16, a church pastor who knew martial arts and now this dude.

"Anyway, Pastor Woodway wants you riding in the bus, says he thinks you'll probably be pretty good in a pinch." Larry pointed back over his shoulder to the center of the camp, "I'm going over to check on my bus now, you wanna come along?"

"Sure, got nothing else to do." Kathy followed Larry to the bus and stepped inside while he checked the oil and coolant.

"Say, is this seat behind you taken?"

"Wait a minute," Larry yelled from under the bus hood. "I can't hear you under here. Let me finish up." Wiping his hands on a soiled once tan cloth, Larry came to the bus door, "Now what did you ask?"

"I asked if this seat was taken." She sat behind the driver seat, using a large black metal 4 D cell flashlight to illuminate the inside of the bus.

"No, the kids say I block all the view."

In a deep smoker's laugh, Kathy released some of her pent up tension. She'd spent too many hours in bars and, before it became too costly, had smoked nearly two packs a day. She admired the width of his shoulders, "This will be jus' fine."

"Have to warn you though; it can get pretty noisy in here with all these kids."

"I like kids...little ones at least. Teenagers drive me crazy."

"Sure hope you can sing. We sing a lot of songs to keep the kids happy and I sing a lousy baritone."

"Sing? Sure...but you'll have to teach me the words." Kathy looked about the bus and spotted all the various stuffed animals, assorted dolls and blankets. Piles of coloring books and boxes of crayons were stacked up neatly against the wall of the bus.

"These kids will teach you, you'll fall in love with 'em." Larry went back to the bus engine; he was concerned with a knocking noise he had heard earlier. He first thought a bullet had pierced the engine block, but there was no sign of any bullet holes on the outside of the bus and no evidence of a possible ricochet off the road underneath.

Kathy stepped out of the bus and watched while Larry looked as if he was being swallowed by the bus monster. "Tell me something, Larry, with your wife dead an' all this going on around you, how can you still believe God actually cares?"

Larry knew a serious question when he heard one and decided the bus could wait. He climbed down, wiped his hands off and glanced over at the camp to watch the women herding the children toward bed. A couple of the older ones were making a game of it, running as the adults gave chase. He looked at Kathy, "Do you believe in love?"

"Love? Yeah, I think so...I've thought so a few times, but usually it ended up being only a physical thing."

"I had it once, didn't realize how important it was until I lost it, but I still remember how it feels." Larry continued wringing the rag in his hands; it helped having something in his hands when he talked of serious things. "God gave us the ability to love; we were created in his image. So, if we can love, why can't he?" Larry saw the look of puzzlement on Kathy's face and believed he had only confused her more. "I'm not real good at explaining things, Kathy. Maybe you should talk with Cindy Roberts."

"Who's Cindy Roberts?"

"She's the woman who led the singing tonight, has a beautiful voice."

"You mean that big Black lady?"

Larry was saddened by her remark, "Yeah, but I prefer to identify people by names. Racial differences nearly destroyed us, the few remaining survivors have a second chance; we need to look at people as human beings...not by color or what country their families came from."

"But isn't God white?" Kathy asked. She was going into unknown territory now, but there seemed to be something pushing her and for some strange reason she felt safe with Larry. *He could probably break me in two with those hands of his, yet there is a strange softness about him I've never seen before. I gotta check this out; find out who these people are?*

"Who told you God was white?" Larry asked.

"Look at all those paintings, they show this white Christ...a real skinny guy hanging from a cross. The movies they played at Christmas...he was always this anorexic white dude or some blue eyed surfer bum."

It was Larry's turn to laugh, "First of all, Jesus Christ was 30 years old when He began His ministry; He was a carpenter; a man who worked with His hands. He wasn't no pansy or some blue eyed surfer bum. His ministry lasted three years on this earth while He hiked through some of the roughest desert terrain in the world. Tough and lean, that's the way I see Him. As to color, Jesus was from a desert country off the Mediterranean Sea. Do you think those people look white?"

"So you're saying He was dark, like an Arab?"

"Middle-Eastern, like an Arab, yes...but He could've been light skinned, too or even darker. The thing is, Kathy, no one truly knows what color His skin was, His eye color or even the color of His hair. It's not important. What is important is His ministry, which has stood for over 2,000 years and grown across the world. However, on a personal note, I do believe the skin color of Israelites lightened up some after all those Jewish people from Germany, Poland...from all over Europe and America, went there to populate the land after World War II."

Kathy was impressed, "You know, for a football player you're not too simple minded. I thought all you guys were brainless hunks of beef with big egos and bigger paychecks."

"You weren't too far off, Kathy. I once fit into that category and I can't even remember where I blew most of that money. Now I'm a repentant sinner trying to live my life the way Jesus Christ would want me to. Remember that old logo, WWJD, 'What Would Jesus Do?'"

"No, but I didn't run in those circles." Kathy yawned, "Look, I need to get some sleep. We'll talk some more on the road, okay?" She turned to leave.

"Good night, Kathy Looney," Larry said as he watched her walk away. *Strange girl, strong an' independent...I think I like her! But will the kids?*

After they broke camp early next morning, the convoy headed east toward New Mexico. Point Man and His Misfits had left camp an hour earlier with orders to check out Sun Valley. By mid-afternoon, Point Man reported over the CB that the town was deserted and appeared to have been stripped of anything they could use. "Only a few abandoned cars, but they're all drained of gas and the tires are flat. Store shelves are empty and we've spotted several decaying bodies scattered about. Looks like a riot broke out here, Boss. I don't think you should stop - Over."

"Keep moving then - Over and out," Ed replied.

The rest of the day was quiet as they drove down the highway. There was no traffic coming from the east and this continued to worry Ed. That evening they made camp near Lupton, a small town east of the Arizona-New Mexico border. In the morning he would send Point Man and company in to check out the town, but would back them up with four riflemen. Thick clouds of volcanic ash spread southward darkening more than two thirds of the sky to the north; the night sky was pretty much blocked from view in that direction. Only to the south could they still see a few shining stars, but it was only a matter of time before the sky was completely covered from north to south and east to west. A few of the people in the convoy continued the old tradition of wishing upon the first star to be seen at night. The wishes varied, but they took a back seat to the prayers that were seriously whispered. Because of the angle of the planet and the ash clouds overhead, the Tariq-Leroy Comet was blocked from view. Yet, most everyone left alive on earth knew it was still coming and realized that nothing outside of God could stop it from very probably destroying the Planet Earth.

Taking his turn at guard duty, Larry O' Brian wandered along the south side of the encampment and listened for the warning sounds of a rattlesnake. Since a close encounter with a snake in his young years, he had always had a deep fear of them. Rattlers were at the top of his - 'Things-I-Do-Not-Want-To-Run-Into-In-The-Dark' - list. When he learned that Alaska didn't have any snakes he felt relieved, until Ed started telling bear stories over the late night campfires. *Killer Grizzlies in the Alaska wilderness- thanks, Ed.*

"Larry...Larry, wait up." Kathy Looney appeared with a brown wool blanket draped over her shoulders. The temperatures were dropping and they'd already had a few more snow flurries. "Thought you might want some company an' I couldn't sleep."

"You'll have to stay quiet. There's rattlers out here and I do not want to step on one."

"Big guy like you an' you're frightened by a snake?" Kathy was having fun with him. She actually knew how dangerous a rattler could be.

Larry frowned, "I know it sounds silly, but I do not like snakes, spiders, scorpions or rats. They give me the willies!" Larry looked around, keeping his eyes locked on the desert floor around their feet. He used the illumination of the encampment to guide his steps because a flashlight would give his position away if they were being watched by anyone out there in the brush.

"With all the noise we made setting up, I doubt there's a snake around now. But spiders, those I can't say." Kathy hated spiders too, but found it strange to have a big strong dude admit to his fears. Most guys always liked to brag, but this one seemed... "Larry, I wanted to talk some more about Jesus. I heard a woman saying how He's coming back. What's that all about?"

Though he was speaking to her, he kept his eyes on the desert outside of camp. "God's Word, you'll find it throughout the New Testament. The Lord and then His disciples spoke of how He will return." Larry kicked a pebble out of the way while he cradled his rifle in his left arm away from Kathy. He felt as if he was protecting her, like a gentleman walking a lady down a city street. *Gentleman? Me? It's been a long time since I used that word in connection with me.*

"I remember a little bit of the story, but not much." She smiled up at Larry, "Looking at me now, you wouldn't think I used to go to Sunday school? Back before my parents died." Kathy stepped in front of Larry, blocking his way and waited for his response to what she had said. She hadn't talked about Sunday school days since her brother was killed.

With a 30.06 Winchester in his arms, Larry gave Kathy a studious gaze that started with her feet and went up to her face. *Long straight hair, cold dark blue eyes an' more woman then I've ever seen before. Nearly as tall as me, maybe*

170 -180-pounds, slender in the right places and those other...careful, boy, you're gonna get yourself in trouble here... "You're a very attractive woman, Kathy. Is that what you want me to say?"

Yes...No, I wanted...expected something different, something new. Maybe he is like all the others, he can't see past my body... "Guess it's gettin' late, think I'll head back."

"Wait, Kathy, I'm on strange territory here. My wife's been dead for almost a year and I'm not sure what I should say here. But if it helps any, I've read what's in your eyes...not out here - it's too dark. But in the bus, I've looked at you in the mirror and saw the hurt, the pain you carry. I'd like to help you, even talk about your Sunday school days, but I'm not the one you're looking for. Only the Lord Jesus Christ can heal what's inside you...like He healed me."

"Yeah, maybe so...I jus'..." Kathy stopped, her eyes locked on something behind Larry. "There's a light out there, out in the desert." She pointed with her right index finger.

Larry turned, but he didn't see anything at first, "Probably a star on the horizon."

"No, it's moving...can't you see it?" Kathy continued to point in the direction of the light.

Then Larry saw it, "Hey, you're right!" He brought his rifle up, "Go tell Ed, I'll stay here and keep an eye on it." A moment later, Ed appeared with Joey and two others. All were armed and they watched as the strange single light came closer. There was no engine sound and its swinging motion was confusing them. After a few moments passed, the puzzle was solved when a man's voice called out, "Hello the camp. Can we come in?"

Ed recognized the voice to be that of a young man, but he kept his M-16 locked on semi-automatic. He shouted back, "Move in real slow an' come in with your hands empty and in plain sight." By now most everyone in camp knew something was up and had moved toward the commotion. Except for the guards on the other side of the perimeter who knew this could be a ploy and maintained their positions and vigilance.

As soon as Ed finished speaking, a man's voice spoke from behind a clump of bushes to their immediate right. "Well, young fellow, if I'd been a bad guy, you an' those others would surely be dead by now."

"Who-o-o?" Larry backed up, swinging his rifle around toward the voice.

"Easy, Larry," Ed warned and threw his left arm up to keep Larry from pointing his rifle at the intruder. "...if that man wanted to shoot us, he would've done it by now." Ed kept his own rifle aimed toward the ground, as did the others.

"Ease up their cowboy, ah'm comin' in real friendly like." A tall lanky older man slowly stood up within 10 feet of Larry and Joey. He held his rifle cradled in his right arm with the barrel pointed down. Feeling the tension in the group, the stranger dropped his rifle to the ground and held both hands up, "Take it easy fellas, only me and mah boy out there on his horse. Yuh all got so durn busy watchin' that ol' battle lantern of ours yuh didn't hear me crawl up beside you. Wanted ta listen for a moment, see what kind of folks were a campin' on mah land."

"Your land?" Ed asked, he thought this was federal land.

"Yup, all 20,000 acres, goes right up to within 50 feet of I-40. Mah ranch is back yonder in a small valley, "He pointed with his thumb over his right shoulder and began to brush sand off his pants.

A dark brown horse and rider came into view and they saw a teenage boy sitting in the saddle with a dark colored cowboy hat cocked on the back of his head. An old gray Navy battle lantern hung from the saddle horn, which explained the swaying motion.

"Mah name is Chester Fulbright an' this here's mah son, Matthew. He's 16, but works like a man of 20 years. We lost his maw couple years back, now it jus' be the two of us ta handle the house chores and suffer mah cookin'."

"Well, Mr. Fulbright, you sure taught us a lesson tonight. Pick up your rifle, you're welcome to come in and have some coffee and maybe we can exchange information." Ed led the two guests into camp where the horse was tied up to a vehicle's door handle and several kids got busy petting it and pleading for rides. Smiling, Matthew reached down and picked up one of the smaller lads and put him in the saddle. The youngster's big grin was infectious and the crowd took a quick liking to the young cowboy.

While the Fulbrights warmed themselves by a campfire, some ladies prepared coffee for their guests. Pastor Woodway, who'd been praying, came out of his tent to see what all the commotion was and Ed introduced him to the Fulbrights and their horse- "Pickle".

"Pastor huh? Gotta say you people sure got me confused some. That tent made me think you was a traveling circus. Now it looks like you're some Bible crusade," Mr. Fulbright said. An old cowboy with arthritis, he rubbed his gnarled hands together to get them warm. "Got a chill out there, crawlin' around in the sand and playin' Injun. Ah'm gettin' too old for that kind'a sport."

"Sir, you are nearly correct in your assumption. We are traveling, but we're on our way to Alaska," Pastor Woodway said. He took two cups of coffee from one of the ladies and handed them to the Fulbrights.

"Alaska?" Matthew Fulbright asked with astonishment.

"Yes, young man, Alaska. Only safe place left on this continent of ours." Pastor replied.

"You got any sugar?" Matthew asked.

"Boy, that ain't polite!" Mr. Fulbright reprimanded his son.

"I think we have enough sugar to share with our guests." Pastor looked to one of the ladies and a cup of sugar appeared right away. He offered some of the irreplaceable sweetener to them, delighting the boy and bringing a smile to the father. "As you can tell, been a while, sugar's might scarce in these parts. No more sugar cane an' all those artificial sweetener factories long gone..." Mr. Fulbright slowly sipped his coffee and savored the sweetness. "Pastor, you all still puzzle me a mite. Now I gotta admit it's been a long time since I stepped into any church, but why you headin' out. Times like this... well, I'd think you'd be holdin' fast an' helping those sinners living aroun' here."

"Normally, I'd agree with you, but these are far from normal times. It comes down to a question of faith, sir. The Lord is directing us north, but as to why...I cannot answer that question. Not because you're a stranger, but I truly do not have the answer to give you. I only know this; Alaska is our assignment and our destination."

Ed interrupted, "Mr. Fulbright, have you seen any traffic heading west in the last few days?"

Fulbright gave Pastor a thoughtful eye before turning to look at Ed, "I've seen maybe a hundred cars go by in the las' couple of weeks, all goin' west. Lately though, the highway's been deserted. You've been the first cars I've seen in two days." Fulbright accepted a refill of his coffee, smiling as another two scoops of sugar were added.

"Talked with anyone lately?' Joey asked.

Sitting around the fire on metal folding chairs, Mr. Fulbright looked up at Joey with a threatening coolness to his eyes. Ed recognized the look, but then noticed how Fulbright began to soften, "Don't mean to be rude, mister. I ain't talked with a Black man in some time, but ah guess you must be okay if you'se with this bunch."

Joey started to leave, then stopped and addressed their guest, "Mr. Fulbright, our band is multi-racial. We're trying to leave man's hate behind us. But so you know, a lot of my people died at the hands of hateful whites too." Ed stopped him with a hand on his arm.

"Mister, I mean you no disrespect. Guess losin' mah wife effected mah manners. Your right though, bad people is just plain bad people, color don't mean what's inside a man." Fulbright stood up and offered his hand to Joey. "I'll understand if you refuse it."

Joey stepped forward and the two men exchanged a firm grip, and a warm smile, which spread through the group.

Sitting back down, Fulbright answered Joey's question, "Last person I talked with was better than a month ago. Ah rode down into Lupton to pick up supplies, but the town was all but deserted. Store was cleaned out, 'cept a 50 pound bag of kitty litter."

"What are you doing for food?" Ed asked.

"Well, I sure ain't eatin' that kitty litter," Fulbright said with a laugh, then turned serious, "Mah misses, she spent better than a year cannin' an' plum filled our basement with fruit an' veggies. If I look hard 'nough, ah could probably find my missin' left slipper in one of those jars. When she start to cannin', there ain't nuthin' safe. Makes me wonder if she knew she was goin' ta be leavin' us an' wanted ta make sure we was cared for." Fulbright's eyes misted over, memories of his wife cut deep. "Anyway, she left us with quite a supply of preserves. Got a hundred an' two head of cattle left, but runnin' out 'a feed an' they're starvin'. We used ta shoot one a month, ate pretty good too. But another week, they'll all be dead. Ran out 'a gas last week, so we been ridin' that ol' plug. Not too bad, but Pickle's a little long in thu tooth now. Ah had ta trade mah other horses off to get grain for mah cattle, now ...nothin' left." Fulbright stopped and stared into his cup as if he was looking for a vision in the coffee.

"Have you heard of anything east of here?" Ed asked.

"Las' thing we heard was over thu radio. Somethin' 'bout a radiation cloud movin' up and settlin' over Albuquerque. People runnin' every which way tryin' ta get outta town; lot a' people dead they said. Radio went off thu air las' week. I got windmills at mah place; storage batteries still got power, but no radio traffic." Fulbright looked into Ed's eyes, "You wasn't thinkin' 'bout goin' through Albuquerque were yuh?"

"Not now, thanks to you," Ed said with appreciation. He stood up, needing to stretch his legs and think over this news. He also needed to check his map and find a new route.

"If it was me, I'd head north on old Route 66. Goes right through the Navajo Reservation; ah doubt those people give yuh any trouble. Take you right into Colorado, then you can probably get back on your old route." Fulbright stood up, stretching the kinks in his back and handing his empty cup to the nearest lady, "Thank you, ma'am. That was right nice."

Ed walked over to the ambulance, opened the front passenger door and pulled an AAA road map from the glove box. Laying it on the hood and using a penlight, it only took him a moment to figure out a new route via Route 66. Before returning to the fire, he closed his eyes and prayed, "You did it again, Lord. We were heading right toward death, so you provided us with this old rancher to get us back on the right path. Thank you, Lord." As he walked back to the fire, he noticed Kira sitting with Pastor and smiled at her. Her eyes lit up and she smiled back.

"Mr. Fulbright, you've apparently saved our lives. Is there anything we can do for you?"

"Could use some water, got four empty canteens hangin' on mah saddle...mah well's turned a wee sour for some reason...An' I'd like a word in private with your pastor." Fulbright and Pastor wandered off while Joey and Matthew filled the canteens. A few moments later, Pastor came out of the darkness and waved Ed over.

"Ed, Mr. Fulbright has asked us to take his son with us." Pastor was resting his hand on Mr. Fulbright's shoulder.

"Sir, we can take both of you. I can fix up a trailer to haul your horse too," Ed said.

"Nope, jus' the boy. He don't know it yet, but my ol' ticker is givin' out. Don't have a lot of time left. Ah was tellin' Pastor how I been spendin' many a night prayin' to the man upstairs, askin' Him ta show a way to take care of mah boy. He'd be alone, jus' a lot of dead cows an' a dead horse for company. Pretty soon the water be gone...or contaminated. No, your group is the answer to mah prayer. With you, he's got a fightin' chance. With me...he's got no chance at all."

"Okay, we'll take him with us," Ed said noticing the movement of pastor's eyes and knew he wanted to be left alone with Mr. Fulbright. Back at the fire, Ed asked Kira where the Fulbright kid was.

"Over at the water trailer with Joey, watering the horse." Kira replied. She came to stand in front of Ed and he looked down at her, noticing how the fire danced with a soft glow over her hair and her eyes seemed to sparkle. He couldn't remember where he'd seen such pretty eyes, so innocent...*Hey, what goes here! I don't need this! Thinking these thoughts about some teenage girl.* Ed turned away in a hurry and walked over to where Joey and Matthew were.

A bit later, Mr. Fulbright summoned his son, "Matt, you come over here." Mr. Fulbright was standing beside Pastor, leaning on him for the strength he needed for what he had to do. Matthew stood quietly, listening as his father spoke to him in low whispers, explaining to him what he intended to do.

"What!?" Matthew asked in disbelief. "No! I'm not gonna leave you, Dad!" Matthew shouted and quieted when he saw that discomforting look in his father's weary eyes. "Dad, I can't leave you...this is ridiculous! I don't know these people an' I sure ain't leavin' you alone out here!" Matthew looked at Pastor with hate filled eyes and then stomped off into the desert.

Pastor looked to Ed, gesturing with his head for Ed to follow the boy. Shaking his own head, he was wondering what other type of jobs he'd be forced into before this trip was over. After a few moments of searching, he found Matthew sitting on a sandy knoll, his elbows locked around his knees; his head resting in his hands. He was crying.

Ed wasn't quite sure how to handle this one, with kid gloves or right to the point? "Matthew...can I call you Matt?"

No answer.

"Listen, Matt, your father is trying to do what's best for you."

Ed decided to take the direct approach when Matt failed to respond. As a police officer he'd delivered countless death notifications and never gave it too much thought. Yet, this felt different; he spoke in a soft tone, "Matthew, I'm sorry to be the one to tell you this, but your father is dying. That's why he wants you with us, to make sure you're taken care of."

Matthew looked up in shock and glared at Ed with hard moist eyes. "You're lyin'!"

"No, I'm not. He told us that he has a bad heart and that he's been keeping it from you. With us you have a chance and quite honestly, we could use another good man. If you stay here, when your father's gone, you'll starve to death. It's time to think of your old man, he'll be able to pass on in peace knowing you're taken care of." Matthew stared at Ed with a look of defiance, an expression that told Ed he'd stay with his dad no matter what. "Look, I'm taking these people to Alaska where we hope to find freedom. This land is dying from radiation poisoning. You can stay here and bury your dad and then start digging' your own grave. Or you can honor your dad's request by coming with us and he'll be able to join your mother in peace. Now I'm talkin' to you like a man, so make up your mind." Ed slapped his leg in frustration before heading back to Pastor.

Mr. Fulbright was sitting atop his horse, full canteens hanging from his saddle horn and speaking with Pastor and Joey. Ed shook his head, silently telling Pastor he wasn't able to break through to the Fulbright kid then turned as he heard Matthew coming out of the desert. Passing Ed, Matthew walked up to his father and rested his head against his father's left leg.

Reaching down, Mr. Fulbright pulled Matthew's hat off and ran his hand through his son's hair, "You be a good boy an' pull your weight. Remember, ah'm right proud of you. You've become a real man an' Ah know your mother'd be proud too. Remember the rules an' listen ta Pastor and this Mr. Sawyer fella," He put the hat back on Matt's head, "Ah love yuh, boy...be good." Fulbright nodded his head toward Pastor and turned Pickle toward the desert. With the lantern off and a kick of his old spurs, Mr. Fulbright let Pickle have his head and vanished into the darkness.

While several people attempted to comfort Matthew and welcome him, Steve Agar was planning his getaway. Taking advantage of the distraction, he caught a guard unaware and knocked him out with a rock to the side of the head then made a mad dash for a white CJ-7 Jeep. Making a quick job of hot wiring, a trick he learned in his juvenile delinquent days, Steve jammed the gas pedal to the floor and sped off through the desert. Once he hit the pavement, he left behind several yards of black acceleration marks and headed east for the big city of Albuquerque.

Ed gave chase on foot, '*Who's behind the wheel?*' Seeing the futility of his actions, he stopped and walked back to where Joey was leaning over the unconscious form of Rick Dudley. "He's okay, but when he comes to, he's going to have a mother of a headache."

"Do we know who it was?" Ed asked.

"Yeah, looks like that Steve Agar dude decided to take a powder," Joey answered.

Summoned by others, Doc came running up and following a quick check, called for a stretcher and had Dudley carried back to the ambulance.

Point Man showed up at Ed's side, "Boy's headin' east an' too fast for us ta catch him. You want us to follow him?"

"No...By tomorrow night he'll be glowing like a Christmas tree...the idiot!" Ed said in disgust. Shouldering his rifle, he headed for his tent and left Point Man and Joey standing alone.

ALBUQUERQUE:

Reaching the city limits of Albuquerque, New Mexico, Steve was surprised to find the city deserted. He wasn't aware that over half a million people had been evacuated to escape the radiation. Before him were darkened streets littered with abandoned vehicles and piles of trash. He came upon two white and yellow city commuter buses lying on their sides and was shocked to see a dozen or so bodies sprawled around the buses and on the sidewalk nearby. Like Phoenix, Steve realized panic had gripped the citizens and people had fought for the last remaining seats. Rioting and fires, carnage and mayhem; civilization's last hurrah as man strived to replace God. Looting, arson, murder and rape; it happened here as in every American city that survived the initial missile attacks. A feeding frenzy as fear ran rampant, driving people to do things they would never have thought of doing in a civilized world. Evidence of the Beast was scattered about the city; mangled bodies and smoldering ruins. Now only an invisible silent killer existed; radiation carried along on the wind currents and reaching into every structure and now no one was safe.

But Steve didn't know anything about radiation and he had never heard Mr. Fulbright's warning about Albuquerque. Everything looked peaceful enough, the dead offered little objection as Steve yanked off a gold ring here, a watch there, or even a silver necklace from the neck of a female corpse. It was all free for the taking and all for him. *I'm goin' to be so rich!* By afternoon of the third day, feeling weary and in need of a bed, Steve parked in front of a luxury hotel. He watched the sun set from the windows of an expensive 18th floor suite. Later, as he relaxed in an overstuffed black leather recliner, sipping on an imported bottle of beer, his stomach began to burn. Moments later, he was kneeling beside the toilet struggling to breathe; his whole body afire; blood began to seep out through his eyes and ears. Sweat drenched his body and then his lungs began to fill up and he felt as if he was drowning. The hands on a gold ornamental clock swept past each hour and evening gave way to night and then to a graying early morning. Steve's pleas for help to the front desk went unanswered; the phones still worked, but no one was there to answer and when the final blackness descended, Steve Agar suddenly realized the truth - too late. There is a God, there is a Hell and he was headed for the latter.

7 - EVACUATION DAY

"... 'See, the Lord is coming with thousands upon thousands of his holy ones to judge everyone, and to convict all the ungodly of all the ungodly acts they have done in the ungodly way, and of all the harsh words ungodly sinners have spoken him. These men are grumblers and faultfinders; they follow their own evil desires; they boast about themselves and flatter others for their own advantage.'"

Jude 14-16 NIV

KCVF-RADIO FAIRBANKS - 10:00 A.M., MARCH 25th

"A very chilly good morning, Fairbanks...This is Ron Larson, your favorite DJ, coming to you from Station KCVF Radio Fairbanks." Ron glanced down at his notes, "My trusty thermometer shows a brisk - 42 ° outside, so I hope you're all keeping warm out there."

This would be Ron's final broadcast; afterward he would turn the station's keys over to those stone faced souls in the Office of Information. Within hours, ADF personnel would arrive to strip the station of every piece of usable equipment for transport to Fort Greeley where he'd be issued either a shovel or a rifle. Relieved of his DJ job, Ron would grab a quick bite in the Fort Wainwright chow hall and board a 45 passenger school bus for the long chilly ride to Fort Greeley. Civilians and non-essential military personnel were being transported 98 miles on the Richardson Highway, east to Delta Junction and then right at the junction of the Alaska Highway to continue another eight miles on the Richardson Highway, to Fort Greeley.

"Now before I give you the latest in news, let me remind you once again of our city's evacuation points. Please listen up and make sure you write these locations down. I remind you, if you miss evacuating our Golden Heart city, you'll either be on hand to greet the OAP with a welcome basket or you'll find it a long chilly walk to Fort Greeley." Ron picked up the typed out evacuation order and began reading off all the pick-up points throughout the Fairbanks area. He repeated each of the locations a minimum of three times to make sure everyone would hear and have time to write them down. He didn't want it on his shoulders that someone missed a ride.

Fairbanks Police and ADF military police were also out driving through the city streets, repeating the evacuation order over their vehicle's P.A. systems. Volunteers were out pounding on doors and searching abandoned buildings for street people. A squad of ADF infantry escorted each volunteer team in the event they happened to come upon UWCA members or OAP sympathizers.

As with any war, there were enemy sympathizers that needed to be dealt with. But rather than incarcerate them, General Saunders ordered them picked up to be transported north by enclosed trucks. An armed convoy would travel up the Dalton Highway to the deserted community of Coldfoot located approximately 259 miles north of Fairbanks. Here, members of the UCWA and any other sympathizers were to be dropped off. As a humanitarian gesture, each man or woman would be supplied with a weeks' worth of food and water the use of the abandoned buildings for shelter.

Over 100,000 people were to be moved to Greeley within the next 14 hours; some had already left, but it was still considered a near impossible task in such a short time period and with so few vehicles. Every bus from the Fairbanks North Star Borough School District, city bus line and tour companies and, as they became available, military buses, were put in to service for the speedy round trips to Greeley. Every civilian and military wrecker escorted each convoy in the event of break down. Already, three buses had been towed back to a Fort Wainwright shop for repair.

Each bus carried two armed soldiers to keep order and military police escorted the cavalcade of buses. Check points, controlled by Militia forces, were set up south of Fairbanks – one at Eielson Air Force Base, a second at Harding Lake and a third at Delta Junction. These were to ensure that no one had stopped one of the buses in the thick ice fog and forced themselves on and to ensure that each bus was still moving and had not broken down between check points. In such cold weather, a disabled bus could quickly become a deadly freezer; every one of them carried a large poster board with an identification number which was radioed on to the next check point. If a bus hadn't reached the next check point within an hour and a half, a Militia vehicle was sent out to search for it.

"Remember folks, these pick-up points are all outside. So, please don't stand around arguing over which bus you want to take or which seat gives the best view. Simply board the first available bus and grab the first available seat, before you all get frostbite." Ron sipped hot tea; the dry air was giving a bit of cackle to his voice. "You'll have ice fog nearly all the way to Harding Lake, so the view will be limited; most of these buses are diesel; so the sooner the bus gets moving, the sooner the driver can get the heat going again. Also, this is very important, folks - you may only bring one carry on. I repeat - only one carry on and it will be sitting on your lap all the way. That means no travel trunks, be sensible or the driver will kindly throw your bag out the door. Weapons may be taken with, but rifles and handguns must be unloaded and turned over to the soldiers on each bus. You may keep your folding knives, but all sheath knives and hatchets will be turned over to the driver, who will return them upon arrival at Fort Greeley. There will be no appeal. Drivers and the assigned soldiers for each bus have final say over the weapons and baggage. Any rebellious passengers will be turned over to the police, so behave like ladies and gentlemen and we'll get this evacuation done in good order." Ron imagined that all pick-up points were probably going to be in a state of mass chaos and felt pity for the poor drivers and soldiers assigned this duty. *Some guy's going ta have ta tell some damp eyed homemaker that she can't bring the family trunk with all the family photos, or that one clown who shows up with his full head moose mount with 64 inch rack 'C'mon, guys, I can't leave this! I got it in the Fall of '09, nearly broke my back hauling the darn thing out...'* "And don't worry, folks, there's plenty of room for everyone. No one will be left behind for the OAP." *Hope so! Or some distraught relative will probably come lookin' for yours truly. This will probably come off like when all those parents send their kids off to camp and nothing goes right; kids misbehave, parents argue and the driver sits behind the wheel pounding his head and wondering how he got stuck with this lousy job.*

Ron looked at his news notes and then stared up at the wall clock. He nodded his head in defiance and tossed the notes into the trash, "As you all know, this'll be my final broadcast and since the news isn't all that good anyway, I've decided not to bother with it." Adjusting a few knobs, he inserted a pre-recorded CD, "Time for some music for a change. I think KCVF Radio Fairbanks should sign off in style." Ron began flipping switches, rotating a couple of dials as Exile spilled out over the air with the familiar beat of 'Old Time Rock and Roll'.

Grabbing the microphone, Ron shouted, "Remember people, rock an' roll will never die! Let's boogie!"

Over the next ten minutes, Ron, who was worried either the police or the military would come rushing in to turn him off, played his four favorite rock classics as two large outside speakers filled the dimly lit neighborhood with the legendary guitar riffs of Eric Clapton, the heavy drums of Ginger Baker, the hard driving lyrics of Sludge Pie and his last choice was a classic - "Born in the USA".

North of the station, Sadler's Furniture Store parking lot resembled a gigantic sidewalk sale. In one of the largest parking lots in the city center, crowds of people bundled in arctic gear, waited to board one of a dozen Princess tour buses. Far more comfortable than a school bus, these blue, silver and white buses sat idling as people climbed aboard. Most of the time it was organized and the people polite, but occasionally military police were called when shoving started or an argument broke out over too much personal baggage. Exhaust from the bus's heavy diesel engines added to the ice fog, the smell of it heavy in the air.

Everyone was either wearing a face mask or had scarves draped over noses and mouths to keep the ash from entering their lungs. With so much ash in the air now, everyone had a grayish hue to them and they stopped briefly before entering the bus to brush it off and pound their feet to clean off their boots.

Among the crowd, a saddened Sgt. Brad Sawyer was saying goodbye to his family, "You take care of your mother and sister until I get there," Brad said to his 12 year old son, Bob.

His eyes hidden behind snow goggles and most of his face covered by a medical mask, the boy stood proud, his shoulders back as he replied in a hurried voice, "C'mon, Dad, you already told me all that stuff. I know what to do." He broke away from his father's grasp, ran between several other families and shot aboard the nearest bus. He wanted a window seat and these buses were loading up fast.

His sister, Becky, in close pursuit, yelled, "Hey, wait for me!" And over her left shoulder she shouted, "Bye, Daddy!"

With the kids gone, Brad wrapped his arms around Kathy, "I should be there tomorrow, so quit fretting."

"I'll take care of him," Scott assured her.

"You take care of each other," Kathy said. She turned to put her arm around Scott's neck, surprising him. Then, with a single small suitcase in hand, she hurried off to catch up with her children and yelled back from the bus steps. "See you tomorrow!"

Brad replied with a wave and stayed to watch the bus pull away. He felt a twinge of doubt whether be seeing her again and shook it off with a shrug of his shoulders. He hated those feeling and always discounted them; after all he was still alive. An "All Units" call came over their belt radios and both Brad and Scott made a dash for the patrol car.

"All units...All units! Report of shots fired. Respond to South Cushman and Van Horn. Be advised, this is an evacuation point and ADF personnel are on scene." Susie always broadcasted in a professionally calm voice, whether it was a murder or a simple fender bender. But this time, Brad could hear the fear in her voice and it made him uncomfortable. *Must be all those back to back shifts she's been working…its affecting the officers; not any wonder it would hit the dispatchers too.* Susie's voice came back over the radio, "Be advised additional ADF units are en route from Wainwright and we have a report of multiple wounded and several shooters in the area. Ambulances will be en route, but will standby until area has been made safe."

"Why do people want to cause so much trouble on such a cold day?" Brad asked Scott as they jumped into the patrol car and Brad grabbed the car's microphone to report they were enroute. It took them a moment to steer clear of the people before Brad could accelerate down Cushman Street. Though they were running Code 3; lights and siren; Brad had to keep his speed down because of thick ice fog and so many people walking to evacuation points. A glance at the speedometer showed he was driving 32 mph and it made him snicker.

Scott glared at him. "What's so funny?"

Brad shook his head, "Must be stress... here we are running Code 3 to a reported mass shooting and I'm stuck speeding down Cushman Street at 32 mph. This is ridiculous."

Scott simply shook his head in response as he checked his equipment, listened to Susie on the radio talking with other patrols and then said, "Ain't nothin' been right since those missile flew and now you got me praying."

"Love all around, partner...but keep your noggin down...I got me a feeling we're walking right into a gut twister."

"You know how I hate your hunches...Pop the trunk when we get close." Scott knew they might need heavier weapons for a call like this and was glad he was wearing his bullet-proof vest.

Getting closer to the scene, Brad turned the lights and siren off and slowed to 15. All too soon they could hear the sounds of automatic weapons fire and both knew a full blown battle was raging.

Grabbing the microphone, Scott confirmed the 'shots fired' report as Brad pulled the patrol car into the deserted Tesoro gas station located directly across the road from the abandoned Mobat Tire Company Store. "Unit # 2, we're on scene and advise all responding units we've got automatic weapons fire out there! Use caution and do not fire unless you know who you're shooting' at. We got a whole lot of friendlies out there."

Spotting the first body on the far side of Van Horn, Brad slammed on the brakes, allowing an excited Scott to pop open his passenger door and dive out. He did a shoulder roll across the hard icy ground, hurting his right shoulder. Pistol drawn, he jumped up, nearly losing his footing on the slippery ice and then struggling for balance, made a clumsy dash for the protection of a silver and white MCI tour bus.

Reaching cover, Scott saw two more bodies directly behind the idling bus and was sickened to see two were small children. One still holding a stuffed brown bear in his arms; fiery anger began to grow inside of Scott.

Suddenly, the rear window of the patrol car exploded inward from a shotgun blast, barely missing Brad with a .00 12-gauge pellet. A small shard of glass cut into the back of his neck and he was bleeding slightly. "Look out!" Brad yelled. "You got one coming up on you from your right…one bus over and he's got a shotgun!" He'd seen the man, who was carrying a long double barreled shotgun, come into view from behind a school bus. Brad got a pretty good look at the man, who looked to be 6', stocky and wearing a dark colored heavy insulated one piece snow suit. A golden brown rabbit skin hat was pulled down over his ears and a dark colored scarf around his face.

As Brad jumped out of the patrol car and dove for cover behind the left front tire, a bullet struck the vehicle trunk. Several more rounds impacted the doors on the other side, which caused Scott to call out, "Brad…Brad, you okay?"

"Yeah, but its gettin' kind of tight here…Scott, there's a shooter to our south and another mover to your southeast…Give me some cover' fire!" Brad yelled back and darted to the back of the car in hopes of getting to his shotgun. The trunk lid was already popped and would be easy to pull up. The trouble would be getting there without getting shot. Taking a deep breath, he crawled to the back of the patrol car, slammed his left palm against the center of the lid and pushed upward. The lid flew up and Brad reached inside for the black canvas weapon's bag. A bullet zinged by his head like an angry wasp, while another struck the inside of the trunk hood and got a startled Brad moving even quicker as he frantically searched for his weapons bag. "Me and my premonitions," he muttered and then added, "Like the man said, 'I'm getting too old for this!' " Finding the bag, Brad yanked it out and took cover behind the rear wheel where he unzipped it in haste and pulled out a lethal looking black shotgun affectionately known in certain circles as a "Street Sweeper". It carried a 30 round circular magazine loaded with .00-buckshot. He pulled out a single magazine, inserted it and chambered a round, then cautiously looked each way to see where the bad guys were and hollered to Scott, "You see anyone?"

"Got that one you spotted behind that first bus to my left and there's another behind that Monte Carlo on your right….But he's keepin' his head down. Two more shooters are exchanging shots with ADF troops hiding behind that ADF truck behind us, but I can't see where the other shooters are," Scott shouted back. His heart was racing with adrenaline flow and he was eager to engage the shooters to avenge the people who had been gunned down. By the sound of the weapons fire around them, both Brad and Scott suspected at least four and maybe six unfriendly shooters.

With such fire power and the evidence he had already seen, Brad was fearful of how many dead and wounded civilians he might have. He raised his weapon and took in a deep lung full of frigid air, thankful he was wearing his wool scarf because the falling gray ash became plastered to his face. He rose to a crouched position and fired off a three round burst at the

Monte Carlo. The heavy gauge shotgun ammo blew two of the windows out and made a dozen holes in the side of the car causing the shooter to panic and take off running toward another school bus. When Brad saw that the man was running toward a bus filled with civilians, he pulled out his pistol and dropped him with a short three round burst. With so many civilians close by, he didn't want to use the shotgun in fear of hitting one. Back down on the ground, Brad crawled to the front tire which offered cover from the other shooter. After considering his options, he slithered across the frozen ground to the first bus and cut loose a two round burst of buckshot, which forced the other shooter, a much smaller man in old military garb, to retreat further for safety. He was now taking a play from Brad's game book and was using the heavy bus wheels to for protection.

As the shooter jumped about in an attempt to find a target, Scott caught sight of his legs and put a single pistol round into the man's left ankle. He went down screaming and a nearby ADF soldier silenced him with a long burst from his M-16. After having seen so many civilians gunned down, especially children and older people, this young ADF soldier was not interested in taking prisoners.

Seeing how his partner was pinned down, Scott decided to move and doing so, unintentionally exposed himself to another adversary. As he was turning to advise Brad of his intentions, two .357 rounds struck Scott in the chest, driving him against the side of the bus. Eyes closed, mouth open as cold air escaped his lungs; Scott slowly dropped to the frozen ground and lay still.

Hearing those shots, Brad looked up to see Scott's limp body slide to the ground. "No-o-o!" Brad yelled out and enraged, jumped to his feet and began rapid fire shotgun blasts from the hip. He sent round after round of buckshot at the shooters he spotted across from the ADF soldiers. The first and second round went high, missing everything, but the third one dropped one of the shooters with a bloody wound to his shoulder. Round four and five blasted out small .32 caliber sized pellets, flattening the tire of one bus and killing the second shooter instantly.

"Scott? Scott, can you hear me?" Brad called out, but there was no response. He was unable to reach his partner because another shooter appeared from behind the Mobat Tire building and took three shots at Brad in quick succession with a small Sig-Saur 9mm automatic pistol. Unhurt, Brad unleashed another barrage of buckshot that hit the building and drove the shooter back behind the corner and out of sight. At that moment, another man dressed in woodland camouflage with face hidden by a winter scarf and a black sweatshirt hood, panicked and made a run for it. It was a bad choice. An ADF troop fresh out of basic weapons training, knelt behind his vehicle and using the bumper for support, cut the shooter down in mid-stride with a long burst.

Combating the effects of cold air mixed with adrenaline rush, Brad found it hard to breathe as he made a mad dash for the ADF truck. Rolling in behind two soldiers, Brad heard a radio message over his belt radio; two more FPD units had notified dispatch they were on scene. Immediately, both units came under heavy fire from behind the old tire building. They were little help to Brad at this point. Wishing he had night vision goggles, Brad struggled to scan the area through the thick ice fog. He knew all the civilians here for evacuation were either hiding behind buses, on board and flattened down behind seats, or pinned down in the open and frozen to the icy ground. He didn't know how many were dead, wounded or lucky enough to be out of the line of fire. But he had to do something and these two ADF troops looked too young to have any combat experience.

"I'm Sgt. Sawyer, who's in charge here?"

"Sir, Lt. Bridgewater was in command, but they killed him right off. My name's Atwood, PFC Atwood, we was loading buses and all of a sudden this guy pulls out a pistol and starts shooting. Lieutenant went down first with a head wound. Bodies fell everywhere - kids an' women too," His voice cracked, his hands trembled, but PFC Atwood still held his rifle at the ready. By Brad's count the man had already accounted for one shooter and maybe more.

The second soldier spoke, "Must be fifty...sixty of 'em out there, they got us surrounded."

The young soldier was rapidly losing control and Brad had to quiet him fast. "Take it easy, soldier." Brad grabbed him by the shoulder and looked into his eyes, "First off, they haven't got us surrounded or I wouldn't be here. Probably less than a dozen of them left, if that." He looked to PFC Atwood, "How many in your detail?"

"3rd Squad, nine of us...Not counting the LT. Maybe five left, two of 'em in that bus." Atwood pointed to a gray Army 45 passenger bus parked on the far side of the tire building. "One guy's in the building...if he's still alive. He went over to take a leak when all the shooting started."

Using his belt radio, Brad advised all units to listen up, "Sawyer to all units. There are five or six soldiers and probably some armed civilians here, so confirm your target before firing. If they don't respond to a warning, shoot. Officer Radley is down, I repeat, Radley is down." His voice broke, but he rallied. "I figure maybe a dozen bandits left, but more MPs are on the way." Brad took a deep breath to steady his nerves. His hands were freezing, making it hard for him to feel the weapon or the radio. "Unless you see a civilian in trouble, hold your fire and remain in position. Too many people wandering around is going to spell trouble… Help is on the way."

Who are the shooters? Gangs, afraid to be left an' trying to commandeer a bus by force? No, the shooters I took down were too old to be gang members. UWCA? That's possible. Cause problems, delay evacuation or maybe seize a bus to escape. Brad had a lot of questions and too little time to come up answers. In the distance he could hear the sirens of responding units. His attention was diverted by the movement of four men crawling between school buses to his left. All four were armed and appeared to be headed for a 29 passenger school bus loaded with people. *Too far for shotgun…*Brad looked at Atwood, "Let me see your rifle, son." Without hesitation, Atwood exchanged his M-16 for Brad's sweeper. Brad lifted to use the truck bed as an aiming platform, but his movement alerted them and before he could fire a short burst of automatic fire struck the ADF truck and a frightened troop cried out in pain as he went down with a wound to his right knee. One of the bullets had apparently ricocheted off the ice and hit him, making a nasty wound. Brad returned fire as Atwood grabbed the wounded man's rifle to help. "Be sure of your target, too many civilians out there," Brad said and Atwood nodded in response between shots.

The last two men went down, causing the other two to panic. Both stood up to make a dash for the back of the bus, but Brad dropped the lead one with a shot to the leg and the man tumbled to the ground, hollering as he grabbed his wounded leg. His hat fell off, exposing a baldhead with a large Nazi Swastika tattoo on it. *UWCA!* Brad thought. He took aim at the second man, the heavily attired man, who looked more like a dark colored Pillsbury Dough Boy, who had reached the rear of the bus and yanked the emergency door open. His eyes grew wide in shock as he came face to face with the cold blue eyes of a woman protecting her three children. It wasn't so much the enraged women as the fact that he was staring down the wrong end of a pump action 12-guage shotgun.

Hunters in Alaska have long known there is nothing worse than coming up on a female critter with young. This woman was no different; she let go and the explosive blast drowned the short sound of the man's death scream. He was thrown backward nearly 20 feet and landed in a smoldering heap.

Gunfire tapered off and Brad traded back for his shotgun. Removing his gloves, his fingers nearly white from the initial stages of frostbite, he placed his fingers in his mouth to warm them. Looking at Scott's body, Brad glanced over to Atwood, "Cover me, I'm gonna check on my partner."

"He looks dead from here, Sarge," Atwood replied he busy putting an emergency bandage around his semi-conscious friend's leg. "You'd better stay here until we get some more help."

"He's my partner." Brad didn't wait; he inhaled and exhaled a deep breath and took off running. He made it to Scott's side without a shot being fired in his direction, going around several dead bodies and hurdling over one discarded oversized suitcase. Leaning over Scott's body, checking for a pulse, Brad didn't hear the movement behind him until it was too late.

"Ah, Sgt. Brad Sawyer to the rescue...I'm so happy to find you alive." The tone was threatening sarcastic but Brad recognized the voice immediately. Cautiously, he started to turn to his left, but the next words stopped him, "Drop your weapons, Brad...or I will kill you right here and now." His shotgun was already on the ground, so he un-holstered his pistol and dropped it, then cautiously turned to find two men standing less than eight feet away. The man on the right was a tall, skinny fellow in a black one piece snowsuit. Darken snow goggles and a medical face mask concealed his face. He was also holding an expensive Remington 7mm hunting rifle with a large scope aimed at Brad's head. The second man was short and heavyset, wearing clear goggles, a blue wool scarf over his face, a navy blue parka over insulated coveralls, holding a Smith & Wesson .357 revolver leveled at Brad's nose.

"You!?" Though Brad had recognized the voice, he was none the less stunned to see that the man holding the revolver was City Councilman Robert Hodgekiss. The man was an outspoken supporter of the police department and had been for years.

"I'm surprised, Brad, amazed even, that an officer with your experience never saw it. Yes, I run the UWCA...but I hate using acronyms. I represent the new world order, a servant to our beloved Emperor and Supreme Leader of the Unified World Church Alliance."

Brad started to shift his position, the ground was cold, but it made the guy with the rifle real nervous, "Please don't move, Brad. Jack is a bit strung out with all that's occurred here today. I planned to simply steal a bus, head north for Circle and cross the Yukon. I had planned to set up a small community in one of the empty villages. The OAP wouldn't even bother with us, but with all good plans there is always someone to screw things up. I really didn't want to kill all these people, Brad, but my boys...well, things got out of control when that stupid lieutenant demanded their weapons."

"Bob, give it up," Brad hoped one of the MP units or one of his own patrols might be getting within range to take out this Jack. He figured he might be able to handle Hodgekiss, but not both of them at this range.

"Can't do it, Brad. I only wanted you to know it was me before I killed you. You were one smart cop, but sadly such an honest one. All this Christian baloney you preached. It just made me sick to listen to it and see how you bought in to so many lies...Oh, one other thing," Hodgekiss gestured with his revolver at Scott, who lay behind Brad, "I was the one who shot your nigger partner. Felt good...In the New World Order his people will know their place...But now I guess it's time to finish this..." Four quick shots rang out. The revolver slowly dropped from his grasp before Hodgekiss clutched his chest and fell forward. Behind him, a dumbfounded Jack simply collapsed over him like a deflating balloon as his hunting rifle slid across the ice.

Jumping to his feet, his own pistol in hand, Brad glanced at the two bodies and turned around to look at a grimacing Scott.

"Politicians!" Scott said in disgust. "Sure glad he kept talking his jive, took me bit ta lift my arm. Mah whole chest is on fire. But thank the Lord for this here vest." Scott lowered his arm, his pistol resting loosely in his hand upon the ice.

Brad knelt over Scott and opened his coverall. He saw the two .357 slugs stuck deep into the bulletproof vest. He may have sustained a couple broken ribs, but Officer Scott Radley was alive. While Hodgekiss conversed with Brad, Scott was able to lift his arm high enough to put two bullets in Hodgekiss' chest and then two more rounds into a very surprised Jack. Brad believed Jack must have thought those first two rounds were coming out of his boss's pistol and reacted too late when the Grand Poo-Pah of the local chapter of the UWCA dropped dead.

"I thought you were dead," Brad said.

"Next time you hear me complainin' about these vests..." Scott said in pain, "...remind me of today." Scott's voice was a dry whisper as each rise of his chest brought on shooting pains through his upper body. "Now find me a nice warm place ta pass out." Scott dropped his head, unconscious, but alive.

An ADF company moved in to pick up the rest of the UWCA. Without their leader they gave up without firing another shot. The wounded were immediately cared for at an aid station set up inside the Mobat Tire building where a dozen blast heaters provided warmth. The dead were placed in dark green body bags, keeping the UWCA members separated. Captain Susan Riley arrived to supervise the MPs as they moved the bodies to a cleared area where she could gather information off the UWCA bodies.

"Sure glad to see you, real iffy there for a moment," Brad said to Captain Riley. He stood towering over her as they looked down upon the row of civilian body bags lined up in front of them.

She couldn't speak for a moment, watching as a soldier zipped up a body bag containing the body of a small boy of possibly 6 or 7 years. "We were caught off guard...we weren't expecting this kind of attack."

"Don't blame yourself, Susan. Our Intel didn't have anything either."

"53 dead men, women and children, Brad...five dead MPs and two buses shot up so bad they're out of service." She turned to look at Brad, "This was my watch and I blew it!"

"How many enemy?" Brad asked, hoping to change the subject to lesson her pain for the moment.

"15 is the count...But, we don't know how many might've escaped." Susan looked around the area; civilians were filling every bus of which all but two were spotted with bullet holes.

"Do we know who they were? Who was leading them?" Susan asked as she rubbed her mittens together to keep her hands from freezing.

"Confirmation. They were members of the Unified World Church Alliance; the leader was City Council Member Robert J. Hodgekiss. Weird, you know, he was our strongest supporter on the council. I never for the life of me suspected he was part of the UWCA."

Captain Riley shrugged her shoulders and pointed to the bodies of the enemy, "The UWCA...that makes sense. At least we got them and hopefully all of them, but all our evac points need to be reinforced in the event there are others out there." Susan began to turn away, her gray face mask covered with a fine layer of ice crystals, "Oh, I forgot, welcome to the officer corps. I heard today you were being made a militia captain and assigned to our Intel Section...Good luck, Brad." With that she walked away, her head low and shoulders bent over as if she carried upon her back the weight of all the dead and wounded.

"God bless you, Susan," Brad said loudly and she turned to smile back at him.

He looked down at the body bag by his feet, sighed deeply and walked towards the building to check on Scott. He found his partner leaning against a wall, grimacing from pain as he shifted his weight.

"What did the Doctor say?" Brad asked.

"Couple ribs broken, but not bad," Scott said as he tossed two misshapen .357 slugs to Brad, who caught one in his gloved hand and had to pick up the other from the floor. "Present from me to you."

"Thanks...An' thanks for saving my life back there. I imagine Kathy will have another hug for you when she hears about our...guess you could call it an old west style shoot out. I've never been in anything like that before and hope I never have to again."

"Partner, with what's coming our way, we only got a little taste of gunplay," Scott said as he leaned on Brad's left shoulder.

"You're probably right and it's not something I'm looking forward to. But when it comes, I want one of those M-4's or even an older M-16 in my hands."

"Heck with that, I'd rather have a quad-.50 caliber machinegun or even a battery of howitzers."

"You always like to think big," Brad said. "Come on, let's get out of here." Brad helped Scott walk out of the building and headed for their shot up patrol car.

"Wow, you think this thing will make it to Greeley?" Scott, leaning against the car, was cautiously examining the bullet holes and blown out windows. Every movement was painful, but he wanted to tough it out until he could collapse in the front seat of their car.

Brad shook his head and grinned with relief, He couldn't believe he hadn't been hit. One of the EMT's had put a bandage on his neck, but that was it. "We'll drive it to the shop if it starts. We can get some plastic and tape to cover the windows. We've got a lot of equipment to haul and I sure don't want to have to carry it." Brad helped his partner into the car and kept the wisecracks to a few as Scott winced and uttered a few curses against the UWCA. He walked to the back to close the trunk and discovered that it wouldn't close; the lock mechanism had sustained too much damage. Brad walked about searching until he found a piece of yellow rope in the back of a school bus. He startled several kids when he opened the rear door, but when they saw his badge, calmed down. He chatted with them for a minute and then returned to his patrol car. He tied the trunk down and climbed in behind the wheel. To his surprise, the engine started on the first attempt, "Least they didn't hit the engine."

"They hit everything else...Take me home, Sarge...I need a long holiday on a real warm beach and add a beautiful woman to soothe my wounded pride." Scott closed up his parka hood to keep the cold air from coming in and freezing his face. Poor Brad wasn't so fortunate; without a windshield, the wind chill factor he was facing as he drove to the shop was in the -75 range and only his goggles kept his eyes from freezing solid.

Brad radioed Susie he was coming in and13 minutes later, pulled the shot up patrol car into the heated garage and turned off the engine. Looking over at his partner, he could hear the sounds of light snoring. When he pulled himself out of the car wincing from a sore back, Brad was startled to see Chief Bob Osborne observing the battle damage and shaking his head. But when he looked up at Brad, there was a smile of relief on his face. "I got the numbers and heard about Hodgekiss. That was a real shocker, Brad." Osborne looked down at Scott, "How is our warrior?"

"Two ribs, a lot of pain...but he survived two .357 hits."

"That's why I made you guys wear those vests," Chief Osborne said with satisfaction.

"What now?" Brad asked.

"We're done here, Brad," Bob said in a tone that expressed his sadness. He felt like he was deserting a sinking ship and it only depressed him. "The city is being evacuated. So, if you can patch that thing up, take it to Greeley. I think we may have another windshield over there in back, probably have ta use good old duct tape to hold it in place; I'll try to find someone to help you." Osborne shook his head as he looked the car over. "Good car, at least she's going out in style."

Chief Osborne helped Scott out of the car and led him into dispatch where he could sit with Susie while Brad worked on the car. Once a windshield was found, Brad used plastic sheets to cover the shot out windows and secured everything with a massive amount of duct tape. He then filled the gas tank, checked the fluids and loaded the car with everything he could find that might be useful later, including an unopened case of duct tape. Alaska's number one piece of survival equipment…worth its weight in gold…no, make that sugar. A lot of people joked about how Alaskans used the gray plumbers duct tape for just about everything, including designer clothes and putting up cabins, but the fact was this tape was reliable and stuck to just about anything. Some people even used the durable tape to hold vehicles together, and a few - the ones who lived in tent cities outside the canaries - used it to hold their summer homes together. Brad felt fortunate to find a whole box of the stuff. *Wonder what I could trade some of this for?*

Chief Osborne stepped back into dispatch, "Susie, call all units in for equipment pick up and refueling. No sense leaving anything for the OAP. Also advise them they'll be escorting some of the last buses to Greeley and I want you on one of those buses or in a patrol car." Rubbing his temples, he returned to his office for some badly needed pain relief.

When Brad and Scott left the station, the new windshield was firmly in place with the famous silver tape holding it in place. Brad had loaded the patrol car down with everything he could stuff into the tied down trunk and back seat. A mile out of town, Scott drifted off to sleep and Brad didn't have the heart to awaken him for the slow ride. Brad had taken up a rear guard position staying at least a mile behind a caravan of 14 buses and two dozen large truck and trailer vans of supplies. He was glad the car's ancient heater was still working. Even with the duct tape in place, the icy wind whipped through the patrol car from several small openings and reduced the car's interior to a - 5 °or colder. Only Brad's balaclava and Scott's hood kept their ears from freezing. Brad continued to glance over and check on Scott's position. He had to wake him up twice to keep him from slipping over too far to the left. Held in by his seat belt, which caused him a lot more pain, he growled through clenched teeth. Brad finally got him shoved over to the right, leaning up against the door and glanced over every moment or so to make sure he was still alive. His breathing through his wool scarf was easy to see as the icy cold turned his breath into a fine mist, making the car's defroster work overtime to keep the windshield from frosting over.

DELTA JUNCTION

When they drove through Delta Junction, Brad was amazed by the extent of activity taking place; thousands of men and women worked closely together filling sandbags with a mixture of ash, dirt and snow. Others were busy building a series of massive walls across the highway. Not counting the check points before Delta Junction, Brad and Scott were stopped four times for identification and each time the guards were amazed by the number of bullet holes in the patrol car. Brad had visited Delta Junction a couple hundred times in the past but had never seen such activity. There were hundreds of vehicles of all shapes and size, military and civilian, and people everywhere - all of them busy as they prepared for war.

He was able to spot the ADF troops right off, but most of the Militia forces were dressed in what uniform items they could scrounge up and personal arctic gear. Brad noticed how the ice fog was thickening, caused by so many vehicles left idling to keep people warm and he knew this could be a major problem when the OAP ground forces arrived. It's hard to shoot at the enemy when you can't see him coming. That was a real problem back there at the evac station...I hope Fort Greeley isn't as bad. But it was.

By now the tale had spread throughout Delta Junction and Fort Greeley of the shoot-out with the UWCA and the bravery displayed by members of the ADF and FPD. The casualty count shocked everyone, but with war about to begin, they all knew it was only going to get much worse.

FORT GREELEY

A short time later, the convoy slowly passed through the front gates of Fort Greeley; each vehicle waved on by a squad of ADF Military Policemen. Once the identification process was completed each vehicle headed for the main base. When it was Brad's turn, the senior MP shook his head in wonder. He counted the number of bullet holes on the police cruiser and through his black balaclava he said to Brad, "I count 17 bullet holes, Sergeant, not to mention the fine new windshield you got there. Ain't duct tape grand?"

"With a roll of duct tape I can conquer the world, Corporal," Brad said with a grin before he was finally waved through.

Once all the buses were unloaded, the occupants directed into the Base Gym for processing and room or house assignment, Brad and Scott were able to break away. With the help of two on duty MPs, Brad was able to learn where his family was put up.

"What happened to your car, Dad?" Bob Sawyer asked in bewilderment unaware that Scott had been hurt.

Bob wore his parka over light blue flannel pajamas and his feet hurriedly shoved into unlaced winter boots. He should have been in bed, but he was 12 and much too excited to sleep after hearing through the rumor mill of the great Fairbanks gun battle. When Bob heard voices inside the barracks talking about the Fairbanks police car parked outside, he leapt from bed and ran out into the hallway, then to the front door of the barracks building. As soon as he saw it was a Fairbanks patrol car, he rushed back to his room and climbed into his winter gear, then ran out to welcome his father and when he got close he stopped abruptly, startled by the amount of battle damage.

Inside the foyer of a large barracks building, now used to house dozens of families, Kathy stood before both men with her arms crossed and a single raised eyebrow; her look of agitation darted back and forth between the two men, "Gentlemen, please explain, how in the last 12 hours of your police careers, you two get involved in the worst shoot out of your lives?"

"Shoot out; what shoot out?" Brad smiled sheepishly with wide innocent eyes and reached out to grab his partner, who suddenly fell against Brad nearly unconscious, not so much from pain, but reaction to all his pain drugs.

"Dad, what's the matter with Scott?" Bob asked, noticing the droopy - eyed look on Scott's face and his faltering stance.

"I got to get him to bed; Kathy…the boob was wounded saving my life… We'll talk later."

Scott looked up at Kathy and through the pain, he whispered, "I thought it was a real quiet shift," he glanced up at Brad and added, "I think he slept through most of it."

Three men stepped up and carefully took Scott and half carried him to Sawyer's room to lay him down on Bob's bed. Scott was down for the count.

"Okay, big guy, now please explain that!?" Kathy demanded as she pointed to the patrol car, which now resembled Swiss cheese.

"Oh that…umm, would you believe termites?" Brad said, fighting to hold back a smile and relief at seeing his family again. Okay, okay! We got into a shoot-out with the UWCA." He pointed a thumb over his shoulder and said, "Scott got hit twice, but his vest saved him. He's got a couple broken ribs and he'll need to sleep for about 18 hours." Brad glared at his spouse, "And for your information, Mrs. Sawyer, Scott saved my life today and you owe him a big hug and maybe a kiss."

Kathy dropped her arms and stared at her husband, but she was getting cold and decided it was time to end the game. She had heard the whole story earlier anyway and decided she wanted to torture her husband for getting into the battle. That is until she saw how Scott was hurt. She would reserve one hug and a kiss for Scott when he woke up, adding a big, "Thank you, Scott". Kathy hugged her husband and held him tightly once they were inside the barracks and her eyes began to tear.

After they ensured Scott's comfort and moved Bob to a mattress on the floor beside Scott's bunk, Brad decided on some sleep before trying to unload the patrol car. Before he could close his eyes, Kathy insisted on a full detailed story of the battle. They followed this with a prayer for those who were hurt in the attack and the families of the dead. Only then did they offer up to God a prayer of thanks for keeping both Brad and Scott alive. Stripped down to his long underwear and forced to share a single bunk which Kathy was comfortable with because she needed to hold him, he finally closed his eyes to sleep. His last thoughts were of the future, what's going to come next?

ADF INTELLIGENCE MISSION, CANADA - MARCH 25TH

Waking up to sub-zero temperatures, both men having been too tired to stay awake on guard and keep the fire going, Jeb and Wayne were soon back on the road again. Though seriously stiff from cold joints, they became exhausted quickly as they snow-shoed through two miles of crusty gray snow, before stumbling upon a small occupied cabin. Built of spruce and birch trees, the cabin was comfortable for one or two, but somewhat crowded for more. They were made welcome by a lonely and quite talkative old trapper. It didn't escape either of the two men that the talkative trapper happened to have a dog sled and eight sled dogs. Though both Wayne and Jeb felt bad about it, especially after eating a meal with the man, they were forced to borrow the dog sled and dogs for their journey. The trapper, a long bearded older fellow, had quite a profane mouth when angered and he released a tirade as Jeb loosely bound and tied him, and then placed him by the warm fire. With such a vile outburst, they decided to leave him gagged to quiet him down. But he continued to snarl and growl through his gag, especially when Wayne found his precious maps.

Wayne had searched the small cabin and located the trapper's hand drawn maps, which, when unrolled had shown most of the trails through British Columbia and further east. It had taken the trapper most of his 50 years living in the wild to locate these old trails and knowing he was about to lose his treasure turned him frantic, forcing Wayne to walk over and use a sleep hold on the old gentleman to quiet him. "He'll wake up in a couple hours and be able to untie himself. By then we should be several miles down the trail."

"I hope so, I sure wouldn't want to tangle with that old man again," Jeb said.

Fortunately, Wayne was knowledgeable on the use of dog sleds, having used them on other Special Forces operations throughout Alaska and Canada. The difficult part was getting the strange dogs to heed his orders. Jeb was of a mind to shoot the lead dog, after he was bitten twice while hooking him up. Only his heavy mittens kept him from a serious wound. Wayne doctored Jeb up, checked on the old man and tossed a couple pieces of wood in the old geezer's wood stove to keep him from freezing. Then to Jeb's surprise, Wayne issued a few simple sledding commands in French and they were off.

The first mile was difficult, especially for Jeb, who had to ride in the sled and suffer every bump and bounce of the trail. It was faster than going by foot, but Jeb would have been more than happy to jump out and run behind to escape the beating he was receiving. Sitting on top and behind several bags of dog food, a camp cook stove with sharp edges that stabbed into his side, and several cast iron pots, Jeb used the dog's reindeer skin bag of booties to soften the blows to his poor backside. On these icy trails, the dogs required booties on their feet to protect them from frostbite and knowing this, Wayne stopped every few hours to change the footwear. At these times, Wayne attempted to reassure Jeb that they were making good time and how, by using these old trails, they could bypass the checkpoints and probably reach Calgary in time.

Oddly enough, it was Jeb's body warmth that actually warmed up the old booties. Wayne found this amusing, but Jeb didn't and after traveling approximately 20 miles, Jeb toyed with the idea of shooting the dogs and possibly even Captain Wayne Roberts for coming up with this hair brain idea. *I'll never be able to walk again...I really hate these dogs and all I can see in front of me is dog butts!*

ON THE ICE PACK EN ROUTE TO SAVOONGA

With several miles of rough traveling behind them, nothing but ice in front of them and a dark gray sky above to look at, Captain Myers struggled with boredom. He had learned early on to ignore the sounds of his mukluks crunching the crusty surface and even the many grumblings of his troops. As he preferred to travel for six-hours, followed by a six hour break, Myers pulled down his arctic mitten and checked his watch. They still had another two hours and 16minutes to go before the next break. *Colonel Freeman expects the attack to commence today, meaning we're now under ADF Command Fairbanks for orders. I sure hope this hike was worth it, or my troops are going to drill a big hole and use me as bait as their ice-fishing.* Through the graying light of a new day, where visibility on the ice was extremely limited, he looked back at the men marching in single file behind him and noticed they were spreading out too far, "Close it up some, no more than 15 feet from the man in front of you."

The close interval was necessary. He had already lost four of the 96 troopers he began the long march with. They had simply wandered off during the long tiresome dark stretches and failed to respond to shouts or shots fired into the air. MSgt. Iukapah was of the opinion the ones missing had probably fallen through the ice. Several times the point element had given word of patches of open water ahead and they were forced to change direction to bypass the dangerous areas.

The night before they had spotted a polar bear with infrared binoculars and Myers sent out a single squad to hunt the bear down. Two hours later, they returned triumphantly with over 400 pounds of bear meat. The bear's great white cape, which contained the fresh meat, was draped over a sled and for a short time the men and women appeared happy, talking of the courage and spirit of the great bear. MSgt. Iukapah, who went with the squad, estimated the bear to have stood over 9 feet and was possibly 7 to 8 years of age.

"This was a great bear, Captain. His meat and spirit will nourish us," Iukapah said. He then turned to make sure their rear guard was still with them.

They continued to march, slapping one foot after the other upon the ice and only stopping for short 10 minute breaks every hour. During this time Myers took compass readings to insure they were staying on a direct westward course for Savoonga. *If everything goes well and we don't lose any more troops, or meet up with a large body of water that will need bypassing, we should reach Savoonga by the 2nd of April.*

The troops alternated between pulling sleds and walking flank, rear guard and point duties. This meant with six hour break times between shifts, a troop would only have to pull the heavy sled once every two days.

Quiet came to an abrupt halt when a man on the right flank heard the sound of an aircraft in the distance to the north. A second troop and then another reported the sound of jets and soon, they all begin to see the white powdery contrails from dozens of jets flying low beneath the dark gray clouds of ash. It had stopped snowing; increasing visibility and Myers saw the enemy aircraft heading east.

"The invasion is on, so stay alert. Now let's get a move on!" Captain Myers ordered and hustled to where MSgt. Iukapah was making contact with ADF Command-Fairbanks. Once the notifications were made, Myers looked to his company and in a weary voice, hollered, "One more hour to go… keep moving!"

The sleds were heavy, weighing close to 1500 pounds or better and it took a lot of muscle power to get them moving again. Two men were in front pulling, others were on each side with ropes and two more were pushing. Icy conditions had caused one sled to tip over and it took an hour to get it righted, repacked with the items that had come loose and back in motion.

Between large patches of stark whiteness and larger patches of dirty black ash on the ice, bitter cold and freezing winds, Captain Myers could truly understand his company's poor attitude. Lesser men and women might have deserted, but not these Eskimos and Athabascann troops. His respect for these people grew with each step he took across the ice and he was deeply sorry for his negative thoughts when ADF Command had first told him he would be taking over a rifle company in the 1st Division. His thoughts abruptly disappeared when he spotted the point man signaling frantically and pointing to the north. Then Myers heard it too, the sound of a low flying helicopter. Grabbing a spotting scope his radioman carried in his backpack, Myers located the oncoming helicopter. "Looks Russian… Everyone drop down!" Myers ordered. He turned to MSgt Iukapah, "Get the heavy weapons platoon up here and have 'em standby to fire." He hoped the pilot would fly over them as they were wearing white camouflage in order to blend in with their surroundings. Unfortunately, the size and color of some of the sleds and equipment would standout on this huge sea of white ice.

"Protect the radios!" Iukapah ordered and several of the men threw their heavy packs over the communications gear.

A long moment passed and then the OAP observation helicopter was almost directly over them; every member of the company held their breath and pointed their rifles at the enemy bird. The helicopter, which did appear to be Russian, began a wide banking turn to the left to fly in a large circle. Myers pointed and ordered his heavy weapons squad to open up. There was nothing to hide behind and Myers knew from the missile pods hanging from the skids, that the OAP observation helicopter was armed with air-to-ground rockets that could destroy his whole company. His troops would have to make a stand right here in the open; there was no other choice.

"Fire!" Captain Myers ordered, which was echoed by MSgt. Iukapah, and a company of troops armed with M-16s and newer M-4s, opened up with full automatic fire on the attacking helicopter.

8 - THE NAVAJO PEOPLE

"He must turn from evil and do good: he must seek peace and pursue it. For the eyes of the Lord are on the righteous and His ears are attentive to their prayer, but the face of the Lord is against those who do evil."

Hebrews 3.10-12 NIV

NAVAJO RESERVATION, ROUTE 66, NEW MEXICO, USA - MARCH 26

The convoy traveled for 73 miles through the Navajo Reservation without seeing a single Indian, teepee or roadside tourist trap. Two of the smaller vehicles; a Ford Explorer and a Jeep Wagoner, were beginning to look a little worse for wear. Ed was pretty sure they would have to abandon both of them soon and that meant shifting some people and gear around to other vehicles.

Their journey came to halt when they reached the San Juan River. Point Man stood in the middle of the road in front of the remains of a massive concrete and steel bridge. The bridge's center span lay at the bottom of the river gorge, but torn pavement and massive blocks of concrete rubble blocked the highway.

"Smells like dynamite," Point Man told Ed after checking the debris.

Ed examined some of the rubble and agreed with the big guy then ordered camp to be set up on the east side of the highway, where the state had maintained a large parking area for visitors to park and see the gorge. He called out a dozen names and those called were sent out in two scouting parties, one to the right and the other to the left, in search of a river crossing. Point Man, who was driving a Dodge Durango 4x4, led one party to the west over a series of low hills that followed the river. Joey, in charge of the other party, drove a one ton Ford 4x4 stake truck and headed eastward across the desert flatlands.

"Don't get lost," Ed told his two leaders.

"Ed, we've got a river on one side…how can we get lost?"

Ed grinned, "With you two in charge, I …just go!" Ed waved them on, hoping he might have a chance to get an afternoon nap. With the two teams gone, Ed assigned Larry to supervise setting up camp and placement of guards. "You make sure they stay alert, someone blew up that bridge and that someone could still be around." He walked to the tent site he'd chosen and spent the next 15 minutes setting up and checking for scorpions then laid down on his black air mattress and quickly nodded off for a well-deserved nap.

Men and women working together erected the large circus tent, tying the flaps up to allow air to pass through. Water coolers were pulled out of the trailer van and set up in convenient locations, while younger teenagers began a game of capture the flag to keep the children busy and out of everyone's hair.

The area was searched for rattlers and one, found underneath a large flat rock, was killed with a .22 caliber pistol and skinned. The meat was cleaned and roasted for dinner, allowing many a chance to taste rattlesnake for the first time. The six foot long skin was stretched out to dry, but no one was quite sure what to do with it after that. Pastor suggested they use the skin for hat bands, a gift for Point Man and His Misfits; a way of saying thank you for their hard work and vigilance on this journey, and everyone agreed.

Unable to sleep more than a half hour, Ed got up and stepped outside his tent to watch the children run about the parking lot. Lost in memories of his nephew and niece, he didn't notice Kira come up behind him until she spoke at his side, "Are you worried?"

"What? Oh, hi...No, I'm not worried. And don't sneak up on me like that!"

"Sorry, but you sure fooled me. I saw how you were looking at those kids and you looked worried."

A disgruntled expression appeared on his face, "For your information, Miss, I was wondering what sort of world we've left for those kids to grow up in."

"If Pastor Woodway is right, they'll have a beautiful new world to explore," Kira said. She disappeared for a moment, but reappeared shortly with a cup of water. "Here, you look thirsty."

"Thanks." Ed gulped the water and glanced down into Kira's eyes. He was thirsty. *Girl's got pretty eyes...* "Now, what can I do for you?"

Before Kira could answer, Larry O' Brian began excitedly hollering out Ed's name.

"Over here, Larry!" Ed shouted. He handed the cup to Kira and rushed over to his large bus driver. Larry's big frame stomped across the sand covered parking lot, leaving massive sized footprints in his wake, "Point Man's back an' he's brought company."

"Company?" Well, if they didn't shoot Point Man on sight, they must make for some interesting people.

Ed walked alongside Larry to where a crowd had gathered around a dozen American Indians on horseback. Several of the riders held rifles, barrels pointed to the sky, but two carried compound bows with fiberglass arrows notched on the taut string and in quivers strapped to their backs. Gun belts around waists held an assortment of holstered pistols. Several had newer sheath knives tucked into the belts. Most had long black hair over their shoulders and decorative head bands. They were shirtless or wearing dark tank tops, and well-worn blue jeans. Some wore tennis shoes and others mid-calf leather moccasins. All were riding strong looking horses and Ed was envious. A few of the breeds were highly sought after; gray appaloosa with black spots, solid brown and one black one that Ed thought to stand 18 hands. Beneath expensive western leather saddles were handmade multi-colored Navajo horse blankets.

"Hey, Boss," Point Man said as Ed approached. "I brought some new friends home for dinner. Met with 'em up river…they were hunting deer." Point Man lowered his voice so only Ed could hear, "Had a few nervous moments, but we got ta talkin'. They was even nice enough to show me a shallow spot where we can cross."

"What can we do to return the favor?" Ed asked as he studied their guests.

No one answered right away, so Point Man interjected, "They need a doctor, Boss. They got a lot of sick people." He pointed toward the riders, "Story is, when the missiles hit, they left the main reservation and headed north to the land of their ancestors and they're having a tough time."

"Who's the leader?" Ed asked as he admired the beautiful horses. He recognized the Appaloosas and recalled how he had always wanted one.

"The dude sitting on that gray… the one with all the spots," Point Man said pointing to a handsome young man in his early twenties mounted on a beautiful gray mare with a long black mane and tail. His long black hair was held back in a ponytail by a flowery yellow bandanna. He had a golden brown complexion and intelligent dark brown eyes. His face remained expressionless as he held an older model Winchester lever action 30-30 across his lap and studied Ed closely.

Putting on his best State Trooper smile, the one he normally used when dealing with politicians and wealthy property owners, Ed walked up and offered his hand in welcome, "Ed Sawyer, I want to thank you for showing my friend a river crossing. The bridge seems to be out."

"We did it to keep city people from the north out of our town. Some men came down and raided the northern part of the reservation and hurt a

217

lot of real nice people before we chased them off. We thought you might be more trouble for us, until we talked with your big man." The Indian smiled and added, "Big man has a strange name, but honest eyes. My name is Joseph."

Ed smiled at the comment, "I understand you need a doctor?"

"Yes. My people are very ill and no one seems to know why. We have three who are qualified EMTs, but that's it. Big Man said you have a good doctor."

"How far to your town and has anyone died?" Ed asked, concerned the sickness might be the Plague.

Joseph laid the rifle across his saddle and dismounted, which put Ed at ease. Though he did notice Joseph was carrying a large caliber revolver in his holster and if anything did go wrong there was enough fire power there for a large scale battle. "No one's died yet," Joseph said. "This isn't the plague...but something else that began five days ago." Joseph glanced about the crowd and smiled when he saw the looks of joy upon the faces of the children. This was the first encounter with real Indians for some of them and they all probably wanted to ride a horse, just as he had as a youngster.

Ed knew how most people died within 24 hours of contact with the plague and mortality was 99%. Ed asked Joseph again how far to their town.

"Not far, I only hope your doctor can help." The Indian looked over Ed's shoulder; the diversity of racial groups surprised him. "You sure are a mixed group, sort of a United Nation's road show instead of a church." He pointed to Point Man, "Big man here told where you're headed - Alaska...that's a real long way."

Ed knew he would have to speak to Point Man about giving out so much information to complete strangers, "Let's go find, Doc." Ed gestured toward the ambulance and Joseph followed. Others began to dismount and were almost immediately besieged by several children who ran forward to see the animals. Once permission was granted, they were each lifted on top one of the horses and led around the area, with the reins in the hands of the horse's owner to ensure safety. With so much unfriendliness in the country, neighbor firing on neighbor for survival, the sharing of names and a simple thing as a horse ride was a welcome change for both groups.

"If you have some sugar to trade, I can offer you some fresh Whitetail Deer we took down only a couple hours ago."

Ed's eye brows shot up, "Fresh venison, sure." He licked his lips and waved O' Brian over, "Larry, would you go get a 10 pound bag of sugar from the trailer. We're going to have fresh venison for dinner tonight."

"Now that sounds great!" Larry answered as he turned to carry out the request.

"You've got a lot of big men in your party," Joseph said as he watched Larry walk away.

"Larry was All Pro with the Arizona Cardinals," Ed said. "Now he drives our school bus and protects the kids."

"I can't imagine anyone wanting to mess with him, much less your big man and his friends," Joseph said with admiration. He yelled out orders for his men to unload the deer. They could hunt others, but sugar and other spices, once easily found on a store's shelf, were now priceless.

"Joseph, it's getting late. Do we have time to make the crossing before dark, I hate losing any time?" Ed asked as he waited for Larry to return.

"One hour, no more," Joseph said as he looked at the sun. The clouds from the north were coming closer, now taking up nearly two thirds of the sky. He and Ed knew that before long they wouldn't be able to see the sun or the stars and it sent cold shivers up their spines.

"Well, we're already set up here, so we might as well stay and cross in the morning. After we cross, we can get back on the highway and proceed north. I'd be happy to have you and your men join us for dinner."

"I'll leave some of them with you, to ensure you are not bothered by some of the other Navajo in the area, but I must return home." Joseph pointed to the north, "You see how the darkness draws closer. Each night we see fewer stars and I do not know how much longer we will see the sun. One of my men, a former professor at ASU, says the volcanic ash may cover the entire northern hemisphere and there will be no crops. Humans will go the way of the dinosaur and we've done it to ourselves."

"I'm afraid he's probably right," Ed agreed. "I only hope we make it to Alaska before it's too late."

"The farther north you go, more of the sky will be in darkness. Alaska is so far north, I believe it is already covered and possibly buried by ash. I've read of all the active volcanoes in Alaska, I'm sure the ash has covered the ground and what was white is now black."

"I hope you're wrong, Joseph" Ed said. "But that's where we're headed." He led Joseph to the ambulance to meet Doc and Nancy.

After talking it over, Ed remained reluctant for Doc and Nancy go to the Indian village alone, but Doc remained equally adamant, "This could be something contagious, Ed; there's no sense losing more of us. Nancy and I can handle it; you take care of the others. If we don't make it back, I've trained several good EMTs to help get you north."

"Doc, you're really making it hard to let you go…but, I guess it is the Christian thing to do."

Joey returned, unable to locate a crossing and surprised to find Navajo in camp. One of his kids was mounted on a brown horse and he grinned, knowing he was having a memorable experience.

Ed came up, briefed Joey and they began planning the move west. There would be some difficulty in making the crossing; the river, though shallow, was wide and muddy. The heavy wrecker had to be set up on the far side, stabilized by huge steel plates and its winch used to pull half a dozen of the heavier vehicles across. They would most likely fight a tug-o-war getting the double tanker across, but George Washington believed he could carry it off.

They ended up trading salt and other spices for two more deer. The hardest part was selecting the right cook to barbecue. Twenty volunteered, but the job finally went to two men who held master degrees in backyard barbecuing. It wasn't long before the odor from the fire pit was driving everyone crazy as they waited impatiently for the dinner bell. One or two teenagers tried to swipe a cut of cooked meet only to be chased away by the head cook with threats of them going hungry.

Before the sun vanished behind rolling hills to the west, Ed looked toward them and wondered about Doc and Nancy. Though he had four of the Indians in camp, enjoying music provided by the worship team and his two friends made radio checks on the hour, Ed was still concerned for their safety. *Suppose they don't let 'em leave? Doctors are apparently real scarce in these parts and I get stuck with four Indians and their horses to feed - not a great deal!*

NAVAJO LAND

Handling the old ambulance through the rocky hills was a real test of Nancy's driving skill - she often winced in sympathy as Doc groaned with nearly every shake and rattle of the ambulance. "Should've tied you down in back and gagged you," Nancy complained while she ground gears to climb through a steep pass.

"These old bones of mine can't take this kind of torture. Don't these people believe in roads?" Doc reached up to prevent a bottle of sterile water from flying off the shelf; he'd already lost one earlier in the trip.

For two hours they followed the Indian band, crawling through a series of rounded hills, over patches of bleached white sand and passing by near impossible rocky terrain where the trail was barely wide enough to fit the ambulance between two monstrous boulders. Near the end of the third hour, Nancy spotted the Navajo town and alerted Doc. Her first impression was one of disbelief; if it wasn't for the fact she knew it to be the 21st Century, she'd have thought they'd gone back in time to the mid to late 19th Century. White single story adobe structures and several old trailers were spread out over a small valley, shaded from the late afternoon sun by a tall rocky bluff.

Dozens of women and children were gathered around large outside cast iron or handmade hard baked clay stoves. Curious at the sound of a vehicle approaching, they turned to watch. It wasn't every day a World War II Army ambulance drove into town with a frenzied wide eyed white woman behind the wheel.

They drove past corrals made from Joshua Trees and chicken wire. Some held burros, while others held horses and goats. There was a small herd of sheep running loose. When she drove through town, chickens scattered to keep from being run over. But Nancy was too busy rubber necking to worry about chickens. She couldn't help but admire the colorful clothing the people wore: purples, yellows and reds, bright and dark blues that made her envious as she looked down at her own drab clothes.

Coming to a stop and turning off her engine, she heard raised voices and noticed a couple of apparently angry women having trouble with their stoves. One was smacking the top of hers with a large stick, while another tossed aside a cast iron pot to have a few choice words with her husband before storming off toward the house.

Seeing the curious expression on Nancy's face, Joseph, who was riding in the front passenger seat as guide, enlightened her, "Some of our women haven't learned to cook in the old ways. In the lower reservation they used microwaves, gas ovens and watched the soap opera on large screen TV. It's been hard on them to come back here and learn to rough it, especially with no hot showers...not yet anyway."

"Someone's dinner gonna be late," Nancy said, as she watched the woman with the stick turn from the stove to berate her husband. The woman grabbed up a small child and walked off to take comfort with her neighbor, the one who had already expressed her feelings for antiquated utilities.

"It will take time, but we are safer here. Our people have lived off the land for thousands of years and we must learn to do so again," Joseph said.

Doc came out the back of the ambulance with his medical bag in hand, "Where's my patients?"

Having listened to his complaints for most of the drive, Joseph was surprised by Doc's energy. "This way, please." Joseph directed them toward the largest building, where a very short old man in a blue jean coat, red flannel shirt with a missing button, faded blue jeans and extremely old brown leather cowboy boots, met them. With a weathered look of tough leather to his face and deep wrinkles around heavily bloodshot brown eyes, Nancy thought the man could easily be 100 years old or more. "Doc, he makes you look like a kid."

Joseph smiled, "This is my grandfather, William Henry Salcedo and Chief of our tribe." Joseph spoke in Navajo for a brief moment before he turned back to Doc, "I apologize, but my grandfather, who speaks fluent English, refuses to use it. He blames the world's situation on everyone but us Indians."

"Sure hope he isn't one of the sick ones?" Doc said, exchanging a raised eyebrow with the old man.

"No. They're all inside here. Come." Joseph walked past his grandfather and led Doc and Nancy into the Navajo Meeting Lodge. In the largest room were eight wooden rope beds, each with a patient while three ladies handled the nursing chores.

'These must be the EMTs', Doc thought as he followed Joseph into a smaller room and discovered seven sick children laying on air mattresses.

"How long did you say this has been going on?" Nancy asked, with a note of concern as she looked down on the unhappy faces of the sick children.

"Started five days ago, but no one has died so we know it isn't the plague," Joseph reminded them. He made sure to wrap a clean bandanna around his nose and mouth before he went any closer.

"How about your medical supplies, what have you got on hand?" Doc asked. He handed a facemask to Nancy and donned one himself.

"Only what we could grab from our homes before leaving. We've been giving 'em Aspirin, anti-acids for cramps and anything and everything we could think of to help with the diarrhea. Mostly, they complain of headaches, dizziness and stomachaches. Some fever, but not very high."

"Let me start examining the children first," Doc said. He opened his bag and removed his aged stethoscope. An hour later, Doc and Nancy stepped outside to compare notes, "Nancy, if I was ta hazard a guess... I think what we got here is food poisoning."

"You may be right, Doc... nothing else seems to come to mind," Nancy said.

Doc asked Joseph to lead them to where the food supplies were stored and he led them to a large adobe building behind the meeting lodge. Examination showed one open barrel of dried deer meat to be tainted. "That's your culprit," Doc said.

Joseph asked around and discovered the meat from this barrel was used for a birthday celebration a week ago and leftovers were being used to make a broth for the people who had become ill.

"Another day or two and your young people would've started to die from dehydration," Doc said. "You're lucky those ladies kept pushing fluids down them. But even that won't help if you keep putting spoiled food into them." Doc pointed to the spoiled meat, "Burn the meat, don't leave it for smaller animals to consume and… get rid of that broth." IV fluid, full of medication and vitamins was pumped into the patients, making a large dent in Doc's dwindling supply. But there was little else he could do, these people needed it right away or risk death. When the children showed signs of coming around first, the whole tribe wanted to celebrate.

With the patients on the mend, Nancy spent time with the women teaching them better hygiene practices for surviving without electricity. She learned from listening to their complaints that going back to nature was not brought about by a unanimous vote. They all missed modern kitchens, cell phones and on down the list of conveniences. At the top of the list was modern plumbing and Nancy could only sympathize. She really missed having her daily hot shower.

Notifying Ed via radio, Nancy advised him they would be spending the night and not to worry. "We're okay, it was only food poisoning an' we'll see you in the morning." Doc didn't mind staying the night; the thought of driving back in the dark was not something he looked forward to.

That evening, Doc and Nancy found themselves the guests of honor at a tribal celebration. Even the Chief thanked them in English, but then reverted back to his Navajo tongue for the remainder of the night. Navajo dancers, dressed in ceremonial garments, performed several traditional dances. One of the tribal elders, a man with long graying hair, who looked to be as old as the chief, told an ancient story about one of their famous medicine men. Gifts were presented to the two guests; men presenting Doc with various items and Navajo women presenting an Indian doll and a beautiful Navajo blanket to Nancy. This would be a night Doc and Nancy would never forget.

BACK AT CAMP

Seeing Ed sitting alone on the outskirts of camp, Kira gritted her teeth and walked over to join him. Her footsteps in the desert sand alerted him and he turned to see her approach. "Yes, Miss Woods?"

"Thought you might like some company?"

Ed decided he'd better take the bull by the horns and get this over with, "Kira, you need to find yourself a nice young man to spend this kind of evening with…not an old duffer like me." That was about as far as Ed got before Kira stopped him.

"You listen to me, Mr. Ed Sawyer. I'll have you know that in the old days, women my age already had a second or third child by now. Like I told a certain person already, the marrying age policy of the modern era died with the onset of World War III. So…Oh-h-h, never mind! Maybe you are an old duffer." Kira glared at him and stomped off, leaving Ed with a confused expression on his face. *Lot of fire in that little gal…* Then he remembered what she said, *marrying age…Second or third child?*

Well-fed and content with his life, Larry O' Brian lay under the bus to change the oil and hummed an old song his wife had liked while he watched the old oil drain out. He was surprised when someone gently kicked his foot and he heard a female's voice, "Hey there, Big Guy," Kathy Looney said.

"Hello." Larry knew the voice, but was surprised by how excited he felt in hearing it.

"With those Navajo warriors about, you might wanna be a little more alert," She warned.

Larry slid out and sat up to look up at her, "Aw, you know those people are peaceful. Besides, I don't think I ever heard of the Navajo being a warlike tribe."

"Don't fool yourself. They had to fight off the white man and the Apache to survive on this desert. Everyone wanted their land, but you notice they held on to it."

Slowly, he stood to his feet and wiped his hands with a soiled rag. "Such a great night, almost makes me want to build a house right here. Then again, I guess lumber might be kind of hard to come by."

"Thought you was headin' for Alaska?" Kathy asked, her eyes studying a few visible stars to the south.

"Ed told me about the Northern lights, how they dance around and light up the sky. I'd like to see that…if the ash clouds ever leave. But I'm sure not looking forward to those cold nights he's talked about; how temperatures can get down to 50 or 60° below zero. Too cold for this city boy, gonna have to skin me a whale to use the blubber to keep me warm."

"Do you know anything about whale hunting, Larry?"

His face broke out into a big smile, "About as much as I know about bear hunting, which isn't much outside a few of those hunting magazines Ed has."

"I was up there once…six weeks one summer. All I got ta see was Fairbanks though. A pretty nice place, people were friendly like, but prices were really high."

"I didn't know you were in Alaska. How come you went up there, vacation or a job?"

Kathy wanted to kick herself. *Why'd I have to mention Fairbanks?* She remained quiet staring off into the desert as she fought the urge to leave and those painful memories from those old days. It was a strange tug-of-war and poor Larry didn't know the rules.

"Did I say something wrong?" Larry asked, but Kathy wouldn't answer him. So, he shrugged his shoulders and slid back down under the bus. He still needed to replace the filter, replace the plug and pull the pan out. When he came out from underneath the bus, Kathy was gone. *What'd I say?*

Walking alone, Kathy recalled that particular summer in Fairbanks. A six week contract to dance six nights a week at a bar called Reflections. Living in a dorm over the bar, she took her meals in several different beer joints around south Fairbanks. She never saw the great Alaskan pipeline, Denali Park or stayed in a single campground. She never fished for salmon or rode on the Alaska Railroad, and never even saw a moose or bear. Awake before work, she only saw the sights of South Cushman; three bars, two gas stations, a thrift store and a row of pawnshops. Then she spent 9 to10 hours dancing in front of intoxicated young servicemen and filthy minded old dudes with pawing hands. The $4,000 she made during those six weeks helped pay her brother's tuition, but she never went back. *How can I ever tell Larry who I am or what I've done? No, I can't trust anyone. They'd toss me off like unwanted trash if they knew.* Kathy remembered contact with other Christians, the ones who picketed the dance clubs she worked at. *All those hateful words they used in the name of God. People preachin' God's love one day an' smackin' girls around with their signs the next. Bunch of hypocrites!*

Early next morning, the ambulance rolled into camp and a very relieved Wagon Master met them. Doc and Nancy showed off all the lovely gifts they had received until Ed finally broke things up, "All right everyone, we leave in 30 minutes. Get yourselves ready."

Before the Navajo riders left, Pastor Woodway presented them with a ten pound bag of garlic salt, "To help with smoking and storing your meat." They thanked everyone, gave a final wave and rode off into the hills, stopping once to look back before disappearing over the ridge.

"Hey, Doc, did they make you an honorary member of their tribe?" Joey asked after the riders left.

"I'm not exactly sure, Joey, those people said a lot of things last night I couldn't understand. Nice people though and I really hope they make it." Doc wandered off to check on patients wounded in their battle with the Disciples. It had been a long time since he had taken bullets out of people and wanted to make sure he still had the skill for leaving small scars.

An hour later, spurred on by Ed's constant badgering, the convoy had made the river crossing with little difficulty and was back on the highway heading north. Ed had high hopes to hit Dove Creek, Colorado before nightfall but was concerned with how eerie the dark sky to the north was looking. In days past the dark clouds resembled a thick wavy blanket, but now it had a different look, much more ominous and it worried him.

Point Man, wearing a heavy fur parka and leather Thinsulated gloves to keep warm in the harsh wind chill he rode against, was out front on his hog and reported over the CB that the next 50 miles were clear. Ed was troubled with the idea they had to travel so close to Hill AFB, Utah. According to last reports, Hill had taken a direct missile hit and was probably hot enough to scramble eggs.

From the Navajo they learned that Salt Lake City, home of the Mormon religion, was a ghost town after clouds of radiation killed thousands of dedicated followers who refused to leave their historic temple.

Every five miles or so, Point Man stopped to pull out his Geiger Counter, which was kept strapped to the side of the gas tank. Riding north, the needle hadn't budged and once more he sighed deeply with relief as he looked at the lonely road ahead. Every other mile or so, they came across an abandoned or wrecked vehicle which His Misfits checked. He radioed Ed to advise him of the find and whether or not it was worth stopping to siphon fuel or load salvaged supplies. However, most of the vehicles were already stripped and several contained dead bodies. Point Man relayed this information and left it up to Ed whether or not to stop the convoy for burial duty. It was a hard decision, but after conferring with Pastor Woodway, they opted to keep moving unless it involved children. Then Ed would assign several men in one of the rear escort vehicles the gruesome task of burying the young. He knew the smaller vehicles could catch up with the convoy pretty quick once the grizzly task was completed.

Riding in the back of the bus with the children, Pastor Woodway engaged old Charlie White Ear in a theological discussion. A full blooded Apache, Charlie White Ear had avoided contact with the Navajo riders. Somewhere back in his ancestral line, a Navajo tribesman had killed a family member and the Apache were known to carry a grudge for a long time. He did not want to dishonor his new friendship with Pastor Woodway by assaulting a guest. Though he did accept a plate of venison during mealtime deciding that feuds were one thing and the taste of fresh deer meat another.

Bouncing along on the over taxed springs of the bus driver's seat, Larry glanced up into his rearview mirror to see if Kathy was awake. She was and he offered his apology in a whisper he hoped only she could hear, "Sorry 'bout last night."

Kathy looked up from the magazine she was reading and saw Larry looking back at her in the mirror, alternating between the road ahead and the mirror he used to keep an eye on the kids, "You didn't say anything wrong, Larry. I've just got things in my past I can't talk about...that's all."

"We've all got anchors that tend to drag us down; at least I used to let 'em. Then one day I gave them all over to God and now they're covered by the blood."

"Covered by the blood? Now what's that supposed to mean?" She asked with a sarcastic bite.

Larry ignored her tone and kept his voice low, "I confessed my sins, Jesus forgave me and my past sinful acts were thrown into the Sea of Forgetfulness."

"Give that to me again in plain English," Kathy leaned forward in order to keep their conversation private. Most of the kids were busy listening to a story, while others were playing games with each other and the young women riding along with them.

"Look, it's real easy...Once I repent of my sins, I'm forgiven and the Lord never remembers it again. He doesn't hold my forgiven sins against me...It's His promise. Unless I sin again of course... but then I repent again. Lord says in His Word to forgive 7 times 77 and that on a single day."

"An' you really believe that?"

"Of course I do. If you can believe in God, you can believe in His promises. The Lord knows we're not perfect and we will often stumble along, breaking one of His commandments or another. The important thing is that we come to Him to ask His forgiveness and demonstrate a change of heart in ourselves."

Kathy stared at him in the mirror, "I didn't say I believed in God."

"So, you do believe in God?" Larry looked into the mirror to see her expression.

"We talkin' the Big Guy, right? Numero Uno... the God who created everything an' now watches as his world blows up. If this God cares so much, why doesn't he lift a hand to stop all this bad stuff from happening?"

"Sounds to me like you're pretty mad at God," Larry said. "That's not disbelief, but anger and that's a good start."

"What are you talking about?" Kathy raised her voice, which caught some of the kid's attention.

"If you're mad at God, then you've admitted He exists. Kind of hard to be mad at someone who doesn't exist, isn't it?"

"I can see why you played football."

"Hey, I'll have you know I carried a 3.0 grade average in college," Larry said in mock defense.

"What was your major?" She asked with a smirk on her face and a raised eyebrow.

He hesitated at first, but then said defensively, "Physical education."

"Enough said." But Kathy was smiling when she looked up into the mirror.

"Can you talk with me about some of the things bothering you? These big shoulders of mine's gotta be good for something."

"Listen, I appreciate the offer, Larry, but I'm not ready for an episode of True Confessions..." Kathy stopped when she saw the hurt in Larry's eyes. "You didn't deserve that, I'm sorry. But Larry, I haven't had a friend in a long time...let's let it lay for a while, okay?"

"Okay by me, but I'm here if you need me. Best listening chauffeur in the southwest."

"Thanks, I'll see if I can find you the cute little black cap to go with the job."

Ed gave into his gut feeling and decided to bypass Dove Creek; instead he directed the Convoy on to Rico, Colorado. As they passed small roadside communities along the way, they saw several structures on fire or burned to the ground, some still smoldering. Point Man reported hearing gunshots from some of the smaller towns and that others appeared deserted. A few of the locations were nothing more than roadside truck stops, a few gift shops and cafes. But they were all destroyed, a dead body lay here and there, and it made Ed wonder who was up ahead and who had caused such carnage. He didn't want to risk stumbling into an ambush or coming across a contaminated settlement, so he ordered Point Man to drive by all questionable sites.

Setting up camp outside Rico, Ed changed his mind and had Point Man, Joey and several others drive two 4x4's and a supply truck into Rico to check out the town. They come back within an hour and Point Man had bad news. "Town's deserted, Boss. There's a lot of smoldering ruins and we counted at least 68 bodies. We didn't get very close though, that town gave me the creeps. Reminded me of...another place" Point Man wandered off, his memory filled with the burning ruins of Somalia and all those dead women and children gunned down by rebel soldiers.

The next day they passed by Ophis and Point Man reported it was much the same as Rico. War was moving through the land, but Ed wanted to know if an organized unit was carrying out this carnage or was anarchy the rule of the land? He thought of the Devils Disciples and wondered if there was something similar out in front of them. Since the outbreak of World War III, civilized rules of conduct had ended abruptly. Everyone seemed to be out to protect number one, either individually or in small armed groups. With this scale of damage and so many dead, Ed suspected militia or an active military unit was conducting a cleansing. He didn't know how far ahead of him they were or how fast they were moving and there was no indication of what their numbers might be. He hoped the survivors, if there were any, in the smaller towns had fled to cities in search of government assistance. After witnessing what happened in Phoenix, however, he doubted they would find any such help.

When they approached Norwood, Point Man glanced at his Geiger-Counter and was startled to see the needle climbing, *'That little needle's movin'!* He slammed on the foot brake and down shifted leaving nearly 60 feet of skid mark on the road surface. His quick actions caught His Misfits by surprise and they had to maneuver quickly to avoid hitting him or each other. "We're hot! This is a hot zone!" Point Man shouted. He waved at them to turn around and head back toward the convoy. Returning to the intersection of Highway 145 and Highway 62, the needle on the Geiger-Counter returned to normal. When the convoy caught up to them, Ed was startled to see Point Man and His Misfits stripped down to underwear and scrubbing each other with rags and water from their canteens.

"What happened?" Ed asked as he climbed out of the ambulance. *Man, these guys are some hairy dudes...* Ed yelled back over his shoulder, "Nancy, get on the CB and tell everyone to stay with their vehicles."

"Sorry, Boss man, I didn't wanna use the CB in case there were too many ears listening." Point Man pointed to the convoy. "We ran smack into a hot zone up north on Highway 145, scared the Hell outta me. Hopin' this spit bath washes the rads off, but you let me know if we start glowing in the dark."

Doc came up and took over the clean-up detail. He put on a thin lead lined apron, which Ed didn't know he had; a mask and lead lined gloves and began issuing orders. The five bikers were quickly led over to the first water tanker, where Joey unrolled a length of two inch hose and commenced to wash them down, while all the women were told to look the other way.

Point Man and his buddies thought Joey was enjoying this a bit too much, but stood for it until Doc ordered their underwear off. They started to protest until Pastor came to support Doc's orders. Several men, trying not to snicker for fear of facing the anger of these giants, held up a wall of blankets to keep the very embarrassed bikers from public view.

Each one of the bikes had to be cleaned like they had never been cleaned before. Every surface was scrubbed down, nearly bringing tears to the biker's eyes as old grease spots and stickers were scrubbed away. A few paint chips drifted to the ground too and then the motorcycles were drained of all fluids and sprayed off again before they were loaded into the back of two trucks. Doc didn't want to take a chance and insisted the bikes couldn't be used for at least 24 hours and only then after a complete check was done with a Geiger counter.

Disgruntled at losing their bikes for a while, Point Man and crew, now in clean clothes and scratching their heavy beards, took over a large six passenger Ford F-350 4x4. Staying on Route 62, he took off ahead of the convoy and drove to Placerville. They found it utterly deserted; picked clean of food and gas. But not burned to the ground like the other communities and there were no dead bodies to be seen.

From Placerville they drove to Ridgeway, where Highway 550 intersected with Route 62 and it, too, was stripped of supplies. But an hour later, Point Man stumbled across a treasure. Lying in a deep ditch, flipped over on its side and nearly full of fuel, was an abandoned 4,000 gallon gasoline tanker truck. The convoy reached them 20 minutes later, and the fuel was transferred into George Washington's gas tanker. Before they pulled away, Ed left a note on the vehicle's dash, "To Whom It May Concern - if payment is required you may contact Pastor James Woodway in Fairbanks, Alaska for reimbursement. Thank you and God bless."

CITY OF RIDGEWAY, POPULATION 457

Point Man suspected their good fortune was bound to run out sooner or later and at Ridgeway, it did. He slowed down to a complete stop; the His Misfits had their weapons ready. Ahead was a huge roadblock which spanned the entire width of the highway and was extremely unusual in its make-up - crushed cars, piled 12 to 14 high. A single lane on the right side allowed access, but it was temporarily closed by a large Bluebird RV. A large party of men at the roadblock was armed with rifles and most were wearing cowboy hats. From the painted signs in front of the roadblock, Point Man realized these people had set themselves up a toll gate. Each sign was painted white and lettered in foot high black block letters, which simply stated- "YOU PAY TO PASS OR GO AWAY".

Not wanting to start any trouble, Point Man decided to wait for Ed and turned off his engine to conserve fuel. One of the Misfits needed to relieve himself, climbed out of the truck, held his arms up so the people at the roadblock saw that he was unarmed and went to the back of the truck.

This was one time Point Man was glad not to be riding his hog, five bikers would have made good shootin' practice for that bunch of rednecks. They would'a shot first an' then identified the bodies. Point Man glared at two of the taller men. Both of the men wore black cowboy hats and carried rifles over their shoulders, *God forgive me, but I still have trouble dealin' with rednecks!*

Once the convoy caught sight of the roadblock, Ed ordered all vehicles to stop. He wanted to keep the vehicles back at least a half mile in the event shooting started. A moment later, Ed, Point Man and Pastor approached the roadblock unarmed and on foot. Point Man was carrying a white handkerchief tied to a long branch to show they were peaceful. The two men Point Man had studied, both holding Ruger 30.06 caliber Model M-77 bolt action rifles, stepped out and stopped a few feet away. Ed introduced himself and the others. The two men appeared to relax somewhat when they heard Pastor's name and title, and saw he was holding a Bible.

"Gentlemen, we have women and children with us and we're just passing through on our way north. We picked up a high radiation reading near Norwood and were forced to detour this way. Will you please let us through?" Ed asked.

The taller of the two men replied, "We got 457 people here in Ridgeway, Mr. Sawyer, everyone else is either gone north or dead. So we operate this toll gate to help us survive." The man cradled his rifle, the barrel pointed down now and it helped Point Man relax.

"Things have been mighty thin lately; you're the first traffic we've had in three days." The man whispered something to his friend, who nodded his head in agreement and then the first man spoke up, "Sure, we'll let you pass but you gotta pay our toll."

"How much is your toll?" Pastor asked in an even tone, he understood the reality of simple survival.

"We can see you've got a tanker truck, so we want 1,000 gallons of gasoline and 200 gallons of diesel, if you have it. We also want one quarter of your canned goods and meat, and 1,000 rounds of ammo. Mostly we need 30-30, 30.6 and 7 mm, and some .45 ammo too."

"Hefty toll," Ed replied. "But we have no choice." He glanced at Pastor and then Point Man before he made his decision, "I'll give you the gas, but no diesel...we're low on that. In exchange, we'll throw in an extra 20 cases of assorted canned goods and 25 pounds of dried meat and 250 rounds of assorted ammo. That's the best I can do, or we turn around an' find another route."

The two men looked at each other and then the taller one said to Ed, "Wait a moment here, we gotta talk with some of the others."

"Ed, you think they'll fight?" Point Man asked, as they waited.

"I don't think so," Ed replied. "They don't look that hard, mostly family men trying to survive this madness."

After a few moments of talking in raised and heated voices, the taller man returned and offered his hand, "You got yourself a deal, Mr. Sawyer. Welcome to Ridgeway."

"Thank you." Ed shook hands; Point Man and Pastor Woodway responded in kind.

As soon as the fuel was transferred and supplies unloaded, Pastor Woodway was happy to conduct an evening service in a nearby church. The Ridgeway clergy were all gone, having taken their flocks north in hopes of finding safety; most of the people left wanted to hear the Lord's Word spoken again by an ordained preacher. Pastor gratefully accepted the invitation and even performed a marriage as the convoy members spent a relaxed 19 hours in Ridgeway.

The next evening, the convoy set up the big circus tent near Malta, Colorado and the following day, they jumped to Highway 91. From there, it was Highway 70 and on to Highway 9, where the community of Kremming, Colorado lay. The town wasn't deserted, but no one came out to greet them or attempt to throw them out. Several shadows were seen darting about inside buildings and on Pastor's advice, camp was set up several miles north of town on the chance some of the townspeople changed their mind and became inhospitable.

Next day, they used Highway 40, until they switched to Route 14, which joined with Highway 125. One highway looked like another as they drove through Colorado, but it was the darkened sky to the north that concerned everyone. The father north they drove, the worse the sky appeared until they found themselves underneath dark gray clouds of volcanic ash and the occasional spot of new winter snow.

Up to now, the Colorado landscape had been free of winter snow and ice. Some members of the convoy feared this weather condition was due to the heat released by nuclear weapons, but the Geiger Counter wasn't ticking and Ed's standard reply to these rumors was, "Road's dry ain't it? I'll leave the rest to the Big Man upstairs."

WYOMING

On April 3rd, the convoy crossed the Wyoming border at 9:43 p.m. and ran into a dark gray wall of heavy snow. Everyone was ordered to either put on masks or wear bandanas across their faces while the convoy moved through the falling ash/snow mixture. What concerned Ed was the air filters on most of the vehicles, he was worried the falling ash would clog them rendering them useless and sure enough, during the hard drive through Southern Wyoming they lost two pick-up trucks.

Retired silk stockings were used to cover the air filters and these needed to be changed often. With deeper snow/ash, the heavy wrecker was placed out front to make a passable roadway. Point Man's truck stayed on the road, but wasn't nearly wide enough for the large vehicles to use. Within a day, the Great Alaskan Wagon Train was now down to 22 vehicles and they had nearly 3,000 miles of deep snow and falling ash to contend with. Ed estimated the depth of the snow to be approximately 9 inches and it was still falling when they made camp beside the Platte River that night.

Tensions were high; no one wanted to have a snow ball fight with the blackened snow and now all the stars were hidden as the volcanic clouds covered the sky completely. Several people squabbled over the dwindling supplies and one man was stirring things up with talk of mutiny. Eli T. Bain was a mid-sized heavy set man with a full beard of grayish brown hair and heavy black colored glasses. He wore a fur lined brown leather vest over a dark blue flannel shirt with sleeves rolled up to reveal his muscular forearms. His blue jeans were new, but his logger style work boots were scuffed from years of use. White snow goggles and face mask hung around his neck and he was sitting on the end of wooden bench while he addressed a large group of people, "Folks, I talked with some of those men in Ridgeway and they heard it on the radio… Alaska's under attack. By the time we get there, the place will be overrun with slant-eyes from China." Eli Bains was an uneducated man who had sold used mining equipment in the southern part of Phoenix and was well known for his intolerance of anyone not in agreement with him on just about any issue. A new member to the church and unmarried, he had a salesmen's voice that could come out smooth as silk until riled.

Recognizing the kind of man Steve Agar was, Eli had hoped to use him as an ally, but Steve had jumped the gun and was now lying dead in a hotel room in Albuquerque, New Mexico. Even without Steve, Eli made sure he was backed up when it came time to make his play. He had convinced six other men to stand with him and they were behind Eli, rifles slung over shoulders as he made his case, "We go up there an' we'll be either taken prisoner or killed right out and I just don't see no reason to make that long drive when we could make a home back there in Ridgeway." He glanced about the crowd and focused on the family men, "We passed a lot of deserted towns along the way, some of them untouched, and I say we move into one if you don't cotton to Ridgeway...Wait an' see what happens to this here United States, it'll come back." Eli pointed outside the tent to the falling snow, "Why risk getting bogged down, freezing to death in some God forsaken piece of nowhere. No, I say we stay here in the good ol' USA." He pounded his fist on a tabletop. "We're a democracy, so let's put it to a vote... Split up if need be."

Walking through the crowd, Ed tossed Point Man and Joey a slight nod of his head before he approached Eli. He waited for a pause in the man's speech and then stepped out from behind Larry O' Brian to address Eli "You've got 'em listening, Bains. Frightening people usually works, gets them to think and wonder." Ed looked over the crowd of people and then gave Eli a hard look, "Now how about explaining to these people how you'll survive the radiation? By summer, the whole United States will be covered with radioactive fallout and everyone who stays here will be DEAD!"

"How duh yuh know the radiation will get us. Mr. Ed Sawyer? You're no scientist, you don' know that fer sure. But we know the slant-eyes are in

233

Alaska. That's fer sure. Then there's the Canuks…they got the border closed. How yuh gonna get past the Canadian Army…you tell me?" Bains looked around the group, nodding and hoping to see some glimmer of support. But what he saw were people beginning to step back. Most realized that taking on Old Man winter would be rough, and facing the Chinese doubtful at least, but it was a no win situation with radioactive fallout. Besides, these were men and women of faith and they knew the Good Lord wasn't taking them north just to die an unpleasant death.

"Bains, you're an idiot!" George Washington Sr. said before walking off to check his rig.

Several men stepped forward with Joey, each with a rifle at the ready while Point Man and His Misfits came up behind Eli's men and requested weapons be handed over for safe keeping. They did so without a problem. Ed stepped forward and before Eli could react, quickly removed a revolver from the man's belt holster, "Mr. Bains, you made an agreement with this group to follow Pastor Woodway to Alaska. I remember when you signed on with a lot of 'Amen's' and 'Praise God!' coming from your mouth. Now you take it upon yourself to bust this group up without even coming to Pastor or me with your concerns before riling these people up." Ed handed Bain's gun to Larry O'Brian. "You want to leave, that's fine with me. Take your personal possessions and I'll have Point Man take you to one of those deserted towns you spoke of."

Bains' eyes grew wide as his face flushed a crimson red, "Look here, Sawyer, I put food in that trailer and that water trailer belongs ta me too. What about that?"

"Water trailer stays; you donated it to the convoy." Ed glanced around. Most of the people were gone now. "I'll make sure you have food and water, enough for 2 weeks." Ed turned to look at the other men; Eli's six supporters, "Anyone of you want to go with him, I'll give you each 2 weeks provision too. Just remember you all made an agreement before we began and I took you at your word. But Mr. Eli Bains is right, we still live in a democracy and you are free to leave. The choice is yours to make. But make it right now."

One after another, the men shook their heads and slowly backed away to follow the others who believed they had something else to do at the moment.

"You can't do this to me, Sawyer!" Eli yelled. "I got rights! I'm an American citizen an' yuh can't treat me this way. One way or 'nother, Sawyer, I'll get you for this."

"I'm sorry you feel that way, Mr. Bains." Ed summoned Point Man forward with a gesture of his hand, "Mr. Bains, you have one more chance. Stay a part of this body and behave or leave… now!"

"I know mah rights! You think you'self some kinda king, a dictator. No…sooner or later I'm gonna find some law an' I'll charge you with…with stealin' an' …with kidnapping." Eli Bains was so upset at this point, he was spitting out his words. Joey and Point Man knew it was only Ed's size that kept Eli from attacking him.

"You give me no other choice." Ed lowered his head and kicked a stick into the fire. "Eli, you speak of rights, but we no longer have the rights provided by our US Constitution or the Bill of Rights. The United States Government ceased to exist as a lawful body an' those rights you so readily speak of, vanished with the first missile impact. What rights you now have come from being a member of this group." Ed glanced at Point Man and then to Eli Bains, "But your own statements put this convoy at risk." Ed looked back to Point Man, "Escort Mr. Bains to the nearest town and leave him with an unloaded rifle, a box of ammo and two weeks supply of food, and water."

Eli Bains, trembling with anger, was speechless. Turning his back, Ed walked away as two Misfits grabbed Eli by the arms. He resisted, crying out for help and when no one came, shouted obscenities and cursed Pastor and Ed Sawyer for all to hear.

Ed thought it strange that Pastor seemed to be absent and later located him alone, standing over a small cook fire, a cup of hot coffee in his hands. "Where were you? You must've heard what transpired after dinner with all of Bains' shouting, but I didn't see you." Ed was not so much angry as he was confused.

"Ed, you are in charge of this group in areas of logistics, defense and all matter of other duties, one of which is discipline. For the last couple of nights, I've been hearing rumors of Mr. Bains desire to split the group, but I also knew this was a matter you would have to handle to maintain a proper balance in our leadership. I handle the spiritual side, you will handle the material side and this is the way it must be."

Ed looked down into the fire as he thought that over and then replied, "Okay, but…well, did I do right when I had Bains escorted from camp?"

"You did what you felt was best for the group as a whole. Bains was causing dissension and we both saw enough of that back in Phoenix. He had an agenda and you stopped him from hurting the flock."

"What do you think will happen to him, Pastor?"

"That is not in our hands, Ed. He made his choice and must carry the weight of that choice around his own neck."

"You're beginning to sound all King James again."

"Sorry, my friend, I've spent the last hour deep in prayer with the Lord. It happens to me." Pastor placed another piece of wood into the fire. "I'm going to bed, good night."

"Good night, Pastor." Ed watched him walk toward his tent and wondered how Bains would fare.

A TOWN OF DARKNESS

An hour and ten minutes later, Point Man and two Misfits dropped a very angry Eli Bains at the center intersection of a small darkened roadside town. They removed the handcuffs Joey had loaned them and left him with food, water and an unloaded rifle.

"Ammo's in the bag with the food, make it last. Now you could waste a round shooting at us as we leave, but you might not want to do that," Point Man said in a threatening tone as he began to back away.

"This is what you wanted, Bains, now it's all yours...you could even run for mayor," One of the Misfits said.

The other pointed to the abandoned buildings around them, "You can rule it the way you see fit."

Power was off, but snow would provide water and the empty buildings would provide an ample supply of tinder for a fire. The two Misfits and Point Man climbed into the truck and slowly pulled away, watching the hate on Bains' face.

Shoulders slumped in despair, Bains' hate gave way to fear as the truck vanished from view and he looked around at the darkened buildings. Alone, more alone than he'd ever been before, Eli Bains' heart skipped a beat and began thudding hard when the surrounding silence was suddenly broken by the sound of laughter. In the distance, the laughter sounded maniacal and as it came closer, others joined. Bains was frightened, but remembered what Point Man had said about ammo for the rifle. Dropping to the ground, he fumbled with the food bag and spilled the box of 30-06 bullets out on the pavement. Pulling one bullet out he attempted to load his rifle, but his hands trembled and he dropped the bullet; it bounced off his boot and rolled into the darkness. From behind him, came a low sinister chuckle, followed by an eerie cackling and as he fumbled with another bullet the air was split with a high shrieking voice that sounded like a wounded animal. His body shook in fear; his hands trembled so badly he could barely hold his rifle and nearly dropped it. He looked up to see several shadowy forms moving toward him. Rushing to load his rifle, he clumsily jammed a bullet in the wrong way and it slid off the side of the weapon. As it vanished at his feet, he wished he had remembered a flashlight; right now he would even beg for one from Mr. Ed Sawyer, but in his anger he had completely forgotten it. The dark figures drew closer; insane laughter driving him to panic. He dropped to the snowy ground, scrambling madly for another bullet. With his bare hands he clawed at the snow searching for the box and finally felt a third bullet. With freezing hands, he quickly rammed the copper colored round into his rifle before slamming the bolt forward. But Mr. Eli Bains was too late. Two sets of withered hands shot out from the darkness and violently jerked the rifle from his trembling grasp. Dark, ghastly wraiths, driven to desperation by starvation to acts of inhumanity, drug him to the ground to smother his screams.

Driving north with the truck's four headlights illuminating the snow covered roadway, Point Man and his two friends, listening to a Jazz CD, never heard Mr. Bains' pleas for help. They couldn't hear the strangled screams as bony hands closed around his throat and they would never know that the town's remaining residents were busy making Eli Bains feel quite welcome. For tonight, he had become the guest of honor for dinner.

A COMING STORM

9 - SPIES, GENERALS AND WE'RE HOMEWARD BOUND

"But do not forget this one thing, dear friends: with the Lord a day is like a thousand years, and a thousand years are like a day. The Lord is not slow in keeping His promise, as some understand slowness. He is patient with you, not wanting anyone to perish, but everyone to come to repentance.

2 Peter 3:8

IN JERUSALEM

Satellites had been rendered useless either by orbiting clouds of radiation or newly acquired high-tech anti-satellite warfare, and as a result, most of the world was unaware of the Biblical prophecies unfolding in Israel. For the last 1220 days, two unnamed men of towering stature had held an endless audience in Jerusalem. For days without end, they had prayed, prophesied to the masses and healed the sick, while staring down the enemy forces. Thousands of people had come great distances to witness these two beings' mighty spiritual ministry.

Muslim fanatics attempted to stop them - first with gunfire and, finally, with suicide bombers; all failed. The men were protected by an invisible barrier; a strange radiant obstacle which no bomb of bullet had been able to penetrate. In bright sparkling colors, the barrier, a mighty act of God, was seen as more undeniable evidence of His existence. Strangely, the omniscient presence guarding the two was visible only to those who had come with deep and genuine faith to witness God's glory. The Children of God, deeply anchored in faith were the only people able to see the great white warrior angels guarding the two Chosen Ones. Christians began sending word to outlying communities, spreading the news that the men were truly the Witnesses foretold in the Book of Revelations and that their 1240 day service, was about to end.

OUTSIDE CALGARY, ALBERTA, CANADA - APRIL 3rd

Captain Wayne Roberts commanded the dogs to halt and dropped the sled's braking hook. The grueling trip, which had lasted 47 hours and 19 minutes, was behind them. The fear of breaking through ice covered streams, the struggle of helping the dogs haul the sled through mountainous terrain, the constant barrage of chunks of ice thrown up by the feet of the sled dogs, the stinging of flesh slapped by low hanging branches, the bitter cold and biting wind – it was behind them. They were outside Calgary and badly in need of rest.

His whole body one big painful muscle, Major Jeb Stewart carefully poured himself out of the sled and knelt for a moment, the desire for retribution written on his face as he glared at the wagging tongues of the nearest dogs. "Only the fact that I know this trip is important to the survival of Alaska, prevents me from shooting you foul beasts… and then enjoying the sheer thrill of roasting your skinny remains over a fire and devouring every morsel with pure joy!" He cringed as his spine cracked when he cautiously stretched to his full height, stopping in mid-stretch as his body complained and looked at Wayne, "My legs are numb from the hips down and my face feels like it's been blasted with birdshot." A thousand sharp needles stabbed him from his neck to the bottom of his feet as blood circulation returned to cramped muscles. With each minute that passed, the pain lessoned and he was able to move without gritting his teeth.

Though burnable wood was scarce, Jeb managed to gather enough to get a small fire going to cook the last of the dog food. Wayne looked over the trapper's map with a small flashlight. "If I'm reading this right, this trail parallels Highway 93 right into Calgary and I estimate we have about 9, maybe 10; miles left to go. Of course this gentleman's handwriting isn't the best and we could be headed for his favorite booze-barn."

"Sounds great to me, Captain, I wouldn't mind a drink right now. I'm sure you've read it right and Calgary isn't too far away and I got to admit, I am looking forward to a hot meal and a warm bed."

Wayne folded the map and shook his head as he shot a raised eyebrow in Jeb's direction, "Think again, Major, we'll probably end up getting water boarded for torture to see what secrets we carry in our heads, then afterward, if we're still alive, thrown into an icy cold jailhouse with nothing to look forward to except a morning firing squad to welcome the new day." Wayne began feeding the dogs, while Jeb considered the thought of being tortured. After a moment of deep thought, Jeb shrugged his shoulders and nodded, as he conceded to the possibility of death. Knowing there was nothing he could do about it now, he slapped his left leg as if to say, Oh well and went about changing the dog's booties - except for the lead dog. After being bitten twice, he left the old devil eyed half malamute/half McKenzie River husky for Wayne to deal with. Looking at the lead dog, Jeb estimated the brute's weight at 140 lbs., which was highly unusual for a sled dog. But he had to admit the dog was the most intelligent of the group and did a pretty good job leading them on the trail, not that he wouldn't mind using a strong stick on the canine's head.

"We'll let them rest for an hour while we finish off the rest of our grub an' warm our feet." Wayne smiled as Jeb avoided going near the lead dog. "I don't know why he doesn't like you, Major."

"Maybe he can read my mind," Jeb answered, as he glared at the beast.

Back on the trail, the dogs seemed to sense the trip was drawing to a close and rushed into a quick stride. With tongues hanging and tails wagging, they headed east and poor Jeb was bounced about like he was on Disneyland's Space Mountain without the safety bar to hold him in. Wayne wasn't having it much easier running behind the sled to help push it up the hillsides and then struggling to keep a hold of the runaway sled for the quick downhill sprints.

Reaching the top of a high treeless ridge, Wayne brought the sled to a halt in deep snow and with a sigh of relief, gazed down on the bright lights of Calgary. If it hadn't been for the use by other dog teams and the occasional snow machine on this trail, their journey would have proved impassable. Even sled dogs have an impossible time traversing 4 to 5 foot deep snow, but the path was reduced to a mere six to eight inches with recent traffic. Thankfully, they had not encountered anyone along the way.

"Well Miss Dorothy, it does look like we've finally reached the Emerald City of Oz," Jeb said. He was greatly relieved to know this insane trip was finally at an end and ignored the disgruntled glare in Wayne's eyes for being referred to as Miss Dorothy.

"And you know what you can do with your little dog Toto, Major," Wayne added in response. He left off the reference on where the major could put Toto, out of respect for his rank.

"Touché!" Jeb replied, with a smile on his face. He was feeling good for the first time in several days. He pulled his frosty black Balaclava and goggles down from his unshaven face to wipe the weariness and a handful of dirty ice off the front of him.

Wayne stood beside the sled and gazed down on the city. The great expanse of lights had surprised him. Even though a thick layer of patchy ice fog hung over the city, like a moth eaten blanket, bits of illuminated buildings popped up here and there like a thousand small islands.

"I remember watching the Winter Olympics on TV when they were held here. I was only a kid, but I dreamed of the day I could represent the United States and win a gold medal," Wayne said.

"I know, you could've entered the dog sledding event," Jeb said sarcastically.

"You can joke, Major, but have you any idea how we're going to carry out the rest of this mission. My assignment was to get us here, now it's your turn to make the decisions."

Jeb pondered that for a moment and then replied, "First, we release the dogs. As much as I dislike these beasts, I wouldn't want to see them end up on somebody's dinner plate. Food's getting scarce and in some countries, dog is considered a delicacy." He pointed to the lead dog, "But him, you can shoot."

Wayne smiled and went back to the sled to begin releasing the dogs. When all of the dogs were unharnessed, the remaining dog food was poured out to be left for them and the sled was pushed beneath the branches of a huge spruce tree. Jeb turned to Wayne, "We'll have to leave our weapons here too, Wayne. I suspect it's better to go in unarmed and not risk being shot by a trigger happy sentry." Jeb explained that the quickest way to see the General was to turn themselves over to the Canadian Army.

"What about our uniforms?" Wayne asked as he watched the dogs, happy to be loose, ran around them like small children. Wayne and Jeb had no choice but to chase them off with threats of mayhem and a few well-placed snowballs. The message got through and the canines gobbled up the food and disappeared over a far hill.

"Wayne, we've got no choice… I'm not about to walk through Calgary in my underwear and we'd freeze to death without them. I'd rather be shot as a spy then look like an idiotic simpleton…We'd never see the General that way." They stashed their firearms near the sled, hoping to return for them. Then, with packs slung over their shoulders and snowshoes on their feet, they trudged through deep snow and made their way towards the outer perimeter of Calgary.

Ahead of them was a gradual sloping treeless hillside of some 200 yards or better, a perfect ski hill in Wayne's opinion and at the bottom lay a long row of sentry posts. Illuminated security points were positioned 100 yards apart with 10 feet high triple strand concertina barbed wire strung between them. Light poles every 20 yards gave sentries enough illumination to see any intruders coming within 150 yards of the perimeter.

"Looks like they've enclosed the entire city in wire," Jeb said. "I can't even see a main gate."

"Let's aim for that nearest sentry post, I'm cold and even a prisoner deserves to be warm," Wayne said as he headed down the hillside in hopes some half asleep sentry didn't start taking potshots at them before they could get close enough to speak.

PERIMETER SECURITY POST #38, EARLY MORNING HOURS - APRIL 3rd

As of midnight, Corporal Scott Wellington figured he had served with the elite Canadian Army Military Police for exactly 3 years, 4 months and 18 days. All of which time he had been puzzled why the Canadian Army always referred to the MP's as being elite. Because during that time, he had worked only guard duty at one stationary post or another around Calgary's perimeter and saw nothing elite about it. He thought about his lack of sleep and struggled to stay awake every night. No matter how much sleep he got during the day, each night was a fight, simply because nothing ever happened out here in this desolate section in Calgary's backyard. The minutes passed ever so slowly; he was not allowed to read anything but his post's General Orders, or to listen to Calgary's only radio station. No, he was to spend every moment observing the area around his post. There were times his eyelids began to weigh more than his rifle and on several occasions he had gone outside to pick up a chunk of snow to rub his face in order to keep awake.

Wellington had high hopes of reaching the rank of sergeant before his 4 year anniversary. Then he could be one of the privileged, able to ride in a warm patrol car and leave these guard posts to the lowly corporals and privates. More than once he had seen one of the sergeants riding in the patrol car dozing and he so wished it was him getting away with it, instead of that over-weight, foul mouthed Sgt. Joe C. Webster. Wellington thought Sgt. Webster looked like a dwarf from the Hobbit books, not that he would ever say such a thing out loud and land himself in the regimental kitchen on permanent KP. He knew those clowns were pulling 18 hour shifts and the little gate shack of his was far better duty than that.

Post #38 happened to be on a section of perimeter that was farthest from the center of the city. This was a cold boring site and sadly, one of the last on the list to be relieved for guard change in the morning. The guard shack; made of plywood, with double-paned windows all around and a metal roof now holding up over 4 feet of snow was not insulated. Measuring with his size 12 EE boots, he estimated the shack to be 8 feet wide and 10 feet long. Furnishings were limited to a 3 foot tall metal stool and portable floor heater and a single burner hot plate on top of which was a small dented blue enamel coffee pot, a Christmas gift from his parent's two years ago.

He'd used the same grounds three times this night, but it was hot and kept his stomach warm when the outside temperatures were -30 and below. When the winds came up, temperatures dropped rapidly and he had already seen wind chills lower than -70. The only good benefit to the winds was that it made the ice fog patchy and occasionally completely blew it away which enabled him to see parts of the city. Not that he could see the stars or the moon anymore, the night sky was one big blanket of black, but when the fog lifted he could see the limits of his post under the bright security lights and this included the hillside above him.

He dug uncontaminated snow from layers deep beneath the black ash outside the shack, melted it on the single burner and boiled it in his coffee pot before he poured in three tablespoons of wet, dark mushy grounds. Wellington was about to fill his mug one more time, when he glanced up to see two figures coming out of a wall of ice fog under the outside lights. Having never seen anyone walk down from this particular hillside before, the area being off limits; Wellington rubbed his eyes to make sure they were real. *People!* Startled by their sudden appearance, he hurriedly unplugged his hot plate, simply an act of nervousness and grabbed his rifle; a British Enfield bolt-action relic. First making sure he had a round chambered, he cautiously walked out to meet the two strangers.

Because of the perimeter's pole lighting, which stood 18 feet above ground and two security lights mounted on the shack, the shadows behind the strangers were the size of giants, which only added to Wellington's jitters. When they were close enough for him to recognize as Army officers, he straightened up.

"Stand to be recognized!" Wellington hollered as he brought his rifle up waist high and pointed his bayonet tipped weapon at them. Though he had practiced the challenge numerous times in training or during exercises, this was the first time he had ever used it in real life and as a result his voice came out a bit squeaky and he repeated his challenge a second time after clearing his throat. His challenge quickly got the attention of the two guard posts 100 yards on each side of him and a moment later, two other MPs were running over to give a hand - anything to break the monotony of a long boring night.

"Your papers please, Gentlemen," Wellington said. He kept his rifle at the ready, level at the officer's waistline. *What are they doing out here? Is this another exercise to ensure we're on our toes?*

"Corporal, please inform your superior..."Jeb glanced at Wayne before continuing, "...inform your officer in charge, that you are detaining two Alaska Defense Force officers...men who have shown up at your post wearing Canadian uniforms." Then added, "But please advise your officer that we are not spies."

Puzzled, Wellington again asked for their identification. Dealing with officers always left him on the cautious side and he still wasn't sure if this was some crazy exercise. By this time, the other two guards had arrived and stationed themselves behind Jeb and Wayne, with their rifles, also with World War II style bayonets, leveled at their backs.

"Corporal, I really hate to be rude, especially since I am an unwanted guest in your country and it's so very cold out here, but I must insist you contact your superior. This is extremely important! I need to speak with an officer immediately." Jeb let out a deep sigh and shook his head when he saw the look of confusion on Wellington's face. "All right, we're spies, okay, and you caught us! Now please give your ...sergeant of the guard...whatever you call him, a call and report this. You have no idea how important this is."

Not sure what he'd gotten himself into, Wellington gave Jeb and Wayne a good looking over and glanced at his buddies, "I really hope this isn't an exercise, Sir, or someone's idea of a prank?" Wellington asked.

"No!" Wayne exclaimed. "And who'd pull a prank in this weather?"

"You're a hero, Corporal. You and these men have caught two foreign spies; they'll make you a sergeant at least. Now please give your CP a call and inform them...Please!" Jeb was getting impatient, but he also took notice of how close the tip of that bayonet was to his chest.

Finally, Wellington made his decision, "Yes, Sir." He left the other two MPs guarding Jeb and Wayne, while he went into his guard shack and picked up the telephone. The ground line ran directly to Security Command and no dialing was necessary.

"Report," a grumbled voice said from the other end.

"Sergeant, this is Corporal Wellington at Post #38, Section Foxtrot-One. I'm detaining two army officers in uniform at my post. They showed up here on foot a couple minutes ago, coming down from the hillside above my post. Both appear to be unarmed and sober, but they've advised me they're Alaska Defense Force officers and demand to speak with an officer." Wellington listened to the sergeant for a moment and then replied. "Yes, Sergeant, they're sober and on foot, no others with them and they simply demanded to see an officer." Wellington leaned through the doorway and studied Jeb for a moment. *Looks like a nice enough chap, quite polite, but the other one looks like he could break me in two without giving it much thought.* "No, Sergeant, I haven't been drinking any hooch. Private Lupac and PFC Gordon are holding the two men under arms, while we speak. Right, I know what you're thinkin', sergeant... last week we had guards reporting UFOs buzzing their guard shacks." That prank spread like wildfire and before long, dozens of guards were reporting little green men running through the perimeter wire. The next night's coffee ration was taken away for that little joke. Hanging up, Wellington walked back out to Jeb, "Sir, I was told an officer is en route."

"Thank you, Corporal. Do you suppose we could wait inside your shack, my nose is about to fall off," Jeb pulled his balaclava down and smiled, which caused Wellington to grin back in response.

"Yes, sir. Might be a bit crowded though and I'll need to search you." *He may be an Alaskan officer, but an officer is an officer an' you'd better sir 'em or hear the worst otherwise.*

It was over 30 minutes later before a Canadian Army armored personnel carrier showed up, the wide treads cutting through the snow and its big diesel engine bellowing out a plume of dark smoke into the frigid air. Corporal Wellington had everyone step outside, mostly because there wasn't enough room for everyone inside with the arrival of the others.

While the vehicle idled, demonstrating a need for engine work as it spat and lugged now and then, 1st Lieutenant Archibald Bitney carefully climbed out of the heavily-armored front passenger door and stood on the ground for a moment, while he adjusted his coat and pistol belt, and then placed a rabbit fur cap on his head. Only then did he come forward with a distinctly perturbed look on his face for having to come out in the icy cold. He was immediately under escort by three rather large Military Policemen; each in a thickly insulated one-piece dark green hooded snowsuit and armed with an Uzi 9mm machineguns.

Wellington stared at the Uzi Machineguns. *Sure, his personal guard gets to carry those and we're out here with these museum pieces.* His thoughts of displeasure shattered when Lt. Bitney approached 5 inches from his face and burst out, "Explain yourself, Corporal. I do not like having to come out here on such a pitiful cold night. For your sake, this had better be important." He shot a beady eye to first Jeb, who was wearing the Canadian Army winter issue captain's uniform and Wayne in the 1st lieutenant's uniform. Seeing that they appeared sober Lt. Bitney put his left hand up for Wellington to wait and then hustled everyone inside the crowded shack with a wave of his right hand. He also ordered two of his MPs to remain outside on guard.

Inside, Lt. Bitney shot a curious stare at Jeb and then ordered Wellington to make his report, but before Wellington can reply, Jeb stepped forward, "Lieutenant, before you berate Corporal Wellington any further for doing his job, I might add in a commendable fashion...."

"Identification!" Bitney demanded, cutting Jeb off.

Neither officer complied with the order. Mainly, because they didn't think too highly of this upstart and both men were simply too weary to put up with his arrogance. "As I was saying, Lieutenant," Jeb's voice went from calm to a commanding tone, which caused Lt. Bitney to take a step back, " ...your Corporal here has done a fine job, he has our ID in hand and has searched us for any contraband or weapons. To which we had neither." Lt. Bitney, his well-practiced icy glare having returned, was about to interrupt when Jeb stepped closer to him. With his right hand up, palm facing Lt. Bitney, Jeb said, "Lieutenant, I have been riding in a dog sled for two days across some of the most unpleasant and treacherous ground I've ever been forced to see through the back end of a pack of dogs. So please, if you do not mind, keep your mouth closed until I have finished speaking."

Bitney was shocked into silence and a couple of his enlisted men had to bite tongues to keep from laughing. Considered a jerk by the men under him and known to be one of those officers who harassed lower ranking enlisted men, Lt. Bitney was also known for his arrogance and was currently under investigation for reports of sexual harassment of enlisted women.

"Lieutenant, we're here to contact General Howard-Wright on an extremely important and urgent matter, one in which..."

"The General?" Lt. Bitney looked as if he was seeing Jeb and Wayne for the first time, "Just who in the heck are you two?"

"As I've tried to explain, Lieutenant, my Alaska Defense Force ID in Corporal Wellington's hand identifies me as Major Stewart and this gentleman standing beside me is Captain Roberts. We are staff officers in the Alaska Defense Force and have come here to speak with General Howard -Wright on an important matter and time is of the essence."

Lt. Bitney's hand rested on the butt of his personal Beretta 9 mm semi-automatic pistol, and his face reflected contempt for Jeb and Wayne. Jeb reached under his shirt very slowly, to insure Lt. Bitney didn't suspect him of going for a weapon as he pulled out his ADF dog tags. He held the tags up and jingled them in front of the lieutenant, which caused Lt. Bitney's jaw to drop, his eyes to bulge and his Beretta to suddenly appear in his right hand, "You're both under arrest!"

"Yes, we know that, Lieutenant. Corporal Wellington has already advised us of this fact and he should receive full credit for having taken us into custody," Wayne replied. He had taken a liking to the young guard, especially after he had offered sharing his pitiful supply of coffee. Wayne felt sorry for these enlisted men, seeing how incompetent Lt. Bitney was as an officer.

Orders were issued and both Jeb and Wayne were handcuffed with hands behind their backs, loaded into the back of Lt. Bitney's vehicle and transported to Security Command. When the vehicle vanished into the darkness, Corporal Wellington returned to his duties. With so many people going in and out of his shack, he struggled to get the room warm again and sipped a cup of weak coffee while he logged the events in his notebook. Every few minutes or so, he glanced up the hill, wondering what or who else might come down his way.

Security ordered a Canadian Air Force Blackhawk helicopter up to ascertain if there were other ADF troops in the area, but they found no sign of additional personnel. However, the co-pilot did report the infrared scopes had picked up a pack of either dogs or wolves running through the hills in that general area.

OFFICE OF CANADIAN ARMY INTELLIGENCE- CALGARY

Captain Upton York, on duty Intelligence Officer from Montreal, was on the 16th hour of an 18 hour shift and nearly bleary eyed when he picked the phone up. He had already violated General Orders by falling asleep at his desk and was none too happy to wake up to the desk phone ringing. He sat back up in his high-backed leather chair, brushed his thick brown hair back with a sweep of his right hand and worked a kink out of his neck with a quick head jerk before he spoke into the phone, "Captain York speaking, how may I be of service?"

Lt. Bitney identified himself and spent the next few moments attempting to make himself sound good as he informed Captain York of the events that had transpired at Post #38, then waited for Captain York's instructions.

"Lieutenant, transport your two prisoners to the Command Post. I'll meet you there in about 30 minutes." York hung up and rubbed his eyes. A severe headache caused by too much work, too little sleep and extremely bright overhead office lights forced him to seek relief with the aid of three aspirin tablets. He pushed himself back from the desk, stood up and pulled on his thickly padded gray arctic officer's coat. Quickly, he checked his appearance in a ¾ length narrow mirror attached to the back of his office door, and satisfied, went out the door.

Surprisingly and probably due to his weariness, Captain York was halfway down the hall before he realized exactly what Lt. Bitney had said over the phone - two ADF officers were here to see the General and carrying an important message from General Saunders...*Wake-up, York, this could be important enough to get a day job, maybe a possible promotion to the General's staff and some decent chow!*

By 0740 hours, Jeb and Wayne were both feeling the effects of too little sleep and the warmth of the Command Post was not helping any. There were repeated questions in a dark windowless interrogation room with a solitary light overhead. They were questioned twice together and then separately three times by Captain York and another unnamed female Intel Officer. Against Jeb's advice, Captain York had ignored the "EYES ONLY" stamped on the document pouch and reviewed the documents intended only for General Howard-Wright.

By 0930 hours, both ADF officers had been fed a hot meal of lumpy oatmeal and powered eggs, and then transported to Canadian Army Headquarters with an escort of six MPs in a warm 15 passenger van. Captain York carried the pouch addressed to the General with an arrogant smirk on his face as if he expected a big reward for these prize prisoners. He didn't believe a word of what was written in the documents and remained convinced these two men were assassins from either Quebec or possibly even England who entertained hopes of killing their top general. At this point, both Jeb and Wayne could have cared less what Captain York thought and they would have taken great pleasure in knocking his block off.

Inside the building and still under heavy guard, Jeb and Wayne were handcuffed to a metal and plastic cushioned couch, with the MPs under strict orders to keep a close eye on them or face assignment in the Northwest Territory.

They listened through closed door as an apparent higher ranking officer quickly dislodged the smirk from York's face with a loud tongue lashing. For nearly ten minutes, York was turned inside out, accused of acts bordering on treasonous conduct and simple acts of plain stupidity unbecoming of an officer. When Captain York came out, his head bowed, Jeb thought he resembled a boy who had just seen the vice principal after getting caught for something despicable, and receiving two hard swats to the backside. Jeb's dad had received such a painful and embarrassing fate in his early school days and had reminded his son of it on several occasions.

Captain York walked by Jeb and Wayne without saying a word or even looking at them before he exited the room. Shortly afterward, an attractive female Major in a green uniform dress appeared at the door that Captain York had walked out of and ordered the MPs to remove the handcuffs. Relieved, the two men rubbed their wrists thanking the major.

"This way, gentlemen," the major said. Her black hair was extremely short, but it was her very large green eyes that caught Jeb's attention. She stood 5'6", weighed 115 lbs., with a narrow waist and very nice legs beneath a knee length skirt. Jeb decided he would like to get to know this major better and with his best wolf smile, passed by her into the next office. But his smile turned to one of surprise when he saw who was waiting for them; they both snapped to attention and rendered crisp salutes to a very stern looking General Howard-Wright. The Old soldier seemed to be scrutinizing them from head to toe with a slightly distrustful look in his aged eyes. He didn't return their salute, not yet anyway, as he stood behind a rather large black metal desk and studied the two officers standing at attention before him. His wide shouldered, 160 lb. frame reached a height of 5'9". He was nearly bald, but what was left of his red hair was turning gray which gave the 73 year old General a distinguished look. Oval shaped gold wire glasses perched on his large nose. There was, Jeb thought, still a sparkle in his bloodshot blue-green eyes. Beyond a neatly groomed mustache which was formed to the exact corners of his mouth, he was clean shaven with no sideburns and no beard.

General Howard-Wright wore the stiffly pressed red tunic of a Canadian Mountie, with four gold stars on the shoulder epaulets and a fastened high mock turtleneck collar, with dual collar brass shields of the

Royal Canadian Mounted Police. A glossy black pistol belt with golden brass buckle held a Smith & Wesson Model 66 .357 revolver with the holster's leather flap in the RCMP traditional way. He carried neither extra ammo, nor handcuffs on his belt, but Jeb knew a senior officer of his rank wouldn't need these. The red tunic, black pants with yellow stripe down the outside of each leg and tucked into knee high glossy black leather riding boots, was the same style uniform he earned as a young Mountie lieutenant and had insisted on wearing when he assumed command of all Canadian military forces from the Province of Ontario west. Nine rows of multi-colored ribbons adorned his left breast, several showing acts of bravery during his 42 years of military and RCMP service to his beloved Canada.

For the last 3 years and 7 months, it had been the attractive Major's duty to keep the old man's uniforms spiffy enough to meet his standards and have plenty of extra eyeglasses on hand because he was always misplacing them. As to shinning his riding boots, General Howard-Wright preferred to do this chore himself, advising the Major how it gave him some quiet time to think. She hadn't said anything, but was relieved not to be responsible for his footwear, simply because in her nine years of military service she still couldn't grasp the technique for creating a high gloss spit shine.

"Knowing how thin that door is, I gather you heard my rather unkind remarks directed at Captain York?"

Jeb and Wayne, who had expected a return of their salutes, lowered their hands. They were unsure exactly how to answer the General, but Jeb was in command, "Yes, Sir, and I must admit I feel he deserved every word. We've wasted a lot of time because of him and his foolish interrogations and of course there was a certain Lieutenant Bitney who is one of the most arrogant officers I've had the displeasure to meet."

"Yes, yes, I've been informed of all that transpired since your arrival at Post #38... I was quite upset to see Captain York and Lt. Bitney had taken it upon themselves to open General Saunders' document pouch and review the classified documents. I gather you will, in some way, have the ability to convince me you are indeed representing General Saunders, and not spies from Eastern Canada sent here to, should we say, confuse the current state of affairs by killing me?" Jeb and Wayne glanced at each other, they hadn't even conceived the idea that they would be looked at as assassins and now realized why the officers interrogating them were so deliberate in their duties. "This is what my two young officers were thinking and why they held you for so long. Thankfully word got to me and I was able to review the documents and have you delivered here before too much more time had passed."

"Sir, I request permission to stand at ease?" Jeb asked. He disliked having to talk while standing at attention.

"Of course, please stand at ease, Gentlemen. But, also understand my loyal aide has a 40mm pistol pointed at your backs....at least until I'm satisfied of your identities."

"Thank you, General." Jeb turned, looked over his shoulder and grinned at the major, who did in fact have a pistol aimed at them and clearly looked as if she knew how to use it.

The Major was an expert in the Canadian army's issued pistol and rifle weapons, as well as being a third degree black belt in Jujitsu. Not only an aide, she served as General Howard-Wright's personal bodyguard.

Jeb did all the talking while Wayne watched the General's facial expressions and body language. If this was going to turn sour, he wanted a chance to get them out of here. Being Special Forces, Wayne felt he would rather go down fighting then be stood up before a wall and offered a cigarette and a blindfold. But so far, General Howard-Wright was being very courteous.

Jeb cleared his throat, "I ask your pardon, General, according to my instructions, General Saunders asked you to recall a certain United Nations' function where the two of you first met in New York. General Saunders was a Lt. Colonel at the time and Assistant Division Commander for the 173rd Airborne. You were in your first tour of duty as Commander for the Royal Canadian Mounted Police for the Northwest Territories. On this particular night, there was a small wager made between the two of you over a certain number of drinks a certain officer could drink and still stay on his horse, while riding through an RCMP obstacle course. The two of you went AWOL, boarded a military plane by threatening two young pilots with dire consequences and were flown to Quebec. There, you used your authority to borrow a couple of mounts, taking long enough to finish off a second 5th of Jack Daniels whiskey and commenced to hurt and embarrass yourselves in front of an audience of several stable workers and one RCMP sergeant, who had known you for some time and was good at keeping a secret."

"Almost made it too, my horse spooked and we never made it back to New York in time for next day's meetings," Wright wiped his mustache to hide his smile. He remembered that night all too clearly and his long friendship with General Saunders. "How is the old far... the General?"

"He's doing fine, sir, though weary and stressed out with concern over our current state of affairs. Still, his health is holding up and his troops love him. So, I can honestly say, morale is high, even though our future is in doubt.

The General turned to his aide and dismissed her, but before she left the room he reminded her, "Would you see to those two officers, please...I think a bit of soul-searching time in charge of some meaningless detail will do both of them some real good and keep those presumptuous gentlemen from doing any more harm."

"Yes, General," she replied, "we've had more than a few complaints about Lt. Bitney's mistreatment of troops under his command. I have an idea of a particular duty, one that might put his miserable self in order." She smiled to both Jeb and Wayne before leaving, carrying her pistol in her right hand.

"I pity Lt. Bitney, the Major is not a person I would want for an enemy," Wayne said.

General Hoard-Wright grinned and ran his right index finger over his moustache, "Yes, she has a way of straightening up some of my more wayward officers." The General's expression became one of seriousness and the tone of his voice turned harsh, "Though I'm happy you made it here unscathed, I must ask if you have caused harm to any Canadian citizen or committed theft of property, while making your way here."

Jeb hesitated briefly, then admitted to what they had done in order to complete the journey, "Sir... well, Captain Roberts was forced to render one sentry unconscious so we could steal a military vehicle and we were forced to leave a trapper loosely tied beside his wood stove to stay warm while he untied himself when we stole his dogsled and eight dogs. We're not proud of this, but steps had to be taken to get us here in time. These Canadian Army uniforms we brought from Alaska, as was all of our equipment."

"All right, you can advise my aide later of the trapper's location and we can send someone to make sure he was able to free himself and why it was necessary for you to take such extreme actions. I'm not sure if we can replace his dogs, but ...she'll see what can be done," Wright smiled, visualizing the old trapper's attitude when an army patrol showed up to check on him, knowing how angry the man would be and he pitied the officer or non-com in charge of the detail. General Howard-Wright knew he would have done much the same thing to carry out this sort of duty and he gestured for Jeb and Wayne to be seated, "Have you heard what's happening in Alaska since you crossed our border?"

"No, sir," Wayne answered.

"First let me order us some coffee and then we can continue," General Howard-Wright sat down behind his desk, pushed a button on his phone and summoned his secretary from a side office and when she arrived, he ordered a coffee service for all three and some of his favorite crackers.

"Coming right up, sir," she replied as she stepped out of the room, ever so quietly and Wayne noticed she was wearing running shoes.

Mrs. Stephanie Osgoodly was 64 yrs. old, with graying brown hair pulled back in a bun tied in place by a royal blue ribbon. Wrinkles surrounded dark brown eyes and high cheek bones accented her narrow face. She wore black frame glasses with lenses so thick her eyes looked larger than they actually were. Unlike the General's aide, Mrs. Osgoodly wore civilian clothes - a dark blue pantsuit, with an expensive looking gold broach pinned to the left lapel of her suit coat. Wayne had to smile when he saw that her running shoes were color matched to the pantsuit and imagined she had other shoes to match different attire.

General Howard-Wright's expression soured a bit, "The enemy has launched an invasion and has secured a foothold on the western shores of your Seward Peninsula. I was informed that your 1st Division put up a gallant stand, but was forced to retreat before overwhelming numbers. The enemy is moving east toward the Yukon River with numbers estimated in the hundreds of thousands, if not millions. Our intelligence..." Wright stopped. "Sorry, gentleman, we're not quite allies yet. However, I do feel Fairbanks will be under ground assault within three days."

"Sir, is there any news on our 1st Division's commander, Colonel Freemen?"

"Nothing, but our intelligence is limited for Northwest Alaska." Wright didn't want to tell them he had forward observers in the Alaskan interior to monitor the OAP's advance into the massive Tanana Valley; which was larger than either New Mexico or Arizona. General Howard-Wright had lost contact with all but two of these Intel teams and suspected the others had either suffered communications problems or worse.

"What about Prudhoe Bay?" Wayne asked. His best friend was working as a bolt turner on an oil transfer site at Prudhoe.

"At last report, Prudhoe Bay remains untouched, however I am sad to say Barrow was hit hard with multiple bombings; a lot of people are dead. Deadhorse was only strafed, most likely by the same bombers, but they expect worse to follow if Prudhoe Bay falls to the enemy. It appears the OAP wants your oil and its facilities and will not risk an air attack on the fields. No one wants to deal with an oil fire, especially one that could consume the whole field. I've seen photos of their heavy tanks and in my opinion, gentlemen, they should be considered mobile artillery platforms. From their monstrous size, I fear they will be nearly unstoppable with conventional land weapons."

Jeb didn't want to hear any more about the OAP, he wanted to return home and get ready for the fight. "Sir, have you had time to review the letters from General Saunders? If Possible, Captain Roberts and I would like to be on our way home with your response."

General Howard-Wright stood and began to pace the room. He was silent for a moment, then turned to face his guests, "You two risked a lot coming here in those uniforms… you could've been shot as spies."

"We know, Sir," Jeb replied. But, it was the only way to get here."

"Of course," General Howard-Wright replied. He walked around the room asking questions, "What are your personal feelings about an alliance with Canada? Do you feel together our two forces can defeat the OAP? Is Fort Greeley defendable?" and "What is the shape of Fort Greeley's airstrip? Can it handle fighter jets and my heavy transports?" He took in a deep lung full of air, slowly released it and then asked, "How many Divisions will the ADF have in place at Fort Greeley in 15 days?" The aging officer returned to his desk and reached down into a bottom desk drawer to pull out an enormous cigar, "Excuse my inhospitable act, gentlemen, my one vice and I have so few left. They were exported from South America; I find them to be superior to Cubans. But, I have to keep them hidden. One of my junior officers might take it upon himself to lighten my dwindling supply and, sadly, we do have thieves amongst us." He clipped one end off of the cigar and used a silver cigar lighter from off his desk top to light it as he waited for Jeb's reply. The side office door opened and the General's secretary entered carrying a silver tray holding a coffee service for three and a small bowl of the General's crackers.

While waiting for the coffee to be prepared, Jeb noticed the large Bible on the General's desk and how much wear it showed, *He's a Christian too…so many Christians…*Jeb remembered the General's question and asked, "Sir, may we speak in front of this nice lady or should we wait?"

"You hear that, Steffy?" General Howard-Wright turned to Jeb, "Steffy's been with me a long time, nearly three decades and she probably knows more secrets than I do. So you go right ahead, she'll be typing up the recordings anyway." He pointed to a barely noticeable pencil thin microphone hanging from the center of the ceiling. "Everything said in here goes into a private eyes-only file, even that lashing down I gave Captain York will get typed up. But in his case, a copy of it may end up in his personnel file, along with a Letter of Reprimand."

Jeb nodded, thanked Steffy for preparing his coffee with three sugar cubes, and sipped the extremely hot beverage. He was surprised by the kind offer of sugar and continued after sharing a small grin with Wayne, "Sir, we have five Divisions in the field, backed by somewhere between 150,000 to 200,000 civilians. Not all of them are trained, but they're Alaskans and that means they can most likely shoot straight."

General Howard-Wright put his coffee cup down, "Major, my country is involved in civil war, much like your North and the South of the 1860's. To make matters worse, I have learned the Eastern Canadian government has now officially allied themselves with that fiendish European Emperor." He spat out a wad of cigar juice, missing his trashcan and staining the floor.

Steffy shook her head, frowned and left the room. She'd leave the messes for his aide or one of his junior officers. Her days of cleaning up after him were over long ago and he knew it.

"I must also advise you that I and others in my staff consider this Emperor to be the Anti-Christ foretold in the Book of Revelations." The General reached down to lay his left hand upon his aged Bible. "We have no elected president here because our former president elected to remain in Ottawa and is now our enemy. In protecting Western Canada, I have declared martial law in all Canadian provinces west of Ontario's eastern border and assumed leadership responsibilities. As you can understand, defeating Eastern Canada's puppet government is my primary objective and like your President Lincoln, I grieve over the taking of fellow Canadian lives." General Howard-Wright saw the sadness come to their eyes and held his hand up, "Relax, gentlemen, I won't let my old friend down… I'll be sending you back with my decision to support Alaska with what forces I can muster to assist you in defeating the OAP. You will fly first to Whitehorse by my personal military jet, then by helicopter to Beaver Creek. From there under armed escort, you will be transported by armored personnel carrier to the Canadian-Alaska border. You will carry with you letters for President Andrews and my old friend, General Saunders. I expect Steffy'll have them ready by this afternoon." General Howard-Wright inhaled deeply and released a sweet smelling cloud of smoke which made Wayne envious. He fully understood why the General didn't share his limited supply of cigars, but would have enjoyed smoking one. Not a cigarette smoker, he enjoyed a good cigar now and then, but hadn't had one in a very long time. "You will please have General Saunders make arrangements to have your border open for our arrival and very possibly a large scale air drop at Fort Greeley. Once we defeat the OAP or chase them back across the border with their tales between their legs, the two of us will kick that phony Emperor right off that golden throne of his." General Howard-Wright studied his cigar for a moment and continued, his voice rising in indignation, "Can you believe the audacity of that man? They built him a throne over 9 feet tall out of solid gold. Then, these stupid people actually put a crown of diamonds… I think it was the King of England's crown, on top of his pointy head. Such an ignoramus…such pure gall… No, that pretender needs to go back into the hellish flames he came from." He pointed to the floor with his right index finger and looked at Jeb and Wayne, "I apologize, gentlemen." He walked around the desk to stand before his new allies, "It just angers me to think some of my fellow Canadian officers are cow-towing to this…" General Howard-Wright shook his head, struggling to control his temper and gritting his teeth to stop further outbursts. Composed again, he continued, "Excuse me, gentleman, I do get a bit riled at times." The General brought his cigar up in his left hand and puffed on it before he went on, "I heard he has a so called miracle worker performing sleight of hand parlor tricks in hopes of duping people to have them forget what is occurring in Jerusalem with the Two Witnesses foretold in scripture." Wright reached around and picked up his Bible, "Word of God foretold this very thing and it's as if those people over there in Europe, England and my beloved Eastern Canada are all illiterate!"

The General seemed to suddenly notice how weary Jeb and Wayne were, "You'll have to forgive an old man's ranting …You need some rest. I'll have those letters prepared while you get a few hours' sleep. Please, step outside and take advantage of the coffee service. My aide will be there shortly to take you to a room where you can get that sleep I promised you."

"Thank you, Sir," Jeb said as he and Wayne snapped to attention with crisp salutes and made a fast exit. This time the General returned their salutes and added a smile.

Three hours and 47 minutes later, Jeb and Wayne were transported by Military Police car to the flight line where they boarded a Canadian Air Force V-20 jet which was so plush they felt like celebrities. Before the flight, both men observed a sudden flurry of activity around the base, to which Jeb had commented, "Looks like orders are already coming down."

"The General doesn't waste much time," Wayne said. They were flying at 1200 feet aboard a blue and white aircraft with Canada's maple leaf painted on the tail. When they reached cruising altitude well below the ash clouds, Jeb was tapped on his shoulder by the aircraft's crew chief/ flight attendant, Corporal Smitty Hasseloff.

"Sir, the General thought you might be more comfortable in these flight suits." He handed a new gray one-piece flight suit to each officer. "The General thought the possibility existed that one of your own men might take a shot at you since you're wearing Canadian Officer's uniforms. Hope I got the sizes right."

Jeb and Wayne were asleep when the crew chief draped wool blankets over them. Before leaving Calgary, he'd received special instructions from the pilot, "These two are VIPs - special guests of the Commanding General. Take good care of them, Smitty, from what I've been told, they're carrying our future with them and we're to ensure their safety above all costs."

"Funny, I always thought the Alaskans were like brothers. I never thought we should've closed the border with them...I've got a sister there; she an' her husband, an' a couple rug rats live in Delta Junction."

"What's he do there?"

"Used to be with the US Park Service...some kind of ranger, but now, I imagine he's either in their ADF or with the local militia."

"Well, you might be seeing him soon if the scuttlebutt is right. I'm betting our cushy days of flying the General around are about to come to an abrupt halt. Hope you remember how to handle a rifle, Smitty."

Stunned by the thought of becoming a ground pounder and lugging a rifle around or digging foxholes, Smitty stared at his pilot for a moment and remembered how badly he had fared on the rifle range back in his initial training. "You think the General can pull some strings and get me a job behind a desk? I don't do so great with a rifle."

"Smitty, from what I understand about what's coming our way, they're won't be any desk jobs. I'll probably be carrying a rifle before too long... but I can ask the General for you next time we chauffer him around."

"Thanks... I think." Smitty went back to check on his passengers. Afterward, he sat down and thought about his future and he wasn't too optimistic.

OFFICE OF THE PRESIDENT, ANCHORAGE, ALASKA

General Glenn Saunders was beginning his daily briefing with President Andrews when the subject of Major Stewart and Captain Roberts came up, "Glenn, have you received any word from those two officers you sent to Calgary?"

"No, sir," Glenn replied. "Major Stewart and Captain Roberts were my first team; I sent two back up teams to ensure success. But I've received no word from any of them as of this morning."

President Dave Andrews nodded, understanding the implications of losing communication with those three teams. They were either dead or being held prisoner and their message had probably not reached General Howard-Wright. "What's our current status?" Dave was sitting behind his immense desk, a black spiral notebook in front of him to keep private information handy. For these daily briefings, he preferred no one in the room except General Saunders and himself, allowing them to complete it in a more relaxed atmosphere.

Glenn put his own notes down and sat down in one of the cushy easy chairs in front of Dave's desk, "At the moment we're mining all runways at Fort Wainwright, Eielson and Fairbanks. Except of course for what we need to continue using up to the last moment. We're also mining Stevens' International Airport, Fort Richardson and Elmendorf. The earthquake damage made most of the runways unusable, but we want to ensure all airfields are useless to them. Elmendorf only had the one active strip open and that took a lot of work on the part of our Civil Engineers. Some of them really wanted to get their hands on the enemy when they watched the Explosive Ordinance Disposal troops show up. I sympathized with them; all their hard work only to see it blown up by our own people to keep the enemy from using it. The OAP will find a big surprise waiting for them when they attempt landings at any one of those closed fields, but it cost us nearly all of our usable explosives.

Northern Wing Command will operate out of Fort Greeley and Delta Junction. Southern Wing Command will continue to operate out of Elmendorf for now, but they'll be kept ready for evac to Fort Greeley. As I said, the Civil Engineers at Elmendorf were able to keep one runway open, but the hangers were all considered unsafe from quake damage and the aircraft were moved to outside revetments. This keeps the troops busy around the clock with snow and ash removal to have the aircraft ready around the clock and the single runway open."

"What about OAP airborne units?" Governor Andrews was concerned the OAP could air drop troops north of Anchorage or into the Interior, to block an evacuation.

Glenn sighed and flipped open his note book to review his notes. Satisfied with what he had written earlier, he looked up, "Intel says their intended campaign for our side of the world involves only ground units supported by heavy armor. Our last Intel from the United States showed the OAP to have only a single airborne division, but not enough cargo aircraft to support them. My think tank feels the OAP will most likely use airborne troops for their strike against Israel and parts of Northern Africa."

The briefing went on for another 20 minutes. Afterward, General Saunders left to attend another briefing with his senior commanders. Leaving a lonely President behind to stare out over the fog and pray he was making the right decisions. Off to the north he could see flashes of lightening in the black volcanic clouds. In his private moment, he began to wonder how much worse it would get before the big day of impact, or the return of the Lord Jesus Christ.

EAST OF THE CITY OF WALES - OPERATION BREADBASKET

Reminiscent of America's D-Day on June 6, 1944, a massive array of OAP armored units swept over Little Diomede Island like an incoming ocean tide, setting off the demolitions left to explode and in the process, warn the troops in Wales of the invasion. Fiery explosions filled the night sky with showers of bright sparkling lights and pillars of fire. More than a hundred men and women were killed or wounded by traps left behind for the enemy, but it didn't stop or slow the invaders because they abandoned the bodies of dead and never stopped to care for wounded.

The mighty dreadnaughts, armed with an array of weapons and weighing over 30 tons continued to crush the ice under dual six foot wide treads. 300 heavy tanks were accompanied by line after line of lightly armored vehicles, each carrying a rifle squad. As far as the eye could see from northern to southern horizon, huge diesel engines produced a thunderous roar which carried across the ice like hundreds of howling lions. The near deafening sound was easily heard by the defenders in Wales. Such an impressive sound sent cold shivers into the waiting young troops of the.

As they came across the ice, Colonel Freeman received reports from forward units who estimated the OAP spearhead to be led by hundreds of heavy tanks supported by infantry. Troops were riding in armored personnel carriers; others lead the armored units on foot in search of dangerous thin ice or open spots in the ice pack.

"Colonel, they're like nothing you've ever seen. They're coming on like a plague of locusts and those tanks, Colonel. They're like huge monsters in your worst nightmare, some of them have huge white teeth painted on the front…like gigantic sharks."

"I doubt our AT-4s can stop them or even slow 'em down," a Special Forces sergeant reported over the radio from his forward position five miles from Wales. Ten minutes later, all communications with that post and others was lost.

Colonel Freeman glanced about his command tent, reached over his comm. Officer to pick up another microphone and contacted an Air Force forward observer in Nome. "Lieutenant, I am ordering in Baby Huey. Implement Operation Breadbasket - Over."

"I copy, sir… I'll get it done… and good luck, Colonel - Over and out."

Orbiting well above the ash clouds for the last seven hours at a height of 27,000 feet to avoid detection, a bluish gray and black camouflaged C-5A Galaxy had waited for the command to commence Operation Breadbasket. Captain Rick Johnson and Captain Sally Shields, former US Air Force officers, now members of the ADF, prepared their jumpy crew for first war.

One of the few young officers to be designated lead pilot in the former US Air Force; Captain Johnson was 34 yrs. old and a proud Yankee from Boston. He had been a transport pilot for over seven years and had, though a bit reluctantly at first, learned to love his Big Bird. The one piece flight suit hung loosely off the drooping shoulders of his 6'2" frame. Badly in need of washing and pressing it was baggy over his narrow hips and skinny 164 lbs. Two day's stubble of dark brown facial hair covered his narrow face; bloodshot eyes gave evidence of lack of sleep since joining the ADF. A set of infrared goggles were pushed up on his forehead. For now he was flying with his own eyes and his aircraft's radar system.

A COMING STORM

Captain Shields sat comfortably in the right seat reviewing a blue covered notebook containing the written plans for Operation Breadbasket. The 110 lb., 33 year old half white, half Cherokee Indian from Little Rock, Arkansas had short black hair with a large clumsy looking headset holding it in place. Deep brown intelligent eyes darted across the pages. She, too, badly needed sleep, but that would have to wait. She put the notebook aside to help Captain Johnson maintain tight control over Baby Huey as the aircraft began its mission.

The only C-5A Galaxy in the ADF inventory and possibly the only one left in the world had been en route from Germany to Edwards Air Force Base. Flying over the North Pole to save time and fuel, they had planned to change flight crews at Edwards and pick up a classified cargo - a new high tech test aircraft designed for the Navy's future. The C-5A, with a new crew, was to fly the cargo and support crew to the east coast for flight tests over the Atlantic Ocean. The commencement of World War III on Christmas morning caused the huge aircraft and stunned crew to divert to Eielson Air Force Base where Captain Johnson and his flight crew had been placed, if somewhat reluctantly, under the command of the ADF. Due to its monstrous size, the C-5A could only land and take off at Fort Wainwright and Eielson or Elmendorf Air Force Base. Ted Stevens and Fairbanks International Airports had runways of suitable length for the aircraft, but the ADF was in the process of mining them to prevent their use by the OAP. The largest plane in the US Air Force, the Galaxy, which looked too heavy to even get off the ground, could carry two full flight crews, 70 troops in passenger and a large array of cargo in the massive hold. The aircraft was capable of hauling two Abrams tanks with support troops, or two companies of combat troops and all needed gear.

Unfortunately, flying in from Germany it only carried 14 Army and Air Force personnel on leave catching a hop home aboard the nearly empty plane in hopes of being home for the Christmas holidays. While en route, the senior loadmaster had pulled out a box containing several footballs, some Frisbees and two leather baseball mitts and a ball. When the aircraft was empty there was a lot of room to play, but when word came of the OAP attack, everyone stayed glued to the cargo bay's radio for any news coming over the radioman's link to the Alaska Air Command.

Nicknamed Baby Huey after the old Saturday morning comic book cartoon character - a gigantic baby duckling - the aircraft also carried two very large, extremely lethal 2,000 lb. bombs. Held in Air Force inventory and only recently found, they were to be stored in Eielson AFB's old bomb dump. Experts quickly went to work to ensure the 2,000 lb. bombs were still functional for use in Operation Breadbasket. Each bomb was the size of a large 12 passenger van and painted black with newly added white graffiti;

some in not-so-nice, often highly profane messages directed at the OAP. The bombs were very cautiously loaded aboard the C-5A, leaving Captain Johnson uncomfortable with these nightmarish beasts in his airplane. Each bomb was placed on a moveable metal pallet with hydraulics to pull the bombs to the back of the aircraft. When the order was given, the back doors would be opened and both bomb and pallets would be jettisoned onto a selected point on the ice pack. The bombs were expected to explode forming massive holes and weaken surrounding ice with spider web stress fractures. Experts had high hopes this would slow the enemy's advance and possibly sink heavy armor.

When the order was given to commence Operation Breadbasket, a flight of four F-22 Raptors were readied for flight. These 21st Century fighters were kept on Nome's tarmac under white camouflage sheets, loaded for bear with multiple air to air missiles and 30mm cannons. Support crews hastened to make them ready for take-off and once they were in the air quickly boarded a Black Hawk helicopter that had been kept in a privately owned hanger to avoid detection by OAP recon birds. Eight minutes after launch, thrust from the Raptor's extremely powerful twin engines on full afterburner had the F-22s in the assigned area waiting for Baby Huey to break through the clouds. With all the radar problems the ash was causing, Captain Johnson only hoped he didn't plow into one of those F-22s when he came through the black clouds at over 400 mph.

IN WALES

Back in his Command Tent in Wales, Colonel Freeman had hoped the sudden appearance of the C-5A shooting down through the dark clouds of ash, would terrorize the enemy by its sheer size and sudden ominous presence. He knew the plan called for the F-22's to be on hand in order to keep the enemy fighters off the C-5A while it delivered its deadly load and dealt a deadly blow against the OAP spearhead. But if the fighters did come in, Colonel Freeman was worried the Raptors could be badly outnumbered and he whispered a prayer for both the pilots of the fighters and the crew of the C-5A.

ABOARD THE C-5A

For nearly 35 seconds the only thing Captain Johnson and Captain Shields could see was black, with a sporadic bolt of lightning shooting across the windshield and through the ash clouds. Then they were through and Captain Johnson let out a deep audible sigh of relief when he saw four friendly fighters suddenly appear on his right wing. The volcanic ash made it nearly impossible to rely on his aircraft's radar, but once through, his relief was short lived. Lt. Riggs, the navigator/radar operator excitedly announced over the intercom, "Sir, we got 12 bogies coming in from the west at an estimated Mach-2. From their signature, I believe they're Russian MIGS most likely armed with air-to-air missiles and 30mm cannons …and with our name on 'em."

"Okay…well, that's the fighter's problem. We've got to drop these bombs where they will do the most good and hightail it out of here before we get our tail shot off."

Captain Shields glanced at her pilot and shook her head in disbelief, "We may be big and strong, but we have all the speed of a little old lady walking her three legged dog… So, you'd better hope those Raptors keep those MIGS off our butts or we're going to become the largest flaming snow sled ever seen."

"Oh, you of little faith," Captain Johnson replied. "It'll take a lot to take this bird down and those Raptors will make short work of those old MIGS."

"I sure hope so… It looks real cold out there and the thought of hiking back to Fairbanks just makes me feel cold all over."

Captain Johnson grinned back at her, "No sweat, half-pint. You help me keep our Blundering Bessie in the air and we'll make it home… to Fairbanks." I only wish it was home… our home and not this frozen pancake below us.

Odds by the numbers were in the OAP's favor, but the Raptor was a highly superior aircraft compared to the Russian MIG and the Alaskan pilots were better trained, so Captain Johnson felt the ADF were better than 2 to 1 in favor of winning the air battle. He put the fighters out mind for the moment and concentrated on his first ever bombing run, not something he thought he'd be doing in his flight career and especially not with this gigantic C-5A Galaxy. Oh, he'd worked it out on paper, but realized how different real flight operating was compared with a table full of diagrams and simulator time. On paper he didn't have to fight winds coming in off the ice pack to keep his massive bird level while maintaining the low operational level of 300 feet. From the cockpit, Captain Johnson felt as if he could reach down and touch some of the spiraling ice peaks shooting up from the ice pack and it made him so uncomfortable that he had to fight to descend the last 100 feet. He needed all the physical help his co-pilot could give to keep the bird from buffeting too much and possibly shaking a bomb loose. The big plane liked height - demanded it, and this low level stuff made the whole bird shake like a thrashing 70 lb. King salmon on the hook. It was a fight that strained every muscle in the body as the two pilots struggled to keep it from plowing up the ice below, making the largest crop furrow in history.

Major Bob "Doozer" Ashcraft, 32, who had been a member of the US Air Force's Alaska Air Command, was in command of a flight of four F-22 Raptors and was extremely glad to be back in the air. They'd been sitting at Nome for the last three days and he had grown weary of playing cards, telling stories; avoiding those tales of people they had recently lost with the onset of war and either jogging or walking up and down the runway for exercise. The residents had been evacuated before their arrival and they were under orders to avoid searching the town for souvenirs and to remain at the airfield to await the order to fly. Doozer loved flying the Raptor, finding it a far superior aircraft to the F-15 Eagle he had trained on. Originally assigned to Nellis Air Force Base in Nevada, he'd been reassigned to Elmendorf Air Force Base nine months earlier to fly the Raptor in the Alaskan skies and was now one of the senior pilots in the new ADF Air Force. He knew his family, whom he had moved home to San Francisco were gone, so he had channeled his grief and anger into flying. He devoted all his time to flying the aircraft and carrying an avenging desire to kill as many of the enemy as he could. But for right now, the primary responsibility of this mission was to ensure the C-5A could complete its assigned task.

Nine minutes later, Doozer's flight of Raptors engaged the enemy with their initial release of air-to-air missiles. From 17 miles away, three of the MIGS fell from the skies in fiery deaths. Doozer then ordered the other three Raptors to engage the remaining MIGS, while he stayed with Baby Huey.

The dog fight didn't last long, especially with the limited air space. No one on either side wanted to shoot up through the clouds and risk clogging turbine engines with ash and before long only the three F-22s remained on Doozer's radar. But within minutes, his radar and the radar onboard the C-5A, picked up a second flight of aircraft coming in fast from the west. Based on their supersonic speeds, these planes were not the older MIGS and he feared his three Raptors pilots were about to enter a fight for their lives.

Doozer worked his radios with nimble fingers to maintain contact with his flight and talk with Captain Johnson as they flew over a seemingly endless length of ice pack.

"Breadbasket, this is Raptor 3. Over," Doozer said into his oxygen mask. He preferred using the basic call signs because Raptor sounded so lethal in nature and he knew from intelligence reports that the OAP had a great fear of this aircraft. Raptor 1 and 2 call signs belonged to senior ADF flying officers and they were covering the skies over the Tanana Valley at this moment.

"Raptor 3, this is Breadbasket. Over," Captain Johnson replied. He had earlier advised his radioman that he would be talking directly with his fighter cover to lessen the time between traffic.

"Raptor 3 is staying above and behind your right wing; remaining Raptors will engage 2nd flight of fighters. By their speed I strongly believe these are either SU-23 Russian or newer JL-20 Chinese fighter/bombers. I guess their stealth technology isn't working up to par. Over," Doozer advised. He watched his radar and was able to identify a third flight coming in from the west, but couldn't see how many aircraft there were. Not that it mattered, he knew they were about to be overwhelmed by the enemy and the only thing in his favor was there wasn't enough room in the skies for so many fighters to be engaging in dog fights.

"Raptor 3, I request your flight rejoin us to keep those vultures off. We only have one pass to make and then we can disperse and head for the clouds for cover. Over," Captain Johnson said.

"Raptor 3 agrees...let me know when you're ready to make your bomb run. Out," Doozer said and then advised the other three Raptors to join him and take up positions behind Baby Huey, "We'll break off when the enemy engages, but we have to keep the enemy missiles from knocking the Big Bird off. So, prepare to hang back until you know the enemy has a missile lock and lead those things away from Baby Huey. Once she drops her eggs, we'll shoot for the skies and risk it by heading for 25,000 feet and make our way home."

It didn't take long before the Chinese fighter/bombers began making their attack on the C-5A. They were unsure what the massive cargo bird had planned, but they knew it wasn't carrying tourist gifts to welcome the OAP. In the next seven minutes the skies were filled with dozens of air-to-air missiles of various types and sizes accompanied by extended streams of 30mm cannon fire. Five of the Chinese fighters went down, not able to maintain the speed and turning ability of the Raptors, but the OAP finally scored and knocked two of the Raptors out of the sky in fiery explosions. One Chinese fighter was knocked down by a comrade's missile, but the odds were still in their favor as they now concentrated all their fire power on the C-5A.

Doozer, whose aircraft had already sustained battle damage from enemy cannon fire, observed a Chinese fighter move into weapons range of Breadbasket, but he was out of ammo and had no more missiles. He looked about the skies and saw his wing man engaged with two enemy fighters to the south and knew this situation with the enemy fighter ahead was all in his hands. "Breadbasket, you got a bogie coming in hot on your tail. Start wagging your tail while I move in...and guys, good luck! Raptor 3, out...so long dudes," Doozer glanced down at the photograph of his beautiful wife and three kids stuck behind the altimeter gauge. He smiled, "Be seeing you real soon guys...I love you." Seconds before Doozer was able to ram his fighter jet into the cockpit of the Chinese fighter, the enemy pilot was able to fire off a lone missile, which covered 2,712 feet of air space in seconds and struck the massive outer engine of the C-5A's right wing and exploded.

Doozer never saw the explosion. He closed his eyes at the last microsecond, with a tender thought of his family and rammed into the enemy plane at 550 mph. The two fighters exploded in one yellow and black fireball. Being only 300 feet above ground, it was only a matter of seconds before the two dead pilots and their burning aircraft collided with the ice pack. Fiery debris rained down on the ice and spread fire across the icy wasteland, while overhead, the remaining Raptor began rotating in a spiraling fall from the skies to crash within two miles of Doozer's wreckage. The four Raptors were gone and the ADF had lost four courageous pilots.

Captain Johnson, frantically shutting off fuel lines and flipping emergency switches as fast as he could, fought to keep the airplane in the air. Meanwhile, a severely wounded Captain Shields, her body covered in blood, broken glass and shrapnel from the engine's explosion, struggled to maintain consciousness and help out as much as she could.

Lt. Tommy Riggs, a young 2nd year navigator from Tulsa, Oklahoma, heard the explosion and quickly moved into the flight deck. He saw the rough shape Captain Shields was in and began carefully removing her from her seat so SSgt. Larry Reeds could start emergency first aid on her on the cabin floor. Twice she screamed, but then passed out, which rattled Lt. Riggs who tossed aside her bloodied oxygen mask knowing he wouldn't need it at this low level. After brushing the glass aside, he took over the blood stained flight chair and began following Captain Johnson's hand gestures, pointing to various switches and ensuring he had his feet on the pedals. Highly nervous, Lt. Riggs nodded excitedly and following Captain Johnson's instructions, took over Captain Shield's blood-stained flight controls.

The cargo crew was far too busy with the payload to come to the flight desk, so it was up to Captain Johnson and Lt. Riggs to handle the bleeding Bird and keep it in the air.

"How much farther we need to go with this," Riggs yelled. The intercom was down and the head sets were no longer useful. Wind howled in through the holes in the fuselage and the two pilots had to shout to be heard.

"Not far, I can see the enemy right up ahead and they look like an army of ants... I doubt these two bombs are going to do much," Captain Johnson hollered, then over his shoulder to SSgt. Reeds, "I she going to be okay?"

SSgt. Reeds looked down at Captain Shields' lifeless body in shock and disbelief and then remembered Captain Johnson's question. He had never been in combat before or seen a dead body and was teary eyed, when he looked up into the worried eyes of his pilot, "She's dead, Captain... nothing I could do...too much bleeding!"

Captain Johnson closed his eyes for only a brief moment and then gestured for SSgt. Reeds to approach. When he did, Captain Johnson grabbed him by the shoulder and pulled him closer, "Put a blanket over her. Then I want you to go back to the cargo bay and tell them our intercom and radio are out and I'm not sure our hydraulics is even working from up here. Give me four minutes and if the back doors haven't opened, you guys take over and do everything yourselves. Open them up, use a pry bar if you have to, but drop those bombs one after the other. Then you get up here and let me know they're out and then I'll try to fly us out of here. Got it?"

"I gotcha, Captain... Good luck!" SSgt. Reeds slapped Lt. Riggs on the shoulder, grinned at him and began to make his way back toward the cargo bay. But he stopped briefly in the vacant extra-flight crew's area to secure a blanket for Captain Shields. Once she was covered, he muttered a very quick prayer and dashed for the rear of the plane.

Captain Johnson gazed once more at the body of Captain Shields, now covered with a thin green blanket, but had to break away from his thoughts when the aircraft began to shake violently and a frantic looking Lt. Riggs motioned for his assistance.

The flight deck's cargo bay controls didn't work, but the controls in the back of the plane still did and after four minutes, the massive rear hatches on the C-5A slowly opened. Icy cold air filled the interior of the aircraft, turning to fog as it met the warm temperatures inside, but the men had their parkas on and were prepared for it. Not waiting for further word from up front, MSgt. Bob Hightower, an Afro-American senior loadmaster from San Bernardino, was only three credits away from earning his Bachelor's Degree in History. Before the missiles flew, he had high hopes of obtaining a lieutenant's commission. He punched the hydraulic controls, relieved to see them working and watched as the pallets moved toward the back. MSgt. Hightower estimated the time of drop off to be 40 seconds for the first bomb and 55 seconds for the second. SSgt. Reeds worked his way forward to advise Captain Johnson of the updated times before impact.

The bird had slowed from battle damage; dropping to 230 mph and Captain Johnson was fearful they might not be able to avoid shrapnel from the blast. He grew concerned for the other crewmen on board; Major Oscar Whitney- a weapons expert, Captain Lacy Upchurch - Office of ADF Intelligence and Sgt. Brad Railsback - assistant loadmaster.

When the first bomb dropped from the rear of the C-5A, it looked as if Baby Huey was popping black eggs out. No one thought to add cargo shoots to the loads, so the first bomb smashed through the ice and didn't explode until it had plowed through 18 feet of icy water. But then the explosive power lifted a huge sheet of rugged ice the size of a football field. Cracks formed immediately, causing further massive gaps until an area big enough to hold the entire Rose Bowl Stadium was open ice.

The second bomb behaved quite differently and exploded upon impact with the ice, which may have been caused by the difference in thickness of the ice for the 2nd impact point. But the reaction was much the same, causing a massive hole in the ice and sending out a spider web of cracks in all directions.

Captain Johnson couldn't see the results and he wasn't about to turn the aircraft around for a better look, not with all those Chinese fighters still in the area. He had to rely on his crew to take plenty of photographs and make visual reports into the handheld tape recorders they were provided with before the mission was launched. Everyone had one, but Captain Johnson and Lt. Riggs were too busy to use theirs at the moment.

Before the C-5A could gain attitude and 25 seconds after the second bomb was away, a Chinese air-to-air missile flew in through the open cargo doors and exploded in the rear of the aircraft. Everyone in the cargo bay was killed and the destruction made it impossible for the pilots to hold the aircraft in the air.

"Hope you enjoyed the flight lesson, but we're going in!" Captain Johnson shouted to Lt. Riggs.

With both gloved hands wrapped tightly around the icing up controls, Lt. Riggs could only nod in understanding. He glanced back down at Captain Shields, wishing he could've gotten to know her better and then in a loud voice he shouted, "Can we take a few of them with us?"

"Don't see why not...Shields said she thought this would make a lousy snow sled," Captain Johnson grinned as he fought to control the slant on the huge wounded bird.

A third Chinese fighter was lining up for a kill shot, but was forced to move out of the way to avoid a collision when Captain Johnson brought the throttles back to slow his plane down. It was shaking so badly, Lt. Riggs wasn't quite sure if the plane might fall apart before they could get it lined up with the front line of the enemy spearhead.

The punched holes and cracks in the ice had accounted for the sinking of 19 mighty dreadnaughts, 92 armored personnel carriers and the deaths of more than 1400 OAP soldiers. But when Baby Huey plowed into the ice and became a battering ram into the front ranks of the OAP spearhead, total chaos erupted and the ensuing destruction destroyed 48 additional dreadnaughts, 76 armored personnel carriers, 52 light armored trucks and 658 soldiers.

The C-5A Galaxy had indeed been a lousy snow sled, but had covered more than a mile of ice, slamming into OAP hardware along the way, breaking off its three remaining engines and then its huge wings, until the C-5A finally came to a fiery stop and exploded in an eruption of towering fire and bellowing plumes of black smoke.

It took the enemy another three hours to four hours to organize its forces and get the invasion back on the move, but the enemy was stunned by what had occurred on the ice outside of Wales. They had thought the pitiful few numbers of Alaskans would run like the frightened Russians had, but clearly this wasn't the case and now they were gravely concerned with what they might find when they made landfall.

HITTING THE BEACH AT WALES-

When Colonel Freeman lost all radio contact with the C-5A and the four Raptors over the ice pack, he feared the worst and whispered a prayer for the brave air crews. When he received word they had lost contact with all forward observation posts, he knew the enemy was all too near and gave the order to prepare all forces to implement their operations and prepare for battle.

The OAP came on like a steel tsunami, wave after wave of unstoppable armor supported by a 3rd and 4th flight of 12 MIGs each. There was nothing Colonel Freeman and his 1st Division could do, but fire off volley after volley of 105 mm and mortars, while the rest of his division bugged out. Only then could the artillery and heavy weapons platoons, operating as rear fire support, leave their positions. By then most, if not all, of the bunkers were destroyed and most of the men and women who had bravely manned them, dead or wounded.

OAP fighters strafed ADF positions with heavy machinegun fire and bombed the fleeing Alaskans relentlessly with 500 lb. bombs. When the first wave of OAP land forces came off the ice pack, they found a coastline that resembled a moonscape; huge bomb craters concentrated throughout the ADF positions. Bodies and destroyed equipment scattered everywhere, fires burning and the remains of several track vehicles smoldering. OAP soldiers began searching ADF positions for survivors and in doing so were severely maimed or killed by booby traps left behind for them.

Taking heavy casualties from MIG attack and barrage after barrage of tank fire from the dreadnaughts, the Fighting First Division was cut to pieces before most of them could escape. Entire companies were eventually taken prisoner, but most of them, especially the wounded, were executed on the spot. Those who could still walk were herded into hastily built POW camps. With such an overwhelming invasion force against them, the First Division had held off the OAP armored spearhead for less than an hour.

Surviving elements were scattered, running for their lives in small groups as the OAP pursued them. Colonel Freeman and some of his staff survived the attack and with a small force of two platoons, headed southwest.

ADF COMMAND-COMMUNICATIONS, FORT WAINWRIGHT - APRIL 4th 1118 HOURS

A bleary-eyed and exhausted sergeant stood in front of a Plexiglas strategy board and used a black grease marker to show Lt. Col. Wardly, Senior On-Duty Communications Officer, the enemy's current positions and last known coordinates for the survivors of the 1st Division.

Lt. Col. Wardly stiffened when he noticed General Saunders' sudden appearance beside him and knew he was waiting for an update. "Good morning, General. We've received a second confirmation of enemy units crossing the Yukon River approximately three miles north of Major Blackstone's last known position. With the bridge out, the OAP are crossing the ice with light equipment, setting up a heavy concentration of anti-aircraft batteries and building bridges on the ice for their heavy tanks."

"Did Blackstone have anything else to report?" General Saunders asked. He looked over the board, while waiting for a response.

"He was taking heavy fire from forward armored units. The OAP have one brigade of light tanks, supported by light armored personnel carriers and a regiment sized force of infantry across the ice. They appear to be headed for the old town of Minto. But as I said, the big tanks are still held up by the terrain; Blackstone believes the OAP will be bringing up road equipment to build a road for the heavier tanks and artillery units. He reported earlier seeing road graders and bulldozers, but they haven't put in a road to the Yukon River yet...Blackstone is on the move again and making a run for Fairbanks."

"What's his vehicle status?" General Saunders asked.

"Most of his command is on foot, General. They're using what few vehicles they have left to carry wounded, keeping them out in front. However, he reported the terrain is making it near impossible for the light vehicles to make much headway through the deeper snow, Sir, and they may have to abandon them."

"Blackstone sounds like a good officer, Colonel. I expect he'll bring his troops through. What is the status of Juliet?" Saunders asked. Juliet was the code name given to Delta Junction's airfield. For the last two weeks, working around the clock, ADF engineers were lengthening the field to handle ADF fighter aircraft. Following the task of knocking down more than a thousand trees and cleaning away the debris, snow removal came next and then ground ice was scraped down to a hard flat surface. Special dozer blades were put into service to make a usable surface for aircraft to land on and traction was the key. Another five hundred man force was given the duty to erect dozens of steel hangers and dirt revetments to protect the aircraft arriving from Eielson and Elmendorf Air Force Bases.

"Your construction OIC says he'll have everything ready, Sir. What materials we didn't have, they're scrounging from other buildings and farms."

General Saunders studied the board, making Sgt. George Greer slightly nervous, "Sergeant, I don't see anything new on here concerning our 1st Division Headquarters' staff?"

Wardly gestured to the sergeant to take a seat and let him field the question, "General, all attempts to make contact with Colonel Freeman have met with negative results. Our last report, 20 hours ago, had him engaging the enemy near Koyukuk... Not a sound after that." Lt. Colonel Wardly shook his head slowly and lowered his eyes, "Sir, I fear the worst."

"Let's not give up on them yet, Colonel. Radios break down and things happen that could prevent him from making contact. Colonel Freeman is a fine soldier, a man who would never give up and his Eskimos and Athabascann troops are some of the best fighters in the ADF."

"Yes, Sir, we'll keep trying to make contact with Colonel Freeman."

"General," Lt. Nilick, communications officer, walked up to General Saunders, stood at attention three feet from the senior officer and waited to be noticed.

"What is it, Lieutenant?" Saunders asked in a tired voice.

"Sir, we've just received an unusual flash message from our border post on the Alcan... a Major Stewart and a Captain Roberts send you regards. The Major in charge of the border post reported both officers were escorted to the border by a Canadian unit under a white flag. Fortunately, the Major recognized Captain Roberts and had this coded message passed on."

"What's their ETA, Lieutenant?" Saunders asked as he read the short coded message.

"They're aboard a Black Hawk, General," Lt. Nilick checked his watch, "ETA 37 minutes from now with good flying weather."

"Thank God!" General Saunders exclaimed. He smiled at everyone in the room, surprising all of them and then walked out of the Comm Center leaving behind a very startled staff. Few of them could remember seeing the General smile before.

ADF COMMAND HEADQUARTERS-FORT WAINWRIGHT

General Saunders was in his office, packing up his desk when his secretary notified him that Major Jeb Stewart and Captain Wayne Roberts had arrived.

"Show them in."

Wearing the flight suits provided by the Canadians, Jeb and Wayne marched in and saluted, "Reporting as ordered, Sir," Jeb said as the senior man.

"I am very happy to see you both, gentlemen. Your message says General Howard-Wright is joining us. What else?" The General was standing behind his desk, which was cluttered with cardboard boxes.

Jeb reached into a leather courier pouch and pulled out several sealed documents. "These are from General Howard-Wright, Sir. One is a legal document giving him the legal authority as Acting Prime Minister for Western Canada. The other papers cover his decision to aid Alaska in their fight against the OAP and form an alliance with us."

"Praise God!" General Saunders exclaimed and bowed his head to whisper a prayer of praise. Afterward, he looked up and directed the men to have a seat, "I need to make a call to the President." Saunders buzzed his secretary and asked her to make a call to President Andrews, "Tell me when he's on the line." Then turned his attention to Jeb and listened as he related some of their tale about the journey to Calgary. They were interrupted when the call came through from the President. Once the phones were confirmed as being secure, both Jeb and Wayne sat quietly as General Saunders read off some of the more important details from the documents.

"General Howard-Wright is offering us four Combat Divisions...four Divisions! And he's sending us his own regiment of Royal Canadian Mounted Police as a point unit. That's 600 hundred men mounted on some of the most beautiful black horses you've ever seen! Gentlemen, for the first time I really feel we have a fighting chance here. Now, please continue on with your story about the trip to Calgary."

Over the next few moments, Jeb and Wayne shared their ordeal, nearly bringing the General to tears of laughter from hearing about the foul smelling cook and their dog sled ride. He then buzzed for his aide and a moment later, Captain Eugene Ward stepped in from the outer office. "Have a coded message sent to the Alcan border post...effective immediately our borders are open to all Canadian military traffic. No civilian traffic from either direction will pass until notified. Be advised Western Canadian Army now our ally and will be treated as such. Next, notify Delta Junction with the same information and have a large area prepared for the RCMP Regiment near the air field. The tarmac will give them some open space to exercise their horses. They should be arriving within 24 hours and we'll need feed and bales of hay for the horses, and most likely extra provisions for the men.

Lastly, advise Command they can expect two Canadian airborne divisions to be parachuting in within 48hours. Expect coded traffic to prepare for same and keep all traffic on scramblers." Then as an after-thought he added, "Have one of our Special Forces units work with them." General Saunders studied Ward as he clicked off a list in his head. "Oh, get me that logistics officer...can't remember his name at the moment, but the Canadians will need space for four divisions on Fort Greeley. We can open up that area where those worthless missile silos are." Saunders looked at Jeb. "Wasted space now, all the missiles were fired leaving only holes in the ground... they didn't hit a thing. Waste of money!" General Saunders shook his head in bitterness, recalling how much money went into the production and testing of those anti-missile missiles. He looked back at Ward, "Should be enough room there, if not, we'll find it elsewhere. One good thing about Fort Greeley, there's a lot of open space!"

"Yes, General." Ward saluted, did an about face and left with his notebook in hand.

"He's good kid. I stole him out of Intel last week and promoted him. If we survive this thing, he'll probably be sitting in my chair someday."

"Sir, what do you have for us now?" Jeb asked.

"I thought that would be obvious. You're both back in the Intelligence game. One of you gets to stay here and the other moves on to Delta Junction. Want me to flip a coin on who goes where?" Saunders said with a smile.

"If the major doesn't mind, I'd rather stick it out here for a while." Wayne suggested and then glanced at Jeb, "I got a few friends here I'd like to keep an eye on."

"Okay with me, Captain Roberts knows the Fairbanks area better than I."

"It's so ordered then. Major Roberts, you are assigned here and Lt. Colonel Stewart, you will accompany me to Delta and then on to Fort Greeley as new commander for that Intel Section." Saunders grinned as he saw the look of surprise on both men's faces.

"You earned these promotions and probably a lot more for what you accomplished in Calgary. Too bad we no longer have the salaries to go with it."

"Thank you, Sir!" They replied in unison, stunned by the promotions. This moved Wayne into field grade rank and Jeb to command his own section.

"Sir, what's the latest from Colonel Freeman?" Jeb asked.

"I'm sorry, Colonel. We lost contact with the 1st Division when they engaged the enemy in Koyukuk. The Yukon River Bridge was blown and Major Blackstone and his unit are retreating from the enemy toward Fairbanks."

"They were good soldiers, General. Maybe some of them have survived," Jeb said. Speechless, General Saunders could only nod his head in agreement.

YUKON RIVER SHORELINE, APRIL 4th

Bone weary cold, an exhausted Colonel Freeman gazed down at his frostbitten hands and stomped his feet in a futile attempt to get feeling back. Gathered around him were some of the surviving members of the 1st Division: 73 men and three women huddled together like penguins to retain some level of warmth. They were in arctic survival conditions, while a blizzard protected them from enemy aircraft. But severe cold sapped their strength. Without a working radio, they still had some ammo for their rifles and a dozen or so grenades between them.

Directly in front of them lay the Yukon River; 100 yards wide at this point and covered in solid ice, making it a dangerous crossing for his band of tired followers. Behind him lay the blackened ruins of the Nulato Township and eight new graves for brave men and women killed in battle with an OAP recon unit. It had been 24 hours since the Battle for Koyukuk - a fierce engagement after which Colonel Freeman was able to escape with only a few troops. The rest of the 1st Division was either killed or captured, and even Major Brockmire, whose artillery battalion pounded the enemy to a standstill along a narrow valley, eventually fell before the OAP's onslaught. When their ammo had run out, it was to hand-to-hand fighting until OAP forces rushed forward in a human wave to slaughter Brockmire and his valiant command.

An embittered Colonel Freeman had watched much of it from a ridgeline far to the south, but there was nothing he could do but stand to attention and salute his fallen comrades. Too worn out to offer up a single tear and too empty of feeling to grieve anymore, Colonel Freeman ordered his remaining command to continue south. Their uniforms soiled and in tatters, they ran all day and into the night, trying to stay one step ahead of the OAP advance units. No one had eaten for the last 53 hours; their supplies had been captured before the last battle, but water was abundant. Simply scoop up a handful of snow and let it dissolve in their mouths - then keep moving.

Eyes nearly frozen shut, Colonel Freeman sent his weary band toward the river, where they stumbled upon a company size OAP Recon Unit. The enemy had been resting and were caught completely by surprise. Colonel Freeman had lost several troops in the firefight, but his command buried the bodies in the snow to hide them and waited to see if other enemy units showed up.

Letting his force rest and guards posted, Freeman forced his mind to work through the cold mist inside his head.

The 1st Division, over 20,000 men and women, was reduced to Major Blackstone's force and the 70 survivors Freeman had around him. He was in a state of total disbelief of the last 24 hours. *My orders were to withdraw, I did. To engage the enemy, we did. What now? I've got 70 troops, no food and little ammo. We won't surrender, but a troop of boy scouts could probably whip us right now. Where do we go from here? So many dead an' still the enemy keeps on coming...*

10 - NEW CAREERS AND RELUCTANT VOLUNTEERS

"I tell you the truth, whoever hears my word and believes him who sent me has eternal life and will not be condemned; he has crossed from death to life. I tell you the truth, a time is coming and has now come when the dead will hear the voice of the Son of God and those who hear will live. For as the Father has life himself, so he has granted the Son to have life in himself. And he has given him authority to judge because he is the Son of Man."

John 5:24-30 NIV

FORT GREELEY, FAMILY QUARTERS - APRIL 4th

Shortage of living space caused families to be herded like cattle onto Fort Greeley. The first to arrive were first housed in several dozen long abandoned two story army barracks. These rooms, 14 by 10, had once held two enlisted men or women, but with the influx of refugees each room was reassigned to a complete family. Sometimes that family numbered up to as many as 10 people. Paint was peelings off walls and woodwork and mold had built up around a single, often cracked outside window casing. Each room was furnished with two sets of aged wooden or rusty metal bunk beds stacked three high and secured to the wall by metal brackets. Two cots were provided as needed. There were no couches, no chairs, tables or dressers. In the older barracks there were two large bathrooms with showers on each floor shared by all. In some of the newer barracks, two rooms were connected by a small bathroom with a telephone booth sized shower stall. Here too, wall paint was peeling and mold and rust stains were found everywhere. High iron content in Fort Greeley ground water had stained the old porcelain sinks and tubs and most of the bathroom mirrors were cracked, rusted or missing. Tiled bathrooms floors were damaged and ancient plumbing was in a bad state of disrepair. It had taken work crews several days to get the water turned on, fighting broken lines and frozen pipe. Hundreds of plumbers, handy men and assistants were busy around the clock to make the extremely cramped, living arrangements suitable - or at least bearable for now.

Fort Greeley had a reputation for being the coldest army post in the world with winter temperatures in the Interior of Alaska, sometimes dropping below -80°. Barrack rooms were built off a communal center hallway to keep icy cold air from entering individual rooms. This hallway quickly became a social corridor and children's play area. Anyone walking the hall had to be aware of the hazards under foot - dozens of toy cars of all makes, colors and sizes, multi-colored bouncing rubber balls, an odd Frisbee, plastic toy soldiers and cowboys & Indians play sets. There were Barbie dolls and piles of doll clothes and any number of Disney characters scattered about the floor to help keep children busy and not wondering why their parents looked so worried or even frightened.

Providing housing for so many people was a monumental task that the staff at Fort Greely met by looking at every possible solution. They sent people to open up and clean out long abandoned office buildings, unused warehouses and set up row after row of tents on just about every piece of open space on Fort Greeley's main post area. The tents came in all sizes and colors, but the main problem was always keeping people warm. The post fire department, with increased numbers from militia volunteers, had already responded to more than 100 fires in the tent areas. Thankfully, only a few people were in need of medical attention, mostly for minor burns. Still, the post Fire Marshall was prepared for a major fire and staged drills every day.

ROOM # 218

With an appraising wink and a leering raised eyebrow, Kathy Sawyer admired her husband in his new ADF uniform, "You're looking pretty snazzy there, Captain." She popped him a playful salute and went up to hug him.

A recent volunteer to the Alaskan Militia, Brad was puzzled to find he was being immediately transferred to the ADF for the duration of hostilities, but he didn't share this confusion with his wife; she had enough to deal with.

He stood before her in his new green leaf camouflage fatigues, a new set of black captain's bars on each collar point. A green web belt wrapped snug around his waist held a newly issued Model 1911 .45 caliber Colt automatic pistol in a hard canvas holster. Army green canvas combat suspenders over his shoulders connected to his belt by clips took some of the weight when a soldier was lugging around 50 lbs. of ammo magazines, triple canteens, knives and a bayonet on his canteen belt. Brad added an Army green canvas first-aid pouch to his suspenders and had planned to add his K-Bar knife as well, but hadn't gotten around to it yet. His white bunny boots were bloused a few inches above the ankles according to ADF regulations, though Brad thought it looked a bit lame. He had thought only Airborne troops bloused their boots, but had seen the ADF Military Police doing it and now everyone in the ADF had followed suite.. Once a tradition for elite troops that everyone else had picked up. *At least I don't have to wear one of those silly looking berets - I'd look like a sissy!*

"Honey, I feel like some kid playing soldier," Brad complained.

"Wish they'd let you know what you'll be doing," Kathy said. She stood back, examined him and then pulled a loose green thread off his collar.

"I'll be told..." He glanced at his watch, "...in about 30 minutes. I gotta go, Babe. The military doesn't look kindly on its new officers showing up late for appointments."

"You'll do great wherever they assign you." Kathy hoped it wasn't with a combat unit. She felt he had seen enough bloodshed and wanted him closer to home. She picked up his new fatigue hat, with attached black captain's bars and placed it on his head. "My, how dashing you look," She raised an eyebrow, a wild gleam in her eyes.

"Whoa, woman, I don't have time for that now!" Brad playfully pushed her farther away and pulled his cap down for a proper fit. He looked into the mirror hanging from the opposite wall and said, "I look like some kid playing soldier."

"You look handsome, Captain. Now go kiss the kids goodbye," Kathy said pointing outside into the hallway, where the kids were playing a game of Scrabble on the floor with three other children.

GREELEY BASE GYM

Used to his roomy apartment in town, newly commissioned 2nd Lieutenant Scott Radley slept the night in his sleeping bag on a cushion of thin rubber matting on the hard wood floor of the base gym. It was not the best thing for his injured ribs, but he didn't want to complain too much; especially since he was sharing the wood floor with more than two hundred other new Militia officers. They also shared a community bathroom with 12 sinks, one of which was broken, 12 mirrors, with three of them cracked and one missing its glass completely and 12 badly stained showers with rusty plumbing fixtures and little hot water. With such a crowd, first to rise in the morning meant first to get hot water before the supply was used up. Morning rush, and that's exactly what it resembled, usually added up to a random supply of bruised elbows, more than a few shaving nicks and toothbrush poked in the eye or shoved partially down a throat. There were more than a few words of profanity thrown in as tempers flew and an occasional punch thrown.

Outside the Base Gym were hundreds of 20 man canvas tents shared by the ranks of lowly Militia enlisted men and women. Each tent was heated by either a coal or wood stove in an effort to keep the troops from turning into Popsicles. This meant massive loads of coal and wood being brought in and troops for work details to lug the needed fuel around to the tents.

Mostly new arrivals, the Militia volunteers had shown up with their own firearms. Each weapon had to be examined and if found acceptable, ammo provided for shooting practice and later, combat.

Scott smiled when he saw one young man walk by with a pair of western style pearl handled revolvers tied down gunfighter style. Another sported a long, well-groomed black beard, cradled an expensive over-and-under shotgun in his arm and was even wearing a vest with an assortment of goose and duck calls hanging from it. *One guy thinks he's Billy the Kid and this dude looks as if he thinks we're going on some goose hunt? And these are supposed to be officers?*

One very heavyset woman with long blonde hair tied back into a single braid and tied off with a thin leather ribbon, was armed with a well-used 30-30 Winchester rifle, and the tall, very thin but handsome man walking with her had a newer model AK-47 slung over his shoulder. Some of these new Militia officers carried various types of shotguns and others were armed with high caliber, bolt action Kodiak bear killer guns- mounted with expensive high powered scopes.

Finally in front of a sink brushing his teeth with jerky movement to avoid hitting other men crowding in for a piece of the mirror or some hot water, Scott heard his name called out from the gym. He turned around with a mouthful of toothpaste froth to see Brad smiling back at him above the others. "Good morning, Lieutenant, and how are you on this bright an' shiny day?"

Scott held his right hand up to say hello, then lifted a finger of the same hand to say he'd be with Brad in one minute. He turned to spit the froth into a sink, barely missing the arm of another new militia officer. Finished, he fought his way through the waiting crowd of men and found Brad standing outside the bathroom entrance, "Brad...ah mean, Captain Sawyer an' no disrespect intended, but I do hope someone shoots that silly grin off your face," Scott remarked with a touch of noticeable sarcasm to his tone.

"Now, now, Lieutenant, remember you are now an officer and a gentleman." Brad glanced around to see if he recognized anyone else, but he didn't and figured most of these men had come in from the bush communities. "So, how's the ribs, buddy?"

"Not bad, but the next jerk to elbow me is gonna get it right across the..." Scott stopped when he saw the look of disapproval on Brad's face.

"Keep that temper in line, Scott. Remember, they don't fire you in the Army. They court-martial you and then use you for bayonet practice."

Scott shook his head in disbelief and used his towel to wipe off his face and then asked, "What's up...Sir?"

"I have to report to ADF Headquarters, what about you?"

"What happened to you being in the Militia?"

"They transferred me over to ADF and made me a captain. So where are you headed?" Brad asked.

Scott was disappointed, he had hoped he would work with Brad again, but then shrugged it off and replied to Brad's question, "I'm supposed to report to some captain at Building #53 at 0800 hours."

"Scott, I know you have a problem with navigation, but you are an officer now and should learn to read a map."

"What's that supposed to mean!?"

"Scott, this is building #53."

"Great, then I don't have far to walk then," Scott ignored Brad's rebuff and placed his bathroom supplies into his black canvas equipment bag. He looked back at Brad, "From what I've learned I'll probably be commanding a platoon of new Militia volunteers, running them though basic training." He glanced around and drew closer to Brad, "Tell you the truth, Brad, some of these white folks don't seem to cater to seein' a black man in an officer's uniform. Gotten some real cold eyes this morning an' ah tellin' you I don't like it much either."

"Have you had any real trouble?" Brad asked. He glanced around the gym and noticed there were a few looks of contempt directed at Scott and a couple of other Afro-American officers.

"No real trouble, but I've seen that look before…Don't worry, Brad, I've lived with it before in the Army… and before."

"You're a good man, Scott. Any platoon should consider themselves blessed to have you as their lieutenant." Brad patted his friend on the shoulder, "I've got to run. I'll see you tonight if I can. Kathy's in Room 218, Building 114."

"Don't let 'em give you no desk job," Scott said, then added, "I hear those forward observers have a nice cushy job, you'd like that."

"Thanks, I'll let Kathy know you recommended it too."

"Don't do that, she'd kill me." Scott tossed his friend a casual wave, which made him wince from pain and watched as Brad left the gym.

ADF COMMAND- FORT GREELEY

Wrapped up in his newly issued Army Parka and struggling to make his way through knee deep snow and freezing temperatures, Brad left the fort's parade grounds and climbed the icy steps of the Headquarters Building. He was stopped by two heavily armed MP's and showed them his orders and police photo identification. Having not been issued an ADF ID card yet, his police ID was accepted, but only after a phone call.

After receiving directions twice from two administrative aides sitting behind desks, Brad finally stood before a door with "LOGISTICS" painted in three inch glossy black letters. He was puzzled to find two good sized white-helmeted MPs, wearing neatly pressed camouflage fatigues stationed at the door inside the office. Both armed with M-16's, held at the ready and holstered side arms on canteen belts, with extra ammo pouches and pouches for M-16 ammo. *I'm not sure what they're guarding, but these two look like they could handle anything coming their way.*

"State your business, Sir," one of the MPs ordered in a brusque tone.

"I'm reporting as ordered, Sergeant." Eye to eye, Brad handed him his orders and again showed his police ID and badge.

"Yes, Sir," Sergeant O'Harrell's tone softened. "Through this door, make an immediate left and follow the hallway until it makes a hard right. Knock on the fourth door down from that corner, right hand side."

"Thank you, Sergeant." Brad walked through the door and gazed down a sterile light green hallway, with dark green doors on the right side. Numbers were painted on the doors but there was no other designation for office identification.

Brad turned to Sgt. O'Harrell, "What's the room number, Sergeant?"

With a straight face, Sgt. O'Harrell replied, "Fourth door on the right, sir." He closed the door and left Brad standing alone in the hallway.

"Wow, I wonder which door leads to the tiger to gobble me up and which one leads to the princess?" Reaching the fourth door, he counted them off again to make sure and knocked twice and waited. There was no response. He knocked again, this time a bit harder. He didn't have to wait long before the heavy wooden door was unbolted from inside and opened a mere crack. Brad heard the sound of three locks being released and wondered what he was getting himself into. The door swung open slowly and he looked down nearly a foot to see a single dark brown eye staring back up at him. The barrel end of a large automatic pistol was pointed at his mid-section.

"Business, Captain?" The smallish man inside the room asked in a terse tone.

"Captain Sawyer. I was told to report here." *This guy can't be ADF - he's only an inch taller than my son.*

"Present your ADF card and orders, Captain."

Brad pushed his papers through the narrow crack in the doorway, "Here are my orders, but you'll have to accept my Fairbanks Police ID to confirm identity since I haven't been issued a military ID yet." Brad was startled as the door closed in his face and paused in mid-knock when the door swung open and the little man gestured him through, "Please step through, I do not like to keep the door open."

Inside, Brad watched as the man, who wore no uniform or other identification, slammed the heavy wooden door closed and slid three dead bolts into place.

"I do apologize for my abruptness, Captain Sawyer, but security is a touchy business and one I take very seriously. Have a seat; the Colonel will be with you in a moment." The little man, who was wearing a heavy blue wool sweater, a pair of tan jeans and leather slippers was about to walk away, but turned to face Brad, "Pardon my manners, Captain…my name is Jefferson P. Lanly…Captain Lanly if you please." Lanly nodded once before turning around to leave the room. He disappeared through another door closing it behind him.

Strange little man, must be some administrative officer, Brad took a seat and waited. He would soon learn that Captain Jefferson P. Lanly was anything but an administrative officer. Until recently, Lanly was a college professor at Georgetown University with a PHD in Languages. He was fluent in 14 oriental dialects including two Vietnamese and nine Montegnard, along with Thai and Burmese. He spoke French and Spanish, with a little street Mex thrown in from having spent six months in Tijuana, Mexico. Credited with an IQ of 190, Lanly had finished high school through a home school program at age 12, received his first BA from the University of Alaska/Anchorage at 14 and was awarded his PH.D at the young age of 17. He had then traveled to Washington DC to accept a position as one of the youngest instructors to ever be employed at Georgetown University. There, his aptitude for oriental languages was noticed by the US Army and in particular, General Saunders. Soon after finishing his second year at Georgetown, Lanly received an immediate summons to the Alaska Army National Guard. He could have side-stepped the summons, but serving in the military was something he wanted to do and height had kept him from. After reporting to General Saunders, he never returned to the college campus and a month later, reportedly left Alaska for an unannounced trip to Europe. In actuality, Lanly proudly accepted a commission as a captain with the US Army and took on a top secret assignment to go undercover in mainland China. The job and assignment was actually ordered by the CIA, working in conjunction with US Army Intelligence. It was General Saunders idea to work through the Alaska National Guard, to keep Lanly's identity unknown to the US government's Oversight Committee for Intelligence. General Saunders suspected the Chinese had greased the palms of a few politicians and didn't want to take any chances with Lanly's life and the valuable intelligence he would provide.

Lanly underwent minor cosmetic surgery at a CIA safe house in Europe and then traveled to the orient by way of aircraft, boat. Once there, he enlisted in the growing ranks of the newly formed OAP. After earning a citation for bravery, when his unit encountered the Vietnamese army, he was assigned as an assistant to a Divisional Intel Officer. The man had learned of Lanly's ability to interpret Vietnamese and other oriental languages and thought the young man would be of value to a particular OAP Warlord General. He dropped information to CIA operatives located throughout the orient who sent it on to the ADF through secret couriers. Some of the information he committed to memory and upon his return home, these facts and figures were found to be priceless. For his service, Lanly was awarded the Distinguished Service Cross and later transferred to the ADF and assigned to the Office of ADF Intelligence. Several months after he came home from China, the OAP launched nuclear war against the USA. It was General Saunders who knew how valuable Captain Lanly was to the Alaska's defense and made him the number two man in Fort Greeley's Intel Section. Now 28, Lanly stood a short 5'1", suffered from premature balding and weak eyes. Resting on the tip of his somewhat pointed nose was a pair of black rimmed coke bottle glasses, giving him a distinct middle-aged professor look.

Footsteps echoed down a hallway, a door open and Brad looked up from reading a 15 year old copy of Reader's Digest to see a uniformed Lt. Colonel approach; he stood to the position of attention. Besides the Lt. Colonel rank on his shirt's collars, the nametag over the left pocket of his urban camouflage uniform identified the officer as STEWART. Over the right breast pocket was an ALASKA DEFENSE FORCE tag, where it had previously stated, US ARMY. *Must've kept women with sewing machines busy changing uniform tags much less changes for official headings on government paperwork. Can't understand why they just didn't leave it as US ARMY and US AIR FORCE.*

Lt. Col. Jeb Stewart stood before him and began reciting from memory, "Captain Brad Sawyer, former sergeant of the Fairbanks Police Department and son of a retired Fairbanks police sergeant. One brother, Edward, last known to be an Arizona State Police lieutenant. Married; your wife's name is Kathy; two children; Bob and Becky. Reports show you to be known and respected by members of the ADF staff, which included high praise from Captain Susan Riley of the Provost Marshall's Office." Lt. Colonel Stewart offered his hand and introduced himself. "Brad, I'm OIC of Intel for the Northern Area Command. I have counterparts in Anchorage and a small unit at Fort Wainwright. From this point on, you work for me and alongside that impish character that let you in. But don't let his size or manners fool you, Captain Lanly is one heck of a soldier."

"Yes, Sir." Being only his first day, Brad was not used to all this military stuff and didn't know what else to say.

"Okay then, let's step into my office where we can be a little more comfortable," Jeb led Brad down the brightly lit hallway, through a door that opened into a fairly large office and took a seat at an old large gray metal desk with many small dents, scrapes and scratches centered in the room. The metal chair he sat upon was as old as the desk and it protested as his weight came down and the wheels whined and groaned as it moved. There was a battered brown leather couch with arms covered in cigarette burns and ancient coffee stains; one wall was lined with locked white five drawer file cabinets. The green walls were mostly blank, the exception being a newly acquired large colored map showing Alaska, Western Canada and Eastern Russia. On the map were several thumbtacks in various colors with small ID tags marking locations which Brad wasn't close enough to read.

Jeb gestured for Brad to have a seat, "First, let me tell you something about the man you'll be working with. When I first heard his story, I was dumbfounded, but it did provide me some insight into the character of the man."

Listening to Lanly's story, Brad was as awestruck by the little guy's courage to enter the lion's den, survive and return home unharmed with hidden treasure. "Makes me think of the Hobbit... facing the dragon and...well, it was a cool movie, but I don't think it should've been made in three parts...Sorry, Sir...I'm a bit nervous right now and not sure what you expect of me...I'm a street cop, Colonel. I've never gotten into the intelligence part of the job or worked undercover."

Jeb smiled and walked over to the map, "He's much too shy to ever tell you his story which is why I wanted to brief you. To begin with...well, intelligence work is, of course, somewhat different from police work. You weren't aware I was watching you, but we keep a hidden camera in our waiting room. It's important to get an impression of everyone who comes into this office - comes with the job; I saw your eyes and recognized the look you gave Lanly as he walked away. Your first impression wasn't favorable. So tell me, what did you first think of Captain Lanly?"

I'd better not go into the Hobbit thing. "Sir, I thought he was just another one of those admin officers and it wasn't until he told me he was an officer that I gave him that much credit." Brad was ashamed to say and then added, "I didn't think he was tall enough or in good enough physical shape to be in the ADF. I think I know what you're getting at, Colonel. All isn't what it seems to be in the Intelligence world," He was embarrassed.

"Exactly, I knew you'd catch on right away." Jeb pointed to the City of Fairbanks on the map. "Another thing I admired about you, Brad, was even after you were promoted to Police Captain, you preferred to wear your sergeant stripes and the badge your father wore. To me that displayed integrity, a sense of pride for what you've earned-yet humble too, loyal to family and fellow officers. The bravery you showed at the evacuation point would have earned you at least a Silver Star in the army. These are the reasons you're here and why I needed a man of your high caliber."

After so much praise, Brad was extremely nervous to learn exactly what he would be doing for this man and the ADF. *He's showered me with rose petals, now comes the moose droppings.*

Jeb looked down at his watch, "Brad, I won't keep you on the edge...I've selected you for a very dangerous assignment. One that I feel only you can accomplish."

Brad studied Jeb for a moment and looked into his eyes, expecting an offer to buy a bridge or swamp land in Florida. *This guy must've been a used car salesman or an insurance salesman in the old days, he has that look.* But Brad also knew that with the invasion and the comet's impact immanent, he couldn't think of a job that wasn't dangerous. So, he asked the big million dollar question anyway - "Okay, Colonel, you have my interest peaked...what's my dangerous assignment?"

Jeb took a seat in the chair beside Brad and glanced at his watch before he began, "Captain, in six hours and...14 minutes, you're to be flown by Black Hawk Helicopter to Fort Wainwright. There you will be met by a Major Wayne Roberts, who will brief you on your mission."

"I knew a Captain Wayne Roberts on Wainwright. He used to work Special Forces; my men had a few martial arts training days with him and some others in his squad. We, I mean the Fairbanks Police Department, also had a few shoot-offs with the MP's and Special Forces guys, came out about even usually."

"Same one," Jeb said. "He received a promotion to major for a little job we did for the General." Jeb stood up, walked over to the map and mentally traced the route they had taken to reach Calgary. After a brief silence and a shake of his head as he recalled the adventure, he sighed and pointed to a red flagged pin indicating the Yukon River Bridge. "OAP advance units have reached about here, which is why we blew the bridge. I expect they're already crossing the river in great numbers and on their way to the Tanana Valley." He looked over at Brad, "I won't lie to you, Brad. This is going to be an extremely dangerous job. One you've been personally selected for and it could very well cost you and Major Roberts your lives." Jeb let that sink in for a moment before continuing, "General Saunders and I feel you two are the ones for this job, but final decision is yours. You must volunteer, as Major Roberts did, because you'll be going behind enemy lines with absolutely no support from us."

"Behind enemy lines? Why me?" Brad asked in astonishment. "I don't have any spy training, no real combat skills...Sir, you sure you got the right Sawyer?"

Jeb nodded, understanding how Brad felt. He had felt much the same way when the General had ordered him to Calgary. "Your knowledge of Fairbanks will be one of the main things that will help keep you and Major Roberts alive. We need eyes and ears in the city after the OAP moves in to occupy Fairbanks. Numbers, morale, supplies...anything and everything you can report. You are not there to engage the enemy, but to report on them."

"Talk about Daniel and the lion's den...Kathy's gonna kill me," Brad said in disbelief.

Jeb offered Brad his hand, "I gather you mean you'll accept the assignment then?"

"I have no other choice, Colonel. If my participation helps stop the OAP, then I'm fighting for the lives of my family. Will I have some time to say goodbye at least?" Brad asked as he shook Jeb's hand.

"I can give you five hours. Then you're to report here for final briefing and equipment issue."

Five hours! Better not waste any time then. Brad saluted and left Jeb's office, his mind full of thoughts of how to best break this new assignment to his lovely wife. Captain Lanly, now in uniform, was waiting by the outer door. Brad only glanced at him, nodded once, but said nothing as he walked by and began to jog down the hallway.

ROOM # 218- FAMILY QUARTERS

Heated words were bantered about and tears flowed from both sides until there was nothing else to argue about. Once the discussion was over between Brad and Kathy, the kids were allowed back into the room and the family huddled together on the floor between two sets of bunk beds. Brad said his goodbyes to a confused Bob and Becky and then a couple of neighbors came by to pick the kids up at Kathy's request to spend some private time with Brad alone. For the people who needed to know, Kathy told them Brad was about to leave on an important assignment for the ADF, but nothing more. Yet by the argument and tears, these people knew this may very well be the last time Brad and his family might be together.

Whispering words of love to each other, Kathy held her husband tightly as minutes ticked by all too fast. When the hour finally came to leave, the kids returned and they shared a quiet moment of prayer as a family.

Hugs and kisses behind him, a distraught wife held up by caring friends, a tearful daughter, and a young son standing bravely as his daddy went away, Brad left Family Quarters behind and went to locate Scott. The door closed behind him leaving Bob and Becky to comfort their mother and themselves.

BASE GYM

Bedrolls and sleeping bags stacked against a sidewall, four new platoons formed up in the center of the gym for introductions to their new platoon sergeants and platoon leaders.

Scott wasn't happy - 15 minutes after talking with Brad, he found himself standing at attention in front of his new company commander, Captain Oscar C. Buford. An intolerable bigot, the 24 year old stood 6' 2", was extremely overweight, had bleached blonde hair and blue eyes. In deliberate rudeness, Buford refused to return Scott's salute, "Just gimme your orders, boy!" Buford demanded and then ripped them from Scott's hand. "Can't understand they makin' you an officer... you must know somebody or have some kind of pull in Anchorage."

It took every ounce of will power Scott could pull upon not to reach across the desk and throttle this man, or at least belt him on the side of his head with the flat of his hand. Scott stood silently while Buford reviewed the papers with an endless stream of profane words to show his contempt for the Militia promoting a black man to the rank of lieutenant. "You stand there; boy...I'll be right back." Buford grabbed his fatigue hat and stomped all the way over to Battalion Headquarters to see his uncle, Lt. Colonel Chester C. Middleston. After a10 minute wait, Buford was finally shown into his uncle's Office and got right to the point, "I don't care where you send him, but I don't want no nigger officer in my company!"

Middleston's eyes widened with anger and he slammed his fist down on the top of his desk, "Oscar, you are one sorry example of an officer. For your mother's sake I got you commissioned and I took you into my Battalion. That's as far as I go for my sister. Now what officer are you referring too?"

"That Radley... I don't want him!"

Lt. Col. Middleston shook his head in aggravation and disgust for his nephew, "Now listen up, dear nephew, Lt. Radley is a good man and he may even teach you something about how an army should work. Get out of my office before I bust you down to private and make you Lt. Radley's runner!" Lt. Col. Middleston bellowed. Red faced, he jumped to his feet and pointed toward the door with his left index finger. "Now get out!"

By the time Buford returned to his desk, he had already developed a plan for getting rid of Lt. Radley. A new bunch of men and women had recently arrived and some of them were from Buford's old drinking hangout in Delta Junction. He knew these men, who shared similar dislike for the colored race, would work out just fine for what he had in mind. Buford smiled at Scott, "Boy, it looks like I'm stuck with you for now, but I've got jus' the job for a man with your vast experience. A new platoon of raw recruits arrived last night and they're yours to mold into real fighting men...women too. I know how you Blacks like ordering your women around. Important thing to remember is - this is my Charlie Company, but I'll give you 3rd platoon to see what you can do with it. Follow me...lieutenant." Buford walked out and Scott followed.

Buford and three other company commanders were using an old athletic room as an office and it didn't take any time at all for the other officers to have a strong dislike for Buford. Watching Buford's mistreatment of the new Lt. Radley, they shared a silent glance among themselves and felt some sympathy for the new officer.

In the gym, 34 men and two women sat on a section of wooden bleachers and as Buford approached, several shouted out boisterous greetings for their old drinking buddy. Buford ignored them and addressed Scott, "Lieutenant, have your platoon form up."

Scott took a deep breath, relaxed his hands, which up to now had been balled into tight fists and addressed his new command, "All right, quietly form four lines facing the wall behind me and listen up," Scott ordered.

Slowly and casually, they began to stand up and formed several uneven lines. Not what one could consider a true line, but acceptable for the moment since they were raw troops.

"For those of you, who do not know me, my name is Captain Buford and I am your Company Commander. This is Charlie Company, commonly referred to as C Company. The rest of your chain of command will be covered in due time." Buford smiled at his friends and walked behind Scott, who remained at parade rest while the captain spoke. "You are designated as 3rd Platoon. I'd like to introduce Lt. Radley, your Platoon Leader. A credit to his race I am sure, he will instruct you in the finer parts of military life." Buford gave his buddies a knowing look, "Now you be sure to make him feel at home, won't you." Buford walked away without another word.

Scott was at first surprised and a bit suspicious of Buford's brief address to the troops, but he stepped right in, "Let me have your attention," Scott ordered. Some of the men conversed among themselves, others sat down. "Remain standing, please," Scott requested. "I will select four squad leaders for A, B, C and D squads. You will hold a temporary rank of Private First Class. Assistant squad leaders will be assigned later. One of you will be made platoon sergeant, also known as platoon NCOIC for Non-Commissioned Officer-In- Charge and he...or she will assist me in training you." He gave them all a hard look, hoping to see if one might show some

287

sign of military bearing. *I'll even take a Boy Scout…a Girl Scout…* But so far all he'd seen was a group of undisciplined reindeer herders, potato farmers and a random selection of professional bar hoppers. "At my command, you will assume the position of attention." Scott demonstrated the position. "This means standing straight, stomach in, chest out, legs together, eyes looking straight ahead and chin tucked in." Scott looked up and down the line and bellowed, "Attention!"

He learned quickly why DI's from his Boot Camp days yelled so loud. Most recruits thought the position of attention meant not sitting down, a few stood looking at one another rather than straight ahead. *This is going to take some time…* His new command did everything but drop to the floor as he issued his first series of commands. Simple orders such as right face and left face created minor chaos, as it was made apparent they either didn't know the importance of discipline or were making him a fool for tolerating their rude conduct.

Scott took notice of their uniforms, or what was passing for Militia uniform; some had on ADF camouflage shirts and faded blue jeans or tan slacks, while others had on desert or urban camouflage picked up at second hand stores before hostilities began. Three men were decked out in expensive hunting leaf camouflage with padded red felt or tan leather at their elbows. One of these was the man he'd seen earlier wearing all the duck calls. *I've gotten stuck with a bunch of cowboy couch potatoes. Share a keg and catch a football game between drills…or during drills. These jerks don't have a clue an' I'm supposed ta get 'em ready for war?*

"First off, lay your firearms on the bleachers…carefully. Make sure they are not loaded…And point the long guns to the ceiling while you unload them. All side arms are to remain holstered. If you're carrying a semi-automatic, point the pistol downward and not at the troop in front of you and ensure a round is not chambered." Scott waited as they accomplished this and was thankful no one was shot in the process. He ordered them back into line then demonstrated the proper stance for attention and walked up and down the line as each demonstrated understanding by coming to the position. During this, Scott heard the word "Nigger" spoken in a whisper from several feet away. Stopping abruptly, he spun and glared at the man he suspected of making the remark. As he scanned the group, he saw looks of defiance, smirks, and sneers. Everyone heard it, but no one owned up.

"Captain Buford has left, so I would like to take this moment to get to know you better. You may address me as Lieutenant, LT, Lt. Radley, or a simple…Sir. But if ah hear the word nigger again I will make sure you was wishin' you was fightin' for the other side. For those of you who haven't gotten it yet, it's not us niggers, you honkies or some poor ol' nates and a few spics fighting this war. This is Alaskans against the OAP for survival. Either follow me or take a chance on getting killed the first time we engage the enemy." Several smirks disappeared, but not all of them. "Now let's try it again, shall we?" Scott ordered, "Attention!"

Brad found Scott in the gym with a rag tag assortment of men and women lined up in front of him. He stood back and listened to some of the backtalk Scott was getting from several Delta Junction good old boys. He knew that Scott was struggling to keep his temper and knew these people had no idea what they were up against if Scott decided to let go on them.

"When's the last time you fired your rifle?" Scott asked a bearded man in front of him, wanting to learn how proficient his platoon might be with their weapons.

"Let's see, last time...I think it was when I took mah boys out coon hunting, Lieutenant...sir." The man shouted over his shoulder, "Wasn't it coons we were after, Charlie?"

"Sure was, Bert... Big black ring tailed coons." Charlie was in the back row, a big grin on his face. A good 240 lbs. or better, Charlie was larger than his buddy, Bert, both in bad need of a shave. Based on heavy bloodshot eyes, Scott thought both men could use a couple of weeks in detox to dry out, apparently having spent too many afternoons drinking home brew. There were no raccoons in Alaska; everyone knew these were racial remarks and wondering how their new lieutenant would handle it.

"You are all at attention and will speak only when spoken too." Scott heard someone coming up behind and was somewhat startled to see it was Brad. Remembering to present a crisp salute, he addressed his old friend in the proper military manner, "Good afternoon, Captain Sawyer." Scott was also surprised at seeing Brad in civilian clothes.

"Lieutenant, may I have a moment of your time?" Brad walked over to the side of the gym and waited for Scott.

Scott ordered his platoon to the bleachers, hoping he would be able to get them up again without having to kill one or two as an example. He approached Brad with 500 pounds of woe weighing him down. "What's with the civvies?"

"Can't say, but you look like you have your hands full?"

"Misfits, farmers, couple drunks an' don't let me forget to add a couple members of the local KKK chapter...Brad, ah'll never have 'em ready when the shooting starts." Scott kicked the wall to let out some of his frustration.

"I need a big favor," Brad said to get Scott's attention. "I'm leaving in a few moments, can't tell you where, but I might not be coming back." Brad stopped as he saw the look of shock come over Scott's face.

"What do yuh mean yuh might not be comin' back?"

"Good chance this is a one way trip, buddy." Brad reached across and put his hand on Scott's shoulder, "Listen, no time for that now. I need you to look after Kathy an' the kids. You know, watch over 'em."

"You got it," Scott assured him. "But I wish I was goin' with you. Got a bad feelin' about this bunch an' my bigot captain thinks I'm jus' some uppity nigger."

"They'll learn to respect you. You were a good cop, best I ever worked with. You have the military training and more importantly, the ability to lead. So give yourself a chance and ignore the racial stuff." Brad slapped his friend on the shoulder, "One other thing… an' it's a tough one to ask." Brad moved closer and his voice dropped to a whisper. "Scott, my family can't be taken alive. Do you understand what I'm asking here?" He looked deeply into his friend's widening eyes and knew Scott understood what he was asking of him.

Scott nodded, unable to say the words.

Brad smiled and shook his friend's hand, which quickly turned into a quick hug between old friends. Stepping back, Brad nodded once at Scott and then walked over to where 3rd platoon was sitting. "I'm Captain Sawyer, late Fairbanks Police Department. I want you to know how fortunate you are to have Lt. Radley as your platoon leader. He was my patrol partner. We've been through some tough scrapes together. A couple days ago he saved my life, killing two men that were about to gun me down. And that was after he'd been shot twice. Thankfully he was wearing his bulletproof vest and only suffered a couple broken ribs. That's a lesson in itself, use your equipment properly and it might very well save your life. Lt. Radley is former US Army. He doesn't give up on a friend, or one of his soldiers. A lot of people would've died at the South Cushman Evac Point if he'd laid there feeling sorry for himself. Do him a good turn and he'll do his best to keep you alive." Brad slowly scanned the group with a glare in his eyes, "I warn you; if I hear that one of you got him killed...I'll hunt you down and kill you myself." Brad turned, nodded again to Scott, winked and walked away.

Still stunned by Brad's request, Scott was moved by the speech and stood silent for a moment to watch his best friend walk out of the gym. Then he returned his attention to his platoon, "All right, let's try this again...form four lines." Scott saw one of the men raise his hand and gritted his teeth when he saw that it was Charlie, one of the jokers.

"What's your question?" Scott asked, knowing he was about to be hit with another bit of witty racism.

"Lieutenant, my sister and her three kids were there...on South Cushman. She told me last night that Fairbanks Police arrived in time to save them...and quite a few others. I just wanted to say...thank you... Lieutenant...You'll have no more problems from us."

Scott bit his lip as he nodded thanks, he truly didn't know what to say in response. "Okay, let's form those lines and start from the beginning."

During break, Charlie and Bert came forward and offered their hands in friendship and Scott shook them. A couple of others, friends of Captain Buford, held back, but with Charlie and Bert backing him, Scott no longer had problems with racial tension in the 3rd Platoon.

Captain Buford was dumbfounded when he came out of his office to find 3rd platoon sitting in a circle around Lt. Radley who was teaching them combat shooting techniques from the prone, kneeling and standing position. Blood pressure rocketing, language in the gutter, Buford returned to his office and, much to the distaste of his fellow officers, slammed the outer door.

ADF HEADQUARTERS-INTEL SECTION

A blank expression on his face, Captain Lanly quickly closed the door and dead bolted it after Brad stepped in. "Colonel Stewart will be right back; he had an errand to run. Would you like some coffee while you wait?"

"Sounds good, thanks," Brad replied.

Sitting in Lanly's office and sipping from a white ceramic coffee mug, Brad admired some of the photographs on the wall behind Lanly's desk. There were three 5x7 silver framed black and white photos and an 8x10 color print in a gold frame. The first black and white photo showed four OAP soldiers standing over several dead bodies; like big game hunters. Another showed five laughing OAP officers in an oriental bar; the third was of a soldier standing at what appeared to be an awards ceremony. But it was the fourth photo, the color one that caught Brad's attention. It was then Governor Andrews pinning a medal on Captain Lanly's chest. General Saunders was standing directly behind Lanly in a manner that gave Brad the impression he was holding a gun to Lanly's backside to keep him from running. Having a trained eye for detail, Brad continued studying the black and white photos and then it came to him. Captain Lanly, in oriental disguise, was in each photograph. "I'm impressed."

"You're the first one to recognize me," Lanly said. "I bow to your observational skills."

"Care to explain those three photos?" Brad asked.

"We were in the Philippines and those dead men were blood thirsty bandits, enemy to everyone. The firefight was nick an' tuck for a moment, but we carried better weapons. I kept the photo to remind me how close I came to death that day." Lanly pointed to the next photograph, "That one was taken in a Tokyo Bar, celebrating my promotion to 1st Lieutenant. I get quite a lot of enjoyment out of that one in particular, especially after they all had to forfeit their beer ration for my party."

"And this third one?" Brad asked.

"That is my promotion to captain and also our first issue of the new OAP winter uniforms. They issued black and brown uniforms to every soldier from the Philippines to Siberia. Coarse material, no matter how many times you washed it, it didn't matter. Those things stayed uncomfortable all the way through Siberia."

"You've led a very interesting life, Captain," Brad said with admiration. "The one with the new uniforms, you're also receiving a medal...right?"

"Yes, I was presented with the Chinese Silver Medal for Bravery...equal to our Bronze Star."

"So...?" Brad inquired.

"During the first Battle for Siberia, I pulled some wounded men out of a burning tank. Couldn't let them burn, not then. Now...after what happened later, I might have."

"You were in Siberia? You're rapidly becoming my hero, Captain," Brad stood and raised his coffee mug. "You might appear short in stature, Captain Lanly, but I know of very few men who could accomplish what you have."

"Would you please tell the General that?" Lanly pleaded, and pointed to the ceiling, "I've requested an infantry outfit, assignment as company commander...even platoon commander for a front line Militia outfit... anything to get me out of here."

Before Brad could respond, Lt. Col. Stewart appeared, "Step into my office, Brad. I have a few things for you." On a large folding table in Jeb's office were several items that caught Brad's attention. "I feel much like "Q" in those James Bond movies, always handing out some new exploding briefcase or poison pen."

Brad picked up his new ADF ID card and a light blue ADF Intelligence ID card; the photograph apparently taken from his Alaska driver's license.

"You're cleared up to a Level Five Security clearance, only I and a few others have higher than that," Jeb said.

"Now I know why I was asked all those questions before leaving Fairbanks."

"You've been checked and cross checked to ensure you don't have any skeletons in your closet. Now this little item," Jeb held a small brown disc the size of a U.S. quarter. "This is simply a bug; a tracking device. You are to keep it with you at all times, put it in your shoe or in your wallet - but don't lose it. Hopefully, we'll be able to track you and know where you are at all times. Range on it is about 12 miles from the Fort Wainwright trans-metering tower." Jeb looked at the Glock pistol Brad was carrying in a well-worn brown leather shoulder holster. "I see you're armed already, that's good. Pick up extra ammo on Fort Wainwright. Jeb handed Brad the next object which was not much larger than a cellphone, "This is your radio and it has your call sign written on the back. Normal range is also about 12 miles, but don't count on anything over 10 miles with current temperatures staying in the minus levels. Something about ice fog jams the radio signal over some distances."

"Extra batteries?" Brad asked.

"Captain Roberts will have plenty. Here is the belt loop holder, whole thing weighs 8 ounces and the attached antenna is flexible."

Brad turned the radio over and saw that his call sign was India-5 - *easy to remember.*

"Okay, now for the fun stuff, right out of James Bond and Captain Marvel." Jeb picked up a silver colored ink pen. "This is not a pen. Push down on the top and a thin needle shoots out the bottom. Jab it in your arm, your leg, it doesn't matter. You'll be dead in under three seconds, so please be extra careful with it."

Brad took possession of the pen and studied it, "To keep me from being captured?"

"Right!" Jeb picked up several other items and identified them, "One lock pick set, a small flashlight with extra batteries, a miniature infrared scope and this little honey…" Jeb presented Brad a small square black box about the size of a four ounce juice container with a small antenna wire hanging from the bottom and a small glass lens on the opposite end. "…this is the latest in digitized mini-cams. This beauty can transmit a black and white picture to a receiver within a five mile range. We've already hidden a receiver on Fort Wainwright that will relay the message through another hidden receiver on Eielson Air Force Base. Eventually, we'll get the message here. Scientists say it takes about two to three seconds from camera to here and goes through three other sites along the way."

Carefully examining the camera, Brad hoped he was better with this then his own 35mm. His photos always came out wrong, either forgetting to take the lens cover off or holding his thumb in front of the lens to block the picture. He never did figure out how to use the cellphone to take photographs and let Kathy take all the family photographs.

"I want pictures of everything you can get; tanks, armored personnel carriers, troops and officers. This doesn't use film and you'll have plenty of power with these special batteries." Jeb handed Brad a small box containing 20 watch sized batteries.

"Do I need to sign anywhere for all this?" Brad asked as he placed everything into a small black canvas belly pack. First he made sure to remember to place the pen in his shirt pocket with a thin plastic lid on the bottom to cover the needle.

"No, I hate additional paperwork. But don't pawn it off to some OAP trader."

Brad smiled, but then his grin vanished and he asked, "When do I leave, Colonel?"

"A Blackhawk awaits you on the roof. Captain Lanly will show you upstairs." Jeb shook hands with Brad, holding his hand for a brief moment in a tight grasp. "Good luck, Brad."

Fifteen minutes later, Brad was aboard a UH-60 Black Hawk Helicopter flying over Fort Greeley's outer perimeter, and skirting a thick blanket of ice fog. *I should've told them I was a pen pal to Castro, a closet pervert...anything. But no, I gotta volunteer for this secret agent stuff.*

Brad felt like he needed to throw up, his stomach was struggling with stress and to make things worse, he usually got airsick.

11 - THE COURAGE OF TIGER FIVE

"In your unfailing love you will lead the people you have redeemed. In your strength you will guide them to your holy dwelling. The nations will hear and tremble..."

Exodus 15: 13-14 NIV

ADF HEADQUARTERS CONFERENCE ROOM, EIELSON AFB - APRIL 6th

At the request of an equally exhausted President Andrews, four very fatigued men and one woman, four of them in two day old uniforms and one in a wrinkled white shirt with sleeves rolled up to his elbow and blue tie hanging loosely about his aged neck, came to Eielson Air Force Base to exchange views about the war and debate what actions should be taken next against the advancing OAP. And not too surprisingly, only the female officer bothered to take the time to put on a clean pressed uniform before appearing before the new President. The two senior air warriors were quite comfortable in Air Force flight suits, while the ADF soldiers felt their urban camouflage fatigues were suitable for this meeting of the minds.

They all sat around a large oak conference table cluttered with notebooks, loose papers and scattered pens, white ceramic coffee mugs and full ash trays, discussing the various intelligence reports and operational plans for the next stage in either their defense of Alaska's largest city or the possible decision for total withdrawal of Anchorage's citizens to Fort Greeley. With the help of several assistants, they made use of maps and graphs spread about the floor, a large Anchorage city map held between two female sergeants and Alaskan maps of varying sizes tacked to the walls.

Four senior military aides and the President's two Alaska State Trooper bodyguards remained outside the room and exchanged yawns. Each one was struggling to keep his eyes open, even after finishing off several cups of coffee, as the long hours slowly passed without let up from their bosses inside.

Weary from the long hours this meeting had taken, President Dave Andrews stood at the head of the table and attempted to emphasize a point he had concerning the problems for the defense of Anchorage. The great North American earthquakes had caused severe damage to the city, killing over 2,500 people and injuring four times that many. It was still unknown how many people were still trapped inside all the buildings, due to all the visitors in the city. The list of missing residents continued to grow and the current number was reported to be 6,857 and it was feared that the number of fatalities would climb to over ten thousand. Any structure over two stories tall was either damaged to some degree or worse; reduced to rubble. Most roadways were initially blocked and within moments following the first major quake, a 200-foot tsunami swept up the Cook Inlet and had caused great damage to shoreline structures and harbors of South Anchorage. Southside neighborhoods were still under three and four feet of water, but waters were receding and rescue operations were underway. Waters from Cook Inlet were reported to have surged northward to O'Malley Road and to the east as far as the Girdwood cut-off. Earthquake Park had dropped and slipped into the Inlet. Buildings on the north end of Steven's International Airport were damaged when land dropped and slipped. Two of the major runways were severely damaged.

The Towering British Petroleum Building and Sheraton Hotel and Alaska USA Federal Credit Union Building were all severely damaged and partially collapsed, losing one or more floors to the violent tremors. The badly damaged Captain Cook Hotel stood precariously close to the edge of a new cliff created when land north of it dropped and slip out toward the Inlet. The Hilton Hotel lay in a heap of rubble where the depot had once stood. The railroad buildings and the Comfort Inn were nowhere to be found. Other multi-floor structures were damaged in the many aftershocks that ranged as high as 9.6 on the Richter scale. Diamond Mall's office center collapsed upon the ice rink and city engineers were forced to condemn the entire mall. J.C. Penny's top floor crumbled and its attached parking garage collapsed, which trapped over a hundred customers. 253 customers were eventually evacuated from 5th Avenue Mall; 78 of them with injuries and 5 fatalities. All but the top level of the attached garage withstood the quake, but due to cracks in the structure it was condemned by city engineers. With all the cracks and breaks in the downtown roads, no vehicles could be removed from the garage. State, city and private road crews working alongside each other shoved damaged vehicles aside to open streets for emergency vehicles to use. This was proving to be a monumental task as large portions of third and fourth avenues had dropped as much as ten to fifteen feet with some portions slipping downhill to the railroad industrial area. The C Street Bridge had collapsed and disappeared in the rubble of wrecked buildings and moving earth. The New Seward Highway from O'Malley north to the Glenn Highway was eventually opened to two lanes of travel, but it took an extra three days to get the Glenn Highway open to the Palmer/Wasilla cut-off. Civilian and military helicopters were working around the clock to deliver injured people to local hospitals able to take patients. The most severe cases were flown to Fairbanks. Area wide high schools and college campuses were set up and manned by volunteers to handle lesser injuries and the homeless.

Colonel Raymond Hightower was General Saunders' second in command of all ADF and Militia forces in South Central Alaska. A handsome Black man, Hightower stood a muscular 6'4" and at his last physical weighed 200 pounds. A graduate of West Point, Class of 1994 and former Lt. Colonel in the U.S. Army, he had once commanded a battalion in the 82nd Airborne at Fort Bragg, Kentucky. He was on a one year assignment to Fort Richardson to review the Army's arctic training programs when the balloon went up. While assigned to Fort Richardson, which bordered on the city limits of northeast Anchorage, Hightower was overwhelmed by the size of Alaska's wilderness and puzzled by Alaska's easy going lifestyle. When World War III broke out, General Saunders located him on Fort Richardson and selected him for a position as a full colonel and his present command with the newly formed Alaska Defense Force. Worn from far too many hours of squabbling, he remained quiet as a heated debate broke out between two senior staff officers over the President's ideas.

One officer was Colonel Tom "Tex" Watson, who was recently made commander of ADF Northern Wing and stationed at Eielson Air Force Base. His Command was in the process of being moved to Fort Greeley and he was not happy with the order to abandon Eielson. A graduate of the Air Force Academy, Class of 1991, he was on his feet to better voice his opinions and had little problem with interrupting the President over several key issues. Watson never liked civilians, especially politicians and in particular, a state governor recently made US President and without a popular vote by the citizens. He also personally thought, but did not voice it, that General Saunders should be running this whole mess.

Watson, who was built like a fire plug, had the wide shoulders of an NFL linebacker and stood a compact 5'10". His gray hair was cut in a military style buzz, his normally clear blue eyes were bloodshot and except for a thick gray moustache he was clean shaven. His gray flight suit was adorned with numerous multicolored flight patches; one small patch on his left shoulder identified him as an F-15 ace fighter jock which he had gained while flying with the Israeli Air Force against the Syrians. A major at the time and on loan to the Israeli Air Force as an advisor and to gain combat experience, Watson, who was flying a new F-22 Raptor, shot down seven Syrian fighters over a five day period.

Like Hightower, Watson had fallen in love with Alaska when he assumed the position of Executive Officer for of the 358th Combat Fighter Wing at Elmendorf. When the OAP attacked the United States, Watson was newly and was one of the first senior officers to place his entire command under the newly formed ADF. He also accepted command of the ADF

Northern Wing at General Saunders' request and moved his family, reluctantly, to Eielson Air Force Base.

His wife of 33 years preferred to remain in Anchorage close to church friends, but as usual, she went where her husband's orders directed them. Their son, who was engaged to a local young lady, elected to join the militia and remain in Anchorage. Watson's oldest child, a daughter, was also serving with the ADF Air Force and assigned to Elmendorf Air Force Base as an F-15 pilot.

Watson had flown an aging F-15 to Elmendorf for the meeting, with plans to trade it in for one of the new F-35 fighters, thinking General Saunders would be chairing the meeting. He found himself in a heated argument over a particular point of aircraft deployment with Colonel Brady "Ape" Wilcox.

A fellow pilot, Wilcox had no prior military training, but had logged over 30,000 flying hours in various propeller and jet aircraft. He had worked as a test pilot and later, senior pilot for General Dynamics and had left them to accept a position as one of three Vice Presidents for Alaskan Airlines and happened to be in Anchorage when the Christmas morning attack occurred. With his knowledge of aircraft, flying experience and running a large company, General Saunders convinced him to accept command of the ADF Southern Wing, over the objections of Colonel Watson and other flying officers, who were not happy to have a civilian placed in a major command position. But unlike the Northern Wing, made up of active duty Air Force pilots, the Southern Wing consisted mainly of Militia, Reserve and National Guard pilots. Businessmen exactly like Wilcox, who put in one weekend a month and two weeks every summer. General Saunders knew he had picked the right man for the job.

Ironically, President Andrews thought Wilcox and Watson were nearly mirror images of one another, from hair color to body size. The exception being Wilcox's piercing brown eyes, a trunk load of crow's feet and wrinkles about the face and a jutting block jawline. "Excuse me, gentlemen, I think we're losing focus here." President Andrews said loudly. "We're trying to decide if it is best to deploy the 93rd Squadron against the enemy now or hold off for either the protection of Anchorage or Fort Greeley." President Andrews sighed with relief when both Colonel Wilcox and Colonel Watson returned to their seats. "Colonel Wilcox feels we should commit the 93rd now, hit the enemy as they proceed south towards Fairbanks," President Andrews quickly reviewed his notes. "On the other side, Colonel Watson defends his plan to hold the 93rd in reserve at Fort Greeley until the OAP makes their attack on Delta Junction and later, Fort Greeley." He looked around the table, "Do we have any discussion from other members present?"

From the other end of the table, George Maconnel, Senior Advisor to President Andrews and a newly appointed Colonel in the ADF Militia, remained silent with a whimsical, 'Don't you involve me in this, Mr. President' look on his face. A former U.S. Senator representing Alaska in the US Congress, Maconnel retired from politics to start a small hunting and guide service near Talkeetna, approximately 70 miles north of Anchorage. He hoped the business would provide for his elderly years, but that was before General Saunders came to visit.

Colonel Maconnel, overweight by a good 25 pounds, balding gray/brown hair and droopy dark brown eyes preferred to wear civilian clothes. He often wore a dark brown Fedora hat and carried a beautiful diamond willow walking stick; a gift from his wife. He thought wearing a uniform at his age was simply plain foolishness, but obeyed orders to wear silver eagles pinned to his shirt collars, though he flatly refused to blouse his boots. It was Maconnel's keen mind and ability to stay calm during heated moments such as this that made him invaluable to President Andrews. In congress it was his resemblance to a used car salesman that often caught his opponents unaware and with a hungry look as if he was about to make a quick sale, Maconnel, who was of Irish decent, would more often than not, surprise his opponents by winning the day.

When action began, Colonel Maconnel planned to be dressed in his favorite hunting clothes, armed with a Smith & Wesson Model 29 .44 caliber revolver worn in a shoulder holster and carrying a Remington 12-guage pump shotgun. With his aged eyes failing him, he thought a shotgun was better for him over one of his high powered rifles.

Recognizing Maconnel's look of non-committal, President Andrews turned to address the stalwart Colonel Hightower, "Your opinion please, Colonel?"

"Into the lion's den Daniel was thrown," Hightower said and received a respectful chuckle from all present, "Mr. President, as I see it, those A-10 Warthogs, ugly brutes as they are, armed with 30mm cannon capable of cutting a tank up like Swiss cheese, is an Air Force problem to deal with." Hightower ignored President Andrews' disgruntled look and continued, "From a ground pounder's view, they fly as slow as a one winged goose and I strongly believe any pilot who chooses to fly one is straight suicidal by nature." Hightower gestured at Watson, "I'll have to agree with Colonel Watson, we should keep the wing at Greeley for now or take the chance on losing them to the OAP's superior air cover. These A-10s of ours cannot out fly the OAP fighters. " Hightower looked into the unhappy eyes of Colonel Wilcox, "The Air Force made a big mistake when they shipped the A-10's out of Alaska in the first place, but once the Intel boys saw the OAP build-up and knew what was coming, the decision makers at the Pentagon at least sent us back this one squadron. We have to use it wisely. So, I'm sorry, Brady, that's as I see it. "

"I should expect such from a dumb old flat footed ground pounder," Wilcox said in jest. He nodded to Watson, "You win this one, but the war isn't over yet."

Present Andrews turned to Colonel Archie Olson, former Lt. Colonel of the Alaska Army National Guard and full blooded Athabascann Indian. A tribal leader, Colonel Olson had worked his way up through the National Guard ranks for 41 years, having started out as a private from Arctic Village. At 60, Col. Olson was selected for his position by Colonel Hightower, who promoted him to full bird and his Executive Officer. Light brown skin, narrow dark brown eyes and heavily wrinkled face, Col. Olson knew just about everything there was to know about the Tanana Valley terrain. For years he had hunted, fished and conducted guard drills throughout the valley. Lt. Colonel Olson was 5'7" and weighed 138 lbs., which meant he didn't take up a lot of room in the cushy conference chair he was sitting in. He listened and watched the others and only commented when called upon.

"Colonel Olson, your input please," President Andrews asked.

"Sir, I'm a grunt or ground pounder if you prefer and I know little about the capabilities of the A-10. But I can say, that if I was on the ground facing one of those OAP dreadnaughts you've shown us photographs of, I would want one of those A-10's covering my behind...I am in agreement with Colonel Hightower."

"So, the A-10s will remain at Greeley to cover our infantry when the time comes. Is there anything else?" President Andrews asked. He reached for his coffee cup, only to find it empty. A steward, seeing the disappointed expression on the president's face quickly moved in to refill it from a silver coffee carafe. A large 33 cup coffee urn was in the corner of the room and it was the steward's chore to ensure everyone's mugs were kept filled with steaming hot liquid.

"Yes, Mr. President," Col. Hightower said, "...I plan to move the 2nd Militia Division into position tonight to reinforce the beachhead." Hightower pointed to the map of Anchorage and indicated the position he was referring to along the southern boundary of the old Anchorage Shooting Club rifle and pistol ranges. "I recommend we abandon Fort Richardson and Elmendorf within the next 48 hours."

"So soon?" Colonel Maconnel asked.

An attractive brunette wearing black major leaves and dressed in a well-pressed set of clean urban fatigues, stood to her feet and replied, "Yes, Colonel...and for the same reason we've moved President Andrews from his fine penthouse apartment; our intelligence people believe OAP bombers will begin hitting our southern bases within the next 48 hours."

Major Ruth Judge was Colonel Hightower's Chief of Intelligence and present at this meeting by Col. Hightower's request. At 34, she was still quite beautiful, green eyed and nearly model thin at 6' tall and 126 lbs. Single, she was a former Criminal Investigator with the US Army assigned to Fort Richardson CID unit and had been employed by the Anchorage Police Department as an Intelligence Officer. When hostilities broke out, Colonel Hightower had learned about her and brought her on board as his Intelligence Chief.

"Mr. President, the OAP now have control of the airfields in Nome and Kotzebue, and they are ready to handle air traffic from Eastern Russia."

"Do you still have men in the field up there?" President Andrews asked in surprise.

"Eskimo scouts, Mr. President - small two man radio units from the 1st Division who volunteered. They're quite good at staying hidden in the bush, able to move around in the dark and live off the land."

"Still no word from Colonel Freeman?" Col. Maconnel asked, his face showing concern for the valiant men and women of the 1st Division.

"No contact," Hightower replied. "With remorse, we now consider the 1st Division to be lost...with the exception of Major Blackstone's unit, who are at this moment moving toward Fairbanks in all haste."

"Can't we get them picked up by helicopter?" Wilcox asked.

Major Judge resumed her chair and replied, "Negative, sir. The OAP air cap covers that entire area and they will shoot down any rescue force we send in."

Colonel Watson spoke up quickly. "But, if some bad weather sits in, grounding the air cap, I've got some hot Black Hawk pilots willing to give it a shot. They'll move in at tree-top level, buzzing the ice fog and staying well below enemy radar. The other difficulty will be is if the ash begins to fall again. That heavy black ash can fowl up an engine pretty fast and drop a bird right out of the sky."

"It's still hard to believe a whole division could be destroyed so quickly." Colonel Maconnel said.

"From what we picked up over the radios, the OAP came across the ice in a three-mile wide front. It was like...well, like our D-Day in 1944 or when Hitler's armored units counterattacked and sent the allies running for cover during the initial stages of the Battle of the Bulge. Using tanks with motorized infantry support, the OAP hit hard and our beach positions on Wales couldn't stand up to them. On top of that, the OAP Air Force strafed and bombed the beach defenses until the only thing left of Wales was a smoldering ruin and a hundred deep bomb craters."

"We also lost four of our Raptors and our only C-5A, which from reports did a great job carrying out Operation Breadbasket," Colonel Wilcox said with admiration.

Colonel Hightower then added, "Some of Colonel Freeman's units were able to retreat and set up an ambush at Koyukuk, hammering the enemy with artillery until every round was used up. After that, we have no idea if any of our troops survived." Following a moment of silence, he asked, "Mr. President, I have a lot of civilians to train over the next 72 hours and some of these Anchorage city dwellers don't seem to know which end of the rifle to shoot with. I'd like your permission to leave; Colonel Olson can field any more questions you might have."

"Be patient with them, Colonel," Colonel Maconnel said. "Most of these fine people have grown used to a 37.5- hour work week, barbecuing hot dogs and burgers on Saturday afternoons and attending church services on Sunday mornings. Before this, the only guns most of them handled were on their TV arcade games or the occasional moose hunt." Colonel McConnell stood to his feet and offered his hand to Colonel Hightower, "Good luck, Colonel."

"Thank you...and good luck to all of us." Hightower shook McConnell's hand, nodded to Watson and Wilcox, before he saluted President Andrews. He gave a raised eyebrow expression to both Colonel Olson and Major Judge before he headed toward the door.

"Please give my regards to General Saunders and inform him I will be leaving for Greeley within the next 48 to 72 hours," President Andrews said.

Colonel Hightower turned in the doorway, faced the president and replied with a quick, "Yes, Sir".

After Hightower left, followed by one of his waiting junior officers, Colonel Wilcox turned to the President and asked, "When can we expect the Canadians?"

"General Saunders reported the first airborne units have already dropped on Greeley, tractor trailers are passing through Delta Junction as we speak... And believe it or not, General Howard-Wright has sent a force of 600 mounted RCMP's, who are apparently the lead element and honor guard for General Howard-Wright's Western Army." President Andrews pushed a buzzer and another enlisted steward appeared almost instantly. "Would you please ask the cook to send in some sort of finger food?" President Andrews requested. "I've got the munchies."

"Yes, Mr. President," the man in white coat, white shirt with black tie, and black pants, replied as he disappeared through a side door.

Colonel Wilcox stood up to stretch his legs, "Horses? What good are horses against tanks?"

"It seems they are a morale factor for the Canadian Army and General Howard-Wright's personal favorite," President Andrews replied. "He was with the RCMP before the army and won a Bronze Medal when he rode in the Olympics held in China... And I sure wouldn't want to face 600 galloping horsemen coming at me with the 8 foot long pig stickers they carry." He smiled at Colonel Wilcox and said in a pleasant tone, "Please remember, gentlemen and my dear Major, the Canadian Army is offering us four Divisions of combat troops. With our combined force, we stand an even chance of defeating our invaders or at least forcing them back across the ice."

"Mr. President, while we're waiting for those munchies, could you update us on our Navy's condition?" Watson looked down at a sheet of paper with numbers and names of vessels assigned to the ADF and a second page showing those recently confiscated for the war effort. Not all Alaska fishermen were agreeable to giving up their fishing boats, pleasure craft and barges for the war. In a few cases, they had to be seized by force and some people were hurt. Fishermen were known to be a hardy lot, especially those who faced the deep turbulent blue green waters off Alaska's shore. They were known as quite an independent lot, especially those who had lost most of their livelihood because of the ongoing tightening of federal fishing regulations. As a result, some of the fishermen, crabbers and charter boat captains had lost homes and marriages and blamed Uncle Sam. Others freely volunteered vessels and labors to help protect and feed the Alaskan people. This wasn't an easy chore for the best of ocean going crewmen since the waters off Alaska's coast and south of the icepack had turned dangerous with waves reported to be more than 60 feet up to a possible 90 feet.

Major Judge addressed the room, "As you all know, our statewide defense system was tied into the NORAD Network. When NORAD was knocked out and all our satellites were rendered useless by layers of volcanic ash or suspected Star Wars activity, we basically lost our eyes in the sky. This also meant all GPS systems were useless as well. Our only working long range radar is at Clear Air Force Station south of Fairbanks. Part of the DEW line system, the site is currently manned by volunteers guarded by Militia. With little threat of missile attack, the site is about useless, but we continue operating the facility to monitor enemy Air Force activity and in the event OAP forces change strategy and launch ICBMs our way." Major Judge paused as two stewards brought in two silver trays; one holding quartered tuna sandwiches and the other chicken salad sandwiches. Another coffee urn was wheeled in and all the mugs were topped off and ash trays emptied. Once the stewards left the room, she continued. "From the south, we have surface radar units effective to approximately 120 miles by line of sight and a limited naval force to warn of enemy approach. This force consists of mostly fishing boats and large trawlers patrolling the Aleutians. There are observation posts on offshore oil rigs in the Cook Inlet, three State Fish and Wildlife boats patrolling south of Kodiak Island, and four Coast Guard vessels patrolling the Bering Sea well below the ice shelf and so far they have not been attacked by OAP Air Forces. Several Coast Guard C-130s, used to operating in bad weather with high seas, are busy with search and rescue operations. None of our vessels are heavily armed with the exception of the Coast Guard Cutters, which carry single 30mm guns, supported by M-60 Machineguns," Major Judge said in her strong briefing voice. She pointed to a large wall map displaying the Gulf of Alaska, "With these weird storms popping up and the massive waves they produce, we've lost nearly half of our fleet in the last month, but these have been mostly smaller boats."

President Andrews dropped his eyes, extremely saddened as he thought of the number of crew members who had given their lives to maintain vigilance and then he took over the briefing as Major Judge returned to her seat. "So, gentlemen, this is the current condition of our navy...we have nine vessels equipped for limited combat, 126 boats for recon, harbor guard and fishing... and 19 barges for transporting goods as need arises." President Andrews took his coffee cup and walked over to a large framed photograph of the Denali Mountain Range and began to recall his fishing trip last summer. He was in Bristol Bay, near Dillingham fishing for silver salmon. With him were several political friends; he had paid $215.00 a day per person for the six day charter to catch a total of 26 silver salmon. It was well worth it. The sea was calm and the sun was shining for 21 hours...Oh, to go back in time.

Colonel Maconnel took a bite of chicken salad sandwich and closed his spiral notebook. He knew this meal would be considered his ration for the day, so didn't mind wrapping another in a napkin for later. He then addressed Colonel Wilcox in a direct tone, "Colonel, just what steps have you taken to ensure the safety of the citizens of Anchorage if the city comes under attack?"

Colonel Wilcox was taken aback by Colonel Maconnel's tone, but then he remembered the man was a lifelong politician who knew from long experience that military and politics never mixed well, not even during time of war. Colonel Wilcox presented his best smile and in a calm voice replied, "Following established procedures, set down by General Saunders and in which I am full agreement with, I have implemented a 24 hour air cap over this city. I am keeping two F-22 Raptors or F-15 Eagles airborne at all times. Two F-35 fighters are lined up for immediate launch as back up should the need arise and a full air squadron of either F-15s or F-22s are ready on 15 minute alert status. We have a shortage of F-35s and needed parts, as you know, so I am using them sparingly. Besides ADF ground units, we also have Militia forces preparing to defend the beaches along the northern end of Cook Inlet, supported by four batteries of artillery and two batteries of anti-aircraft guns, which also guard the coastal refinery. But once the President and General Saunders make the final decision as to whether or not to evacuate Anchorage, our air and ground forces will be reduced for the withdrawal to Fort Greeley. We already have bus convoys running around the clock to evacuate citizens to Fort Greeley. Hospital patients and in some cases elderly are now being flown by transport on to Fort Greeley, mainly because the bus trip could be too hard on them. Until action is imminent, almost all personnel are involved in search and rescue operations, or the clearing of roadways."

President Andrews also added his two cents, "Our main problem is simply the numbers; we have over 300,000 people to move and time is limited. As to whether or not we keep an adequate fighting force in Anchorage…that will be finally decided upon within the next 24 hours. We've mined the harbor with what few anti-ship mines we had, providing a safe corridor for our fleet and General Saunders has placed Seward, Homer and Kodiak on 50/50 alert status."

"I thought we were only worried about the OAP coming in from the west?" Colonel Maconnel asked.

Major Judge spoke, "General Saunders' Fort Wainwright Intelligence Section learned through overseas sources that OAP purchasing agents have bought an additional one dozen super tankers from the Middle East oil cartels. These vessels, similar in size to the ones that were used to sneak the OAP submarines into the Gulf of Mexico, were last reported at the docks of Cam Ranh Bay and Danang, Vietnam. Both are deep water ports and one of the reasons we feel the Chinese attacked Vietnam, along with the vast wealth in rice paddies. The major took a sip of coffee and from her notebook pulled out a photo of one of the super tankers being flagged out of Iran. "The General believes and I tend to agree, that OAP naval yards are most likely converting these super tankers into troop carriers for an invasion of the Middle East. We believe they used this strategy to convert those tankers to carry at least two missile subs across the Pacific."

"I read that report, Major," Colonel Wilcox said. "Based on their incredible size these tankers can probably take on a full battalion and maybe more. Still, I wonder how they'd get the men and equipment off quickly enough for a beachhead assault?"

"I was thinking much the same thing…until I remembered seeing one of those very same James Bond flicks General Saunders spoke of!" Watson exclaimed.

"Landing craft, most likely on two levels and loaded with troops. The doors will open and first one level and then the next can peel off… That's exactly how they'll do it!" Wilcox exclaimed and then added, "Ingenious!" Excited, he grabbed up the coffee carafe to top off his cup. "Wonder if they got the idea from the movie?" Wilcox poured coffee into Watson's cup.

Least they're agreeing on something. "Okay, enough with the spy thrillers. I'm getting bleary eyed and if I drink anymore coffee I'll be floating. So, the General has ordered we keep an eye on the eastern edges of the Gulf of Alaska. The radiation from their missiles will keep them from traveling too far into the Gulf, so if they come at us from the south, we should be able to pick them off. Now is that all? Anything else we need to cover before we break up this little party?" President Andrews asked as he looked at the other men.

"One last item, Mr. President…and I should have brought it up while Colonel Hightower was present," Watson said with slight hesitation and then continued, "Back in the 1970's, the Air Force tested the probability of using a C-141 as a weapons platform for the release of cruise missiles. We have two C-141's at Elmendorf, being used by the Air National Guard, that were supposed to be on their way south to the bone yard when all this blew up in our faces. I know for a fact we have four cruise missiles stored at the launching facility at Kodiak. They were part of the testing program for the anti-missile defense system on Shemya, for all the good that did us."

"Go on, Colonel," President Andrews said.

"My geeks tell me they can convert one of our C-141's for this task in 48hours. Not to safety standards, you understand, but they could launch the missiles."

"What about guidance systems?" Colonel Wilcox asked.

"Not a problem for short range low altitude. We have two conventional warheads, enough high explosive to take out a large city block…but…we also have two nuclear warheads in the 10 kiloton range stored at Fort Greely," Colonel Watson advised.

"Nuclear? Here in Alaska?" Colonel Maconnel shot to his feet. "You'd use a nuclear device on our own soil?"

"Only as a last resort, Colonel," Colonel Watson said in quick response after observing how upset Colonel Maconnel was getting. "We'd detonate a conventional warhead on Fairbanks to hurt the enemy's supply line and save the nuclear weapons for a last ditch effort if Greeley becomes surrounded and we have no other options." then added, "It might be the only way to save Canada from invasion."

"Last ditch effort…weapons of last resort…this sounds like a scene from some Peter Seller's sci-fi flick," Colonel Maconnel raved. He addressed the President, "You must not allow this, Mr. President! We already have a comet coming at us and we still have no actual idea how much damage it will cause upon impact. The Lower 48 is glowing in the dark, India plastered Pakistan and now most of the Middle East is unlivable…But to purposely use a nuclear device on our own beloved land…that's preposterous!"

"Where did you say the aircraft are now, Colonel?" President Andrews asked.

"Elmendorf," Colonel Wilcox replied attempting to ignore Maconnel's reddened face and hoped the old man wasn't going to have a heart attack.

"I'll discuss this matter with General Saunders. But I must admit, gentlemen and dear lady, I tend to agree with Colonel Maconnel over the use of nuclear weapons. Up to this moment, I didn't even know we had such weapons in our inventory," President Andrews glanced back at Maconnel, "Still, the thought of leaving my beautiful Alaska for the OAP to rape and plunder will cause me to think this matter over seriously." The President paced the room while the others remained silent; tension between Colonel Maconnel and Colonel Wilcox was evident by the way they glared at each other. He turned and faced Colonel Watson, "For the present, have the C-141 fitted for the conventional weapons. We will probably have to use them to defend Fort Greeley or possibly Anchorage if the OAP drives further south…or they come in by the sea. This meeting is over; we'll meet again in 24 hours or earlier if the situation changes,"

As the meeting broke up, Colonels Wilcox and Watson simultaneously released a tired groan as they stood to their feet and stretched to get the kinks out of stiff muscles and help their aging backs loosen up. With aides following, the two men walked down a long lighted cement corridor which ended at a double flight of gray metal stairs. Taking one step at a time they climbed upward to a set of heavy metal double doors that led them outside. April temperatures at Eielson had risen above zero and with no ash in the air, it possible for the two commanders to enjoy a breath of cold fresh air.

Eielson was a landscape of deep white snow, covered in black and gray ash, scattered bare trees, aged gray buildings, large and mid-sized hangers, office buildings, barracks, warehouses. In the center of the base were three tall flag poles; the center one holding the Star and Stripes of the United States, a lower one waving the blue and gold flag of the State of Alaska. On the third was the new light blue, green and white flag of the Alaskan Defense Force with a grizzly and an eagle in flight to signify the air and ground forces.

A COMING STORM

The air was filled with the noisy sound and flashing white and yellow lights as hundreds of people rushed to and fro preparing the base for war and eventual evacuation. The ice fog was thinning and patchy with the warmer weather. With the recent snow and ash fall of nearly nine inches, heavy equipment operators were busy cleaning the runways and tarmac, and only afterward would they start work on the roadways.

Following a low and fast Blackhawk helicopter ride south to Elmendorf Air Force Base and upon arrival, Colonels Wilcox and Watson were startled to step out of the bird to the squealing sound of the base's alert siren. It was immediately followed by an excited voice shouting over the base public address system, "Red alert! Red alert! All personnel report to combat stations. All personnel report to combat stations. This is not an exercise!" The warning was repeated three times; men and women began running in all directions for assigned shelters or battle stations. A few moments later, Wilcox and Watson, noticeably out of breath and somewhat rattled, ran into the Command Post. Colonel Wilcox located Major Anders, the Officer of the Day to get an update. All around the CP trained enlisted technicians and officers were going about their jobs, manning communications booths, status boards and radar screens.

We practiced this a hundred times, now it's for real and the practice is proving itself. "What have we got?" Colonel Wilcox asked Major Anders.

"Eight bogies, sir," Anders reported. "We show them at 120 miles out and coming in from the southeast at approximately 540 mph."

"Where's our air cap?" Wilcox asked.

"They're currently over King Salmon; the farthest point of our coverage. I've sent out an RTB, (return to base), but its' unfortunate timing for us." Anders looked at the nearest radar screen and saw the eight blips slowly drawing close to the Alaskan shoreline. "It appears they're headed for Anchorage, Colonel. They've bypassed Kodiak completely and staying to the eastward side of the Kenai Peninsula."

"Launch the alert birds!" Wilcox ordered. He was surprised with himself for not already having done it. *I was a company VP, not some combat commander.*

"Yes, sir...two F-35s are ready to roll," Anders replied.

"Bring Tiger Squadron up to full combat readiness and launch them in 15 minutes," Colonel Wilcox ordered. "There may be others enemy planes coming in behind those eight bogies and I don't want to be caught unprepared. Contact all squadrons, bring them to combat alert status and have them stand by." Colonel Wilcox walked over to the nearest radar screen, put his hand on the enlisted man's shoulder to reassure him.

Meanwhile, Colonel Watson approached an MP Lieutenant standing by the door to the CP, "Make sure the President is safe. Don't send just anyone; I want you to do it yourself and then report his location and status to me."

"I'm on my way, Colonel."

Colonel Watson returned to Colonel Wilcox's side, ready to be called upon for advice, support or whatever.

Complying with his colonel's orders, Sgt. Oshkik lifted a plastic cover and pressed a red button, triggering a second siren and an air blast horn inside the alert hangers. The 2nd siren accompanied by four blasts of the alert hanger's air horn signaled permission for the two alert birds to taxi. An additional siren mounted atop a hanger where Tiger Squadron waited, notified them to prepare for the launch of their 18 remaining aircraft.

Pilots pulling alert, one of the most hated duties in the Air Force lived in their flight suits and practically slept in their birds. On a 24 hour rotating schedule, the two F-35 pilots and their assigned planes were replaced by two other crews and planes from the same squadron. Following seven days of alert duty, the squadron was replaced to ease the tension; as alert status meant a state of living and breathing combat readiness.

Only six F-35 fighters were assigned to Elmendorf; another six were assigned to Eielson and on their way to Fort Greeley. The number of pilots qualified to fly the F-35 was limited, not to mention qualified mechanics, parts and high-tech electronics needed to keep these new birds in the air. As a priority, Colonel Wilcox assigned two of these F-35s to alert status and rotated the planes, qualified pilots and ground crew every 24 hours. Knowing the capabilities of the F-35, Colonel Wilcox felt sure his two birds could easily handle the eight bogies coming at them. But he was still concerned with where they had launched from and this would be the next priority, once his pilots had splashed the eight bogies into the cold and unforgiving Alaskan ocean.

COMBAT ALERT REVETMENT

Lt. Joe "Pappy" Amstead nearly jumped into the cockpit of his F-35 when the first siren went off. He knew the order to launch would soon follow. He slammed his knee against the ridge of the cockpit, but his surging adrenaline flow was enough to hold off a scream. To his right, 2nd Lt. Barbara "Goldy" Moxie had gracefully climbed into her F-35, waiting as her crew chief readied her parachute harness for hook up. When the second siren sounded they were both ready to taxi toward the runway. 21 seconds later; cockpits closed, all equipment strapped down for launch, Pappy and Goldie kicked in afterburners and were suddenly shoved back hard against the back of their seats. With a thunderous roar, they both raced down the runway at 220 mph and still accelerating.

The F-35; the latest fighter in the US Air Force inventory, smacked full of the latest high technology and greater flying capability than the F-22, had been sent to Alaska to conduct arctic training with both the Raptors and the F-15 Eagles. 12 F-35's were flown up from Nellis Air Force Base, Nevada and as far as anyone knew, were the last 12 F-35's in existence. Pappy and Goldie had come up with the aircraft, having already been trained on them and sent through the Air Force Red Flag school. Stuck in Alaska after the missiles flew, all 12 of the US Air Force fighter jocks had immediately joined the ADF and hoped for a chance to engage the OAP with their hot rides.

Pappy and Goldie remained below the ash barrier; at 1100 feet and approaching Mach 1, they were headed south through the darkening sky. Unless ordered to break through the ash clouds and reach for the clear heavens above, which seldom if at all happened, they'd keep it fast and low to the ground. They both knew that once a fighter went through a cloud of ash, it would be down for a week as mechanics cleaned the aircraft's insides for every single particle of ash. From vacuums to tooth brushes, the tiresome chore of cleaning the turbines was extremely laborious.

TIGER ALERT FLIGHT

"Echo Tower, this is Tiger 5, alert birds are in the green. Over," Pappy said flashing a thumbs up sign to Goldy, which she actually couldn't see from her vantage point. She slowly moved up into position on his right wing, excited to the point of trembling, but thankful with goggles and oxygen mask in place, Pappy couldn't see her nervous smile.

"Roger, Tiger 5. Switch frequency to 103.5 and contact Echo Base for further orders. Good hunting, Tiger 5. Out," the control tower radio operator said.

Pappy reached down and dialed up the new frequency, knowing Goldy was accomplishing the same thing. "Echo Base, this is Tiger 5. Over," Pappy said.

"This is Echo Base, reading you 5x5, Tiger 5. Go ahead…Over."

"What's on the menu tonight, Echo Base…Over?" *I can feel in my bones, this is the real thing. Its shoot 'em up time and we're getting the first bogies.*

"Be advised you have eight bogies… I repeat eight bogies, coming in from the southeast flying at 14,000 feet and descending fast. Range is eight…zero miles and speed five…six…zero and slowing…Over."

"Are we free to engage, Echo Base…Over?" Pappy felt the adrenaline pumping through him. This is so hot, no more exercises…the real deal and I got this beautiful bird to play the swan song with. Time for some sweet revenge!

"We show negative signature for friendlies, but you are ordered to confirm identity before combat engaging…Over," Echo Base advised.

"Copy that. Have we got any other friends coming to this party…Over?" *Eight to two is not my best choice of odds, especially if these clowns are flying those new JI-20 interceptor bombers we were briefed on. We can beat them on turnings, but we're matched for speed and armament.*

"Air Cap coming in from the west, ETA 11 mikes but they will remain on station. Tiger Squadron is preparing for launch, but will be 15 mikes behind you…Over." The female air controller spoke in a calm voice and Pappy thought she sounded sexy, making him wonder what she might look like? *That kind of thinking is gonna get me in trouble…settle down, boy…You got a war to fight and this plane to fly!*

"Copy, I request clearance to 15,000 feet…Over."

"Negative, you are to stay beneath cloud cover…remain at your present 1100 feet…Over."

"Copy, Echo Base. I will remain at present height, direction and speed. I will contact you again in 5 mikes…Out." Pappy looked up at the strange ash clouds above. The swirling black mist reminded him of a nightmare he once had as a kid; where he was swallowed up in this black churning substance never to be seen again. His mother would dash into his bedroom to shake him awake and then hold him until he was able to fall asleep again. Pappy could make out lightning flashes in parts of the clouds and seriously hoped he wouldn't take a lightning strike on this flight. He was not looking forward to getting into a dogfight with a ceiling of only 1100 feet or at best, 1200 feet. He glanced to his right to make sure Goldy was where she belonged. She was.

"Check your guns, Goldy," Pappy said over the ICS system - plane to plane contact.

"Copy, Pappy." She fired off a quick burst of 30mm cannon fire.

"Guns all working, Pappy… did you remember to check yours?"

"Mine are A-Okay, Goldie."

"Everything is in the green, so let's go a huntin'," Goldie said and nudged her plane ahead of Pappy's wing by a good 100 feet.

"Remember your place, Lieutenant or you'll be scrubbing down my plane for a week and shining my flight boots."

Goldie slowed up just a hair, resumed her proper place and glanced below to see lines and lines of white breakers in the stormy seas below. They were flying over the Gulf of Alaska and she could see this was one nasty spot. Goldie sincerely hoped she'd never have to go swimming here - especially paddling a little yellow one person survival raft in the event she was shot down praying a rescue chopper was en route.

"Pappy, how tall do you think those waves are down there?"

"One of my surfer buddies from Hawaii would probably tell you they were 60 - 70 feet...but I think they could reach right up here and wash off the bottom of my bird."

"I'm hoping we don't have to find out...Is that five minutes up yet?"

"Having patience is the sign of a good officer, Goldie, so sit back and focus your mental energies on the job up ahead...I want to drop as many of those..." Pappy didn't get to finish because he was receiving radio traffic from Echo Base.

"Be advised, your eight bogies now at 1200 feet and slowed to 420 mph. You are on a direct path with them and should have them on your radar screen in six minutes."

Pappy looked back toward Goldie's plane and said, "You ready for this?"

Goldie nodded nervously, "I've got your wing, let's go party!"

BACK AT ELMENDORF

"Echo Tower, this is Tiger-1 requesting permission to launch 18 Eagles in two sections," Captain Susan "Mother" Watson, daughter of Colonel "Tex" Watson, said over the radio. She held her bird ready at the south end of the runway; lined up behind her was Tiger's Alpha section in flights of two F-15 Eagles. Behind that Bravo's section of nine Eagles was holding back on the tarmac until Alpha section was airborne and the runway was clear.

"Tiger -1 you have permission to launch. No other traffic in the immediate area-over. Be advised our air cap is currently 22 miles to the southwest and remaining at 1100 feet."

"Copy that...I'm rolling now." Kicking in afterburners, Watson's petite frame was slammed back into her seat as a rumbling roar blasted her off the runway at 170 mph accelerating to 340 mph. She didn't want to lose any time in catching up with her two alert bird chicks and wasted little time as her Eagle shot up into the sky.

Once Alpha Flight was in the sky, turning to the south, Bravo flight moved up to the active runway ready for launch. The two birds assigned air cap duty, were ordered to maintain station once they were back over the Anchorage area. Both pilots reluctantly agreed, but expressed feelings at being left out of the fight. One slammed his fist against the canopy and the other inadvertently spoke a few chosen words of profanity over the radio.

He would be reprimanded about it later, but right now there were other priorities to handle.

The Alaska Air Command renamed the ADF Air Force, consisted of former US Army helicopter units, US Air Force and Alaska Air National Guard aircraft. The fighter squadrons, three of which were assigned to Elmendorf and three to Eielson were now on their way to fort Greeley. The ADF Air Force consisted of 12 of the new F-35 fighters, 22 of the F-22 Raptors and 80 F-15 Eagles and 24 A-10 Warthogs. There were six C-122 and 14 C-130 cargo aircraft, several dozen UH-1 Huey and UH-60 Blackhawk Helicopters. 12 Chinook double rotor cargo helicopters previously assigned to the US Army to haul cargo and 105 mm cannons were being used for air evacuation of hospital patients. The ADF also had nine H-53 Rescue Helicopters once used to pull injured climbers from the sides of towering mountains now being used for recon and supply drops to forward units. The Air Force at Elmendorf also had two massive aged C-141 cargo jets and three VC-20 executive jets. Twelve KC-135 Tankers stationed at Eielson and Elmendorf on 30 day TDY rotation from the Lower 48 were in the process of being moved to Fort Greely. Two of them were on 24 hour stand by in the event they are needed to refuel any of the fighters. Parked at Fort Greeley were six F-16 Falcons up from the Lower 48 for Arctic training held back to be used as interceptors in the event Canada had chosen to attack across the Alaska border. Now they were being prepped for a similar interceptor role in the event Fairbanks was not fully evacuated when OAP bombers arrived. Added to this inventory were over 600 privately owned aircraft of various sizes, shapes and makes; some with skies were being used for courier duties throughout the state.

Unfortunately, when Elmendorf was taken by surprise by the eight bogies to the south, the KC-135 alert tankers were already landing at Fort Greeley in need of refueling themselves. The ADF had been caught with its pants down and it made General Saunders wonder if he had some OAP sympathizers in his ranks. With the fuel trucks, or yellow backed lumbering beasts as they were sometimes called, still on the highway en route to Fort Greeley from Eielson, it would be nearly impossible for the Tankers to be able to assist Tiger Flight, if and when they needed fuel. There was still one KC-135 on the ground at Elmendorf, but it was down for repairs. Frantic ground chiefs began shouting at crews to get repairs done in haste as the plane was badly needed. A line of refueling trucks waited for the ground chief to signal them it was okay to move in and start refueling, but it was going to take time and the Tiger Flight crew chiefs knew their precious birds were going to be running on fumes when and if they made it back to Elmendorf.

Someone had really dropped the ball on this one and Colonel Wilcox wanted to know who it was, but as commander he would have to take the blame. Like Colonel Watson, he simply wasn't expecting an attack from the south and wondered where these enemy aircraft were coming from. As far as they knew the only air fields to the south with runways large enough to handle jet fighters were Dillingham and Dutch Harbor; both of which were last known to be in Militia hands and mined.

Transferring frequencies from tower to Command Post, Captain Watson headed Southwest to rendezvous with her two chicks, "Pappy, this is Mother Hen at 800 feet heading your way, how do you read...Over?"

"Mother, how nice to know you're in the neighborhood...Over."

"All right, Pappy, keep your mind in the game and your fingers off those triggers until you confirm these bogies are enemy aircraft. I don't want any accidents due to pilot twitters...Over."

"Tiger-1...Mother, you know I never get the twitters...Stand by, I'm picking up those bogies on my radar...they've accelerated to Mach one." Pappy quit talking for a moment as he devoted all his attention to flying and bogies screaming at him at 550 feet.

ADF COMMAND POST

Listening in on communications between aircraft, Colonel Wilcox spoke with Colonel Watson and commented on how well his daughter was working out as a squadron leader, "Her pilots think pretty highly of her and so do I."

"Thank you, Brady, but her mother deserves all the credit. I wanted my little girl to marry, have babies and play house. But her mother listened to her pleadings and signed her up for flight school when she was 14, while I was off defending the flag. I never had a chance after that."

"Don't short change yourself. She's inherited your fighter skills." Wilcox turned to Sgt. Armstrong, "Sergeant, do you have any idea where those fighters came from?"

"No, Sir. They popped up on our screen from the southeast...Too far south to have come from Nome or Kotzebue and at last report we still have control over the fields at Dillingham and Dutch Harbor. Personnel there have mined the runways and are currently being evacuated by boat, not that I'd like to be out there on those seas right now."

"I agree with you, but we couldn't risk flying them out," Wilcox said as he walked over to Watson and whispered, "I suspect we have an enemy task force to our south, too far out for coastal boats to see, but close enough to send in a recon flight to view our shoreline defenses and test our strength."

"If that's so, then they most likely bypassed the Aleutian Islands, swept around to the southeast and are coming in from the Gulf of Alaska. Only the OAP would risk the Northwest radiation and our recent sea storms." Watson added. "We really need to know their strength to be better prepared."

"I agree," Wilcox said and returned to listen to crew chatter over the radios. Colonel Watson looked at the area map imprinted on a six ft. square piece of clear plastic, studied it and then summoned one of the communication officers, "Lieutenant, I want you to make contact with Colonel Hightower, advise him of our situation and that we may have an enemy fleet to our southeast. I recommend he prepare beach defenses for an invasion within the next 48 hours. We'll keep him advised as we learn more."

"Yes, Colonel," Lieutenant Miller said and stepped over to a sergeant manning a table burdened with radios and proceeded to have him make contact with the beach CP.

TIGER FLIGHT

"Tiger-5 this is Tiger-1...Over."

"Tiger -5 go ahead Mother Hen...Over." Though her call sign was Mother, most everyone referred to her as Mother Hen after she took over the squadron; a practice she didn't seem to mind. She had earned the name Mother in appreciation for her helping several cadets make it through senior class academy finals with a week of unauthorized all night study periods.

"Pappy, can you identify those bogies yet...Over?"

"I was about to call you, Skipper. Negative friendly ID, they appear to be MIG 34s in two flights of four. Requesting permission to engage...Over?"

"Use your Hawkeyes first, Pappy," Captain Watson said. "We should be up with you in nine mikes; please try not to run into us on the turnaround...Over."

Smiling at Mother's last remark, Pappy advised Goldy to arm Hawkeyes. "Fire as soon as you get a lock on, then we'll see about breaking 'em up and going to Sidewinders."

"Copy that," Goldy replied. She armed her heavier missile and went hunting with her weapons computer, making sure to stay close on Pappy's right wing.

"Launching Hawkeye...Fox-two!" Pappy felt the missile drop away and heard it blast forward. A micro second later he could see the missile's fiery exhaust as it shot out toward the enemy.

Goldy's missile was only seconds behind. She got a lock on her own MIG -34 and her eyes lit up as her missile shot forward. She actually had a hard time believing it, here she was in a real war and flying one of the most advanced aircraft in the world.

Since the OAP pilots were flying the newer Model 34s, Pappy suspected the planes were captured from the Russians during the Battle for Siberia. He couldn't help but wonder how good these OAP pilots might be, but realized he was about to find out.

Goldy's warning systems activated first, "Pappy I got one...no two launches. Make that three!" In her excitement, Goldy's voice climbed up an octave making her sound like a squeaky teenage girl.

"Pappy, could these be carrier planes?" Goldy asked. She had not been briefed on any OAP forward operating bases in the Aleutians and since the Western United States and Southeast Alaska were highly radioactive, she figured this was the only way a flight of enemy fighters could get so close to Alaska. She knew Elmendorf Command Post would be wondering the same thing. In a few seconds they would engage a force of superior numbers in close air combat and there wouldn't be time to check for carrier hooks.

"No idea yet, Goldy, but we'll know soon." Pappy shouted out a hit when his radar lost one of the oncoming bandits. Goldy's missile chased another MIG until the pilot was able to out maneuver the lethal projectile and it slammed into the sea. But the pilot lost control and ejected from his fighter only a moment before it too crashed into the frothy blue green stormy waters of the Gulf of Alaska.

As the enemy aircraft drew ever closer, Pappy advised Goldy, "I'm taking on the lead aircraft...launching sidewinders now." He switched to guns and dove from 800 feet, grinning as he watched the lead aircraft explode. The enemy flight began to split up into smaller groups of two in hopes to gang up on the two ADF fighters.

"Hot Stuff!" Pappy shouted and released a burst of 30mm, which raked the fuselage of a MIG-34 and a heavy concentration of black smoke began bellowing out of it.

Goldy was not as fortunate as to get by playing tag with the enemy planes. The MIG-34 was a superior fighter in its own right, but a lot of air combat had to do with the training of the pilots, and in this air battle, the Alaskans had the OAP outgunned. After Goldy sent a Sidewinder up the right engine of one MIG, she was chasing down another keeping Pappy in view. Her main assignment as wingman was to ensure Pappy was not being pursued by an enemy fighter. But as long as he was the aggressor and she believed there was no aircraft on earth equal to the F-35, she was free to pursue her own targets.

On the flip-side, Pappy knew Goldy's flight skill limitations and was keeping one eye on her and the other eye on the enemy fighter he was chasing across the wave tops. His onboard radar showed him the 7th Cavalry had arrived and Goldy was now in good hands.

"Tiger 5, this is Tiger 1, have you in visual. Alpha Section, split into two's and swing wide before engaging. Bravo section, maintain air cap in case they have friends coming to the party...And keep an eye out on Goldy, that girl wants to make Ace too quickly!"

"Tiger-2 copy...Out." 1st Lieutenant Bob "Hair Lip" Beigh acknowledged. As Bravo Section commander, he would over fly the enemy and keep his chicks below the limited ceiling. *There's not a lot of air space up here and those clouds look as if they want to suck us in.* A bolt of lightning shot out and came all too close to one of his fighters, sending a cold chill up the pilot's backside.

Over the next 90 seconds, the darkening skies over the Gulf of Alaska were filled with the roar of climbing, diving and swerving aircraft. Unlike modern day dogfights where enemies shoot missiles at each other from as far away as 20 miles, these brawls were going on within rock throwing distance as OAP 30mm and ADF 30mm and 20mm rounds were exchanged.

"Eject-eject-eject!" An ADF pilot yelled out. Instantly his cockpit exploded upward as his ejection seat propelled him 80 feet above his exploding aircraft. He had lost a wing to enemy fire and within seconds his entire aircraft had turned into a fireball. A chute opened at 450 feet and a frightened pilot slowly floated down to a cold churning sea. A rescue helicopter was dispatched from Elmendorf, but with the turbulent seas and frigid waters, waves reaching 60 feet or more, there was little chance the man could survive before the helicopter would arrive on scene.

Pappy and Goldy had downed three aircraft, but enemy 30mm bullets had raked the rear fuselage of Goldy's F-35 and she was trailing black smoke. She was still in the air though and wanting to continue the fight. When Tiger's Alpha Flight engaged, both Pappy and Goldy had to change air combat tactics to avoid a collision with their squadron buddies. With only 1200 feet of clearance between a cold watery grave and clouds of volcanic ash, there wasn't much room to allow for error.

Finally, their force decimated, the last two surviving OAP fighters broke off and headed for the wave tops. They were making a speed run toward the southeast and seeing them, Pappy and Goldy gave pursuit.

"Pappy, don't shoot 'em down... let's see where they lead us," Goldy suggested.

"Say your fuel status?" Pappy asked.

"About like yours, bright boy... maybe a couple drops left for the return trip."

"Echo Base this is Tiger 5, requesting a tanker out here ASAP!"

The comm. Sergeant looked over his shoulder at Colonel Wilcox. Both of then knew the one KC-135 was still being worked on and there would be no refueling for some time. Colonel Wilcox shook his head and the comm. Sergeant nodded in understanding, not that he liked it any. He knew those pilots were badly in need of fuel and it wasn't coming.

"That's negative, Tiger 5... no tanker available at this time."

Pappy thought about it for a moment. "Echo Base, we need to locate possible task force... requesting permission to follow those fighters...Over." *It doesn't take both of us to follow those clowns...Goldy needs to go back!*

Wilcox looked at Watson, knowing this could well be a suicide mission; the pilot was just as aware of that, but was willing to take the risk in order to send back vital information. "Advise Tiger 5, he has permission." He turned toe controller, "How long before that tanker can be airborne?"

"Ground chief says a minimum of 40 minutes for repair and another 45 to refuel and that's with violating safeguards."

"What about a tanker from Fort Greeley?" Colonel Watson asked.

"Same problem, sir... it will take nearly an hour to get a tanker in the air and on location. By then, Tiger 5 will be in the water."

Colonel Wilcox slammed his right fist into his left palm and blurted out, "Why didn't we plan for this!?" He glared at Watson.

"No one expected them to be coming out of the Gulf. It's a hot zone, far too dangerous for sane people and they've risked their invasion force to catch us napping," Colonel Watson said in response.

"And now I have to send a good man to his death!" This was part of the job Wilcox hated most and knew he was far from being done with giving other such orders. He took the microphone from the comm. Sergeant's hand, "Tiger 5, that is affirmative, you may proceed. Stay in radio contact...Over."

"I copy," Pappy replied and went direct to Captain Watson and kept it simple, "Mother, this is Pappy, we only need one aircraft for this mission. Would you please order Goldy to RTB (return to base)...I know she won't do it if I tell her." Pappy didn't have the guts to glance back over at Goldy, who was shooting daggers his way behind her helmet visor.

Captain Watson was not only furious that someone from the CP would order one of her pilots on a one way trip without conferring with her, she was heartsick it had to be Pappy. Struggling to maintain control, she contacted Goldy, "Tiger 7, this is Tiger 1, join on my wing and that is an order...Over."

318

Goldy was of two minds, one to ignore the order and follow her stupid big brother- buddy, or obey and abandon him. She was leaning toward disobeying the order when Pappy called her, "Goldy, there's nothing you can do up here that I can't do with one plane. I wouldn't want to see you falling from the sky and wasting a valuable aircraft. Every bird is going to matter now, we can't throw away one out of loyalty. I can gather this intelligence by myself. Obey Mother's order, we'll see each other again ...that's a promise."

She hesitated, but finally relented, "God bless you Pappy." She banked to the right and slowly turned to rejoin her flight. Six MIG 34's were destroyed and an F-15 downed with the pilot missing. Everyone hoped that he was sitting in a life raft waiting for pick up.

"Tiger 1 to Alpha section, RTB...I repeat RTB. Bravo Section, join up and follow us home." Captain Watson wiped tears away from her eyes and went direct to Pappy, "Pappy, you find out what we need and then skedaddle back! You hear me? Make for Kodiak if possible, otherwise eject near a shoreline. Do you copy?" Her voice was breaking.

"Okay Mother Hen, I copy. Take care of Goldy, she's a good stick and got a clean kills today."

"Affirmative... Keep the faith, Pappy and remember...I love you." Captain Watson's heart was breaking, knowing she'd probably never see Pappy again and didn't really care if she broke with radio procedure. No one suspected their involvement, but she and Pappy had been an item for the last seven months. They talked of marriage, waiting to see if the world survived World War III and the coming comet. Now, everyone would know how she felt about one of her pilots.

"Back at you, Babe...I'll see you sometime," Pappy replied then concentrated on flying, diving for the water to escape enemy radar.

COMMAND POST

Colonel Watson, an expression of surprise on his face, stared at the ceiling speaker with his mouth open. He never knew his daughter had found someone and now, he was helping to send the poor guy to his death.

TIGER -5

Staying low and barely missing the gigantic wave tops, Pappy, using advanced radar, tried to keep the engine flames of the two fighters in view, as they flew deeper into the Gulf of Alaska. Below him, 60 foot rollers and category two hurricane force winds did not appear to be optimal weather for ejection. It took all of Pappy's flight skills to keep his aircraft in the air; buffeted about like a child's toy and pelted non-stop with golf ball size hail after they entered the storm front. Pappy had once worked as a bush pilot in southwest Alaska and it wasn't hard for him to recall bad weather at times he ferried hunters back and forth. Back then he'd also flown with the Air National Guard, becoming familiar with the F-15 Eagle and after seven years with the Air Force he was selected for the F-35 program. Before the F-35 and prior to the outbreak of World War III, he was contemplating leaving the military because he'd become weary of playing the officer politics game. Even being a hot shot pilot, he knew he'd never make field grade. As a bush pilot he would be making three to four times the annual salary of a 1st lieutenant or even a captain. When they enrolled him in the F-35 program and put him into the seat of this hunk, he knew he had never felt such poetry in flight, such power and the plane had become like a drug in his system. When he wasn't flying, he thought about flying and being stuck on the ground was pure torture for him. The knowledge of losing his new love life was bad enough, knowing his flying days were about to come to an abrupt end and looking down at his fuel gauge dropping steadily and seeing himself taking a fateful swim in the icy waters below only depressed him further. "I got about 25… maybe 26 minutes of flying time to find the enemy fleet an' then, hero, your options are few and far between."

"Say again, Tiger 5…Over," Echo Base radioed.

Dang, forgot I was on radio… "I have 25 minutes flying time and still heading southeast into the Gulf. With monstrous seas below me and the wind picking up, I'd sure hate to be a sailor on a boat out here. The hail stone are looking more like baseballs now…Glad they built this cockpit glass so thick."

Pappy's plan was to fly another 20 minutes at low altitude and then shoot up to the ceiling for a final look. Only then did he notice he had lost sight of the enemy fighters and he radioed in, "Echo Base, Tiger 5, I've lost the enemy fighters in the storm… and my radar is malfunctioning due to the storm. Do you have them on radar…Over?"

"Negative. Storm is causing too much interference for our system too and you're also leaving our radio range…Over."

"Then you might say I am flying on a wing and a prayer, so poetic." Pappy didn't bother to say anything more, he was thinking of Mother as he soared ahead at 600 mph leaving a white frothing wake along the rolling wave tops. *We should've got married…but then again, I'd be leaving behind a widow.* Watching the storm clouds swirl about and the sporadic bolts of lightning shoot across the nose of his aircraft; Pappy could almost feel those monstrous waves reaching up to rip him out of the skies. After a moment of eerie silence, keeping to his same heading, Pappy surprised himself when he began to mutter a prayer, "Lord, I sure hope you still remember me. Been awhile since we talked last and I was wondering, hoping you might say, if our previous agreement was still on? I'm probably going to die here today… hope its quick, Lord…that water looks really cold down there and those waves…well, Lord, they remind me of some surfer's worst nightmare…like a huge wall coming one after another and slamming down on top of itself. " His voice was beginning to quiver, "But God, I'm really hoping I've still got a place reserved up there…even if it means I have to sweep those golden streets or polish the gates. I really like fluffy white clouds, Sir… an' stoking some furnace down under doesn't seem to sound all that great. Anyway, as you know, I've done my share of stupid things and committed some real serious wrongs…an' I'm not too sure how you feel about those pilots I killed? Maybe we'll get to talk about that if you give me time to make my case. But now that I got you on the line, I have two favors to ask of you. First, you take care of Susan for me because she'll need some comforting and her old man, though a real stand-up guy and a great pilot…well… he has trouble with the love part with his daughter. Secondly, Lord, I'd surely like to find that enemy fleet before I run out of fuel and take a big splash into…" Pappy stopped praying when a red light started flashing on his board.

"Fire, I GOT A FIRE!" Pappy shouted. He was trying to turn his head in a 360 degree loop, struggling to see where the fire might be coming from. "Lord, are you listening to me?" Pappy said in tone of desperation. It relieved him somewhat not to see smoke, but he knew a burning wire wouldn't always produce visible smoke until the aircraft suddenly blew up right from under him. His training told him to eject, but the white tops below quickly quashed that idea. *I wouldn't even have time to inflate my raft before I was pulled under or one of those rollers crashed down on top of me and squashed me like a bug.* "Lord, there's things happening kind of fast up here right now and I really hope this is only a short in my fire light. But the ol' fuel gauge tells me my time is about up anyway. I gotta climb out of here and take a look, get some sky under me and maybe I can see the enemy fleet sailing our way." Pappy raised the nose of his aircraft and quickly ascended until the altimeter told him he was passing through 1100 feet. Directly above him, close enough that he felt as if he could reach out and touch it, were the swirling dark clouds of ash and sporadic lightning flashes. With the barrier of blackness above him, bright flashes of lightening racing across the sky, heavy winds and massive hailstones pummeling his cockpit, and towering seas below, Pappy had a sudden memory picture form in his mind from his old Vacation Bible School days when he was 11 years old. *Just like that picture in the teacher's huge Bible, where Noah's Ark was being carried through the rough seas and the Heavens were emptying a deluge on the earth to make the flood…funny to think about that now.*

COMMAND POST

"He's praying, Colonel," Major Anders said to Colonel Wilcox.

At the mention of Colonel Watson's daughter and his inability to make a parental connection with her, several people in the Command Post looked to him. But he avoided their gaze, fighting to keep his eyes from tearing up and wondering what he would say to her when she landed. She didn't even know he was here from Eielson and to be honest with himself, he probably wouldn't have taken the time to locate her for a few minutes of family time.

Colonel Wilcox looked across to Major Anders and said, "If it were me, Major, I'd be praying too. In fact, I think we all should be praying right along with him. We need to know where that fleet is, how big it is and what kind of surface craft. So, Major Anders, you'd better start praying right along with me because we need all the help we can get right now." Colonel Wilcox walked away to be by himself to say a couple of his own prayers for a brave man, his courageous act and in dire hopes Pappy was able spot the enemy fleet.

Colonel Watson stood off by himself too, also whispering a prayer and listening to the words from the man that might have become his son-in-law.

TIGER- 5

Pappy began to level off at 1150 feet and quickly noticed his fuel gauge was registering only fumes to fly on at this point. Having never flown with so little fuel in his tanks before, he wondered how large his reserve supply actually was, how long it would carry him aloft and did not want to believe what the manual had said. He glanced around, but all he could see was thick gray and black clouds, balls of ice pelting his cockpit canopy like .00 buckshot pellets and only darkness below. When the lightning flashed overhead, accompanied by roaring thunder, he could just make out the white froth of the monstrous wave caps below and Pappy once more wondered what death was going to feel like. He'd turn his radios off when the engines died; he didn't want anyone to hear his screams in those last terrible seconds; especially not his beautiful lady. Suddenly his eyes filled in wondrous awe; he saw a miracle unfold before him. Miles ahead, a break in the clouds began to widen, allowing a ray of sunlight to shoot through from the heavens above and grow in size. Pappy raised a clinched fist and shouted in joy, "Thank you, Lord!" He forgot all about his dwindling fuel supply or what the people back in the CP might think of his spiritual exclaiming and made contact with Echo Base, "This is Tiger 5, I've got a break in the clouds and I'm riding an actual sunbeam up for a look...Stand-by!"

Ascending right up to 6,000 feet, Pappy observed the ash clouds were surprisingly broken up and the sky was opening up in all directions. It was right then he spotted the first enemy ship and he exclaimed, "I've got 'em! I've got 'em!" Pappy banked to the right, shocked by the number of ships below him in calm seas and began to circle the massive fleet. He wasn't a Navy man, but this had to be the biggest group of ships he'd ever seen before. Pappy wasn't aware of it at the moment, but he had entered the eye of the storm and for a brief moment all was calm and the sky appeared clear. He didn't have a lot of time to think about that anyway; the engines sucking up the last few drops in his wings and a sudden drop in altitude loomed ominously in his near future.

"Echo Base, how do you read...Over?" Pappy asked excited, as he stared down at the vessels and began to count and attempt to identify types. He had studied OAP ship identification weeks ago, but his mind seemed to be blank all of a sudden.

His cockpit radio came alive, "Echo Base is reading you 5x5... go ahead, Tiger 5...Over." Both Colonel Watson and Colonel Wilcox were beside the Communication Officer, ready with note pads as Pappy began his report.

"I can see four, I repeat four aircraft carriers. They look equal to our Enterprise-class, but they must be Russian. There are dozens...I counted nearly 50 before I stopped, of smaller vessels escorting them. There is one light navy cruiser...Russian or maybe Chinese... I think. Storm did some damage, I make out at least a dozen capsized boats...I see two battleships...big honkers with at least 18 inch guns...New Jersey class or like the old Japanese Yamato." Pappy was silent for a moment. He couldn't figure out how the OAP was able to build up such a navy without the US military knowing about it. "I've got fighters heading my way...not much time left anyway." Pappy checked his weapons status and wasn't happy. *Spent too much ammo on those bogies... never learned to reserve my weapons and this is what I get for it!*

"Echo Base, be advised I see very large ships on the horizon...they look like...yeah, super tankers, like the Exxon Valdez that went on the rocks long ago...Maybe even bigger. I count six of 'em...no...seven super tankers to the rear of the fleet and what looks to be a very large cruise ship...probably for senior officers." Pappy tried to get a position from the map board attached to his right leg, "I'm flying directly east of Kodiak Island, about 140 to 150 miles off shore. Massive...I repeat this is one massive fleet." Pappy heard an alarm in his cockpit and shouted, "Gotta go now... they have missile lock. So long!" Pappy dove for the waves, riding another sunbeam down before banking right and swerving left to escape the missiles fired by enemy aircraft. He didn't know how many planes were trying to burn his tail off; his defensive weapons system was overwhelmed and he reached over to shut off the on board alarm because it was driving him crazy. The fuel gauge reading dry, Pappy unzipped his left arm pocket, pulled out a small snapshot of Susan and himself and slid it in to the cuff of his right flight glove, tossed her a loving wink and smiled. "I love you, lady."

He had decided minutes earlier to try a Kamikaze dive and use his aircraft for one good hit against the nearest OAP carrier. Three enemy fighters were on his tail and a missile climbing up his jet exhaust; Pappy fired his guns until they were empty and then released his two remaining Sidewinders. He was holding his breath, when, only 200 yards to go for a score, an enemy missile hit the F-35 and it exploded in a fireball. A valiant pilot and his beloved aircraft were lost; the OAP fleet continued north with only minor damage. One Sidewinder took out the bridge of a light cruiser; the other detonated on the lower flight deck of the targeted carrier. Pappy had scored.

Within moments the weather began to close in, the seas rose and the winds sent all OAP personnel below decks to weather out the storm. Five of the 12 OAP aircraft launched to intercept Pappy never had time to make it back aboard and splashed down into a tempest in the making.

COMMAND POST

"Sir, we've lost all contact with Tiger 5," Sgt. Armstrong reported in a sorrowful voice.

"Thank you, Sergeant." Colonel Wilcox looked over to Colonel Watson, "A very brave man."

Colonel Watson nodded in agreement, then looked over at the ready board and saw that his daughter was next to land. "Before this is over, we're going to lose a lot of brave men and women. Now you'll have to excuse me, I have to go tell my daughter that her pilot fulfilled his last mission."

"It's a good start, Colonel...maybe Pappy accomplished more here today than carrying out his flight duties. Maybe it's time you remembered to be a father first and an officer second...and maybe she'll forgive you? I hope so."

"Thanks, I hope so," Colonel Watson replied.

12 - A CHAPLAIN'S CALLING

"'Woe to the obstinate children,' declares the Lord, 'to those who carry out plans that are not mine, forming an alliance, but not by Spirit, heaping sin upon sin.'"

Isaiah 30:1 NIV

OAP PRISON CAMP, CITY OF KOYUK, ALASKA - APRIL 7th

Blowing at near gale force strength; icy winds created a chill factor of -70° below zero. The frigid air was cold enough to instantly freeze unprotected flesh and easily sapped strength from exhausted wounded prisoners held in a barbwire fenced compound. To keep his thoughts focused and hopefully bring some degree of comfort to his fellow prisoners, Chaplain Doug Packa cleared his voice to speak. Through rattling teeth, he recited a few words of scripture from memory and struggled to remember the Words of God he had once memorized and known by heart. Chaplain Packa's pale face and week's growth of beard were white with frost; his voice raspy from a near frozen throat. He stuttered out the words, stomping numb feet in three feet of crunchy snow and black ash to keep circulation moving. Grimacing from piercing pain, he stopped every few words to suck on his stiff frozen fingers and rub the blowing ice from his squinting eyes. He knew he was suffering from 2nd and 3rd degree frostbite, dehydration, starvation and a festering bayonet wound to his right shoulder, hypothermia and most likely pneumonia. During his pitiful five hour class on Arctic Survival, he learned how hypothermia sneaked up on its victim, coaxing a person to believe in a false sense of warmth and followed with a sleep of death. Doug Packa looked around and saw how the other prisoners were huddled to maintain some degree of warmth, while others were alone; already in deaths embrace and thankfully, no longer in pain.

The ADF prisoners were given no wood, nor shelter; the OAP was not a supporter of the Geneva Convention and its civilized rules for the treatment of prisoners. All shelter, food and wood or oil to burn went to OAP units, while prisoners were left to care for themselves within a barbed wire enclosure, exposed to the harsh elements. Disgusted with their treatment, Doug struggled with a burning hate for the oppressors. But with so little time left, he didn't want to appear before the Lord with feelings of bitterness so fresh in his soul. Yet, it was a hard task when he was forced to look upon the frozen bodies of the dead and observe the bitter suffering of his comrades. When a soldier died, his clothes were quickly stripped off and handed to ones in need of some covering. Occasionally a struggle broke out between two or three prisoners for a garment and it usually fell upon Doug's weary shoulders to break it up. The dead were covered in fresh snow and Doug whispered a few kind words of funeral ceremony spoken from frozen memory. Shivering, knowing it was a good sign that the deadly hypothermia hadn't taken a death grip on him, he limped from one body to the next. When needed, Chaplain Doug knelt down and tenderly closed lifeless eyes and, finished with his words, covered faces with handfuls of snow. This provided a symbolic gesture of burial. Frozen ground, painful wind chill and exhaustion kept the troops from burying the bodies of their comrades and their presence added to the depressing scene. Not that the OAP would allow them to be buried; they had other plans for the ADF prisoners.

A loud commotion that erupted from the nearby field kitchen caught Doug's attention and he turned around to see what was happening. Groups of men and women in uniforms so reduced to rags that a few wore ADF parkas to stay warm, were unloading large metal cook pots from a flatbed trailer pulled by a captured Trak. They carried the pots to the kitchen area where several cooks used blackened wood salvaged from the Koyuk ruins to rekindle cook fires. When the fires were blazing, several large pots were hung from large metal spits placed over the open flames. They were slowly filled with shovels of snow dug from below the ash. Several soldiers, struggling against the harsh winds, stumbled forward with frozen roots they had found after digging deep into the icy surface. They had even used grenades to blow ice at locations they suspected might reveal hidden treasures to fill their shrunken stomachs. Frozen roots and an occasional dead shrew or vole was tossed into the simmering vats. The soldiers fought one another to remain near the cook fires to warm frozen hands and it took a large cook swinging a massive metal cleaver in a threatening manner to chase them away so he could have room to work.

"I...I sure don't get-t-t their lingo, Chap-p-plain, but I don't think it-t-t sounds friendly," Corporal Ron Milke stuttered between clenched teeth. Glued together by necessity, he shared Doug's tattered parka after losing his own in the Battle for Koyuk and helped Doug, whose left arm was all but useless from the bayonet wound, move about to pray over the soldiers of the 1st Division.

Outside the kitchen area and prison enclosure, over a thousand OAP soldiers were jogging in large circles or exercising to stay warm. Not everyone had a tent; the enemy had lost a lot of equipment in their forced march to the east and most looked upon the prisoners with a seething hatred in their eyes for the severity of the discomfort they were forced to experience.

"Hey, Doug, look at that-t-t guard-d-d over d'ere..." Milke said. He pointed to the man and added, "...he's chewin' on a boot-t-t. Boy, they mus' be real hungry to do that-t-t."

"Don't-t-t make eye con-n-ntact with-h-h 'em!" Lt. Okupah ordered, struggling to spit the words out. "They-y-y sh-h-hot-t the las-s-s' guy." Lt. Okupah was unable to walk because he suffered from severe frostbite to more than 50% of his body and no longer had any feeling in his arms and legs. Doug had leaned him up against three other soldiers and told the ranking sergeant to ensure the lieutenant shared in their slight degree of warmth.

203 prisoners somehow remained alive out of 429 from the day before. Maintaining some degree of humanity, men kept the severely wounded inside the circle, but they too were dying rapidly. Those who could still move traded places every half hour or so, taking turns for the inner warmth. The outside circle of prisoners risked the danger of torture from OAP guards walking around the fence line. With long bayonets fixed on rifles, several of the guards entertained themselves by stabbing at the prisoners through the wire. Never fatally, only to hear a man cry out in pain was enough to satisfy them - for now. Doug had been a target; four inches of bayonet steel had pierced his side, but he was able to bite off the scream and in the process, gained some degree of respect with the non-Christian prisoners.

Looking to the dark heavens, Doug had sudden knowledge of what was coming and started to pray aloud with renewed strength, "Our Father, hallowed-d-d be your name, Your Kingdom-m-m come..." Doug's heart sang out as a few other men joined in. By the time they finished almost all of the men capable of speech were praying and some of the weaker ones, unable to utter a sound, slowly nodded in agreement. Even under such harsh conditions there were men who remained lost to the Lord's message of salvation and Doug hoped he would have time to bring these few to Jesus before it was too late.

Scanning the wire, he noticed a strange expression on one of the guards and wondered, Sympathy? Compassion...Are there possibly some Christians among these men? He saw similar expressions on three other guards and it gave him hope. Their eyes...*These men truly know the Lord and are shamed by what they've been forced to do.*

His face all but frozen, Doug was able to form a small smile at these men on the other side of the wire and once more looked upward, *Dear God, how many of our enemy are your children? What evil has forced them to engage in such a conflict against their Christian brothers? Why have they invaded when we might have openly shared with them the room and food to survive the coming catastrophe?* Doug spoke to the men, "No matter what happens to us, believe in the Lord Jesus Christ an' this-s-s day you too will join Him in Heaven. He is with us-s-s today an' sees-s-s the price you pay," Doug pointed to one of the OAP sergeants, a man whose expression displayed the evil in his heart. "...for these are people led by false gods-s-s an' evil men," He reached down to place his gloved hand upon Okupah's head. The lieutenant's cap was gone to one of his soldiers, his black hair frozen, his eyes locked in death. Doug closed the lieutenant's eyes then addressed the men, "Speak-k-k to one another, let-t-t no one sleep. Comfort the wounded an' pray...pray. This is one weapon they can't take away from us-s-s." Doug fell to his knees, dragging Milke down with him. They both know they'd probably never get back up, simply because they had no strength left.

Spotting a female guard, Doug was forced to think of all the female prisoners, separated from the men in the beginning and dragged off kicking and screaming. Their terrified screams and later; painful moans, had lasted through the night and continued to haunt Doug's thoughts. He knew rape and death, had befallen these valiant ladies and he had cried out to God in anger for His wrath to fall down upon those who did these fiendish things. The icy wind blew and his men continued to die.

Captain Clark, the senior prisoner, went crazy when the women were dragged away and lashed out at the nearest guard, "Animals! You're all animals!" For this, Clark received a bayonet in the chest and Doug found himself the ranking officer.

Moments passed before Doug looked into the wind and saw a group of soldiers moving through the crowd. They wore different colored uniforms; black arctic gear more suitable for these frigid conditions. Other OAP soldiers backed away with looks of fear or open disgust. Something in Doug's spirit stirred. With an exhausting effort, he forced himself to his feet, bringing a startled Milke with him. Taking a stance of defiance, he glared at the new detachment as it encircled the enclosure and a small party separated to approach the gate.

Milke released a death sigh and collapsed at Doug's feet, pulling out of the parka the two shared. Another soldier, lying on the snow, reached over and gently closed Milke's eyes and then began to strip him. Several others joined in while Doug fought to ignore them. This was survival; he knew his friend no longer needed them, but his heart missed a beat as he watched them shove Milke's body away from the huddle. Lt. Okupah had died moments before and Doug had stretched him out on the snow beside Milke. As he knelt down beside them, he covered their faces and whispered, "Rest, my friends...my brothers...The Lord will welcome you this day."

Doug didn't notice it at first, but he no longer stuttered from the cold, a flame was burning from deep within and his strength was returning. *Is this my time, a final flare-up before I die?* His thoughts turned to those officers in black standing at the gate, waiting for the enclosure to be opened by two enlisted men. *Something very different about these men...their uniforms...that patch on their shoulder shows a black dragon holding a white knife...Even their own men cower from them... why?* Then it awakened him, cleared his thoughts; he could see a shimmering of true evil surrounding these men. Doug suddenly felt the dark vileness they carried swarming around him and his men. *Yet, I'm not afraid...I don't even feel cold anymore...Is this truly the presence of God!* "Hallelujah!" Doug shouted, "Hallelujah!" His exclamation surprised the OAP Secret Police, especially when Doug began singing a song of praise with renewed strength. One by one, some of prisoners began to join in with whispers and then voices grew louder as the Spirit of the Lord moved through them. Soon, some of the stronger ones were standing, ignoring the wind as they stood tall and moved closer to Doug. In a miraculous sign of faith, 28 clear voices joined together singing Amazing Grace.

An OAP Secret Police major, a sub-commander for the Black Dragons, was seething with contempt for the Alaskan's display of faith. He shouted out his orders in English, demanding they cease singing but they refused and their reaction threw the major into a violent rage. Once the gate was opened, he entered the enclosure with four regular bodyguards to protect him, while the contingent of Black Dragons stood silent and observed their commander in action. With a well-used leather whip in his right hand, the major struck out wildly at the prisoners, but still the men continued to sing. He attempted to get closer to Doug, who was surrounded by ADF soldiers holding ground, taking a painful beating to protect their chaplain as they continued to praise God in song as each had never done before in such degree.

Fearing for this senior officer, two of the bodyguards, dressed in black parkas and black rabbit fur winter caps, stepped forward and were forced to grab and drag the near maniacal major outside the enclosure. In response, the enraged major turned his insane anger on the two men beating them with his whip until they were forced to flee. A look of pure sadistic pleasure lit his face as he barked commands to his men who stepped forward with AK-50 rifles ready. He shouted one more order, "Fire!"

The voices inside the enclosure continued until only a faint echo moved down the valley, followed by an eerie silence. Satisfied, the major entered the enclosure and walked over to the body of Chaplain Doug Packa. He looked down and suddenly, the Major's eyes grew wide with a mixture of surprise and confusion. The Chaplain's face wore a genuine smile and lifeless dark brown eyes stared back at him. Frightened, believing this man with the Christian cross on his collar was staring directly into his soul; the little major backed away and tersely ordered his men to remove the officer from the enclosure, "Do not strip him. Do not touch anything of his. Carry his body far away from here and burn it completely until even his bones are ash. Then you cover his ashes with deep snow and report back to me when the chore is complete." He turned away, hesitated and gazed down once more upon the body of the chaplain. Once more he felt a strange sense of utter fear grip him; something he was not accustomed too. He glared at the men he had given the assignment to, "Do it now!" He stomped off and left those officers closest to him wondering what had shaken up their commander so? Outside the enclosure he regained some of his composure and shouted orders for the men to strip the remaining bodies of all clothing and valuables and then carry them to the kitchen. The cook was ready; most of the men and women were visibly shaken that the prisoners were to be prepared for the cooking pots. But here in Koyuk and along the OAP's frontlines where food supplies were extremely low, deceased prisoners were to become food for the starving OAP troops. Cannibalism was spreading throughout the army and the OAP warlords were concerned.

COLONEL FREEMAN, YUKON RIVER

Under cover of darkness and heavy snow mixed with ash, Colonel Freeman and the remains of his command crossed the frozen river ice on foot. Upon reaching the far shore of the Yukon River undetected, they spent the rest of the night huddled together in small parties inside hastily built survival shelters; snow caves and a half dozen lean-to's slapped together with the few poncho liners they still had and tree branches cut from standing spruce.

With wind chill factors dropped to -40 ° and colder; the soldiers were suffering from frostbite, hypothermia and extremely low morale. At a time like this, Colonel Freeman was glad his troops had listened to every boring lesson they received in Arctic Survival School and lessons in surviving Alaska winters learned from fathers and grandfathers. He was only wishing one of those instructors was standing around with a thermos of hot coffee for the Old Man. Older soldiers like him were often pampered in the field during training, a practice he so dearly missed at this moment.

Four guards were posted on one hour shifts to avoid anyone falling asleep on duty the rest of the troops were unconscious in shelters; Freeman held a short staff meeting inside a snow cave with his two surviving officers and one senior NCO. "Our orders were to slow the enemy down, but as an effective combat unit the 1st Division no longer exists to carry out those orders. We're running for our lives and now our job is to keep these troops together, and alive."

"What are were going to do, Colonel? If we can't fight an' don't want to give up, what's left?" MSgt. Manning asked.

"If memory serves me, Shageluk is about 30 miles southwest of here and that's where we're headed, Sergeant. We might find supplies there and hopefully some people who will help care for our wounded."

"Troops should be ready to move by morning," Lt. Mayo said. "Thirty miles isn't that far." He hoped by saying so he could believe it himself.

"I have a feeling, Lieutenant Mayo, every inch of those thirty miles will be a struggle for even the best of us. Get some sleep, all of you. We leave in just over five hours."

NEAR SHAGELUK, 23 HOURS LATER

His mittens in tatters and his hands blistered and burning from 2nd degree frostbite; his head throbbing from the intense cold, Colonel Freeman stopped on the trail to make a clothing adjustment. Shivering, his teeth clinched, he removed his coat first, then his wool scarf and then pulled off his sweater, followed by his shirt. He jerked off his T-shirt and, shivering from head to toe as the snow assaulted him, tore his T-shirt into two pieces. Others were watching him wondering if their commander had lost his mind; Colonel Freeman ignored them and started putting his clothes back on. Finished, he carefully and painfully used the t-shirt material to wrap his hands before painstakingly shoving them back into torn mittens. Without uttering a cry, he bit off the pain and fumbled to pull his parka hood back up. The fake wolf hair trim could be closed tightly to form a small funnel, which ever so slightly warmed the air a few degrees before it reached his lungs though the wool fibers of his scarf.

After watching their commander, several of the others followed suit and within moments, the line of men behind him once again put one numb foot down in front of the other to continue on through knee deep snow. Tattered mukluks, fatigue and deep snow made for a disastrous combination and it was roughest on the two men pulling point duty as they painstakingly broke trail. No one could feel their feet and only mental discipline kept them trudging ahead; each man following the man in front of him, refusing to give up, to lie down and die. Right behind the point and struggling to remain in the lead, MSgt. Manning pushed himself forward, one more hill, another valley...*We gotta be close...gotta be close...*

ADF COMMAND-ELMENDORF CP - APRIL 8th 0714 HOURS

Between 0001 and 1200 hours, Major Brad Davis performed duties of Officer Of The Day inside the Command Post. Sitting back in a metal folding chair, a cup of hot coffee in hand; one of the perks of working in the command post, Davis was savoring his last cigarette. He would have to barter for more as soon as he got off duty, but he wasn't sure what he had for trade. Thinking about it, he looked over to the radioman and noticed an incoming message. Sitting his coffee cup down, Davis stood up and walked over to see what had come in. "What have you got, Sergeant?"

"I'm not really sure, Major. Somebody calling themselves Sierra 1 reports they've arrived on station, but nothing more."

"Doesn't sound familiar...Well, put it in the box for Intel, maybe they'll know what it means."

"Yes, Sir."

Soon afterward, President Andrews walked in to the CP to check the overnight reports. "Good morning, Major Davis. Anything new?"

Major Davis was startled by the President's early arrival. He still wasn't used to the senior politician coming into the Command Post, especially at this time of day. But he stood to his feet, straightened his shirt and replied, "Strangely quiet, Mr. President. Beach defenses are coming along, Seward and Homer report no signs of the enemy fleet, nor have there been any air attacks to our south." Per policy, the Command Post was never called to attention when a senior officer or the president entered the room.

"Any messages from outlying commands?" President Andrews turned to study the situation map board, which made a couple of young airmen nervous being in such close proximity with their new President.

Major Davis remembered the recent radio message, "Sir, we did receive a rather odd message only minutes ago. Someone identifying themselves as Sierra 1 reported on station. We have no listing for a Sierra 1 so I had the message put in the outgoing box for Intel."

President Andrews grinned in response to the information, "Major, will you please contact General Saunders and advise him of this message?" Andrews did an about face from the board to look at Major Davis with an expression of wide eyed excitement. *They made it! At least one of our plans worked... now I pray the Lord will watch over these men and women for what lies ahead.* Captain Myers and his company of Eskimo and Athabascann Scouts had made landfall on St. Lawrence Island and were setting up home in the abandoned community of Savoonga.

"Yes, Sir," Major Davis said. "Right away." Major Davis now knew this was a top secret matter and turned his attention to his RTO Sergeant, "Radio the General, give him the message and make sure he gets it...send it in code. I do not want it lost by some...Just make sure he received it and demand certification of same."

ADF DEFENSIVE PERIMETER-DELTA JUNCTION

Once a quiet farming community, Delta Junction had welcomed a growing tourist industry in the latter part of the 20th Century. Besides a large number of Russian families, who had fled the east to find freedom in

America's democracy, there were several communes in the area, which enjoyed the quiet remoteness of Delta Junction. One of these groups had set up a profitable potato chip business and prior to the Christmas morning attack on the Lower 48, had shipped their chips throughout the USA. To the north side of town was a thriving reindeer farm with more than 300 animals and eight miles to the southeast of Delta Junction was Fort Greeley. As was the rest of the USA, Delta Junction was hit hard with the recession; high jobless rate, mortgage foreclosures at an alarming rate and travel dropping off as the US dollar steadily lost value.

Delta Junction had experienced increased unemployment in 1997 when the U.S. Army closed Fort Greeley. Nearly overnight, Delta Junction's population dwindled to less than 2,000. Scores of businesses closed and boarded up windows, but the farmers still had land to work. They continued to plow their hay fields and work their potato farms and for a brief spell the economy came back. This was brought about mainly because the U.S. Government had selected Fort Greeley as a missile defense base. But when the attack came from the Gulf of Mexico these protective missiles so far north in the interior of Alaska were fired with little or no effect. With the silos empty, Fort Greeley was eventually transferred into the hands of the Alaska Defense Force. Officially known as the north end point for the Al-Can Highway, Delta Junction's well-known "Y" intersection converged with the Richardson Highway which extended from Valdez on the coast to the intersection with Airport Road in Fairbanks. Originally a native trading trail, known as the Valdez/Fairbanks trail it had been improved and graveled and renamed the Richardson Highway.

The Al-Can, originally built by mostly Afro-American and white Canadian troops during World War II, was a way of getting supplies into Alaska. The Japanese had invaded Alaska's Aleutian Chain and it was feared they might reach mainland Alaska unless stopped in the islands. Once a single lane dirt road forged through some of the harshest terrain in North America by men fighting long bitter winters, knee deep summer mud and attacked by blood hungry mosquitoes and swarms of black flies, the highway eventually became a two lane hard top road which ran through some of the most beautiful scenery Canada and Alaska had to offer.

Change uprooted the Delta Junction community again as thousands of soldiers and hundreds of pieces of heavy equipment poured into town to begin transforming the land into an extensive series of fortifications. Artillery emplacements were excavated. Anti-personnel and tank mines placed by the thousands into the frozen ground, while troop bunkers and trenches of all sizes were placed over the landscape where tourist buses had once parked. Heavy construction dozers, front end loaders and graders worked around the clock, shoving brown dirt, black ash and dirty white snow to form defensive barriers. In some places dynamite had to be used because the earth, frozen by the harshest of winters, refused to give under the steel blade. Besides the equipment, men and women withstood sub-zero temperatures and quickly used up a dwindling supply of elbow grease and sweat to fill sandbags with fresh snow and dirt, or take on the chore of digging trenches to connect the troop bunkers.

With traffic backing up at various security checkpoints, MP's, resembling polar bears from standing outside in the blowing snow so long, were forced to use green and white camouflaged HMMWVs, (high mobility multipurpose wheel vehicle - also known as Humvees or hummers), as pilot cars to lead convoys from Fairbanks along a specially marked path through newly placed mine fields.

Too large to place in Delta Junction, two batteries of 155mm artillery pieces were positioned inside Fort Greeley, while three batteries of M-119 105mm howitzers were spread across Delta Junction. Anti-aircraft batteries, which were mostly made up of 12 quad .50 caliber machineguns mounted on the back of two half ton M-series trucks to remain mobile, while eight 20mm rapid fire mini-guns were positioned around Delta Junction's airfield, on newly constructed concrete bases and surrounded by a six foot tall wall of sandbags. All of the air defense weapons were supported by M-60 machineguns placed in squad sized troop bunkers around the airfield or kept mobile on either Humvees or Delta Junction's older M1-51 Alaska Army National Guard Jeeps.

General Saunders had a single brigade of M1-A1 tanks, which had recently been assigned to Fort Wainwright and two companies of M-2 A-2 Bradley Fighting Machines in reserve as a mobile force. All 16 Strikers vehicles, less than a third of which had been originally assigned to Fort Wainwright, were positioned around the inner perimeter, or downtown business district of Delta Junction. The majority of the Striker vehicles were sent overseas in support of United Nations troops in the Middle East and hadn't returned home before World War III broke out. It was believed they were most likely lost in the nuclear exchange between India and Pakistan, which bathed most of the Muslim world in radioactive fallout.

The biggest task at the moment was preparing five crescent shaped earthen walls on the west side of the city. 300 yards long, 10 feet high and 16 feet wide at the base, these walls were placed 100 yards in front of each other. Tank traps were made up of the largest logs they could find in the area and were set up between the walls, along with hundreds of mines. Pathways are designated by flags for personnel and vehicles to travel through, and evacuate by if and when necessary.

By order of General Saunders, the farthest wall out was to be unmanned, but covered with Claymore mines to be remotely triggered against OAP infantry. Triple strand barbed wire was spread out along the top, with trip wires connected to hidden grenades and trip flares to illuminate the enemy. The next four walls had entrenched emplacements for .30 caliber and .50 caliber machineguns, supported by M-60 light machineguns with crisscross fire patterns. These were further supported by troops armed with M-249 SAW weapons and AT-4 shoulder fired anti-tank weapons. There were even some ancient Vietnam era LAW rockets and 40mm M-79 grenade launchers, which were spaced every 20 yards. 200 yards behind the inner wall closest to the city center were three 60 mm and four 81 mm mortar pits ringed with 5 foot walls of sandbags, also supported by personnel armed with SAW weapons.

Though this was the 21st Century, Delta Junction began to resemble a page out of a World I history book; trench warfare from the muddy plains of Europe and even a mounted cavalry unit of 600 RCMP horsemen awaiting the call to arms. Yet, with all this manpower and weaponry, Alaska remained a very small David against the OAP Goliath.

MAJOR BLACKSTONE'S COMMAND, LIVINGOOD - APRIL 8th

Remaining prone on a small snowy ridgeline, Major Blackstone watched through glare resistant binoculars as the enemy's point element continued to advance slowly south on the Elliot Highway. He lowered his binoculars, glanced over his shoulder to view the terrain behind him, and estimated the distance to Hill Top to be less than 30 miles. Every foot of the distance would be covered on foot, trudging through knee deep snow or even deeper. Hill Top Service Station and Café had once been a favorite eatery among long haul truckers on the way north to Prudhoe Bay. Sadly, the cafe was abandoned when the bottom fell out of the market and now sat empty with a partially collapsed roof under deep snow and ash.

Speaking through his wool scarf, Major Blackstone issued orders to his radio man, "Sergeant; advise Command of the enemy's progress. Remind them this will probably be our last contact and that we're heading for Hill Top. By going cross country, we should be able to beat the enemy at their current rate of travel. I am requesting helicopter pick up for 57 troops in…" he thought for a moment as he estimated distance and their own slow rate of travel, "… 24 hours or they can forget about us. After that, it won't matter much and no sense endangering any rotor-heads."

"Yes, Major." With the radio's batteries so weak, the RTO had to send the message three times with a special code before Command understood. Once completed and with Blackstone's okay, the RTO smashed the radio with the butt of his rifle and threw the used up batteries into the snow. "I can't say I'll miss lugging that thing around anymore, Major." Even at only 14 pounds, the radio became a heavy burden for a man suffering from weakening muscles, dehydration, frostbite and the first stages of hypothermia.

"You make sure you tell them I ordered you to do that. Some admin clerk might want you to pay for the thing with your cigarette ration," Blackstone said. He wanted to grin, but refrained because it would've hurt his near frozen face. He had remembered his RTO didn't smoke and his ration went to his appreciative friends. That was until they all ran out of cigarettes. "Okay, let's move out!" Major Blackstone ordered. "Keep in line and no one gets left behind." *I can't afford to lose any more troops and I dearly hope the ones that drifted off are lying under a pile of snow. I wouldn't want to be held prisoner by the likes of those people…no sir, I'd rather be dead!*

PASTOR WOODWAY'S CONVOY ENTERS MONTANA - APRIL 8th

With the exception of viewing a panoramic landscape of snow covered mountains and great wide plains, and having sustained a broken axle on one of the trucks, driving through Wyoming was pretty much uneventful. But crossing the state's border into Montana made up for it. Unhappy about having to change from motorcycle to the Brinks armored car, Point Man was abruptly stopped at a roadblock on the sprawling outskirts of Billings. The locals, hidden behind steel barricades; 55 gallon drums and car bodies, didn't even wait for a chat before they began shooting with automatic weapons and shotguns. A deadly firefight broke out, forcing Point Man into a 100 foot skid and some quick action to keep the back door of the vehicle away from the roadblock and allow him and His Misfits a chance to climb out and take cover behind the heavily armored truck. But they were pinned down because the truck was disabled from hits to the front tires, radiator and engine block. The windshield was cracked badly with bullet impacts, but the bullet proof glass had protected Point Man and His Misfits from being hit. A shot to the radiator had caused a geyser of steam to erupt and cover one of the Misfits with near to boiling coolant.

Hearing Point Man's call for assistance over the CB radio, Ed and eight volunteers arrived on the scene within minutes and parked their vehicles behind a curve in the road, where they were shielded by some brush and an old road sign advertising an upcoming tourist joint. When Ed saw the danger his friends were in, he left three men with the vehicles and led a five man assault team forward. Seeing them coming up from behind, Point Man and His Misfits blasted away with covering fire. Point Man even used his M-79 grenade launcher, which seemed to have surprised the people at the roadblock and for a few moments firing had ceased.

When Ed reached Point Man, he asked, "What did you lead us into now, Big Guy?"

Point Man glared at him, "Well, it sure ain't no church group with an offer of love and peace on their minds...Those dudes opened up on us as soon as we came around the curve, never even gave us a chance to say our piece."

"What's the shape of the truck?" Ed asked.

"She done for... we'll have to leave her here."

The people at the road block resumed firing and bullets bounced off the side of the Brinks truck and hit the pavement all around the men. Ed knew they had to get out of there or risk injury and maybe death.

"I guess a white flag won't help?" One of the Misfits asked.

"Not with this bunch... they're down right unfriendly," Point Man said.

Ed looked about the area, "Okay then... Big Guy you get your men moving back while we cover, then you and I will bring up the rear. Hit 'em with another 40mm round, just before you and I take off."

Point Man looked to his buddies, "Take off as soon as we start shooting...once you get to the other vehicles, set up a defense for the rest of us and keep an eye out on the hillside to our right just in case they send a flanking force over to ambush us."

They continued to use the Brinks armored car for cover, while two men jumped inside to remove anything of value. Once that was done and the Misfits made their way back, Ed sent the other five men, who were loaded down with extra ammo and supplies from the Brinks truck, back towards the rear.

Ed was lying on the snow beside the Brinks' left rear tires shooting from under the truck; Point Man removed a high explosive 40mm round from his bandoleer, loaded his M-79 and told Ed to get ready to run. He aimed in the direction of the road block and fired; when the round exploded in the middle of the roadblock it sent 55 gallon drums in all directions and ignited a secondary explosion. Point Man and Ed ran to escape the shooting. Ed hated abandoning the Brinks Truck, but he saw no other way and wasn't about to risk bringing up the wrecker to salvage the truck and risk the lives of his people.

For nearly a minute the shooting ceased, then started up again as the people at the roadblock saw two men fleeing the truck heading for the curve in the road. Thankfully the snow hadn't been very deep through this part of the state and both men were able to run at a pretty good clip, but after covering only 20 feet or so, Ed suddenly went down and skidded on his face across six to seven feet of snowy road surface.

Point Man hadn't heard Ed call out, but something inside told him to turn around and he spotted Ed lying face down, blood forming around his head. Knowing how often head wounds were extremely critical or fatal, Point Man yelled out for two Misfits to come a running. He returned to Ed's side, checked for a pulse and was greatly relieved to see that his friend was still alive. Carefully, he turned him over onto his back and examined the nasty wound on the right side of his head. The bullet had entered the rear of Ed's head and slide along the skull before exiting above his right ear.

While his two Misfits provided cover fire, Point Man removed a battle dressing from his canteen belt and carefully wrapped it around Ed's head wound. Satisfied, he ordered his two buddies to pick Ed up cautiously and hustle him back to the vehicle. Angry at seeing his friend hurt so grievously, Point Man selected a white phosphorous round, (also known as a Willy-Peter round), loaded it into his M-79 and fired it off toward the roadblock. He waited for a brief moment listening for the explosion. The burst of white phosphorous and the screams that followed seemed to satisfy the Big Guy - *you could've talked…even showed us another way around your damn town…you didn't have to cut loose and turn the road into a battle field. No, you got what you deserved, but if my buddy dies I may just have to come back and light up your world,* he turned and ran back to where they were loading an unconscious Ed into the back seat of a Ford Expedition.

With all the bullets flying around Doc was surprised to learn that besides Ed there were only two other injuries. One Misfit had suffered 1st and 2nd degree burns from steamy coolant and another member of the rescue party had suffered a minor bullet grazing across his left forearm.

Reluctantly, Point Man left Ed to Doc's care and at Pastor Woodway's order, took over temporary command. Nancy drove the ambulance while Point Man took the right front passenger seat and directed the convoy around Billings by using a series of deserted access roads that bypassed the roadblocks. Ed's old AAA Map showed Point Man the access roads, but they needed the plow truck to clear the way on numerous occasions. They had jerry-rigged a heavy steel snowplow on the front of their two and a half ton flatbed truck to serve this purpose. Two of the Misfits, in their best foul weather gear, volunteered to ride in the back of the truck to keep the driver safe. A few random shots were reported, but the convoy didn't meet any further resistance. Apparently, the people who remained in Billings had decided they didn't want to engage in a major gun battle with such a large well-armed party.

For the next 31 miles, they drove a single lane of cleared snow as fast as the snow plow could go; holding at 25 – 30 mph. Several times they had to stop while the heavy truck battled deep drifts across the road. But the driver knew what he was doing; he had worked for the Arizona Highway

Dept. for nine years and on several occasions was sent to Flagstaff to help when heavy snowfall closed roadways. During one winter storm he had worked back-to-back 18 hour shifts for more than six days; the overtime paid for a family trip to Disneyland.

Believing they were safe, Point Man finally brought the convoy to a halt and made camp 42 miles north of Billings. Several vehicles required maintenance; two were overheating and, much to Kathy's amusement, Larry O'Brian was fit to be tied to find a flat inside right duel. His precious bus had been wounded and even worse, his children endangered by some clown with a rifle. He slammed his strong right fist against the outside wall of the truck, amusing the children inside and demonstrated to Kathy that even a saint could get riled up. Realizing how serious it could've been if one of the kids had been hurt, she helped by grabbing up a five lb. lug wrench and went to work trying to loosen the huge lug nuts.

When Ed woke up, he was confused to find himself strapped down to the ambulance gurney with an extremely piercing, skull bursting headache. A tearful Kira was hanging over the top of him when he opened his eyes and brought them into focus. "What's going on?" Talking almost made his eyes cross as a jolt of pain zapped through him.

Hearing Ed's voice, Doc gently shoved Kira aside. "Hold still," Doc ordered curtly as he propped Ed's right eye open with his fingers and directed a bright light into it to check for pupil response.

"Hey-That hurts!" Ed exclaimed as he fought against his restraints.

"How do you feel?" Doc asked with a bit more concern in his voice then a few seconds before.

"I'd feel a lot better if you'd get that dang light out of my eyes."

Doc ignored his request and checked the other pupil. "Lay still, Ed. You got shot... nasty greaser right above the right ear. You lost a lot of blood, but the bullet actually did little damage. That hard head of yours and Point Man's quick action saved your life." Doc sat back and slid his penlight back into his right chest pocket.

Ed slowly moved his head from side to side and grimaced from the pain, "Feels like I got kicked by an angry mule...Anyone else hurt?"

"You were all lucky, only two other minor wounds. One of the gorillas got burned some by hot coolant and another bullet grazing. From what your men have said, you were truly testing your angels today. Those people back there were down right inhospitable." Doc looked over at Kira and handed her a dry tissue to wipe her eyes. "You can release the big lug now," Kira moved up and began to undo the straps.

"Why was I strapped down?"

"Head wound. I didn't want you moving around. We have no X-ray machine available and you might have...It doesn't matter now," Doc said curtly. "I'm the doctor and I had you strapped down. Now get off my gurney so I can change the sheets...this little lady here will help you to your tent."

"Where are we?" Ed brought his right hand up to brace against his wound. He was dizzy when he sat up and was forced to lean against Kira's right shoulder. Not that she minded one bit.

"Point Man said we were about 42 miles north of Billings," Kira said. "Quiet spot, no one's around and the snow has stopped." Kira helped him as he put his legs down and tried to get his balance. There wasn't a lot of room in the back of the ambulance so Kira stepped outside first to help Ed down.

Doc stood in the doorway and pointed at Ed, "Keep that bandage on your head until I pull those stitches in a couple days. Take those four Tylenol #3 tablets I gave Kira. Two now and two more tonight. Come see me if you need more in the morning."

"Thanks, Doc." Ed took the two pills Kira handed him, swallowed them down with a gulp of water from Doc's canteen and slid the others into his shirt pocket. As he did so, he noticed a large splatter of dried blood on his favorite shirt and sighed.

"Find Point Man and thank him...Seems that big brute saved your life. He pulled you out after you went down and applied the bandage. It will make for a great story you can tell around the camp fire to the kids."

Feeling like a force four hangover was slamming his brain against his skull Ed cautiously leaned on Kira's shoulder for support as he took his first few steps. Once he felt steady, Kira put her arms around him and hugged him tightly with her head against his chest.

"I'm okay, girl, it's nothing to fret about." He tried to push her away, but she wouldn't let him go. "C'mon, Kira, ease up a bit. I gotta go find Point Man."

Kira let go and used the dampened tissue to wipe her eyes, "I thought you were dead...an' I didn't wanna lose you... I...I love you, Ed." She suddenly looked shocked for revealing her secret and then glared up at him, "There! I said it an' I'm not sorry."

"Look, can we talk about this later." Ed's head wanted to blow and he knew it was going to take ten of those pills to relieve the throbbing pain. *He said two more for tonight?* "Look, Kira, I really don't have time for this!" Ed shouted, gaining the attention of the camp.

Her eyes full of hurt and her lips in a pout, Kira turned from him and stormed away, leaving Ed standing with a dumbfounded expression on his face. *I can't win...I jus' can't win! I'm the one who got shot and now I look like a creep for getting her mad and probably have most of the camp upset with me for yelling at the poor girl. Lord, it's been a very rough day an' now I have to find a clean shirt.*

Ed bumped into Pastor Woodway behind the cook's area and gratefully sipped from an offered canteen to wash the second set of pills down. Then, after finding two fold out chairs to sit on, he took a moment to discuss what had happened. They spoke of dwindling food supplies, vehicle conditions and morale. It was about then the four tablets began to hit and Ed felt a strange cozy calmness come over him. "Pastor, I think I need some sleep. Would you ask Joey to set up the guard roster for tonight?"

"Point Man's already taken care of it," Pastor said. He helped Ed to his feet. "Ed, you need to apologize to Kira and straighten out whatever there is between you two."

"Pastor, I sure don't need any woman problems right now. Not with all this to handle." Ed waved around to take in all the tents and vehicles.

"Moses had a wife and he was responsible for hundreds of thousands, maybe millions...you only have these few lambs to lead."

"Lambs...sheep...C'mon, Pastor, I'm too old for that girl. We're friends and that's all there is to say about it." Ed walked away, using the sides of a couple of vehicles to steady himself. He was hoping to find Point Man and after that, his tent before he collapsed. He found the big guy standing by his precious Hog, "Tinkering with your toy?" Ed asked, as he came up behind Point Man.

"Hey, Boss Man!" Point Man dropped his ratchet and gave his friend a good once over. "Glad to see you up an' around."

"Doc told me what happened. Thanks." Ed offered his hand and Point Man shook it in a firm grasp.

"No sweat. When I saw you guys coming, you looked like the 7th Cav to the rescue." Point Man reached down to his huge tool box and picked out a smaller wrench.

"How's the little lady?" Point Man asked; a smirk on his face and laughter in his eyes.

"You, too!" Ed walked off, leaving Point Man shaking his head in amusement.

Not knowing what else he could do, Ed, still with a throbbing headache, went looking for Kira. Unable to find her, he headed for his tent in hopes of fighting off the touch of dizziness with a nap. But he stumbled upon Kathy Looney, who with icy cold eyes shooting daggers into Ed's heart, said in a sarcastic tone, "Why it's Prince Charming." Too dark to see

Ed's bloodshot eyes or realize what poor shape he was in, Kathy lit into him like a protective she beast, "What'd you tell that girl? You don't think she's had enough misery in her life already?" Kathy shook her right finger at him, using it like a teacher's pointer. "She paced around the fire waiting to hear if you were all right an' then, you...you great big lout, you blow her off because she cares too much for your sorry hide. Some big hero you turned out ta be!" Kathy sidestepped Ed and walked on, shaking her head in disgust and mumbling a few profane words under her breath.

Apparently like most everyone in camp, Ed could only shake his head, which hurt entirely too much, so he kicked the crusty snow at his feet. When he reached his canvas six man wall tent, he wandered in and found one of his tent mates, Larry O'Brian looking up at him under the bright glow of a kerosene lamp, "Ed, you'd make a great extra on some zombie flick."

Ed, still struggling with some degree of dizziness, plopped down on his cot, draped a wool blanket around his shoulders and glared at Larry, "Just shut up, unless you wanna pull some extra guard duty!?"

"Ease up, Boss. You're looking a little played out...worn out...exhausted...a bit on the touchy side."

Ed started to growl, but then backed off and said, "Sorry, Doc gave me some pills but they don't seem to be helping any. Maybe I only need some sleep. Tomorrow I'll be my ever cheery self again." He slid his feet into his sleeping bag and turned his back to the world.

"Good night," Larry whispered and grabbed up his bath towel, walked out of the tent and headed for the water wagon for a spit bath. Approaching the water wagon, Larry found someone ahead of him and was surprised to see Kathy Looney washing her hair. She was wearing a man's white t-shirt and faded form fitting blue Levi's. Her parka was draped over a water can and she was trembling from using icy cold water in such low temperatures. Larry estimated the current temperature was in the high 20's, but cold enough to freeze a woman with wet hair quite rapidly.

"Evening, Kathy."

"Who? Oh, it's you." Kathy replied gruffly as she turned to face him. "I had some soap in my ears, didn't recognize your voice."

"You're up mighty late," Larry grinned; admiring the domestic scene before him brought back nice memories of normal time. He had watched his mother wash her hair in the kitchen and then mix a strange potion of mayonnaise and olive oil to stay in her hair for 30 minutes before rinsing. His wife had washed her hair in the shower, but he didn't want to dwell too long on those old memories. He missed her so and still kicked himself for how badly he had screwed up his marriage.

"Hold it a minute. Let me finish rinsing my hair." Finished, she dried her hair, shoulders and face and then wrapped her hair in a towel. She pulled her parka back on and her new red wool gloves; a gift from one of the ladies in the convoy. "Okay, now I can talk. What's up?"

Larry noticed there was something different about Kathy and his strange expression made her uneasy.

"Did I grow a third eye or somethin'?" She asked, hand on her hip and hit him with her best icy glare.

"Sorry," Larry smiled. "I think this is the first time I've seen you without all that outlandish make up you normally wear."

Her defenses sprang up instantly and she was one second away from blasting him with a string of profanity that would have probably striped the paint of the adjacent water trailer and left him bald. "You got something else to say to me?"

"Hey cool down, I didn't say that to be mean. I was trying to say I think you're much prettier without all that war paint. It makes you look...hard. I like this look much better."

"A lot of men will argue that one with you." Kathy stomped off, heading for her tent and leaving another shaken male in her wake. Back inside her tent sitting on her bedroll, Kathy pulled a small mirror and brush out of her shoulder bag. Looking at herself, she studied the lines in her face and the clearness in her eyes. She was unable to remember when her eyes were without the redness that came from working too many smoky bars, smoking cigarettes and living around cigarette and cigar smoke, and drinking down too much booze to escape her miserable life. She also noticed another thing; how clean she felt inside. This is new. She looked over at Kira, who shared her tent and listened to her petite snores. *Girl, you've been through a lot, but you got real guts. With all you've gone through, you still have faith in God. An' these people, taking a trip like this all because of one man's vision. If it wasn't for the times and the messes we're in, I'd have said I was on one big glorious LSD trip. But acid hasn't been around for quite a while, so this is all too real...* Dropping her mirror, Kathy felt something strange come over her, a tingling sensation from the tip of her toes to the top of her head. She remembered feeling the same excitement as a child; someone had called it the "Holy Spirit goose bumps". She recalled her younger years and then suddenly, a giggle, much like she expressed as a young teenager, bubbled up out of her. *What's going on?* Kathy lifted the mirror up and examined her reflection. A woman with clear eyes looked back at her and a single tear slid down her cheek. A voice began to speak inside her head, a voice she remembered hearing once a long time ago; she listened. More than a voice, it was a sensation, reminding her that she was no longer the girl who danced topless to pay for food and rent, who talked men into buying expensive house drinks and stole their money when the opportunity presented itself. A rebirth was taking place, but something was still lacking and she knew it had to do with her relationship with Jesus Christ. Closing her watery eyes, she whispered, "Lord, I...oh, God forgive me...." Cleansing tears began to wash away the sin, the bitterness and the pain. Later, her child-like laughter woke Kira and some of the other ladies. At first they told her to quiet down, but then one and then another sensed something was going on with their new friend and they began to realize what was happening in Kathy's life. One of the guards on his rounds walked by and thought it sounded like a teenage slumber going on inside.

With morning, Kathy was out of the tent and looking for Larry. Sure enough, she found him with his head under the hood of the bus. "Can we talk?" Kathy asked.

"Hand me a Phillips screw driver," Larry said without looking at her.

"I wanted to say I'm sorry about last night. You struck a nerve an' I bit back. Will you forgive me?"

Larry pulled his head out from underneath the hood and noticed a difference in her this morning; a new freshness; and she wasn't wearing all her war makeup. "We all need to explode now and then." Larry climbed down and wiped his hands with some anti-grease goop and a clean rag Kathy offered him.

"You're a beautiful woman, Kathy." Then before either of them knew what was happening, the two of them kissed. Not a long kiss, but not a sister brother kiss either.

"I'm glad we did that...spontaneous like. It might have taken me another week or two to get the guts up. I've wanted to tell you how I felt, how quickly it happened, but something stood in the way." Larry's smile was nearly ear to ear.

"I know...me too. Funny what a little hair washing will do?" She smiled and her expression turned serious. "I need to tell you about myself before we go any further, Larry. Okay?"

"Sure, if you feel you need to. We all have pasts, but I'm here to listen to whatever you've got to say."

"Thanks...I lost my only brother during the riots...he was killed out in front of our apartment. It was always just the two of us, he went to school while...well, while I worked as an exotic dancer." She stopped and shook her head. "Exotic... that's what we say to cover what we're really doing... I danced topless, but never full nude, I had a line and never passed it. But that doesn't matter, I wasn't a good person back then, Larry and that's how I knew about Fairbanks. I spent six weeks up there, dancing topless in one of the clubs... I did it... the dancing, for quite a few years. I met some real creeps and that's why I've never trusted any man...until I met your group."

Larry nodded, but continued to hold her hands in his own until he thought she had finished explaining. "Kathy, I don't care. When I first saw you, I knew you'd had a rough time...you wore it like a badge of honor. My background isn't much different except I was on the other side. I went to those clubs, whistled at the girls and bought those expensive watered down drinks. Drugs, booze an' women, but the Lord gave me a second chance. Maybe that's why I drive this bus, helping these kids to heal my wounds. Pastor is one smart hombre. He knew what I needed to work my head out."

"That's what I need to tell you... I recommitted my life to Jesus last night and the ladies in my tent... well, they were real nice to me."

Larry's expression beamed, "Let's go find Pastor." Before she could ask why, Larry hustled her towards Pastor's tent. There, they spent more than an hour with Pastor Woodway, alone and without interruption. Before breaking camp, Pastor announced Kathy's rebirth and her engagement to Mr. Larry O' Brian.

Heading off down the road, the convoy came up against another heavy snowfall and Ed brought them to a halt on Highway 19, near Boxelder Creek. Camp was set up in snow that floated in the air with the softness of goose down. Ed walked up to where Pastor was building a fire, "I think we got about 150 miles to the border."

"158 miles to be exact," Pastor said. He remained kneeling and pointed back to a partially buried road sign barely visible through the falling snow showing the distance to the Canadian border.

"I stand corrected." Ed knelt down and threw a few sticks on the fire. "I'm sending Point Man ahead with the plow, all the way to the border on a recon."

"That's probably best...How's Kira?" Pastor asked; a hint of a smile in his eyes.

"She's ignoring me." He tossed another piece of wood into the growing fire. "I've tried to apologize, but she walks off and I don't have time for kiddy games." Ed stood up and kicked at the snow in frustration and nearly put the fire out.

"Did you ask God about her?" Pastor asked as he cleared the snow away and laid fresh tinder on the growing flames.

"No! I haven't asked God." Ed looked upset. "Look, Pastor, I know what I need to do and when I have the time I'll do it. But I'm still twice her age and some people might not like this. I mean, look you're our pastor, you know old men don't belong with young girls. It just isn't done!"

"There's no need to be upset Ed, you apparently have feelings for this young lady. But do not treat the Lord like a bothersome bill collector. He's a jealous God and should always be first in your life. Not someone you can make time for when you see fit."

"I didn't mean it that way." Ed looked confused. "Oh, I don't know what I mean." Ed shifted the balaclava on his head, adjusted the bandage and walked away, leaving Pastor by his fire with a gleeful look in his eyes.

MAJOR BLACKSTONE, BELOW HILL TOP - APRIL 9TH

Exhausted and barely able to think straight as the cold sapped the life from him, Blackstone had to face a hard fact; there were no helicopters waiting for them at Hill Top. *No rescue, we've been abandoned...This will be our dyin' ground, this frozen wasteland will become our graves.* Feeling a tug on his leg, Blackstone reached down to help one of his men to their knees.

Unable to remember the date, he had only nine men and one woman left out of a unit with over fifty troops. A few had died in a brief firefight with a small OAP scout element, but most had simply wandered off in the darkness to find a place to sleep the frozen death. Suffering from mental fatigue, he couldn't even remember their names. Weapons and field packs, anything of weight, was dropped along the trail. Their only thought was to forge ahead, to make Hill Top, but the deep snow and icy cold, added to fatigue, continued to cut their numbers down until it was only the eleven of them. He had 40, maybe 50 yards to reach the top, to walk out on level ground and possibly find shelter inside the old restaurant building. *We'll make our final stand there. I can make it...we can make it. We can rest there; build a fire...get warm again.* Turning, he looked down the hill and forced himself to count the remaining soldiers. Covered with ice and snow, his frozen command near death, ten still remained with him.

"Major Blackstone!" A loud voice called out.

My name, someone's shouting my name...up ahead I think.

"Major Blackstone!" The voice was louder.

Gotta climb...one foot an' then the next...Climb...climb...climb. Blackstone ran out of gas and fell face first into the snow, he couldn't go on. Numbness spread from fingertip to elbow on both arms and his feet felt like frozen clubs almost all the way to his hips. Lying in the deep snow as the wind swirled above him Blackstone remained motionless and waited for the Angel of Death to seek him out.

"Blackstone...Major Blackstone!"

Hearing the voice so near, he shook his head to clear his vision and lifted his head up out of the snow and with a strength he thought had left him, he pushed himself up to his knees. He glanced up ahead and was surprised to find he was only an arm's length from the Hill Top parking lot. Pulling crusty snow and ash towards him, Blackstone called upon every ounce of energy in him to propel himself forward and out on to the old Hill Top parking area. Though covered in deep snow, with splotchy ash, it was open level ground. He looked up to an utterly black sky and struggled to grin through open sores on cracked lips, his face dangerously pale white and fell unconscious onto the snow.

Only twenty yards away, three Black Hawk helicopters were sitting with their rotors slowly turning, just enough to keep their batteries charged. The rescue party had arrived hours before and was about to leave when one of the crew chiefs happened to spot a few snowy shapes coming up the hillside. While men ran down to help; two of the pilots and a medic went to assist Major Blackstone.

"He's coming around," The medic had taped an IV needle onto Major Blackstone's arm and packed warm-up pouches around his underarms, crotch and chest and stomach. He didn't want to take the Major's boots off until they were back at the hospital, but he wrapped them in layers of blankets. "Major Blackstone, you're safe now. I'm Lt. McCoy and we're here to pick you up." McCoy helped Blackstone to a sitting position. "Is this all your men, sir?"

"Yes...nine men...one woman an' me," Major Blackstone whispered. Talking through his lips was almost too painful, but they needed to know the price his command had paid to carry out orders and reach here.

Helped into the Black Hawks, the men and one woman were wrapped in wool blankets and given warm coffee to sip as the medics in each bird checked them over. The medics knew their job and avoided serving hot coffee to patients with facial frostbite and cracked lips. The first priority was hypothermia and then the frostbite, but the medics already knew these men were going to be spending some time in the Fort Greeley Hospital.

Lt. McCoy gave the signal to lift off and as soon as they did, ground fire from another OAP scout element opened up on them. The door gunner in each bird returned fire and miraculously, not a single round hit the birds; a moment later they were out of range.

The light snow grounded the OAP, but ADF Black Hawks with all volunteer crews had made it by contour flying above the tree tops. One of the crew chiefs thought for sure his bird had caught at least one tree top from one of the few remaining tall spruce, (most had been cut for fire wood), but his pilot ignored his petty complaints. "When it goes THUNK I'll worry!" On the return flight, the helicopters flew at 400 feet on a route that allowed them to fly over the city. They were advised to see if anyone was signaling for rescue and if so, another chopper would be dispatched.

Major Blackstone groaned in pain, but sat up to look out the helicopter's window to see Fairbanks pass by below. They saw no one. The city looked strange with no moving traffic, no pedestrians, no lights and no smoke from chimneys.

Major Blackstone smiled at the bird's crew chief and whispered a raspy, "Thank ...you." Unable to stay awake any longer, he lost consciousness and almost an hour later awakened and cried out when they placed him on an ambulance gurney at Fort Greeley.

"You've arrived at Greeley, Major," General Saunders said. He was there to meet the rescue birds and give out hardy, "Well done!" Saunders stood aside as they wheeled the injured soldiers to waiting ambulances. With the exception of Captain Myers' command, these 11 were the only known survivors of 1st Division. *20,000 men and women...gone...Dear God.* General Saunders pulled his scarf back up to cover his mouth and nose and walked to the side of the hospital's helipad. He looked up to the dark heavens, while light snow, mixed with black ash, continued to fall and cover him.

"Lord, what now? How many more must fall before you return?" His questions unanswered, General Saunders walked back to the helicopters to thank the crews again for a successful rescue operation.

Passing Hill Top, enemy scouts in white camouflage suits, soon came within sight of the community their maps identified as Fox. They knew they had only six miles of rolling hills to go before reaching the northern city limits of Fairbanks; second largest city in Alaska.

The Tanana Valley, massive in size, was mostly rolling hills, vast plains, famous rivers such as the Yukon, thousands of miles of creeks, and countless lakes. Bordered on the south by the Alaska Range and the north by the Brooks Range, the great flat moist plains of the valley were large enough to hold the State of New Mexico or Arizona. From tundra flats to marsh lands, from historic gold fields to a land covered in white birch and green spruce, and Denali towering in the distance; the Tanana Valley was a sight to behold. But the OAP had not come as happy tourists. No, they were here to plunder, destroy and ravage.

Word passed rapidly back through the ranks of cold, weary soldiers that Fox had been sighted. Two hours after reaching Hill Top and leaving the abandoned café a smoldering ruin, the men of OAP's lead element fell on Fox like a wave of locusts. They needed food, but there wasn't even a crumb to be found. In heated anger, the arsonists set every structure on fire; the smoke could be seen for miles in all directions. They enjoyed the temporary warmth but a few of the more intelligent soldiers saw shelters going up in smoke and their complaints were drowned by loud angry shouts from crowds of starving troops.

So close to Fairbanks, only the threat of death from warlords kept the OAP from sweeping out of the hills to invade the city. The Warlord Generals were a cautious lot that used the Black Dragons to keep their soldiers in line. As more time passed without provisions, outbreaks of mutiny against the Black Dragons were popping up more often along the front lines. The Warlord Generals, prominent men with lengthy military records appointed by the OAP War Council, knew their only hope in keeping their commands together lay in finding needed supplies in Fairbanks.

Spies and a few scattered sympathizers had supplied limited information on food storage before evacuation of the city. Recon over flights had left the OAP with the belief that Fairbanks had been completely evacuated. The warlords, however, couldn't believe Alaska would actually desert their second largest city. Fearing a trap, they wanted to send infantry patrols to guarantee the city was free for the taking.

One such patrol was made up of nine battle hardened men who saw action from the rice paddies of Vietnam to the invasion of Russia and then Alaska. They were transported to the outskirts of town by armored personnel carrier. From there, they were to hike until they reached the city center. According to their maps of the city, they were to rendezvous at a place identified as the Bentley Mall's massive parking lot on College Road. Here, they were to meet other patrols coming in from other sectors and send reports back to the main force. After hiking across Vietnam, Siberia and North Western Alaska and surviving bitter cold weather and often the whip lashes of sadistic officers, veterans likened the short hike through the hillsides north Fairbanks to entering Disneyland for the very first time. Metal snowshoes were bent and worn to the point of falling apart from the long laborious trek.

The first patrol left their vehicle to trudge through deep snow over treeless hillsides surrounding the city. They were ordered to bypass all individual dwellings, so as not to waste time, but to radio back any contacts if they came under fire. Not a shot was fired and not a soul was seen, but as they hiked down the hillsides they entered a thick layer of ice fog that blanketed the city and made the men extremely nervous. The thick ice fog covering the valley floor provided such an ominous setting that some of the men were spooked when they entered the deserted city.

Only the NCO's iron will and ready pistol kept each of the patrols in check. Empty homes and stores were tempting. When the first patrol spotted the towering McDonalds sign, all military bearing was lost as every starving member of the patrol, including the grizzled old sergeant, rushed forward in hopes of finding something to eat. Instead, a booby trap in the walk in freezer ended the hunger pains for half the squad. Two others were severely wounded later by a second booby trap; a trip wire with a grenade nestled next to a Holiday gas station's partially filled popcorn machine. The man couldn't resist a handful of stale popcorn and two of them paid dearly for it.

By the time the first patrol reached the western end of the Bentley Mall, only the sergeant and one slightly injured man remained. Their radio was damaged beyond repair and they were afraid to touch anything for fear of other booby traps. Looking down at his injured men, the Sergeant wondered how well the other patrols were doing. Almost immediately, he heard an explosion nearby and the distinct sound of an older AK-47 being fired on full automatic. Clutching his assault rifle, he lowered his head and wished he was back home fishing with his father and brothers in the South China Sea. What worried him most was having to make his report before an abusive Japanese captain; an officer who was too fearful for his own career and held little regard for those under him - especially a Chinese non-com whose ancestors had once been victims in the rape of Nanking so many long years ago.

13 - THREE LOST SHEEP IN THE MIDST OF WOLVES

"Listen, I tell you a mystery: We will not all sleep, but we will all be changed in a flash, in the twinkling of an eye, at the last trumpet. For the trumpet will sound, the dead shall be raised imperishable, and we will be changed."

1 Corinthians 15: 51-52 NIV

THE POLARIS HOTEL, FAIRBANKS - APRIL 9TH - 1005 HOURS

A thin wisp of ice fog swirled back and forth like an ocean wave and guided by cold arctic winds, the frigid crystalline vapor surged through deserted city streets and washed up against the frosted sides of abandoned buildings. Overhead, a dark ominous presence loomed; a ceiling of black volcanic clouds and bright flashes of lightening. This was nature's response to man's foolishness, which brought forth a blanketing of dark ash covering the Northern Hemisphere, mixed with falling snow. Mankind welcomed its first nuclear winter and found it pretty unfriendly.

The enemy came from the north with the sound and fury of sheer power and might. OAP dreadnoughts, powerful weapons with a growing sound of clanking metal and deep rumble of large diesel engines sent fear into any enemy. A light brigade of mighty beasts; 22 heavy tanks cautiously moved through a hillside pass above the city accompanied by a regiment of near frozen infantry. With wary alert eyes, they sought out any sign or sound of ambush or more importantly, something to fill their starving bodies. These half frozen soldiers, weary of roots and repulsed by their own acts of cannibalism were ready to kill each other over a single scrap of food.

Hundreds of dog sled teams and domestic animals had been left behind; all had been killed to feed the starving men and women of the OAP. Any wildlife found along the route they traversed was shot and consumed by hungry troops, more often than not still raw. Soldiers ravaged what they could find not bothering to build a cook fire that might attract an officer or senior non-com. The order of the day was to send all animals back to main camp, to be shared by all, but the troops hadn't seen any of the meat and knew it was being kept for the senior staff. The infantry soldier realized it was safer to eat it raw or not have anything in their stomachs at all.

It had been weeks since the OAP forward units had seen even a spoonful of rice. All OAP supplies were being diverted to the main army which was headed for the Middle East and the Alaska forces were left to forage for themselves. This made for angry soldiers and only the presence of the Black Dragons kept them from revolting and deserting the ranks. Firing squads for quarrelsome soldiers were becoming all too numerous and it had the Warlords greatly concerned.

ADF FORWARD OBSERVATION POST- FAIRBANKS

12 stories above the city and 30 feet above a gray sea of ice fog, Captain Brad Sawyer, newly appointed ADF Intelligence Officer, stood shivering, while he kept himself concealed under a gray plastic poncho as he watched the OAP enter the city. Brad's all to thin poncho matched the building's aged paint and kept the volcanic ash off him as he watched through binoculars and counted the enemy's heavy tanks cross the pass and it concerned him how fast they had vanished moments later under the fog. *That is a whole lot of fire power coming against my town. Each one of those beasts could probably take out a small city by itself and no AT-4 is going to do much harm to those big babies. An A-10 might take one out, but even then it could be iffy. They make Hitler's Tiger Tanks look like a Hot Wheels toy...Just one long line of monstrosities, each one a serpent of death to kill Alaskans.*

He watched and noticed that several of the tanks still in view had begun to spread out across the upper hillsides. He knew they were using snow covered roads through the residential areas of Fairbanks. First, they checked out the side roads, searched the remaining houses for people or possible supplies. Soon...they would be on the Johansen Expressway. *Probably take them about two days to search the city and once they find it empty, there's gonna be a lot of angry troops in town - hungry ones too.* Brad's hands tucked into heavy gloves trembled from the bitter cold as vapor cloud from his frosty breath escaped from underneath his protective cover. He only hoped the enemy didn't have any thermal imagery equipment aimed his way.

IN FOX

Six miles north of Fairbanks, in the rural community of Fox, the main body of the OAP point element had set up a massive defensive ring. Unable to believe the Alaskans had abandoned their second largest city to the enemy, Warlord General Mei had sent in a reinforced armored probe to investigate when his small infantry patrols had failed to report in. The officer commanding the probe reported back thick ice fog, an eerie silence and deserted buildings and streets. This lack of action confused OAP Command, which brought General Mei and his staff into a long and heated debate on what the ADF had planned for defense. Without satellite communications, or better weather to get an observation aircraft aloft, he was blind until one of his spies or an OAP sympathizer reported back with the location of ADF defensive positions. He knew the highway between Fairbanks and Eielson Air Force Base was over 22 miles long and at any point the ADF could have set up an ambush. From old satellite photographs General Mei could understand why the ADF might abandon Fort Wainwright, as it offered little or no protection with the way it was spread out around the runway. But he was baffled at the idea that they would leave Fairbanks which offered tactical strategic points from which to conduct ambushes to decimate his men. With thick ice fog and limited visibility he had no air support and this also concerned him. His request and later demand for air recon was put on hold by higher authority back in Siberia until the current snow storm ceased and the skies cleared. After the losses they had suffered on the Seward Peninsula from an Air Force which supposedly didn't exist in great numbers, OAP Siberian Command was reluctant to send out advanced squadrons from Russia until Fairbanks was taken and the three airfields; Fairbanks International, Fort Wainwright and Eielson, ready to receive OAP fighters. Inflight refueling was required to cover the distance the fighters had to fly and snow was preventing that for now. This meant he had to have the Fairbanks area runways, munitions for the fighters, fuel and a secure maintenance area. His units must take the city, the airport and Fort Wainwright within the next 72 hours or he risked being relieved of his command and most likely executed. OAP command had little patience for generals who did not secure their objectives in the required time period.

OAP TANK COLUMN

Sergeant Nishehi commanded the lead tank; a dreadnaught that weighed nearly as much as a diesel locomotive and carried the firepower of five WWII Sherman tanks. With him was a dedicated crew of seven who much preferred the warmth of their huge diesel engines to being a frozen infantrymen walking alongside.

A young man from a small town near Beijing and son of a music teacher, Sgt. Nishehi was following his senior officer's armored personnel carrier. Nerves on edge, he grew more fearful with each passing moment and rotated the turret of his tank 360 degrees in search for any sign of the enemy. Ice fog and lack of opposition had put him on edge and he recognized the look of jittery nerves on the faces of his men. His stomach no longer grumbled from lack of food even though he had eaten nothing but some boiled roots in over a week. He had reached the point where his stomach had shrunken and his body was beginning to consume what little supply of fat he still had. He and the members of his tank crew laughingly called it the Alaska Diet Plan. He suspected his 158 lbs. had dropped sharply since they had left Siberia; if not for suspenders he would have trouble keeping his pants from falling down. Nishehi was revolted by the thought of partaking in the human stew some of his comrades had shared earlier. No, he had not reached that point yet and considered those who had as less than human and tended to shy away from them.

The tanks crews were usually able to keep tolerably warm inside their beasts as long as they kept it buttoned down tight. But Nishehi had to open the exhaust ports on his every 15 minutes to keep his crew from succumbing to the thickening multi-engine fumes. In Siberia, the equipment had performed well, but after their last battle with Russian armor, several of the tanks were experiencing mechanical problems. His needed to be vented so often the inside temperature fluctuated between 25 and 60 degrees. This meant moisture accumulation on everything including electronics and the communication's private was skittish about handling his gear. Sgt. Nishehi had to use a hand operated wiper blade to clean his view plate to look out through his overhead hatch window and study the ominous sky overhead. Those strange black clouds frightened him. Ash and snow mixture blocked his vision in less than a minute. He could only hope the enemy wouldn't risk fighters in such foul weather.

Thick icy fog didn't help either; his ultra-bright head lamps seemed to bounce off the swirling ice crystals. Not only must he be concerned with tank traps, he had to be wary of running over one of his infantry squads in the intolerable ice fog. Nearly invisible in white snow suits, some of the foot soldiers were walking as if drunk; one man had fallen below the tracks of a tank only moments before. He knew the poor foot soldier was suffering constant bitter cold and lack of food. There was a great lack of concern for the troops as they were ordered relentlessly to drive on in conditions of such privation. Since leaving the all too sparse island of Big Diomede, they were in a constant state of vigilance, going with little or no sleep which caused disunity between dismounted motorized infantry and tank crews. Even among the infantry units, fights had broken out until units of Black Dragon Secret Police were ordered to escort each unit to handle any break down of military decorum with quick and deadly punishment.

On the jittery edge of sanity, Sgt. Nishehi could imagine hearing strange spooky voices in his headphones as he looked out through the front view scope. Turning his massive turret from right to left and back again, he noticed there was not a bird in view, no warning challenge from an angry squirrel for daring to approach his territory or even a household dog racing out to defend his owner's property. This strangeness, this thickness to the air, this absence of any life was more terrifying than a firefight. He remembered seeing huge black ravens to the north and thinking it was good fortune. He'd listened to the challenge of a small titan of a squirrel when Nishehi's tank brushed its tree and knocked its nest to the ground. His outside listening devices allowed him to hear the squirrel, but back then he didn't think twice when his dreadnaught crushed the brave little warrior and his home under its massive steel treads. But with no sound outside, other than the noise of a fellow dreadnaught or the grumbling of a nearby infantryman, he wished he could hear one of those uppity squirrels now. He knew the rest of the crew were hoping for a firefight, his main gun had a young trigger happy soldier tapping his greasy finger on the heavy steel triggering mechanism; he had already warned him a half dozen times to keeps his hands away until the order came to ready the weapon. Sgt. Nishehi hoped for something to happen, anything, to break this strange tension they all felt as their monstrous beast carried them further into the city.

FROM THE POLARIS BUILDING ROOF TOP

"So, those are the soldiers who conquered Southeast Asia and Siberia, who swept over the Philippines, Australia and now reign over nearly half the world." Brad whispered out loud. "Judging by your infantry's condition, you guys looked pretty pooped out." Brad often talked to himself at times like this; it was his way of dealing with the knee knocking fear clutching his chest. *Or it might be just the cold?* "Who am I fooling?" Brad asked himself. "I've faced gang warfare, barricaded subjects by the dozens and way too many crazies armed with all kinds of weapons… but I've never had to face tanks the size of … what would I compare you with? You're unlike any tank I've seen before… more like a wide-body big brother to a Bradley Fighting Machine with two walkways for exterior Gatling-gun positions… a tank turret three times the size of an Abrams tank which supposedly carries a 105mm cannon… How can you survive such recoil being inside? You've got rockets, anti-aircraft missiles and dual treads over six feet wide. Some of you even have cow catchers…I guess it's to scoop up people or debris blocking your path. But how you ever got across the tundra with so much weight… no wonder you attacked in the winter. You would've got bogged down in the summer and probably sunk, but then, there wouldn't have been an ice bridge to cross on… Makes me feel I'm living out some futuristic battle. I've got no idea how we're going to stop your machines." Brad let out an audible sigh and then said sarcastically, "Maybe our cold germs will kill you!"

Using his special James Bond camera, he attempted to film the closest tanks as they continued through the pass. The Richardson Highway ends at the intersection with Airport Road at the entrance to Fort Wainwright. The Steese Highway begins at this intersection, crosses the Chena River and skirts downtown Fairbanks before entering a pass in the hills north of the town to drop into the Goldstream Valley and Fox then continues north through Central and ends at the small town of Circle on the banks of the

Yukon River. The Elliot Highway intersects the Steese at Fox and continues north to the old mining town of Livengood and then to Manley Hot Springs. The Dalton Highway, built as the TAPS Road (Trans Alaska Pipeline Systems Road), takes off from the Elliot at Livengood and continues north to Coldfoot and Prudhoe Bay. It was this highway the OAP had used, but were forced to build bridges to traverse the frozen Yukon River.

"Sure hope you can see this, guys?" He began snapping photos with the camera equipped binoculars he had been issued before leaving Fort Greely.

GENERAL MEI'S HEADQUARTER'S TRAILER IN FOX

Still puzzled by the retreat from Fairbanks and unable to get satisfactory answers from his staff, General Mei suddenly pulled his pistol; a souvenir he'd taken from a captured Russian colonel prior to the man's execution, and killed the nearest staff member. Disgusted with how long it was taking the man to die, Mei stepped over him and issued orders for the probe to continue deeper into the city. "Find me prisoners!" Mei shouted to his stunned staff. "Only then may you search for food."

Shock turned to fear seeing one of their own killed; staff members turned away from the body of their dead comrade and bowed their heads as General Mei walked by. He left the Command trailer headed to the communications trailer to send a report to his commanding officer in Siberia and he wasn't looking forward to it. The Warlord Generals wanted results and could care less about the condition and morale of their troops. They had millions of soldiers and a few thousand cold hungry soldiers meant little to them.

ROOF TOP

Brad's hands were aching from the bitter cold so he decided it was time to go. Snow and ash was coming down heavier, giving off a pungent odor that made him cough, even through his scarf. It was also making it more difficult to observe the unwelcome visitors coming through the pass. Flashes of lightning made Brad extremely uncomfortable; his roof top position was far too close to radio and TV antennas.

Although it was April, Fairbanks temperatures continued to hold at sub-zero. Brad didn't have access to an outdoor thermometer, but he believed the temperature to be somewhere around 35° below zero. He knew that even with an arctic parka and snowsuit, standing in one place too long could turn a person into a Popsicle all too quickly.

Checking his watch, he confirmed 43 minutes had passed since he'd come up to the roof. "Long enough for government work 'cause I sure ain't gettin hazard pay for this." With the enemy this close, Brad knew all of the deserters, stragglers, OAP spies and sympathizers, European spies and old-fashioned gang bangers and their youthful wannabes, had scurried off to find a hole to hide in until the shooting was over. Those who had stayed behind, having heard about the events in Siberia - OAP spies and sympathizers alike - felt that once the first OAP units entered the city, they were likely to shoot first. They believed they were probably much safer hiding in some basement or underground storage facility - at least until the city was occupied. It was for this reason that the Warlords did not receive intelligence they needed

Brad took one final look; the sheer gargantuan size of the enemy tanks continued to awe him. The only thing missing was torpedo tubes and a flight deck. He used an iron ladder riveted to the inside elevator shaft to descend to the 12th floor, then climbed down three flights of red carpeted stairs to the 9th floor with his pistol ready in one hand and flashlight in the other. He proceeded cautiously down a darkened hallway. He passed by the open door of a room and saw the unmade bed, a bath towel on the floor and remembered a much happier time when tourists poured in and out of these rooms like clockwork staying on schedule for some tour departure. Tourists who had arrived or departed in fancy tour buses and airport taxis. He thought they were treated more like cattle by the different tour companies and grinned as he recalled they always had the same tourist questions, but were always in too much of a hurry for the answers.

He thought of the Ice Palace Restaurant, once located on the 12th floor, "Food was all right, turned out a great steak...Steak?" Brad whispered and then added, "Don't go there, boy, think about something else...like C-ration pork chunks smothered in grease. Filling, yes - but oh man, what a foul taste"

Entering another stairwell at the other end of the floor, he carefully walked down another 10 flights of stairs to reach the basement level. Making sure to stay clear of glass doors and windows, he walked over to a locked brown door marked 'Employees Only'. He unlocked it with a key provided by Colonel Stewart, opened it, stood on a metal grate landing and locked the door behind him with a deadbolt . He climbed down a narrow metal stairwell to the custodian's shop, side stepped several patches of ice on the cement floor and into a small supervisor's office littered with old job orders, used coffee mugs, paper cups, newspapers and scattered debris. On one wall hung an old employee duty roster and on the opposite wall an old Hot Rod calendar with a picture of a fancy painted 1932 Ford Coup.

Brad's prior knowledge of this building's layout had come in handy. In the old days, an after-hours gambling house was located here in a large secret room off of the super's office. It had been frequented by many of Fairbanks' elite crowd of partiers, including a former State Commissioner of

Public Safety, a Lt. Governor and even a visiting US Secretary of the Interior. With such a cliental, it was never raided, but as the good old boys died or became too old to move about, the location was abandoned. A hidden latch inside a fake wall switch cover activated a large, double door wall locker which swung out to expose a pathway into the former gambling den. Smaller side rooms offered players more privacy for other sinful desires. Brad's father was the first to tell him about the secret place having caught an intoxicated city councilman and deputy mayor leaving the basement after a late night of roulette. From then, he learned of other city leaders who often ventured here for clandestine rendezvous with ladies of the night or a friendly game of poker. Secrets and the Good Old Boy network was kept quiet and in return, police budgets were passed with little debate. The Hole in the Wall Club had a new secret – providing a secure hiding place for Brad and Captain Wayne Roberts – keeping them safe from the enemy.

"I'm home, Lucy," Brad said loudly as he pulled a curtain aside to keep light from escaping the room through the open front door and then pulled down on a rope to swing the lockers back into place. Turning around with gun still in hand, Brad was startled to find Captain Jefferson P. Lanly standing behind a concrete pillar with an, M-4 rifle aimed at Brad's midsection.

"You were up there long enough," Wayne said. He lowered his own rifle and leaned against the wall.

"Hey, Jeff, when did you get here?" Brad asked as he holstered his pistol and came over to shake hands.

"Snuck in a half hour ago, Wayne nearly tapped..." Jeff pointed to his forehead, "...me twice until he remembered who I was."

"No one told us you were coming," Wayne said as an excuse. "You're lucky I'm the curious type and didn't shoot first."

"Colonel Stewart thought you might be able to use my language skills. But actually, I think he really wanted me out of his hair."

"You're welcome here," Brad said with a beaming smile, "You're also just in time, OAP tanks are moving down the Steese Highway as we talk."

Wayne shouldered his rifle, "In that case, it's time to pull another gopher routine and move to our next apartment. I don't want to be trapped here."

Brad was in agreement, "Before long, this place will be infested with little oriental faces and we won't be able to move an inch. Let's pack."

"I remember how they work," Jeff said. "...they won't be looking for the usual towels and ashtrays to take back home for the wife. These guys are probably starving by now, so they'll be checking every drawer, every cupboard and wall locker for something to eat." His remark caused both men to smile. Several of those cupboards and drawers were booby trapped for the wayward tourist.

Brad thought for a moment and then asked, "Did you happen to pick up any souvenirs on your journeys, Mr. Lanly?"

"I received a sweet deal on a Thai elephant sculpture made from teak wood."

"What happened to it?" Wayne asked as he shoved equipment into his pack.

"I had to leave it in China," Jeff said with a note of sadness in his voice. "I was in a bit of a hurry at the time, some of those pesky Black Dragon types were nosing around and it was time to switch identities - again."

"So, how many personalities did you carry off, Jeff?" Brad asked.

"One Burmese private, a Thai corporal and three separate Chinese; one enlisted and two officers."

"Do you ever wake up wondering who you are?" Brad asked. But Jeff only replied with a big smile.

Under the Polaris Hotel was a tunnel, part of a system that ran under the city streets built originally by the military for transferring steam heat between buildings and the Main Steam Plant on Fort Wainwright. Until recently, they were hooked to the city's steam plant and maintained by the city to provide heat for the downtown area, needed businesses and warehouses, ADF assigned apartment buildings and the police and fire departments. These tunnels were large enough for access when repairs were needed on steam lines and Brad had used them on several occasions; working surveillance and moving confidential informants in and out of the police department building.

Loaded with gear, the three men left the basement by way of a short climb down a black iron ladder bolted to the wall and soon found themselves in an access tunnel. They walked cautiously along a lengthy concrete corridor with only flashlights for illumination chasing the occasional shrew off. Lunch? Brad wondered. They stopped to read metal wall plates at tunnel junctions to confirm their location.

"We're here," Brad said in a loud whisper.

"You're sure?" Wayne asked then added, "I hope so, 'cause this place smells like..."

Brad cut Wayne off with a childish voice, "Be nice now, this will be our home for a while and you should be respectful of the neighbors and their young ones."

"Neighbors?" Wayne asked in disbelief.

Brad pointed his flashlight at a dozen or so shrews scurrying along in the dark and a single nest where tiny eyes were glaring back at them. "Besides, it's either here or someplace not so nice. So hold your nose and maybe we'll be lucky." Brad climbed up a short iron ladder and with some effort slid aside a heavy metal manhole cover which allowed them access into the basement of Fairbanks City Hall.

Built in the early part of the 20th Century as the Main School Building, the building was condemned and later designated as a City Landmark. In the 1990's, it underwent extensive renovation and reopened as the New City Hall and Boy & Girls Club. Three stories high and built of rebar reinforced enforced poured concrete, the building had walls 12 inches thick and quite massive for the time period it was originally constructed. Much later, the new Fairbanks Police Department was built adjacent to it, joined by a hallway which unfortunately provided the mayor direct access to the police chief.

Brad worked his way through the huge basement, nearly half the size of a standard football field and immediately went to the door leading to the 1st floor. He took a six foot length of heavy metal chain from his pack, picked up at the previous location, and wrapped it around the inside door lock to prevent anyone from opening it from the other side. "This should hold it until I can get it welded shut. I'll have to hustle over to the Police Shop to find the stuff I need." When things began turning sour, the police officers and a few volunteers began doing their own vehicle work. They had scrounged what they could from the City Shop and this included a couple of welders; one small enough for Brad to lug back to their hiding spot.

"I wouldn't bother, if they get curious enough they can always blast it open with one of those tanks of theirs," Wayne said.

"They'd have to run the tank through most of the building to be able to make the shot, but okay," Brad said. "We'll use the tunnels for access and hopefully the OAP will kindly ignore 'em for a while." Brad began setting up house, while Wayne hauled Claymore mines out of his pack and positioned them to take out any enemy force coming through the door or the tunnel entrance they had just used.

Jeff laid a length of trip wires set with fragmentation grenades in the tunnel. Afterward, he helped Brad unload the remaining equipment, "I doubt the OAP will be searching the tunnels for a while. Those men are too hungry... they'll be foraging through every neighborhood house and store to find food. Then they'll begin looking for stragglers in old government buildings. Most if not all of the man hole covers are buried by snow and ice and unless one of them simply happens to stumble upon us, we should be safe." he selected a corner for his bed, used some cut up cardboard boxes for a mattress and undid his arctic sleeping bag. "I sure prefer our bags to theirs. I nearly froze to death using their Barbie Slumber Party bags."

"Where did they get a …" Brad realized he had been had.

"Sorry, Brad, but the OAP's bag is two threadbare wool or cotton blankets sewn together with a poncho liner wrapped around it to keep you dry. Anything below 50° above zero and you get cold."

"What about the officers?" Wayne asked.

"They usually had shared a tent and sometimes a stove. But Russia changed everything. We lost thousands to frostbite and we only survived by using Russian equipment. From what I understand, the arctic gear and equipment we should've had went to other armies and we were left with the castoffs." Jeff was silent for a moment as he thought about it and then added, "Maybe it was their intention from the beginning for their army to survive off the land and what spoils they could claim from the enemy. Such barbarism did cause the soldiers to fight harder."

"You mentioned other armies…what other armies?" Brad asked.

Jeff glanced over at Wayne who nodded his permission, "I'm sorry, Brad, I've forgotten how little time you've been with us. It must be the cold… the OAP has three distinct armies that I know of and the army facing us here in Alaska is their second or third largest depending on casualties."

"Second or third?" Brad asked in amazement.

"Yes," Jeff replied. "The OAP's largest army was trained and equipped for conquering the Middle East. They will be the ones who sweep down upon Israel. According to the Word of God, as I understand it in the Book of Revelations, they will also be the ones destroyed by the Hand of God."

"What of Army number two then?" Brad asked as he tried to visualize God's destruction of such an army.

"All I know for sure is how this army was used earlier for the seizure and occupation of Australia and much of Southeast Asia. I was with them for a while, but had to switch identities to avoid detection. This last time I was also forced to switch armies. It's really not all that hard to do when you think about it, not with so many nationalities walking about and all of them of an oriental lineage. All I did was change shoulder patches, rank emblems and my location. I also put several hundred miles between my former commands… I didn't want to take any chances of running into a former comrade."

"You really led an exciting life, Jeff. I think you're my new hero!" Brad said.

"Thanks, Brad…But who was your old hero?"

"My Dad, he was a very courageous man who raised two wild rebellious sons."

"Then I'm truly in great company," Jeff said in admiration. He smiled when he saw the look of appreciation on Brad's face.

"Can you two stop palavering? I'm freezing to death here!" Wayne said.

Besides getting a small fire going with smoke channeled out through the building's old heat vents and concealed by ice fog, the next thing on the agenda was a full equipment check. Next, they conducted a search of the basement for anything they might be able to use and to their great surprise they stumbled upon a pre Vietnam War reserve of emergency food supplies. According to attached paperwork, these supplies were put in place on October 2, 1957. The water containers were useless; frozen solid and spoiled. Some of the nutritional wafers were still edible with lots of water added from their own supply and pieces of ice boiled for removal of impurities. They hit the treasure trove when they found two boxes containing U.S. Army green wool blankets sealed in plastic wrapping. Though a bit smelly, each man now had soft bedding and at least two blankets for added warmth. When it was time to turn off the lights, Brad was assigned to stand first watch and in the peaceful silence, he remembered to thank God for these blankets and prayed for his family's safety.

Moments before Jeff was to relieve him, Brad heard the sounds of heavy machinery moving around outside and knew the OAP was nearby. *We're sure not going anywhere now! The Indians got us surrounded... No 7th Cavalry to the rescue this time...And this is their third largest army?* Then Brad recalled that his dad had once said about the Chinese, "Son, they could put 100 million into the field. If it came to it, the only way to stop them would be with a nuclear bomb and God forbid we would ever have to use that against human beings ever again."

"They beat us to it, Dad," Brad muttered then ambled over to make sure Jeff and Wayne were awake - they both were.

FORT WAINWRIGHT

Once known as Ladd Air Field, Fort Wainwright previously housed the U.S. Army 6th Light Infantry Division. Though the runway was long enough to handle a C-5A Galaxy, the base was most often used for the army's various helicopter squadrons: Black Hawks, Huey's and Chinooks which supported both infantry and air rescue units. At one point, Fort Wainwright had a population of over 20,000, but with the outbreak of war and the impending invasion of Alaska, the post and Fairbanks became temporary home to more than 190,000 men, women and children from communities of the Seward Peninsula and the Interior, and this is what Warlord General Mei had expected to find. He had received word of the Alaskan President's refusal of surrender and had expected a fight for Fairbanks. Incensed, General Mei now stood before his 5 foot square city map and studied the Chena River. This meandering body of water, often narrowing to only 30 feet wide, traveled through the interior of Alaska and right through the middle of Fairbanks, before emptying its waters into the much larger Tanana River.

Upon finding the city apparently evacuated, he suspected and was proven correct in that the ADF had booby trapped many buildings. He was enraged to learn his men had stupidly blundered into these causing the seven bridges across the Chena River to blow up in their faces and kill and wound more than 100 of his soldiers. To make matters worse, in his haste to control Fairbanks, he failed to listen to squeamish staff members who had suspected the ADF had also booby trapped the Wainwright runway and several flight line buildings.

THE THREE SHEEP

Wayne inspected Jeff's cooking and frowned, "What is it?"

"Savor the smell, relish the taste, but never ask." Jeff used a wooden spoon he pinched from the hotel basement supply room to stir his simmering cook pot, adding a bit of salt and wishing he could have brought some of his other oriental spices.

While Jeff cooked, Brad and Wayne decided to take a chance and make a fast recon of the building upstairs before the OAP took ownership. They also needed wood for the fire and anything else they could scrounge. Brad was hoping for reading material, anything to keep his mind busy and he seemed to recall the mayor was a western fan.

An hour later, Jeff was relieved when the two men returned with arms full of fire wood and a couple old Fred Meyer's shopping bags hanging over their shoulders. They'd broken apart wooden chairs from the city council chambers and brought back all they could carry. "Now we can have a real fire," Brad dropped the wood near Jeff's feet, reached into his bag and pulled out two Elmer Kelton paperbacks, a famous author of western stories, which he had borrowed from the mayor's desk.

"Keep the fire small," Wayne ordered. "Wood will last longer and less chance of discovery."

"I know how to build a fire, Wayne," Jeff said in a cutting tone. "Is there anyone around up there, yet? He reached for the new wood and fed a couple of small pieces into the fire cherishing the warmth it quickly produced. When not cooking, he was busy boiling water on a steel spit he had constructed. With all the ice in the basement, Jeff figured they would have enough water to last for several months. But heat was also important.

Without fire, they would be dead within 24 hours from hypothermia and they still needed to worry about dehydration.

"No, not a soul...yet," Wayne plopped down on a pallet of blankets beside Jeff to warm himself. "Brad took a few photos from the top floor, but the fog is hiding the tanks.

"Hope the Colonel can make out what I'm sending him," Brad said as he pulled out the camera, "Kind of dinky for my tastes."

"Next time we'll have Colonel Stewart issue you one of those 1970's shoulder mounted news jobs to make you feel more like a man." Jeff commented and then announced, "Dinner's ready; bring your own silver... and please, make sure to tip the cook. Chocolate or coffee is preferred, but refraining from unkind words of an unsavory nature reefing to my culinary abilities will also be appreciated."

Brad had to smile even though he was cold and hungry, "I can sure tell you went to college, using all those big words... sure hope you cook as well as you talk."

Jeff pointed the wooden spoon at Brad, "If you dislike my preparation you may assume the chore of head chef for this outfit."

"No offense, Jeff. I know my limitations. Kathy always said I was the worst cook in the neighborhood, except for barbecuing. She loved my ribs and barbecued chicken." Smelling the food and looking down at his plate of camper's Mulligan stew, Brad wondered how his wife and kids were doing and when he might see them again. All three men picked up a plastic sealed bag containing plastic utensils and prepared to consume Jeff's appetizing meal.

"Hey, this isn't too bad... you got a future as a cook, Jeff," Brad said.

Jeff shook his head, "I'd rather be leading a company of soldiers... but we all must serve where we can do the best for our country."

"Well said," Wayne offered.

"I told you... he's an educated man," Brad added as he shoved another spoonful of stew into his mouth and nodded his acknowledgement of a good tasting meal.

OFFICE OF ADF INTEL, FORT GREELEY

"Colonel Stewart, we're getting another feed in from Fairbanks." 1st Lt. Ashgok appeared in the doorway of Lt. Colonel Jeb Stewart's office wearing newly issued urban camouflage fatigues, black leather boots and a brown leather shoulder holster under his left arm. Civilian issue, the holster held a black Glock 10mm pistol. He carried two extra loaded magazines on the shoulder rig's right side for easy access.

Previously assigned to the Provost Marshal's Office, Ashgok was Captain Jeff Lanly's replacement. Ashgok, an Athabascann Indian raised in Arctic Village, had served as a Village Public Safety Officer after high school, spent four years as a hunting guide for rich out of stater's and then served nine years with the Alaska State Troopers. When hostilities broke out he was one of the first Alaska State Troopers to be transferred to the ADF mostly due to his language skills and knowledge of Alaska's rugged terrain. Of small stature, with short black hair and dark brown eyes, Ashgok had a natural aptitude for the spoken word and had learned all three Eskimo dialects, several Alaska Indian languages and a smattering of Russian.

Jeb stood up, grimaced as his spine complained, and with a somewhat weary stride followed the much shorter Lt. Ashgok down the hall into the room where a monitor was set up on a six foot tall stand on four metal wheels. Two eight foot long gray metal tables each with three gray metal folding chairs were in the center of the room. The monitor was set up to receive video feed from India-5 which was recorded on a device below the monitor. There were no speakers since Brad's camera wasn't capable of recording. On the monitor's 27" flat screen, Jeb got his first look at an OAP heavy tank and was greatly impressed by its size and the raw power it displayed. "You'd better make some still copies of the best photos and send them by courier to General Saunders."

"Yes, sir," Ashgok replied. He continued watching the feed, while Jeb returned to his office.

In his new office, the light green walls were blank with the exception of dirt free spots where pictures or plaques from the former occupant once hung. Jeb sat uneasily behind a US Army metal desk, circa 1960's, cluttered with papers and reminder notes. He felt as if the walls were beginning to close in on him; he was having difficulty with his decision to send India 5's three man team to Fairbanks. He knew there would be no way to rescue them and having lost the entire 1st Division, his depression over losing so many friends was making it difficult for him to keep his mind on the work ahead. Jeb knew he should be with Lt. Ashgok watching that video feed, but all he wanted to do was close his door and try to keep the world out.

He opened the top center drawer, removed a necklace that had been made for him, examined each of the polar bear claws and recalled the night he'd wrestled that big white bear and nearly died. He struggled with the wish that he could have remained in Wales and fought and died alongside these courageous men and women of the 1st Division.

Jeb's thoughts returned to the present when he heard a spurt of radio traffic coming in from India-5. He perked up and rushed to the radio room, where Lt. Ashgok was answering the call, "India 5, this is Golf Base, reading you 5x5. Over."

"Are the pictures coming through? Over," Brad asked.

"A bit grainy, but we can make them out. How's everything going? Over."

"A-Okay… Better sign off soon before they pick up our signal. Any new instructions? Over."

Jeb relieved Ashgok of the microphone, "Keep your heads down and no heroics...That's an order! Over."

"India 5 copies…Over an' out," Brad said and signed off.

BELOW FAIRBANKS CITY HALL

"Maybe you should've ordered a pizza?" Wayne suggested. Though Jeff's meal tasted all right, it wasn't very filling.

"Probably be cold by the time they deliver it. Besides, I don't have any money for a tip." Brad placed the radio on top a metal toolbox, looked around the room and with arms spread wide, said "All the comforts of home."

"Remind me never to visit you for the holidays," Wayne said.

ADF INTELL

"How long do you think they have, Colonel?" Lt. Ashgok asked. He was working with the office machines to prepare copies of the best photos for General Saunders.

"I've got no idea, Lieutenant," Jeb replied. "Depends on how soon the enemy begins searching the buildings… Once they go into the tunnels, the game is up."

FORT WAINWRIGHT

In preparing for the OAP Air Force to arrive, ADF engineers had plowed the runways prior to setting explosives. To an approaching fighter, the runways would appear safe enough to land on. Shortly after the first tanks rumbled through the center of the city, an OAP SU-27 fighter pilot declared an emergency; one of his foot pedals was not functioning properly and he attempted to land on Fort Wainwright's long runway. A three man OAP Forward Observer Team hastily set up two rows of temporary runway lights and navigational beacons to bring the fighter in through the ice fog. The aircraft touched down and had traveled less than 100 feet when over 200 pounds of C-4 detonated beneath its wheels. The pilot, a 25 year old college student from Beijing, nephew of a prominent political member of the Communist Party, never had time to eject. The explosion could be heard across much of the town. The burning fuselage and the dead pilot rolled across the pavement to block the runway. A cloud of black smoke rose into the air, the dark plume unnoticed as it mixed with the blackened clouds above. Ironically, the Forward Observer Team had parked their truck near that spot and the bodies of the men were vaporized in the blast.

A second aircraft, another SU-27 escorting the disabled fighter piloted by a 31 year old Vietnamese pilot from Hanoi, barely escaped the explosion and reported the incident immediately to his flight leader. Within 10 minutes, General Mei learned Fort Wainwright's runway was temporarily shut down. Engineers would have to be brought in with heavy equipment to repair the damage and search for additional explosives. These events and others about to occur; would give General Mei quite a large headache and a dangerous political black eye in the view of OAP Command-Siberia. Not to mention The Communist Party big wigs of Beijing, China.

FAIRBANKS

The next incident to occur happened in the snow covered parking lot outside the massive Wal-Mart Store on Johannsen Expressway, when a small mutiny broke out among an armored unit of motorized infantry. Supported by a platoon of Dreadnaughts; OAP troops had discovered a highway lined with businesses; retail outlets, restaurants and fast food joints, hotels and banks. They saw signs for Home Depot, Wal-Mart, Barnes & Noble and the Sportsman' Warehouse, and behind these the new Fred Meyer store. Beyond the huge Fred Meyer store and across the railroad tracks was the Bentley Mall, with an attached Safeway Grocery Store. Considered to be North Fairbanks, these businesses were located north of the Chena River and west on the New Steese Highway.

In an attempt to contain the crazed soldiers, three officers were gunned down with machine gun fire as one rifle squad took it upon themselves to break loose and drive their APC through the front windows of McDonalds. Under their tracks they left shattered plate glass and crushed booths and tables. But the building was found empty of all food and drink. Two of the great dreadnaughts then plowed into the Wal-Mart Store, the crews and attached infantry hoping to find food and liquor. Instead, after doing extensive damage, the starving men and women found spring time gardening supplies on sale, an assortment of toys that needed batteries to operate, pastel colored dishware, clothing, greeting cards scattered about and several shelves of Alaska souvenirs to search through. Sportsman's Warehouse was all but empty; nearly everything had been turned over to the Militia and the angry OAP used heavy machine guns to wreak havoc inside the store. They knew they'd find nothing consumable inside the Barnes and Noble Book Store, but they were surprised to find most of the books missing. They didn't know the reading material was boxed up and removed to Fort Greeley. But maniacal soldiers and Dreadnaughts crews turned their guns on the building anyway. Dozens of cannon rounds were shot into the building, until it collapsed inward and eventually was set afire.

The troops knew they had disobeyed orders, abandoned their equipment and killed their officers to search the stores and restaurants for food. Yet, the rioting continued as soldiers ran amok. They searched banks and even used a dreadnaught to blow a vault open, but it took several NCOs to explain to the thieves that paper money was useless. All the silver and gold was gone, transported to Fort Greeley.

Other squad sized units, broke away from the large mobs and ran south toward Fred Meyer and the Bentley Mall smashing through Boston's Pizza on the way. Their APCs soon followed and smashed through the front of the Safeway Store. Again they searched for food and liquor and again they found none. Enraged, the PAC drivers took their vehicles down the length of the mall in search of anything useable. But chaos erupted, as all of the stores on the northern side of Fairbanks were put to the torch. Starved, cold and weary, the troops reached the point of hysteria and destroyed everything in their path. They used the massive power of their dreadnaughts and APCs to reduce the city's multi-million dollar buildings to fiery rubble. What they couldn't burn, they flattened under the tracks. Within hours, every neighborhood north of the Chena River and west of Fort Wainwright came under fiery attack by vengeful troops. They even turned on one another as troops were shot down in the streets or inside the houses. Three civilian stragglers, who claimed to be OAP sympathizers, were found hiding in Seekins Ford Dealership. Their cries could be heard throughout the display room as they were clubbed to death by the soldiers and left for the cook.

General Mei heard of the disturbance and ordered in a senior officer and two companies of his Secret Police to correct the problem. The officers in command of the dreadnaughts and armored personnel carriers were ordered to cease fire and await the arrival of the Black Dragons. Fearful of the General's wrath, the big guns fell silent. But a large scale firefight broke out between mutinous soldiers and Mei's Black Dragons: wounding or killing dozens before the riot was brought under control with the assistance of loyal OAP troops brought in from Fox to assist the Black Dragons.

Within hours of the riot, a series of explosions went off along the Chena River as underwater mines placed under the ice by ADF engineers began to detonate. Dozens of OAP troops who were in the process of laying their own bridging equipment were swept under the ice and drowned. But within hours, new equipment had arrived and OAP forces began constructing them on the Chena River's northern shoreline.

A very nervous OAP captain appeared before General Mei to report more than a hundred OAP soldiers were dead, 226 wounded and another

47 missing from the riot and Chena River explosions. Three light tanks, mainly used for anti-aircraft, sank to the bottom of the Chena River. General Mei didn't shoot the messenger; instead he turned to the Command Engineer Colonel, pulled out his pistol and in front of several witnesses, shot him in the forehead.

The next mishap of war sent General Mei into a fitful rage; a patrolling MIG- 29, performing air cap duties and low on fuel, attempted to land at Fairbanks International Airport. Though orders were given to avoid using the runways for fear of more mines, the pilot, who didn't want to ditch his bird and aware of the order, took a chance and landed on a lengthy stretch of tarmac. His life ended in fiery death. Racing down the snow covered tarmac at 190 mph, his nose wheel suddenly dropped into a massive hole, the first in a series of large trenches camouflaged by frozen canvas and made to look like ice covered asphalt. The MIG tumbled down the tarmac until its burning carcass came to rest with a huge pillar of black smoke filling the sky. Fairbanks International was also closed to air traffic for the moment.

The ADF Engineers weren't done yet; two tanks rolled through Fort Wainwright's Main Gate and proceeded toward the Post Commissary. In the entrance to the parking lot they struck partially buried 105mm pressure detonated artillery rounds. The ADF had discovered the one soft spot on these powerful dreadnoughts - their belly, where, as in other tanks, the emergency hatch was located.

FOX

General Mei stormed into the radio trailer and ordered all vehicles to stop where they were. All aircraft were ordered back to Nome or Kotzebue, or if they had enough fuel to Siberia. He sent his infantry into Fairbanks in mass searching for mines, booby traps and anti-personnel devices left behind to maim of kill his troops. But the traps had done their job well - OAP forces ground to a halt in Fairbanks and General Mei was seething dangerously. Unseen by his staff and underneath his hard exterior, General Mei was a trifle bit afraid. With these recent events, he would have to answer to his superior, an older Chinese gentleman who took no excuse for failure and all too often, demanded the life of the one who failed to perform to expectations. General Mei, waited word on whether to report to Siberia and truly hoped his war record fighting the Russians and the conquest of Wales, would provide him immunity from the old man's wrath. It didn't. Within 24 hours of receiving his orders to return to OAP Main Command in Siberia, General Mei was executed by a firing squad made up of his own Secret Police. His remains were left exposed to the icy winds of Siberia and some of the Black Dragons suspected he'd end up in a boiling stew pot.

THE VILLAGE OF SHAGELUK - APRIL 9TH

An exhausted Colonel Freeman lay on his back, his brain foggy as he tried to recall the last time he had felt this whipped. Cold air filtered through his scarf and with every breath, an intense pain came with the expansion of his lungs. His fatigue was made worse by lack of feeling in his limbs. Life had become a duel of sorts between his will to survive against nature's elements and a failing body. Each step, however small, was a victory. He was down to climbing by inches as he made his way up a small bluff. Behind him came a staggered line of frozen zombies spread out over a hundred yards or so. Colonel Freeman fell, his face deep in snow, before he was able to force himself to roll over. His face covered in snow and ash, his cheeks, nose and mouth badly frostbitten, a whimper escaped through chapped and bleeding lips as he the tasted bitter defeat. His beloved division was gone, so many dead or made prisoner, and here he was, running for his life. *Why? Why should I go on?*

Twisted in knots, his stomach couldn't even groan in complaint. Only pain, emotional and physical torture told him he was still alive. This kept him inching along to this point. Muscles, not yet frozen, cried out in pain. With goggles lost, icicles hung from his eyebrows, bloodshot eyes were dried out from cold and he displayed a look of impending death. Then a flicker of grit began to shine deep within him and with his last ounce of will power, he pulled himself up to a kneeling position and began to pray, "Lord, I don't have anything left. So tired, if I fall asleep now...too easy...I'll die, Lord, help me! My soldiers... they need help...I don't know where we are... and we're so...so tired." Using his rifle for support, the barrel pointed upward to keep snow and grit out of it, he gradually and painfully rose to his feet. At a low crouch, struggling to straighten his backside, he suddenly heard the voice of his old DI yelling at him, "Never give up!", "When the going gets tough, the tough get going!"

Freeman actually grinned a little, remembering how the guy thought he was Vince Lombardi of the Green Bay Packers and always repeating Lombardi's well-known points of encouragement. But right now, he was way past encouragement or even a DI's threats. All he could feel was a strange darkness surrounding him, a whisper of a voice summoning him as a sense of warming spread throughout his body. "Sleep-p-p."

Crossing over the bluff, mostly on his stomach, dragging his dead legs behind him, Freeman dropped in and out of consciousness. Taunted by the Angel of Death, he could feel every bone in his body cry out for him to lie down in surrender.

Behind Freeman, Corporal Samuel Joseph, a riflemen and only survivor of his platoon, uttered a mournful cry and fell to his side. Lifting his head, he shook it twice to tell the Colonel he was done. He pointed his rifle to the sky out of anger and fired off three single shots before he passed out.

In the Village of Shageluk, people heard those three shots and recognized it as a long honored call for help. They came out of their warm homes, looked to one another to see if there was a problem in the village. Satisfied that no one in the villager fired the shots, they looked to the surrounding area and sent out scouts to investigate. Within moments, one of these scouts found Colonel Freeman and most of his men unconscious. Litters were either made or men and women carried between two or three rescuers in chair fashion. Word spread through the village and blankets and food were brought to the main community hall. On the verge of a freezing death, Colonel Freeman and his valiant men and women, survivors of the Battle of Wales and numerous firefights afterward, found themselves saved by the caring people of Shageluk and offered sanctuary.

SAVOONGA, ST. LAWERENCE ISLAND

Captain Myers' company regained some of their lost strength with the harvest of three reindeer and a joyful barbecue. Though three men were killed in the battle with the OAP helicopter, spirits were lifted to solid ground again with the fulfilling feeling of having roasted meat in their stomachs. After a day of rest, the troops split into groups and attempted ice fishing on the coast. Those who knew the island left to hunt for small game and forage roots from the hillsides. There was no way to test the fish for radiation but life had come down to a simple choice of eventual starvation or eating what food they could find. The village was empty, the villagers having gone to Fort Greeley, but a dozen skin and aluminum boats lay on the beach and they could be used again once winter ice went out - if it went out.

Each man lived with one tormenting fear - tsunamis. When the comet hit, great waves would sweep north and probably destroy Savoonga - possibly covering the entire island. Captain Myers needed to find a spot on higher ground to build a temporary camp. They'd see the Comet's arrival and would have time to move to the new camp. He'd sent three two man patrols to wander the hillsides to look for such a place, while also hunting game. They needed to keep the reindeer for a growing herd. Captain Myers knew there would be others following if the island survived impact and the reindeer could save a lot of lives if raised correctly and only partially used for consumption.

Some soldiers walked along the beach and two were sent to high ground looking for any sign the OAP helicopter might have radioed in the ADF Company's position before being blown from the sky with an AT-4 anti-tank round. Staying by the radio much of the time, Captain Myers was happy to see his men sharing an enjoyable moment as barbecued reindeer was handed out and old stories told of better days. He had learned to truly love and respect these people, his new family.

Standing in the doorway to their new radio hut with a paper plate of barbecued reindeer meat in hand, he looked to the dark sky and wondered how many days they had left before impact? Then glanced to the low hills in the middle of the island and wondered. *Will they be high enough when the waters come?*

3RD PLATOON, C COMPANY, FORT GREELEY

In the short span of a couple of days, Lt. Scott Radley had transformed his platoon of weekend warriors into a real fighting unit. Captain Buford, C Company Commander, refused to look at the progress they had made and felt only contempt for his Black platoon leader. Other platoon leaders in Buford's company and two other Company Commanders sat in on Scott's briefings, causing Buford's redneck to turn even a darker shade of crimson. He couldn't order them not to, that would get back to his commander, but he suspected Radley would soon be commanding C Company if he couldn't do something to stop him. Making matters worse, Scott was able to wrangle an issue of older M-16 rifles for his platoon, something Buford hadn't been able to do The newer M-4s were being issued to ADF active duty troops, leaving personal firearms for Militia. He knew giving a weekend hunter an automatic weapon was comparable to handing a football fan two tickets to the 50 yard line for the next Super Bowl. From that point on, 3rd Platoon was extremely devoted to their platoon leader.

A runner brought word that Scott was needed at Company Headquarters. When he arrived, Scott found Captain Buford waiting for him with a nasty smirk on his face that shouted out, 'WARNING '. "Boy, you tellin' me those men and women in your platoon done fired the qualification course for the M-16 an' they all passed!? You expect me to believe that!?" Buford sat behind his desk, with only the company 1st Sergeant in the room.

"Their scores are on file with the Range Master, Captain. I've already submitted the company's copy to your admin clerk. Some of the men had trouble with the cold, but they did all right after calming down and getting their breathing under control." Standing at parade rest, Scott's eyes were looking straight ahead over the top of Buford's round head. Not since his old boot camp days had he had to put up with so many racial slurs and contemptible attitude. But he kept his temper; he wasn't going to let this man get to him.

"You think you're a pretty smart boy, don't you?" Buford pointed at Scott's chest as if to make his point.

"I'm carrying out my assigned duties, Captain."

"Well, I got another assignment for you, one that'll get you out of my hair for a while." Buford gestured for the 1st Sergeant to hand Scott his new orders. "Battalion's been asked to furnish a platoon for patrol duties. You got it! Take this 'dead-eye' platoon of yours over to 2nd Division Headquarters and report to the Division Adjutant. We'll see how well you do out on the front line with your sharp-shooters."

"Am I dismissed, Captain?" Scott took possession of the orders and nodded to the 1st Sergeant. *How can you be around this clown all day and not want ta throttle him?*

"Get out of my sight!" Buford said raising his voice. His eyes bulging and body language loud with contempt for Scott; he sincerely hoped he'd get his butt shot off.

"Captain, it has been a real experience serving in your company." Scott snapped back to attention, popped a salute that would make any DI happy, negotiated an about face maneuver and marched out of the office. Had he looked over his shoulder, Scott would have seen Buford's face turning a dark shade of purple.

2ND DIVISION HEADQUARTERS, OFFICE OF THE ADJUTANT

Entering the office and finally locating the right desk, Scott reported in and presented his orders to a tall major dressed in crisp pressed ADF urban camouflage; checkered shades of light and medium dark green. "Sir, Lt. Radley reporting as ordered," Scott said.

"Reporting from where, Lieutenant." the Major returned Scott's salute.

"3rd Platoon, C Company, 2nd Militia Battalion… sir. I was sent here by Captain Buford for patrol duties." Scott saw confusion in the major's eyes and then recognition

"Oh, I remember now. General Saunders issued orders for two platoons to set up an observation post near the river. You'll be second in command under 1st Lieutenant Owenby, Alpha Company, 1st Battalion." He stood up and pointed to a map pinned to the wall beside his desk.

"Step over here to this map…What was your name again, Lieutenant?" The major stood by the map board and waited for Scott's answer.

"2nd Lieutenant Scott Radley, Sir." Scott read off the major's name from his nametag, *Jenkins…Major Jenkins?*

"Do I know you from somewhere?" Major Jenkins asked.

"I'm not sure, sir… Did you live in Fairbanks?" *Oh great, probably some business man I issued a citation to.*

"Yes, now I remember. You are...were, Fairbanks Police ... am I right? We crossed swords once. I was a court appointed lawyer to defend a man you arrested. It was about 2 years ago."

A lawyer! This is going downhill fast. "I'm sorry, Sir...I don't recall." *Oh yes I do, you defended one of those wife beating scum sucking dogs but the jury knew the type an' he ended up in jail... probably working a coal heap now.*

"Right... a felony case. This jerk tried to kill his wife with a golf club. You broke through the door in time to save her life."

"Your defendant smacked her around a few times before we got in."

"I'm glad the jury put him away, never liked wife beaters or any form of domestic abuse... especially sexual assault. And don't get me going on crimes against kids! I wouldn't have taken the case except the judge ordered me too. From what I remember, you handled yourself pretty good during cross examination. Kept your temper when I tried so hard to make you lose it." He offered his hand to Scott, "I'm happy to have you with us, Lieutenant."

Relief flooded over Scott as he shook hands. Major Jenkins pointed to where he and his platoon were headed. "You'll be positioned on this bluff, eight miles west of Delta and across the river. You're to hold there until sighting the OAP scout element, hopefully to give us some warning they're coming and then we blow the bridge."

Scott had a lot of questions and Major Jenkins answered most of them. Before they were finished, Lt. William Owenby reported in and was introduced to Scott. *He's only a kid!*

1st Lieutenant Owenby, 22, had held rank as Lt. Colonel during his senior year at North Pole High School JROTC and a Major's gold leaf in the Eielson Civil Air Patrol. He surprised everyone when he turned down a chance for the Air Force Academy to accept a full scholarship at the University of Alaska/Fairbanks. Standing 5'11" and 170 pounds, Owenby had sandy red hair, a face full of freckles and light brown eyes. He reminded Scott of Tom *Sawyer*. *I'm taking orders from some kid...makes sense like everything else these days.* Outside the office, Owenby stopped Scott for a quick word, "I heard what you did in town and I'm really glad to have someone with your experience beside me. Only reason I'm in command is my rank; I have no combat experience, not even a fight in school."

"Call me Scott." *He's not a bad kid; we'll get along all right.*

"What's the average age of your men?" Owenby asked.

"About 35 I think, the oldest guy is a salty dude of 60. I've also got two women, both tough as nails and could shoot the eyes out of a squirrel at 20 yards."

"Mine run between 18 to 32, most under 25 an' six of 'em are young ladies. You can call me Bill." Owenby shook hands with Scott again. First time was formal introduction in front of the Major; this was forming a new friendship. "We'll have a meeting with all the troops in 60 minutes. Afterward, we'll be trucked through the perimeter's mine field. After that, we walk."

"My troops are green, all weekend warriors, but I believe they're ready." Scott turned away; he needed to get his platoon ready to meet their new company commander and members of the other platoon. They weren't going to be happy to hear about this assignment. Most of them were hoping to fight alongside relatives and friends in Buford's company. But, Scott knew the job was a lot better than sitting around under Captain Buford's scrutiny.

Once they finished griping with a few threats to tie Buford up and bring him along, 3rd Platoon loaded up, met new comrades and made the cold drive to Delta Junction. Sitting hunkered down in the back of open trucks in wind-chill of -65°, they were frozen together like a sculpture when they arrived to join Lt. Owenby's troops. 1st Lt. Owenby was upset when he found out Captain Buford had refused permission for Scott's platoon to use a bus for transport to Delta Junction. He even went so far as to file a written complaint with headquarters after seeing that three of Scott's men had to be treated for frostbite. Both Owenby and Scott saw this new assignment was not a match made in heaven, as the two platoons eyed each other with suspicion. The ADF troops were better clothed and armed; carrying newer M-4's. The Militia looked like old geezers, weekend ruffians and bar flies.

When Sam, the oldest member of Scott's platoon, spat out a wad of ground coffee on the boot toe of one of Owenby's corporals, it took both Scott and Owenby to keep a brawl from braking out before they got them herded on to the trucks. This time the trucks were closed in with canvas tops, which reduced most of the wind-chill, but it was still freezing and the troops huddled together for warmth.

45 minutes later, the two platoons, burdened by 90 lb. field packs and lugging heavy weapons and ammo, were on foot making their way toward the bluff. They had an eight mile hike in front of them and Scott hoped his older guys could keep up with the ADF platoon. With Lt. Owenby's permission, Scott took up position in the rear of the column to ensure they didn't lose anyone along the way. He didn't let on, but the straps of his field pack; heavier by an additional 15 lbs. of extra ammo, was cutting into his shoulders. As he walked, occasionally yelling at one of his troops to keep up, he wondered what Brad was doing that sounded so dangerous. Whatever it was, he doubted that Brad was lugging a combat field pack

through deep snow. *My platoon is now… well, along with Owenby's people, the very front of the entire ADF Northern Army. Bet you can't beat that, Brad!*

OFFICE OF THE PRESIDENT, FORT GREELY, ALASKA - APRIL 10TH

President Dave Andrews and General Saunders were sitting in President Andrew's new office on the 2nd floor of Fort Greeley's Main Headquarters' Building. Having been served coffee, General Saunders was dictating to a uniformed admin clerk:

"In agreement with the President, the following full colonels are promoted to the rank of Brigadier General; Colonels Watson, Wilcox, Hightower and Maconnel. This order is effective immediately." General Saunders looked over to the President, "I know the stars will feel good on their shoulders, but sadly it doesn't come with any pay or benefits. Still, it will allow them to work well with the Canadian generals coming to our aide."

"You really think it would be a problem for them to work with our colonels?" President Andrews asked.

"We used to say, 'A colonel is an officer, but a general is a general.'"

"You carry four stars, Glenn…what's that make you?"

General Saunders grinned, "To the enlisted men and women or our junior officers, I'm considered as the one who sits at the right hand of God and carries a bolt of lightning to ensure those under me carry out their duties."

"Wow… what's that make me then?"

General Saunders lost his smile, took a sip of his coffee, glanced at the admin clerk and said, "A civilian… a politician… sir. A man who is usually out of office after four years, writing a book and making a fortune on the lecture circuit."

"But, I'm still able to give you and your new generals, orders while I'm in office."

"That's how our government works, Mr. President. Between the three of us sitting here, I'm glad it's you sitting in that chair and not me."

"So, I don't have to worry about a military coup then," President Andrews asked tossing a small grin at the clerk.

General Saunders set his coffee cup down on the President's desk, nodded to the clerk in dismissal and waited until she had left the room before answering, "Dave, the only thing you need to worry about is a million Orientals coming our way, a burning comet falling from the sky and 400,000 starving Alaskans… you needn't worry about us military types."

"Want to change jobs?"

"Not on your life...Mr. President."

A COMING STORM

14 - GRAMPS & JAKE

"Blessed is the man who perseveres under trail, because when he has stood the test, he will receive the crown of life that God has promised to those who love him."

James 1:12 NIV

KENAI PENINSULA, ALASKA - APRIL 11TH

With striking swiftness, the armies of the OAP descended on the Kenai Peninsula with overwhelming numbers and invaded the coastal communities of Homer, Kenai, Soldotna and Seward. With very little defense, these towns of less than 5,000 people each, quickly fell before OAP's massive war machine and many of the people died horribly. Coming northwest out of the gulf of Alaska, two gigantic supertankers, escorted by OAP Navy Destroyers, parted company and one sailed into the deep blue-green waters of Resurrection Bay to attack Seward. The other slowly lumbered into Kachemak Bay to attack Homer. Both ports were ice free and deep enough to handle the tankers; the military opted not to bomb the port cities to prevent loss of supplies on shore. Instead they launched huge landing crafts capable of carrying troops and combat vehicles up to the size of the OAP dreadnaughts. Landing crafts, combat vehicles and thousands of troops were ferried across the Pacific Ocean inside the supertankers. When the supertankers came to a gradual halt yards off shore, massive bow doors nosily opened like the gaping mouths of a mythical sea beast and the invasion was on. Coastal defenses were unable to stand against such numbers; the OAP surged over Homer and Seward and moved up the Sterling Highway to conquer Soldotna and Kenai.

While defenders in Seward stood rooted in awe, stunned by the sheer gargantuan size of the red and yellow supertanker moving through their bay, the great mouth-like bow of the vessel slowly opened wide and extended downward. The first of dozens of landing crafts carried thousands of fresh OAP troops ashore. A valiant defense was made, but the people of Seward were no match for the OAP and were completely overwhelmed within the first hour of the attack.

The destroyer escort moved to within a hundred yards of the 4th of July Creek ship building and dry dock and opened fire with mighty 5 inch guns and 30mm Gatling cannons in a violent barrage that lasted 30 minutes. Every boat in dry dock and the one boat being worked on in the ship builders massive work garage were utterly destroyed. Fires burned among large craters and bodies were scattered about. Afterward, the destroyer moved off to patrol Resurrection Bay, while the landing forces continued to disembark and move ashore.

Having sailed in secret from the deep water ports of Vietnam escorted by OAP naval forces with no fear of detection from above, OAP troops had no knowledge of the hardships endured by comrades marching across the frozen wastelands of Alaska. Concerned with troop morale, the Warlord Generals kept quiet concerning the acts of cannibalism carried out among the ranks of the Siberian Combat Command. Nor was word shared with the fighting troops that food supplies would not be forthcoming once the current supply on board support vessels lying off the coast was used up.

Based on reports filed by OAP spies, OAP Headquarters Command in Beijing, China, had hopes that forces in Alaska would seize massive food caches in Anchorage. Spies had reported dozens of warehouses stocked to the ceiling there and in Fairbanks. They hadn't expected the ADF to abandon positions in Fairbanks, Fort Wainwright and Eielson. But the Alaskans had and the food was all moved to Fort Greeley. This left only an extremely limited supply for those who had not yet been evacuated or those who chose to make a stand for their homes and property. As the OAP moved closer to Fairbanks, the vast majority of stragglers headed east for Fort Greeley where they were escorted through the minefields in Delta Junction carrying their food supplies with them. When they arrived, supplies were turned over to the Commissary Officer

ON TOP OF MARATHON MOUNTAIN, ABOVE SEWARD, ALASKA

Assigned as a two man Forward Observation Team, they wore white snowsuits over arctic clothing and kept themselves concealed on the eastern side of Mt. Marathon underneath a white tarp. The snow was at times six to eight feet deep; travel was extremely tiring as they made their way to the summit, using overly large snow shoes and lugging 100 lb. packs on their backs. Their orders had been brief and to the point - they were to observe the enemy and report everything to ADF Coast Watcher Command-Anchorage over a large radio which was linked to a series of radio towers along the Chugach Mountains. MSgt. Bradley Oshmak, a 64 year old Eskimo from Kaktovik; a small island community northeast of Prudhoe Bay, had a hard time obeying such an order as he observed the invasion unfold below their position.

He stood in a small foxhole they had dug out in the snow holding a powerful set of binoculars in his hand with a good view of Seward. Their position was covered by an eight by eight foot white tarp with one side facing Seward held up by a two foot length of branch to give them a good view of Resurrection Bay. He was the first to spot the huge OAP Supertanker as it slowly entered Resurrection Bay escorted by a single destroyer. He woke up his RTO, SSgt. Jake Mayes of Seward and told him what was happening below.

As soon as the landing craft launched gun crews on the massive deck began to fire on the city's defenses with 30mm Gatling guns. Seward was under heavy attack and people were dying.

SSgt. Mayes radioed a warning to Seward when the destroyer was first observed coming through the narrow passage and he felt a surge of pride as they watched ADF and Militia units rush to their assigned beach defenses.

When Oshmak spotted the Supertanker, which was nearly too large to enter Resurrection Bay, his heart had nearly stopped and he dropped his binoculars. Although he hadn't been briefed earlier; no one from Militia Command had confirmed to the Coast Watchers that these were troop carriers; he suspected this mighty ship was bad news for Seward and he was sadly proven right. Both he and SSgt. Mayes stood silent and watched the great bow doors open and the first landing craft surge toward the beach.

There were more than two dozen armed helicopters carrying rockets and 20mm Gatling guns; some were captured Russian birds and there were even four older American Hueys left behind from the Vietnam War and later captured in the Battle for Vietnam. MSgt. Oshmak reported the helicopters to Coast Watcher Command and then was forced to observe their lethal attack on the city, destroying vehicles and gunning down fleeing civilians attempting to flee. The heavy 20mm rounds wiped out beach defenses, riddled parked vehicles in city parking lots to prevent them from being used for escape and fired upon the vast array of boats moored in the Seward Boat Harbor.

In the hours to follow, tears ran down the deep creases of MSgt. Oshmak's brown cheeks. His comrades had fallen before wave after wave of invaders, supported by heavy gunfire from the supertanker, landing crafts and heavy armored vehicles coming ashore. Protected from above by helicopter gunships; MSgt. Oshmak knew his friends had no chance at all to stand up against such an invasion force. It reminded him of seeing a horde of black ants storming out of their nest to sweep over their prey by sheer weight of numbers.

Oshmak wanted to climb down Mt. Marathon, to run and leap down the old Marathon trail which runners from all over the world had once used when running the famous 4th of July Mt. Marathon Race. A hundred runners or more would leave downtown Seward at the corner where the famous Yukon Bar stood, dash up the side of the mountain to reach the towering summit and return to the downtown finishing line. The race had supposedly begun when two old codgers sat at the Yukon Bar and one bet the other that he could reach the summit of Mt. Marathon in under an hour - he didn't make it. It became a yearly event on the 4th of July, but it was years before the one hour mark was broken by a runner. MSgt. Oshmak recalled that when the race was run for the last time, the winning time by a male runner was 42:31 minutes set by a 23 year old kid from Soldotna; the female runner from Seattle had set a record of 43:42 minutes in the woman's race. He didn't remember the teen race, although he had a grandson running in it.

But MSgt. Oshmak knew his orders were to be obeyed and remained atop the mountain to keep an eye on the enemy and send reports on. He had to keep his companion from doing the very same thing he so wanted to do himself.

RTO SSgt. Jake Mayes was grief stricken to watch friends and family members sacrifice their lives for Alaska. But a stern faced old Eskimo reminded him, "We can do more for our Alaska, for our family and friends, up here in the mountains then wasting our lives down in city," Oshmak said. "I want to be down there too, but we'd only be killed or captured and the ADF would not have our Intelligence."

Even without binoculars, Jake could see large parties of prisoners being herded away from the beach like cattle. The downtown area was on fire and prisoners were forced to form fire brigades to save what buildings they could to house the army.

Landing craft returned to the supertanker and loaded back aboard, the bow doors were closed and the vessel slowly turned around with the help of three ocean going tug boats seized from the Seward Boat Harbor. Left at anchor, the supertanker would eventually leave Resurrection Bay for duties elsewhere. For the men and women on the beach, this meant no escape; the only direction they could travel was north to Anchorage.

A teenage juvenile delinquent who gave the Seward Police Department a lot of problems with minor thefts and acts of vandalism, Jake Mayes, now 25, continued to behave childishly and was quite disgruntled when his Lt. assigned him this duty with an Eskimo Guardsman. He seldom referred to MSgt. Oshmak by rank - instead he often used a sarcastic tone and called him either Old Geezer or Gramps. Jake was assigned to the Seward Militia by the local magistrate during his last court appearance for a Disorderly Conduct charge. He was a reluctant draftee into the ADF and was promptly assigned to the Coast Watcher Program because of his familiarity with Resurrection Bay. The son and grandson of local halibut fishermen, he refused to work in the family business and after two years of college, called in some family favors to wrangle a bartender's job at Seward's Tony's Bar. A job that lasted until money gave out and Jake found himself standing in line for a militia posting so he could eat.

Always slender, but rapidly becoming downright skinny at 5'10", Jake's dirty long blonde hung hair over his shoulders. His blue eyes were bloodshot from too many nights working smoky bars and getting high on the last buds of marijuana in the city. A long thin face showed an attempt to grow a beard but a roguish mustache hung past the corners of his mouth and ended beside his too narrow chin. His long thin nose made his face thinner and his chin appear to end in a point. Both ears were pierced with an assortment of small gold rings. On his left arm was the tattoo of a belly dancer, most of her face covered by a wide long scarf that flowed around his arm. A series of tattoos went the length of his right arm: a dragon in flight fighting with an enraged bald eagle. Below this was a 3 inch standing rat with extremely long whiskers and two overly large front teeth; he didn't remember having that one done; he was intoxicated at the time.

MSgt. Oshmak wore his grizzled black hair in a buzz cut, ADF style. Jake thought he resembled a beardless Gimli from Tolkien's Lord of the Rings. His arms looked like they could handle Gimli's axe with no trouble. His face and narrow brown eyes showed the effect of many years fighting the elements while hunting walrus, polar bear and whale.

The younger soldier may have known Resurrection Bay and Seward, which no longer mattered, but he knew the older one could survive in a hostile environment. Their winter camouflage white blended in with the snow making them almost invisible; they strapped their insulated white bunny boots into metal frame snowshoes and MSgt. Oshmak urged Jake north, "We go now, there's nothing we can do down there... but die."

An hour later, the two exhausted men stopped for a breather, slipped off their heavy packs and studied the landscape ahead. The plan was to remain parallel to the Seward Highway; a 120 mile stretch of paved two lane road that extended from Seward to Anchorage, and report the enemy movements. They needed to avoid detection when they came back down the mountain to cross the ice covered river at Mile 3.4 and Exit Glacier Road; which was a single lane roadway. Both of these obstacles had to be crossed before they could make it back up into the mountains to the north. Exit Glacier Road was approximately eight miles long and ended at Exit Glacier, one of the few glaciers where tourists could get close enough to touch the bluish glacier ice. Tourism had declined and most travelers didn't travel past the 3 mile marker where the houses ended and only nature's landscape continued for the next 5 miles. MSgt. Oshmak estimated they were still a good two hours from the river, "We stay back from road, maybe one mile up river from the bridge and then we cross the ice. This way we'll be hard to see."

"Right, except they'll probably send a scouting party up Exit Trail Road," Jake said. He remembered the homes and abandoned businesses on

Exit Glacier Road, which included a steak house he had often visited. He knew these buildings would be of interest to the OAP. "We have to cross it, I agree, but I think we should wait until dark."

Jake was winded and panting, but he noticed the old man simply breathed in and out through his nose as if he was out on a country walk. They were warm enough; temperatures on the coast were running above zero; their only problems were avoiding avalanches and staying dry as they struggled through wet mushy snow.

"We need to cross when we get there. No time to wait, they won't see us if you follow me and do what I do."

"Listen, Gramps, let me lead on this...I'm younger an' stronger. Don't want you burning out on me trying to impress me with your Eskimo stamina." Oshmak ignored Jake and started out. As soon as Jake realized Gramps was moving; he let out a deep sigh, hefted the heavy radio and backpack onto to his back, gave the countryside behind them one last look and followed the old man.

"Young people, you have no respect for old ones," Oshmak grumbled over his shoulder. "You always use expensive snow machines to cross snow, no snow machines now." With his Winchester 7mm rifle wrapped in a white sheet for camouflage, slung over his right shoulder, he pointed north with a gloved hand, "I show you how to walk like Eskimo people. No noise, slow...easy...no hurry. You follow and maybe you live." He took slow easy strides through the deep snow breaking trail for the young city boy. Twice, during the next three hours, the old man stopped to relieve Jake of the radio pack, but nearing the river, he handed the heavy burden back to Jake. "Wait here," MSgt. Oshmak ordered. He knelt down to a low crouch and crawled forward to the top of a small rocky bluff which overlooked the frozen river. Formed by glacial runoff in the spring, the ice covered river was nearly 200 yards wide with numerous dry sandbars dividing a dozen or more ice covered channels. Chunks of dead trees stuck up into the air like guardians of the river and there were hundreds of large gray rocks and larger boulders which had been carried down by surging high waters during spring runoff. With the long winter, water was still frozen which was a good thing for the two men.

Pulling out his binoculars and moving ahead a few yards, Oshmak scanned the opposite shoreline to look for any traffic on Exit Glacier Road. Exit Road was mostly hard packed dirt and gravel but the long winter had covered it with deep snow and there were no road crews to plow it. He hoped that OAP intelligence would have reported there was nothing of interest on Exit Glacier Road and they would ignore it. A quick scan showed he could be right - there was no traffic in sight. He returned to find Jake leaning against a snow covered ridge gulping water from his canteen like a foolish teenager with a soda.

"No more water now, Jake, "MSgt. Oshmak ordered. "Wait, we stop after we cross the river. But now we rest here 10 minutes. You make radio contact with Anchorage. Give them our position, but keep it short. The enemy may have big ears. Then we move fast." Oshmak studied Jake's eyes, recognized the contempt Jake held for him and shrugged his shoulders. "When I say drop, you drop and no move until I do. Understand?"

"No problem, Gramps. You lead, I follow," Jake said. But Oshmak saw the condescending look in his young eyes. He had seen much the same look in the eyes of his son and grandson and was wise enough to know he probably had at one time carried the same resentment for his own elders when ordered to do this or that. *Young ones always think they are wiser then old ones, why is that so?* The river crossing took some time, but was uneventful and soon they were climbing back into the safety of the lower hillsides to the north. High above them waited towering Alpine mountains, which swept up until their jagged peaks were hidden by thick heavy black clouds.

At 17:07 hours, Oshmak heard the sound of heavy machinery from somewhere below and found an icy abutment to observe the Seward Highway. A column of enemy tanks and armored personnel carriers were moving north. He pulled back into the tree line to make radio contact with Anchorage.

"Bravo Delta One - Fiver, this is Mike Sierra Five... Over," Oshmak said. He had pulled the radio pack off Jake, so the young man could rest his sore shoulders.

After a second attempt, an Anchorage radio operator replied, "Mike Sierra Five, this is Bravo Delta One - fiver....Over."

"Oscar Alpha Poppa armored column moving north on Seward Highway at Mile six. Speed estimated at 15 ...Over." Oshmak stood and dragged the radio pack with him as he moved to the edge of the tree line for a better view. He brought up his binoculars and focused on the lead tank.

"Get down, old man!" Jake shouted. "They're gonna see you." He pulled on Oshmak's pants leg, but the older man simply ignored him.

"Identify vehicles and number of infantry... Over." The RTO's voice sounded so calm on the radio and this angered Jake. "She sound like she's talking to her mom on the phone... so how's pop? The kids are fine-blah-blah-blah."

"Be quiet!" Oshmak ordered, his hand clamped over the microphone. Ignoring Jake's glare, he gave Anchorage the information, "Four medium tanks, three armored troop carriers on tracks ... six...no, seven covered trucks. They look Russian, possible troop carriers." Oshmak lowered his binoculars "OAP unit will be busy searching houses for several hours in Bear Valley and Camelot subdivisions. ...Over."

"Continue to move north. Unless you encounter trouble, contact again from Twelve Mile Hill...Over."

"Copy and Out." Oshmak secured the microphone to the radio pack, snapping the canvas cover down to keep snow from damaging the circuits. He looked down at Jake's pouting face, "They cannot see us, but can hear loud voices. Time we go." He waited until Jake stood up and then helped him lift the radio pack onto his back.

"You'd think wouldn't you, that with all this modern technology, they'd make a lighter radio. Why can't we just use cell phones?" Jake was grumbling as he trudged forward following MSgt. Oshmak up the hillside. The old geezer was cutting trail and that was fine by him.

During the slow tiring climb to a higher elevation, MSgt. Oshmak offered Jake a piece of dried Salmon to chew on and Jake shot a look of disgust in response. "You no like smoked salmon?"

"I prefer it cooked and on a plate, thank you very much," Jake said sarcastically.

"No stove, no plate. What you going to eat?"

"I've still got two MRE's (Meals Ready to Eat) left. You do remember we were supposed to go back to town when we were relieved. I wasn't planning on this pleasure journey through the mountains." Jake stopped to catch his breath and leaned against a towering spruce tree. They were nearing the top of the tree line and Jake wondered how high his elderly companion was planning on going.

"This no mountains, Jake." Oshmak pointed to the perilous mountainside above them, "Those Mountains!"

"Funny, Gramps... real funny," Jake replied. "How come I got hooked up with you anyway? This is a young man's game." Jake opened a large canvas pouch on his web belt and pulled out a small package of hard crackers. He finished the six crackers quickly, without bothering to offer Oshmak one.

It was noon next day when the weary twosome reached Twelve Mile Hill and stopped to rest beside an old cross country ski trail overlooking the highway. While Jake finished off the last of his MRE's, Oshmak made radio contact with Anchorage to report they had not seen any sign of the enemy for some time. Moments later, an OAP recon helicopter flew right over the top of them and began to circle their position; their radio signal had been picked up by the enemy. "Jake, they found us. We must climb to clouds." Oshmak grabbed the radio pack and his rifle and pushed Jake to his feet.

"That way!" Six hundred feet above them floated a layer of snow and ash clouds where they would be invisible to the enemy. If they could breathe that is.

Machinegun fire raked the hillside, missing Oshmak and Jake by more than several dozen yards. "Not sure where we are, so they just fire," Oshmak said. He brought his rifle up and using a Leopold Scope, sighted on the Russian helicopter. The bird was similar in shape to a US Black Hawk with two door gunners who were busily firing off short bursts from mounted automatic weapons. The pilot continued to circle, searching for whoever was using a radio.

Seeing what Oshmak was doing, Jake fell on his back in the snow and brought his Vietnam era M-16 up to shoulder level then waited for the helicopter to swing back over them. The tall spruce trees gave them only a small window of opportunity to shoot at the bird.

Long a hunter of both polar bear and seal, Oshmak was an excellent marksman. Adjusting his breathing, he applied pressure very slowly to the trigger and followed the helicopter pilot. He waited with an experienced hunter's patience and watched as the helmeted man banked the bird to the left. At that moment, he applied gentle pressure to the trigger and as soon as the bullet fired, he quickly pulled back the bolt, re-chambered a second round and fired again. From beside him, Jake fired off an extended burst on full automatic into the side of the helicopter.

MSgt. Oshmak's heavy grain 7mm bullet entered the pilot's left upper arm and traveled directly through the man's left lung and into his right lung, killing him and forcing a terrified co-pilot to assume control of the helicopter. Most of Jake's shots missed the helicopter completely, but two rounds went into the main compartment and a single ricochet struck a door gunner in the back. Only his security sling kept him from falling out of the bird, the second gunner had his hands full trying to keep his friend alive, while the crew chief was struggling to pull the dead pilot out of his seat to keep the man's hands and feet off the helicopter controls.

With one man dead and another wounded, the trembling co-pilot, who had less than 100 hours of flying time and on his first combat mission, had little choice but to swerve the helicopter into a hard banking right flare and fly out of range as fast as he could get the bird to move.

Unfortunately, MSgt Oshmak knew the OAP had their approximate location and would be sending another helicopter with a squad of infantry to track them down. If a larger force was deemed necessary, the OAP had the numbers and equipment to launch a major search for them.

"We climb…only choice." Oshmak first untied and then unsnapped his snow shoes, strapping them to the back of his field pack, while a jittery Jake did the same. This had been his first time in battle and right now, he couldn't remember if he had hit anything. But he knew enough to change magazines. He removed the more than half empty one and inserted a full one into his rifle.

Oshmak took the lead as the two left the tree line behind and began pulling themselves up along the steepening rocky and icy surface of the upper ridgeline. MSgt. Oshmak tied a 15 foot length of rope between them, in the event one of them lost their footing. Within an hour of making their way across an unforgivable terrain, MSgt. Oshmak discovered a Dahl Sheep trail and began following it upward in hopes he wouldn't run into a grizzly bear. He hoped they would still be in dens, but with such a long winter he knew it was possible they were out hunting to fill empty stomachs. The trail was tough and exhausting work and before long, Oshmak was once again carrying the radio pack, while Jake struggled to keep up with him.

How does Gramps do it? I feel like I've been fighting a 300 lb. halibut for hours, every one of my muscles hurts and he looks like...I don't know what he looks like...I'm too beat and he still goes on.

CANADIAN BORDER STATION - APRIL 11th

Wary of the ominous scene before him, Ed Sawyer approached the deserted Canadian Customs and Immigration Station with his M-16 held ready for any surprises. They'd found the US Customs station abandoned two miles back, but Ed fully expected to find Canadian military units guarding their border.

"Looks like they left in a big hurry," Joey followed Ed through the abandoned station checking each office, room and closet as two extremely cautious police officers would.

Official papers, files and forms, old magazines and office supplies were scattered about on tables, desks and floor. Items of clothing were left on hangers or lying across fully made beds in the bunkroom. There was a half pot of hot coffee still simmering in a white Mr. Coffee Maker. But the sugar and creamer dispensers were empty. All the lights inside and the outside security floods were on, powered by a large diesel generator in a metal shed beside the station. A 500 gallon tank fed fuel to it through a long one inch line. Most surprising was the discovery of an unlocked rifle rack on the wall with four fully loaded .308 Caliber H&K assault rifles standing beside four empty slots. "H&K 31's. Carries an 18 round magazine and fires a .308 mm round. Canada bought thousands of 'em back in 2015... it was H&K's last year of production," Point Man said. He hefted one of the rifles to make sure it was chambered and on safe. "Always liked 'em. We'll add 'em to our arsenal. Hopefully, I can find more ammo for 'em." He eventually discovered eight more fully loaded magazines and three boxes of .308 caliber ammo.

Walking through the 2nd floor bunkroom, Ed counted six beds with two of them unmade. "Looks like someone just got out 'a bed."

"Something sure spooked them...but what?" Joey held his pistol in a two handed grip until they completed the search and then he relaxed enough to holster his weapon. "They even left food on the table," Joey said.

Ed picked up a half-eaten peanut butter and jelly sandwich and noticed the bread was still fresh. "They couldn't have been gone more than an hour or two."

"Hey Ed, the gas pumps are still working...should we borrow some?" Larry O' Brian asked as he walked into the Customs Station holding a 12-gauge pump shotgun.

"Drain 'em, Larry," Ed ordered. He turned to Joey, "Let's get some guards posted, this place gives me the creeps. I keep expecting some giant bug or something even worse to come leaping out of the woods."

"Well, this is Big Foot country," Pastor said to lighten the moment. He walked inside and helped himself to a cup of hot coffee. From his coat pocket he removed a small plastic bag of white sugar and added three teaspoons to his coffee, which got a grin from Ed.

Within moments, work crews were organized to scrounge every drop of fuel and usable supply items from the premises. From food to blankets, paper plates to tiny personal sized mustard packets, everything was stacked neatly into one of the travel trailers or food van. Point Man handed out the four rifles to men who knew how to use them, replacing the bolt action ones they had carried. The older rifles were secured inside the food trailer, because nothing was discarded.

The highway had been plowed recently, and Ed suspected it was probably the vehicle used to evacuate the station. 35 minutes later, Point Man and his Misfits were headed north, while Ed and crew continued to loot the station. This time, instead of the plow truck, the point team was driving an older model Chevrolet Suburban with a 16 foot long yellow canoe tied down to a roof rack on top.

A few moments later, the sound of gunshots could be heard in the distance. Running for the ambulance, Ed threw open the passenger door and grabbed the CB microphone. "Point Man, do you copy?"

"Point Man's down, Boss...we need help like yesterday!" The voice belonged to one of the Misfits, but at the moment Ed couldn't remember which one.

"How far up the road and what are you up against?" Ed got Joey's attention and signaled for him to come quick with an up and down motion of his left forearm and closed fist.

"Unknown numbers, but they're all around us like flies. We're maybe four miles up the road. Point Man took one in the shoulder and plowed us into a ditch. We could use some help on the double!"

The sounds of heavy gunfire could be heard over the radio, "We're on our way!" Ed tossed the microphone down and slammed the ambulance door shut. Joey was at his side with several others. "20 volunteers fast an' bring up the wrecker. I want two men inside with me, the rest 50 yards behind in the school bus. I want everyone armed to the teeth. We're going in hot and heavy!"

Standing near Pastor, Kathy Looney had her right arm draped over Kira's shoulder quiet as they watched Larry get the kids off the bus. Then Larry joined the volunteers armed with his shotgun and a huge Bowie knife on his belt.

Pastor said a blessing for the men as the two vehicles sped down the road to rescue their friends. Driving the wrecker, Ed kept the barrel of his M-16 pointed out the window ready for whatever awaited them. Within moments, he spotted Point Man's Suburban sitting partially off the road and the Misfits shooting from behind a natural fort of two crossed over fallen trees. He couldn't see Point Man, but figured his friend was on the ground, protected by the Misfits.

A couple dozen men were running through the woods, trying to encircle Point Man and company, one armed with an M-60 Machinegun. As they came into range, Joey, sitting in the passenger seat opened fire with an M-16 on full auto. From the bus further back, fifteen additional shooters began targeting the ambushers and with the element of surprise, they caught the enemy unaware.

Bullets bounced off the sides of the heavy truck, leaving gashes in the metal frame, penetrating the hood and cracking windshield glass. Surprisingly, no one was hit; Ed skidded to a halt and pulled up close to the wrecked Suburban and jumped out. Joey and two others jumped out the side door and hurriedly took up positions behind the Suburban and the wrecker.

When the bus pulled up, men dashed out the front door and rear emergency exit to take up positions and form a defensive ring around the wrecked suburban. Two of the Misfits grabbed Point Man and half carried/half dragged the wounded gorilla into the back of the bus. It was a tight squeeze through the door, but with all the adrenaline pumping they got him loaded pretty quick.

For a brief moment, the attackers thought they had an easy score: a bunch of cowboys heading north in a beat up Suburban with a canoe on top. They weren't expecting to find these cowboys so well armed, or backed up by a platoon sized armored unit. Not liking the odds, the attackers began falling away, fleeing deeper into the woods. Some made it, but others didn't as Ed's crew cuts the enemy's number down by at least a third.

Ed took aim on one party of men in heavy civilian parka gear suspecting they were the leaders by the way others were looking to them for orders and began to pull his trigger. But instead of going for a quick kill, he shot three of them in the legs and watched as they collapsed. He had remembered his father saying that it took at least two men to carry a wounded soldier from the field. Six men came running back to rescue their buddies using the quick under arm carry method to drag them off into the woods. As they disappeared, the sound of enemy gunfire tapered off.

When the firing dropped off, Ed waited a moment and then walked over to inspect the Suburban. It was a total loss. The vehicle was riddled with bullet holes, at least four struck the engine block and three of the four tires were flat. All the windows were shot out. "A miracle you guys survived," Ed said to one of the Misfits, "How's Point Man?" Ed wondered if the Misfits used their real names when they were by themselves. He'd never heard them say anything but, "man" or "dude" when making reference to another of their tight lipped clan.

"Dude's got a hard head, saved him when he hit the steering wheel. He took one in the shoulder, a through and through, but he's okay. Joey's inside workin' on him." Joey was in the back of the bus, splatters of blood over most of his chest, but he was doing a fine job of emergency trauma repair to hold the big guy until Doc got his hands on him.

Ed posted four guards in case the enemy came back for another round and then ordered the rest to scrounge what they could off the Suburban, "Okay, strip what we can off the Suburban an' then back in the bus. Load the canoe onto the wrecker and tie it down good because we still have a long way to go. When you're done we're heading back to the convoy...but watch the woods on each side and sing out if you see any movement. No sense getting sloppy, those clowns might be back." Ed climbed into the bus and told Joey they were getting ready to move out. When they were ready, Larry negotiated a difficult series of turns to get the bus turned around. He moved slowly in an attempt to keep from juggling a groggy Point Man.

Besides closing the gunshot wound, Doc removed three double ought buckshot pellets from Point Man's left shoulder, wrapped his arm and secured it in a sling. He also bandaged his head where he struck the steering wheel, "Keep it there until I tell you otherwise."

"Sure, Doc," Point Man replied grimacing through clenched teeth as Doc tied off the last bandage on his arm, "I went through Somalia without a scratch and I get blown away in Canada."

Ed checked on him afterward, "Now we know what spooked the Customs people. They must have gotten word they had some thugs in the neighborhood and deserted their post." Ed looked over Doc's bandaging job, "How do you feel, big guy?"

"Like I been shot, stupid! What idiotic question is that?" Point Man grinned, "Thanks for savin' our bacon back there."

"I owed you." Ed suddenly felt tired and sat down on a metal medical supply chest beside Point Man.

"Did we lose anyone else out there?" Doc asked. He put the rest of his supplies away and discarded the bloody bandages and Point Man's shirt and sweater.

"No, just this lunkhead," Ed answered. "With all the bullets zinging around, we were real lucky."

"How many of them did we get?" Point Man asked.

"Didn't stop to make a body count, but we hurt 'em." Ed laid his head back against the side of the ambulance and closed his eyes for a moment, while Doc changed his bloody shirt and Nancy straightened up the front of the ambulance. The temperature was dropping and they all noticed the amount of falling ash was increasing the further north they traveled. Dismounting the ambulance behind Doc, Ed glanced around the convoy and wondered how many more vehicles they might lose. They already had several more adults riding in the bus and now he needed another scout vehicle for His Misfits to use.

Doc came up beside him in a clean white shirt, a wool sweater and an open unzipped heavy parka, "You had better notify everyone to begin breathing through scarves outside their vehicles. This ash will cause breathing problems and our oxygen supply is limited."

Ed nodded and turned to Nancy, "Please put it over the radio, just as Doc said it.", He pulled his scarf up to cover his mouth and nose and realized that it needed a real good washing. He wrinkled his nose at the smell.

After a short rest, Ed decided to put more miles on the road before making camp for the night. He didn't know if the thugs had vehicles or not, but he wanted those extra miles between them to prevent another firefight. He ordered the Misfits ahead in a dark blue Dodge Ram six pax pickup. "Stay about five miles out, no more than that."

"You got it," the larger of the Misfits said. He tossed Ed a casual left handed salute and climbed up behind the steering wheel.

With Point Man reluctantly riding in the ambulance so Doc could keep an eye on him, the convoy proceeded north without further incident. Ed drove the wrecker truck in the lead, with Pastor riding in the front passenger seat. They approached a road sign and Ed read it out loud - Moose Jaw 118 K." He turned to Pastor, "How many miles is that?"

"Roughly 76, give or take a few hundred feet if I remember my high school math."

Ed smiled, shook his head and slowly applied a bit more pressure to the gas pedal. "Sign also says we're in the Province of Saskatchewan. Once we reach Medicine Hat, we'll be in Alberta." He kept a roving eye, looking at each tree as if a shooter was hiding behind it. "I sure hope the Canadians let us through," Keeping it slow as they forged ahead over a single lane of snow covered road, Ed wrestled with the wrecker's steering wheel and four speed shifter. The clutch was acting up and he was forced to double clutch each time he shifted the beast. He suspected a bullet might have hit the transmission housing or clutch plate assembly.

Further down the road, Ed slowed to a crawl at 10 mph and listened to the grinding of gears. Suddenly he spotted the Misfits pulled into a clearing waiting for the plow truck to arrive to clear off a wide enough space for the convoy to rest for the night.

"Yeah, this looks good," Ed yelled out the window and proceeded to drive off the road into the cleared spot. They wouldn't be able to form their ritual circle, but they could line up in twos to offer some protection. Outside of posting guards, his next priority was having one of the men look at the wrecker's transmission. He didn't want to wrestle with the gears all the way to Alaska and he really didn't want to lose the wrecker since it was the closest thing they had to real armor.

Later, Ed walked back to check on Point Man's condition. He arrived in time to watch Doc climbing out of the back of the ambulance with a look of disgust on his face, "What's the matter, Doc?"

"That big galoot, he wanted to know if the road was clear enough for him to ride his Hog!" Doc pulled out a clean white handkerchief from his back pocket and wiped his brow. "Bikers! Think more of their scooters then they..." Doc looked at Ed, "He'll live."

"Probably too much pain meds...You might back off a bit," Ed suggested.

"Who's the doctor here, Mr. Sawyer?" Doc asked in an agitated tone.

Ed's hands flew up in surrender and he trudged off through the recently plowed snow to find Joey. He realized everyone was on the edge right now and he needed to think of something to calm his people before someone really snapped. Between the long road, the constant snowfall and thickening ash and the occasional sniper, he was surprised he hadn't had another mutiny on his hands.

There was no room to set up the circus tent, but an energetic work crew had used chain saws to clear a small area to the left of the vehicles and strung tarps up in a large rectangle shape to provide a roof for the evening meal. Food was prepared and a long line of hungry people formed with the oldest members of the flock to the front of the line, then came the children and the rest of the adults filled their plates afterward. It was a quiet supper with people sitting on fallen trees, freshly made stumps and some of the metal folding chairs they dragged off the truck. Everyone tried to crowd in under the tarps to avoid the black snow; one man strummed his acoustic guitar to provide gentle background music for the end of a long day.

The strange dark snowfall stopped around 8 p.m., and after the evening meal, Ed took advantage to escape alone and walked into the woods outside of camp for a moment of peace. He kept his rifle slung over his shoulder in case he discovered some unwanted guests about. He was also curious if there might be bear or moose about. A few moments later, he stopped in his tracks when he heard the sound of crunching snow behind him. One hand holding his rifle and his finger on the trigger, Ed quickly turned and brought his flashlight and rifle up to catch Kira approaching. *Now what?*

Blinded by the sudden light, she put her hands up "Want some company?"

Ed lowered his rifle and flashlight. "Sure," he sighed. *Not really, but… maybe this is a good chance to make amends.* "I can offer you the world, the sky, one lousy comet and…" Ed pointed to a large log, "… even a snow covered log to sit on."

"I'll take the log." Kira walked over to a large fallen evergreen and after wiping off the snow, she sat down on a thick brown wool blanket she just happened to have draped over her shoulder.

Standing his rifle against the log, after making sure the weapon's selector switch was on 'safe', Ed looked toward the clouded sky. "Pitch black and nearing subzero temperatures. No stars out to wish by and the air smells like sulfur. Otherwise, I'd say it's a real nice night out." He expected a laugh, but she was quiet for a moment and Ed didn't push it as the two of them sat in silence. Uncomfortable, Ed began to hum an old tune, not knowing what else to do.

Kira broke the impasse by blurting out, "I'm sorry I threw myself at you." She looked at her boots, borrowed from one of the other ladies. "I've been acting childishly… probably hoping you might fill the void my parents left an' that's not fair to you." Ed could only look at her in response, unsure what he should say, so Kira continued, "You don't have to worry about me anymore. I'll behave. You've got enough troubles to deal with and you sure don't need me hanging around." She slid off the log and started to walk away, forgetting the blanket.

"Kira, wait...Please?" Ed waited until she came back and stood in front of him, the top of her head reaching the bottom of his chin. "I'm confused...Not sure how I feel right now about anything. I thought it was our age difference, then my job came into question an'... you're right, I don't need any more complications in my life right now." Ed saw the tears welling up in her eyes, he could feel her pain striking him deeply, "Yet, right now...this moment, I suddenly realize I've had feelings for you an' I don't know what to do about it. I mean, I used to put guys my age in jail for..."

Her eyes brightened and she interrupted him, "You...you do?"

"Yes, Miss Kira Woods, I do." Ed glanced around, hoping they could remain alone. "This age thing is still a problem with me though."

"I turned 17 yesterday, kept it quiet with all that was going on." She smiled up at him. "17's a whole lot better than 16, isn't it?"

"Yes, even another year helps out." Ed put his arms on her shoulders, " Look, time's running out, we don't have a lot of time for a long romance and no matter what we do, we'll offend someone." He stepped back, holding her hands and smiling at her, "So, if Pastor Woodway gives us his blessing, would you consider becoming my wife?"

"YES!" Kira jumped into his arms and for the next several moments neither of them said much of anything as they exchanged first kisses.

A short time later after Ed dropped Kira off with Kathy Looney, Ed appeared outside Pastor's tent, "Pastor, can I come in, we need to have a long chat about proprieties?"

That evening, just before lights out was called for the children, a double wedding was held in camp as Pastor Woodway married a very nervous Ed Sawyer to an excited Kira Woods and a bubbly Larry O' Brian to a speechless Kathy Looney. Wearing borrowed dresses, Kathy's altered for her height, the two brides shone like glimmering stars, but the grooms showed definite signs of nervous insecurity as they listened to Pastor's words and stammered through simultaneous outbursts of, "I do-o-o."

After an extra helping of refreshments, hugs and back slaps all around, the wedding reception was deemed a big hit, which was exactly what the camp needed to break the tension. As everyone said goodnight, the brides and grooms retreated to honeymoon tents set up on the other side of the school bus, far enough away to allow a small measure of privacy. Joey even agreed to pull guard, ensuring privacy in the event someone wanted to pull a few pranks on the newlyweds.

Early next morning, camp was struck without fuss and the convoy headed northwest along a deserted stretch of Canadian highway. Shortly after 5 p.m., the convoy pulled into Moose Jaw and found it deserted. Several buildings had been burned to the ground; there were a few notices warning citizens to evacuate and head north. With OAP missile impacts in North and South Dakota and enemy warheads dropped on Strategic Air Command missile bases, concern was given to the threat of radioactive fallout. By the looks of the town; abandoned overturned vehicles, fire scarred brick walls and broken windows, Ed and Pastor Woodway both suspected a riot had broken out in the closing moments of evacuation.

"We'll make camp north of town. There's no telling who might be left," Ed ordered. The convoy moved another five miles to a good location and the plow truck cleared a space large enough for them to use.

It was another quiet camp that night, temperatures were turning much colder and most of the people were exhausted with the constant day to day traveling and the occasional gun battle. With the exception of guards, most everyone was in their tents by 9 p.m. snug in sleeping bags as portable kerosene heaters attempted to keep the tents warm. Ed hoped they made it to Alaska before the fuels gave out, especially the kerosene, or the people would be lying around open fires when the temperatures approached the extremely dangerous zone where an open flame offered little heat. Snow fell during the night, dumping eight inches on the tents and vehicles. One tent collapsed, rudely awakening the occupants and people crammed into other tents for the next few hours.

Because of ash, drivers, in the moments prior to breaking camp in the morning, changed air filters or the nylon mesh used to cover the air filter. Most of the mesh had come from women's nylon stockings, but it worked.

When everything was cleaned and packed away, the convoy headed out with hopes of reaching Medicine Hat by nightfall. The road was rough road and progress slow following the snow plow truck. Ed set the pace holding the convoy at 25 to 40 mph. The slow speed was driving Nancy right up the wall as she followed right behind Ed with the ambulance. Several times she thought of playing bumper cars with the wrecker to speed thing up. Doc, in the front passenger seat, relaxed her by telling some of his old medical stories, or singing one of his favorite songs. Truth be told though, Nancy had to bite her lip to keep from telling Doc what he could do with a few of those bawdy songs of his.

Point Man returned to his duties and talked Ed into allowing him to ride with his Misfits. The transmission in the wrecker was looked at and sure enough, they discovered a bullet had done a fair amount of damage.

They also discovered damage to the plow truck and it took most of the night but they got both vehicles fixed. However, they had to keep the snow plow blade locked down a half inch above the road surface. It bounced some with its shock absorbers but they could no longer lift or lower it.

With Point Man back in the lead, Joey took shotgun position with Ed and a much relieved Nancy was at the wheel of the ambulance with Kira keeping Doc busy in the back involved in a serious game of rummy. Driving north through some of Canada's most beautiful countryside, Ed felt content with life for the first in a very long time. He only hoped the feeling would last. But it didn't.

Hearing the CB come alive with static, Ed reached for the microphone as Point Man's excited voice came across, "Point Man to Wagon Master - Point Man to Wagon Master...Over."

"Go ahead, Big Guy...Over." Ed looked over at Joey, who was bouncing up and down and sideways to all the bumps in the road.

"I've been up and down this highway, Joey and never had a smooth ride. They call it frost heaves caused by freezing of the ground beneath the road... then melting with summer and freezing again the next winter. We'll have this all the way to Alaska."

"Great!"

Point Man's voice came back over the radio, "We got us a bit of a problem, Boss Man. Switch to scrambler."

What now? Ed tossed the switch, "Okay, what's up... another toll gate?"

"We found the Canadian Army, Boss, and they've jus' taken us prisoner," Point Man said. After giving that a moment to set in, he continued, "They want you ta come in real slow like. Tell everyone to keep their hands off their weapons, better have all of 'em put on safe to make sure we don't have a problem. And Boss, these boys have tanks, lots of nasty looking tanks with real mean lookin' machineguns poking out everywhere."

"Tell them we're coming in real friendly like, Big Guy...we don't want any troubles."

"I already told 'em that, Boss... but they're kind of skeptical. My Misfits are on their knees with hands behind heads and a lot of rifles in their faces. You'd better make sure no one has a jittery finger or it's gonna be short and sweet and our trip is over."

"Tell them I need a minute to ensure I have all my people ready to surrender. We should be at your location in 20 minutes. Play nice, Big Guy."

"Oh don't worry... my arm's in a sling, all my weapons have been taken and I got this 12 year old lieutenant here with a .45 in my ear. See you soon, Boss."

21-MILE SEWARD HIGHWAY WITH GRAMPS & JAKE

They had to cross the highway because the Snowy River entered the Kenai Lake under a lengthy bridge right below them, with both waterways cutting the valley in two. One valley angled north up through Moose Pass and then to Anchorage along the Seward highway; the other valley faced west toward Sterling, Soldotna and Kenai, along the Sterling Highway. The path they needed to follow was on the eastern side of the Seward Highway and this meant scrambling through thick brush, scurrying across the ice and acting much like mountain goats as they climbed up the steep mountainside on the east side of the highway.

MSgt. Oshmak and Jake lay concealed below a rocky ridgeline. Frozen and hungry, the tips of their leather gloves rubbed bare and sliced open by sharp rocks; they were huddled together for warmth in fresh deep ash covered snow. In the distance, they heard gunshots and the booming thunderous sound of tank fire, "Must've found someone in the Primrose area," Jake said in a raspy voice as he blew warm air on his exposed fingertips. Pieces of coat lining had been ripped away and wrapped around their hands, but to climb they had to use their hands and Jake's fingertips were white and bloody from 2nd degree frostbite, working toward 3rd degree. Oshmak was on the radio, keeping his message short, "Enemy below 20 mile, shots fired in Primrose; ...Out." He checked the battery level and knew it was time to change batteries again. "How many batteries left?"

"I don't know. Cold keeps sappin' 'em." Jake reached over and opened a pouch on the side of the radio pack. "One...We got only one battery left."

"Change it now. After that goes bad... we won't have to carry this anymore."

"Then what, Gramps?" Jake asked. "What are we goin' to do then?" Jake's voice filled with the fear he felt and the weariness of his frozen body. "We've got nowhere to go...Maybe we should surrender, Gramps."

"No. We do our job." MSgt. Oshmak didn't wait for Jake to carry out his order. He pulled out the old battery and put the new one in. He slid the old battery back into the pouch and snapped it shut. "We can still use it in case of emergency."

"Emergency? What do you think this is, you old fart? No one's comin' to rescue us and the enemy is nipping at our ankles. Sooner or later another helicopter is going to locate us and we're finished...Finished!" Jake was heartsick unable to speak further because his throat hurt. His eyes welled up with tears and turning his back on MSgt. Oshmak, he closed his eyes and wept.

Oshmak squinted his eyes against the wind, leaned forward and whispered, "We go on, our battle not over. We must live for those who fell before. Now get ready, we climb." Wiping snow off his white camouflage liner to reduce weight, Oshmak slung the radio pack over his field pack and began to climb up through a narrow ravine. Behind him, Jake bitterly accepted his fate and followed. After climbing, slipping and struggling for footing at nearly every rock ledge and tree trunk, Oshmak stopped for a long rest and took another sighting of the highway below. Catching up with the old guy, Jake nearly fell on his face as he climbed in beside him.

"Are you happy?" Jake asked in an angry whisper. His face was glowing from a high fever.

"Happy?" Oshmak looked south with his binoculars.

"Yeah, I said happy... you old coot!" Jake said in a strained voice. "We've got no food an' we're freezin' to death. I figured this must be like some Eskimo religious thing...You know, rights of manhood an' all that. You're getting to relive a cherished moment from your life...But you're killin' me in the process." Jake put his wrapped hands under his arms, afraid to look at their condition because he no longer felt them or his feet.

"No understand you. We're alive, so we go on. No surrender to those animals. I hear the stories...No!"

"What stories?" Jake cleared the snow away. Making a small depression he could huddle in for protection from the wind. His lips were dry, chapped and bleeding again, making it painful for him to drink the icy water as the snow melted in his mouth.

"They eat people."

"They eat people?" Jake was horrified at the idea. "Where'd you hear that?"

"No food up north, Jake...OAP army eating prisoners."

Jake thought he might vomit as his stomach reacted, but nothing came up. Seeing the poor condition of his partner, MSgt. Oshmak opened his field pack and pulled out their single miniature stove. Jake had thrown his away after he burned the last of his fuel, but Oshmak held on to his and rationed his fuel for survival. To Jake's surprise, MSgt. Oshmak removed a single fuel pellet from his pack, cupped a wooden match in his hands to protect it from the wind and lit the stove. Without a word, Jake slid forward and placed his hands close to the small flame and then asked, "Why didn't you tell me you still had fuel?"

"Eskimo people survive. We wait until we need... you need now." MSgt. Oshmak pulled out several pieces of dried salmon. "You eat."

Seeing the dried fish, Jake yanked a piece out of Oshmak's hand and with his own hands shaking, warmed it over the flame while Oshmak heated a tin cup of snow. He bathed Jake's face with warm water then carefully dampened his frostbitten hands. Jake grimaced with pain, as circulation returned for a brief moment. Afterward, Oshmak carefully wrapped the injured hands with somewhat clean material from his own coat lining. "We rest now."

Only a short hike later, they contacted Anchorage again to report that the OAP point element had moved past them on the Seward Highway below their position and had proceeded north.

MSgt. Oshmak and Jake couldn't see it, but from the shooting up ahead, they both knew a brief firefight had broken out when citizens of Crown Point had attempted to put up a defense. With only hunting rifles and pistols, they couldn't stop the tanks from braking through their road barrier.

Several hours had passed since the last shot was fired and from their hillside position overlooking the Seward Highway at Mile 24, Oshmak cradled a dying young man in his arms. His chest filled with fluid, his limbs frozen, Jake could not continue on. Over the next few hours, he wandered in and out of consciousness, while MSgt. Oshmak struggled to keep him warm inside a small emergency shelter he constructed from branches. Oshmak thought of going down to locate an abandoned house in the Crown Point area but the enemy was still all about. He made a final contact with Anchorage, "Enemy destroyed Crown Point; now headed for Moose Pass. My friend Jake in final sleep," MSgt Oshmak said. He gazed down into Jake's lifeless eyes, "Last message... God be with you... Out."

Laying Jake's body aside and closing the young one's eyes, MSgt. Oshmak climbed out of his small shelter and looked into the distance toward Anchorage. The massive Chugach Mountains and a foul smelling cloud of ash prevented him from seeing it, but he knew where the great city lay. Icy gusts of wind struck the old man, but Oshmak stared into the face of it and didn't bend. Skin frozen, limbs no longer feeling, lips cracked and bloody; he took a moment to make peace with God. Encircled by majestic mountain peaks and the panoramic view of the Upper Trail Lake valley, MSgt "Gramps" Oshmak, raised his arms and yelled at the top of his voice, "God, I welcome you today. Now I ready to die an' join my people who have gone before!" Then with respect to his ancestral beliefs, he slowly nodded to the mountains in each direction before climbing back into the shelter and lying beside his teammate. Getting himself comfortable, Gramps folded his arms over his chest and drifted off to last sleep.

15 - ULTIMATE GLORY-ULTIMATE SACRIFICE

"Dear friends, do not imitate what is evil but what is good. Anyone who does what is good is from God. Anyone who does what is evil has not seen God."

3 John 11 NIV

DOWNTOWN FAIRBANKS - APRIL 12TH

Towering flames of vibrant orange and translucent yellow shot upward hundreds of feet into the air releasing a fiery demon to dance upon the city's rooftops. Within a short time period, enraged arsonists ran through city to set fires in dozens of subdivisions leaving Fairbanks wrapped in a fiery embrace. Soldiers sought to vent anger and rage in willful acts of complete and utter devastation against the Golden Heart City. With torches, grenades and tank fire, they reduced the city to smoldering timbers. The first fires began with small mom & pop businesses, which became piles of concrete rubble and twisted metal. Then the armored units joined in, shelling larger businesses and releasing a constant bombardment of fire upon furniture stores, discount outlets and banks. Fast food joints quickly became targets only after searches revealed nothing to eat. Heavy and medium tanks moved through homes after the infantry had conducted searches for food and crushed everything before them. Buildings that could not be smashed, were blown apart by the OAP's weapons of doom. Emaciated OAP soldiers, pale from severe cold and hunger, displayed a maniacal rage, born of relentless warfare and false promises of the food they would find in Fairbanks. Booby-traps took the lives of more than 100 soldiers and not a crumb of food was found; the soldiers began to turn on their officers and opted to release their wrath upon this accursed city. They went house to house only to find all the cupboards bare. If some item of food was found; a single piece of dried bread or a nearly empty bag of crackers, a desperate fight ensued. Men and women fought hand to hand, using knives, knuckles or guns and often the matter was settled with severe wounding or death.

In some businesses and homes, ADF demolitions people had left food behind as bait for a well-placed booby-trap. Starving soldiers refused to wait for Explosive Ordinance Disposal teams to clear the location, not wanting to share in their prize and lose the food to an officer. They paid with their lives.

401

Senior officers ordered in other infantry units to restore order, but the soldiers sent in from Fox soon joined in the revolt and clashed violently with OAP Secret Police in the crowded streets throughout the downtown district. All around them the city burned. Here, where once thousands of tourists passed through gift stores and restaurants every summer, only ruins lay, where dozens of mangled bodies were left to lie as filthy snow soaked up their blood. Watching the horrific scene played out through a narrow basement window, tears ran down Brad's cheeks. To see his beloved city die such a death at the hands of the OAP had overwhelmed his emotions. Not a single structure within his view was left untouched, even the building above them had been hit countless times by tank fire, but the thick concrete walls of City Hall protected the structure from collapsing too easily.

The three men hidden in the basement were nearly deaf from the explosions above them and their clothes covered by a thick layer of concrete dust from the ceiling above. They considered themselves lucky; the ceiling had remained intact - for the moment.

"There must be thousands of 'em out there... the noise is ear shattering. They're all crammed together in this one spot like sardines in a can," Brad said. With a quick jerk of his right hand, he pulled the lower part of his black wool balaclava down and used the back of his hand to wipe his runny nose.

"I say we should nuke the place, wipe them out with one blow," Wayne said.

Brad was surprised by this and said, "We got nukes?"

Wayne could only nod his head up and down, while he adjusted his scarf over his balaclava and wiped some of the concrete dust off. He turned to Brad, "I don't really know if we have any nukes or not, but 500 pounders would do quite a job if you're thinking what I'm thinking." No one answered for a moment and a strange stillness settled over the three of them while they contemplated the action Wayne was suggesting. Calling in fire had been considered a last ditch action done in the past by a lot of people in America's wars. They all knew one of those bombs could land right in their laps, but they also realized how badly they could hurt the OAP and possibly save people in Fort Greeley.

Concrete dust in the air forced them to wear scarves or in Jeff's case a cloth painter's mask, under the wool headpieces. Brad found a case of the cloth masks while searching through supplies in the basement and could only guess they had been there since the City Hall had been refurbished in the late 1990's. The Hall's exterior walls were pounded again by 105m and 90 mm tank fire, leaving even more gaping holes on every floor. Nearly every window was broken out by concentrated bursts of machinegun fire and the top floor had finally caved in on the front and north sides.

Downtown Fairbanks was reminiscent of World War II Dresden, Germany, after the Allies' massive bombings had leveled most of the city.

Still struggling to hear, Jeff cautiously raised his voice so the other two could hear his ideas, "From what I can see, no one appears to be obeying orders up there... I saw a dozen soldiers machine gunned down by their own guys... must have been the Secret Police... they're called the Black Dragons and most of them are criminals." Jeff looked at his friends in disbelief. "I hadn't expected this, but they're falling apart out there."

"Good!" Wayne exclaimed. "Colonel Stewart needs to get the word out; they've got to bomb the city right now. Streets are packed with tanks and trucks... they couldn't ask for a better target or a better time." Wayne climbed down from the nearest basement window and looked to Brad and Jeff for their replies.

"I think you're right," Jeff agreed. Brad nodded his endorsement, his head was ringing and he thought his eyes might be bleeding. He wiped them with a semi-clean white handkerchief, saw a couple small blotches of bright red blood and showed them to Jeff.

"We can expect that with the shelling we took... a result of a concussion. You'll be all right...until those bombs fall at least."

"Thanks!"

"We should use the radio, but not from here," Wayne said. "They might triangulate on us. We'll head down the tunnel as far as we can go and then contact Stewart."

"Right," Brad replied then looked to Jeff, "You stay here and keep an' eye on those jokers outside while I go with Wayne." He picked up the radio and slung his rifle over his shoulder.

Jeff shook his head in frustration, "I'm always left behind while you guys seek out the glory. I think I'm beginning to suffer some sort of complex." He grinned under his mask and waved them on.

"When this is over, Jeff...I'll pay for your therapy," Wayne said. Then with a casual wave by both men, they left the little man alone - surrounded by tens of thousands of OAP soldiers.

"You'd better let me lead," Wayne suggested. "I know where all the trip wires are and with your big feet, it could ruin our heroic attempt."

"Lead on, *MacDuff*." Brad pointed toward the door which led down into the tunnel and then bowed slightly to let Wayne pass by.

Nearly an hour passed for them to work their way northeast through the darkened tunnel, bypassing the Polaris Hotel, they stopped when a metal sign told them they had reached a junction beside the Chena River.

"This should be far enough," Brad said. Crouching in the tunnel, he pulled down the bottom of his balaclava to expose his mouth and brought the radio to his lips, "Golf-One this is India-Five…Over."

Following a second try, a strange male voice responded, "This is Golf-One, go ahead India-Five…Over."

"How do you read? Over." Brad looked over at Wayne, suspicious of the voice. In the darkness it was hard to read Wayne's eyes through the flashlight's glare.

"I am reading you 5 by 5, state your location…Over."

Already wary because of a voice he didn't recognize, Brad eyebrows popped up when the unknown person asked for their location. He held his hand over the microphone and whispered to Wayne, "We're being put on, this isn't Greeley."

"Ask for confirmation," Wayne said in a low whisper.

Brad nodded his head in agreement and said into the microphone, "Authenticate India-Adam 1…3…8…Over."

"India 5, state your location…Over."

"It would appear we have a party line," Wayne said. Brad had again covered the mike. With this new radio and the enemies advanced electronics, they both suspected the OAP could pick up their voices even if the microphone wasn't keyed.

"They must be overriding our radio signal to Greeley." Wayne looked up the tunnel as he thought over their options.

"I've got an idea." Brad pulled the camera out of his shoulder pack and said, "Look for a clean spot on the wall… something I can write on."

"Don't you think they're jamming everything?" Wayne asked.

"India 5, I say again… state your location! Over."

"Golf-One, I'll be with you in a moment…Hold your horses…Over." Brad dipped his finger into the muck on the tunnel floor. "This'll work…But I'm really glad I've got gloves on." He went to where Wayne was standing by a semi clean piece of tunnel wall and as Wayne held the flash light, Brad used the muck to write out, "OAP has freq. City center jammed with tanks and men - bomb ASAP!"

"At least you can spell," Wayne said in jest.

"My old man was a stickler for correct spelling… worse than my English teacher in high school. He even sent one of my papers back, dropping my B minus to a C because I had misspelled half a dozen words on a four page report the teacher didn't catch. The woman was humiliated and took it out on me for the rest of the semester."

Wayne had to laugh, but managed to hold the two flashlights up to light the wall, while Brad turned the camera on and filmed the wall for 20 seconds. They used more mud to smear the message out.

"Maybe we should've left it up… could've been a piece of history for some archeologist to discover," Wayne said.

"Forget it, they'll be happy with our bones. C'mon…let's boogey!" Brad said loudly. He led the way with Wayne right behind him.

Brad came to an abrupt halt, with Wayne nearly slamming into him. "Sorry, I forgot something." He pulled the radio off his belt, yanked the bottom of his balaclava down and said into the microphone, "India 5 to Golf One… Over."

"Go ahead, India Five… Over," the same known voice replied.

"Put us down for an order - six number ones and five number two's, heavy on the sweet and sour sauce. And don't forget the fortune cookies. Bye now." Brad smiled when he saw the confused look on Wayne's face. "I didn't want to leave them hanging. It's not polite."

"That was stupid, they'll probably be able to triangulate on us."

"We won't be here," Brad said. "… Lighten up, I've got to have some fun or I'm liable to go batty down here. Not only am I scared out of my mind, I'm freezing, the food is lousy and I feel like General Custer at the Little Big Horn."

"Actually he was only a Lt. Colonel when he was killed, but they buried him at his Civil War rank of General," Wayne said.

"I did not know that."

"I saw the movie…the one with Errol Flynn," They continued down the tunnel.

ADF INTELLIGENCE, FORT GREELEY

After only three hours of sleep, Jeb was in no mood to be awakened when he heard someone knocking at his door. One eye open, the other feeling as if it was glued down, he glared at the wooden door and mumbled a profane word; one his mother would have washed his mouth out with soap for. Tossing his green wool blanket aside and climbing off a very uncomfortable metal cot, Jeb lost his balance when he reached for his boots and stumbled headfirst to the floor. Mumbling another string of profanity, his face locked in a snarl and his other eye now open wide, he pulled himself up off the cold tile floor and slowly ambled over to the door in his bare feet, "What?" He roared as he swung open the door - only to look into the smiling face of his Commanding General. "Uh-h-h…um, sorry, General… I thought it was…never mind. What can I do for the General?"

Stifling a laugh, General Saunders shook his head as he remembered several of his own past rude awakenings, "I really dislike bothering you, Jeb, knowing how little sleep you've had, but we need to talk."

"Come in, Sir." Jeb turned the overhead light on and as the General walked in, he made a mad dash to a green metal folding chair, grabbed his uniform pants off the seat and quickly pulled them on. He slid an olive green T-shirt over his head, not wanting to expose the General to his wild array of chest hairs.

Tired from many long hours, General Saunders put aside military protocol and carefully lowered himself down on the foot of Jeb's bed, surprising his young officer. "Jeb, I was next door when India Five's latest TV message came in and thought we should talk about it."

"I apologize, sir, but I'm not aware of a new message. The lieutenant was under orders to wake me up when one came in..." *I'm going to wring his neck for this!*

"Don't blame your lieutenant, Jeb. I happened to be in there, reviewing messages and film when this newest one came in. I directed the lieutenant to stay with the monitor, while I woke you. We needed some privacy and I think your room will work fine, so why don't you have a seat and let me talk for a minute."

"Yes, sir."

"It seems OAP communications has discovered our radio frequency and are overriding it. I imagine after this last broadcast they'll be jamming our Micro wave TV transmissions too." Saunders glanced around the room, noticing how bare the walls were - no posters or other artwork, not even a photo of his girl or family. In fact, the room's furniture consisted of only a single metal bed frame with a reasonably new mattress, a metal double wall locker and one metal folding chair, a green metal nightstand with a black folding lamp and Jeb's bags by the door. There was one small window with dark green black out curtains over it for day sleepers. "They probably didn't suspect we had this capability in place, but they know now," General Saunders added.

"We knew it would only be a matter of time, General." Jeb finished dressing, sat down on the chair and started pulling on his socks and then his boots.

"I'm not sure what they used and don't want to know, but our three geniuses wrote a message on what looks like a sewer wall. Pretty grainy picture, but your new man, Lt. Ashgok, was able to clean it up at our end." General Saunders waited patiently while Jeb tied his boots. "They've recommended we bomb Fairbanks immediately and I wish to discuss this with General Howard-Wright. So, please be in my office in say...ten minutes." General Saunders didn't wait for a reply; he simply stood up and left the room without another word.

"Yes, sir," Stewart replied as the door closed before him, left alone to contemplate what the General had mentioned. Jeb visualized the faces of Jeff, Wayne and Brad and the knot in his stomach tightened another turn. He knew any bombing could very well lead to the death of his three operatives and that thought didn't leave him overjoyed. Walking into the bathroom, he downed two small 1ounce cupful's of a pink anti acid, raked a razor over his face and strapped on his shoulder holster. Grabbing his parka and a fur hat, he made sure his door was locked behind him and left for the meeting.

GENERAL SAUNDERS' OFFICE, FORT GREELEY

General Howard-Wright was wearing RCMP dress riding uniform: a bright red tunic with yellow braid and black riding pants with yellow stripe, a 2 inch wide brown leather belt with matching flap over holster holding a Sig Sauer .40 caliber semi-auto pistol and knee high black leather boots. He was standing leisurely in the center of the room when Jeb was ushered in by General Saunders' aide. Though surprised by the General's formal appearance, Jeb knew better then to remark on it. He looked at General Howard-Wright and struggled in vain to keep a hint of smile off his face.

"I can see by your expression, Colonel, that you might be wondering why I am attired so formally. To satisfy your curiosity, as I so dearly hate to leave a young officer hanging over the precipice, I was pulled away from a new colonel's promotion party by your illustrious General Saunders, who felt this meeting was most urgent."

"You look very elegant, sir," Jeb said.

"Thank you, Colonel." Then turning to General Saunders, "May we get down to it then, I do so hate to miss out on the good booze!"

"You don't even drink anymore, you old fraud," Saunders replied. "Please have a seat, General...You too, Jeb." General Saunders gestured to a coffee service on a side table, "Help yourself."

Jeb declined when he noticed General Howard-Wright was not having any coffee or tea.

"All right then." General Saunders looked to his Canadian counterpart, "Earlier I advised you that Colonel Stewart has a three man Intel team inside Fairbanks. Volunteers known as India Five. They tell us the city is jam packed with tanks and men. We presume this means dreadnaughts and armored personnel carriers. They've called for an air strike which would provide us an opportunity to severely cripple the OAP and I feel we shouldn't pass this up." Saunders stood up and walked over to a wall map displaying the City of Fairbanks and some of the outlying areas. He had only moments before directed his aide to pin the map up and had circled the position of City Hall. "I am planning, with your agreement, General, on sending a flight of F-15s in for a strike on Fairbanks. Loaded with 500 lb. bombs, I believe a quick raid could profit us with some badly needed time and reduce their numbers. The basic plan is for the aircraft to leave Fort Greeley, fly below enemy radar and make their attack from the northeast dropping the payload on city center... from the Chena River to the southern edge of the city." General Saunders pointed to the bombing points on the map and glanced over his shoulder to General Howard-Wright, "I'd like your opinion, General?"

General Howard-Wright walked up to the map and studied it for a moment and then replied, "With an OAP air cap in the area do you really believe you can get your fighters close enough to Fairbanks to be effective?"

"Sir," Jeb spoke up. "If discipline has broken down as our men have reported... well, Sir, maybe their whole command structure has collapsed. They can't use our runways yet and an air cap is limited by fuel usage for any aircraft on station. True, they have a quick response time from Nome, but this would be 30 minutes at best."

"Still, this could be suicide for your pilots," General Howard-Wright said. "The OAP could have hundreds of anti-aircraft guns set up for such an attack." Clearly, General Howard-Wright wasn't sure this was a good idea and it saddened him to think of how many pilots they might lose in such an attack.

"General, with the congestion of vehicles in town...as India Five reports, this could be like dropping grenades on a pool stocked full of trout." Jeb knew he was right; they needed to go on this one. He was groggy when the General woke him, but before coming to the meeting he reviewed the message and agreed with his three men in the city.

"Trout don't shoot back, Colonel." Howard-Wright walked around the room for a moment, while the other two officers waited in silence. "Still, now or later, it matters little if we can't stop their armor... I agree with your plan, General."

General Saunders nodded and turned to Jeb, "Colonel, contact Brigadier General Watson. I want him here in my office ASAP." He walked over and shook General Howard-Wright's hand in a strong grasp. "One minute after midnight I will have a flight of avenging Eagles over our city. 500 pounders can do an awful lot of damage to the enemy's spearhead."

"I sincerely hope so, Glenn. I will offer a prayer for your pilots. They will need the Lord's protection for a mission such as this."

INDIA FIVE

A teeth chattering cold front had moved in over the city, bringing temperatures down to -48° and a thicker ice fog reducing visibility to less than 20 feet. Reminiscent of a meat locker, basement living was growing real old for the three men who waited to hear if their message got through to Fort Greeley. Feeding pieces of wood onto the fire, Brad felt a thickness in his chest and fought to stifle a cough. A fever had grabbed hold earlier, but he didn't want to say anything to the others. *Really doesn't matter much, a few hours...maybe a couple of days an' I won't have to worry about some silly cold.* Actually, it wasn't a mere cold. Brad was suffering the initial onset of pneumonia and his fever was climbing, while the infection worsened.

"What's all the noise upstairs?" Jeff asked.

"You know I can't understand the lingo," Brad complained. "Why don't you climb up to the window and see what's up?"

"Hate to leave this cozy bed." Jeff pulled himself to his feet, wrapped another blanket around his shoulders and made his way over to their observation window; one of the few pieces of glass still untouched. He kept a second blanket wrapped around his waist and made his way to a pile of wood crates they had stacked below the window as a makeshift ladder. Heavy bombardment from OAP tanks had created several large cracks in the foundation, making it easier for them to hear the ruckus going on outside. For several minutes Jeff watched and listened, his heart and stomach sickened by what he heard. The men outside were celebrating at some sort of gruesome banquet. When he climbed back down, he looked to his friends and slowly shook his head, "They've become animals!" He spat out in disgust. "They're not soldiers! They're not even men...just...demented beasts." He pointed to where he had observed the enemy, "Hundreds of them out there worshipping some ancient demon. A new general arrived with a group of prisoners...deserters it sounds like. I listened as they beheaded them before the general...now they're... barbecuing..." Jeff struggled to control his upset stomach.

Fighting down the bile in his throat, Brad remembered reading about cannibalism; Old Testament Biblical days, the Donner party in the 1800s and some soccer team lost in the mountains. But to have it going on right outside...he forced himself to think of something else and sincerely hoped Scott would carry out his last wish if, and when the need arose. With midnight approaching, Brad's fever continued to climb. He could no longer hide the cough from his friends and as he lay under a pile of blankets, chills racked his body. Seeing how sick his friend had become, Wayne had taken a seat beside him and began using a damp cloth to wipe Brad's brow. "Sick call's in the morning, but a bit of walk I'm afraid," Wayne said as he tried to make Brad comfortable.

"Too…too bad we don't have anything more powerful then Aspirin," Brad said in a whisper. He smiled at his friend, grateful for the attention. The smile quickly faded, replaced by a clenched jaw as another attack of tremors struck his body.

Feeling abandoned, cold and missing family and friends, they were not aware a flight of F-15's was closing in on Fairbanks to carry out the mission they themselves had suggested.

PROSPECTOR FLIGHT-

Maintaining 370 mph at tree top level to escape OAP surface radar, Prospector flight split into two sections of eleven F-15's each. Armed with either two 500 pound bombs or four 250 pound bombs and an assortment of missiles for air-to-air combat if needed, they were capable of dropping close to 22,000 pounds of high explosives on the OAP lead element. During pre-flight briefing, no one wanted to talk about the damage they would be causing to one of their own cities, but each pilot wrestled with his own thoughts as their target grew near.

"Prospector One to Alpha and Bravo, we are 20 miles east of target. Bravo will remain in reserve, staying southeast over North Pole. I will lead Alpha in on the first run. Prospector Five stay back unless you sight bandits… At which time you are free to engage. Once they pick us up on radar, we will have approximately 30 mikes before bandits arrive on station from Nome…Over."

"Five copies," Prospector Five replied.

"Alpha, follow my lead northeast to southwest at 600 feet. We will be observed by enemy units in Fox, but our mission is Fairbanks. Maintain assigned interval to avoid secondary explosions. Once you clear the city, ascend to 900 feet and form on me in attack flight formation, while Bravo goes down. Drop bombs on center of town with first run, use blocks between Chena River and Airport Road as aiming marks," Captain Mark "Red" Hansen said over the plane-to-plane intercom.

A city boy who was raised in Upland, California, he always felt a bit cramped in his Eagle cockpit. At 6'4", 230 pounds with the broad shoulders of a former college defensive end he was large for a fighter pilot, but had grown accustomed to the tight fit. He often got the attention of other pilots when he slowly uncurled himself out of his Eagle. It was for his capable flying ability and accuracy on the range that newly promoted Brig. General Watson named him Prospector's squadron commander. A graduate of Cal Poly, San Luis Obispo; Hansen accepted an Air Force Commission and was flying F-15's out of Eielson Air Force Base when the missiles hit the lower 48 on Christmas morning. His curly reddish blonde hair, blue-gray eyes and lack of facial hair made him look much younger than his 28 years. Hansen looked above and saw Prospector Five and Bravo section moving off to his left, "Alpha, check in."

"Two," Lt. Howards radioed back. He was busy glancing over his shoulder to observe the OAP's destruction below.

"Three," Lt. Brittick said next. He checked all his gauges one more time and made sure the master arm switch was thrown.

On down the line the pilots reported ready status until all 10 birds had checked in for the action ahead.

"All right, we're looking good. Switches on hot an' wait for my word," Hansen ordered. Like most pilots, Hansen carried a photo of his family taped to his control board. In his case it wasn't a wife and kids, but his dad and mother. He had never married; his last girlfriend wasn't that much of a catch and they had broken up before he was shipped to Alaska. He knew his family was gone; they were spending Christmas with his aunt in Oakland on Christmas. But he also had the relief of knowing they were all Christians and he would most likely be seeing them soon. They had seen the glow of light off the black ash clouds from a ways off, but as they came closer, the burning city startled them. As those startled voices came over the radio, Hansen broke in and ordered everyone to cease transmission. The sight sickened him, too, but they had a job to do; he dropped the nose of his bird and focused on his revenge. The load his Eagle had to deliver would rake this enemy with 500 pound talons.

Zooming in under radar at nearly 410 mph, the thundering roar of eleven F-15s finally caught the attention of the OAP anti-aircraft gun crews in Fox and then in Northern Fairbanks. But it was too late. By the time the warnings came over the radio, the first bombs were impacting the center of town and mass chaos broke out as explosive flames ripped through the layers of ice fog. Without warning, more than two thousand soldiers were consumed in a fiery death as bomb fragments shredded heavily armored tanks and troop carriers like a knife cutting through warm butter. Portable fuel storage tanks, dragged on tracks and sleds from as far as Northern China, burst and their contents set ablaze. Ammo storage areas, only recently built up, exploded and in an instant the center of Fairbanks erupted with flaming liquid and debris that resembled an emerging volcano. A three story tsunami wall of fire engulfed vehicles parked on Nobel Street and Cushman Avenue; long narrow roadways running parallel north to south through the city's business center.

Coming off his run, Hansen was astonished to have found every roadway in the city center packed with armored vehicles. The glow of a thousand fires had illuminated the downtown area, making it easier to see the streets as intense heat from OAP destruction had actually driven some of the crystalline ice fog away and made it easier to find the target points. "This place looks like one big parking lot," he muttered to himself.

Hansen continued to climb and then held his section over the low foothills to the southwest, while Bravo did their stuff. One of Hansen's Eagles was assigned the duty of photographing the city with her nose camera and a digital camera she carried in the cockpit. She had not joined up yet and was making a large loop of Fairbanks to carry out her assignment, but she was biting at a chance to attack the OAP.

Since the Eagles had arrived, not a single missile was fired at the ADF. They had received only sporadic fire from outlying anti-aircraft guns and not one of the Eagles had received battle damage. First and second runs by his squadron were completed without a single loss and it made Hansen wonder how much longer their luck was going to hold. "Prospector Five, this is Prospector One...Over."

"Go ahead...Over."

"Ascend to 900 feet and take southern route back to base at best possible speed. I'll take Alpha section for one final run with guns...Over."

"Request another shot at 'em, Red...Over."

"Negative, Prospector 5," Hansen ordered. "RTB and that's an order...Over." Hansen understood the desire for one last shot, but right now it was important to keep crews alive and these valuable Eagles in the air for another day.

"Roger that, Red. We are returning to base...Over."

"Keep the coffee hot, Joker...Out." Hansen watched the aircraft lights in the distance as Bravo formed up behind 1st Lt. Ted "Joker" Littleton and headed southeast for Fort Greeley.

"Alpha, we are going in with guns. Save your missiles in case we get jumped by bandits and keep an eye on your radar," Hansen said into his microphone. "We will make one run and one run only. Complete your run, than peel off for a quick dash to home plate at best possible speed on my wing in loose attack formation." He looked straight ahead. With so many fires burning, the city resembled a massive forest fire and he had seen enough of those since moving to Alaska. "Must be a thousand tanks down there crammed together like sardines. We can't miss. Good luck to all of you and keep the chatter down."

Alpha followed their leader at an attack height of 300 feet, making sure to miss all the power lines and cell telephone towers. They hit the northern outskirts of the city and dropped to 200 feet to come zooming in at over 200 mph. Using Cushman as a flight corridor, they blasted away with 20mm cannon fire and stitched a lethal line of thread across the OAP spearhead.

INDIA FIVE

Ground concussions shook the City Hall building and it gave Brad, Wayne and Jeff the feeling a great quake in the 9.8 magnitude had struck the city. The three ADF operatives were tossed around like toy soldiers and helpless to a man, they bounced off walls and storage crates, and they struggled to breathe as thick clouds of concrete dust showered down on them from above. Brad was hurled violently from his bed to smack head first against a wall, temporarily knocking him unconscious. He didn't feel the 3 foot piece of steel rebar that impaled his upper right shoulder - not yet anyway.

Jeff was thrown through the air like a man shot from a cannon and sent bouncing off the basement floor like a rock skipping the surface of a lake, until a stack of wooden crates stopped his flight and collapsed upon him.

Wayne was the fortunate one. He was buried under a mountain of volleyball nets, boxes of deflated basketballs, volleyballs and ping pong supplies that once belonged to the Boys & Girls Club. Still conscious, he closed up into a fetal position while the basement continued to dance around him.

Matters took a turn for the worse when the first floor of the building began to give way, sending tons of concrete debris down into the basement and three helpless men. In spite of all the secondary explosions outside, Wayne was still able to hear Jeff's blood curdling scream.

ALPHA SECTION

"Missiles! We got Missiles!" An unknown pilot shouted over the radio.

From countless hours of training, Hansen automatically looked behind him on both sides. Only to find the night sky clear below the ominous ash clouds; there were no warning lights flashing or tones activated from his weapons system. *Where? Who?* These were the questions that raced through his mind after he completed his run and ascended to 900 feet to watch his flight in action.

Snow and ash had ceased to fall, but the dark ceiling above frightened him. Hansen felt like it was going to smother him as he narrowly missed flying right into it. He recalled how many lectures he'd received on what the ash could do to engines and he breathed a sigh of relief once he had the aircraft leveled off. Seconds flashed by, then he saw a bright flash over the river and knew one of his birds was hit.

"That's Hot Dog!" An excited voice called out over the radio, followed by a second pilot in a mournful voice, "No chute; no time."

"He didn't eject. All I saw was a fireball."

413

"Keep off the radio!" Hansen knew Prospector Nine was the one hit and 1st Lt. Jimmy "Hot Dog" Royal was gone. *Nice kid...*

Before he could dwell anymore on Hot Dog, a second fighter burst into flames before the pilot could finish his run. Prospector Three had lost its right wing and was spiraling out of control. Unable to escape her Eagle due to an ejection seat malfunction, 1st Lt. Emily "Green Eyed Lady" Moxie rode her burning Eagle right into a car sales lot packed with heavy tanks. The initial explosion instantly turned five tanks and a fuel trailer into melted metal and caused waves of burning fuel to spread throughout the immediate area. This in turn ignited a series of secondary explosions which added to Moxie's kills.

Everyone was awake now. Anti-aircraft and tank fire filled the night sky reminding Hansen of old war movies when English anti-aircraft fire attempted to knock out German bombers and filled the skies with illuminated tracers. Hansen would later advise his debriefing officer that Prospector Flight had blown open a wasp's nest. He knew it was time to skedaddle. "All planes on me," Hansen ordered. "Climb to 900 feet, stay below ceiling and let's boogey the heck out of here." Hansen looked in every direction to make sure all his surviving birds were closing in on him. "Report any problems."

"Prospector Four, I'm leaking fuel badly."

"Got enough for the return flight?" Hansen asked.

"Hope so. If not, I'll get out and push."

"Prospector Flight, this is Shadow-One, you have multiple bogies coming in from the northwest at 12,000 feet...speed is Mach-2; they are zeroing in on your current position...Over. "Hansen wasn't quite sure who Shadow-One was, but he was grateful for the timely update. "Identify yourself, Shadow-One...Over," Hansen said.

The airwaves were silent for a moment then a female voice advised, "We're a friend, Bub and we don't want the OAP to know too much about us...Now get your butt home before some MIG burns your feathers off."

Shadow-One was a Canadian RC-135 Recon aircraft, once used for anti-submarine warfare. Having flown out of Eielson AFB between 1970 and 2009, two of the "Hog Nose" aircraft were sold to Canada prior to breakdown in communications. Able to fly at a great height and use their powerful radar systems, the 21 crewmembers aboard the aircraft were able to observe OAP aircraft the minute they lifted off from their new bases at Nome and Kotzebue.

"Kick your birds into high gear and let's get some space between us and those OAP fighters. I don't know what those bogies are, what they carry an' right now I don't care, so head for home...Out." Hansen changed frequencies and contacted Tangle Control at Greeley. "Tangle Control, this is Prospector One…Over." He lifted his oxygen mask to wipe a buildup of sweat away.

"This is Tangle, reading you in the clear. Go ahead…Over," Sgt. Arthur T. Jarson responded in a squeaky voice. He was only 19 and very nervous at the moment into his 2nd week of training.

"Be advised, mission completed, but we've got some bad boys on our tail. Flight split into two sections. Bravo should be on station by now an' I've lost two of my birds…Over."

"Have both Alpha and Bravo on screen. Bravo will be landing in approximately 11 mikes. We've heard of your visitors from Shadow-One; you have other team by large margin, but they are closing. Standby!"

Hansen waited as the scenery below him passed by in the dark. He kept an eye on the ground, the sky, his controls and the aircraft around him. Now wasn't the time to fly sloppy.

"Prospector One, be advised visitors have broken off pursuit. You're clear for landing at Tango in 23 mikes. Good job, guys."

Good job? Whoever you are, I lost two good pilots tonight…Now I wonder how many more before this is over? Hansen focused on his flying and tried not to think about tomorrow.

INDIA FIVE

Bleeding from more than a dozen cuts and abrasions, his body one massive contusion and his mouth filled with the taste of concrete dust, Wayne forced himself to stand. At first there was a seemingly near endless struggle to unravel him from volleyball netting, but he finally cut his way free with his boot knife. He stumbled over blocks of ceiling debris to reach Jeff's side and found him unconscious with a large block of jagged concrete across his legs. Frothy blood coming from his mouth led Wayne to suspect that Jeff had internal injuries and quickly went to work trying to move the concrete off, but he couldn't budge it. He estimated the weight at better than 500 lbs. He finally gave up, winded from his efforts. Leaving Jeff's side, he crawled over to where Brad was trying to sit up.

Brad's shirt was torn open, exposing dark bloodstains on his upper chest and a deep laceration that exposed ribs. In desperation Brad had jerked himself free of the rebar and the severe pain nearly knocked him out again. When he looked up to see Wayne hovering over him with a large compress bandage from his first aid pouch, he tried to smile, but everything just hurt too much.

Wayne offered a caring smile and began to clean off some of the blood seeping from Brad's mouth. "I think you're busted up inside, Brad." Wayne listened to Brad's worsening cough and identified the bluish color to his lips as a lack of oxygen, which caused him to suspect Brad could be drowning in his own fluids. Tying off a bandage, which caused Brad a good deal of discomfort, Wayne braced him against a wall and wiped his face off again with a torn piece of blanket, "Don't move, sit still or you'll probably bleed to death."

"Maybe…maybe this wasn't such a hot idea we had," Brad whispered.

"We hurt them…we hurt them good!"

"Hope so… How's Jeff?" Brad asked. He went into another coughing fit and the pain made him moan loudly. Wayne held him up until it was over and then wiped the blood off his lips.

"Legs crushed, I can't move him. He's unconscious, thank God."

Brad whispered, "You look like you've been in a scrap with a long clawed she cat."

"Not too bad, most of the ceiling missed me." It was then that Wayne looked up and saw the roof was gone, leaving them open to the world. The fire was snuffed out and cold night air was setting in fast. "How do you feel?" Wayne asked, trying to ignore the openness above and the frigid air all around them.

"Not too good as a matter of fact." Brad whispered. "Hard to breathe…must be a bad cold. Feel like I have an elephant on my chest and we're sitting in a freezer."

"Based on what I can see, you were stuck with a piece of rebar and you pulled yourself free. But it looks like a piece of ceiling bounced off your chest too."

"To tell you the truth, I've felt better than this… But give me a few minutes and I'll be back to my old self." Brad went into another coughing fit and Wayne gave him one of the wool blankets to hold against his chest. With each attack of coughs, Brad thought his rib cage was trying to blow up; the blanket helped some.

"I'll be right back." Wayne crawled over to check on Jeff, only to find the little man had died. Lowering his head, he gently caressed Jeff's forehead and whispered, "You were one of the bravest men I've ever known and I am proud to have served with you." Wayne found a blanket nearby, shook the concrete dust off and covered Jeff's exposed body with it.

Hearing Brad's racking cough, Wayne went back to him and held a canteen to his lips. "The first aid book says I'm not supposed to do this, but what the heck…it can't hurt much now."

"Thanks, my throat…dry." Brad opened his eyes and looked up. Seeing through the open ceiling gave him a sense of peace. The fires outside provided a glowing background and his mind drifted and he thought of the camp fires he and his brother had shared with their father. Then he suddenly remembered where they were, "Wayne, get out of here... get into the tunnel." Brad fought for air. "Not long before they come."

"Never told you before, but I hate tunnels. Figured I'd sit here with you and see what happens."

"Contact the Colonel," Brad suggested. He was struggling to stay awake, afraid he might not wake up again.

Startled by a noise from above, Wayne looked up to see the glow of a flashlight moving above. The bombing had left a hole in the ceiling large enough to drive a car through and OAP Soldiers were looking for survivors. He knew they would stumble upon their secret lair within minutes. Looking around for Brad's rifle, he spotted it several feet away and recovered it. After checking it, he loaded a fresh magazine and placed it in Brad's hands before he went looking for his own. It was mixed in with the volleyball netting and it took him a moment to pull it free. Slapping in a fresh magazine, he crawled back to Brad's side and they waited together.

Suddenly, Brad went into another coughing fit, one loud enough to get attention from above. Words were shouted out in a tongue neither man understood, but Wayne suspected they were calling out to find their own men. Wayne quickly glanced around the basement to see if an enemy soldier had fallen down into the room, but he couldn't see anyone.

Frozen, too afraid to move and draw a grenade, they listened as the words were repeated several more times. Without a response from below, the enemy suspected there were stragglers or possibly the radio team they had diligently searched for. One of the sergeants fired a short burst down through the hole to see what kind of response they might get; the bullets ricocheted off the floor, concrete debris and walls, coming all too close for Wayne's liking. Revived by a rush of adrenaline, Brad hoisted his rifle with one trembling hand and fired off a quick three round burst up through the opening. At the same time, Wayne sighted in on a dark figure leaning over the opening and pulled the trigger. A single soldier was hit and fell through the hole to strike the concrete floor with an audible thud. After firing off a second burst, Wayne grabbed Brad's uninjured shoulder and with some effort dragged him behind a large piece of concrete slab. The pain nearly caused Brad to pass out, but he bit his tongue to keep from screaming.

An exchange of fire went on for several seconds before a second body fell through the hole and landed a few feet from the first one, than all became quiet. Wayne changed magazines in both rifles and checked his ammo supply. They had each carried several full magazines, plus there had been an ammo pack, which held additional 20 loaded magazines. But the ammo pack was now under a pile of concrete blocks.

Noticing how weak Brad was growing, Wayne braced him up against a cold slab of concrete and used a damaged wooden crate to support the rifle. Brad now had help to aim his rifle toward the opening in the roof.

"Just pull the trigger, short bursts," Wayne advised.

"No problem," Brad replied through clenched teeth. The pain was burning through him like fire.

Within moments, more than 50 soldiers had encircled the opening and aimed their rifles down through the openings. But they were ordered to hold their fire because the officer on scene wanted prisoners to interrogate.

"Use camera, not…not much time," Brad suggested in a low strained whisper.

Realizing what Brad meant, he nodded in agreement and looked around the basement for the camera. He finally spotted the dust covered camera lying by Jeff's body. Miraculously, it was undamaged by the large pieces of concrete landing only inches from it. Staying low crawling around rubble and keeping an eye on the enemy above, he reached the camera and quickly saw that it still functioned. "It works!" Wayne exclaimed.

First he photographed Jeff to show how the gallant little man had perished and then scanned the hole above displaying images of enemy soldiers looking down at them. Wayne turned the camera on himself, hoping it was in focus and mouthed the words, "Tell my wife I love her." He waved with his free hand to say goodbye. Focusing on Brad, who tried to smile, but didn't seem to have the strength, Wayne watched as his friend nodded twice with eyes closed. Finally, not knowing what else to do, he set the camera up behind them in hopes it might catch the forthcoming action. Not wanting to sit there and freeze to death, Wayne assumed a crouched position beside Brad and raked the rim of the opening with a long burst of automatic fire. He heard two or three screams and the enemy responded in kind.

"Better than freezing!" Wayne yelled at Brad.

Once again the firing stopped and then a voice called out in English, "You surrender, be warm and not die!"

Wayne shook his head at Brad, "Promises, promises, that guy must be a politician." He lifted his rifle once again and fired off an extended burst which rewarded him with the screams of two men. Right then, things took a serious turn to bad when several grenades were dropped through the opening. With a big smirk on his face, Wayne grabbed Brad by the hand and squeezed, "It's been an honor." Brad could only nod in return, a grim look of desperation on his face as he pulled the trigger on his M-16 and held it down as thunderous explosions filled the basement.

FAMILY BARRACKS-FORT GREELEY

A gentle knock on the door and a young Bob Sawyer leaped from his bunk to open it, "Hi, Pastor." Bob didn't know who the other officer was but recognized the silver leaf of a lieutenant colonel.

Chaplain Knight smiled warmly at the young boy and looked to see Kathy Sawyer, who sat on the floor reading to her daughter. "Please, come in." Kathy said.

"Kathy, this is Lt. Colonel Stewart...Brad's boss. He wanted to have a word with you and I thought I'd take the kids out for a walk, okay?"

Her jaw locked, a knot growing in her stomach the size of a soccer ball, she had noticed Knight's watery eyes and knew right off why Colonel Stewart was here. Forcing herself to act, to move, she nodded and gestured Jeb toward a metal folding chair, "Please sit down, Colonel." Fighting back tears, Kathy looked to Chaplain Knight, "Go ahead, Pastor...they need the exercise." She waited as they put on their coats, helping them with their boots and then slowly closed the door behind them. Turning around, braced against the door, she glared at Jeb, "He's dead." It wasn't a question.

Moments later, Jeb opened the door and stepped in to the hallway. He didn't have the courage to look back into the room, but quietly closed the door. Chaplain Knight was waiting outside in the hallway and after patting Jeb on the shoulder, he entered the room to comfort Kathy. The kids were with a neighbor, they'd be told shortly. Through the closed door he could hear Kathy's grief stricken cries and was glad he thought of locating Pastor Knight to accompany him. It was one of Brad's requests if the mission turned sour, to have Chaplain Knight there when Kathy was notified and Jeb honored it. There was one more death notification visit to make to the wife of Wayne Roberts, Jeb zipped his parka up and walked out of the barracks. He stared straight ahead, ignoring the confused expressions of the people in the hallway and focused his attention on the task ahead.

A COMING STORM

16 - SIGNS AND WONDERS

"I watched as he opened the sixth seal. There was a great earthquake. The sun turned black like sackcloth made of goat hair, the whole moon turned blood red..."

Revelations 6:12 NIV

For the first time in nearly four months, the sky miraculously opened up over the Northern Hemisphere to reveal radiant stars and a nearly full moon. It also provided a frightening view of the Tariq-Leroy comet almost one quarter the size of the moon; its fiery tail stretched out behind it. Nearly everyone had their own ideas, rumors circulated faster than office gossip, but it seemed no one could offer up a plausible explanation of why the dark black clouds of ash and falling snow had simply disappeared in what seemed to be almost the blink of an eye. The ash clouds didn't move south or east or west; they just simply, completely disappeared; there one moment to darken skies and send ash downward with a pungent odor of sulfur and then gone the next. But few people were complaining. Once again they could admire the heavenly bodies and in truth, knowing the comet still had a ways to come helped quite a few of those close to near maniacal fears. People all over the globe were still nervous and jittery; panic still existed, but for the people in Southeast Asia they now knew they still had time to flee and for the people in Fort Greeley, Alaska, they still had a few days left to reinforce their defenses.

Tariq-Leroy, its tail visible to the naked eye, appeared to be passing by the earth and this offered some hope until those who were knowledgeable of such things, explained this was only an optical illusion having to do with orbital bodies. Tariq-Leroy was still on a collision course with Earth and there was nothing man could do to stop it.

Most everyone remembered the blockbuster movies where astronauts flew up to the oncoming rock and blew it up with buried nukes. But with the loss of the United States and the space programs of England and Russia closed down due to budget cuts, no one was flying to this rock. Impact was set for 19:39 hours or 7: 39 p.m., April 29th.

WESTERN CANADIAN ARMY PRISON CAMP, CALGARY, ALBERTA-CANADA - APRIL 14TH -1912 HOURS

The next strange event occurred at exactly 7 p.m., Alaska Time, when darkness enveloped the entire planet. Some thought God had covered the Earth with His two mighty hands or wrapped it in a thick black wool blanket. There were no stars, no sun; not even the comet could be seen. And once again, it happened in the blink of an eye and one frightened Canadian soldier was heard to say, "God flipped a light switch off, what's He got planned next?"

Private Archibald C. Albright, a frail young man of 18, suffered a traumatic episode in his younger years when an older brother locked him in a dark pantry for hours when their parents were away. This left Albright with a terrible fear of the dark and he always had a flashlight in his possession. Young Albright's chest tightened as he struggled to breathe. Before he could even grab his flashlight, he lost his footing as the world swirled around and he stumbled blindly into a barbed wire fence. Archie Albright dropped his rifle, a sudden reaction to having his face and hands pierced by steel barbs. In panic, he thrashed about in an attempt to break free from the wire's grasp. Screaming for help, thinking the world was ending and sickened by the taste of blood on his lips, he collapsed to the ground and lay whimpering like a small child with his bloody face cradled between trembling hands. It was how his mother often found him on the floor of the pantry; shaking and sobbing.

It was not only Archie. From all around camp, possibly the world, billions of terrified voices cried out in fearful anguish. Yet, there were some who understood the sign; these were the ones who remembered their Sunday school Bible scriptures of how God caused total darkness in the Last Days.

"Get up, Archie," a man's voice said.

Slowly, Archie lifted his head thinking it was his mother, but then remembered he was in the army. He winced when a bright light shone into his eyes and asked, "Is that you Zack?"

"Looks like you cut your face up, kid," Zack said, using a soiled handkerchief to wipe his young friend's face.

"Where's your flashlight?" Zack asked. Hoping to keep from getting cut himself, he helped Archie to his feet and cautiously pried his feet loose from several strands of barbed wire. He picked up the young man's rifle off the ground and made sure it was clear of ash and snow with a quick rub down.

With Zack's handkerchief, Archie carefully blotted his cheeks and forehead. It stung, but he bit down on his lower lip to keep from crying out like a child. When he checked the handkerchief for blood in the illumination of Zack's flashlight, Archie realized he wasn't nearly as hurt as he had first thought. He unclipped his flashlight from his web belt and after taking off his gloves, shined it at his hands, one at a time to check his wounds. When he found he had sustained only minor injuries, where the barbs had pierced his gloves, he aimed the flashlight around to get his bearings.

All around the encampment, hundreds of flashlights were being waved about and then he noticed how all the perimeter security lights, camp lights and vehicle lights were going back on again. First, there was only the cloud cover, then suddenly the stars and the moon, and then this eerie nothingness.

"Zack, what happened?" Archie asked. "All of a sudden everything went dark... It felt like the very air turned black, I couldn't even breathe for a moment."

"I know. We all felt it...But you don't look too bad for someone who tangled himself up in barbed wire. You might need a stitch or two, though. Good thing it wasn't razor wire or you'd be in slices right now."

"Should I go see the med-tent?"

"I'll get you relieved as soon as I can, kid, but right now you'd better get back to your post before Sgt. Bickers catches you. You know how he's a bit of a jerk about his posts and if he finds you screwing off, you'll end up pulling extra duties."

"But what happened, Zack? Where'd the moon go...and all the stars?" Archie's voice was weak and he was busy shining the flashlight toward the sky above.

"The comet's gone too."

"Sorry, kid, this is too weird for me," Zack said. "Maybe some kind of new weapon the boys from the East came up with. We're still here, so it didn't kill us." Zack made sure his young troop was okay before moving on to check on the next man; Private William Smedley. The young private was dancing around in panic and waiving his flashlight, yelling, "Corporal of the Guard...Corporal of the Guard!"

Idiot! Maybe I could shoot him an' blame it on an intruder. That Smedley will never make a soldier. The recruiters really scraped the bottom of the barrel this time...a real momma's boy...And they gave him a loaded rifle to boot.

Holding tight to his flashlight, Archie resumed walking his post with his rifle slung over his shoulder. Nervous, he glanced around the perimeter and felt reassured to see the big security lights illuminating the camp's perimeter and prison compound. Yet, even with man's illumination filling the area, he was still frightened by this catastrophic event. Whether a secret weapon or nature, he couldn't get over how heavy the air around him felt.

A COMING STORM

No sun, no moon...no stars... where'd it all go? This is really creepy, someone's gotta know something. Moon jus' don't turn off like that...And I feel like I'm breathing through a blanket of wool. Archie, nervous to the point of jitters, kept glancing around as he paced out his post. His heartbeat slowed from 120 thumps a minute to a reasonable 88 beats, but any strange sound sent it right back up again. *Mom told me about this...something about the day God blocked out the stars. She was a real Bible thumper, always worried about me... maybe I should have listened more.*

It took some doing, but Zack got Smedley calmed down, at least enough so he could continue to man his post and let Zack check on the others in his assigned area. He was frightened too, his mind asking a thousand questions about this strange occurrence and like Smedley, he would've liked to dance around in panic. But Zack was a corporal and corporals were expected to maintain themselves and he did his best to do so. Biting his lower lip and hiding his trembling right hand behind him, he walked between posts with a flashlight in his left hand to reassure his squad of sentries. "No, the world is not coming to an end," he repeated over and over. "Man your posts and quit acting like a bunch of frightened children. I'll get some coffee out here as soon as I can, but stay on your post!"

After checking in with Sgt. Bickers, Zack was back to relieve Archie to allow the young soldier the opportunity to have his wounds looked at by a field medic. "You'd better hurry back, Archie, I don't want to be here longer than I have to."

Zack began walking the post, back and forth along an eight foot section of wire fencing which consisted of chain link. On both sides of the fence were multiple strands of barbed wire supported by thick wooden 4x4- poles placed every 10 feet. Archie's sentry post covered exactly 12 poles, for 120 feet or roughly 40 strides. Zack turned and walked back to the starting point to find a very nervous Smedley waiting for him.

"Keep moving, kid! Standing around won't help and you've got a job to do," Zack ordered.

"Yes, Corporal." Sulking, Smedley turned around and marched off.

Inside the main camp, off duty Christian soldiers formed prayer circles. Hundreds of non-Christians watched and a few decided that the strange events meant it time to approach these men and women and inquire into this whole Christianity thing.

On the other side of the fence, Zack observed a large group of American prisoners, being held in confinement while they waited processing. From inside the enclosure, Zack began to hear singing; something he didn't expect from prisoners. Usually they just complained, shouted out curses and threats. But this group was different. It took him a moment to recognize the songs: *Hymns, they're singing hymns. Who are those people… and why are we holding them prisoner? This eerie darkness doesn't seem to frighten them… they actually seem excited by it… What do they know that I don't?*

Gradually, panic and chaos gives way to enforced army discipline as tough NCOs kept the younger enlisted troops from deserting posts. In a few cases they were forced to slap the face of a couple of young privates to get their attention. The two men had deserted their post for the confinement area and were chased down and wrestled to the ground by other soldiers. One of the deserters was a drafted older gentleman of 53 years, who was new to the Army and the other one was a three year veteran up for his Corporal stripe. Each man was marched off in handcuffs to the med-tent for a quick observation and later, placed in the stockade. Panic on one's post was not to be tolerated in the Canadian Army, but an understanding Commander would later release them after a couple of days in the stockade. Events such as this strange darkness went beyond a man's ability to show reserve and he was surprised he had only two deserters from the 18 guards.

But the confinement area wasn't the only effected area, hundreds of soldiers and civilians had panicked in the Calgary area. Three men and a woman were shot down during a wild melee which had broken out in a temporary servicemen's club. Within four hours, stockades were full of terrified servicemen and women. Even the Military Police, who guarded prisoners were fearful and the unexplainable heaviness of the air wasn't helping any. There were concerns a gas had been released by the OAP and hundreds of old fashioned gas masks were donned, but air sampler devices reported no toxins present.

While the officers were huddled around camp, conferring and conferring again, Zack stood Archie's post and listened to the singing from inside the confinement area. As the strength of those voices grew in volume, he began to relax as if someone or some strange force was comforting him. The more he listened and the more he thought about it, Zack looked to the dark heavens above and whispered into the night air, "God, did You cause this event? Are You trying to get our attention… well, I think it's working. I know I'm not a strong Christian, I've done my share and have led a sinful life, but Lord…all I can ask is that you forgive me of these sins and…and comfort these soldiers who work under me…they're a bunch of kids and they're scared…Amen."

INSIDE THE PRISONER COMPOUND – 30 MINUTES EARLIER

Taken into custody for illegally entering Canada, Pastor Woodway's band of Americans was escorted under heavy guard to Calgary. Here they were placed inside an enclosure temporarily, while Calgary Western Command Headquarters tried to figure out what to do with all these people.

Shortly after arrival, Pastor Woodway and Ed Sawyer were taken before Colonel Jonathan Oswood, Military Police Commander for the Calgary Zone and Captain Stephen Bisbain, Regimental Intelligence Officer. Colonel Oswood was a seasoned veteran, a former commando who fought in both Iraqi Wars in black operations, when no one thought Canadians Special Forces units were even involved. Later, as a Division Commander, he lost a hand in a brief skirmish with Quebec Freedom Fighters only moments after the Canadian Civil War erupted. Colonel Oswood was a solidly built man of short stature, with short light brownish gray hair and hazel eyes. He wore thick black glasses and walked with a slight limp from a second wound to his right leg. He used a handmade willow cane for stability. Rather than wear a prosthetic device for his missing hand, he used a leather fingerless glove to cover his scarred wrist.

Unlike Colonel Oswood, who was a humble and thoughtful man, Captain Bisbain was an extremely arrogant, forceful and intelligent young man from Victoria. Half white and half Haida Indian, he made no attempt to hide his anti-American feelings. He wore a regimental black beret that didn't quite fit on top his head over a buzz cut of black hair. Much taller than Colonel Oswood, Captain Bisbain stood nearly six foot, with drooped shoulders and very long arms and fingers. His waist was narrow enough to make any woman envious and his sinister looking eyes, almost coal black, could often intimidate a prisoner with his icy glare, or entrance a lady with a leering look.

Ed wasn't buying the man's glare and struggled to keep from grinning. He knew this Captain Bisbain was one of those people who should never wear a beret, as it made him resemble a grown man with his daughter's Girl Scout beret on. Finally, unable to keep it back, Ed's expressionless face broke into a big grin. Captain Bisbain, who had up till now kept his best wary gaze upon the two prisoners in front of him, was clearly offended by Ed's smile and his hard line gaze quickly transformed to a look of bitter hatred. Ed could read those eyes, knowing the Canadian officer was secretly wishing one of them might try to make a break for it, so he could shoot them in the back. In response to Captain Bisbain's beady eyes, Ed shook his head from side to side in disdain for the Canadian officer. This caused Captain Bisbain a high level of confusion, wondering if this American was capable of mind reading. Captain Bisbain simply wasn't aware of the many long hours Ed had spent in training and his thousands of interviews and interrogations. With far more experience sitting across the table in face offs with criminals and reluctant witnesses, Ed could read Captain Bisbain's body language and had no trouble reading the officer's cold dark eyes. In fact, he was hoping the Canadian was capable of reading Ed's body signs.

Colonel Oswood was sitting behind his large wooden desk; a gift from his men, which had been removed from a school principal's office. The Canadian flag was posted to his right and the Division colors to his left. They had taken possession of a large furniture store to be used as headquarters, so there was no shortage of chairs, recliners and beds. Upstairs, the large room had been sectioned off for the men and women on the staff to use as bedrooms.

Pastor Woodway and Ed Sawyer were sitting in two very fine wooden dining room chairs, while Captain Bisbain remained on his feet. Two very large MP's stood behind the prisoners, in the event they became troublesome. There was a chalkboard on one wall which displayed the command organizational chart. Another wall held a gold framed copy of a famous painting, where a beautiful 1760's era sailing ship fought against the elements. This was one of Colonel Oswood's favorites and he was fortunate to find it being displayed in the furniture store and borrowed it for his office. He needed something with color to decorate the former manager's office. With complete access to all the company's furniture, Colonel Oswood was known to have the most comfortable command center, conference room and bedrooms. He only lacked in the kitchen department and had to walk over to the army's kitchen for his chow.

Captain Bisbain pointed his right finger at first Ed and then Pastor, using it like a sword as he grilled the two men. "You're telling us, that all these people with you are part of some church group?" His voice was dripping with sarcasm. "That they're following you because of some ludicrous vision of yours? Let's get real, gentlemen!"

"I see you're not a religious man, Captain," Pastor Woodway said. He turned to Colonel Oswood and asked, "Sir, do you really think we're some invading force? With women and children...You actually believe we've come north to conquer Canada?"

Colonel Oswood looked down at the table top and struggled to stifle a grin. He knew this party was not an invasion force, but they did interest him and he was actually enjoying this interview watching the contemptuous Captain Bisbain put in his place by this Mr. Ed Sawyer.

"You say you're headed for Fairbanks, but are you aware that Fairbanks and most of northern Alaska and parts of south-central Alaska are currently occupied by OAP forces?" Colonel Oswood asked.

Upon hearing this, Ed sprang up from his chair and before Captain Bisbain could draw his pistol, two large military policemen grabbed Ed by his shoulders and forced him back down. Ignoring the MPs, Ed glared at Colonel Oswood until Pastor was able to quiet him down.

"Ed, this isn't helping us any," Pastor said.

"What about survivors? There had to be survivors?" Ed asked, fighting to keep his emotion in check.

"Please excuse us, Colonel, but Ed's family lives in Fairbanks." Pastor had his hand on Ed's arm; the MPs released their hold with a nod from Colonel Oswood.

Colonel Oswood was dressed in Canadian Army fatigues, the black eagles of his rank displayed on his collar points, the patches of his command on his shoulders but he was not armed. "My apologies, Gentlemen, I was not aware of your connection with Fairbanks. Had I known, I would have first told you that the city was completely evacuated before the OAP moved in. With the exception of Anchorage, most Alaskans are now in Delta Junction or Fort Greeley." Colonel Oswood looked into Ed's eyes with a glint of compassion, "I'm sure your family is safe, but at this moment the situation in Alaska doesn't appear very favorable." Colonel Oswood stood up, walked around to the front of his desk and casually leaned back against the desk top. This move seemed to upset Captain Bisbain, who briefly glared at his Colonel with wide cold eyes and then forced his lips to tighten even more as he turned his attention to the two prisoners.

"We know the OAP has a large force moving in from Siberia, but we've also learned they have a naval invasion task force preparing to hit Anchorage even as we speak. If that city falls, the Alaska Defense Force in Fort Greeley will be facing two fronts; one from the northwest and one from the southwest." Colonel Oswood looked to Pastor Woodway, "Can you please explain to me why you think God has called you and your followers to Alaska at a time like this? What do you expect to accomplish there, Pastor?"

Pastor Woodway gazed deeply into Colonel Oswood's eyes, "Colonel Oswood, God provided the vision and we have faithfully followed his direction. During our long arduous journey we have overcome many great obstacles and have witnessed many miracles to bring us this far. It is not for me to ask why He wants us there. Only that we obey Him and go."

Pastor eye's seemed to light up almost unnaturally, making Captain Bisbain very edgy. He began to suspect this man was a witch doctor attempting to hypnotize them and he quickly spoke up to break the spell, "Colonel, you can't believe this mumbo jumbo jazz. They're probably spies for Quebec waiting to get behind our lines..." Captain Bisbain didn't get to finish.

"That will be enough, Captain," Colonel Oswood ordered.

"Sir?" Captain Bisbain was breaking with military decorum standing only inches from the Colonel's face, "These people are dangerous, sir. You must let me..." Again Bisbain was silenced by a curt hand gesture in front of his face.

"Captain, you are dismissed," Oswood ordered in a commanding tone. When Captain Bisbain hesitated, Colonel Oswood added, "Now!"

Captain Bisbain reluctantly left, closing the door behind him. Pastor began to tell Colonel Oswood their whole story - how God had protected them in Phoenix while the men, women and children prepared for the journey. "No one touched us...we were protected and I can only believe it was by the Lord's angels," Pastor said.

"They walked right by our supplies, our vehicles and never gave us notice. It was as if an invisible barrier protected us from these gangs of looters," Ed added.

Colonel Oswood nodded and brought one hand to his chin, presenting a look of understanding. "And you now sit here in front of me, convinced it was God Almighty who did this?" Colonel Oswood had a calm voice, his eyes darted back and forth between the two men seated before him and the two MP's standing behind them.

"God brought us out," Pastor replied. "The Great I AM led us out of that burning city and for a reason only He knows, delivered us into your hands."

Colonel Oswood sat in silence for a moment and then spoke to the two MPs, "Please leave us alone...wait outside."

"Yes, sir," the senior MP said. They took up position in the outer room.

Leaning against a far wall in the secretary's office and hoping to speak to the Colonel again, Captain Bisbain looked up from cleaning his nails when the two MPs came through the door. He expected to see the two prisoners come out and when they did not, he approached the MP's, "What are you doing out here without the prisoners, Corporal?"

"Captain, the Colonel ordered us to take up position out here."

"Well, you'd better let me back inside then. The Colonel shouldn't be left alone with those two...people." He began to step toward the entryway, but the MP who stood to the right of the door put his hand up, "Sorry, Captain. Until the Colonel advises us otherwise, you were ordered to leave his office."

Captain Bisbain glared at the Corporal, "I'll have your stripes for this, Corporal."

"Yes, sir, you may get them, but only if Colonel Oswood wants to give them to you. Now please move along, Captain."

Colonel Oswood shook his head and returned to his chair behind the desk, "I imagine Captain Bisbain will probably forward a report to higher command reporting that I've lost my mind. But, I've decided to forward your travel request on to General Howard-Wright, my Supreme Commander. Right now he's in Alaska supervising our recent alliance with the Alaska Defense Forces. I'm sure he'll consider your request thoughtfully. In the meantime, I ask that you keep your people on their best behavior. I'd hate to have some sort of incident..." Suddenly everything went pitch black and everyone in the room froze. At first Colonel Oswood thought he had passed out, but within moments the camp lights began to come back on and then the ceiling lights inside the office blinked once and were back on. The two MP's rushed back into his office and stopped behind the prisoners with guns drawn when everyone heard the shouts and screams from outside.

"Stand easy," Colonel Oswood ordered. "Holster your weapons." He walked to the nearby window and through frosted glass looked outside and saw only pitch darkness above. Somehow, the lights in the sky had simply turned off again, but this time it was different from when the layer of volcanic clouds had hidden the stars. Colonel Oswood, with his MP escort stopped first to don arctic clothing then led the two prisoners outside to view the overhead sky. After a moment of silence, he turned to Pastor Woodway, "I imagine, Pastor, being a follower of the One True God and a man of vision, you do remember your scripture concerning the foretelling of such an event?"

As camp lights continued to come on all around them, dozens of frightened troops ran around in panic, others screaming out orders. Ed, who felt the strange weight in the night's cold air, turned to see Pastor Woodway smiling as he gazed upward toward the heavens.

"Yes, Colonel...it is one of the signs He foretold would happen. We are close."

Inside a large canvas mess tent, heated by four large cast iron wood stoves, over 180 people gathered together to lift their voices in praise. Having not much of a singing voice, Ed sat back in a metal folding chair with a blanket draped over his legs, and listened to his young wife sing. He glanced over to the entrance and saw a distraught Captain Bisbain standing there with a mixed expression of disdain and fear. Ed tried to sympathize with the man, *tell you what, Bisbain, if it hadn't been for Pastor teaching us Revelations, I'd be one rattled dude myself.*

"What are you thinking, my dear husband?" Kira asked after they finished the song.

"Just wondering about my brother an' his family... It's been a long time since we saw each other... My nephew was a new born cub and now they

430

have a daughter too. But between you an' I, honey, what I'm really struggling with is why us?"

"Why us?" Kira was confused.

"Why did Pastor receive his vision? Why did God spare us in Phoenix and safeguard us on our way north? What's His purpose?" Ed looked uncomfortable asking these questions, he didn't want the Lord to think he doubted His wisdom.

"These are big questions, my troubled husband. Did you ask Pastor?"

"Oh yeah and he replied in that King James voice of his, 'We are to follow where the Good Lord leads. And that God will reveal at His appointed time.'"

"Sounds like we need to wait then," Kira said. She had grown a lot in these last two months. From a pampered teenager she had transformed into a wife and a strong believer in the Lord's ways, while all around her most of the world had gone insane. When she saw the serious expression on her husband's face, Kira decided to deal with it by plumping down on his lap and snuggling. With a loud grunt, his stern expression changed to one of surprise and then broke into a grin as he wrapped his arms around her. They held each other close, while others around them began to sing another song of praise.

Off to one side of the tent, Pastor Woodway, Joey and Cindy Roberts prayed together while Larry and Kathy O' Brian stood a few feet away holding hands and whispering to each other of their love for one another like a couple of young adults attending a church camp meeting. Shaking his head in frustration, Captain Bisbain stomped off and nearly plowed over an enlisted woman. Without apology, he uttered a few unkind words and hurried off, while two soldiers quickly moved in to pick up their female comrade, and dusted snow off her.

COLONEL OSWOOD'S OFFICE

"Colonel, this came in priority," a young female 2nd lieutenant from communications said. She handed Colonel Oswood the message and he read it loud, "To All Commands - Eastern Army attacking with major force. Forward observers along our lines estimate strength eight Divisions of armor and supporting infantry. No report of air support at this time. We are in full retreat. Request reinforcements be sent immediately." Signed by Colonel Jared Austin, Commander, 11th Infantry Division.

Colonel Oswood studied the message for a moment and then said, "Colonel Austin is not one to panic easy. However, I am surprised Quebec was able to get rolling so quickly with a force that size. We can barely see in this muck and they launch another offensive..." Oswood walked over to a large map pinned on the wall beside the organizational chart showing all of North America, from Mexico to the Arctic Ocean. Colonel Oswood turned to his assistant, "Officer's Call in 15 minutes. Advise the Operations Officer to have security doubled on all posts."

"Yes, sir."

Though Colonel Oswood's primary responsibility was command of all Military Police, General Howard-Wright had left him in Command of all Calgary forces. His current authority, prompted by the existing emergency, also granted him the provisional rank of Brigadier General and with it all duties as temporary Post Commander for the Calgary Zone. Though Colonel Oswood was entitled to wear a General's star, he preferred to wear the silver eagles of a full colonel. He did this for the simple reason he believed he had earned the Colonel's eagle the hard way and would wait for his General's star when it came as either a battlefield promotion for heroic actions or his name posted on the regular promotion roster for his time in service and agreed upon by the current political power. When the troops under him learned of his decision, their respect and fondness for the old man greatly increased.

ADF COMMAND-DELTA JUNCTION

General Saunders' newest aide, Lt. Jane Kelly, was in awe of her boss and her shy manner showed it when she stepped into General Saunders' office to announce General Howard-Wright's arrival, "Sir, General Howard-Wright is requesting to see you."

"Jane, unless I'm in a meeting, General Howard-Wright has an open door in this building. Please show him in."

Walking past Jane, General Howard-Wright stepped in and shook hands with his old friend, "Good evening, Glenn."

"More like the stroke of midnight if you ask me," General Saunders complained. He gestured to an ice covered window and the pitch blackness outside. As morning came and weather experts predicted sunrise for 9:23 a.m., the sky maintained complete darkness with not even a shimmer of daylight on the horizon.

"The Word of God speaks of a time when He would blot out the sun. I imagine that is exactly what is occurring over Israel too," General Howard-Wright said.

"You're probably right," General Saunders said, "Any answers to your prayers that I should know about?"

"Only that He is God," General Howard-Wright replied in all seriousness. "But, I have no answers for you, my friend."

A moment later, Jane walked in with a coffee service for the two generals. Handing a full cup to both men, each prepared exactly the way they liked; she left and quietly closed the door behind her.

A graduate of ROTC at University of Alaska/Anchorage, Jane, a tall slender brunette with green eyes was a star basketball player and upon graduation, she had enlisted in the U.S. Army with a chosen career field in Command/Administrative. She dreamed of one day wearing colonel's eagles like her father, Colonel Alan Kelly, who was reported missing in action and presumed dead. Her father was stationed at NORAD when the OAP missiles flew; she knew this base would have been a priority target for the OAP. Growing up a dependent brat, her mother dead when she was only 12, Jane knew about security and protection of her general. She kept a loaded .45 Colt 1911 Automatic pistol in a Velcro holster attached beneath her desk and knew how to use it. She had qualified as an expert on the Division pistol range.

"What's on your mind?" General Saunders asked, as he tasted his coffee. He usually made his own, but was getting used to his new aide's pampering.

"Status reports on our enemy. My Intel section is playing catch up; one moment I have them preparing for action against the east and now I pull them out of Calgary with orders to prepare against the OAP. I can understand their grumbling, but as a famous soldier once said, 'War is Hell'."

"You're still a poet." Saunders said in jest. Then he got down to business. "There's nothing knew on Fairbanks. However, we believe OAP support elements are moving in from the Seward Peninsula and there's a rumor of them carrying needed supplies... this could also mean heavy artillery. The spearhead has to be low on tank ammo and fuel, especially after the job they did in Fairbanks." General Saunders set his coffee cup down on his desk and picked up an Intel brief prepared by Lt. Col. Stewart. "Colonel Stewart believes their morale factor is weighing heavily against them, a plus for us. India 5 reported acts of cannibalism being carried out and that's got to do something to the troops."

"Morale doesn't stop tanks!" Howard-Wright grumbled. He apologized. "Sorry, Glenn...I haven't had much sleep since we left Calgary. You know I'm a believer, but this strange darkness and the heaviness in the air has me on edge and to make matters worse, Quebec is launching another offensive in Ontario. We're spread very thin right now and they're going to take a lot of ground."

"I've lost a whole division in Wales... I understand all too well." General Saunders walked over to a map hanging from the wall. "Our last report has the OAP surface fleet sitting at the mouth of Cook Inlet. We've lost all communications with the oil rigs and we now suspect they're waiting for a plus tide before attempting to bring their ships up the inlet." He glanced at a paper in his hand, "Volunteers have flown south by helicopter and used heavy demolition to bring down a series of avalanches along the Seward Highway, mostly between Mile posts 74 and 112. Though the quake and following tsunami transformed Turnagain Arm into into an End of the World disaster zone, their heavy tanks can probably still make it across by staying close to the mountainsides. This should block most of their ground forces from coming up from the Kenai Peninsula by foot or in trucks. Ice on Turnagain Arm is also simply too risky to cross on foot and thankfully, we never built a bridge across the Turnagain Arm. So, until they hit the damaged harbors and docks, and torn up tide flats of South Anchorage, with their main landing force, I'd say we're at a brief standstill for now with their Southern Invasion Force."

"I cannot understand why they're waiting." General Howard-Wright said. "Cook Inlet is deep enough to allow most of their vessels to proceed north. They could use this continual darkness as a natural ally to strike at our beach defenses and weaken them. Then they can bring up their heavier ships with the next plus tide." General Howard-Wright studied a wall map of Alaska; principally the Cook Inlet and was silent for a moment.

Sitting at his desk, General Saunders gestured toward the door with his right hand and said, "My think tank...my Intel Section...suspects this unnatural darkness has them shaken up pretty bad too. I'm not sure how many Christians are in their army, or Bible scholars, but this new wrinkle has probably scared them silly." General Saunders picked up his Bible, "You and I both know who caused this darkness; it was foretold right here in the Book of Revelations." General Saunders laid his Bible back down and looked at his friend, "Though I have to admit, I was beginning to have some doubts on how this was going to turn out, but not now. We're on God's timetable...I only wish I knew what the rest of His agenda was."

"I can imagine there are a lot of frightened people out there," General Howard-Wright said, as he pointed outside. "When the clouds cleared and a millions stars sparkled overhead, a breath of life renewed my command. But then the sky suddenly turned off and my soldiers began to panic. It took good officers and dedicated NCOs to hold them in line. Fortunately, the majority of my command is Christian and the chaplains are out among the force counseling and leading services." General Howard-Wright glanced at Glenn's Bible, "Strange, I've read Revelations 6:12 over and over throughout my life and for some reason I always expected some eclipse...nothing like this. The moon over us simply blinked off and I imagine the sun has done the same thing. God is truly an amazing...God!"

"Your troops getting taken care of?" General Saunders asked, as he refocused on military needs.

"You have quite a friendly bunch here actually." General Howard-Wright's expression changed, which gave General Saunders the idea his friend had forgotten something. Sure enough, General Howard-Wright reached into his upper right breast pocket and removed a piece of paper, "Oh, by the way, I received a rather unusual message from Calgary. Some of my armor units along the southern border picked up a group of Americans... attempting to make it to Alaska. Colonel Oswood, I promoted to Brigadier General before I left, finds them a very interesting group. There are 180 or so men, women and children of mixed racial background - all Christians. They reportedly fled Phoenix as the city was burning down around them and traveled north to Canada. They spoke of run-ins with motorcycle gangs, battling bandits, miraculous escapes from radiation contamination and various other assorted thrills." General Howard-Wright folded the paper, put it back in his pocket and sipped his coffee, enjoying the warmth as it passed over his lips. "Colonel Oswood is a good man, Glenn. I made him Military Police Regimental Commanding Officer and left him in temporary Command of all forces in Calgary. He was Special Forces; saw action in Iraq, Afghanistan and was severely wounded in our first battles with the East. According to my information he is quite taken with this Pastor Woodway, the apparent leader of this strange group... strangest of all, Colonel Oswood says he believes in Woodway's vision...that's the word Oswood used...vision... to make this highly dangerous journey. Colonel Oswood has asked me to pass them through to the Alaskan border."

General Saunders nodded several times as he took this all in, "To think, the whole country swarming with bands of survivalists, self-appointed governments, mobs and gangsters striking out everywhere and against everyone, these 200 Christians make it through to Canada from Phoenix, Arizona. Not to mention bypassing the hot zones... it is hard to believe." General Saunders looked down at his Bible, "Unless, God was truly leading them and protecting them... A small exodus if you may."

"I'll get word to Calgary, have these people added to one of our convoys if you like?"

"In a few days we'll be engaged in the largest battle ever fought in North America. I think you and I agree, only through the good Lord's grace will we survive. As to why 200 people would make a difference, I will leave that to God. We have to remember, His Word says very little of what occurs outside Israel in those last few days."

General Howard-Wright put his coffee cup down and said, "Personally, I would like to meet this Pastor Woodway. Maybe he can shed some light on the shape of the United States and my southern border region." He stood, shook hands with General Saunders and left the office and stopped briefly to thank Jane for the coffee as he walked by and pulled on his arctic gear.

ON THE RIVER BLUFF, 8 MILES WEST OF DELTA JUNCTION

Jerking back the frost covered tent flap, Lt. Scott Radley scurried inside to keep the cold out and closed the flap behind him. Lt. Owenby, surprised by Scott's entrance, glared at his second-in-command with rifle aimed in his hands until he identified the intruder. Lowering his rifle, he went back to warming his hands over a small fire and in a tone intended to display his foul mood, said, "If you're selling Girl Scout cookies, Avon products, Tupperware or even encyclopedias, I already gave my orders to Miss America over there." Owenby gestured to his platoon sergeant, SSgt. Lansky.

Sitting on the other side of the tent, SSgt. Roscoe Lansky ignored the lieutenant's lame attempt at humor, nodded once to Scott and continued sharpening his 15 inch Bowie knife. He moved his foot to a folded green wool blanket on top of a white snow cover to keep the blanket dry in the snow. Though the two platoons had brought tents, sleeping bags, an extra supply of white camouflage shells and army blankets, they had no flooring for the tents and only the white camouflage shells protected them from the frozen ground. As the tents warmed up, snow and ice melted and would've left the soldiers in mud if not for these shells, but still there were puddles. Soldiers voiced their complaints first to individual squad leaders, then to platoon sergeants and from there, complaints about camp conditions made their way to Lieutenant's Owenby and Radley. Their replies were always the same and SSgt. Lansky thought Lt. Radley's was the best, "Tell 'em this ain't no Vacation Bible School for little kiddies who need their noses wiped. They can toughen up and live with it, or walk back to Delta Junction as a damn deserter."

Regarded as a top NCO, Roscoe Lansky had spent eight years in the U.S. Marines, as a Force Recon sniper with 19 confirmed kills before receiving a Bad Conduct Discharge and six months in the stockade for assaulting an officer. He could read the signs and knew what the world's situation was shaping up too. Moving to Alaska in 2009, he attempted to join the Alaska Army National Guard, however, his prior record prevented him from being accepted. Later, when NATO fell apart and the United Nations collapsed, Roscoe requested and obtained an appointment with the newly appointed General Saunders. Roscoe described the circumstances involving his conviction by court martial and requested the General investigate his claim. He stressed to the General his desire to serve and never denying what he did, explained the reason behind his actions.

Letting Roscoe know he'd get back to him as time allowed, General Saunders called in some favors and learned that a young arrogant captain led his company into an ambush during the Iraqi War in 2003. While attempting to flee and abandon his company, Sgt. Lansky decked him with a hard right cross and turned the captain over to the medics. His quick action prevented the company from being overrun and many of the men from being killed or taken prisoner. Unfortunately, the young captain was the son of a U.S. Senator and a former Marine general officer. The captain would later resign his commission to pursue a career in politics, but not until after the court martial of Roscoe had taken place. As with all too many military court cases, Roscoe's army defense attorney, a newly commissioned 2nd lieutenant with only two other court-martial's behind him, talked Roscoe into a plea bargain. Roscoe accepted the Special Court Martial decision of six months confinement with hard labor and Bad Conduct Discharge, rather than a General Court Martial with a possibility of life imprisonment and a Dishonorable Discharge.

Three weeks later and four days after the Christmas Day attack; Roscoe received an appointment to the newly formed ADF with the rank of sergeant. Shortly afterward, he was promoted to staff sergeant and assigned as platoon NCO for Lt. Owenby.

Roscoe, all of 44, was considered by his young soldiers to be a bit of an old grunt. A knife scar from an Iraqi bayonet marred his left jawbone and two AK-47s bullets had left scars on his left shoulder. At 5'9" and 170 pounds, he was built solid; Lt. Owenby often referred to him as an old fashioned lean mean fighting machine. With the attack on Alaska immanent, Roscoe had shaved his head and several of his men had followed suit. He carried a confidence about him that reassured his troops and they either respected him or feared him, but often both.

By the light of a small campfire built in the center of the tent with smoke vented out through a small whole cut out by Roscoe, a weary Scott sat cross-legged holding a plastic coffee mug in his gloved hands and admired the gleaming edge on Roscoe's knife. According to Lt. Owenby, the knife was carried by Roscoe's grandfather when the then 19 year-old Marine was island hopping the Pacific in WWII. It was then passed on to his father, a Marine Recon grunt, who had served during the latter part of the Vietnam War. With the noticeable wear, Scott could only imagine how many times that knife had been sharpened in the nearly a decade of use. *I'd sure hate to get stuck with that Arkansas toothpick.*

Making room for Scott to have a place around the fire, Roscoe accidentally kicked SSgt. Joshua Howard's leg.

"Hey! Watch your feet...I sure don't need any more bruises than I already got."

"Sorry," Roscoe said as he spit coffee grounds into the fire and returned to his sharpening.

Scott's new platoon NCO was a direct opposite to Roscoe. SSgt. Joshua Howard had worked as a salesman in a Fairbanks gun store before his assignment to ADF and Scott had remembered him from the few times Scott had bought ammo at the store. Howard was a member of the Alaska Army National Guard and spent his weekends at the guard armory cleaning weapons and over the years had worked his way up to staff sergeant. Under Scott's brief tutorship, Howard learned what being an NCO meant in the real army and took to it like a natural. A tall lanky fellow of 6'4", with reddish brown hair and a drooping moustache he was extremely proud of, Howard had hazel colored eyes, a pronounced Adam's apple, long thin legs and the biggest feet Scott had ever seen. The Alaska Army National Guard had to special order Howard's footwear, size 20 EEEE. Howard was known more often as *"Ichabod Crane"*, referring to the Walt Disney cartoon character in the Legend of Sleepy Hollow.

The two platoons, made up of 66 men and women sat in moist white camouflaged tents and arctic survival shelters on a tall steep bluff overlooking the Richardson Highway. They had been sent out as a heavily reinforced listening post to watch for the OAP's advance.

"See anything, Lieutenant...any stars or maybe some flying saucers?" Howard asked Scott.

"Not a single point of light or even one of your little green men, sergeant. Weirdest thing I've ever seen. If it wasn't for our orders to stay concealed, I'd order up some illumination flares just to settle the troops down." Scott pulled his gloves off and held his palms before the flame. A rock outcropping protected them from showing a heat signature to the west where the OAP were coming from. No one expected the enemy would be up flying in this strange darkness.

"You want first or second shift?" Lt. Owenby asked Scott.

"If you're asking, Joshua an' I'll take second shift."

"Okay." Lt. Owenby nodded at Roscoe, who responded by sheathing his knife and pulling out the logbook. Lt. Owenby made sure everything was logged from duty assignments to suggestions from the troops and even hourly radio checks with Delta Junction.

0224 HOURS- APRIL 15th

"Look!" Private John Sands hollered from his sentry post. "There's something in the sky." In his excitement he completely forgot about security procedures.

"Keep your voice down, Sands," Scott ordered in a low voice. He was already outside with his flashlight illuminating the pathway in the snow hurrying to Sands' position on top of the bluff.

"Sorry, sir...but look, Lieutenant, I can see the moon...At least I think it's the moon." Sands pointed off to the southeast over the distant Alaska Mountain Range. No one talked for a moment as they stared in bewilderment at the sight before them. High above the mountains to the southeast was the moon, but unlike any moon they had ever seen before. The moon, full in size, was blood red.

CANADIAN ARMY MILITARY POLICE PRISON CAMP-CALGARY

Pastor Woodway and Ed Sawyer were summoned to Colonel Oswood's office by a very nervous MP Corporal Jefferson of Ontario. As the three of them walked together, they couldn't help but notice that everyone's eyes were on the red moon. People were scared, for far too many things had happened in such a short time and with no explanation. Oh, the Christians offered up explanations and there were some of the troops who listened, but there were still others who scoffed at the whole Biblical thing and blamed it on an OAP secret weapon. Men and women of different religions blurted out that this was foretold in Hindu, Buddhist or Muslim faiths, but their voices fell silent after a while. An eerie silence hung over headquarters when Pastor and Ed entered Colonel Oswood's office. Ed noted that several of the admin clerks and various MP's smiled as they walked through the old furniture store.

"Have a seat please." Colonel Oswood gestured both men toward the same two dining room chairs positioned before his desk. "Pastor Woodway, I have good and bad news." Colonel Oswood stopped talking when an admin clerk came in with a wheeled service tray of hot coffee and tea. "Please, help yourself, gentlemen," Colonel Oswood offered.

Ed filled a Styrofoam cup with coffee, as Pastor selected tea; both men were visibly thankful for Colonel Oswood's hospitality.

"Now then, I'm happy to inform you that your convoy has been granted a green light for travel through Western Canada and on to Alaska. Military authorities at the border are expecting you and I have you scheduled to join one of our convoys moving equipment and men to Alaska tonight. I imagine you'll be there in approximately three days."

"Praise God!" Pastor exclaimed.

Ed was happy, but then remembered Colonel Oswood mentioning some bad news, "Okay, Colonel, drop the other shoe while you've got us smiling and full of hot liquid." Ed stirred sugar into his coffee and thanked the clerk.

"Our forces are currently under attack on two fronts. The Eastern Army - the Army of Quebec - has launched a new offensive against our force in central Ontario. Our army is in full retreat at the moment attempting to reorganize before we lose all of Ontario." Colonel Oswood walked from behind his desk and stood before the two men. He stretched out both hands to signify the two fronts, "On our other front, we have allied ourselves with Alaska against the OAP. With the addition of the southern fleet outside of Anchorage, we estimate they out number us at better than 20-1 in combat troops." He dropped his hands. "At this moment, that OAP invasion fleet is entering Cook Inlet and we've learned they have secured the Kenai Peninsula as a base of operations. We expect an all-out attack against Anchorage sometime after dawn...that is if we have another dawn."

"Is that all the bad news, Colonel?" Pastor asked. He sipped the hot tea slowly; English Breakfast Blend and a favorite of his.

"My God, man, do you understand what I've just said?" Colonel Oswood raised his voice, "You're taking your people right into a ground war! One you have little chance of surviving."

"Yes, I understand you, sir. But you also must understand me, Colonel... I'm not taking my people anywhere. We're only following where the Good Lord leads us. I am not the shepherd, only another lamb in His great flock." Pastor set his tea down after taking a last sip. "Thank you, Colonel for your kindness and concern. Will there be anything else?"

"I've said my official piece, but personally, I wish I was going with you."

Pastor stood and offered his hand, "Thank you again for your hospitality, Colonel."

"One other thing, Pastor, please keep your civilians out of my hair until you leave. Your vehicles are being topped off and returned to you along with your weapons. But, those weapons are to remain unloaded unless the convoy commander grants you permission to load them. Is that understood, gentlemen?"

"No problem, Colonel," Ed said. "I'll keep our folks in line and promise you that all weapons will be kept unloaded while we remain in Canadian territory or the convoy commander requires our assistance."

"I wish you a safe journey, gentlemen." Colonel Oswood shook hands with Ed and a second time with Pastor. Before they left his office, Colonel Oswood spoke up, "I must admit, Pastor, I cannot understand why our Lord would bring your people to Alaska. But, I sure don't want to be the one to stand in His way."

Pastor studied Colonel Oswood for a moment while Ed stood by the door. "Colonel, I sense you are going east," Pastor said. His statement surprised Colonel Oswood.

"Can you tell me where you heard that?" Colonel Oswood asked.

Pastor grinned and said, "God spoke into my heart, Colonel. He values you and your commitment to Him and your men."

Colonel Oswood was speechless for a moment, but surprised himself by actually sharing his secret orders. "Yes, you're right. I am to assume command of an ill equipped understaffed armored division and drive east at all possible speed. Within the week I will be engaging the enemy at my eastern borders, probably somewhere near Winnipeg… I hope. It's a shame, Pastor, to think of Canadians fighting against each other… much as your own civil war and such a bloody waste."

"We will pray for you and the men and women you lead into battle, Colonel." Pastor stepped forward, laid both of his hands on Colonel Oswood's shoulders and quietly prayed over the man, who had bowed his head and closed his eyes. Afterward, Pastor and Colonel Oswood hugged one another and then both Pastor and Ed left the room.

THE CANADIAN ARMY CONVOY TO ALASKA

At 0430 hours, an Army convoy traveling at 45 to 50 mph moved out with a lengthy single file caravan of 241 vehicles. The trucks were hauling medical supplies, crates of ammo and miscellaneous automotive parts, 55 gallon drums of fuel and boxes of rations, radio equipment and hundreds of extremely nervous troops. The convoy was protected by 43 armored personnel carriers; each carrying a Browning .50 caliber machinegun and a 7 member rifle squad. Colonel Oswood also sent along 25 low to the ground M1-51 jeeps armed with M-60 machineguns for added support. Tanks couldn't go because they traveled too slow for this convoy and were moving up at their own pace to reinforce Fort Greeley.

At the rear of the convoy came the Americans in their bizarre mixture of vehicles. They were on their way to Alaska traveling under the protection of the Western Canadian Army. For the first time in weeks, members of the American convoy felt safe.

THE DEEP WATERS OF COOK INLET, ANCHORAGE, ALASKA - APRIL 18 0500 HOURS

Far off the rocky ice packed beaches of South Anchorage, The Teeth of the Dragon, a massive black and gray battleship, much larger then the USS New Jersey, opened fire on the city. Bellowing fire burst forth from new massive 20 inch guns. The ship was supported by several escort cruisers and destroyers, who launched rockets against the city and cruise missiles against Elmendorf and Fort Richardson. Some of the cruise missiles overflew the bases and impacted communities north of Anchorage - Eagle River, Palmer and Wasilla. The OAP attack on South Central Alaska had begun with a thunderous bombardment on Alaska's largest city and surrounding areas.

For hours, General Wilcox's ADF's Southern Wing flew combat sorties against the OAP fleet, only to be fought off by an overwhelming number of OAP fighters coming in from carriers moored off Kodiak Island and airports in King Salmon and Kenai.

During the initial bombardment of the city, the red moon returned to normal and to the east a new day's sun began to rise and bathe the town in a glorious bright golden dawn.

For a single day, the gallant, outnumbered defenders of Anchorage seemed to hold the OAP forces at bay. But the battleship's gigantic rounds, each equal in power to a 500 pound bomb or more, rained down upon the northern parts of the city and reduced skyscrapers and famous landmarks to rubble. What the successive earthquakes hadn't accomplished, the bombardment completed. Buildings badly damaged in the quakes, toppled or broke apart with tremors created by explosions. Subdivisions were afire with huge craters left where houses had once stood. The University of Alaska/Anchorage and Providence Hospital were hit hard with two cruise missiles, but both had been evacuated and only concrete, sheet rock, steel, wood and glass were reduced to waste. Fires were spreading out of control and the bellowing smoke made it appear the entire city was ablaze. Smaller OAP vessels breached the defensive obstacles so painstakingly put in place and platoon sized units of elite combat troops began to storm ashore. Meanwhile, enemy aircraft pounded beach bunkers with relentless precession to knock out antiaircraft guns and heavier fortifications before the Alaskans could return fire against the advancing enemy.

Two miles south of the city, north of the last oil platform, four super tankers stood ready in the deep waters of Cook Inlet to unload enemy landing craft. When the order was given, the great bow doors of the supertankers slowly open to admit a great wave of frothy white ocean water before allowing landing craft the ability to float free. Although they had practiced the drills countless times, soldiers and sailors are thrown into the sea and dozens are crushed between the various craft. Once the waters settled and the doors fully opened, thousands of soldiers, fresh from many weeks at sea rushed to load assigned craft on multiple levels inside the tankers. Attack helicopters: Chinese, American left-overs in Vietnam, and captured Russian; lifted off the decks of the great tankers and proceed north to protect the landing craft.

ADF artillery batteries struck out against the invasion fleet and an ADF 155mm cannon scored a direct hit on the bridge of an enemy destroyer and a second round exploded in its' magazine. The resulting fiery blast lifted the broken ship out of the sea, its hull ruptured and seconds later it splashed back down to sink with almost all hands on board going to a cold watery grave. Waves from the dying vessel spread out to swamp many smaller boats and landing craft. In water of 34 to 40 degrees, a man does not last very long. A few survivors from a swamped attack boat crawled up on floating ice in an attempt to survive, but soaked in frigid seawater, they quickly succumbed to hypothermia.

Ship's cannons fought a duel with the ADF's limited number of shore batteries, exchanging hundreds of rounds over the next hour - a sight that hadn't been seen since the Pacific island invasions of WWII. Snow and ice bunkers on the beaches, built by freezing men and women to stand against the enemy, simply vanished in flaming explosions. Great craters spotted the beaches creating a moonscape, while behind this three mile stretch of battered shoreline, a once proud city burned to the ground.

A pair of F-15 Eagles broke through the protective ring of OAP fighters to make an attack on one of the supertankers. 1st Lieutenant Chad Leaders, a 30 year old native born Alaskan from Moose Pass in his 3rd year with the Alaska Air National Guard assigned to the ADF, suffered battle damage to his right wing when he dove on the nearest supertanker and raked the ship's bridge with 20mm fire. Coming in right behind him, 1st Lieutenant Mark Milligan, a full time church pastor and part time US Air Force reservist, also from Moose Pass, dropped two 500 pound bombs directly forward of the ship's super structure and into a large open bay. The explosion rocked the tanker and a fiery blast erupted from the hold. On fire from the crippling air attack, the disabled supertanker was forced to run aground on the northwestern shore. Unable to believe it was happening, the 71 year old Captain of the vessel stood frozen in shock, while his wounded First Mate issued orders to abandon ship. The bomb had miraculously struck a landing craft loaded with 105 mm ammo for the OAP's dreadnaughts. The power of the explosion set fires across the entire hold, forcing men and women to abandon their landing craft and dive into the waters to escape the flames. Disabled landing craft fell from rails they were perched on and secondary explosions filled the hold until the ship would no longer answer to the bridge. Thousands of troops and sailors jumped from the ship into the freezing waters and more than half perished in the icy cold without ever reaching shore.

A third ADF F-15, the pilot mortally wounded; his Eagle nearing flame-out, delivered a lethal blow, when Captain Paul Holmes of Fairbanks, dropped his remaining two 250 lb. bombs on top the Dragon's huge forward turret. A massive explosion rocked the great ship, sending debris skyward as the turret was blown completely off its deck mount. Shrapnel broke out nearly all the glass of the battle bridge, killing three senior officers and wounding the captain. Over a hundred tons of thick steel plummeted into the sea, along with Captain Holmes' Eagle, which resulted in a 20 foot wave that capsized two full landing craft and slammed a third one into the side of a burning destroyer. Left with only three mounted turrets, the massive battleship, under orders of the ship's executive officer, began to maneuver the Dragon into a new fighting position giving Anchorage a brief respite from heavy shelling.

Overhead, the sky filled with a 3rd squadron of F-15 Eagles, who engaged OAP attack fighters. When a loser fell, winners barely had time to catch a breath before they engaged the next opponent. Aces, quickly born in this battle, lost their lives the same day in a fiery death. The ADF Air Force, no matter how gallant and brave, was losing the air battle due to the enemy's sheer numbers.

The majority of the OAP attack helicopter forces splashed down through the efforts of Eagle pilots, but there were more of these attack birds on board the remaining tankers. These were held in reserve for the drive north, along with several fighter wings and ground support birds. The OAP southern invasion fleet had committed only a third of its' Air Force for the initial attack, knowing it would need the majority of aircraft for the drive north to Interior Alaska. The OAP were using captured Russian MIG aircraft, US F-4 Phantom Aircraft left to the Vietnamese as far back as 1973, Japanese Defense Force F-15 Eagles and Thai F-16 Talons, French high tech fighters purchased by the Chinese and various smaller aircraft seized when the OAP marched through Southeast and Central Asia. Once the airfields at Galena, Dutch Harbor, Kenai and King Salmon were ready, several squadrons of fighters were either brought in by aircraft carrier or shuttled south from Siberia for the invasion of Anchorage.

The ADF estimated the OAP had better than 20-1 in number of fighter aircraft over the ADF's Air Force. The warlords had no qualm in sending their pilots out in apparent suicide missions if it would help win the war for North America.

When able to do so, ADF pilots either dove to the treetops or climbed to escape to Elmendorf Base for fuel and rearming. The runway at Elmendorf had taken too many hits, the hangers were on fire and ADF Command-Anchorage had to look to other possible landing fields in Wasilla and Palmer; though the strips were considered too short for the fighters to safely land on. Two F-15 Eagles had run off the end of the runway at Wasilla and resulting damage kept them from returning to the battle.

General Saunders was forced to give the order for all fighters to break off the attack and make an attempt to return to Fort Greeley. He couldn't afford to lose any more birds, especially to lack of fuel or running out of ammo. He didn't believe in suicidal attacks and had stressed that to his pilots more than once. He also could not risk putting their few precious KC-135 tankers into the air at this time, although Colonel Wilcox went so far as to demand he do so. General Saunders knew the tankers would be an easy target for the enemy fighters and that he would need them when the OAP made its attack on For Greeley. He didn't have the aircraft to keep a flight of Eagles to guard the tankers and his air cap consisted of two F-35's. He sent what he could - two undermanned squadrons of F-15s from Elmendorf. They didn't have the fuel required to go nose to nose with the OAP Air Force for the defense of Anchorage. A well-guarded convoy of 15 ton Kenworth and Peterbuilt semi-tractors were pulling loaded double tanks from Anchorage to Fort Greeley for the war operation yet to come. They were also expecting a hundred-thousand gallons of avgas from the Canadians, but it hadn't arrived yet.

Similar to the Battle of Britain in the early days of World War II, weary pilots become locked into a series of deadly duels. By late in the day, Colonel Wilcox's two squadrons of 37 Eagles were reduced to 11 flyable aircraft. Several ADF and OAP fighters had crashed into the city and three OAP SU-27 fighters had made fiery dives into Cook Inlet.

Enemy hovercraft, capable of carrying a platoon sized force armed with 20mm cannon, sailed over the ice pack to unload men and equipment further up the Inlet. It was their assignment to attack the city's business center from the west. Best comparable to the attack on Omaha Beach on June 6, 1944, it was D-Day all over again. Hundreds of landing craft surged ashore, knocking out bunkers and other shore emplacements with heavy fire. General Hightower, wearing two of General Saunder's first silver stars, had no other choice but to issue the order for a full retreat. He shook his head in dismay as he watched larger landing craft coming ashore with light and medium tanks aboard.

Hearing the roar of a jet directly overhead, General Hightower glanced up to see an ADF F-15 making a non-approved suicide run directly into the open doors of the 2nd supertanker. The resulting fireball erupted out through the great doors and engulfed more than 20 landing craft loaded with troops. The selfless act had set the ship afire.

To save as many of his command as possible, General Hightower committed a reserve brigade of mixed Bradley Fighting Machines and Strikers to cover the massive retreat. A fierce battle was fought on the beaches by the reserve force, attempting to give the beach forces time to withdraw, but sheer numbers carried the battle. One by one, General

Hightower's armored cavalry was destroyed with the help of off shore fire. Escaping into the suburbs on any available vehicle, ADF defenders headed for secondary positions. From there, a second brigade of older model APC 113's and APC 706's armored personnel carriers, each one armed with either an M-60 or .50 caliber machinegun, moved out from underground parking garages to surprise the enemy. They eventually engaged the OAP front line force along Diamond Blvd, in the southern part of the city. Over the next several hours, a ferocious battle was fought from house to house, business to business. The huge Diamond Mall and other shopping centers were turned into blackened rubble and fiery debris. Neither command gave way, nor was there any quarter given, as the fighting left city streets littered with burning armor and dead infantry.

OAP MIG 34 fighters from King Salmon arrived to support forward units, strafing targets and occasionally killing their own men in an attempt to stop the ADF retreat. Under a smoke filled sky, ADF's last remaining armored unit; nine APC 113s and approximately 200 soldiers both Militia and ADF made a courageous stand on 15th Avenue and fell before the awesome might brought against them. With OAP controlling the air, General Wilcox ordered his few surviving F-15's and seven F-22 Raptors to Fort Greeley and in a fateful decision, committed his newly arrived A-10's to save remaining troops fleeing the city for Eagle River. A sacrifice had to be made and 12 Warthogs with volunteer crewmen were called upon to make it. To save the lives of several thousand troops, General Wilcox had no other choice but to ask his Warthog pilots to volunteer; 10 men and 2 women ran for the readied 12 birds.

General Hightower waved to an A-10 pilot as the ugly thing buzzed over the top of his head, its thundering roar nearly knocking him to the ground. The pilot engaged a row of OAP tanks with 30mm cannon fire, using depleted uranium shells to destroy three OAP light tanks before circling for a second round.

Retreating toward 6th Avenue, Hightower helped a young man operate a .50 caliber machinegun against a diving MIG-29. Standing amid the rubble that had once been his city, he hoped they might have scored a hit as the aircraft buzzed by. But neither of them saw any smoke. Spotting a major he recognized, General Hightower yelled, "Have you seen General McConnell?"

"He's dead!" The major yelled back. A former Anchorage Police Officer, who boasted of his bravery to whoever would listen, kept running north without offering to assist the General. Shrugging General McConnell's death off for the moment with a shake of his head and a tight closing of his eyes, knowing this was no time to grieve, he opened his eyes and ordered his troops to keep falling back. He yelled to the young soldier he'd been assisting, "Bring that gun with you...I'll get you some help." Behind him, the Warthogs engaged the landing force like a pack of half crazed wolves. Still, the outcome was assured before they even took off from Elmendorf, having to use Tarmac for runway. One by one the A-10 pilots lost the air battle to superior faster fighter aircraft flown by the OAP. The A-10 hadn't been built to go nose to nose with an enemy, it had been constructed for ground support and killing tanks. They gave a good accounting of themselves taking out 19 medium and six heavy dreadnaughts, 11 armored personnel carriers, hundreds of infantry, and a slow moving F-4 Phantom Jet. These pilots had given up their lives to provide time for their army to withdrawal from the city.

With carnage strewn across the beaches, boats and landing craft sinking in the inlet, or disabled on the shoreline ice pack, enemy battalions continued to storm ashore over the bodies of fallen comrades and enemy. No prisoners were taken; if an ADF soldier was found they were executed on the spot. Overhead, OAP fighters searched for targets of opportunity until low fuel sent them back to their airfields.

Some retreating ADF-Militia forces sped north to take up positions along 5th Avenue in upper downtown Anchorage. With enemy attack helicopters and some remaining fighters overhead, General Hightower knew escape was impossible. *We'd be sitting ducks on the highway. No, from here we'll make our last stand. Hopefully we'll be buying more time for those of us who got out of the city and our forces in Greeley.*

Along 5th Avenue, inside stores, offices and two motels in the city's core, retreating Alaskans prepared for a final battle against an oncoming horde of enemy troops. An armada of light and heavy tanks and armored personnel carriers carried an advance element forward to engage these few surviving Alaskans. Though intense as grenades and machinegun fire met tank rounds and 20mm cannon fire, the battle was clearly one sided and all but over within seven hours. Most of the ADF-Militia command was either killed or wounded; their bodies littered snow covered streets or left to rot inside buildings. Pockets of resistance, a squad or a platoon hidden here or there, ambushed enemy scout units. But they were crushed within moments by heavy shelling from the dreadnaughts and merciless air cover, or even newly installed beach batteries.

General Hightower wounded and winded; his uniform in tatters and suffering from frostbite to his face, ears, feet and hands, commanded an undermanned platoon of women and men. They hid inside the ruins of the 5th Avenue Mall with a few stragglers; three women from a militia artillery battery, a civilian EMT-2 medic, two admin supply clerks from General Hightower's headquarters and two military policemen. One of the MPs was wounded in the arm; the EMT treated it and placed it in a sling. Remaining silent, they listened as OAP heavy tanks approached from the south and began a barrage against the upper levels of the mall. Pondering his options, General Hightower spotted blood dripping on his right arm from a minor head wound. He stood on the fifth step of an inoperative escalator and looked over his last pitiful command. Frightened and weary, 38 souls grouped below him and he saw them as extremely brave men and women. In their ranks he knew he had 28 privates, 1 corporal and a very young looking 2nd lieutenant. There were also a few stragglers and they all looked to him for guidance. *Now I know how Davy Crockett felt at the Alamo.*

"I'm sorry, I wish there was more I could do, but there appears to be a lot more of them against the few of us. We can't go any further and they've got us nearly surrounded by the sounds of things. Speaking only for myself, I refuse to surrender and be executed like some cowering dog. But I won't make the decision for you. Each and every one of you must decide." General Hightower glanced around the mall, hoping for some sort of miracle.

"I say let's make it quick…let's take out as many of them as we can, General," the wounded MP suggested.

Several others nodded in agreement and General Hightower asked, "How about it, people? Do we go out there like lions or remain here like chickens to be slaughtered?" He looked into the frightened bloodshot eyes of dirty faced kids. But only a few nodded back favorably in response - not the reaction he'd hoped for.

"Okay, you make up your minds. But I'm going out." General Hightower held up his rifle, ejected a nearly empty magazine and slapped in a full one. His gloves gone, fingers and tips of his ears badly frostbitten, his lips cracked and bloody, he looked to these people, some in even rougher shape, and said with all the enthusiasm he could muster, "You've done a great job. I'm extremely proud of every one of you and all those we've left behind." General Hightower headed upstairs to the 2nd floor exit of the mall. Rifle in one hand and a grenade in the other, he was committed. Slowly, one by one, the group quietly followed. Choked with emotion, the General could only smile through those cracked lips. He wiped his eyes with the back of his numb left hand as every one of them joined him for this one last fight. Before initiating his attack, General Hightower, a devout Southern Baptist Deacon, bowed his head and offered up a short prayer for the protection of his beloved Alaska and asked God to welcome these brave men and women around him.

Outside the main mall exit stood an idling medium tank. The sergeant manning the turret gun was taken by surprise when a small force charged out of the mall to engage him and his small force of supporting infantry. Before he could swing his turret gun around, General Hightower ignored the pains of his wounds and jumped up on the tank, shot the sergeant through the chest and dropped his grenade down through the turret.

A valiant stand against superior numbers, these men and women briefly brought the OAP spearhead to a halt. For a little over 14 minutes an intense firefight between outmatched forces was fought on a short snow covered stretch of 5th Avenue that ended when the last soldier, a woman, wounded by rifle fire, bleeding from her face and head, charged an OAP machinegun with a hand grenade. She got her gun, but was riddled by automatic fire from an approaching tank.

After the lead element continued on, an OAP Intelligence officer, Major Nun from Northern China, knelt beside the body of General Hightower. Going through his soiled uniform for papers or anything of value, Major Nun noticed the silver chain around Hightower's neck. He held the General's dog tags and a small silver cross in his hand and he studied it momentarily. Making sure he was not seen nor heard, Major Nun whispered in Cantonese, "You fought bravely, my brother. May I die as well as you have when my time comes, and may our Lord Jesus Christ hold you now in His great arms."

Keeping his Christian beliefs secret, along with hundreds of other soldiers from underground Christian churches in China, Major Nun was one of many forced into the OAP Army by threat to family or at the point of a bayonet. A graduate of Washington State University, Major Nun was selected for Intelligence work. Still, he was under constant scrutiny by his commanders because of his schooling in the USA. Returning the cross and making sure to hide it under Hightower's uniform, Major Nun went on to locate the other officer killed in the fight. Back in Beijing, Major Nun's wife and children were under protective custody; a nice word for an OAP prison camp. This was to ensure Major Nun's and other married officer's complete loyalty for the war across North America.

In less than 24 hours the Battle for Anchorage was over. OAP Army and Naval forces slept in Alaska's largest city. A massive search would be underway for food storage areas and by mid-morning, OAP advance elements would be passing through Palmer on the way to a fateful meeting with ADF forces at Fort Greeley.

They found little in the way of food which concerned some of the soldiers but they still had the rations brought with them from the ships. Unfortunately, this would only last them another three days and then the soldiers of the Southern Invasion Army would begin to starve.

A few skirmishes were fought along the highway as locals made a stand for their homes and property, but no one was able to prevent the OAP from moving forward. Outside of Eagle River, one dozen Musk Oxen were discovered at a privately owned farm and a big barbecue was given. But with more than 100,000 troops, there was very little for each man to have and most of it was consumed by the officers and members of the Black Dragons.

OAP naval forces had another scare; some personnel on board were showing symptoms of radiation sickness from having sailed through Gulf of Alaska hot zones in their attempt to surprise the ADF. They were sailing into Prince William Sound where the Exxon Valdez Supertanker went aground in 1988 and shocked the world when over a million gallons of crude oil leaked into the ocean. Another OAP landing force assaulted the beaches at Cordova and then Valdez. They met no resistance, except for some barking dogs. The great oil refineries were abandoned and the city empty. The Division Commander positioned his occupation force in the city while the vessels were left at anchor. A large armored force moved north over Thompson Pass to rendezvous with the Anchorage OAP army in Glennallen. The Anchorage invasion force had twice the distance to travel; approximately 180 miles from Palmer to Glennallen.

The temperature was -15°, the air superbly clean. A local force of 307Militiamen and women waited nervously in Glennallen to slow down the advancing OAP Army and give the people in Fort Greeley more time to prepare for the last battle.

17 - HOGS TO THE RESCUE

" 'See, I lay a stone in Zion, a chosen and precious capstone, and the one who trusts in Him will never be put to shame.' Now to you who believe, this stone is precious. But to those who do not believe,' The stone the builders rejected has become the capstone,' and, a stone the causes men to stumble and a rock that makes them fall.'"

1 Peter 2:6-8 NIV

THE CURRENT WORLD SITUATION - APRIL 19

While the world was locked in global warfare, Southeast Asia and Southern China was abandoned by multitudes escaping the Tariq-Leroy Comet's point of impact. Finding any means of transportation or simply fleeing by foot, the lion's share head for the sea to find a boat for a fast escape to Australia under OAP control, the African continent or South America. Northern Africa was overcrowded with fleeing Muslims, trying to escape radioactive zones created by the nuclear exchange between Pakistan and India while further south, war broke out across the land with tribal conflicts. In South America, racial warfare divided the continent once more and millions died from the rapidly spreading plague. Those involved in the mass exodus for the South China Sea or the Indian Ocean faced large scale riots in every seaport. Border check points were overwhelmed, roadblocks completely overrun; very little could be done as governments lost control of the situation. Not even OAP troops could stop the population from running for their lives. Many of the OAP troops abandoned their posts and joined the dash for safety.

Arriving in massive vehicle convoys thousands of terrified Thais, Laotians and Cambodians, Burmese, Vietnamese and Southern Chinese attempted to force their way onto boats and cargos ships in port. As the numbers of fleeing Orientals grew, gun battles broke out and ship captains raced to leave port before their vessels were swamped with the sheer weight of frightened people. Behind them, they left docks and harbor businesses in smoldering ruins. Every roadway was jammed to a standstill with simply too much vehicle traffic. Cars and buses broke down or ran out of gas and the people abandoned them to block another stretch of road. All escape routes were blocked.

Trains ceased running when mobs overwhelmed stations and engines were damaged in riots. One locomotive escaped with 23 passengers cars filled to standing room only; people sitting side by side on car roofs. Before it could go 68 miles, a large trestle over a deep gorge was burned to the ground by fanatic cult followers who felt mankind needed to be sacrificed for its many sins and the train was forced to stop.

In the closing days, fear had become the overriding force and common sense and logic left standing beside the roadway with the crippled and dead. Even in OAP held Southeast Asia, cities were besieged by rioters or under the control of vicious street gangs, who had taken advantage of the opportunity to prey upon those too weak to escape the coming calamity. Gangs, mostly youth, felt the old adage of "let's live for today, for tomorrow we die" was the code to live by.

There was no military or police to assist the populace; all government agencies had already taken flight. Millions of people had nothing more than their own feet, maybe a bicycle or handcart, or a hand-made raft to use. Some of these first arrivals ended up paying a staggering price to secure a standing room only spot on one of the many large cargo ships and barges that were able to get underway. The captains of these vessels, each out to make a quick buck in the midst of this calamity, allowed their holds to be filled with frightened people shoving them together like cattle. These transporters of human cargo resembled the slave ships of the 1800's where there was barely enough room to breathe, much less to survive in blistering airless holds.

Loyal border police in India had tried to remain on posts to protect their lands from the invading onslaught, but undermanned, they were quickly overwhelmed when a flood of thousands broke through barriers of barbed wire and wood. Indian soldiers were rushed in to stop the masses, but these men of compassion are unwilling to fire upon women and children and the tide of people surged westward.

There wasn't enough food for everyone and clean drinking water was extremely scarce. Soon the countryside was covered with the rotting bodies of those who had starved to death or killed for possessions. Many fell from drinking contaminated water as a massive cholera epidemic spread across the land and in some cases the plague struck hard and whole communities were decimated. The massive army of refugees met continual rioting from township to township, with panic spreading faster than a classroom rumor; a countrywide panic left its people in a landscape of blood.

In the Middle East, Israel, one of the few democracies still standing, found itself surrounded on land by the armed forces of Egypt, Iraq and Iran, Jordan, Syria and Turkey. But Turkey and Iran's mighty armies had been greatly reduced in size by the nuclear war between India and Pakistan. A huge OAP Army was bound eastward through the Mediterranean Sea and a smaller naval task force headed for the Suez Canal.

Jerusalem Radio reported the OAP had engaged Afghan and Arabian ground forces to the north driving both armies from their positions, while defeating their air forces with an overwhelming number of victories.

The ocean to the west of Israel had begun to resemble a gigantic shipyard with the arrival of the great ships of the New European Empire task force. Like vultures, they laid siege to Israel's shoreline and the Emperor's representative's issued demands to God's chosen people to surrender. He not only desired access through Israel to the great oil fields of the Middle East, he also demanded the Jewish Nation pay homage to him when he sat upon a golden throne in Jerusalem while his army defeated the OAP on the plains of Iraq.

Ironically, each foreign army dared the other to attack Israel first, waiting to see who would risk the wrath of Israel's God or her nuclear arsenal. None of them would make the first move and before long, border battles and long standing tribal feuds broke out between the Islamic Armies.

From the west, NEE sea planes reported the presence of an OAP naval task force in the Mediterranean Sea. Within hours, OAP and NEE carrier planes launched a sea attack against one another's Battle Fleet. The largest naval battle in man's history was fought south of the Island of Sicily. The toll to the OAP Navy was staggering: five OAP aircraft carriers, seven missile cruisers, 17destroyers, 21 support vessels and troop carriers destroyed or sunk. Three supertankers were disabled with two of them beached and 59 carrier aircraft and 41 attack helicopters lost. An estimated 109,000 OAP men and women were reported killed or wounded in the two day sea battle.

The NEE suffered a similar fate: three aircraft carriers, nine missile cruisers and ten troop carriers sunk; one battleship disabled and sinking, and 12 destroyers and 27 support vessels disabled or sunk; 68 carrier based aircraft and 14 attack and rescue helicopters lost. More than 100,000 men and women were lost or wounded in the epic battle. Finally, too crippled to continue, both battle fleets withdrew.

Egypt sent its huge army to the border with Israel and combined forces of Sudan, Chad and Libya attacked Egypt's ports leaving major cities in devastation. A vengeful enemy pounded Egypt's great pyramids to the sand with constant artillery fire and cruise missiles purchased from a dying Soviet Union.

In the Western Hemisphere, the United States, Mexico and Central America remained under a continuous onslaught of radioactive storms. The number of survivors was unknown as all commercial communication had ceased.

Across the globe, millions succumbed to the deadly Plague, leaving a blanket of death in its wake. The Plague had taken a third of the world's population.

Miraculously revived from a near fatal head wound at the hands of a paid assassin, the new Emperor of Europe had personally led his New European Republican Empire ground forces away from a ravaged Western Russia. In a surprising move, he sent his armor and infantry units southeast toward the Mediterranean Sea only to find his great fleet in shambles. Flown out to his new flagship, he orders his surviving to cease their withdrawal He sent them eastward to bombard Israel's shores. Soon, unless the OAP moved in to block him and continue their sea battle, he planned to storm the beaches of Israel with 100,000 troops. Once he had defeated the Jewish coastal forces, he would enter Jerusalem and declare himself Ruler of Mankind in a newly built temple.

Meanwhile, on the shores of Israel, Jewish coastal units had suffered so many casualties positions were now manned by reserve forces. OAP naval guns had given a good account of themselves before the sea battle with the NEE. With the return of the NEE fleet, the first ships to arrive were up against Israeli shore batteries. Hour upon hour, warships and aircraft pound the Israeli beach defenses, lighting up the horizon with fiery explosions. Israeli anti-aircraft guns filled the air with explosive charges, while beach artillery took a heavy toll on the NEE destroyers.

Palestinian military and civilian forces fled homes and land to avoid being caught between Israel and all its enemies.

In the Ontario Province of Canada, a battle of heavy and light armor was underway between former countrymen, as Eastern and Western Canada clashed in civil war. Keeping his commitment to Alaska, General Howard-Wright split his forces to alley himself with General Saunders' ADF and simultaneously, drove back the Army of Quebec. With forces weakened by the alliance, General Howard-Wright's army was losing ground to the Quebec force and soon began to withdraw from Ontario to a second line of defense.

As the Four Horsemen of the Apocalypse rode hard, mankind was doing its level best to destroy the world. Weather systems were running amok; in areas of the Atlantic and Pacific great tempests brought forth winds reaching over 250 mph driving forth towering waves. Seas reached 70 feet and more to pound beaches and drive wrecked ships and debris far inland. Great quakes of 9.7 magnitude and worse continued to shake continents around the world causing massive destruction to parts of Africa and South America, Russia, China and the Korean Peninsula. The great skyscrapers of

Hong Kong fell into the sea, when a great quake rocked the region. Volcanoes erupted around the Pacific Rim sending huge volumes of volcanic lava into coastal communities and heavy black ash into the skies preventing hundreds of aircraft from flying. Tokyo was completely decimated by fires set by anarchists. Nearly all radio services were off the air, the few survivors gave attention to the strange occurrences being reported by short wave radio and word of mouth from Israel.

Foretold in the Book of Revelation, God's Word was being revealed daily. Over a period of nearly 1260 days, two witnesses stood at the Temple wall in Jerusalem and brought forth miraculous healings and prophesied. Once protected from attacking Muslim fanatics by an invisible force, they were shockingly gunned down on the 1260th day by Muslim clerics. For three days the bodies lay untouched, left as an example to others. The Word of God foretold these two mighty heralds of God would rise up on the third day and strike terror into the hearts of the oppressors.

The people of Alaska knew nothing of world events or what was occurring just outside their borders. They only knew that two of their largest cities were in shambles occupied by OAP forces and nearly half the population, some 150,000 men, women and children, had been killed.

From Delta Junction and Fort Greeley they prepared for a final battle against the evil forces of the OAP. With the help of the Western Canadian Army the people of Alaska awaited the enemy as he approached like a vicious storm.

ON THE BLUFF OVER THE RICHARDSON HIGHWAY - APRIL 19TH -1323 HOURS

The ever growing Tariq-Leroy comet shared an early afternoon sky with a fiery late April sun. Alaska was beginning to see evidence of a seasonal change; daytime temperatures slowly rose above freezing and snow began to melt on the open fields. For the soldiers on the bluff this meant wet tents, muddy ground during the day and iced over pathways at night. In Alaska, this was commonly referred to as break up.

Pulling the 1200 to 1800 hour watch, Scott was summoned by word of mouth down the northwest side of the bluff to a forward listening post manned by PFC Joseph Ohtapieu of Tanana and PFC Bobby Redner of Delta Junction. PFC Ohtapieu had reported hearing metallic like sounds coming from somewhere to the west. "Honest, Lieutenant, I really thought I heard something. Would you listen for a minute, please?" PFC Ohtapieu pointed to PFC Redner, "He thinks I'm losing it!"

"What about you?" Scott asked PFC Redner. "You didn't hear anything at all?"

"No, sir," PFC Redner glanced over at PFC Ohtapieu, "...but I'm not too great at hearin' things, sir... especially with my earflaps down." PFC Redner confessed this uneasily, but then added, "I got great eyes though, Lieutenant."

Scott shook his lowered head, fighting to suppress a smile. "Okay sure, we've got nothing else to do. Might as well take a moment and see if we all hear it again." Scott got himself comfortable in the camouflaged foxhole, placing his rifle across his legs and remained silent with two very nervous and very cold soldiers. "Redner, this time keep your earflaps up."

Redner glanced over at his partner, giving him a hard look that said, 'You'd better be right, buddy, or I'm gonna make you regret it for embarrassing me in front of the lieutenant.'

Working a security post on the steep bluff 20 feet above the Richardson Highway, PFC Ohtapieu and PFC Redner were required to stay on 100% alert in the event an OAP scout unit might suddenly appear. As the long hours crept by, boredom and anticipation were key factors in helping a man be anxious to hear something when it wasn't there or see something moving in the shadows. After a few moments of hearing nothing but the wind, Scott began to get restless and whispered to the two PFCs, "You're sure it sounded like a tank?" Scott looked into PFC Ohtapieu's eyes and added, "You know those big monsters the OAP have make enough noise to be heard from a mile away."

"All I heard was a metallic like sound, sir," PFC Ohtapieu whispered back then suddenly popped his head up, but all he could see was the curve in the highway ahead which vanished behind yet another ridgeline of black spruce buried under heavy snow.

"Okay, no sense waiting here." Scott unlimbered himself and climbed out of the hole. "We'll take a patrol out and take a look see." *Besides, these guys could use a patrol to stay sharp. Too much sittin' around is takin' their edge off an' that ain't smart soldiering.* Pulling a handheld radio out of his coat pocket, Scott contacted Lt. Owenby, "Lima Poppa Two to Lima Poppa One...Over."

"Say again...Over." Lt. Owenby's sleepy voice replied.

"This is Lima Poppa Two, how do you read now...Over?" Scott asked.

"Clear... Go ahead...Over." Lt. Owenby rubbed sleep from his eyes. Nearly to the point of dropping off, he had grabbed the radio before Roscoe could.

"Sorry to wake you. One of my guys heard something up ahead and I'd like to take a squad out to investigate. I'll leave Howard here to ramrod...Over."

"Sounds good, but keep me posted...Out." Lt. Owenby grabbed the logbook and made a quick entry with a well chewed pencil. He would let Roscoe return to his snores, but with Scott off the bluff, he would need to stay awake in the event Scott found himself in trouble.

"You two stay alert, while I assemble a squad," Scott ordered. "Then we'll take a walk down there and have a gander."

"Sir, could two others hold the fort down so we could go with you?" PFC Redner asked.

"Sure." Scott left and a few moments later returned with an eight man rifle squad. One short and stocky man carried an M-60 machinegun and another soldier, a female PFC, carried a LAW. No sense taking any chances if there is a tank out there. Scott pointed to the last two men in line and told them to replace PFC Ohtapieu and PFC Redner.

"All right, let's take it real slow going down the hill single file and try to be quiet...no talking," Scott whispered in an authoritative voice. "We'll cross the road, keeping five yard intervals...that's 15 feet for those of you who didn't finish high school, and maintain absolute... complete silence." *By the looks in a couple of faces I'd better tone down my vocabulary and keep it simple. Maybe some of these guys didn't finish high school?*

Reaching the Richardson Highway, squad members struggled across the slippery ice and the crunchy snow along the embankments. On the opposite side they traversed a five foot embankment of hard packed ice and stepped into waist high deep snow. Without snowshoes it was quite the exercise as they trudged ahead to enter the tree line. Scott wished he could have stayed on the road, but they made too good a target if the enemy was actually up ahead. He was forced to leave his side of the road since the bluff dropped off sharply over a 100 foot drop and left only a steep embankment for the next 100 yards or more.

Corporal Isaac Plumber, an Athabascan Indian from Salcha, was on point staying at least 20 yards in front of Scott. He was forced to break trail through deep snow and numerous times had fallen when he lost his footing. 55 minutes later, after they'd covered about two thirds of a mile, Scott found Corporal Plumber kneeling behind a thick spruce tree, with his fist raised halfway up in the air.

Contact! Thought Scott and he immediately moved his rifle's selector switch from safe to semi-automatic fire. Holding the squad back with a hand signal, Scott moved up through Corporal Plumber's foot path in a low crouch. When he reached Corporal Plumber's side, the man held a single finger in front of his mouth advising Scott to remain quiet. He then pointed the same finger through a thick growth of dead trees toward the road and gave Scott a brief wave indicating 'follow me'. The corporal began crawling across the snow, sinking seven to eight inches as he worked his way forward. Scott let him go about five yards and slithered through the snow behind him. Corporal Plumber moved silently, demonstrating his 16 years of moose and bear hunting throughout the Alaskan Interior and sneaking out of his home when his wife was having one of her temper tantrums. They stayed behind the larger spruce trees nearest the highway's embankment, which had been cleared by ADF snowplows. He stopped behind a large tree and waited for Scott to catch up. When Scott reached his side, Corporal Plumber cautiously pointed out five enemy armored personnel carriers painted in OAP Black and Green. Each was armed with a heavy machinegun and parked on the far side of the road end to end facing west toward Delta Junction. To the rear of the lead vehicle, Scott could see 10 men involved in a heated discussion in a language neither Scott nor Corporal Plumber understood.

Grabbing Corporal Plumber by the shoulder, Scott gestured back to where the rest of the squad waited. The two of them cautiously belly crawled from tree to tree along their path until they were out of sight of the roadway. Then staying in a low crouch, they hurriedly made their way over the last 20 yards. Scott startled PFC Ohtapieu when he suddenly grabbed him by the arm and whispered, "You got good ears, kid." Then he turned to PFC Redner and in a low voice, "You better get yourself a hearing aid." He addressed the rest of the squad in the same low voice, "We've got company out there... Follow me back to the bluff." He looked at Corporal Plumber, "As a reward for a good job, you've got point again."

Back on the bluff, Scott had the M-60 gunner from his squad set his gun up in PFC Ohtapieu and PFC Redner's foxhole and ordered the rest of the men to dig in. "I'll get you a couple of LAW tubes, but hang loose. No firing unless you get the order or one of those APCs is crawling up your chest. You got that?"

"Yes, sir," they answered in unison.

"Don't worry too much, guys. I doubt the OAP is going to attack with only five APCs," Scott said. With a nod and look of approval, he climbed back up the hill, but along the way he slipped backwards several times on the melting snow and struggled to keep his weapon out of the slimy mud.

Reaching company headquarters; which was two arctic shelters tied together and held up by tree thick branches Scott went inside to brief Lt. Owenby, Howard and Roscoe on what they discovered down the road. "Ah don't understand their lingo, but it sounded like they was sure havin' an argument about somethin'. Ah think we can probably take 'em out if we set the ambush up right."

"You didn't see any other men?" Roscoe asked. "With five APC there should've been at least a platoon of infantry."

"I didn't stay around long enough to take a head count, but ah'm bettin' the others must've been in the vehicles to keep warm. They was lettin' their officers and non-coms argue it out on who had the right directions. Maybe the long road from Fairbanks was too much for them and they've gotten lost on our one single highway?" Scott was trying to make light of the moment to ease the tension, but it wasn't working.

Lt. Owenby grabbed his notebook and turned to the page he used for supplies, "We've got a total of 4 LAW tubes, 4 M-60 machineguns, 4 SAW weapons and only one AT4. We also have a good supply of Claymore mines and two crates of grenades."

"Plus, we don't know what may be behind those carriers," SSgt Lanky said. Lt. Owenby didn't like it and even Scott had to agree.

Scott now wished he had taken a better look to see if there might have been tanks or a larger force hidden in the woods. He knew the whole OAP Army was eventually coming up this narrow roadway with all their armor and this position here on the bluff was feeling less comfortable by the moment. Working as an NCO in the MPs was a far cry from bein' an officer in the infantry.

"I'm going to give Battalion a call, run it by them," Lt. Owenby said. "They'll want to know about this contact anyway." He gave Roscoe the nod to get on the radio, before turning back to his second in command, "Scott, take what demolitions we have and set up some kind of welcoming party for our visitors."

"You got it!"

Once contact was made with the Battalion, Lt. Owenby accepted the field radio microphone from Roscoe and started talking with Delta Junction. A few moments later, Lt. Owenby found Scott down on the highway demonstrating the proper installation of a Claymore mine to several of his men.

"Scott," Lt. Owenby said in a raised voice.

Hearing his name, Scott turned toward Lt. Owenby and addressed his troops, "Don't touch this, it'll ruin your whole day an' we'll be shorthanded. I'll be back in a moment." Scott walked up to the Lt.

"Battalion passed the buck up to Division and they called back. We've been tasked with another recon to establish whether or not we're looking at only the five APC's or a major advance element. You want it, or I could send Roscoe this time?"

"No. Let him help the troops here," Scott said. "I should've done a better job on the first patrol - it was my responsibility. I'll take Howard with me and one of my squads, but you can keep the sixty in position at the bottom of the bluff to cover our retreat if we need it."

Lt. Owenby looked over the M-60 position and then looked at Scott. "Get your people moving and don't waste time sightseeing, or buying up post cards," Lt Owenby said with a grin. He turned away and went to find Roscoe, who took over the schooling on Claymore mines.

Scott grabbed Joshua Howard by the top of his parka hood, "C'mon, Sarge, we gotta take us a little walk in the woods."

"I suppose it's probably too late to request a transfer back to food distribution?"

"You got that right, wise guy." Scott picked his squad of younger men and two women, and headed down the hill. He grabbed PFC Ohtapieu on his way, "Might need those ears of yours. You're on point with me."

"Yes, sir." *I should've never said a thing. They warned me about volunteering, but I didn't think it had anything to do with reporting what I heard...I know better now. For all the good it does... I'm on point...a lamb to the slaughter!*

When they finally reached the spot where the OAP was parked, Scott was stymied by their absence; PFC Ohtapieu was worn out. SSgt Howard moved up with the squad, while Scott thought things through his next move. Tracks on the road showed the vehicles had turned around and headed back down the road toward Fairbanks, but how far they went was the key question.

"I'm betting they probably saw you, LT and withdrew in fear of facin' a Black man with an automatic weapon in his hands," SSgt. Howard said. He hoped Scott would take the humorous remark well and he did. "There are times, Howard, that your estimation of your talents as a comedian concerns me."

"Does that mean we have to follow those tracks?" Howard asked in a disheartened tone.

"Yes, Sergeant, it means we have to follow those tracks...at least for a while," Scott said. He looked from Howard to PFC Ohtapieu, "I'll take point, but Ohtapieu, you're glued to my backside." Scott looked at each of the men and women in his small party. "Do not fire unless your life depends on it. We'd prefer the OAP not know we're out here and call in an airstrike on our butts."

"Lieutenant, sir," Howard interrupted. "What if your life depends on it?"

"Your jokes are trying my patience, Joshua. I may put you on point and let you entertain the Chinese with your one man stage act." This brought a few smiles on the faces of his nervous troops. Scott contacted Lt. Owenby by radio, on PFC Mayo's back, and advised him of the situation. Lt. Owenby agreed he should proceed west for a couple more miles, but to play it safe. "Roger on that...Out. We'll stay in the trees and take it real slow... and keep an eye out for snipers in the trees, or buried in the snow. If they did see us, an officer may have left some of his men behind to ambush us."

After making sure his white cover shell was in place and he had a full magazine in his rifle, Scott led off with PFC Ohtapieu five steps behind him. Unlike before, the squad was now using quick snap snowshoes that kept them on top of the snow and travel was a bit faster. Howard and the rest of the squad waited for three minutes before they followed with spacing intervals of at least 15 feet and no more than 20. With Scott and Ohtapieu breaking trail, they left an easy track for the squad to follow, even for weekend warriors.

Paralleling the highway and staying a minimum of 25 yards inside the woods, Scott and his jittery sidekick trudged through crunchy snow and kept a 360° watch for the enemy. Ducking low branches, they tried to keep several rows of trees between them and the highway and took short breaks at the end of every hour. Snowshoeing was exhausting work and they were nearing their third rest stop when Scott dropped to the ground and signaled for PFC Ohtapieu to do the same. *Oh boy! Looks like we found the hornet's nest!* Scott took his snowshoes off very quietly and crawled forward on his belly to take a better look, while PFC Ohtapieu waited for the rest of the squad to move up. Ohtapieu gave Howard and the squad hand signals to stay low and take up positions behind the trees.

Using his binoculars, Scot took in the scene before him then crawled back to the squad and gestured for them to follow him deeper into the woods. He hadn't put his snowshoes back on and the going was tough, but he didn't want to waste any time. Satisfied they were far enough away, Scott made radio contact with Roscoe and waited a very anxious moment for Lt. Owenby to come to the radio.

"We've found them...Over."

"What is their strength...Over?" Owenby asked.

"Estimate 45 to 50 men, five armored personnel carriers and three...I repeat three heavy tanks...Over." Scott wasn't really surprised to see the tanks, but their sheer size and lethal capability made him shudder.

"Standby." Lt. Owenby switched frequencies and contacted Battalion. A moment later, he was back with Scott, "You're ordered to fall back and don't take too long or you'll end up walking all the way back to Delta. Battalion is sending us some transportation to evacuate. While we're waiting for you, we'll continue setting up surprises for our guests. Make sure you contact me before crossing the road; I don't want you ruining my surprise...Over."

"Copy that, we're on our way. Possible two hours at best...Out." Scott secured the microphone to the radio pack and addressed his squad, "Move out, stay low and we're going to set a faster pace. We have two hours to make it back to the bluff." Scott looked at Howard, "You're on point, sergeant, so you'd better get going. I'll bring up the rear and kick any stragglers in the backside to keep 'em movin'."

"I hear an' obey, Master," Howard said and then smiled. A moment later, he was down the path they had made. Scott hated using the same trail, but it made for quicker travel and he doubted the OAP had time to get behind them and set traps.

While the squad followed, Scott and PFC Ohtapieu had enough time able to get their snowshoes back on.

1820 HOURS- UNDER COVER OF DARKNESS-AT THE BLUFF

One hour and 36 minutes later, Howard emerged from the trees to see Roscoe busy setting up Claymore and tripwire grenade traps. At first startled by Howard's sudden appearance and upset the security watch hadn't spotted the squad emerging from the trees, Roscoe lowered his rifle. He grabbed the nearest soldier, a private, and sent word to Lt. Owenby of Scott's arrival then resumed his work.

When Scott and the rest of the squad caught up with Howard, he was waiting near the embankment for Roscoe to give them the okay. Roscoe ambled over and showed them where to cross without blowing themselves up.

"Right there, but don't stray in either direction or you'll ruin the LTs surprise," Roscoe said. "I've got grenades hidden in the snow to trip wires and they'll blow if you step on 'em." Roscoe wore a smile of pride for his demo work.

Scott was the last to cross and as he did, PFC Ohtapieu's ears alerted him and went to warn Scott, "Heavy vehicle coming down the road, LT."

"Get everyone into position Roscoe, they're here!" Scott sent a runner to warn Lt. Owenby. With a worried look that comes with command, Scott yelled to Howard, "Get our men up the bluff and make sure our 60 gunner has plenty of ammo."

"You got it, LT!" Roscoe shouted back. Roscoe was already moving, shoving soldier's right and left into their foxholes and warning them to keep their fingers off triggers until the order was given to fire. "This is an ambush and we want it to be a surprise. You fire off one round before the order comes down and you'll have me bustin' your head with the butt of my rifle."

Several tense filled moments passed before a lone enemy APC appeared at the bend in the road and everyone held their breath until it ran right into one of Roscoe's larger grenade traps. The resulting explosion from four hand grenades strapped together caused the APC to flip over on its side. In doing so, it set off a Claymore mine, set only 15 feet away. With a resounding explosion, 200 round steel pellets peppered the wounded war machine and cut down two infantrymen attempting to escape the smoke filled APC.

From the top of the bluff, Corporal Gary Wing used a scope to spot enemy tanks coming down the road. Excited, Wing nearly dropped his delicate scope when he notified Roscoe over the radio. "Tanks! Five...no make that six tanks."

"Six?" Scott exclaimed. "I only counted three earlier." Scott shouted down and ordered PFC Ohtapieu and PFC Redner to abandon the lower security post and move the M-60 up the bluff.

"You two get up here... fast... that ain't good cover to take on no six tanks."

Locating Howard, who was helping the other 60 gunners set up on the hilltop, Scott ordered him to get their platoon ready to pull back to the bridge. "Tell our men to grab their gear, but only what they can carry on the run. After I confirm with Lt. Owenby, we'll climb down the southeast face and head for the riverbank. There is no way we're going to stop this bunch." Scott found an excited Lt. Owenby outside the command tent talking with Battalion and could tell he was upset by the tone of voice he was using with Battalion.

"Yes, I'm requesting immediate assistance. I've got six, I repeat Sierra...India... X-ray enemy tanks and five, I repeat five Alpha-Papa-Charlie's moving in on our position. We require immediate transport on the other side of the bridge for two platoons...Over." Lt. Owenby looked up at Scott and waited impatiently for Battalion to respond.

"Stand-by one," a calm female voice replied.

"Roger." Lt. Owenby suddenly felt a surge of anger toward the woman at the other end of the radio. Here he was getting ready to face six ugly monsters and this soldier sounded like he was calling information for a phone number. Lt. Owenby looked up and heard the sounds of the lead tank drawing near. Its heavy treads crushed fresh melted ice and snow, and sent micro-quakes through the surface of the ground.

Within 30 seconds or less, he knew the lead tank would soon be within visual range of the burning APC. Then it's going to be like Saturday night in ol' Dodge City and we'll be using spit wads against that beast. But it didn't take thirty seconds. The lead tank braked to a halt several yards behind the dead APC and within five seconds it opened up with its 105mm gun. Shells the size of a five pint tankard exploded and utterly decimated the near hillsides, while a second and then a third tank moved up to assist in destroying the countryside. Behind them, the three other tanks began a bombardment of the deeper woods, where Scott had taken his patrol through.

Shaken by the heavy shelling, Lt. Owenby grabbed the radio and reported, "We are under heavy fire...Over." Lt. Owenby hoped the increasingly explosive sounds of tank fire could be picked up by the woman at the other end of the radio, showing the need for urgency.

"Be advised, transport and fire support en route. Mark your position with blinkers an' keep your heads down...Over."

"Copy on blinkers...Out." Owenby tossed the microphone back to his RTO and dove into the tent to retrieve his bag of blinkers from a small canvas pack. Battery operated, these strobes put out a bright enough pulsating red light that aircraft overhead could spot them. Handing half of them to Roscoe, they quickly placed the blinkers out to surround Lt. Owenby and Scott's platoons. He then ordered both platoons to ceasefire and withdraw to the top of the bluff. Scott had to bring in all the fire teams from below to keep them from being hit by whatever air cover was on the way. But this took another three minutes and during this time, the OAP recon force was searching for whoever had set the trap.

Below, the tanks had ceased fire, not wanting to damage the highway surface, but their turrets continued to rotate as they searched for targets off the road. Infantry squads disembarked from APC vehicles and began spreading out and stomping through the trees to form a line of defense. Several soldiers tripped over grenade traps, setting off additional explosions which led to an OAP officer ordering everyone back to the road leaving the dead and wounded where they lay because the OAP Commander was unsure what he was facing. He held his scout company behind their APCs while he made radio contact with the OAP spearhead at Eielson Air Force Base.

The OAP Command Center was located in Amber Hall Headquarters Building; formally headquarters for the Alaska Air Command and then the ADF Northern Wing. Booby traps throughout the building and parking garages had accounted for over a hundred dead and 230 wounded before Amber Hall was reported safe to occupy. But Eielson Air Base still held other traps set up in the barracks and housing areas, which the OAP personnel would soon fatally discover.

Even with heavy equipment working 24 hours a day, it took time for the Eielson runway to be made ready for enemy aircraft; the loss of men and equipment was high, thanks to the ADF and Militia demolition crews. The aging roof on the Main hanger at Eielson collapsed when OAP work crews turned on the light switches for the ground floor restroom. A cleverly planned electric spike from the switch plate activated several well-placed C-4 charges in the roof, which caused it to become separated from the support walls. With all the booby traps, OAP troops were soon afraid to touch anything until a demolition crews had cleared the buildings or abandoned vehicles.

BACK AT THE BLUFF

Lt. Owenby slid across the slushy snow on his stomach until he came up beside Scott, "Make sure everyone is ready to bug out quick when I give the signal. I'm not sure what Command is sending for air cover, but as soon as they engage the tanks we boogey for the river."

"Ah'm already ahead of you, Lieutenant," Scott said. "My platoon is ready to move out and I'm bettin' my old dudes will probably outrun your kids."

Suddenly, without warning, the forward tank simply exploded and showered fiery debris on the roadway and the adjoining hillside and woods. Towering flames from the burning APC hulk and the tank lit up the immediate area and caused strange shadows to form on the white landscape. A second tank exploded, followed almost instantly by a third. The metal monstrosities split apart like ripe melons and debris dropped on the hard pavement. Fires had melted most of the ice surrounding the demolished bodies of the OAP dreadnaughts.

Startled by the sudden change of events, Scott rolled onto his back and glanced up as a loud whirling sound passed by and he spotted the running lights of a large aircraft diving on yet another enemy tank. Blue tracers from 30mm cannon blasted into the remaining tanks and supporting APCs, setting off one loud explosion after another to carry through the narrow valley below the bluff. It had happened so fast the enemy tanks didn't even have time to set up an aerial defense.

"Hogs to the rescue!" Roscoe shouted recognizing the aircraft and the job they were doing on the OAP armor.

Two A-10 Warthogs had come in at treetop level to avoid enemy radar and were on station doing the job they were created for. A chore they were accomplishing quite well in Scott's opinion. "Warthogs!" He shouted enthusiastically, his rifle lifted up in celebration. He slapped Howard on the shoulder, "Man, look at them go."

Again and again, the weird looking aircraft struck with a vengeance, thirsting to avenge the loss of half their wing in Anchorage. When they were finished not a single tank or APC was left untouched; fires lit up the valley floor and more importantly, their junk blockaded the Richardson Highway.

Lt. Owenby and Scott ordered their men to open fire on the fleeing infantry, but only eight OAP soldiers were able to escape the lethal air attack. Those eight quickly fell victim to M-60 and M-16 fire, and when it appeared the enemy was destroyed, Lt. Owenby and Scott stood on the bluff with their men and admired the handiwork below. Black smoke and flames rose from the smoldering piles of melted slag, creating rivers of melted snow to run down the highway until it dammed up against deep snow.

"Those are tank killers!" Roscoe yelled out, his sheer joy echoed by two platoons of grateful troops, who jumped up and down as they waved their flashlights at the pilots of the two aircraft.

The two A-10 Hogs did a final low flyover to ensure the enemy force was no longer a threat and then the lead pilot radioed Lt. Owenby, "Lima Poppa One, this is Wrangler Nine...Over."

Lt. Owenby grabbed up the microphone from his RTO, "Go ahead, Wrangler Nine...Over."

"Six tanks and five APCs confirmed dead. No threats in immediate area, but we will stay on station while you cross bridge. Trucks are on the way...Over."

"I copy and thanks, you pulled our bacon out of the fire...Over."

"Hogs cleaned the roads tonight...Over an' out." The pilot signed off, but the two planes continued to fly a low wide loop above the bluff and mouth of the Susitna River.

"Man-o-man, ah sure wish we had a couple thousand of those babies. They sure made fast work of those tanks," Scott said.

"We have twelve here," Roscoe said. "I heard the other half of the squadron was sent to Anchorage." Having been on the bluff, they were not aware of the tragic losses suffered in the Battle for Anchorage.

"Twelve is better than nothing," Lt. Owenby added. "Okay, Roscoe, let's get 'em moving. Make sure they don't leave any equipment up here the enemy can use."

"Yes, Sir," Roscoe replied.

Within the hour, Lt. Owenby and Scott's platoons were picked up by transport; four deuce-and-a-half-trucks, escorted by two Bradley Fighting Machines. Eight miles later, they were all back inside Delta Junction's perimeter. Rather than split the two platoons up and send Scott and his troops back to Fort Greeley, Battalion Headquarters decided to keep Lt. Owenby and Scott together as an undermanned new rifle company. They placed them on the far northeast section of Delta Junction's new perimeter and out in the brush. Since it kept him away from Captain Buford, Scott didn't mind one bit. Lt. Owenby was promoted to captain of F Company and Scott received an overnight promotion to 1st lieutenant and kept command of his same loyal bunch of, "We Dastardly Dudes and Two Dames," as they referred to themselves.

Complaining all through the brief ceremony at headquarters, Roscoe received a battlefield promotion to 2nd lieutenant and assigned command of Lt. Owenby's platoon and a very reluctant Howard found himself assigned as 1st sergeant for F Company. He was responsible for all company needs and the morale of his troops. If it wasn't for Scott's encouragement and threatening to shoot him in the foot, Howard might have been F Company's first AWOL.

ON THE PERIMETER WITH F COMPANY-

During F Company's first staff meeting, Scott asked Captain Owenby why the ADF hadn't simply blown the Richardson Highway Bridge. There were no other bridges spanning the river and Scott thought it would limit the OAP's advance.

"Colonel Ramonski told me they wanted the OAP to use the bridge, hopeful it will keep them bottlenecked and easy prey for our A-10s. The ones they miss will stay on the highway and come down the road right into our ambush." Captain Owenby shrugged his shoulders, "Like all plans, there's a good chance this one will fall through too. They may decide to stay clear of the bridge, expecting we mined it, and build their own bridges across the river ice like they must've done for the Chena in Fairbanks."

"This means of course, the enemy could spread out and completely compromise our newly built defensive position." Roscoe added in.

"River's pretty wide, Lieutenant, be kind of tough to build a new bridge without us knowing about it." Scott bent over to pull a twig out of his bootlaces.

"We're not on the bluff anymore, Lieutenant," Howard said. "We're eight miles from the river. I doubt we'd hear anything if the winds blowing. But I'll keep my fingers crossed."

"First Sergeant Howard, I liked you a whole lot better as a comedian," Scott grinned.

"I'll tell you something, LT, I liked myself a whole lot better being SSgt. Howard, and having a whole lot fewer worries on my shoulders." Howard was hoping to get a few words of sympathy, but no one was buying into it.

They located their new position, a thick stretch of short dead Black Spruce, among taller white birch trees nearly 110 yards long on the far right of Echo Company. Orders were given and troops went to work digging two man foxholes in the bitterly cold hard ground. Once the snow was cleared away, E-tools bounced off the icy surface; it was going to take a lot of sweat and muscle to dig a hole here. The question was asked, but due to a shortage of supplies, Captain Owenby would not grant permission for the men to use explosives to soften the ground up.

A listening post was placed 100 yards out in front of each platoon and the company command post was situated 25 yards behind the line between the two platoons.

While the troops were struggling to dig in, Captain Owenby got word over the radio that Battalion had assigned a 16 man Militia heavy weapons platoon to F Company. They arrived lugging all their armament and Captain Owenby placed their mortar pits behind and within shouting distance of the CP. Four 81mm mortars, supported by a .50 caliber machinegun and three M60 machineguns added some weight to the undermanned company. Accustomed to such accommodations, the heavy weapons platoon began knocking down trees and building three sided walls to surround their weapons. In no time at all, the weapons platoon had eight 10 inch thick walls some five feet high and after seeing what they had done, Captain Owenby gave his troops permission to build barricades, but only if they were able to camouflage them and the trees had to be taken from deep behind their positions.

"I don't want this area thinned out. When the enemy shows up, all they'll be seeing is these little wood forts waiting for them. They'll know right where to lob their grenades, so be smart. I know the ground is frozen and it's breakin' your backs, but try to dig in. When the shrapnel starts flying, you'll want to be below ground level."

60 miles west of Delta, the enemy's forward units traveled east along the Richardson Highway and cautiously moved through North Pole. A heavy price was paid here. Smoke and fires covered most of the land, as homes and businesses were set aflame by nearly maniacal hungry troops. Not a scrap of food could be found among the abandoned homes, but there were booby traps left behind to entertain the enemy.

Santa Claus House was burned to the ground and the 50 foot tall Santa Claus blown apart by tank fire. The OAP was further enraged to discover ADF demolition crews had destroyed the North Pole Refinery, preventing the OAP from using the fuel storage tanks to keep their tanks moving.

OAP command staff was not happy and word coming down of officer executions made many of the colonel's cringe in fear. Added to their concerns were the continual reports of rioting and mutiny spreading through the ranks. It wasn't long before rumors spread out of Siberia and down through the lines that the plague had struck Northern China; warlords believed refugees fleeing the ports of Southeast Asia had carried it into Siberia. OAP Troops were succumbing to the plague by the hundreds and then by the thousands. The plague's Angel of Death was bearing down on OAP forces that were already enduring starvation and freezing to death in an extremely hostile climate. Chinese warlords and their senior staff members were losing control of their rear echelons. Fear of cruel authority gave way to deeper fears of a gruesome death no one had a cure for. Even the ruthless Black Dragons were unable to keep the troops in line once the plague struck the troops in Siberia. Hundreds of the vile Secret Police fell beneath panicking hordes when soldiers threw their weapons down and tried to flee in all directions. Large scale desertion only added further to the spread of the disease, as cases show up in Nome and Kotzebue - even among officers and Black Dragons.

One of the senior OAP warlords had fallen to the plague and 90% of his command staff had died with him. A senior colonel who was not infected stepped in to assume command. But rather than ensure his troops were making their way to Alaska, he had ordered his regiments to stand fast. He didn't want his troops to enter Alaska or proceed south with the armies invading Saudi Arabia. He had other plans and as a new general officer, he issued orders for the burning of every building and all of the bodies in his area of command. He had hopes of stopping the plague, but he also needed to depart the area. He ordered his army north with plans to occupy the mountains of Tibet.

A COMING STORM

18 - REVELATION UNFOLDS

"The seventh angel sounded the trumpet, and there were loud voices in heaven, which said: 'The kingdom of the world has become the kingdom of our Lord and of his Christ, and he will reign for ever and ever.'

And the twenty four elders, who were seated on their thrones before God, fell on their faces and worshipped God, saying: ' we give thanks to you, Lord God Almighty, who is and who was, because you have taken your great power and have begun to reign. The nations were angry; and your wrath has come. The time has come for judging the dead, and for rewarding your servants and prophets and your saints and those who reverence your name, both small and great - and for destroying those who destroy the earth.'

God's temple in heaven was opened, and within his temple was seen the ark of his covenant. And there came flashes of lightening, rumblings, peals of thunder, an earthquake and a great hailstorm."

Revelation 11: 15-19 NIV

FORT GREELEY, ALASKA - APRIL 23ᴿᴰ 1216-HOURS

With relentless determination Ed Sawyer painstakingly searched one side of Fort Greeley to the other in hopes of locating his brother. Unfortunately, with so many thousands of misplaced people from all over the state, finding one particular family was like looking for the proverbial needle in a very large haystack. The sheer overwhelming numbers had brought Ed to the point of frustration. Exhausted and desperately needing a shower, he was struggling with a piercing headache when he collapsed onto a wooden bench in the hallway of ADF Headquarters. His arms draped over the top of the bench and his eyes locked on a faded piece of gray wall, Ed wasn't sure where he should check next. Kira suddenly plumped down beside him, kissed his cheek, wrapped her arms around his neck and laid her head on his shoulder, which seemed to do the job. He felt refreshed and encouraged once more by her presence and simple demonstration of her affection for him.

"No luck, huh?" Kira asked. With a tender hand, she softly brushed his stub of a beard. You need a shave, dear husband…and a shower too.

"Nope." Ed shook his head and winced from the sensation of a drill grinding away through the side of his skull. The strain of responsibility over the last few weeks was taking its toll on his body and suddenly he felt very old. Knowing it was another one of his headaches, she began to rub his forehead and then the tightness on the back of his neck.

He looked into his wife's caring eyes and sighed deeply, "Thank you, honey... it helps. But I've checked with the MP Desk and even Militia Command, but no one seems to know where he is. I ran into some people from Fairbanks, but they were no help either. From what they told me, there was no established system in place for assigning housing and keeping a record of who is where. Everything happened too fast, so people from Nome are housed with families from Tok or Valdez. When the barracks were filled, they put people in tents or whatever shelter they could locate."

Ed pulled out a folded piece of paper from his right coat pocket, "I did learn though that Brad's last partner on the force was a Scott Radley, who's been assigned to a Militia infantry unit. When I locate him, maybe he'll know where Brad and his family are housed."

Kira gave her husband a couple of aspirin, an item whose value had increased as all medication since the trucks quit running up from the Lower 48. He popped them in his mouth and took a long drink from her water bottle. Kira glanced up and down the busy hallway, "I've never seen so many people piled together in one place. It's like trying to leave a big stadium after a football game." She pointed out that everyone was armed, "Everyone seems ready for the big fight. If they're old enough to be armed - they are." She pointed out one teenager in civilian garb, "He looks about 14 and he's carrying a rifle as big as he is!"

"This is Alaska, honey. Kids start carrying guns pretty young up here, especially out in the bush. You need to know how to shoot or a bear is liable to take you home for dinner. Times have changed and from what I've learned we face staggering numbers. Women have joined our forces and a large number of young teens are eager to defend family and home. Boys take up hunting here at an early age and most know how to handle a gun."

She shook her head, trying to understand the Alaskan mindset and then suddenly remembered, "Oh, I forgot, Pastor Woodway said that when I find you, to remind you of our new orders." Kira studied faces in the crowd. What surprised her most was the lack of fear, but she didn't mention it to her husband. She didn't want another lecture on how tough Alaskans were and how rough it was growing up in the frozen north.

"I know the orders. Our group is being assigned to a newly formed Militia battalion, made up mostly of volunteers and National Guardsmen. I just wanted to find Brad first," Ed said in dismay. He folded the piece of paper with Scott's name on it and shoved it into his pants pocket. "Are all our families set up?"

"We've got a small flat area near the flight line. It's noisy, especially when a plane takes off, but open space is extremely limited," Kira replied and then added, "It a bit smelly too."

"You'll get used to the stench, but do we have room for our big circus tent?" Ed looked up and down the hallway hoping he might catch a glimpse of Brad. As large as his big brother was he knew he'd be hard to miss.

"Pastor was told to keep the big tent down, too colorful and too good a target, as if thousands of smaller orange and yellow tents aren't." She shuddered when a cold breeze swept down the hallway and knew someone had opened the big double doors out front. Nestled up against Ed, she asked, "How could you live in this ice box? I'm freezing and we're inside."

"Not so bad when you grow up in it… you just get used to it and the summers make it worthwhile." He stood up, helped Kira to her feet and hugged her tightly, but he got blindsided by a woman in camouflage fatigues rushing between offices. The woman, wearing the four stripes of an Air Force staff sergeant, only turned long enough to give Ed and Kira a dirty look before disappearing into the crowd.

"I guess Alaskan politeness has given way to Lower 48 rudeness," Ed said. Then he grinned and looked into the loving eyes of his young wife. "People up here like to boast how interior Alaska has only two seasons, winter and three rainy months before winter. But it isn't true. Our summers here in the interior are long with lots of daylight and pretty warm after you've gone through a tough winter. When the temperature hits 80°, it compares to 100° for people in Arizona," He shook his head and frowned, "I've been gone too long, my blood's thinned out from all that warm Arizona living, which I seriously miss right now."

Traffic in the hallway was getting worse with dozens of men and women scurrying in and out office doors delivering a form here or there in a steady pace that resembled an old three Stooges cartoon or a Keystone Cop film. Ed was about to escort his wife out of the building when a young officer charged between them and blurted out, "Excuse me!" Even in his hurry, the young man stopped just long enough to look back over his shoulder and give Kira an appraising eye. When Ed's eyes shot back daggers, the man quickly proceeded on his way. "That punk probably thinks I'm your dad, not that I blame him much," Ed said with disgust.

"Aw-w-w… c'mon, Dad," Kira said in jest. "Let's go find Pastor. He told me if I found you before 1 p.m., I was to bring you back to camp. You and he have some sort of meeting with some big shot." Kira checked her wristwatch, "We still have time if you can get those old bones of yours moving, pops."

He shot her a raised eyebrow glare, "How'd you find me anyway?" Ed decided to ignore her comment about old bones, but he'd bring the pops part up later.

"I kept telling all the cute guys I ran into that I was looking for my sickly dear old father and described you." She started to laugh, "They knew right away who I was talking about and sent me here to this very spot. And low and behold I found you draped over a park bench."

"Great... just great," Ed complained. "I'll probably have a line of young men at our tent tonight asking for my permission to date my lovely daughter. You know that don't you?" Ed glared at his wife while people rushed around them. "I'll probably have to kill a few of them in a jealous rage, maybe in a duel of honor. How'd that make you feel?"

"I think I like it when you get jealous, you're a little spryer for a geezer your age."

"Enough with the age bit!" He smiled at her and followed it up with a quick peck, before he led her down the hallway holding her hand.

Before leaving the building, a weary eyed Lt. Colonel Jeb Stewart walked out of a side door and briefly brushed shoulders with Ed, each man saying a polite, "Excuse me" before they continued on their way.

TENT CITY-FORT GREELEY

"Pastor Woodway?" Chaplain John Knight asked. Dressed in arctic gear, he stepped out of his cloth roofed M151 Jeep and offered his gloved hand. A burly looking corporal from transportation sat behind the steering wheel and kept a watchful eye on all the womenfolk walking by. Single and 20years old, Corporal Lance Rogers was a self-proclaimed expert in the study of the opposite sex, especially those ladies in the 18-25 year range - blondes with blue eyes in particular.

"Yes, I'm Pastor Woodway." Pastor was in the process of helping several families with tent assignments when the jeep pulled up.

"Pastor, I'm Chaplain Knight... John Knight. I was given your description and location and sent here by our ministerial association to serve as welcome wagon and taxi, and I am sorry... no food basket."

Pastor smiled, he liked the looks of this Chaplain Knight, "Then, I gather you're here to pick us up?" Pastor spotted Ed in the crowd and waved him over. "And better late than not, here's my right hand man... Ed Sawyer. We referred to him as the wagon master, mostly because it was his responsibility to get our cheery band to Alaska."

Ed, his wife in tow, walked up to Pastor and was about to ask what was going on, when Pastor introduced them to Chaplain Knight. Hearing the last name of Sawyer, Knight's ears perked up but before he could mention his friend, Brad Sawyer, Corporal Lance Rogers reminded Chaplain Knight of the time. "We gotta get a move on, Chaplain...sir. Places to go and people to see... as they say."

"And who is they, Corporal?" Chaplain Knight asked.

"It's a saying...but we need to get going, sir."

Chaplain Knight replied to Corporal Rogers with a look of exasperation and glanced back to Pastor Woodway, "Yes, he's right. We must get going as time is exceedingly short. If you gentlemen would please climb in we'll be on our way." Chaplain Knight turned to Kira, "I do apologize, Mrs. Sawyer, but I was ordered to bring only these two gentlemen." *I sincerely hope she's older than she looks...but they do appear happy and who am I to judge? The world has gone completely crazy. Pastor Woodway said they're married and he certainly feels like a God fearing man.*

"It's not a problem, I've got lots of work to do as you can imagine." She looked at Ed, "Just don't be volunteering for anything, dear husband. I've read about how the Army works, finding brave souls to send out on top secret missions with no concern for loved ones left behind." She waved her finger at him, "You're a married man now, no more of this running to the sound of the guns stuff. Got that, Mr. Sawyer?"

"Yes, ma'am," Ed replied. "Now that you've properly embarrassed me, can we leave?"

Kira kissed her husband lightly on the lips and watched them drive off through the thick crowd. It did not take any time at all before they vanished into the masses and she turned to help out where she could.

There was a marked corridor between the rows of multi colored tents, but with so many sizes and shapes it was difficult to keep a perfectly straight line. When it wasn't a tent, a 55 gallon drum, either full sized or cut in halfway set up as a fire pit to provide some small level of heat or cooking fire. In either case it was making it extremely difficult for vehicles to make it through camp.

Chaplain Knight and Pastor Woodway attempted to hold a conversation, but it was nearly impossible to hear one another with all noises and voices surrounding them: people shouting out or at family members, hammers striking tent stakes, kids running about laughing or playing or looking for parents and tempers flaring between neighbors. Ed thought it was like driving through a busy swap meet or bazaar on a payday Friday as thousands of conversations were going on; sales pitches for bartering, arguments of every kind and the occasional domestic disagreement. But through all the raised voices the subject of conversation between the two clergymen eventually fell upon church services.

Chaplain Knight turned around in his seat and shouted back to Pastor Woodway, who, with Ed, was sitting in the narrow back seat of the Jeep. "We're conducting church services 24 hours a day, Pastor," Knight advised. "You've never seen anything like it. After that black sky and blood moon, we've had hundreds …maybe thousands of conversions every day. I'd estimate that 75% of these people around you are Christians." Knight stopped and held on to his seat as Corporal Lance swerved to avoid hitting a turning ammo truck going the wrong way on a one way corridor. They nearly lost Pastor Woodway in the process, but Ed held on to him by grabbing his right arm and pulling him back.

"The old barriers between Christian denominations have collapsed. Most chaplains and newly arriving religious leaders are working together. It's as if a great famine has ended and the Word of God is feeding the multitudes. A few of the Rabbi have even crossed over to worship the Lord Jesus Christ." Knight tossed up his hands, "So much is happening in so little time. It just leaves me out of breath."

Corporal Rogers drove over a bump and tossed Chaplain Knight into the air, "Easy, son. We need to arrive in one piece and my kidneys are not made of rubber."

"Sorry." Corporal Rogers down shifted and slowed down.

"If I may say, Chaplain, you do look as if you could use a rest," Pastor said. Both of his hands were tightly grasping the back of Knight's seat for support as Corporal Lance negotiated some wild hairpin turns to miss playing children and the occasional new tent.

"Dang, don't those people know this is a road!?" Corporal Rogers blurted out.

With temperatures below freezing, all the children outside were wearing heavy parkas, wool caps, thick mittens, and insulated snow boots and multi-colored wool scarves and a number of face masks hung from necks. The ash had stopped falling, but no one wanted to be caught out in the open without a scarf or mask to filter the ash.

A cold front had moved in that morning from the northwest and the weather detachment was calling for temperatures to drop to sub-zero through the night with a possibility of snow. Puddles of melted snow had frozen over and most of the roadways had become slippery, sloppy and unnerving driving traps. There were even a few dozen people out on ice skates taking advantage of every open spot they could find.

"We don't have a lot of time for sleep, Pastor, too many in need of counseling or prayer… but from what I've learned about your trip north I'm sure you're used to having to little sleep," Chaplain Knight shouted over his shoulder.

Corporal Rogers excited his three passengers when he barely squeezed between two large fuel trucks going in the opposite direction, as he made a sharp left turn without bothering to signal. Chaplain Knight looked over at Rogers and asked him, "Did you ever drive cab in Anchorage? I seem to remember, almost meeting my Savior on a ride much like this on the way to the airport one morning." Rogers only smiled in reply then downshifted again as he negotiated another hairpin turn and everyone heard the grinding of gears.

Attempting to ignore the corporal's driving skills or lack of them, Ed bent forward and asked, "How many people do we have here?" He couldn't help looking every which way in search of Brad.

Chaplain Knight glanced around the camp as if he was attempting to count the crowds and then replied, "No one has a firm count but ADF Command estimates close to 250,000...that includes the newly arrived Canadians. But when you're out here among them, you think it's more like an easy million." Chaplain Knight hesitated as Rogers hit another bump and swerved around a corner to avoid a head on collision with an oncoming bus by only a few feet.

"How long have you had a license, Corporal?" Ed asked, shouting the question into Rogers' ear.

"Got my license last month!" Lance shouted, without turning around. He upshifted and they sped past the intersection, leaving a red-faced bus driver behind them uttering profane words.

"How about supplies, will there be enough or should we be praying for manna?" Pastor Woodway asked Chaplain Knight, patting Ed's knee to reassure him.

"In all honesty, it's looking pretty ugly." Chaplain Knight stopped talking. He had grown nervous and muttered a quiet prayer as Rogers suddenly drove the jeep into a mass of humanity. There were thousands of people standing around hundreds of burn barrels and campfires in an attempt to stay warm.

"We got to get them off the roads, or this is the last time I drive through here, Chaplain. I know I'll be made responsible if I hit anyone!"

"Slow down! Headquarters will still be there and I know the General will understand our late arrival."

"That's fine for you, Chaplain, but I'm the one the captain will yell at if he gets a complaint."

"I'll take care of it. You concentrate on driving and avoid hitting anyone or anything."

Corporal Rogers only replied by shaking his head, a smirk on his face and angrily downshifted into 1st gear to avoid running over a group of kids playing a ball game in the corridor.

Chaplain Knight turned to face his guests, "When the enemy crossed the Yukon River, the ADF Command closed down the Healey Coal Mines. Every available truck was loaded with coal and transported here via Anchorage and Glennallen. I've asked about the prisoners there, but no one seems to know and I fear they may have been left to defend themselves."

Pastor was shocked when they first arrived at Fort Greely to see so many people gathered in one location and he mentioned his concern now "I'm surprised the enemy hasn't bombed Fort Greeley yet. With so many people here, they could do a lot of harm."

Ed nodded in agreement and looked out over the sea of people: Indian, Eskimo, some Aleut, white and black, Pilipino, Hispanic, and East Asian and wondered if his brother or this Scott Radley fellow might be standing around one of those fires.

"The big brass feels the OAP wouldn't take the chance on endangering our remaining food supply. That and a whole lot of prayer cover in hopes of preventing such an action from occurring." Chaplain Knight turned around in his seat to see Corporal Rogers finally pulling up in front of headquarters.

"Safe at last!" Chaplain Knight slapped Rogers on the shoulder, thanked him for the ride and then addressed his guests, "Let's get inside, gentlemen, it's much warmer."

Ed looked at the building and sighed, remembering he had been at this very building when Kira found him and returned at Pastor Woodway's request. *I could've just stayed here and avoided this mad toad's ride through Adventure land!*

ALASKA DEFENCE FORCE HEADQUARTERS- FORT GREELEY

Lt. Jane Kelly was waiting in the outer office to welcome both Pastor Woodway and Ed Sawyer along with Chaplain Knight. After helping them remove parkas, mittens and scarves, and laying them over the back of a near couch, she offered them hot tea or coffee.

"General Saunders will be with you in a moment, so please have a seat."

Behind the door, General Saunders was receiving a scheduled Intelligence briefing from Lt. Col. Stewart. He sat stoned faced behind his desk and listened.

"Sir, our last recon flight over the Tanana River provided us with these photographs." Jeb handed Saunders eight 8 x 10 black and white photos taken from an F-16's camera pod. "As you can see, OAP tanks and support vehicles are moving east along the Richardson Highway. Heavy tanks; two abreast, are followed by armored personnel carriers and a countless line of half-tracks filled with infantry. These trucks are towing either equipment trailers or artillery pieces." Jeb looked to his notes as General Saunders studied the photos. "At this time, we believe the OAP spearhead to be within four miles of the Tanana River with a line of vehicles going all the way back to Fairbanks." Jeb waited briefly as the General passed the photos along to the other officers present.

"Colonel, you're saying the OAP have a line of vehicles 90 miles long?" General Watson asked in astonishment.

"Even more, sir," Jeb said. "We know they have support units, including additional dreadnaughts and lighter tanks still moving into the Tanana Valley from the Seward Peninsula. Hard to believe, sir, but they seem to be sticking to our road system which is helpful for us." Jeb provided additional photographs taken by the last F-16 able to make a speed run over the northern OAP convoy. Of the five pilots who volunteered for the recon mission only one survived to bring these photographs back. The pilots of the other four F-16s were listed officially as MIA. General Saunders, knowing how prisoners are treated, hoped they were all killed on impact. He didn't even want to think of one of his men being stewed in some OAP steel pot.

"Apparently, our air raid did little to prove how accurate our Air Force can be. Either that, or their generals don't mind throwing away the lives of their men." Jeb returned to his notes, "Ice on the Tanana and Susitna is at least 18 inches thick with as much as four feet in certain areas. This makes the river surface fully capable of supporting trucks and possibly their APC units. Our geologists do not believe the thickness of the ice is able to support their heavy tanks." Jeb walked up to a map pinned to a near wall. "At their current rate of travel, I believe they'll be able to cross the river by late this afternoon." Jeb stopped when he saw General Watson had a question.

"Who do we have up front, keeping an eye on their advance?"

"Volunteer elements of the 36th Eskimo Scouts moving in three man units staying in contact with our CP here in Delta via burst radios. We moved these teams into play as soon our company on the bluff overlooking the Tanana got into a firefight with a reinforced enemy recon patrol. We also have some electronic sensors and scattered listening posts on the Tanana River."

"Colonel, you mentioned burst radios. I'm not certain I understand what you mean?" General Watson asked.

"These burst radios are compact electronics, our most advanced communications devices and we feel the OAP will be unable to trace them or compromise our frequency with their gear. Messages are sent out in a digital format in seconds… I can get a comm. Officer in here to fully brief you on the device if you wish, General?"

"That's not necessary, Jeb," General Saunders said.

"Are there other questions, gentlemen?" Jeb asked.

"I hate to be a burden, Colonel, but what about their bridge building equipment? We strongly believe they used their equipment for crossing the Chena after we destroyed all the bridges. Can't they use this same type of bridging equipment for crossing the Susitna? " General Watson asked.

"As of yet, we haven't seen any of their equipment trailers. But that doesn't mean they're not planning to bring their bridging up," Jeb replied. He knew how fast the OAP could set a bridge across the ice but they first had to transport it to the river and there had been no report of it- yet.

With no other questions, Jeb continued his briefing, "Our last report from Valdez tells us a large OAP invasion force, believed to be a splinter off the enemy task force that attacked Anchorage, has secured a foothold in there and was attempting to move north toward Glennallen. Hopefully the heavy snowfall in Thompson Pass will delay their advance and I've also just learned our forces have laid a few mines to cause avalanches along the highway. With General Saunders' permission, the last Militia units retreating from Valdez were ordered to close the north entrance of Johnson Pass with high explosives. Unfortunately, we lost contact with the Valdez force and were not sure this operation was carried out. An F-15 pilot, a volunteer who once lived in Valdez, was ordered to fly recon over the area and confirmed the highway to be closed by avalanche with an estimated 70 foot closure or better. The pilot also reported seeing both OAP and ADF vehicles in Thompson Pass either broken down or damaged in battle with a lot of bodies." Jeb looked at his notes, "I will add, this same pilot had to fight his way out of the Copper River Valley and downed a Russian SU-19 in the process."

"Jeb, any chance on getting another fly over scheduled for Anchorage?" General Saunders asked.

"It would be a suicide mission, General, and we'd never get the photos back," General Watson interjected before Jeb could reply. However, Jeb agreed with General Watson's statement.

"General, OAP Intel must know we're putting all our eggs in one basket, making a stand here. By now, they probably also know the West Canadian Army has joined us."

"What of our people in Glennallen, Jeb?" General Saunders asked. He was looking over the aerial photos from Valdez and sighed when he saw the size of the force coming ashore there.

"Knowing they would not be able to put up any form of defense against such a sizeable force and on your orders, General, we've successfully pulled our people out and destroyed whatever resources we couldn't bring back to Greeley. However, the town did come under air attack from MIG 34's." Jeb stopped to go through his notes until he found the right piece of paper. "Lt. Colonel Randy Wagner, formerly of the Alaska Army National Guard and more recently a member of the Glennallen City Council, fought a running retreat with enemy advance units. His unit of one thousand put up a heck of a fight and saved a lot of good people from Glennallen. Wagner and his command should arrive here within the next two hours. At last report, his force reported 128 wounded." Jeb stopped as he saw the grief stricken expression on General Saunders. More than 60 troops had perished in the withdrawal and Jeb knew some of these people were known to General Saunders, but they were all of his command.

"Sir, I do have some good news though... more than 8,000 civilians survived the evacuation of Valdez and Glennallen. According to Colonel Wagner, among them are several hundred cases of frostbite and hypothermia."

"What was the total number of casualties from our withdrawal of Valdez and Glennallen, Colonel?" General Watson asked.

Jeb studied his notes for a moment before answering, "Sir, our best estimates; 9,300 ADF and Militia troops KIA or MIA and civilians...possibly as high as 15,000-KIA, mostly from our battle for Valdez. We have no definite number on possible prisoners or wounded left behind." The room fell silent as the men thought of those staggering statistics.

"Such high numbers... unimaginable...15,000 KIA...I don't know what to say," General Watson said.

"There's nothing else that can be said, General. We've lost Anchorage, Valdez, Fairbanks and Glennallen. In a short period of time more than 75,000 Alaskans have given their lives for our beloved land. And there is no time to mourn, General, we still have a fight ahead," General Saunders said. "Is that it, Jeb?" Slowly, as if he carried the weight of the world upon his shoulders, he stood and walked around his desk to return Jeb's photographs to him.

"Sir, my last item concerns our unit on St. Lawrence Island. They report zero cargo aircraft flying over the ice for the last four days, which gives us hope the OAP is no longer capable of supplying their forces in Alaska by air."

General Howard-Wright, who had remained quiet through the entire briefing, spoke up. "What of the OAP Air Force... their fighters?"

"Sir, we know they have a sizable force in King Salmon, Nome and Kotzebue, and they've stationed additional aircraft on the Kenai Peninsula. We've seen only two-aircraft carriers, but intelligence reports show they were both sunk by a squadron of volunteers from Colonel Wilcox's command."

Against orders, a flight of F-15's, with two volunteer F-35 pilots and 1 F-22 Raptor, disregarded the RTB to Fort Greeley and flew a low pattern east and into the Gulf of Alaska. They planned to come up from the south of the OAP task force and stumbled upon the OAP carriers sitting off the northeast corner of Kodiak Island. The squadron, under the command of a Lt. Colonel flying the F-35 who had spent his childhood in Anchorage, hit the carriers. Their wave top attack caught them completely unaware.

General Wilcox spoke up, "Sadly, only five of those brave pilots were able to return, General. With a KC-135 tanker standing by to refuel the survivors, our more advanced birds returned, but we lost 16 Eagles when they encountered the OAP wing on their return. Lt. Colonel Troy Sanders accounted for seven victories, making him an instant ace. All total, the AWOL flyers splashed down 34 OAP fighters and sunk two carriers, with an untold number of aircraft still on board."

"Courageous pilots, but I still don't like the trade off or failure to obey orders... You'd better slap Sanders' wrist and promote him to full colonel. Give him a couple of your old eagles to sew on his collar and tell the others they did well."

"Yes, sir," General Wilcox replied.

Jeb waited to see if there was going to be any further exchange between the generals and then continued with his briefing, "At last count the OAP had 12 aircraft carriers capable of supporting fighters. With no other information to the contrary, we can lower that number to 10 and we believe these other carriers were sent into the Mediterranean for an attack on the Middle East. With what facts we do have, I would estimate their Air Force strength to be in an excess of 300 fighters. Of those fighters, our intelligence reports these are mostly older MIG-29's and 31's and some of the newer MiG-34's. They also have the SU-27 and Su-31 aircraft and our 1st Division reported seeing F-16's and F-18's, previously purchased by the Japanese Defense Force and also the Thai Air Force, from US companies... with our permission of course.

"They also have SU-17, SU-19's and a small squadron of SU-21's, and the newer JA-20s from the Chinese and Russian Air Forces," General Watson added.

"One of our A-10's knocked down a vintage F-4 Phantom over Anchorage, probably a leftover from the Vietnam War," General Wilcox offered up.

"Well, with those numbers, why haven't they attacked our position here? They could make quick work of our defenses." General Howard-Wright stood up from the couch and faced Jeb, "Please answer me that, Colonel."

General Saunders waved Jeb to silence, "I'll answer that. They simply do not have the fuel reserves for a full scale operation. I believe the OAP General Staff is withholding their main Air Force until the day of battle. They're waiting until both their northern and southern armies have us surrounded. Then, they'll throw everything into the pot at once while they have fuel to fly and eventually use Fort Greeley to land after they've overrun us. Without re-supply I don't believe they'll be capable of flying more than one or two sorties. Jeb also suspects the OAP is holding off in hopes of taking our food storage with their ground forces. They don't want to destroy buildings on the chance they're full to the brim with rations. Their men wouldn't like it much and from what I've heard mutiny is spreading through their ranks already."

"I wish," General Watson said.

"I do hope you're right, Glenn." General Howard-Wright said. Then with a stern look and a nod, he addressed Jeb, "A very good briefing, Colonel. Thank you."

General Saunders turned to face both his wing commanders, "I will need an update on the status of our Air Force, fuel supplies and armament within the next two hours, gentlemen."

"Yes, General," they replied in unison. Both men were wearing the single stars of a Brigadier General on their collar points. The five pointed silver stars had been gifts from General Saunders who had worn these single stars long ago. When he had pulled them from his personal belongings, he saw they needed a bit of work to rub off the tarnish. Sadly, both newly appointed General Hightower and General Maconnel had paid the ultimate price in the Battle for Anchorage.

General Saunders understood the airfield's mechanics were overwhelmed by the repair work needed to get the surviving Anchorage wing up and running again. After the Battle of Anchorage, several of the aircraft barely made it back to Greeley and one of them crashed on landing; killing the pilot. When the pitiful few survivors returned from sinking the two carriers, the chief mechanic for Colonel Sanders' F-35 had counted seven holes in the fuselage and could only shake his head and thank God for miracles.

After the briefing broke up, General Saunders asked General Howard-Wright and Jeb to stay behind for his next visitors. While Jeb put his papers into a black briefcase, securing it by key lock, General Howard-Wright poured himself another cup of tea and settled onto Saunders' comfy couch. "I so believe this is more comfortable then my cot."

"Will, you can't borrow it. That's where I sleep," General Saunders replied.

Chaplain Knight, Pastor Woodway and Ed were shown in to the office. Both Pastor and Ed felt a bit uncomfortable to be around two such high ranking generals.

"Please, gentlemen, have a seat and relax," General Saunders said. "Can I get you a cup of coffee or tea?"

Chaplain Knight and Pastor Woodway accepted steaming cups of hot tea, while Ed shook his head. "I'm just fine, sir."

"I've asked you here so you could tell us about your trip north. I, for one, am extremely interested in your observations since leaving Phoenix and would like to hear more about this vision that brought you here." General Saunders poured his coffee and sat back down behind his desk. Only Jeb remained standing in the room, glancing at Ed and wondering if or where he'd seen him before.

Pastor studied his tea for a moment before speaking, while Ed suffered a case of itchy pants and squirmed in his chair. Seeing how uncomfortable his friend was and knowing his desire to locate his brother, Pastor gave him a break. "Gentlemen, I'll give you full details, but I believe my good friend here is more interested in being elsewhere right now. You see, he's searching for his brother and I was hoping you might be able to help him out."

General Saunders exchanged curious looks with General Howard-Wright, but it was Jeb who spoke first. "You have family here in Alaska?"

"Yes...my brother, his wife and two children."

"I can possibly put you in touch with the various housing officers... what city did he come from?"

"Thank you, Colonel, they lived in Fairbanks. We were both raised there, but I left to attend college in Arizona."

"My God! Ed Sawyer...of course, you're Brad's brother!" Chaplain Knight said in a squeaky voice that matched his shocked look.

"Yes, Brad's my older brother. He was a sergeant on the Fairbanks Police force and our dad retired from there. Do you know where he is?" It was then Ed noticed the strange expressions on General Saunders and Lt. Colonel's faces

Chaplain Knight looked at Jeb, who studied Ed for a moment, seeing the family resemblance and then looked at General Saunders.

General Howard-Wright was unsure what was happening, so he remained silent and with all the sudden silence in the room and startled expressions, Pastor Woodway suspected there was a problem. He placed his hand on Ed's shoulder, "Is Brad still alive?"

When no one spoke, Ed stood to his feet. "What happened to him and where is his family?"

Jeb spoke up, "Mr. Sawyer, your brother worked for me after leaving the police department. He took on an extremely dangerous job... which cost him his life." Jeb looked to General Saunders, "Sir, may I show this gentleman to his brother's family?"

"Of course." General Saunders stood to his feet, "Mr. Sawyer, I am deeply sorry for the loss you have suffered. I know what a fine job Captain Sawyer did and the sacrifice he made and on behalf of Alaska, I mourn with you for your loss.

"Col. Stewart will provide you with the details of the job Brad was on and I will add, he died in good company as I also hold the other two men who perished with him in highest regard."

"Thank you, General," Ed mumbled as tears welled up in his eyes and Pastor gently walked him to the door.

"Ed, I'll stay here and brief these gentlemen on the events of our journey while you take care of your personal needs. I'll be back at camp when you return, we can talk then."

"Please tell Kira, Pastor."

"I will."

Jeb took Ed to his office and allowed him to see the films shot by India 5, including the last one. Though mourning the loss of his dear brother, he was extremely proud of the job he had accomplished. Jeb escorted Chaplain Knight and Ed to Kathy Sawyer's quarters. It was a bittersweet reunion as Ed and Kathy wept in each other's arms. Ed stayed to meet the children, but Chaplain Knight and Jeb prepared to excuse themselves. Before leaving, Jeb informed Ed that the circumstances surrounding Brad's death could now be explained to the family. Up to this point, Kathy did not have any details because of security. By the time everything was explained, Brad's family was extremely proud of their fallen soldier.

GENERAL SAUNDERS' OFFICE

Over the next several hours, General Saunders' door remained closed as Pastor Woodway told them of their miraculous journey and the ghastly sights of a war torn land. Jeb, who had returned to hear the briefing, was having some trouble with the miracles part, but both Generals fully understood. General Saunders kept patting his Bible as the story unfolded and every now and then General Howard-Wright would pop off with an "Amen".

Sandwiches, fresh tea and coffee were brought in. Happily, with the arrival of the Canadians, fresh flour had made it possible for bread to be baked again. Up till then, troops had existed mostly on various brands of crackers some of which could have been used for skeet shooting, hard enough to break teeth if one wasn't careful.

Jeb repeatedly asked Pastor why he felt his group of people was directed north by God and Pastor Woodway could only shake his head, smile and respond with, "Only the Master knows."

Weary eyed from the briefing, Pastor Woodway finally returned to camp and found Ed sitting at a large communal fire with his new family around him. Kathy Sawyer was sitting between her son and brother-in-law, Kira's lap was filled with her new niece, a pretty little girl who seemed to be enjoying the group's gentle songs of worship.

Chaplain Knight appeared later, bringing his wife and son, and several guitar players. It wasn't very long before the frigid night air was filled with the sounds of praise music, in real old time a hoop-n-holler style.

19 - BREAKTHROUGH

"The noise of the battle is in the land, the noise of great destruction!"
Jeremiah 50: 22 & 23

TANANA RIVER, RICHARDSON HIGHWAY - 0500 HOURS, APRIL 26TH

As the moon disappeared behind the Alaska Mountain Range, leaving the valley in thick clouds of river fog, OAP scout forces quietly moved across the river's long highway bridge. Scouts ensured the area clear of possible ambush, and demolition crews inspected every inch of bridge for explosives. Having found none, the first of a brigade of dreadnaughts supported by nearly frozen infantry was ordered across. Specialized enemy scouts moved ahead and with their almost ninja-like skills, silenced three nearby ADF listening posts without a shot being fired.

Once ice depth was verified on the Tanana River, other points of crossing were made as huge steel snowplows, mounted on dozens of medium weight tanks, cleared roadways across the ice for lighter vehicles. When the field artillery was south of the river, the heavier dreadnaughts were brought up to move cautiously across the ice, which had been reinforced with lengths of steel plating.

Soldiers walked alongside these mighty juggernauts of steel nervously watching for cracks and impending doom. But once across, they breathed a deep sigh of relief and hustled to catch up with the heavy brutes climbing up the river embankments. Lighter tanks began a prearranged plan to crush brush and trees to clear a large section of land as a rallying point for the point element. They operated like massive construction bulldozers crushing blue and black spruce, white birch and alder beneath their treads. Nature's wonder was swept aside as if a kitchen broom had swept dust across floor tile. The point element spread out in a defensive line formation to support other units coming up behind. The OAP armor battalions were made up of combat hardened veterans, men and women who had survived the invasion of Vietnam, the Battle of Siberia and the attack on Wales. They'd also weathered the sub-zero temperatures of interior Alaska and deep snow, while fighting a dozen skirmishes with the retreating 1st Division across the Seward Peninsula. They held a key position waiting for the order to attack.

While OAP frontline forces moved eastward from Fairbanks; the Southern Army easily secured Glennallen. Point units moved north toward Fort Greeley with all possible speed and only the occasional fallen tree felled by retreating ADF forces, or an avalanche brought down with explosives, slowed them down.

An embittered OAP Admiralty Staff found the oil pipeline ending in Valdez already destroyed and no fuel in the huge steel storage tanks to refuel their vessels. They were counting on that oil to be refined for their ships, but based upon the massive oil sheen visible in the bay, they realized any remaining oil in storage tanks had been drained into the ocean before demolitions crews set off explosives to cripple the facility and the pipelines.

Admiral Tobishi, his eyes filled with anger, sat in his bridge command chair aboard his new flagship; a missile cruiser of medium class, having lost his former flagship; an aircraft carrier, only a couple days earlier to an ADF air attack. He glared out upon Valdez and wanted to flatten the entire town with missiles. He thought over the promises given by the General Warlords in Beijing, of how they would have the element of surprise and would positively take the Valdez oil fiends intact. But he had lost better than half of his great Battle Fleet in a surprise attack from their rear, killing thousands of his command, and didn't have enough fuel to return home. Because he was ordered to sail across the contaminated waters of the Gulf of Alaska swinging dangerously close to the Pacific Northwest under the ominous clouds of radiation, his crews were dying from radiation sickness and he, too, was sick.

Admiral Tobishi, a 78, was from a small fishing village in Southern China. He felt the pains in his stomach and knew he too had radiation sickness and his days were numbered. He had not spoken of this to his staff, but most of them showed sign of illness as well. His final order was to anchor all ships outside Valdez harbor and abandon the contaminated vessels. He hoped some of his crew might survive, but these mighty ships would never sail again; every inch of hull and structure plating was befouled by the very radiation they had wrought upon the American people. The irony of the situation did not escape him as he watched the last of his crew; those not yet sick, leave the ship in life rafts and small boats, while he remained aboard to die with what was left of his command. He knew the small boats and rafts were poisonous, but the waters were far too cold for his sailors to swim to shore and he was under orders not to beach any of the boats and he always obeyed commands.

Across Prince William Sound, OAP Sea and Land combat units launched an attack against Cordova, only to find it deserted and empty of supplies. An Alaska ferry and over 50 fishing boats were found tied to docks in the harbor. The Rear Admiral in charge ordered all boats sunk by naval gunfire. Most of the port facilities, the downtown area and some of the homes were destroyed by explosions and fire brought on from the invaders.

A Pilipino family, claiming to be OAP sympathizers, was found hiding in the back of one tourist shop. The shelves were partially filled with gift items from Russia and the Philippians. Soldiers demolished everything in their anger and then took the Pilipino family out into the streets and hung them from street signs.

Unlike other towns along the south central shore of Alaska, Cordova could not be reached by road. The Alaska Marine Highway ferry system provided most of the traffic in and out of the town. A small airfield for prop driven aircraft provided the only other means of transportation. When the evacuation order was given, the ADF used helicopters and C-17 cargo aircraft to move the population. Only the one Pilipino family refused to go and they paid for their misplaced loyalty.

When he realized what was happening to his sailors and soldiers, the Rear Admiral contacted Admiral Tobishi and learned of the epidemic of radiation sickness. Admiral Tobishi ordered the man to abandon his task force and move ashore. He was hoping the survivors of the sickness might survive in Cordova; there was no room in Valdez for more troops.

Grieved by his order, the task force was abandoned by the healthy, while the sick remained aboard. Cordova was still aflame, but there were homes left untouched and the Rear Admiral dearly hoped his people would be able to survive this Alaska winter. He returned to his cabin and shot himself.

Admiral Tobishi waited until the last of his healthy crew had left the ship and then sent those who were sick but still able to do their job to other sick bays in his fleet. They were under orders to shoot every living soul, and then make the decisions on how they themselves wanted to die. He then returned to his cabin and drank poison prepared for him by the ship's doctor. Afterward, knowing the poison would take only a few minutes to work, he returned to his ship's chair, looked out over the crowded shore of Valdez and died. He had spent 10 years in the USA, where he received his Doctorate in Economics at the University of Southern California. He had never wanted this war, but was loyal to his leadership and carried out orders and secretly wished he could've seen Southern California again. Some of his fondest memories were from there and as he closed his eyes for the last time, he recalled some of his American friends and wondered how many of them were still alive.

DELTA JUNCTION- FORT GREELEY AREA

As the morning of the 26th drew near, Alaska-Canadian forces found themselves facing the OAP on two fronts: those coming east from Fairbanks and the army moving north from Glennallen. By order of General Saunders, AK-CAN units were placed on 100% alert at 0500 hours, yet for some reason known only to the enemy, there was no immediate attack. Only small probes were sent out as platoon sized forces moved against Delta's perimeter. With the loss of the listening posts stationed along the Tanana River, ADF Command relied on Eskimo Scout units to locate the enemy's recon patrols. Within moments Eskimo Scouts detected the enemy and reported locations to Command. Surprisingly, the dark early morning skies over the Tanana Valley remained clear of enemy aircraft as a tense silence hung like a heavy blanket over the two armies.

F COMPANY

Positioned between E Company's northern most foxhole; 10 yards away from an F Company position and a half-mile wide anti-tank/anti-personnel minefield to the right, Lt. Scott Radley's platoon was dug in deep with two men sharing a hole. The frozen ground was tough to dig into, but fear brought on the needed adrenaline to get the job done. Chopping down a few dozen trees to the rear and cutting them up to provide a small level of protection in front of their holes, also helped.

Studying his platoon's position on a small map, Scott knew F Company would have an impossible task trying to stop tanks out in the open. This whole area was a flood plain for Susitna River overflow which seldom happened, and was completely flat for miles in every direction. His platoon was covering a position a normal sized company of troops would be hard pressed to handle. *Grounds too flat, no obstacles to stop 'em. They'll role right over us like were not even here. Flatten us like pancakes to be sure...even with those stupid log barriers the troops feel so safe behind.* To make matters worse, thick patches of white birch, brush and alder prevented his troops from having good fire zones for their LAW, AT4 Anti-Tank Launchers and M-60 machineguns. Scott spent several hours helping his platoon clear as much brush as they could and still leave some concealment for foxholes. He wanted it to look natural and several times walked out front of their positions to look back. From this precaution, he made several changes and in one case, two of his men had to dig another hole and he ordered two other men to give them a hand. Scott ignored their gripes and moved on to his next chore.

50 yards behind and to the right of 2nd platoon, Roscoe's 1st platoon finished digging their own foxholes, lining them with snow filled sandbags, branches and camouflaging them with short brush. It was their job to monitor the minefields and support Scott's platoon in case of an enemy breakthrough. 20 yards further back, Captain Owenby set up his company headquarters in a large five man foxhole covered by a roof of freshly cut

white birch branches and packed over with snow. It helped keep in a level of warmth, but it also cut down his visual range.

F Company's new heavy weapons platoon was busy setting up their mortars and their one heavy .50 caliber machinegun. The fifty would be used as a last ditch effort to cover the company's retreat, assisted by several M-60 machineguns. Their fire zones crisscrossed right over 2nd platoon's position and couldn't be brought into play until after the 2nd had vacated their holes. But it was the mortars Captain Owenby counted on most; they were his only real defense against the OAP armored units.

Snug and warm in his recently acquired goose down-filled sleeping bag, F Company's new 1st sergeant was somewhat content with his new home. Tucked safely behind two platoons of riflemen resting on an inflated air mattress, Howard was enjoying the warmth of a small, but concealed fire the company's RTO continued to feed with dried birch chips and small branches.

A two man listening post, placed 100 yards in front of Scott's platoon rotated observers every four hours. After checking in with the LP, Scott handed the microphone back to his new RTO, PFC Jimmy Olsen of Salcha. Freckle faced, PFC Olsen had grown up listening to jokes about his name and how he actually resembled the DC Comic book character who was Superman's pal. Olsen, 19 was the youngest of six sons and his father was in fact a big fan of Superman comics. It only made Olsen wonder even more why his father had waited for him to be born before cursing him with the name Jimmy.

About to leave for a line check, Scott was climbing out of his freshly dug brick-like hole when he was suddenly struck in the shoulder by a golf ball sized object that nearly knocked him to the ground and grunted out a loud, "Ugh!" He was startled and quickly glanced around to see what had hit him concerned that a sniper had winged him, but there was a sore shoulder and no blood.

"That hurt," he complained then spotted a chunk of ice near his feet. Hail? Before he could call out a warning, the area came under immediate bombardment from huge hailstones; marble size to golf ball with the occasional baseball thrown in to make things a bit livelier. "Everyone get your helmets on and take cover!" Scott ordered. He shoved his own hard top on and not a moment too soon, as he felt another hit to his noggin and watched as a ball of ice bounced to the ground. By the bigger than golf ball size of it, he knew his helmet had saved him a really bad headache.

The sound of crashing ice bombs mixed with the cries of men being rained upon by hard ice. Scott watched thousands if not millions of the large hailstones fall on F Company. What Scott did not know was that the same thing was occurring over most North America and yet, there was not a single storm cloud in the heavens above.

One of the men, an older PFC in Scott's platoon, nursing a sore head and a bruised shoulder commented to the platoon medic, "There's an army of angels up there and they're playing pretty rough!"

One man in Roscoe's platoon was knocked unconscious and thirteen others in the company were bleeding from wounds caused by the ice balls. A soldier in the heavy weapons platoon took a good sized chunk of ice to the side of his face when it bounced off a mortar. He looked as if he'd been the victim of a one sided bar fight where the victor wore brass knuckles.

As fast as it came on, the hailstorm took its time tapering off - until the early morning hours were quiet once more. Company medics were busy bandaging the wounded, while Scott counted his injured troops. *Seven! Seven injured troops from a freak hailstorm. Well, at least none of them will have to go back to the aide station, can't afford to leave my perimeter much weaker.*

At 0547 hours, a jittery Captain Owenby approached Scott to check on 2nd platoon's injuries. He advised Scott regarding how the rest of the company had fared, "None too badly, but everyone is on edge because that was one freaky hailstorm." Captain Owenby even displayed his own battle wound; a bruise to his jaw that left him with two loose teeth.

At 0554 hours, Scott's LP reported hearing movement in front of their position. PFC Jack Oakley and Pvt. Sidney Okapuh were manning the post at the time and they were none too happy to be out there. "Fox 2, this is Lima Poppa 2...Over," PFC Oakley whispered over his radio. He was laying in the bottom of his hole in hopes his whispers could not be heard above the rim of their small hole. Pvt. Okapuh regretted not digging the hole a whole lot deeper and adding an emergency exit door. He had his binoculars up and ready, but the river fog was making it difficult to see anything more than 20 feet away.

"Go ahead...Over," Jimmy Olson answered. He handed the microphone to Scott, who was still chatting with Captain Owenby when the radio call came in.

"We got tanks, sounds like a lot of them and from the voices I can hear off and on, they've got infantry support. Estimate the enemy is still 100 yards off, but directly in front of our position...Over."

"What do you hear exactly...Over?" Scott asked. He gestured to Captain Owenby to get his company ready for attack and whispered, "We've got company."

"We've got metallic sounds...like tanks make when they run over snow and those big diesels are thumping away. Like I said, metallic things clanging against each other...Hold it!" PFC Oakley said and after a brief moment, he came back on the radio, "We hear several voices out in front of us; people talking an' it sure ain't no American... Over."

"Grab Okapuh an' head back here on the double...Over," Scott ordered.

"You don't have to say that twice, LT." PFC Oakley rose up from the bottom of the hole, took a quick glance around and grabbed Private Okapuh by the shoulder straps outside his parka and whispered, "Let's move, hot shot!"

Changing frequencies, Scott advised Roscoe of the report and learned 1st Platoon's LP's, posted beside the minefield had reported the same thing.

Captain Owenby quickly returned to his CP and called Command, only to learn listening posts all along the west perimeter were reporting movement toward the ADF perimeter. He dashed back to Scott's position, grabbed him by the arm and said, "Game time."

Scott disregarded military protocol, slapped his commander on the shoulder and replied with a reassuring, "Good luck, buddy... let's kill some bad guys!"

"You too," Captain Owenby said and gave PFC Olson a friendly nod before he headed back to his own position to ensure the mortar teams were ready to go. If it didn't lighten up soon, he'd need a lot of illumination and after that, as much high explosive as the mortar crews could put through their tubes before the order was given to fall back.

No one expected they could make a stand out here; their own plan was to cause crippling harm to the enemy front before withdrawing to Delta Junction. When and if Delta's defenses were overrun, the plan was to withdraw to Fort Greeley for a final stand. In briefing before being sent out, Captain Owenby was shown his positions for Delta Junction and Fort Greeley. Captain Owenby wasn't too happy with his 2nd line of defense in Delta Junction; taking an end of the wall position along the 5th wall and he sure didn't understand his position at Fort Greeley; holding down a southwest flank on an open field of snow. But he would obey his orders and continue to pray most of his command would survive to reach Fort Greeley.

ADF-CAN COMMAND BUNKER, DELTA JUNCTION

Generals Saunders and Howard-Wright stood behind a large three man center communications console and listened as reports came in from the front line. Glancing at General Howard-Wright, General Saunders shared a look of concern and turned to place his hand on the shoulder of a young communications sergeant. Whispering a quick prayer, he issued the order he had been dreading all night, "Contact General Watson and advise him to launch Raven Flight - now."

At Fort Greeley's airfield, power generators were speedily disconnected and a flight of 20 F-15 Eagles were readied for launch. Raven Flight, armed with four 250 pound bombs and four air-to-ground missiles rolled toward the active runway. They woke up nearly everyone within hearing distance as the Eagles engines began to wind up and prepare for takeoff. Overhead, flying at 30,000 feet under the protection of four Canadian F-18 aircraft, a recently refueled Shadow-One watched for enemy aircraft. Kicking in afterburners for take-off, the rest of Fort Greeley was promptly awakened as 10 rows of two Eagles each, ignited engines and released a deep roar as they thundered down the runway at over 200 miles per hour and accelerating. Hundreds of people, seemingly unaffected by the early morning cold, lined the runway to wave with enthusiasm as the fighters raced by. This was an occasion, undoubtedly the only time the military ever allowed civilians to be standing beside an active runway. Not that they had much choice, hundreds of tents lined both sides of the runway and no one was going to sleep through a squadron of Eagles taking off on full afterburners.

General Saunders turned to Major Ransom, a portly gentlemen of medium height, with thick black round eye glasses holding duty as Officer of the Day, "Major, what units man our extreme right flank?"

"Sir, elements of the ADF 2nd Division with a battalion of militia."

"Notify all company commanders on the forward positions to activate security panels... Settings will be blue lights. I repeat, blue lights." General Saunders looked over at General Howard-Wright, "Any suggestions?"

"No. My units are on full alert and I'm sure with all the noise your people are making, I've probably got 600 hundred rather excitable horses stirred up by now too." General Howard-Wright glanced at the position boards again, "We'll see what the enemy does before I commit my troops. This flanking movement to our extreme right could only be a probing action and we do have the minefield there, boarded by a river."

F COMPANY

Fox 2, this is Fox 1...Over." Captain Owenby had the microphone in one hand and a red lens flashlight squeezed under his chin illuminating a map held in his other hand.

"LT, I got the captain on the line," Jimmy Olsen said to Scott and then handed him the microphone and headset.

"Thanks, Jimmy."

"This is Fox 2...Over," Scott replied. With a wary look he glanced around his platoon and the area out front.

"Set up aircraft warning panels, the color is blue. I say again the color is blue. Expect air support within 5 mikes...Over."

"I copy... blue panel lights." He gave the word to Jimmy and then advised Captain Owenby, "We have antitank crews ready, but it's beginning to sound like Macy's Thanksgiving Parade out there...Over."

"Hold the line, Scott...Out." Captain Owenby, hands trembling slightly from adrenaline rush, handed the microphone back to his RTO and looked out toward the direction of Scott's platoon. The rumble of heavy equipment had reached his position, with minor tremors shaking the land. "That's no 10 or 12 tanks on a probe, sounds like a whole brigade out there at least."

He looked to his RTO, "Get me battalion." After making his report, Captain Owenby was ordered to dig in and prevent the OAP from flanking F Company's position. "Flanking? I'm more worried about being run over, Sir." Captain Owenby didn't bother to sign off, he just tossed the radio equipment to his frightened RTO and shouted to the sergeant who ran the heavy weapons platoon, "Its show time! Make sure your tubes are lined up and you've got plenty of ammo." He waited for a count of 50 then issued orders for the mortars to open fire with two rounds each of illumination. Afterward, the mortars would be using high explosive rounds. All fire was directed to a line 200 yards out in front of Scott's position.

Two of Scott's squad leaders set up the light panels directly in front of their position and then quickly ducked when the first mortar rounds sailed overhead and lighted up the early dawn with parachute flares. In moments, HE rounds impacted the woods directly in front of Scott's position and the world exploded. Targeting was made easy, when Scott radioed back one of the 81mm HE rounds had landed right on top of a heavy tank and secondary explosions were still lighting up the sky. By then, even the mortar crews could see the effects of their work and increased delivery speed. Scott was confused as to why the OAP forces still had not opened up with tank or artillery fire. There was automatic weapons fire coming from the tank's machineguns and from infantry support, but the enemy was shooting too high and not one man in the company had been hit so far.

Powered by a plastic block of 9 volt batteries, lighting system for the panels consisted of 10 collapsible metal boxes, each five feet long and nine inches high assembled. Five heavy amp floodlights provided illumination and turned blue after the correct lens was placed over each panel.

They were in the process of setting up the lights when PFC Oakley and Pvt. Okapuh arrived, having crawled most of the way on their bellies. Not so much to escape enemy fire, but to prevent from being shot by their own trigger happy friends.

"LT, there's a whole lot of 'em out there," PFC Oakley said. He crouched before Scott and brushed the wet snow off then pulled his canteen out and took a long gulp of cold water. But he was drinking too fast from nervousness and started coughing. Scott slapped him on the back.

"Easy, kiddo."

"Thank you, sir," PFC Oakley replied. He wiped his mouth with the green wool scarf wrapped around his neck and grinned down at Jimmy Olson.

PFC Oakley's expression turned to one of seriousness, "LT, we ain't gonna stop them... not here and now."

Scott laid his right hand on Oakley's shoulder, "You two stay here with Jimmy and protect this radio with your very lives. Just remember, their snipers will try to take out our communications first, so stay very low."

"In that case, sir, can I go with you and leave Oakley and Okapuh here with the radio." Jimmy Olsen asked with a wide-eyed expression.

"You'll do fine, Jimmy. I'll be back." Scott left to check the line and see what shape his command was in as the sounds of heavy machinery continued to come forward.

PFC Oakley sat down beside Jimmy, while Pvt. Okapuh knelt down beside the radio and wondered if it was worth more than his life and why? He looked up at Jimmy, "Did the LT really mean to protect this thing with our lives?"

Jimmy Olson shook his head in frustration, "Without the radio we can't contact CP and let them know where we are. Our own air force could hit us by mistake. That's why the radio is so important... so sit in front of it and protect it from bullets."

"You're foolin' me right?"

"Look, we just make sure the enemy doesn't get the radio and if we retreat we make sure to take it with us, okay?"

Pvt. Okapuh nodded his head. I hope I don't have to carry it... thing looks heavy.

Jimmy looked over at PFC Oakley, "Where'd you get this kid?"

"Give him some slack, Jimmy... he's only 16 and we're all scared to death."

"Well, I sure hope he can shoot."

"Oh, he can shoot all right... best shot in the family."

"You related to him?"

"A cousin from my mother's family, but he's a good kid."

"We'll keep him with us then," Jimmy said. With a pat of reassurance, Jimmy let Pvt. Oakley know that everything was going to be okay. "You see me get up to run, don't wait for the order. You just follow me and I'll get you out of here."

"Thanks, Jimmy," Pvt. Okapuh said. He glanced over the edge of the log barricade and saw the outline of an OAP dreadnaught coming through the smoke caused by the mortar fire, glared back at Jimmy and uttered, "I think it's time to go, Jimmy."

RAVEN FLIGHT

With most of the original Raven Flight destroyed in the Battle of Anchorage, a newly appointed Major Roger Eskil now led 19 F-15 Eagles into combat. An Athabascan Indian born and raised in Fairbanks, Eskil was the son of a hereditary tribal chief and next in line for the honor of leading his people. At 5'9" and 167 pounds, Eskil fit comfortably into the Eagle cockpit and was surprised how calm he felt as he led his flight toward Delta Junction.

General Watson wanted to lead the flight, but General Saunders reminded him he was now a general and senior officers needed to be on the ground to observe the operation from the command post.

"Raven One Niner to Fox-1...Over," Major Eskil said into his radio mike. After leaving Fort Greeley, he had switched frequencies so he could contact 2nd Division, and was given the call sign for F Company. Though the OAP were approaching all along the front, they seemed to be making a major push along 2nd Division's section of perimeter and General Saunders was extremely concerned about having the enemy outflanking them. He had hoped the minefield would deter them, but if in fact, the OAP was sending an entire brigade against F Company, a lot of OAP tanks would survive to wreak havoc behind his lines.

"Raven One Niner this is Fox 1, reading you 5 by 5...Over," Captain Owenby replied.

"I've got a special delivery coming your way, but could you provide the correct address? Over." Major Eskil checked out each side of his cockpit, looking at the flying lights of the Eagles beside him. A natural hunter who had stalked bears and moose as a young teenager, Major Eskil disliked flying at night or in predawn light where vision was affected. Distances between fighters could quickly change and mid-air collisions resulted if one pilot misjudged his positioning and distance.

"Raven One Niner, your target is 100 yards directly in front of my company. Our position is marked with blue... I say again, our position is marked with blue light panels and my troops have their heads down. No hills or other obstacles in immediate area, light winds from southeast, no trees over 50 feet if I'm any judge of heights. Can you see blue lights…Over?"

Major Eskil glanced over his left shoulder and spotted the blue light panels a few seconds later. "Copy Fox 1, I have your position. Notify your men we're coming in hot, get ready for some earth shaking music…Out." Major Eskil already knew the minefield was to F Company's right, so he had no fears of hitting any friendly forces there. He pushed a button to address his flight, "Switches hot, prepare to engage. I'll make a north to south run with Raven 13 and Raven 5 on my tail to drop incendiaries. We'll pull out to the east and ascend to 4,000 feet. Keep enough distance to avoid secondary explosions… Let's hurt them for Anchorage." Major Eskil wiped the sweat from his brow.

"Raven 7, remain aloft and keep your eyes open for bandits. Report all anti- aircraft positions. Shadow-One will monitor our traffic and keep us advised of unfriendly visitors." He checked his board; everything was green. "Raven One Niner breaking left…now!" Leading the formation into a lengthy single file, each Eagle spaced roughly 500 yards apart to prevent shrapnel from hitting the next fighter, Major Eskil rolled his bird and leveled off at 4000 feet. Less than a minute later, Ravens 13 and 5 were positioned directly behind him.

F COMPANY

Hearing the thundering roar of the diving jets overhead, Scott began to pray the pilots wouldn't under shoot their targets and drop a bomb right on his position. *Lord, it's happened before. Weird how they call it friendly fire, there sure ain't nothing friendly about it.* Major Eskil's jet raced over their position and Scott thought he could feel the heat from the Eagle's engines. Within seconds, the darkness of predawn exploded into bright daylight as 250 pound bombs and incendiaries slammed into enemy tanks and an icy landscape.

The first bomb was too close for comfort; Scott dove down to the bottom of his hole and squeezed in beside Jimmy Olsen. He covered his ears with gloved hands to prevent hearing loss and screamed to fight the pressure closing in as the concussion waves passed overhead.

Explosions hit one after another causing the ground to shake so violently that blasts catapulted his men out of foxholes. Hellish fires lit up the woods in front of them and his troops were plummeted with falling debris. One man was seriously wounded when a large chunk of shrapnel fell from the sky and drove him to the ground.

Illuminated by the burning brush and trees caused by the incendiaries, Scott finally saw the size of the force coming at them. More than a dozen tanks lay burning, reduced to melted hulks, but there were three times that number of dreadnaughts to take their place. He made a quick count of those he could see and didn't like the numbers he was coming up with, but wasn't about to stay around long enough for a recount. He was ready to give the order to fall back when he saw the enemy infantry closing in. Hundreds of ground troops faced his platoon and he knew he had to get his people out of there. Dozens of the enemy were engulfed in flames; some running about, others thrashing on the ground with no one was going to their aid.

"Dear God..." Scott nearly ripped the radio pack off Olsen's back when he grabbed for the radio microphone and headset. "This is Fox 2, we got more than a brigade of medium and heavy tanks moving in on us supported by at least two maybe three companies of infantry and possibly more. No way can we hold."

Captain Owenby gave him the order and Scott, who had handed the microphone back to Jimmy, shouted out, "Pull back!"

As if they had waited for F Company to start their retreat, the enemy opened up with its first volley of tank fire. The first shells landed in line with the very positions his people were running from. Flying shrapnel cut down several, and at least two were thrown skyward from explosive impacts. Within moments a barrage of tank fire and heavy machineguns made splinters of wooden barricades and trees directly in front of F Company. If it wasn't for Raven Flight, he would have been quickly overran as the enemy simply rolled over F Company's position.

As it was, that was still going to happen, but at least now he had a few moments of warning to get his people out. "Everyone, grab weapons an' ammo. Pull back in line with the Company CP to reinforce the heavy weapons platoon." Scott shouted at the top of his lungs and then added, "Four to a hole and be ready to move again."

RAVEN FLIGHT

"Raven lead, this is Raven 7, enemy forces are flanking ground troops to the north. Enemy tanks are in the minefield...several smaller tanks have already been disabled. They are using disabled tanks and bodies to push over mines plowing a path with their dead." Raven 7 was 1st Lt. Andy Salcedo, who reported the strange scene below from a height of 1200 feet. Explosions from the tanks illuminated the area enough for Raven 7 to see what was happening below and he was shocked by what the OAP was doing. Raven Flight's bombing run had set the forest ablaze, and after killing or damaging nearly two dozen tanks and uncounted ground forces, fires illuminated most of the area below allowing the ADF and Militia ground forces to see the enemy. Raven 7's voice came over the radio again in disbelief, "Hold on, we've got additional armor units moving in to support enemy's first line. Be advised, Raven lead, appears a second brigade or better is advancing from the river to force a breakthrough across the northwest line. I'm getting some flak up here, will have to ascend to 2,000 feet to keep my tail from being shot off."

"Raven One Niner to Raven Flight, let's set up for second run. We will continue to attack and keep them off our troops for as long as possible. Raven 7, stay aloft and keep an eye open for bandits... our luck won't last long."

"Remember I've got a full load up here and I'd like to get into the party," Raven 7 advised.

"If bandits show, you'll have enough to do," Raven One replied then prepared for his next run.

With all the armor the OAP was bringing, Major Eskil knew they would never be able to hold Delta Junction and he wondered about Fort Greeley. *They've just got too many tanks, too many planes and too many troops... how'd they get such a large army and we didn't know about it? Someone had to be paying off someone else to turn a blind eye to this and I'd sure like to have that someone in my sights right now.*

F COMPANY

Emptying one 30 round magazine, Scott slapped in a second when an enemy tank round impacted only a few yards away. The concussion wave from a 90mm cannon picked him up and threw him backwards for nearly 10 feet, where he smacked into the smoldering trunk of a standing birch tree. With painful difficulty, he fought off a wave of dizziness and tried to get his breath back with some difficulty. The heat wave which had accompanied the blast concussion left his uniform soaked with a mixture of his sweat and melted snow. When he pulled himself to his feet a bit unsteadily, he looked west where fires caused by the bombing silhouetted the advancing enemy. For a brief moment, as he waited for his head to clear and quit seeing double, he thought he was seeing all the demons of Hell marching toward him. With clarity returning, he realized how close the enemy was and shouted at the top of his lungs, "They're right on top of us! Move back! Move back!" Scott continued to yell for his troops to fall back, bring the wounded and ensure they had weapons. Suddenly he dropped to the ground to crawl forward to locate his own M-16, having dropped it when he was smacked by the concussion wave. He was able to locate his rifle and made sure it was operational before he fired off two short bursts toward the advancing enemy infantry. His ears were still ringing and his eyes burned from all the burned sulfur in the air. People from both sides were screaming, either at one another or for the pain they felt before death ceased their cries.

Scott glanced around to observe complete chaos as fires burned, snow melted to mud and two undermanned platoons supported by a fast moving weapons platoon, clashed with an enemy horde out numbering them by better than 20 - 1. There were still the tanks to consider, coming on like monsters of the deep to consume their human prey. Scott glanced around and wondered, *where's our tanks? Be a nice time to commit them. Maybe save a few lives.* Realizing Jimmy, his RTO, was missing, Scott took off running between trees in search of young Jimmy Olsen. Exchanging shots with the enemy, Scott located Jimmy's body beside a patch of burning alders. Looking down at his shrapnel riddled body, rage began to burn within. He knelt, brought the butt of his rifle to his shoulder and fired off a long burst of automatic fire toward an advancing line of OAP soldiers then stood and in defiance roared out into the night like an angry beast. With a new magazine in his rifle, a wrathful and nearly crazed officer took his vengeance out on the approaching enemy.

Three OAP soldiers burst through a stand of alders and rushed Scott with bayonets aimed at his chest. He didn't know why they simply didn't just shoot him, but firing from the hip, he dropped all three with a five round burst.

He could see some of his people, slowly withdrawing while firing against the enemy and he remembered he had a job to do to protect his platoon. "Fall back! Fall back!" Scott shouted again, his voice hoarse from the smoke in the air. Trying to be heard over the sounds of combat was nearly impossible, but he kept trying. "Bring the wounded and fall back. Don't stop to fight, just run for it! Head for the second line…we'll make a stand there."

Overhead, Raven Flight continued to dive on the enemy with bombs and missiles, and when they were used up, they raked the enemy with 20mm cannon fire until they were to depart. They returned to Fort Greeley for fuel and rearming, but in the meantime there was no air cover.

Snow and ice erupted around Scott as an AK-47 bullet grazed his skull and left him momentarily stunned and bleeding. The world moved in slow motion. All around him blinding flashes of lightening and thundering claps of weapons fire rolled across the valley. Hot air, thick with the pungent odor of sulfur, made him nauseous and forced him to drop to his knees vomiting. A large piece of hot shrapnel from an exploding tank sailed over like a Frisbee barely missing. Whole trees, uprooted by earth tremors caused by Raven Flight and enemy bombardment entrapped both enemy and Alaska troops, while loud crackling fires silenced their cries for help. Scott watched through watery smoke blurred eyes. With both vision and hearing impaired, he became lost in the woods. Ahead, enemy tanks and troops smashed their way through the line like NFL defensive linemen against a high school offense.

With the ADF 2nd Division in full disorganized retreat, Scott stumbled through the woods in search of his platoon, his white camouflage cover soiled with blood and blackened by smoke. After several minutes of looking still unable to locate the rest of F Company, he crouched behind a stand of black spruce trees out of breath and began to wonder where he was in relation to the secondary line of defense, but more importantly, how far away was the enemy?

ADF-CAN COMMAND BUNKER, DELTA JUNCTION

"General, the entire northwestern front is under attack. We can't keep up with the radio traffic, everyone's calling for reinforcements," Major Ransom said. "This isn't a probe, sir. They've committed their whole point to our right flank." Major Ransom held two microphones, one in each hand, a frenzied look on his face. All around him, the communications center was besieged with calls for help from 2nd Division, while several companies of ADF troops ran for their very lives.

"Order artillery units to concentrate all fire on the north and south sides of the highway 100 yards in front of our forward most position," General Saunders ordered. He checked his assignment board to reconfirm unit locations for quick reference. "I still believe the main attack will come down the road, but we better be prepared for a second front along the dry river bed." He studied the situation board for a moment.

"Major, send our own 4th Armored Brigade south along the dry riverbed. I want them backed up by the 6th Cavalry's Strikers. Advise Generals Watson and Wilcox to launch ready flight immediately after Raven Flight lands. General Watson's squadron commander is to go directly with 2nd Division ground controllers to coordinate an attack to the north." General Saunders looked to General Howard-Wright, who was issuing orders to several members of his support staff. He waited until he had the General's attention, "I plan to hold the A-10s until daylight... those boys work better with good visibility."

"Sounds good to me." General Howard-Wright turned to a young Canadian captain, "Send our 102nd Armor Brigade in to support of the ADF 4th Armored Brigade. Put 97th Tank Corps on standby in case they need to handle any stragglers the others might miss." He looked at General Saunders, "The 102nd is made up of Bradley Fighting Machines and what few Strikers we picked up from your US Army's garage sale several years ago. Too bad I had to send all our Tornadoes east; they'd help in the coming air battle."

When the Eastern Canadian Army launched its invasion of Ontario, General Howard-Wright was forced to send his entire Air Force, minus Shadow-One and her four F-18 protectors, to meet their air and ground forces. Reports coming in from the east were not favorable; casualties were mounting at an alarming rate.

General Saunders walked over to where Lt. Kelly was standing and accepted his web gear. Strapping it on, he pulled out his old Colt Model 1911 .45 caliber pistol with real ivory grips, a gift from his wife and chambered a round before re-holstering it.

"General," General Saunders said, "...I feel strange standing here while my troops are out there fighting and dying."

"This is the job of command, my old friend and you know it all too well." General Howard-Wright knew his friend hadn't been in a major engagement before, not of this scale and hoped he could bear up, not act like some heroic bull colonel and go running off to the front lines. "As you informed one of your new generals earlier, we who command stay back, issue the orders, and send our troops to their fate. This is the fate of generals." General Howard-Wright turned to listen to his own communication officers as they talked back and forth with his units.

"Major Ransom, get a hold of the mortar pits. I want them prepared with HE in the event we need to fall back to Fort Greeley," General Saunders ordered.

"Yes, General," Ransom replied and looked for the right microphone. Satisfied he issued the orders and waited for a response as the message was sent out over the radio.

ADF NORTH AREA MORTAR PITS

Sgt. Archuleta threw the microphone and headset down and stared at Cpl. Lewis in frustration, "What do those people think we're doing down here, shooting pool an' playing craps?" Disgusted with the brass, Sgt. Archuleta picked up another 81mm HE round and dropped it into the tube. With the enemy so close, his crews had sent out a steady series of HE rounds for the last few moments to cover 2nd Division's retreat.

F COMPANY

Bleeding from a nasty head wound, Scott stumbled through a gully and was startled to come across some of his men following a badly shaken Captain Owenby through a thick stand of alder. Behind them, an enemy armored personnel carrier, supported by a thin line of infantry pursued them on snowshoes. Without realizing it, Captain Owenby's F Company survivors had run right into C and E Company survivors who were too tired to run anymore making a stand at a frozen creek bed. C and E Companies had let F Company pass, which said a lot for their fire discipline, and then the Alaskans engaged the enemy. The short lived battle was over in moments and the dwindling remains of three ADF companies again fled east.

Wiping blood, dirt and smoke off his face with the frosted back of his gloved hand, Scott counted the survivors of his platoon. *"Nine men...I got only nine men left."* Both of his ladies were dead, but he didn't have time to think about that now. Glancing at his watch, he was stunned at the realization that he had lost 21 men and two women in less than 48 minutes. In that same amount of time, Scott had killed more than a dozen of the enemy and taken out a medium tank with a LAW he discovered in the snow. But still, they kept coming and his supply of ammo was getting low. "Keep to single shots, conserve your ammo," Scott ordered. Roscoe, whose white snow cover was draped in blood from head to toe from several hand-to-hand engagements, spread the word to conserve ammo to the remains of his platoon too.

2nd Division was in full retreat: men and women running, crawling and being carried; rushing to fall back to the next defensive position as the new morning sun rose to breach the horizon. What had been hidden by darkness was now revealed; white snow rapidly turning a ghastly shade of crimson red.

Heavy enemy machineguns, supported by 90 mm tank cannons, swept from side to side, cutting down everything in their path like a wiper blades sweeping rain drops off a windshield. Dead covered the land; wounded lay screaming for help until enemy guns silenced them. No quarter was given, no mercy offered and no honor shown. Men and women simply fought to survive or die.

When he heard a scream only a few feet behind him, Scott turned around in time to see Captain Owenby cut down by a machinegun burst stitched across his back. Knowing his friend was dead Scott calmly knelt on one knee, brought his rifle to his shoulder and fired four quick shots to kill the soldier who had killed Captain Owenby.

"You okay, Scott?" Roscoe crouched beside him.

"Captain Owenby bought it."

"I saw and if you keep sitting around here you'll catch one too. Let's move it, LT!" Roscoe shouted. Then in a lower voice, he added, "What's left of F Company is now yours, Scott."

A few moments later, Scott heard his name called out through the early morning haze. Howard was manning an M-60 machinegun, a belt of ammo looped around his shoulder and into the weapon. He was waving for Scott and Roscoe to join him. But before they could move Howard vanished, replaced by an eruption of dark smoke and flame. An enemy tank round had landed directly on Howard's position and Scott knew his friend never knew what hit him.

"C'mon, Scott, we gotta keep moving," Roscoe said. With a tight grasp around Scott's combat suspenders, he half-dragged Scott to his feet. "More fightin' ta do, buddy…This is far from over."

ADF OUTER PERIMETER WALL ACROSS RICHARDSON HIGHWAY

As the enemy's northern army attacked, sending thousands of OAP soldiers across the Susitna River and east along the Richardson Highway, they came within 200 yards of the first perimeter wall. ADF artillery fire rained down on them competing with the shrill sounds of a hundred Chinese bugles. Led by junior officers and NCOs, the soldiers followed up with thousands of shouts and shrieking screams in an attempt to rattle the ADF defenders. An order was given, and even as the shells burst around them, OAP front lines charged the first outer wall.

The OAP infantry came first up against concentrated machinegun fire from camouflaged bunkers, followed by a field of Claymore mines, trip grenades and showers of heavy mortar fire. Sheer weight in numbers carried them through the first three walls, killing and wounding hundreds of ADF and Militia forces. Then as the enemy climbed up the western side of the fourth wall, ADF forces broke the attack with brutal hand-to-hand fighting on top of the man-made barrier. Standing atop a mound of snow, all too quickly taking on a crimson color, Alaskans used knives, bayonets and rifle stocks, fists and feet, to stop the enemy's advance and slowly the OAP force started to withdraw.

105 mm howitzer crews, already low on ammo, rained a fiery death down on the retreating enemy. Arriving F-15 Eagles and F-22 Raptors strafed the woods and took on targets of opportunity with 250lb bombs until the jets were forced back to Greeley for fuel and rearming.

Major Eskil, flying in low to cover a downed pilot fleeing from the enemy, lost his life when a shoulder mounted missile blew his right wing off and his Eagle cartwheeled down through a thick grove of trees in a blaze of fire. The downed pilot, with only a .38 caliber pistol for defense was chased through the deep snow and caught. But this was not a day for prisoners; he was killed immediately.

Along the dry riverbed to the south, a combined ADF-Canadian armored force ambushed a large OAP tank force in the process of attempting a flanking movement to the ADF's southern defensive perimeter. A fierce battle was fought, as Canadian Bradley Fighting Machines, ADF M1-A1 tanks and Strikers, supported by Canadian light tanks, engaged the mighty OAP dreadnaughts and a company of lighter tanks.

OAP Mechanized Infantry, in support of the tanks, dug in, but came under heavy fire by a Canadian Airborne Unit armed with AT4 tank busters. With the help of the Canadian Tank Brigade, the enemy was held off for a brief spell, except from the north, where without enough armored support, 2nd Division continued to lose ground at a rapid pace.

ADF MOBILE CP

Transferring to a mobile trailer pulled by a monstrous older model green and white 10 ton Kenworth, General Saunders listened as Major Ransom filled him in over the radio with the latest reports on OAP's southern forces. "Sir, our Cavalry scouts report the OAP lead element coming up from the south in striking distance of Fort Greeley by noon today." This was not what General Saunders wanted to hear, but he knew the force coming up from Anchorage and Prince William Sound was due soon and he'd be fighting two armies; one from the south and the other from the northwest.

"Major Ransom, notify Colonel Deekins to move the new Militia division to reinforce our southern perimeter. Advise him, I'll send all possible reinforcements I can spare from the northern perimeter as soon as possible."

"Yes, sir," Major Ransom signed off.

Standing in the back of an overly warm and lightly armored steel sided 40' by 12' trailer, General Saunders stood with his shirt collar soiled in sweat, his face moist and studied the sad state of his army on a situation map attached to a wooden wall section. The driver, accompanied by two soldiers, had moved the Kenworth into a secure position - for the moment. Two APC units with mounted M-60's accompanied the Mobile CP, each carrying a reinforced squad of infantry.

ANGEL & RED BEAR FLIGHTS

With permission from General Saunders, General Watson was airborne at 5,000 feet to observe the battle below. He felt encouraged witnessing the bravery exhibited by armored units engaged with a superior force of enemy tanks in the dry creek bed. Sweeping in from the north, General Watson led a flight of six F-22 Raptors to support General Wilcox's remaining ADF Southern Wing of 20 F-15 Eagles. From Shadow-One, overhead and refueled by ADF KC-135 tankers, they had learned the skies off to the west, were filled with a large scale force of enemy fighters. The OAP was committing their fighters from Nome, Kotzebue and recently cleared Eielson Air Force Base.

With golden rays of sunlight blazing out across a beautiful cloudless sky, General Watson had a very brief moment to think about his daughter. Recuperating in a field hospital after her fighter was shot down she was killed when Glennallen came under air attack. Witnesses reported the field hospital, which had prominently displayed a very large red cross, was hit with two large bombs. General Watson's only hope lay in knowing his daughter was in heaven with her courageous boyfriend and he'd probably be joining them very soon. Her face filling his mind, General Watson gave her small photograph taped to the side of his cockpit a caring wink and turned his attention back to the job at hand.

Shadow-One was speaking into his ear phones, "Red Bear One, Angels One, you've got bogies coming in at 8,000 feet from the northwest. They're just about filling my screen...Be advised I also have a second formation at 12,000 feet coming in from the southwest. At present speed - if they don't run into each other, both flights could be over station in 12 mikes Over."

"This is Red Bear One, I copy, Shadow-One," General Watson replied.

"Likewise," General Wilcox added.

Going direct with each other, Generals Wilcox and Watson decided to engage the threat coming in from the northwest first, assisting the battle already engaged. They would let the ADF field artillery set up a massive flak field for the southwest OAP flight without having to worry about hitting one of the good guys. After notifying Shadow-One and Saunders of their decision, a grand total of 32 ADF aircraft gallantly flew off to face their destiny.

F COMPANY

When he was ready, hand tremors under control momentarily, Scott popped up from behind a fallen tree to fire off a LAW at an approaching APC. Sailing through the air for over 20 yards, the rocket penetrated the machine and killed the crew in a fiery blast. Roscoe, kneeling beside Scott, leapt up and used an AT4 to take out a medium tank that was escorting the APC which Scott had destroyed. Both were glad they were only facing APC units and medium tanks because so far their anti-tank rounds had little effect on the heavier dreadnoughts - other than scraping paint on the massive beasties.

When Scott reached the highway, the sight before his eyes sickened him, and after what he'd been through already he didn't think it was possible to feel any worse until now. For a mile in each direction the battlefield was littered with countless bodies of the dead and dying from both sides. They lay draped over barbed wire; piled two and three deep over sandbagged walls or mangled in shallow holes. With a thick layer of gray smoke hanging over the ground, the Richardson Highway resembled a pock marked dried lava field with thousands of craters in all sizes. The once thick growth of trees that bordered the highway was reduced to smoldering stumps and splinters. Delta Junction had become a no man's wasteland with the first four walls breached and the body count standing in the thousands.

Covered in soot, exhausted and bleeding from several wounds about his body, Scott studied the bleak terrain before him for a brief moment and then issued an order to his small command, "Pick up whatever you need and move back, we can't hold here. If you find a wounded man, sing out and we'll carry him or her with us... but leave the wounded enemy for their own ... and no executions... We don't need that kind of stuff on our shoulders."

F Company was reduced to eight men, including Scott and Roscoe. They had joined the survivors of Bravo, Charlie and Echo companies. Fighting a running retreat, Scott soon found himself in command of a ramshackle greatly undermanned battalion after all other superior rank officers were cut down.

Climbing over a burned out APC, Scott spotted the Delta Junction business district in the distance. He recognized the sign for the IGA Grocery Store and standing there, it had strangely amused him. Such normalcy, when the world bleeds all around it... No Alaska flag in sight, no American red, white and blue waving, but that silly, stupid sign was untouched. *It's like our capitalist America mocking the communists...* "This way, guys...follow me. We'll use the buildings over there for cover."

Before they reached the buildings, Scott spotted a Canadian tank unit moving up from the south and he and Roscoe waved them down. The lead tank slowly came to a halt and the others stopped after forming a defensive line position with their 90mm guns facing the enemy.

A Canadian major, stood in his turret and called down to Scott, "Is this the last of you... is there anyone else coming this way?"

Shaken by the question, Scott muttered to himself, "Are we the last? All those people dead and the enemy still strong..." Instead, he shouted to the major, "Yes, sir, we're the last... there's no one else behind us."

Kneeling on one knee, Scott ordered Roscoe to position their men behind the tanks, drink some water and await further orders. "Give 'em a rest, it won't be long before we start up again."

"I'll see if the Canadians have any food or water," Roscoe said. He started to walk away when the Canadian tank unit suddenly opened up with their big guns and pounded the woods to the northwest where F Company had just escaped. At first Scott thought the enemy was right over the ridge, then realized the tanks were using their guns like field artillery against enemy positions.

ADF MOBILE CP- 0720 HOURS

"General, our entire right flank north of the highway has collapsed. Our troops are holding the line within 300 yards of this spot with the remains of our 2nd Battalion, reported to be less than 100 men. They are supported by a force of 40 Canadian tanks." Mobile CP Duty Officer Major Higgins said.

"We have no other reports from the rest of 2nd Division, but that could be a communication problem. However, that's all we have between us and the enemy and I recommend we move real soon or risk capture."

General Saunders felt the bitter taste of defeat in his mouth and it soured his stomach to give the order, but he had little choice, "All right, Major; pull us back to our secondary position. Have all troops pull back and make sure they bring the wounded."

"Yes, sir," Major Higgins replied and nodded the General's confirmation to retreat to the CP communications officer.

Delta Junction had become a quagmire of blood, mud, melting snow and mangled metal. A once proud tourist stop resembled a no man's land after Pickett's charge on the 3rd day of Gettysburg.

When word came over the radio that OAP Southern Forces were within 10 miles of Fort Greeley, General Saunders could no longer wait and hope for a miracle. He ordered a complete withdrawal; all ADF and Canadian forces in Delta Junction to fall back to defend Fort Greeley at best possible speed. Knowing Generals Wilcox and Watson were committed elsewhere General Saunders committed his remaining A-10s to cover their ragged retreat along a narrow two lane stretch of highway.

F COMPANY

"Are you any good at hitchhiking, Scott?" Roscoe asked when word of the order to withdraw was passed down. He was sincerely hoping for a ride from their Canadian allies.

But before Scott could answer, the Canadian tank unit commander shouted down to Scott and Roscoe, "Do you chaps need a ride by any chance?"

"And all this time I thought you Canadians were an unfriendly bunch." Roscoe didn't wait for Scott to reply, he issued orders for all ADF troops to climb on the nearest tank.

After making sure there was room for the wounded, Scott finally climbed on the last tank to leave the city. He kept turning around, looking to see if there was anyone else coming up behind them needing a ride. But the battlefield was quiet, no one was moving; buildings and vehicles were left in smoldering ruins. Except from above; the air was filled with the thunderous roar of fighter jets, their heavy cannon fire and air-to-air missiles streaming at one another. Riding on the back of the rumbling tank, nursing his many wounds of varying degree, Scott glanced up to see a fighter falling from the skies in death's fiery embrace and wondered, *whose side were you on*? He glanced around at his exhausted troops, thinking about all the men and women who had died in the last few hours and in a whisper of a voice, he asked, "God? Why? Why are you waiting? This can't be what You wanted... so why, Lord? Why don't you put a stop to this? Too many good men and women have perished today and still we fight... Are you even listening, Lord?"

RED BEAR ONE

Clearly the F-22 Raptor was the superior aircraft; General Watson had downed his third MiG in less than five minutes. He put his Raptor into a 3G turn to avoid an enemy missile and leveled off to line up on the tail of an SU-21. But the enemy numbers were staggering; the skies were filled making conventional dog fighting nearly impossible. General Watson felt it was like flying into wave after wave of wasps.

In the midst of the dog fight, General Watson observed numerous enemy fighters colliding with each other as the sky became simply too full to fly in. Watson ordered his pilots to take the low road, while Wilcox took his flight to the upper heavens. After only 46 minutes in the air with only three surviving aircraft left from a flight of 32, General Watson knew he was quickly running out of time.

General Wilcox scored his fourth air victory and was smacked in the side by an air-to-air missile. His plane exploded in a fiery ball of flame. There was no time to eject; General Wilcox rode his fiery Eagle to the ground.

Out of missiles and engaging guns, Watson shredded the SU-21's tail assembly with 30mm cannon fire and sent the enemy aircraft spiraling downward. Seconds later, an air-to-air missile, one of three directed at him, managed to get by General Watson's defenses and struck right below the plane's canopy. General Watson never felt the pain of dying as his fearsome Raptor exploded in a black fiery blast. Less than a minute later, the air war ended over the Susitna River, when the last F-15 Eagle, flown by a young section leader, lost its air battle against three MIG-29 aircraft.

ADF MOBILE CP, EN ROUTE TO FORT GREELEY

"Sir, Shadow-One reports they've lost all radar and radio contact with both Angel and Red Bear Flights. At this time, both Generals Watson and Wilcox, and crews are presumed lost." MSgt. Shirley Mayer, a forlorn look on her face, advised General Saunders.

General Saunders closed his eyes and whispered a prayer for the souls of his men and women who had bravely faced overwhelming odds this day. He turned to face Major Higgins, "Status of Wrangler Flight?" General Saunders felt the tears of an old man come forth, but he fought them off and rubbed his eyes. Losing his friends was hard and thinking of how many others had perished today only made the weight a heavier burden to bear.

"Sir, Wrangler Flight is providing air cover while our forces return to Greeley. So far, OAP air units appear to be returning to their bases and the enemy ground forces are holding positions in Delta."

"Thank you." General Saunders couldn't understand why the OAP wasn't pressing, but he wouldn't complain. Hearing this news, he felt as if a 600lb gorilla perched on his shoulders had transformed into a 200lb chimp. He returned to his chair and studied the plans for the defense of Fort Greeley. With only Wrangler Flight left and some attack helicopters, he was down to a very small Air Force to defend more than 300,000 people. *Lord, if ever we needed you, this is the time. We face such dire odds unless You intercede, why must so many fall before You decided the time is right? Why? Why?*

The Richardson Highway between Delta Junction and Fort Greeley, an eight mile stretch of two land road was a traffic jam. Retreating forces became entangled while overhead, Wrangler Flight continued to provide air cover. But strangely, the skies were clear of enemy fighters. Wrangler requested permission to attack enemy positions in Delta Junction, but were ordered to stay aloft over the retreat; everyone on the comm. circuit chose to ignore the bitter rumblings coming from the 12 Warthog pilots.

Military Police were out in force for traffic control and this small respite allowed ADF-Canadian troops to move slowly down the road and file into Fort Greeley. More MPs were on hand to direct combat units to assigned positions; wounded were taken to over crowded field hospitals. Jet fighter hangers had become hospital wards to deal with the excessive number of wounded troops.

Within hours, Fort Greeley's huge perimeter was manned on three sides by ADF-Canadian infantry supported by surviving armor and artillery units. The eastern side faced Canada, where mile after mile of anti-personal and anti-tank mines were laid to prevent passage. When the mines were used up, the Explosive Ordinance disposal experts used dynamite, grenades and even gasoline bombs to stop the enemy's advance. Guard towers were quickly erected to lace the eastern perimeter every hundred yards to have personnel available to set off the improvised charges; a reserve force of Militia was prepared to take position if the OAP managed to pass through the minefields climbing over their own dead.

Swelled to over 300,000 people, Fort Greeley had become the largest city in Alaska's history. Children were sent to underground shelters with the elderly who were unable to serve on the line or in a supporting role. Nearly anyone able to hold a rifle was handed one; some were sent to the perimeter; others held in reserve for later action.

ADF NEWLY FORMED 8TH DIVISION HEADQUARTERS

Walking through Division Headquarters looking for new orders, a slightly disabled Scott ran into his old company commander, Captain Buford.

"Radley, where you been boy?" Buford, surrounded by fellow officers, asked in his usual sarcastic tone. "I was informed I could expect your company, but yuh never showed up. Guess I'll have to mark you down as AWOL, boy. Ain't that just great?" Buford stood before Scott, his arctic camouflage neat and clean, his boots shining from a recent spit polish. "Aroun' here, boy, going AWOL could get you a firing squad and you'll probably find me leading it."

"I've turned my battalion over to ADF Command, Captain. I haven't been advised of my new orders yet." Scott fought hard to keep his mouth in check, but he sincerely wanted to reach out and knock Buford's head right off and he might anyway. His uniform was torn, his parka heavily stained with blood and soot from battle and his head wound was still wrapped in a fresh bandage, while Buford looked as if he had not even heard a shot fired in anger.

"Battalion? Who'd give you a battalion, Mr. Bright Boy? But don't matter none, now you're back in charge of a platoon of sorry eyed civilians... Not even Alaskans either. Think you can handle that, Nigger boy?" Buford smiled from ear to ear, wanting to impress his fellow officers. The men around him had developed a sour taste for Buford, but remembered who his uncle was and played the political game- at least for now. Feeling too witty with his own voice, Buford never expected he was about to lose several front teeth.

Unable to hold back and forgetting his arm wound, Scott unleashed a powerful right that impacted Buford's mouth. Driven backwards, Buford slammed against the wall and collapsed unconscious to the floor. Ignoring the awe struck stares of Buford's fellow officers, Scott popped a crisp salute to one of the captains, did an about face and walked off.

"About time someone had the guts to deck this clown," Captain Gilderson said with a look of disdain on his face. He glanced down on Buford's bleeding mouth and grinned then looked to his fellow officers and asked, "I didn't see anything... did any of you?"

"He must've walked into a wall while admiring his fat face in the mirror," a young captain replied. A lot of heads nodded agreement and the party of officers left Buford on the floor as they moved along.

FORT GREELEY'S SOUTHERN PERIMETER, 8TH DIVISION TERRITORY

For the latter part of the afternoon, Ed Sawyer, wearing an ADF parka with a white shell cover over civilian clothes, stood in a sloppy mud filled trench and looked out over a four foot stack of sandbags to a large open snowy field. His Sorrel Boots, covered thick in mud and ice, inserts soaked, provided little warmth. His gloved hands trembled from the morning's icy cold. The sky was cloudless and a beautiful blue color, allowing Ed to see the towering Alaska Mountain Range in the distance to the far south running to the southeastern horizon.

Every few moments, his inexperienced company of volunteers, awaiting their new commander, occasionally exchanged a round or two of gunfire with an OAP company on the far side of the field. Out of range for rifle fire, ADF-Canadian artillery units effectively kept the OAP infantry at a distance. But now and then an OAP officer got the nerve up to order his men forward to gain a few feet of snowy ground.

At Ed's right side, Point Man and His Misfits happily manned a pair of well cleaned and oiled M-60s. They had 1200 rounds of ammo for the machineguns, 14 grenades, nearly 300 rounds for their rifles and 60 rounds each for their pistols and revolvers, so the Misfits felt they were ready for the OAP. Plus they had their selection of knives, throwing stars and one ancient Marine Corps battle axe ground down to a short machete.

"You know, Ed, we've come a very long way to get into this fight," Joey Roberts said. He was cleaning his M-16 with piece of an old white t-shirt and checking to make sure the rifle magazines were fully loaded.

"Yeah, but you've got to admit if we had to be in a fight, this is sure the one. Think of the movie we could make… maybe we'd even get Mel Gibson to star in it."

"Don't know, he's a bit old now for action flicks," Joey replied then pointed off to the south and said, "Those people have us outnumbered, outgunned an' everyone on this planet is runnin' low on food. Unless Pastor's got a great Hail Mary pass stored up in his bag of miracles, this little game of ours might jus' go to the visiting team."

Ed grinned in reply and glared down at the thick pudding-like mud in his fox hole. It was over his ankles and keeping his weapon clean was his primary concern, along with providing some degree of warmth for his new wife.

Kira, with an older M-14 which had probably been used by a marine in the Vietnam War, draped over her shoulder, was visibly shivering in the cold temperatures. She had one blanket over her shoulders covered in blotches of mud, and was struggling in vain to keep her feet out of the mud.

Ed followed the narrow trench line between foxholes and made his way to her. He put his arms around her and gave her a tight squeeze. "I'll try to find us some more blankets, but in the mean time you need to keep moving to stay warm. Go back behind that row of trucks and do a few laps in a tight circle. I don't want some sniper picking you off because you popped your head up where it didn't belong."

Kira shook her head, "I'll stay here with you, dear husband. We may only have hours left together and I want every second of them - I'm greedy."

"Okay, but keep your feet moving or they'll freeze…and keep your rifle dry. Those M-14s freeze up especially if they get covered in mud."

"Yes, I hear and obey," Kira replied. She used a part of her blanket to wipe the rifle then looked at her husband with a serious look in her eyes and asked, "Ed, what's it going to be like…I mean when they come across that field by the hundreds?"

Ed looked to the enemy and then with a look of concern on his face, he answered, "I really don't know, Kira. I've never faced anything like this before. Oh, I've had to deal with large mobs and protestors, but never an army of well-armed soldiers. I imagine it could be the worst day in our life… and again, it may be our best. Battles do that to people… it brings out the best and worst in them. Some never want to forget their days in war and others work hard to put them behind. So, I guess we will see what the day brings and pray we can hold them off."

"Ed, don't leave me. I want to be at your side if this is…" Kira couldn't finish. Her eyes teared up; she leaned against her husband and whispered, "I love you."

"I love you too."

INSIDE FORT GREELEY

With Roscoe and his few remaining men following behind, Scott made his way through over crowded streets. Around him, thousands of cold and frightened people pushed and shoved one another to make their way through mobs having nowhere to go. Fear was spreading like wildfire; mass panic was in the makings as some were knocked to the ground and trampled by growing mobs of terrified hungry people.

Seeing three teenage girls fall before a line of fearful civilians, Scott brought his rifle up and pushed them back, while Roscoe and one of his men helped the frightened girls to their feet. It made Scott ill to see how people were behaving, "Don't you people understand, there's no place to run. This is it! We fight an' die on this piece of ground. There ain't no General Custer and his 7th Cavalry coming over the hill and no Georgie Patton...." Scott paused. He was heard a woman's voice coming over the fort's PA system. She was singing and all he could do was simply stand and listen to her captivating voice and the deep emotional feeling her words produced in him.

FORT GREELEY HEADQUARTERS BUILDING

Chaplain Knight, Pastor Woodway and other church leaders tried everything they could think to calm the masses, some of them nearly getting knocked down in the process by angry men and women who didn't want to hear words of faith. "Get out of our way! We're all gonna die and you want to conduct Sunday school," one woman shouted.

"All you holy rollers are the same...pray-pray-pray...and what's it done for you. We're going to die today and you still wanna pray. Go back inside, Pastor, before you get hurt," a burly middle aged man in a thick insulated snowsuit growled, as he shoved Pastor Woodway. The man ended up on the ground before he knew what had happened. Pastor Woodway understood their fears, but he wasn't going to be shoved around by anyone and used a wrist role to put the man on his backside.

"You'll have to teach me that one," Chaplain Knight said to his new friend.

"They're just scared and who can blame them," Pastor Woodway replied.

"Well, we've got to come up with something before this mob turns into a riot."

Standing on the steps of the Main Headquarters Building, Pastor Woodway spotted Cindy Roberts and her kids in the crowd. She had come looking for him. With Knight's assistance, Pastor was able to push their way through the people and bring Cindy to the top landing of the building's stairs. "Cindy, I need you. The Holy Spirit has spoken; I know now why we're here. This is our moment to act and I need you to start singing as loud as you can." Pastor looked at Chaplain Knight, "See if you can get us on the main PA system... locate the communications officer inside and please hurry."

"On my way," Chaplain Knight said and vanished into the masses headed for the front door. He displayed his military ID to jittery military policemen and was allowed entry.

"You want me to sing...now?" Cindy asked; a look of confusion on her face.

"Right now, Sister! As loud as you can!" Pastor exclaimed. A look of compassion on his face, he rested his mittened hand on Cindy's forehead and began to pray for her. Several people nearby, curious by what was going on, stopped to watch.

Chaplain Knight suddenly appeared at Pastor's side dragging an extremely long black cord connected to a large microphone.

"It's wired in and hot," Knight said keeping the microphone away from him so as not to be heard.

Pastor Woodway took the microphone and held it in front of Cindy, waiting as she cleared her throat. Her kids were snug up against her for she was very afraid she might lose them in this crowd. When she opened her mouth there was no hint of fear, no hesitation and she knew what song she was to sing. Cindy released the sweetest sound Pastor had ever heard and he knew it was the Lord using this spirit filled woman to calm these people and send a message out to all the troops.

"My eyes have seen the Glory of the coming of the Lord..." From deep within, Cindy bellowed out like an opera singer, singing the time honored hymn; her voice grew with power as she lashed out in a deep voice she had never used before with the song's memorable chorus, "...Glory, glory, Hallelujah. Glory, glory, Hallelujah..." As she sung, people stopped cold to listen. Soon, they joined in and within moments the song was spreading through the crowds like a massive wave at an NFL football game. It was working too, driving away fears as sweet worship stilled the stormy waters and a massive choir of tens of thousands formed within the perimeter of Fort Greeley. Words of praise spread from one hundred to one thousand and then to a hundred thousand, as voices lifted up to the heavens. More voices joined; the song was sung over and over again. No one tired of the words and the calming, yet joyful effect it sent over the masses.

SOUTH PERIMETER

"Can you hear singing?" Matthew Fulbright asked Kathy O'Brian.

"Yeah...I can. But what are they singing?" Kathy stood beside her husband.

"Hey, I know that song!" Larry O' Brian shouted. "Sounds like the whole fort is singing it too."

Recognizing the song and the words, the troops along the perimeter broke into song. Ed and Kira, Joey, Point Man and his Misfits, Larry and Kathy, Matthew Fulbright and all the others joined in and before long most everyone on the perimeter was singing out loudly. For one brief moment, it was if the cold no longer bothered them and their voices sang out boldly.

Joey no longer wondered where his wife was. He knew she was with Pastor right now leading the largest choir ever seen on this planet.

Pastor walked up behind Cindy, "Keep singing, while I read the Word of God." Chaplain Knight held the microphone for him; Pastor turned his Bible to Psalms 18 and began reading, "I love you, O Lord, my strength. The Lord is my rock, my fortress and my deliverer: my God is my rock, in whom I take refuge..." Over the next few moments, Pastor continued to read as a quiet calm fell over Greeley. The voices inside the fort quieted to hear the word of God spoken, while the troops on the perimeter continued to sing and provide a gentle back drop to Pastor's Woodway's reading. When he completed the last verse of Psalm 18, Pastor said a soft, "Amen", and the entire fort was left in a state of silence

Cued by the Holy Spirit, Cindy took in a deep breath and let out with a loud, "Lift up the name of Jesus, people and let the enemy hear our BATTLE CRY!"

Suddenly, thousands of voices unleashed a rousing chant of, "Jesus! Jesus! Jesus!" Thousands of people who had never given their lives to the Lord asked others to lead them in the Sinner's Prayer. Fear was washed away, hunger pains were forgotten, as the name of the Lord was lifted to the heavens as never before.

Pastor turned to see General Saunders, President Andrews and General Howard -Wright knelt down together at the top of the steps, as they offered up a prayer of thanksgiving. Asking other clergy to help them, Pastor Woodway and Chaplain Knight went to lay hands upon these three men of authority and they prayed.

In the distance, OAP forces who were prepared for the ground offensive heard the song. Some of them, out of fear for their own lives or that of family members had kept their relationship to Jesus Christ hidden, remembered a different time, a better time. The name of Jesus shouted out from the Alaskan encampment touched them with memories. These cold, hungry soldiers paused to reflect on the path before them and quite a few closed their eyes and silently prayed for God's intervention.

A COMING STORM

20 - CATCH A FALLING STAR

"And I saw an angel coming down out of heaven, having the keys to the Abyss and holding in his hand a great chain. He seized the dragon, the ancient serpent, who is the devil, Satan, and bound him for a thousand years. He threw him into the Abyss, and locked and sealed it over him, to keep him from deceiving the nations any more until the thousand years were ended. After that, he must be set free for a short time."

Revelations 20:1-3 NIV

INSIDE FORT GREELEY - APRIL 29TH

This was a time of worship and celebration like no other, an intensity of praise that seemed to hold the enemy at bay, as massive crowds of people continued to lift joyful praises to the heavens throughout the morning and into late afternoon. People who never knew one another linked arms as hundreds of circles were formed. There was no separation by church denomination or ethnic group, this momentous gathering appeared to be as the church scriptures foretold; one body joined together to simply praise the Lord Jesus Christ. People were on their knees, others dancing and even more lifting their hands to the heavens and praising their Lord. Thousands hugged complete strangers; it was as if a veil of selfishness and thoughtlessness had been lifted and nearly everyone had opened their hearts to their neighbors.

Even as at the time of Noah's Great Flood there were those among this jubilant throng who stood in the shadows; people who still refused to believe in anything beyond themselves. Others remained steadfast to their Native American, Jewish, Hindu or Muslim faith. Here, in these last moments, they were left to struggle with what may lie ahead - alone. With bitterness in their hearts, some non-believers held gloved hands over their ears in an attempt to block out the singing and praying. They could be seen standing together in little groups, cringing with locked jaws. Some, more arrogant in attitude made unkind faces to mock Christians celebrating around them. Among them were learned men and women, former college professors and teachers who once spoke out in favor of Darwin, or taught modern day communist doctrine. They attempted to ignore the proceedings going on around them, while they continued to debate creation theories with one another. Yet, they were fearful, even as they lifted their voices in open refute of the strange events going on around them.

"Mass hysteria", "Escapism", "Elitism" and "There is no basis in fact that this Jesus fellow ever existed," were tossed about among them as the chant of "Jesus-Jesus-Jesus" continued to fill the air. But one or two of these pillars of education withered in their hardline stance, as a flame kindled in their hearts, first lit in youthful days of Vacation Bible School, began to grow. Smile formed and gradually they separated from their fellow scholars and join in either a prayer circle or a throng of those praising God. Another lost lamb had returned to the fold and people rejoiced.

OAP SOUTHERN FORCE

South of Fort Greeley lay a vast open field of snow, recently transformed to massive puddles of deep mud. The field was 1600 yards in length from ADF to enemy positions and over a mile wide; bordered by the Richardson Highway and rolling hillsides to the east. This was the free fire zone, to the south of which a thick tree line concealed a steadily growing force of OAP infantry and armor.

In this formidable landscape, the enemy was held together by promises of wealth, plunder, warmth and food. There was also the offer of women for the taking; many of the shivering men looked toward Greeley through lust filled eyes and dreams of the prizes that awaited them. These soldiers age 18 through 65 years, transported to Fort Greeley aboard trucks and APC units, had not endured the torturous march their northern comrades had experienced. They had not participated in the heinous acts of barbarous cannibalism - yet, but in the south supplies were rapidly running low. OAP General Staff headquartered in Anchorage and Fairbanks grew deeply concerned about what might come to pass if sufficient food was not soon obtained for their huge army.

To the north, the Black Dragons had dealt harshly with troops throughout the march from Wales to Delta Junction. Thousands of OAP troops were executed on the spot and Dragons assigned to Southern Army were shooting some of their troops to keep order. Several Christians had refused to keep their allegiance to their Christian god a secret any longer and attempted to witness to others, only to be shot down by the Dragons. But still, those who remained quite had their spirits stirred by the celebration of worship heard coming from the Alaskan camp. Though spoken in a foreign tongue, they understood the name of "Jesus" being raised by tens of thousands of voices and they looked to the heavens for a sign.

In Christian communities and underground churches of Asia, the Word of God was taught; discussions and debates were common place among the people. In churches hidden from the government, they shared even single pages torn from a well-used Bible. But as the OAP closed Christian churches throughout their new alliance and hunted down the underground fellowships, executing the leaderships, these people, through their lessons on the Book of Revelation, clearly believed the End Times were at hand and they prayed for the Lord's Second Coming.

ALASKA'S MILITIA-8TH DIVISION, SOUTHERN PERIMETER - 0750 HOURS

A glimpse of gray from an early morning dawn had revived the perimeter guards; the long night was finally over. Ed stood studying a small fire, stirring the ashes with the toe of his muddy boot. The flames from the previous hours of darkness were hidden by snow filled sandbags and fueled steadily by broken wooden ammo crates. His face very pale from the constant exposure to the icy cold, Ed looked up and saw the concerned expression on his friend's face. Point Man, perched on a blanketed M-60 1,000 round ammo can, frowned as he stared at the toe of his right boot.

"You look like you got something weighing you down, Bro. What's bothering you? I mean besides one million Chinamen wanting to kill you and a comet dropping on our heads?" Ed asked.

Point Man didn't answer right away, but simply continued to gaze at his boot for a moment longer. Then he lifted his eyes to glance back and forth between Ed and the others around him. The four Misfits were still asleep, having worked the midnight to 6 a.m. shift unloading ammo and other supplies along their stretch of the perimeter. This was one of the times their big muscles were deeply appreciated by all and they easily did more than their share of the work. After a moment of silence between them, Point Man looked hard into Ed's caring eyes and said quietly, "Been wondering 'bout something." Point Man lowered his wool scarf to reply to Ed's question in an unusually low whisper. He didn't want to be overheard, not with a subject this personal to him.

"Well, I'm listening," Ed said. "A little conversation might help the time go by." He glanced over at his wife, Kira, curled up beside Kathy O' Brian for warmth as they slept. Ed's sleeping bag and a couple white camouflage shells were below them to keep them from the frozen earth and Larry O' Brian's bag on top. Earlier this morning Larry had draped his plastic poncho over them to protect them further from the morning frost. Larry and several of the others from their church group were on guard duty along their stretch of perimeter wall crouching behind a barrier of sandbags five feet high and double bagged in width. Everyone hoped it was thick enough to stop a rifle bullet, but most of the occasional sniper bullets had sailed overhead, so they had yet to prove the theory.

"You'll think this is silly, but I'm wondering if God has hogs in Heaven," Point Man said in a whisper.

Ed pulled his bayonet out, used it to shift a chunk of wood around in the fire and stuck it in to the snow to cool it off. The question amused him but he had to stifle a smile as to not offend his very large friend, "I gather we're talking about the two wheeled jobs and not the four legged kind...right?"

Point Man gave Ed a hard glare, one capable of making most men wither from fright. "You said yuh wanted conversation. Snide remarks will get you nothin' but some missin' teeth." Point Man rubbed his eyes; the smoke from the fire was warm, but irritating. "Sorry, guess I'm getting cranky. All this cold... I'm not sure I like this Alaska of yours."

"Winter in Alaska always makes people cranky, but the freedom up here has always made it worth it." He looked to the mountains and smiled, happy to be home again and thought of Brad and his smile disappeared. He looked back to his buddy and said, "Well, since you're handling the stress of the moment so well, I can probably say I don't really know whether or not they have Harley choppers zooming down the golden streets of heaven... they do produce a lot of smelly noise pollution."

Point Man ignored the pollution remark, "Be nice, Wagon Man. This is serious stuff ... I need to know so I can answer my guy's questions." Point Man jabbed a thumb in the direction of the Misfits.

"Well then, I'd have to say I still really don't know. Never heard it brought up as to whether or not they have vehicles...or even motorcycles in heaven. Mostly they talk about wings and chariots."

"Chariots...that's right! Maybe I could dig one of those...the guys might think they're cool enough to get by. I remember hearing a song about chariots, Cindy use to sing it real pretty like. Yeah, I could dig a chariot... but what pulls them? Do we got horses in Heaven?"

Too many questions! "I've always hoped there was a special place in Heaven for animals. Favorite pets would mean horses too. Be a lot of unhappy cowboys if they didn't have horses in Heaven. Don't you think?"

Before Point Man could say anything in response, he stopped and looked back over his shoulder to the sound of small vehicle approaching.

Ed looked up and saw it was an older M151 Jeep, swerving and plowing through the snow and slush, as if a teenager was behind the wheel racing with the wind. There was a single lane plowed road between camp and the perimeter positions and the jeep driver was using both sides of the roadway to race forward in an erratic manner.

"He's sure in a hurry, must think the OAP might toss a shell at him," Point Man said standing, his rifle held tightly in his huge hands. His beat up

M-79 grenade launcher was slung over one shoulder, with only four rounds of 40mm ammo left, and his 12-gauge pump shotgun, fully loaded in a handmade leather scabbard attached to combat suspenders on his back within easy grasp. He also carried three knives of various lengths and had a 40mm Glock pistol in a shoulder holster with two extra fully loaded magazines on his belt. His backpack; a leather civilian model from his outlaw biker days, was packed with additional ammo for his weapons, but he sincerely wished he had additional 40mm ammo for when the enemy made their advance.

Ed had to grin when he looked at his buddy, thinking he sort of looked like one of those survivalist soldiers from one of the old computer games his young officers liked to play in the trooper station back in Arizona. *I wonder how many zombies he could get on a good day?* He turned his attention to the approaching jeep with the insane driver, "Driving that way, he's in a hurry to get himself killed real quick! Wonder who it is?" Ed reached inside his pack for his binoculars. Trying to stay below the sandbag wall behind him, Ed took a look see and was able to identify the driver as Lt. Col Jeb Stewart, which surprised him, but he did not know the passenger. "Wonder what Colonel Stewart wants out here?"

"Maybe someone should teach the Colonel how to drive a four by," Point Man suggested. Ed ignored him. "They call it defensive driving, makes less of a target that way, but this road's poor condition is a sure fire way to cause a rollover." The vehicle finally came to an abrupt halt behind a Canadian Bradley fighting Machine. Colonel Stewart used the hulk of metal for cover while he and his passenger dismounted the jeep.

"You stay here. I'll go see what the good Colonel wants." Ed placed his binoculars back into his pack and staying in a low crouch made his way over to where Lt. Colonel Stewart and his passenger were standing behind the Bradley. The Canadian crew was asleep inside, taking advantage of these few hours of rest. They would wake up when the shooting started or when an order from their squadron commander came over the radio.

"Maybe the Chinese have surrendered?" Point Man suggested to Larry O'Brian, who had just walked up to see what was up. With his height, Larry had to stay real low and his knees were covered in mud from the times he slipped in the brown slime at the bottom of their trench.

"If so, those guys out front sure haven't heard it." Larry ducked as a rifle round from the enemy side zinged overhead and pinged off the side of the Bradley causing Colonel Stewart, his passenger and Ed to dash behind the jeep for extra cover.

Scott, his face burning from wind chill, was a bit shaken by the wild ride out to the southern perimeter. He understood the reason behind it and didn't say a word as he unlimbered himself slowly from the front passenger seat; thankful he'd survived the trip. But he still shot Lt. Colonel Stewart a disgruntled look when the senior officer was looking away. Turning around, Scott examined the men and women in fighting positions in front of him and wondered if any of them were experienced soldiers. *Ah jus' don't have the time to get them into fighting shape, not like ah had with my platoon...Lord, I miss that bunch... some mighty brave men and mah two gracious ladies.* He looked over his new command, shook his head and glanced to the Heavens and asked the Lord, *Help me, God... Ah've got to kick this unit into fighting shape and fast, 'cause the war is comin' mighty quick an' all ah may have is hours... if that.*

The sandbag wall, with intermediate .50-caliber and M-60 machinegun positions, supported by SAW, AT-4 and LAW weapons, was nearly a mile in length and manned by men and women of the newly formed 8th Militia Division mostly volunteers from the evacuation of Anchorage and Valdez, not already assigned to a unit.

After experiencing the enemy's armor attack on Delta Junction, Scott knew this sandbagged perimeter had no chance of stopping even the lighter OAP tanks or Armored Personnel Carriers. He struggled with recent memories of the fight in Delta as a soldier walked up to Colonel Stewart and shook his uplifted hand.

"Nice to see you again, Colonel, but if I recall rightly, I'm not supposed to salute you out here on the front lines. Something about it drawing attention to you being an officer and all. But it is good to see you again," Ed said. With a thumb gesture back over his right shoulder toward the perimeter, he asked, "So, what's up? Or are you simply checking out the new division for the General?"

"You are correct about the salutes, Lt. Sawyer; snipers are always looking for an officer to kill. And it is good to see you too, Ed." Jeb turned to introduce Scott, "Ed Sawyer, I'd like you to meet newly promoted Captain Scott Radley, your brother's old FPD partner and recently, one of the surviving heroes from our battle in Delta Junction."

Scott had heard Ed stories from Brad over the months they worked together, but only recently learned of his arrival from Chaplain Knight. He stepped forward and with a surprising passion, broke military decorum and hugged Ed about the shoulders.

When they broke away, Ed grinning in response to Scott's act of friendliness, Scott said to him, "I've heard a lot about you, Ed. Your brother was mighty proud of you... Well, until you didn't come back to Alaska and took to riding Arizona dune buggies. He thought you'd gone insane, choosing the desert over Alaska."

Ed smiled brightly in return, meeting his brother's patrol partner and friend. He knew Brad would've never shared such stories if he didn't like this man and it only made him feel closer to Scott. He remembered all too well what Brad thought about his decision to stay in Arizona and the unkind words they had shared over the telephone on that December night when Ed had told him he wasn't coming home for Christmas and had taken the lieutenant's promotion.

Jeb gave Ed another bit of news, "Ed, I brought Scott out here for more than just a meeting with Brad's brother. Effective immediately he is now in command of Bravo Company, 3rd Battalion-1st Regiment of our new 8th Division. 2nd Lt. Ed Sawyer," Jeb pointed at Ed, "that's you by the way. I wasn't joking earlier. It is official and signed off by General Saunders. You are now a platoon commander."

"What?" Ed asked in surprise. He wasn't expecting rank, thinking he was simply part of a militia group under ADF command.

"You've got the experience and Scott needs good men to handle his platoons. Orders came down this morning and that's that." Jeb smiled at the two men. "You two can figure out your own squad leaders and Scott, you'll need two other platoon commanders."

Scott knew he'd get another assignment, but he was surprised when the orders came down for his promotion to captain and Bravo Company commander. He glanced over at Ed and almost laughed when he saw the look of astonishment on Ed's face when he was made an instant lieutenant. "You're brother would've loved this, him being a captain and all and you a lowly lieutenant. Probably would've had you diggin' ditches or somethin'."

"Yeah, he would've." Ed shook his head, struggling to keep his eyes from tearing.

"Look, I've got to go." Jeb shook hands again with Scott and Ed, "Sorry there's no pay with the rank, Ed - I mean Lt. Sawyer." Jeb climbed into his jeep. "But if you need anything...besides food that is, give me a call on the radio. I'm your new Regimental CO. The General transferred me over… said they didn't have need for Intel OIC anymore.

Here," Jeb said as he tossed a pair of captain's bars to Scott. "Those used to be mine and I'm still alive, so they might be lucky." Starting the jeep, he tossed a quick wave and whipped the jeep around to drive away in the same wild fashion he had arrived. Both men were left standing, watching him slide side to side down the muddy roadway, but it was Ed who still had the stunned expression on his face.

"I guess you'd better show me around, Lieutenant," Scott said. Jeb's jeep had disappeared behind a blur of powdery snow and a thick stand of white birch.

The ADF had concealed a battery of 105mm artillery behind this stand of birch trees, ready to support the militia when the time came. An under strength Canadian brigade of Bradley Fighting Machines armed with an assortment of weapons were also positioned along the perimeter in support of the Militia. But when the OAP dreadnaughts made their move, the ADF had little to stop them with.

Ed pointed to the forward trench, "No problem, Captain, but remember to stay low and on your belly, unless you're in a trench or behind armor. They've got some good marksmen over there and they've come close to clipping my feathers a couple of times."

"Do we have any experienced troops out here?" Scott asked. A group of pale faces in soiled clothes returned his gaze. Between snow, mud and ashes from the fire, fuel and oil from the vehicles, no one stayed clean on the front lines, but it did help with the camouflage effect.

"Most of these people right here in front of us came up from Phoenix with me and they all gained some combat experience along the way. Those big hairy fellows zonked out over there," Ed pointed at the Misfits, "... are manning two- M-60 machineguns and they know how to use them. The biggest dude, the guy by the fire who's staring at us, we call Point Man; he saw action in Somali. I'd like to make him one of my squad leaders; he's a handy guy to have around." They stepped away from the Bradley Fighting Machine; exposing themselves to enemy fire, quickly dropped to a low crouch and made a dash to the nearest trench; where Ed introduced Scott to the rest of his little band.

After making sure everyone in his new platoon was awake, Ed introduced each person to Captain Scott Radley, and then pointed to his wife, "This is my wife, Kira."

"Wish we were meeting under better circumstances, Mrs. Sawyer," Scott said as he shook her hand. He shook hands with Joey Roberts and Matthew Fulbright. Scott remembered seeing Larry O' Brian in action on the football field via television and felt a bit strange, when the big man shook his hand and started calling him "Captain".

Following the introductions, Scott shared a cup of weak, hot coffee with several of his new company as they encircled a warm fire and made small talk. Ed and Scott later sat by themselves to chat about possible candidates for platoon and squad leaders.

Once the positions were filled, startling several of the choices made, Scott crouched behind a stack of sandbags and used a set of binoculars to complete a 360° check of his position. He could see the enemy and was thankful for the flat empty landscape before them. To the east the forested rolling hills were heavily mined with antipersonnel and antitank mines. To the west, the riverbed frozen over, but with steep embankments over 30 feet high prevented any flanking movement by the OAP.

He was relieved to count the line of Canadian Bradley Fighting Machines supporting his section of perimeter and knew that back in a tree line of white birch, a battery of 105mm Howitzers was in place. The perimeter was supported by 81mm mortars and .50 caliber machineguns and a secondary line of defense was to be with the artillery, but it would be a long run in the open for over 400 yards or better. After that, the enemy had a straight line into the heart of Fort Greeley's housing area and the Main Base and airfield.

"Have you met our Battalion CO?" Scott asked after completing his visual check of the area.

"No, but maybe we'd better hustle over and introduce ourselves. From what I've picked up, the new CO is a bit nervous about visiting the front line," Ed answered.

"Great. At least he'll stay out of our hair." Following a series of trenches and meeting the rest of the company, Scott followed Ed over a low ridge line and through a section of thick woods. The area was mined, but a corridor was marked with flags. Once the shooting started the flags would be pulled.

Battalion headquarters was a large green and white arctic camouflage canvas wall tent. A .50 caliber machinegun was positioned directly in front of the only opening; Claymore mines were set up on the other three sides, with posted warnings for anyone who might walk by. Before they walked inside, Scott pinned new rank onto his collar and handed Ed his old lieutenant bars, "Here, I hope they keep you alive as they did me." Scott helped Ed pin one of them on the front of his Parka and the other on his newly acquired rabbit fur hat. Clearing two very large MPs, they walked inside the huge tent and found several officers standing around a large map table. When they came closer, Scott noticed a major who appeared to be the center of attention and Scott reported to him, "Sir, Captain Radley reporting to the Battalion Commander." When the officer turned around, Scott's jaw and his salute dropped; he found himself standing in front of a newly promoted Major Buford, who, upon recognition, glared back at him with bloodshot eyes filled with shooting daggers. When the major took on a frightful grimace, Scott saw that the man was missing two front teeth and another one was broken off. This brought some satisfaction to Scott for a job well done and he shook his head in disbelief finding himself once more under the command of a KKK bigot.

"Well, how nice to see you again...captain." Buford looked to the officers of his battalion staff and dismissed them with a casual wave of his hand then returned his attention to Scott who, along with Ed, remained at attention. "Your orders came down the line earlier today and you have no idea how happy I am to have you in my command again." Buford looked at Ed with a disdainful expression, one he apparently used for those little people in his command and then ignored him. "I seriously thought about having you placed under arrest for assaulting a senior officer, but the thought of you spending your last days in a warm cell made me change my mind. No, I'll keep you out in front where I can keep an eye on you. First to fight as you African warriors like to say and hopefully you'll catch a bullet when the first wave hits."

Scott was biting his tongue, praying he could stifle the urge to reach out and strangle his new CO.

Buford dropped his smile, "You command Bravo Company, mostly new boys and girls from that bunch of Jesus freaks who came up from the lower 48. You'll fit right in with them, boy." Buford stepped closer, glanced about the tent and then whispered, "Remember, nigger, I'm watching you and I do owe you a big one." Buford stepped back, looked at Ed one last time, shook his head and then shouted, "Dismissed!" He completed the exchange with a shower of spittle on Scott's face and chest.

Visibly fighting to keep his temper in check, Scott trembling with rage did an about face and marched out of the tent with a very confused Ed at his heels.

"I gather you and the major are old friends?" Ed offered Scott his handkerchief to wipe his face.

"Thanks," Scott said. "That man is an atheist and probably a card carrying member of the KKK, if not the communist party. He tried messing me over before and a couple days ago I decked him... Thought I'd never see him again, but fate can be so unkind to nice people. C'mon, I'll get this washed out for you...let's get back to the company. I want to check our weapons positioning again." Scott picked up the pace as they followed a well-used trail through the snow covered woods.

A moment later, Richard Knight, son of Chaplain Knight, came running up behind Scott, "Hey, Captain...sir."

"Richard! What are you doing here?" Scott asked.

"I'm old enough to be out here an' all the volunteers are being sent out this way. Can I join your company?"

"Richard Knight, this Lt. Ed Sawyer. He's Brad's younger brother."

"We've met already," Richard said. He stood beside Scott and shook hands with Ed.

"Richard, does your dad know you're out here?" Scott asked.

"He doesn't like it, but yeah, he knows I have to be here. Man's got to do what he's got to do...right?"

"I think it was John Wayne who said that... but okay, you're my runner. No complaints or I'll send you back to wash dishes somewhere."

"Thanks, Scott...I mean, Captain, sir."

Scott reached up and grabbed Richard in a playful headlock, letting him go when they reached the ridge. "Keep your head down and do what we do, or you'll get your butt shot off an' I'll have to explain why it happened to your dad. Just remember, kiddo, buttless boys never find girlfriends." Richard turned around, trying to look down his backside, which caused both Scott and Ed to laugh.

SAVOONGA, ST.LAWERENCE ISLAND-

Full from a meal of freshly harvested reindeer made into sausage and recently caught red salmon cut into thick steaks; Captain Myers pushed himself back from the table and stood up. He had not felt so full in months, but struggled with a sense of guilt knowing what the rest of the ADF was probably eating.

At last count, 812 adult reindeer wandered the hills behind town and they had found 47 calves. A dozen of the adults were shot and processed, and the meat was hanging from rafters inside a small deserted courthouse. Skins were cleaned as a few elders in the company taught the younger ones how old traditional skinning practices were accomplished to preserve the valuable hides. Soldiers lived in 14 modular houses and a communal kitchen was set up in the town's community hall. They had found several dogs left behind that had lived off the few scraps they could scrounge from the landfill south of town and were being used for guard duty.

Putting on his parka, Myers pulled the hood up over his head and stepped outside with a homemade toothpick dangling from his mouth as he looked up and down the snow packed street. Normally about this time of day, Myers liked to take a long walk to work off his meal and check his troops. Yet, this morning...*The air feels so crisp an' clean...but there's something else. A peculiar feeling...my skin's tingling!* A strong gust of wind struck him, chilling him to the bone and Captain Myers looked up at the oncoming comet. The flaming giant, not quite as bright as the sun, looked to be nearly the size of a full moon; its tail was hardly visible, which made him think the comet was coming head on. Captain Myers' new impact was most likely within mere hours and he worried about what would happen to the earth and more importantly, his new island home. Myers also sensed there was something very different about the comet, but couldn't put his finger on it. He noticed there were several of his men coming out of their houses to look up at the ominous sight and he wondered if they too sensed the change in the air. At that moment, the first earth tremors began to build underneath the island and Captain Myers shouted, "Earthquake!"

COMMUNITY OF SHAGELUK

With one eye propped open, Colonel Freeman squinted as he glanced up toward the comet's growing brightness. He knew the rock would soon be breaking into the outer atmosphere which would cause multiple rays of light spreading out like the ripples in a pond from the dropping of a pebble. With friction on an astronomical scale, the comet's icy make up would burn away somewhat but not enough before impact.

Frozen in place, Colonel Freeman, still suffering from the wounds and frostbite injuries he had sustained in the Battles for Wales and the long retreat afterward, visualized several of the scenes from old sci-fi movies. How asteroids descended upon the Earth, such as Final Impact and Armageddon but where civilization was saved in the nick of time by gutsy astronauts. He couldn't help but wonder, would mankind survive and would there be another tomorrow?

Colonel Freeman looked at his bandaged hands and sighed deeply in regret for all the men and women he had lost on their retreat. He had already survived the long bitter trek from Wales to Shageluk, saved from death by the villagers who helped revive them from a possible frozen death. Everyone, villagers and soldiers alike, stood like statues, watching the comet create a massive light show upon entering the outer atmosphere. "Only moments away now and I sure hope the eggheads were right about the impact point. I'd really hate to have that thing fall on us, not that we'd feel anything." Colonel Freeman said to the men standing around him. "Makes me think about all those bugs I stepped on, what the little critters might have thought as my huge foot came down on them. Puts things in perspective… there's always someone with a bigger foot."

Then he too felt the first tremors and stood speechless as they grew in intensity and slammed Colonel Freemen and his soldiers to the ground. The quake caused the house behind him to crumble and he could hear people screaming in terror as the air filled with the sound of an oncoming freight train. Colonel Freeman, lying in the snow, clinched his eyes shut and held his breath, while the world danced to its own beat.

This is it!

FORT GREELEY'S SOUTHERN PERIMETER

Holding a metal canteen cup under his nose to let the hot coffee bring some warmth to his cold face, Ed knelt on one knee beside a small fire while he watched Kira and Kathy continue to add pieces from a discarded ammo crate into the flames. They did this sparingly, because no one wanted the flames to rise above the sandbags, marking their position for enemy mortar fire. But they also needed it hot to chase away the morning's icy cold.

Mealtime consisted of a cup of coffee; no sugar or non-dairy creamer since these ingredients were being saved for the children and seniors.

Joey Roberts, newly appointed 2nd platoon leader sat on his sleeping bag cleaning his M-16 preferring morning coffee with old friends, finished it off and tossed his cup to Kira to refill for Larry's' use. Joey inserted a full magazine and upon chambering a round, let out a sigh, said his goodbyes and crawled off to his new position in the trenches to confer with his new squad leaders. His five minute breakfast time was over.

About to accept his own cup of coffee, Scott clutched the log he was sitting on when the ground began to role under him. Looking over his shoulder as he was slammed down to all fours, he saw dozens of troops pointing to the heavens and looked up to see the comet burning through the sky overhead and he knew their time had run out. It's gonna hit!

He began issuing orders, but the noise was growing too loud for anyone to hear him. All he could do was lay flat on the ground, with his helmet on, eyes squeezed shut and ride a great quake build up to the 10 point range.

People on the perimeter were hurled about, Bradley Fighting Machines flipped over on their sides as the snow covered ground cracked, leaving deep fissures, and behind them in the area of the artillery, trees were uprooted and artillery pieces cast aside as if a giant hand had swept across the ground.

ADF-CAN COMMAND POST, FORT GREELEY

General Howard-Wright felt the earth move underneath him and with a startled expression, looked over to see General Saunders gripping a radio console to stay on his feet.

"Earthquake!" President Andrews shouted. He was sitting in a metal chair and shouted out the warning only a micro second before being hurled backwards to strike against a black five draw file cabinet.

Deep rumblings rose up from the depths and the noise becoming ear shattering. Later, President Andrews would describe the quake as if some mythical hellish creature was breaking out of its pit, splitting the earth apart and it was really mad.

Unable to keep his grip on the console, General Saunders was sent flying and slammed up against the wall. The wind was knocked out of him and he collapsed like a deflated balloon to the shaking floor.

Power failed, forcing the CP into utter darkness until some of the emergency battery operated lights flashed on. Equipment went flying in all directions and two hot coffee pots spilled blistering liquid over the bodies of two shocked clerks, who released screams of pain in unison. File cabinets and desks were tipped over, chairs uplifted and tossed about the room to knock over some of the personnel. Telephones, computers, office supplies, file folders and writing utensils, instantly became dangerous weapons as they became flying projectiles.

Trying to maintain his footing, General Howard-Wright grasped a table top, but quickly lost his hold and slid sideways across the bouncing floor. Striking the wall, he let out a loud grunt of pain, before he was rendered unconscious by a falling book shelf.

Overhead lights fell loose; wires pulled out of the wall and sparks flew everywhere. Then the thick concrete walls began to crack open and building debris crumbled, while the earthquake continued on. Parts of the ceiling gave way, showering people with broken ceiling tiles, broken water pipes and sewage lines, and splashing water all about the CP. Clouds of concrete dust fouled everyone's taste and made it hard to see, as electrical wires dangled dangerously over everyone. Miniature lightning bolts shot out and sparks appeared like menacing fireflies.

Lying on his side, Major Ransom jammed the knuckles of his right hand between his teeth to bite off the pain of a broken leg. Thrown out of his chair and onto the ground, a five drawer filing cabinet had fallen on his left knee shattering it.

Nearly three minutes passed before the earthquake began to subside, the longest three minutes in anyone's life, accept for those who were old enough, to have gone through the Alaska's Good Friday Earthquake of 1964.

FORT GREELEY'S SOUTHERN PERIMETER

Great cracks appeared in the earth, trapping soldiers under tons of dirt, ice and snow. With nothing to secure a hold of, many of the troops were tossed around like toy soldiers in a force three hurricane. Thousands of men and women in both armies lay flat on their backs or their stomachs waiting for the great quake to cease. Left behind were dozens of collapsed bunkers, 100s of yards of trenches, damaged vehicles and weapons, and thousands of casualties along both ADF and OAP perimeters.

As the quake subsided, no one moved for fear the intensity would grow again or an aftershock would occur all too soon. Everyone lay flat or huddled together with the thought of the impending battle far from their minds for the moment.

Protecting Kira with his own body Ed grunted when a small wall of sandbags tumbled down upon them and covered their legs. Point Man bounced on top the fire, giving him 2nd and 3rd degree burns on his backside and arms. Joey rolled across the trench clipping one of his men in the jaw with his boot. Headed for a deep open crevice, Kathy O' Brian screamed out in terror and was saved by her husband, when Larry grasped her left leg with a firm grip and pulled her back to safety.

Matthew Fulbright came within two feet of being crushed by a near Bradley Fighting Machine as the hulking mass was turned on its left side. Inside, the Canadians screamed to get out, but were forced to wait until the shaking had ceased; they used an iron bar to un-jam their vehicle's escape hatch.

Hitting in the 9.3 to 9.8 range, the great quake roared out like a wounded animal and slowly tapered off like a whimpering child. Only then, did humanity look to the heavens and experience the sight and sounds of a great fiery explosion in the heavens as if 100 H-bombs had exploded in the sky, releasing unheard of power and a massive concussion wave that shot earthward, one that again flattened everyone on earth to the ground. With stunned disbelief, people watched stunned as the Tariq-Leroy Comet simply exploded like a helium balloon shot with a fire arrow. In a short span of time, this raging fireball gradually faded into space as a silent flicker of light and then nothing. No one spoke, they only watched in awe as the sky was suddenly filled with sparkling star lights cascading down from the heavens visible from one horizon to the next.

Lying on his back eyes wide open, Ed remembered one of Pastor Woodway's teachings on Revelation and recited what he could remember out loud to his wife, "A third of the stars will fall from the heavens...and that's what's happening here."

Richard Knight was found unconscious, a large bump on the side of his head from colliding with a stationary Bradley Fighting Machine. Once he regained consciousness, they could only provide him with two aspirin to ease the pain and a bag of snow to ice the bump with. The best part was young Richard being mothered by both Kira and Kathy O' Brian, the attention he was receiving was clearly much better for the young man than aspirin.

Many bodies were removed from trenches where walls had collapsed and buried victims. Others were found and pulled out of collapsed bunkers. Dozens of people were reported missing along the perimeter and it was feared they might have fallen into one of the numerous crevices that had opened in the land. Quite a few people stood to observe the light show overhead; others were involved in rescue work and some of the volunteers were lowered into crevices where several bodies were located. But some of the crevices appeared bottomless and no one was going down that far to look for the dead.

Still, the perimeter was manned and once again ready for the enemy, while the sky continued to shower the world with pieces of a fallen celestial body.

INSIDE FORT GREELEY

Concrete buildings and earthquakes make for a terrible mix. Collapsed walls had buried hundreds of people, other buildings were aflame and bellowing plumes of black smoke carried over the installation. Rushing to the main hospital, Pastor Woodway made his way through the fearful grief stricken people. Along the way he had seen mangled bodies, some only recently pulled out from beneath tons of concrete ruble. Some bodies remained buried, with only a leg or arm visible; they would have to wait for the living to be rescued.

Scores of injured people lay on the cold ground, most without any type of covering and only a tarp or poncho lining under them, as they waited to be seen by a member of the medical staff. So filled with grief, all Pastor could do was stand with blood trickling down his face from a minor head wound and stare at the carnage before him.

"Pastor, you've been hurt." Nancy Myers rushed up to look at her pastor, holding a compress bandage in her right hand. With blood and mud plastered all over her face and clothes, Pastor almost didn't recognize her. "My poor, sweet sister...I'm okay. We need to help these others. Where are all the doctors, the nurses?" Pastor asked while Nancy ignored his request, set him down on a metal chair and carefully cleaned his wound with clean water.

"I don't know, but we've got bones to set and people need sewing up." Nancy applied a 4x4 bandage to the wound and wiped the rest of the blood away. "This is all I can do right now, Pastor. You'll need a stitch or two later."

Chaplain Knight ran through the crowd, "Pastor Woodway, I'm so glad I found you. We could really use your help, a lot of dying people out there who need our comforting. Can you lend a hand?"

"Of course," Pastor said and gave Nancy a quick hug. "Thank you and God bless you."

"God bless you too, Pastor." Nancy watched as the two man dashed off to speak final words over the dying and comfort the living.

Turning to her next patient, Nancy found a young boy; his face full of tears, his right leg torn open from knee cap to ankle. "You're lucky, kid. Someone had the sense to use scotch tape to close your wound. They probably saved your leg."

"Hurts," the boy complained as another tear rolled down his cheeks.

"I bet it does," she agreed. "Here, bite down on this until I can find something for the pain, it'll keep your mind busy." Nancy pulled out a piece of surgical tubing from her deep fatigue pants pocket, cut off a piece and placed it between his teeth. "Wish it was candy coated." She looked around for a moment and then said to him, "I'll be right back."

Returning with old Doc in tow, Nancy was first surprised and then deeply saddened to find the boy dead. With nothing to cover him with, Nancy took off her own parka and laid it over him, "I don't want him getting cold, Doc."

He understood. "C'mon, Nancy, we've got a lot of work to do." Doc led Nancy away, there were others waiting for care and mourning for the dead had to wait.

A COMING STORM

21 - JUDGMENT DAY

"Then I saw a new heaven and a new earth, for the heaven and the first earth had passed away, and there was no longer any sea. I saw the Holy City, the New Jerusalem, coming down out of heaven from God, prepared as a bride beautifully dressed for her husband. And I heard a loud voice from the throne saying, 'Now the dwelling of God is with men, and he will live with them. They will be his people, and God himself will be with them and be their God. He will wipe away every tear from their eyes. There will be no more death or mourning or crying or pain, for the old order of things has passed away.' "

Revelations 21:1-4 NIV

ADF-CAN HEADQUARTERS, FORT GREELEY - APRIL 29TH

Covered in a thick layer of gray concrete dust and splashes of sewer water, General Howard-Wright, pasty white and splattered with droplets of blood, resembled the walking dead. With some effort, he painstakingly pulled himself to his feet, clenched his teeth and held perfectly still while Lt. Kelly, who had obtained a black eye and a sprained wrist, used her good hand to pull out small jagged pieces of concrete embedded in his wrinkled forehead. Behind him in mild shock, General Saunders sat back in a dust covered desk chair and watched, with a look of concern on his face, as a dusty medic began to splint Major Ransom's broken leg.

President Andrews, semi-conscious, remained on the floor back against the wall, while his two aides treated him for bruised legs and suspected torn right shoulder from falling debris. His left wrist was broken and he had also received a nasty three inch laceration to his left cheek, but he was very thankful to be alive. Miraculously, both of his aides had escaped major injury; one of them had been a former EMT-2 and was busy giving him a good going over to ensure he had no additional injuries. Within moments, the President of Alaska was wrapped up and with help, was able to get on his feet; though he did take his steps rather slowly.

Once composed and knowing President Andrews was in good hands, both generals stumbled outside through the rubble to get their first look at the damage. On seeing the degree of destruction they were both shocked into a stunned silence. Not a single building in the main post area was left standing intact; hundreds of fires were burning uncontrolled throughout the installation, while thousands of people searched through debris for possible survivors.

Turning to General Howard-Wright, General Saunders asked in a low whisper, "What is God doing, here? Most of these people are Christians, why is he doing this to His people?"

Dumbfounded, General Howard-Wright continued to gaze upon the damage before he finally replied in a failing voice, still dried out by all the concrete dust, "I...I do not know." He could only stand there with a blank expression on his bruised pale face, shock making him feel nearly immune to the icy cold temperatures. As they stood resembling two gray statues, emergency vehicle sirens and massive loud speakers sounded throughout the camp.

President Andrews stood beside an injured woman who lay draped over a radio console and remained silent as a fellow clerk used a damp cloth to wipe the blood spray from her face and neck. The woman was struck by a piece of rebar, knocking her to the ground and rendering her unconscious, but only after leaving an ugly gash that badly needed tending and would forever mark her once beautiful face. Leaving her to the care of others, President Andrews was cautiously helped outside by one of his aides, while the other was requested to stay with the wounded. Upon seeing how his two senior generals had survived, President Andrews approached and quietly embraced the men.

"I didn't know if either of you had survived," President Andrews said. Heart filled emotion coupled with extreme relief, choked him up, while tears flowed down his cheeks. Gazing out on the scene before the headquarters' building, he saw so much blood upon the snow and bodies of men, women and children, killed outright by explosive debris from buildings crashing down.

"Mr. President, we've been informed the comet literally exploded as the great quake subsided," General Saunders said in a raspy voice. He'd be coughing up concrete dust for hours. His lungs and that of others' were most likely caked with the foul powder, which could possibly lead to pneumonia. But right now, the available oxygen canisters were needed elsewhere.

"I...I imagine anyone who was outside saw it happen. Probably the biggest light show the world has ever seen and we missed it."

A Militia major, his uniform in tatters and splashed with blood, walked up the steps to the senior officers and waited while he overheard their conversation and waited for an opening. When the talking stopped, he moved up to get the President's attention, "Excuse me, Mr. President, but I saw it and it was one big WHAM!" He pointed up to the sky, "... Pieces continued to fall for several moments and it lit up the whole sky. It was…it was a miracle. Like God got behind it and kicked a 100 yard field goal."

"Thank you, Major… that's apparently what he did," General Saunders said. The major saluted him casually and walked away to continue helping search parties.

At that precise moment, with the three of them standing at the top of the steps, the valley floor to the south erupted with the sounds of a thousand Chinese bugles, echoing off the nearby hills and sending cold chills down everyone's back; as it was intended to. The comet may be gone, how or why they could only leave to God, but the OAP remained and their attack on Fort Greeley was commencing.

"Excuse me, gentlemen, I must return to my men," General Howard-Wright said shaking hands with General Saunders and President Andrews. Dusting himself off, he turned away from his friends to climb into a waiting Canadian 3/4 ton weapons carrier. Standing up, he saluted the two of them and shouted, "God bless us all." then sped off and vanished behind a massive pile of rubble that had once been the base gym.

FORT GREELEY'S SOUTHERN PERIMETER

For nearly 30 minutes enemy horns had sounded a dirge of excruciating pain to their ears and it was already getting Point Man pretty upset. "If those horns don't stop soon, I'm gonna go right out there and bend a few of 'em around some clown's head." He pressed the palms of his gloves up against his ears to lessen the pain from those ear blasting bugles, which were only 1600 yards away. From the loudness of the horns, Ed believed they were either playing into microphones or the sound was being carried from recordings and sent out over speakers set up along the enemy's position. He remembered hearing how the Chinese used this same effect while fighting the Americans in the Korean War. He had watched the movie, Pork Chop Hill with his father and brother long ago and remembered how the enemy had used this technique to work on the nerves of the American infantrymen. Even the Americans used it, but they substituted the shrieking bugles with badly played rock and roll music to torture people.

"You'd think at least one of them would know how to carry a tune," Scott said. He was responding to Point Man's complaint with a snide remark in hopes of breaking the tension.

Larry O'Brian added in a loud voice, "Yeah, this stuff sounds like some killer clown dragging his nails across a chalkboard and if they're trying to scare us, they really blew it big time. I'm just getting madder by the minute."

The men and women of Scott's company are on 100% alert; no one could sleep anyway with this kind of racket going on. All weapons were loaded and most everyone could feel an itch in their trigger fingers. Scott had made sure his M-60 machinegun teams were placed every 20 yards along his company's length of perimeter wall. Each team was supported by a single SAW and two AT4-antitank or LAW weapons. Lack of experience in men and women of the 8th Militia Division was the only major hurdle and a noticeably low supply of ammo for the M-60's and .50 caliber heavy machineguns. Both of these weapons had become near obsolete by the US Military and new ammo supplies had not been ordered before World War III had broken out. They had to do with what they had on hand and it wasn't a whole lot with the number of weapons being taken from the Alaska Air Force and Army National Guard armories and put into use.

Thankfully, General Saunders had only recently provided the southern perimeter with former US Air Force and Alaska Air National Guard Security Forces personnel, who could competently operate the .50 calibers and M-60 machineguns.

Each M-60 assistant gunner was issued 200 rounds of ammo in two100 round metal cans. Gunners were trained to fire in short three-four round bursts, but everyone knew that when thousands of Orientals rushed the trenches it would be hard to maintain fire discipline. As a result, gunners and assistant gunners were also issued .45 caliber 1911 Colt Pistols or Smith & Wesson .9mm Pistols for back up.

Men and women operating .50 caliber machineguns were issued 500 rounds. Assistant gunners carried an M-16 or older M-14, along with a sidearm.

The SAW weapons had a ready supply of ammo, as well as the AT4 antitank weapons. However, the LAW once used could not be reloaded. There were far too few M-79 grenade launchers to spread across the perimeter so they were held back to defend the artillery and cover any retreat to the second line of defense. The 81 mm mortars were down to short supply after the Battle of Delta Junction, but it was hoped they could maintain a constant bombardment of high explosive for at least the first wave. Once the ammo was used up, the crewmen on the mortars were ordered to destroy the tubes; a necessary prevention to keep the enemy from using them.

Moments passed before the shriek of the Chinese bugles died out. Then an eerie silence lasted for five minutes before a brigade of enemy medium tanks released an opening salvo of 90mm fire. The attack was on.

With the first shots fired, the blasted bugles returned to taunt the ADF-Canadian troops. Listening to the tank rounds whistle by overhead, soldiers on the perimeter ducked down in fear of a short round falling on their lines. Mud and brown water at the bottom of the trench was not comforting for men and women of Scott's undermanned company. Dark clouds of earth and snow erupt into the air, as enemy tank rounds impacted before the ADF secondary defenses, killing dozens of reserve troops and destroying artillery pieces with the first barrage. Rows and rows of craters were left where several tents and aid stations had stood. Some of the rounds carried even further, landing alongside Greeley's old football stadium leaving craters on the 50 yard line.

"Open fire!" Colonel Deekins ordered over the radio to his partially destroyed artillery battery. Positioned in the birch grove behind the 8th Division's position, the men and women rushed from their trenches to man the artillery pieces and return fire. Colonel Deekins had already been given his battle orders by General Saunders and in response, ADF heavy guns: huge 155mm and the smaller, but still deadly, 105mm artillery pieces opened up with a return volley. Immediately west of this position, recently installed newer model M-119 105's retrieved from Delta Junction, began their lethal bombardment on the OAP front lines to the North.

Within moments, concentrated fire from both Canadian and Alaska tanks chimed in supported by heavy machinegun and 25mm cannon fire from Bradley Fighting Machines and Striker vehicles.

A noisy one to be sure, the first battle for Fort Greeley was deafening, as ADF big guns, supported by their Canadian ally, took on the enemy's dreadnoughts and medium tanks. General Saunders with agreement from General Howard-Wright, had issued orders for all ADF and Canadian mortars crews to stand by, waiting to be committed when OAP ground forces engaged the southern and northern perimeters.

With such a volume of fire between the two forces, it wasn't long before the air turned foul with thick black smoke covering the large open fields on the fort's perimeter. Within an hour, the OAP's sharp shooting had left nearly a dozen burning and smoldering combat vehicles on the southern perimeter. From the vehicle fires burning along the OAP perimeter to the north and south, the ADF's war machines had scored quite a few hits. The pungent odor of hot metal, melted rubber and plastic carried over the land while dozens and then hundreds of Alaska volunteers rushed wounded soldiers to the nearest aid station, as others quickly scrounged up weapons and ammo from damaged vehicles.

Miraculously, Scott's Bravo Company was untouched, but death had rained down hard upon those units positioned behind them, causing men and women on the line to dig deeper into holes for safety.

Ed had kept Kira beneath him during the enemy barrage covered over with a flak jacket he obtained from a friendly supply sergeant. In the process of trying to save her, Ed had nearly smothered his young wife and she was fighting for air when Ed propped his head up over the top row of sand bags to take a quick look around to ensure it was safe. He was surprised to see that the enemy's tanks were not advancing and wondered why? He got his answer when he heard the thunderous roar of their powerful engines and then saw the OAP Air Force announce their arrival with a diving attack along the southern perimeter.

A flight of SU-19 fighter aircraft swept down from the skies and opened up with 30mm cannons to literally blast the perimeter foxholes apart. From the air, there was little to no cover and ADF and Militia troops abandoned positions all along the line. Watching the attack move their way, Ed pulled himself into a ball and shoved Kira further down into the hole beneath him as rounds impacted within yards of their foxhole and showered them with shrapnel, snow and dirt. Only Ed's newly issued helmet protected him from a lethal head wound, when a chunk of shrapnel the size of a 50 cent piece bounced off the side of his Kevlar headgear. Had it been one of the older style helmets, Kira would've been a young widow, but she still had an unconscious husband to deal with and getting him out of the way so she could climb out of the hole to aid him.

ADF and Canadian anti-aircraft batteries opened up and sent out a thick wall of flak to fill the skies above Fort Greeley. First one, then another and then five and ten more enemy fighters tumbled out of the sky, as Brave gunners held position to send thousands of .50 caliber machinegun, 20mm and 30mm cannon rounds into the air. With time to man their positions again, these anti-aircraft weapons are soon supported by M-119 105's.

Upon seeing the building support fire from the rear, perimeter heavy machine gunners and even M-60's, returned fire and two more fighters plummeted to the ground on the snowy plain between the enemy positions. Another fighter skidded across the snowy field and the first pilot attempted to make a run for his perimeter from the burning aircraft. Before he could get far from his fighter, the SU-19 exploded and the pilot was caught and killed in the fiery blast.

Taking heavy losses and unable to deal with the heavy concentration of flak, enemy aircraft were ordered to withdraw to airfields in the west for rearming and fuel. Within moments, with their aircraft out of the area, enemy ground controllers sent coordinates to tank commanders of the fearsome dreadnaughts and brought their fire to bear on the ADF anti-aircraft batteries. Within 30 minutes of the brutal assault, nearly all of the aircraft batteries were destroyed; hundreds of crew members killed or wounded.

A new flight of SU-19's launched an air attack; over confident enemy pilots found themselves facing several heavy weapons companies on both the southern and northern perimeters, armed with shoulder firing Stinger missiles. Though they lost more than a couple missiles to poor guidance systems, they still made quick work of the first wave of SU-19s. The remaining enemy birds retreated once more and held over the OAP perimeter to await further orders.

Seeing the brief respite Scott issued orders for all dead and wounded to be removed from the line and the wounded transported to the new aid stations. One aid station was staying mobile by using large flatbeds and lowboy trailers to place stretchers on, in hopes of making them less of an easy target to hit.

Orders come down the line, spread from company to company through radio operators and runners, "Everyone to their positions!" Scott grabbed up his binoculars and lay prone over the southern edge of his foxhole and brought the enemy into focus. From the far side of the field, enemy infantry units were rising up from trenches and he was awestruck by thousands upon thousands of ground troops spreading out over a mile in length. They formed a long impregnable human wall and behind each soldier, like the mouth of a shark, row after row of men and women could be seen forming up. Scott could see even more additional troops emerging from the forests to the south. *Wonder if there is an end to this army?*

At first speechless, Scott wiped snow over his face for shock effect and then called for his new RTO. Within minutes, he found the forward observers assigned to work with artillery were either killed or wounded in the air attack. Scott, who didn't have time to wait around for someone to be assigned to the dangerous forward observer job, quickly sent in a request for artillery. Within moments a single, massive 175mm round landed nearly 75 yards in front of the first row of enemy soldiers, showering them with ground debris. "Drop it back another 200 yards and fire for effect." A second round sailed over the ADF perimeter and exploded in the trees behind the OAP. "Okay, bring it back 50 yards an' pour it on! Sweep the field from west to east! You've got a mile or so to work with an' a whole lot of Chinamen to kill." "Tanks are moving up too," Ed shouted out.

The OAP suspected the snowfields were mined, which they were, but with only a limited supply of anti-personnel mines and even fewer tank mines the ADF still had on hand. So, rather than risk their war machines, the OAP warlords sent forth a human wave to detonate mines and protect their fearsome dreadnoughts. With the enemy's gradual advance of frightened soldiers these cold and hungry troops, knowing they were drawing ever nearer to the enemy's positions, watched in horror as their comrades died and felt the earth shudder beneath their feet from the impact of near misses.

With the heavy artillery bombardment coming from their rear, men and women of Bravo Company couldn't help but notice their own artillery rounds were impacting ever closer to their positions. Shouting to his machine gunners, Scott ordered them to hold fire. Mortar crews were being put into play using High Explosive and White Phosphorous rounds to shower down upon the advancing infantry, while the ADF big guns lifted their range to deal with the mechanical nightmares positioned behind the advancing foot soldiers.

When the enemy reached the posted 1000 yard markers put in place when Anchorage had fallen, Ed heard the awesome sound of Bradley Fighting Machines and a dozen Strikers brought in to reinforce their position, open up with their weapons. Bradley fighting Machines cut into the enemy first line with .25 mm cannon fire, while the Striker gunners blasted away with M-60 and .50 caliber machineguns. Behind the infantry, some of the mighty dreadnoughts exploded into flames from a combined fire of Bradley cannons and field artillery which brought a loud cheer of appreciation down through the line for the artillery and armor units.

Usually there was stiff rivalry between armor, artillery and ground pounder, but not today. They joined together to face a common foe; Alaskan and Canadian armies stood poised to face the largest army on earth; or at least part of it.

President Andrews had only recently received information through Canadian sources that the OAP was moving on the Middle East and Israel from the east, while the Northern European Empire and its Satanic Emperor were moving on Israel from the west. He knew, or at least he prayed, it was only a matter of days, maybe hours before the Lord's return to save Israel. He only hoped and prayed his Alaska would also be saved from the clutches of the enemy before them.

Kneeling atop the steps before the ADF Headquarters building, supported by his aides, he led his people in prayer for Alaskans and the Canadian allies. The flag of the United States, waving in the wind above him with the Canadian and Alaskan flags on each side, President Andrews reverently and loudly sought for the Lord's return to save them before this mighty horde facing them could win the day. He prayed their Lord would bring an end to this enemy and allow these brave people who knelt with him to live.

But for the moment, the enemy was drawing closer near enough for everyone on the main post to see the carnage being caused in the OAP ranks. Bodies covered the field; yet row after row of OAP infantry continued to march over the top of them; spurred on by very vocal and violent officers. When one man went down, another filled the spot and another behind moved up into the second row. Those who failed to move up fast enough were either shot down by an officer or clubbed by one of the senior NCOs.

To the northwest, the OAP held back the infantry and pounded post defenses with dreadnaughts and artillery. The dried up spring bed, covered in ice was littered with the bent and broken remains of still smoldering mechanized monstrosities from ADF, Canadian and OAP armor units. A fierce battle had been fought here and the OAP tanks moved slowly through the valley approaching assigned lines outside of Fort Greeley. Once in position, they pounded ADF positions with hellfire, knock out mortar and artillery units.

Some of the dreadnaught's heavier rounds carried over the ADF/Canadian perimeter and struck the barracks inside the main post area and set them afire. When this happened, the majority of the people left the prayer meeting and fled for the airfield, which was as far as someone could get from the perimeter lines. Buildings already in rubble from the earthquake were blown apart as the massive rounds impacted and dozens of people killed or wounded. Panic returned to the main Alaskan body and there was nothing Pastor Woodway and his new military friends could do to stop them. But the perimeter defenses continued to hold.

Oriental solders shouted threats and waved fists and buglers blew out shrieking calls. Holding infantry rifles waist high, long bayonets pointed toward the ADF line, they continue to trudge forward through knee deep snow. It was slow going, but they didn't stop; going was made easier for the row after row of men and women following behind.

Mines exploded and sections of the human wall disappeared, but only until fresh troops rushed forward to fill the gap. The mines were only powerful enough to kill infantry or damage medium tanks. But Scott and Ed both hoped they might provide a nasty headache to the crewmembers inside the powerful dreadnoughts; when the heavier tanks were committed. But they remained in the trees as field artillery blasting ADF and Canadian secondary defenses.

"They're like a wave of locusts," Joey shouted. He brought his rifle up, fired off a burst and watched as soldiers crowded together fell face first into the snow. Joey's platoon had been hit hard and was down to two squads which Scott had added to Ed's platoon. Between them they had a full platoon which Scott had left Ed in command of and Joey as second-in-command. Ed's platoon was responsible for a section of perimeter nearly 100 yards in length spread out very thin with two soldiers to a hole.

Though the Canadians had supported the ADF southern perimeter with armor units and artillery, they had held back airborne companies to protect the airfield. Infantry was used in northern perimeter positions to protect civilians in the main post area. In the event it was needed, ADF and Canadians would fight a last ditch battle from the main post area. With knowledge provided of what prisoners could expect at the hands of the enemy senior officers were under orders from respective generals that no Alaskan or Canadian soldier would surrender to the OAP. A military police commander was chosen and after a full briefing of expectations, his unit was put under orders to carry out the grizzly assignment for the civilian population.

President Andrews knew that if the Lord chose not to return to save them, the OAP would not find a living prisoner to endure the sheer torture of witnessing family and friends cannibalized. It was such an order as to sicken him and his two generals. While shells fell upon the fort, President Andrews ignored the panic and summoned his newly formed ministerial association to the headquarters building. He released the generals to their jobs, while he and his chaplains, pastors and bishops, rabbi and ministers met in joint prayer. He was a little bit surprised, but he and his fellow Christians and Jews welcomed Muslim, Buddhists and Hindu leaders. He couldn't remember a time in history where such a joint prayer time had occurred and he thought God would sincerely understand because these were all His people out there in battle, represented by leaders in here. It got so big he moved the meeting out of the conference room and into the briefing theater in the basement which seated 200 people. It had suffered some quake damage: large crack from ceiling to floor and some ceiling tiles had fallen to the floor or were found broken in theater chairs, but was suitable for the prayer meeting.

Once everyone was inside the large room and military police posted at the entry, President Andrews with Chaplain Knight and Pastor Woodway addressed the church leaders, "Gentlemen, we come from many backgrounds and the color of our skins may vary, but we have witnessed events never before occurring in our history and foretold to occur in the End Times in the Bible. We have seen the collapse of the world's economy with the sighting of the comet, followed by terrible storms, volcanic eruptions, towering tsunamis and great quakes. We have watched the rise of a satanic Emperor and the miraculous appearance of the Two Witnesses as foretold in the New Testament. No, my friends, I can see little doubt in the return of our Lord Jesus Christ and I believe it is again time to pray to show our Lord our new found unity and demonstrate to Him that we follow the One True King."

Some church leaders squirmed about in their chairs and two rushed to the door where they were released by the MPs. The others ceased their uneasiness as the sounds of battle outside carried down into the theater.

"Now is the time to pray, my brothers and sisters and I ask Pastor Woodway, who has journeyed from Arizona with his flock to share in these Last Days with us, to lead us."

WITH BRAVO COMPANY ON THE SOUTHERN PERIMETER

Lying against the sandbags with only the tops of their helmets visible over the top Scott grabbed Ed by the shoulder strap and pulled him toward him, and still had to yell to be heard over all the noise, "How can we make a stand here against them? It's like stopping an ocean wave...we'll be overrun." His frantic voice surprised Ed, who tried to think of something to calm his new company commander. But for the first time in Scott's life, he felt that he was truly facing impossible odds and it had really rattled him.

"Well, Captain, we have no place to go and you gotta admit, we're in for one history making fight," Ed said in a calm voice." We'll make our stand right here and show those boys what Alaskans are made of."

Bugles blared, artillery and tank rounds sailed overhead and thousands of voices screamed, but Scott ignored all that and stared at Ed, his eyes wide with fear. Yet seeing Ed's courage had its effect and he began to calm down. He nodded, "Thanks." Adding, "You know you're a lot like your big brother. I followed that man into many a bar fight and our last fire fight was a dilly... He'd be real proud of you, Ed."

Ed grinned in response and replied, "Thanks right back at you."

Giving Scott a reassuring pat on the arm, Ed moved a few feet to the right and grabbed Kira by the hand to draw her closer so he could speak into her ear without having to yell, "Things are gonna get a bit hectic here in a moment. I just wanted you to know how much I love you." He squeezed her tight about the shoulder and she rested her head on his chest, which wasn't all that easy with her still wearing a helmet.

"Funny, in this short time we've been together, you've brought so much joy into my life...I only wish you were in a safer place," Ed said loudly.

Kira raised her head and look into his bloodshot eyes ringed in filth, "I love you too, Mr. Ed Sawyer." Kira kissed him and as their lips separated, she buried her face in Ed's chest again and whispered, so he couldn't hear her, "I'm so scared."

But Ed knew what she was feeling and going through her mind, because he felt the same fears; he brought her head back up to eye level, "Listen, honey," Ed pushed her to arm's length and handed her a 9mm Glock pistol, "I've taught you all you need to know about how to use this. It's loaded...Make sure you're not taken alive. I know how hard that is to hear, but don't let it happen. Stay in this hole, if we're overrun...you know what to do and if I'm wounded, you do it for me too. We know what they do with the wounded; I don't want that to happen to us... okay?"

Kira fought to hold back tears, but the dam burst and water flowed down her cheeks. "I don't know if I can, Ed."

"Promise me, you won't be taken alive. Either that, or I'll kill us both right here and now!"

Kira looked into Ed's pleading eyes, his face flush with emotion. She knew she could not allow that, Ed was too valuable to lose. "All right, I promise."

Ed, with a hard look in his eyes, glared at her for a moment and then shook his head, and said, "I'll hold you to it, honey."

THE VALIANT RIDE OF THE 600

Extra ammo was brought up, but as predicted they were running extremely low of M-60 and .50 caliber ammo. Remembering how good Point Man was with a LAW tube, Ed scrounged up a half dozen and gave them to his old friend. "Use them where they'll do the most good, Big Guy."

"Can do, boss man."

The enemy was well within rifle range and the perimeter was getting hit from tank fire. Scott was about to issue the order to open fire when a really loud bugle call rang out from behind their own lines. Spinning around, Scott was startled by the sight of a massive cavalry unit moving up from the secondary positions. With an open mouth of disbelief, he watched speechless as General Howard-Wright, dressed in his finest RCMP red tunic carrying a bright shining long sword at the ready, led his RCMP regiment of mounted horsemen through the line. In matching red tunics, black pants and high calf black boots, they jumped the trenches and sandbagged wall, then cautiously rode out between the breaks of barbed wire to a position out in front of Alpha, Bravo and Charlie Company's positions.

Responding to bugle calls in a highly disciplined manner, the Royal Canadian Mounted Police attired in their finery rode majestic raven black horses which averaged 16 hands and quickly formed into six long lines of a hundred horsemen each. Each Mountie was armed with either an eight foot long lance with a yellow ceremonial flag attached near the tip, or a long sword. They carried a sidearm; a Smith & Wesson .40 caliber pistol loaded with 10 rounds. White frost shot out from the nostrils of these beautiful warhorses, their necks muscles bulging and black flanks glistening, while these highly trained mounts awaited the order to move. In the building excitement, it took real horseman to hold these beauties in place.

The ADF forces along the perimeter were confused by the sudden appearance of this red shirted cavalry, but the enemy was even more in a state of disbelief and halted their advance. The use of a mounted unit in this day and age confounded the enemy completely; they stared with wide eyes and open mouths at the Mounties. Quite a few of them were really impressed, having never before seen such a sight; except in a movie.

"Totally awesome!" Kira shouted, as she waved at the passing Mounties.

"Our 7th Cavalry to the rescue," Kathy O' Brian added.

"They may not be able to stand up against automatic weapons, but those Mounties are sure going out in style," Scott said. He had a lot respect for these men and saluted several of the mounted officers as they rode by. Recognizing Ed, General Howard-Wright lifted his sword in salute and slowly nodded his head as he passed by. Ed returned the salute, feeling a wave of pride wash over him as the beautiful horsemen formed into their ranks. Watching the first rank lead off at a slow cantor, high stepping through the deeper snow, Ed recalled an old poem, "Into the Valley of Death rode the 600."

"Fitting," Point Man added. "…Very fitting."

Scott turned around when he heard General Saunders' voice behind him, "A proud man leading his mounted command in possibly his last cavalry charge and a warrior's death for my very dear friend."

"Sir, you shouldn't be up here," Scott warned.

"Nonsense, Captain. My friend is about to sacrifice his life in such a glorious way in an attempt to give us a few more moments to live. I couldn't be anywhere else. He has the enemy so thoroughly confused; they've actually stopped their advance and artillery fire, as we continue to pound them with our field artillery.

"Sir, at least please move into the trench line. You make too good a target out here. We can't afford to lose both generals." Scott gestured toward the trench where Ed was watching the show.

"You're right of course," General Saunders said in agreement. He shouldered his rifle and followed Scott into the trench. From there, they heard General Howard-Wright issue the order to move out. With his escort bugler blowing strongly, the first line of mounted riders advanced against the enemy at high stepping trot. As the horses moved ever forward, the riders sat tall in their glossy leather saddles and brought either swords or lances up to the ready.

Then came the final command as General Howard-Wright rose up, standing in his silver spurs, raised his long glistening blade into the attack position, with the fine point of the weapon aimed at the enemy, and shouted out, "Charge!"

The bugle call was given lances lowered to a level position, swords held straight out; and the lines moved forward in readiness to impale and or slash out against the first line of enemy troops. The going was slow, but the horses were excited and the ground covered quickly. The second rank of horsemen launched forward followed by the third and so on until all six ranks of brightly colored horsemen and their valiant black steeds were charging the enemy. Centered and out in front, General Howard-Wright's blade would meet the enemy first.

There were no mines this close to the perimeter, but due to his concern the Mounties might come under friendly fire, General Saunders had given orders through his personal RTO for all units along the perimeter to cease fire and artillery fire to impact the tree line behind the enemy's front lines. "They've got heavy armor in there. Make sure the artillery keeps hitting them until they're out of ammo."

Though puzzled by facing a mounted force in this date and time, OAP commanders issued orders for their lines to advance and slowly the enemy continued forward. Yet, up in front, soldiers, facing the onrushing wave of spear carrying mounted troops atop huge black horses panicked. Not waiting for orders to open fire, they dropped to their knees and fired. Others remained standing, shouldering rifles and pulling triggers to stop these horsemen.

From the enemy's tree line came a series of tank salvos aimed at the charging horsemen and barely missing their infantry. OAP rounds impacted the first line of the RCMP Regiment. Waves of snow, dirt and shrapnel blew nearly half of horsemen off their mounts and caused dozens of horses to fall into tumbling masses of horseflesh. But the second rank prepared for this event leapt over the bodies of the slain or wounded to continue their epic charge.

They did not falter and from all along the ADF perimeter, came the shouts of support for these brave comrades. But their yells and applause was drowned out when the crashing sounds of the Royal Canadian Mounted Police smashed bravely into the front lines of the enemy infantry. Horses, enraged by the call of battle, clashed with panicked ground troops, driving them back into the rows of supporting companies.

Surrounded by a dozen of his most trusted officers, General Howard-Wright broke through the enemy forward ranks and slashed at one soldier and then another with his 90 year old ceremonial sword. A weapon his father had carried as a young RCMP captain and given to the General upon his graduation from RCMP Officer School. For the first time the blade had tasted blood and it was against a foe armed with automatic weapons.

Behind the General came the rumbling roar of his second, third, fourth, fifth and then sixth row of mounted troops. When the force hit the enemy front line at nearly 35 miles an hour, nearly 370 Mounties who had survived the heavy bombardment, forced their way through to OAP's supporting elements. A dozen gallant riders made it so far as to actually burst through to the tree line, leaping over the enemy's artillery or riding over the top of the fleeing soldiers, before being brought down by automatic fire. OAP troops panicked firing wildly, trying to bring the horsemen down killing and wounding their own people.

Standing in his stirrups, General Howard-Wright, his shirt bloodied by a single chest wound and his gallant horse wounded several times, lifted his sword to the heavens and without uttering a word, brought it down one final time to slash at an enemy soldier. A burst of automatic fire from a 19 year old Cambodian, who had never seen such a horse, threw him and his mount to the red stained ground. The Cambodian dropped his weapon to the ground staring at the dying horse, wishing he was back home and teary eyed, regretted having to kill such a beautiful animal and his courageous aged rider. His commander down, the regimental bugler, hurriedly dismounted to stand by his dead commander and blew their battle cry until he too was finally silenced with a burst of fire.

With lances aimed low, horsemen continued to impale the infantry in a thundering explosion of clashing metal, and the grunts and screams of man versus beast. Lances, driven with almost inhuman force, slew the enemy by the tens and twenties, and soon hundreds, while even more foot soldiers fell beneath the hooves of those raven black beauties. But sadly, the odds were too great and the enemy encircled the Canadians like a pack of wolves closing in on the kill of a trapped moose.

From less than 300 yards away, General Saunders watched in silence as the last of the valiant horsemen fell before the enemy's overwhelming numbers. With not a single steed left standing and having lost sight of Wright's red shirts, General Saunders gave the order for all guns to open fire.

"Fire!" He shouted in vengeance. "Hit 'em with everything you've got! Avenge the 600!" He screamed.

Machineguns, backed by what few LAW tubes and AT4 rockets they had left, chewed into the enemy, as ADF mortar fire was brought closer and closer to the perimeter. Running up and down the trench issuing orders, Scott returned to find General Saunders knelt behind a pile of sandbags firing an M-16 on semi- automatic. "Sir, you should return to the CP. They're gonna need you there, General."

"No time, Captain. Besides, I'd rather be here with my troops." Changing magazines, General Saunders asked Scott where the Battalion CO was.

"Dead," Scott replied. "His CP took a direct hit." Scott heard, but didn't say anything to General Saunders that Major Buford was reportedly cowering beneath his desk when the first barrage came in.

"How many troops do you have here, Captain?"

"After their last shelling, we're down to less than 100 able to bear arms, General. I've got two undermanned platoons and that was after I broke up my 3rd platoon to add strength to my other two. The other companies are in much the same shape." Scott went eye to eye with the General, "Their air attack and tank fire has chewed us up somethin' bad, sir."

"Who is your ranking man?" General Saunders lifted the rifle to his shoulder and fired off another burst while waiting for Scott's answer.

"I guess I am, sir."

"That makes you battalion CO then. But it may be a moot point. Keep your troops on the line and I'll try to get you some help." General Saunders turned around to find his RTO severely wounded, a medic working on him, and the radio damaged.

"I think I'm going need your RTO, Captain."

"Sure thing, General, he's all yours." Scott looked at his RTO and nodded his head in the General's direction. "You stick with him until relieved. Got it?"

"Yes, sir," the young RTO replied. A bit awestruck at being assigned to the commanding general, he gathered up his gear and stuck close to the old man.

Watching the wall of humanity move toward him, Ed estimated the OAP would be on Bravo Company within moments. Checking his dwindling ammo supply and finding only six remaining magazines, Ed decided it was time for a little rock & roll time to diminish the front lines some.

"If you've got the ammo, switch to full auto! We're running out of time," Ed ordered. The command was quickly echoed down the line and those that could switch over selectors on their M-16s to full automatic fire, did. For some this brought on an elevated level of excitement; they were thrilled to see how many more of the enemy they could drop in these last few moments.

Within 100 yards, the enemy suddenly reminded Ed of an oncoming ocean wave Scott had talked about and knew there was little he could do to stop the tide from coming in. But he popped up over the sandbags directly in front of him to sweep from right to left with an extended burst of ammo. With blazing automatic fire coming from the ADF perimeter, hundreds of OAP troops were dropping, as thunder shot out across the snowy plain and white turned to a dreadful crimson color. But still, the enemy ranks continued to be replaced in an ever steady flow. Ed knew this, but what else could they do and he ordered, "Grenades!"

All along the defensive line, men and women began throwing what few grenades they had left. With such power expended in such close range this number of grenades had the cumulative effect of 300 pounds of dynamite exploding along the perimeter's jagged length. Suddenly, the OAP, ranks forgot about discipline and broke ranks, rushing forward, climbing over wounded and dead, to break through the barbed wire. Claymore mines, a last stop effort, mowed down nearly the complete first line of infantry, but still more came. In the spots not broken up by tank barrage, soldiers in the newly made first row were forced to lie over the razor sharp wire, to make a bridge with their bodies for others to climb over the rows of concertina wire to reach ADF positions. The last few grenades were thrown into the wire, but to no avail as first hundreds and then thousands of enemy soldiers poured into the trenches. Fighting was hand-to-hand with the soldiers of 8th Division completely overwhelmed by enemy numbers. One ADF soldier locked in a life or death situation with four or even 10 OAP troops. But as in the many wars of man's history, a barbaric scene was once again played out on the southern plains of Fort Greeley. It was actually the sheer mass of the enemy force that kept them from simply running over the ADF defenders.

It was like too many people trying to board an elevator with the doors unable to close. The few were keeping the many from advancing by using their bodies to block the doorway. One row of men dueled for survival; the rest remained blocked up and could only wait for an opening. Only when a group of defenders fell was there space for the enemy infantry to advance, but with each moment these openings slowly widened.

Blood flowed through the trenches with men and women fighting for life with knuckles, knives, shovels, rifle butts and the heel of a boot. Very few shots could be fired; the two opponents were too close to bring up a rifle. They slashed at each other with boot knives, driving a knee into a man's chin as they grappled in the mud and tried to drown one another in the bottom of the trench. Ammo cans were used as clubs, M-60 ammo belts used as whips and the noise was deafening.

Bowled over by three enemy troops and pushed back into a crater, Ed struggled to get his K-Bar knife. He pushed a wounded man off his chest and slashed out against the other two. One soldier screamed when Point Man appeared behind them and jerked the soldier off Ed by the scruff of his neck and clobbered him over the head with the barrel of his Colt .45. The members of the Phoenix to Alaska convoy formed into a tight circle and fought back-to-back against this terrible onslaught. But it was not long before Bravo Company's position was completely overrun. Point Man, his arms and chest covered in other soldier's blood, grunted in pain as two OAP bayonets stabbed into his backside. He was trying to help one of the Misfits back to his feet, but the bayonets crippled him severely. When he dropped to his knees, Point Man was able to wrestle both rifles away from the childlike figures before him and used one to club both men to the ground before he collapsed from loss of blood. Swinging the M-60 like an ancient battle ax, the last surviving Misfit dropped four soldiers before taking three bullets to the chest and falling over the chest of one of his old buddies.

The sounds of battle were stifling; extensive gun fire; screams of attackers and victims, and the mournful cries of the dying. Black smoke from countless explosions filled the air with the pungent odor of sulfur and the ground was two, three and even five bodies deep along the trench line. Every foxhole was filled with the dead and dying.

Standing at the backside of a hole created by tank fire, Ed fought to keep Kira behind him and used his rifle to block a bayonet thrust aimed at his heart. Kira reached around him with the Glock and shot the man down. Knowing they had no chance in the trenches, Ed ordered his few remaining friends back toward a collapsed bunker and shoved a gasping Kira in that direction. "Go...go...go!" He shouted.

Joey, Larry and Kathy, young Richard, Matthew Fulbright, and a couple other survivors sprinted for the smoldering bunker, fighting their way through a dozen clashes. They slashed out with knives, stabbed with bayonets, used M-16's like baseball bats and used whatever force was necessary to live. Yet only the seven of them made it to the bunker, where they discovered a single M-60 rested on a bipod. Joey had just reached the corner of the bunker when he went down with several shots to the back and Ed knew he couldn't be reached. To do so he would have to leave Kira, but then he saw that Joey had taken his last breath and ducked back inside the bunker as OAP troops ran past Joey's body.

Ed ordered Kira and Kathy to the rear of the bunker then tossed them what few grenades they had found in a broken wooden crate inside the bunker. "Start lobbing those out the back to keep them from trying to get in." Meanwhile, Ed, Larry, Richard and Matthew Fulbright used the single M-60 to rake rows of oncoming soldiers still in the wire. Everyone knew it was only a matter of minutes; maybe seconds before the end came. But they would go down fighting to the last trooper.

As if by silent agreement, Both Ed and Larry saved their last bullets for their wives, knowing they couldn't allow them to be taken alive and how hard it would be for these two fine ladies to take their own lives. A Slightest hesitation could leave them as prisoners and unspeakable horrors to follow.

30 feet west of the bunker, Scott lay semi-conscious in the bottom of a foxhole. Covered in too much of his own blood, he struggled to keep the darkness away that he knew wanted to claim him. He'd been shot twice; once in the right leg and a second bullet to the left chest. It was the blood loss and the icy cold that was making him light headed. To make matters worse, an enemy grenade had been thrown through the air to land at his feet and he simply wasn't strong enough, by might or will, to lob it back.

FORT GREELEY

With an out and out attack in process, church leaders left the prayer meeting to be with their people. With so many wounded coming in, it wasn't hard to find a need. While praying for a dying soldier injured in the great quake, Pastor looked into the eyes of a man taking his last breath. He asked God to welcome home this brave man and gently closed the man's eyes with a gloved hand. Unable to shed even one more tear, Pastor Woodway moved on to a girl missing her right leg from below the hip and not expected to live. Triage was in place, those not expected to live were placed in a special area where the chaplains and church leaders moved about to offer some peace and compassion before the final moment.

By order of the President, demolitions were in place in enclosures to ensure none of the wounded would be left for the enemy. An action he never thought he would be forced to bring against his own people. By order of the President, all civilians not on the battle line were herded into large groups on the airfield's tarmac and runway. Here, MPs assigned the sad duty of ensuring there would be no prisoners, remained ready to carry out their last order. They would then turn their weapons on each other; two such dire actions they never thought they'd ever be ordered to carry out.

A COMING STORM

Pastor Woodway, his face filled with tension, thought about those of his flock out on the perimeter and all these people before him, forced himself to concentrate on his prayer for a moment before he opened his mouth, when he was stunned into silence by an amazingly powerful sonic boom. Rather than coming from any one direction, the explosive blast of sound had come from directly overhead and seemed to carry across the skies in full intensity to every direction.

Pastor didn't know it, but the deep booming sound had driven every single human to the ground. But it didn't damage a single ear or render anyone unconscious. Lying on his back, his arms outstretched, his heart racing at 140 beats per minute and not even feeling the cold ice and snow beneath him, he looked to the sun and beheld a great sight unfold. The sun's burning light was growing in its intensity and as the booming noise faded and with his mouth hanging open in awe, Pastor watched in near disbelief as the massive sun suddenly separated into two gigantic halves. With this distinct separating a flood of radiant multi-colored lights streamed out in enlarging waves of radiance to fill the entire sky. The center for the two halves had given birth to a universal bridge shimmering rainbow colors that illuminated the heavens. From a point of immense bright and nearly blinding light between the halves of the sun, this beautiful bridge grew forth in length and width to eventually touch the towering peaks of the world's most majestic mountain ranges. Such a point of landfall touched upon Denali, the Great One, or as visitors would know it Mt. McKinley.

Though knocked to the ground, miraculously no one was injured; the concussion wave from the initial booming blast had sent a shudder through Pastor's body, rising from the bottom of his feet to surge to the top of his head. Even his fingertips were tingling, yet with this strange sensation he also felt a warmness bathing him over. He knew this was the presence of the Holy Spirit, for he had felt it once before when he was given his visions to leave Phoenix and take his flock to Alaska. Slowly, Pastor Woodway pulled himself up to stand and watched in silence as others stood to behold the wondrous sight in the sky. No one spoke a word; they remained wide eyed and speechless like small children visiting Disneyland for the first time.

As the boom faded, another sound began to grow in strength; a more beautiful and sweet sound and its one blaring notes carried across the world to be heard by all. It was the sound of a trumpet, or maybe a bugle, but it was no ordinary horn. Pastor stood, his body trembling from hope fulfilled and shouted, "It's the Lord's trumpet! He is returning!"

Pastor Woodway could feel every hair on his body stand up, his heart was beating rapidly; the warm sensation continued to travel throughout his body. His eyes were moist with tears of joy, for he knew what was happening. Like so many others before him, men and women who had waited for more than 2,000 years for the Lord's triumphant return, he did not expect it in his lifetime. Yet, now was the moment, the hour and the day, and he was here to witness this grand event and it seemed to him, he'd been waiting a long time for just this moment in time to occur.

The blast of the horn changed and heavenly musical notes began to carry across the land; so unlike any earthly music ever produced. Everyone heard it, from the Antarctic to the Arctic, and those who knew of the prophecy knew the same thing; this was the proverbial trumpet and its majestic sound was a mighty call to arms. The Heavenly Host with the Lamb of God in the lead, were about to make their presence known to mankind and the Son of Perdition.

Pastor Woodway, his hands still trembling, gazed upon the colored heavens and with arms spread upward and raised in joy, listened in awe to the Great Horn of Biblical prophecy as it released choruses of mighty notes in supernatural power.

"This is it!" Pastor shouted at the top of his lungs. "God's Golden Trumpet, so beautiful in its call to His people." Pastor danced around in his excitement, looking from one horizon to the other, unsure of what he expected to see next. Then from straight overhead, a massive solar flare like no other before exploded in the heavens from between the two halves of the sun, even brighter than before and it washed the colors from the sky to leave only a bluish hue. This explosion of light forced him and everyone else on earth to their knees, as the bright whiteness temporarily blinded them.

When his vision returned, seconds, moments or maybe hours he was not sure, Pastor Woodway saw that everything and everyone around him appeared to be frozen in place. Still able to hear, to see, to breathe, but unable to move or even scratch his head, Pastor looked to the skies in anticipation as the great moment unfolded.

He didn't realize he was holding his breath, but glanced down to the young girl in such dire pain from losing her leg and saw that she was in deep sleep with an expression of peace upon her face. Gone was the pain and gone was the extensive bleeding and she was not the only one. All of the wounded across the camp, across the world, had fallen into a deep trance like sleep, while the trumpet continued to sing out.

In reverent awe, Pastor watched as thousands of shining gold rays burst out from between the two sun halves and as they grew in unimaginable length and width, reached out to touch the earth's horizons. These rays soon become golden highways for the Lord's Heavenly Host to bridge between the spirit realm and the world of man.

With sheer amazement in his eyes wide enough to come popping out of his head, Pastor watched as gigantic towering silver gray thunderheads began to form at the point where the golden highway seemed to grasp hold of the earth. Their massive tops, seemingly flat in nature, soared miles high above the earth and yet, these mighty storm titans cascaded down to within inches above the ground. Here the thunderheads began to produce a fine, silvery mist in great concentration, which began to shower upon the world.

With tears of joy and with only God capable to explain it, he began to feel this strange inner warmth grow in power and radiate outward, to join with so many others, as the coming storm bathed over mankind and returned to it an innocence it had lost.

As the cloud giants drew closer, washing over snowy fields and mountains alike with their unearthly mist, Pastor made out figures atop the clouds and knew in his heart that these were the Heavenly Host; foretold in the Book of Revelations dressed in shimmering white linen from neck to ankles, and riding the most beautiful white stallions this world had ever seen, these mounted troops, numbering in the hundreds of thousands, maybe millions, carried long golden swords and lances. Banners were present amongst the riders, the words written upon them in ancient Hebrew language. As the Golden Trumpet call diminished in intensity, Pastor could hear the angelic riders singing, "Hallelujah! Hallelujah! For we sing praises to the Lamb of God and bring forth victory to our King!"

With the Lord's radiant glory outshining all others, Pastor could easily identify the King of Kings and listened as the heavenly singing continued, "He is the King of Kings and Lord of Lords, who will reign for evermore!"

Then Pastor watched in a daze as spiraling roadways began to form in the clouds. Once completed, the Heavenly Host charged down the thunderheads, riding upon these pathways and dividing into multiple armies. They come well prepared to wage war across the globe against the enemy of man, to slay the Anti-Christ and his minions, and once more imprison the Beast. Humbled that he was present to witness such an event, Pastor gazed upon the Lord and observed how He lifted His left arm and used his mighty sword to create a mighty tempest among these towering cloud giants before riding off for His foretold confrontation in Israel. Other members of the Host took flight to all four winds, riding tempests to their assigned destinations to bring the awesome Power of God against the armies of Satan.

Pastor took notice as a single Host army descended toward the Fort Greeley area, the great Tanana Valley and rapidly all of Alaska. Smaller, but still great in power, bellowing thunderheads merged and the Heavenly Warriors fell upon the ADF and OAP warriors. Within the length of two heartbeats, the Tanana Valley became completely covered in this strange silvery mist and visibility was reduced to mere inches.

Accompanied by a barrage of thunderclaps reminiscent of the sound created by a division of field artillery and shiny silvery lightning bolts so numerous as to make one think he was inside an electrical transformer. Majestic horsemen flew across the blood soaked battlefields to bring forth righteousness against the fleeing enemies of darkness. Unseen by earthly eyes, a great, but brief battle was fought against demonic forces in the spiritual realm; the Armies of the Lamb of God were victorious, as prophesized so long ago.

The Heavenly mist moved across Alaska like an oncoming ocean tide and reached out to utterly destroy all man's weapons of warfare. Everything meant to bring harm in the cause of war vanished as this strange mist consumed it. As if made of paper mighty dreadnaughts, tanks and artillery pieces disappeared into the landscape. Mortar tubes, ammo and rifles were no more, pistols and revolvers faded from holsters, grenades vanished and machineguns dissolved into the earth.

A warm wetness engulfed Pastor as the mist enveloped him, giving him the feeling of being held in the Lord's mighty Arms for the first time. Not only did the mist touch his outside body, he sensed a cleansing of his heart and soul. Physical pain from his old war wound disappeared. Emotional pain from seeing so many suffer, vanished with the strange purification only the Lord could bring forth. Bursting with a new joy, Pastor felt his body freed of restraint, the fog disappeared and he jumped around like a young child in celebration. Below him, the young girl awakened and caressed her new limb before rising to her feet. She was not the only one to do so; where once a field was littered with dying; men, women and children rose to their feet with new healthy bodies.

Pastor stopped dancing and stood stunned with amazement; watching as thousands rose to inspect news limbs. They felt the places where ugly gashes and wounds had simply disappeared. Broken bones were not simply mended; they showed no signs of ever being injured. The blind could see, the deaf could hear; every infirmity was healed with the passing of this strange healing mist.

A boisterous celebration began, but the Lord wasn't done yet. Pastor watched with eyes wide in wonder as people rose from the massive open air morgues. The dead had been brought back to life and miracles continued to multiply. Mortal wounds were gone and horrific memories of death no longer existed.

Pastor stood and once more lifted his arms and cried in praise, which resounded with others through the streets and fields of Fort Greeley. No longer simply a Bible story or words studied in the Book of Revelations, this was real and His promises were fulfilled. "The Lord has returned as promised, the sick are healed and the dead have risen... Glory to God in the highest!" Pastor shouted.

He continued to jump for joy and then he suddenly fell to his knees in reverence and continued to thank the Lord Jesus, while others continued to celebrate His return.

FORT GREELEY'S SOUTHERN PERIMETER

Waiting for the grenade to explode, to end his misery, Scott was startled by a great sonic boom and though still waiting for the grenade to end his life, curious of the intensifying sound of that strange trumpet. *That's one heck of a PA system those dudes got... but this one's so pretty...Ah can almost hear singing.* Then it was as if time seemed to have no meaning. The grenade just sat there and no one was piling on top of him, or sticking a bayonet into him. He couldn't move, couldn't really see anything except for what was in the hole with him and then, he watched this strange blanket of silvery mist wrap around him. His weapons and the grenade near him suddenly disappeared into thin air and for a moment, he thought he was already dead. *I gotta be dead? The enemy ain't got nothin' that can do that.*

Scott suddenly began to feel a strange tingling sensation and somehow, he couldn't explain it, his strength was instantly restored and all his wounds disappeared. He kept checking himself, wondering where all the blood went. When his ability to move again was fully restored, Scott slowly poked his head up and was flabbergasted to see that every gun, knife and machinegun, every mechanical monstrosity of war, had utterly disappeared. All the bodies were gone too, but mostly it was the bodies of the enemy. From the ADF and Canadian side, the wounded and the dead were rising to their feet, and Scott saw confused expressions of bewilderment upon their cleansed faces. Those who were wounded found their wounds completely healed. Even the Mounties were standing out in the field, their horses, lances and swords gone. In clusters and smaller groups they too walked back toward the perimeter in bewilderment.

As if awakened from a deep sleep, General Saunders rose to his feet and began to pat himself down. All the dirt, grime and concrete dust were no longer on his uniform. His face was clean and he couldn't seem to recall what had happened to him, only that he was in a dark place and was suddenly back in the light. Only then did General Saunders realize that all the ice and snow of a hard winter was gone too. The Alaskan countryside had been instantly transformed into a lush green field of summertime; flowers bloomed and the air was comfortably warm as in the month of June or July. Even the birds had returned; a flock of Canadian geese flew overhead; it'd been several months since he'd seen a flight of birds.

"Are you okay, sir?" Scott asked the General.

"Strange, it seems I may have been dead, but now I don't remember any pain." General Saunders looked out over the perimeter. "And where's the enemy? Where's the wire and the trenches? It doesn't even look like we had a battle out here."

"Ah'm really confused about the military stuff and terrain, sir, but most of the enemy is gone." Scott saw some of the enemy in the distance "There's still some out there, sir, but they look unarmed like us and by the way they is walkin', Ah'd say there a bit confused too." Scott raised his arm and pointed out to the field where hundreds of oriental soldiers were wandering about in small groups, unsure as to whether or not they should approach the ADF lines.

General Saunders looked to the sun, took in all the sights going on around him for a moment and made a decision, "Well, Captain, I imagine by all that's occurred... I'm sure you looked at the sun and all those strange clouds, that mankind has just been rescued by our Lord Jesus Christ."

"Sir?" Scott was new to all this, yet he realized a lot had just happened and by the looks of the sun and sky, only God could've accomplished this.

"General, you're sayin' this be His time to return and that's why we're alive?"

General Saunders smiled and patted Scott on the shoulder, "That's right, Captain...mankind has waited more than 2,000 years and we were here to see it happen. I can see it as the only reason why both of us are alive and most of the enemy has disappeared... vanished and most likely gone to Hell."

"What about those men out there, General?"

By now the Mounties had returned to the line and joyous parties broke out between the Alaskans and the Canadians. General Howard-Wright straightened his red tunic and a little put out at first for losing his ceremonial family sword walked toward General Saunders with a smile growing on his face.

"Captain, I believe those gentlemen are our fellow brothers and sisters...believers. We must welcome them. I'm sure they're probably just as confused as we are." General Saunders was still shocked to see how the foxholes, wires, bunkers, and even shell craters had disappeared. Men and women who had been killed or wounded, were either on their knees praising God or whooping it up with their comrades, pointing to the heavens and watching the clouds of mist fade in the distance.

General Saunders watched as the ground turned green under the mist and trees barren from a harsh winter burst out with leaves. "Well, what do you think about that?"

"Go out and get our brothers and sisters, Captain," General Saunders ordered.

"Yes, sir," Scott replied.

Walking out to greet his old friend, General Howard-Wright, who was walking forward with most of his 600 men, General Saunders invited him to help welcome their new oriental brothers.

Meeting in the middle of the field, with only green grass at their feet, all of the parties were greatly surprised to find that there was no longer a language barrier. Everyone seemed to understand what the other was saying, "It's as we've heard so many times before, my old friend," General Saunders said to General Howard-Wright, "... the Lord moves in mighty and mysterious ways."

General Saunders walked up and embraced the nearest oriental soldier and soon, all felt welcome, as the army of men and women headed into Fort Greeley to see what other miracles had transpired.

"Look!" A soldier yelled out and pointed to the sun. With everyone watching, the sun once more returned to being a single very bright orb and this restoration seemed to relieve most of the people.

"Must be 70°," Scott said and then added, "... and no mosquitoes!"

Surrounded by the enemy, no chance of escape and everyone dead except for he and Kira, Larry and Kathy O'Brian, Ed grabbed his wife and yanked her backwards toward one corner of the bunker. He had his pistol out and leveled at the side of Kira's head. Larry was doing the same with Kathy, who had her eyes closed and was waiting for the bullet to enter her brain. Both Kathy and Kira knew why their husbands were going to shoot them and preferred dying this way to be taken prisoner by the OAP.

An enemy soldier entered the bunker, his rifle leveled at Ed. Closing his eyes, Ed began to apply pressure to the trigger, when the sonic boom went off overhead and the enemy soldier was knocked to the ground, his rifle flying out of his hand. Ed held his arm out, his pistol pointed at the head of the young enemy soldier and was about to shoot him when the boom faded, and the might trumpet blew.

Ed felt it come over him and he dropped the pistol. He hadn't realized it, but Larry O'Brian had aimed his pistol at a soldier coming through the roof, and he too had dropped his weapon.

"What's happening, Ed?" Larry asked in a loud voice.

"Hold on, Larry, I think we're in for big surprise!"

When Ed, Larry, Kathy and Kira were able to move again, they were surprised to see they were sitting on fresh green grass, the bunker and everything else military was gone and all their wounds had healed.

Matthew Fulbright and Richard Knight, who had been killed in the battle, were sitting side by side on the ground staring at the sun through shaded hands. Both had big smiles on their faces and eyes filled with bewilderment.

"Yeah, but have you've noticed the birds... Look over there, that's a herd of moose." Ed gestured to a flowing spring bed, where a small herd of moose cows were drinking. One rather large bull moose was offering his protection in the event a predator came near.

Ed had his arm around Kira; they were in joyous celebration with old and new friends, brothers and sisters, "For over 2,000 years man has waited for the Lord's return and we happen to be blessed to actually be alive to witness it," Ed said. He waved his right wide open hand in presentation, "The Lord has returned in all His glory. All our weapons have disappeared, the carnage we've caused is gone and our beautiful land bathed in this lush greenery of summer once again." Ed turned to embrace his wife suddenly feeling like a young kid again. Old pains from bar fights, foot chases and tangling with young healthy offenders, had gone.

With the healing of the body and heart, all bigotry, fear, resentment and revenge was washed away. A place where only moments before deadly combat was being staged had been transformed into a giant social and praise celebration in honor of the Lord Jesus Christ.

FORT GREELEY

Pastor spotted Chaplain Knight dancing with several children, little ones who had died in the great quake. The rubble had vanished, craters disappeared and all signs of battle or damage caused by the great quake nowhere to be seen. Though all the snow had instantly melted away, not a puddle could be seen. Everyone had tossed off their winter gear to enjoy a warm summer day. Added to the people's joy there was the sudden appearance of food and it was plentiful. Bushels and bushels of fresh vegetables and fruit; the supply was immense and estimated to be plenty to feed this great mass of people for quite some time. There were herds of horses, cows, sheep and other animals, and also birds of the air, which were currently filling the skies with song. Here was further evidence of God's love; He had left supplies to provide mankind until man was once more able to provide for himself.

With the strange mist clearing away, Pastor heard joyful shouts coming from the south and turned to see the soldiers from three armies walking together. From the northwest perimeter came even more soldiers, as the battle dead rose up restored to life with no memory of the pain they'd experienced. "No weapons and they all have that childlike look of innocence to them with wide eyes of bewilderment," Pastor said to Chaplain Knight.

Seeing his flock restored, Pastor ran over to meet them and share in this powerful unheard of moment of restoration. Between his flock, OAP soldiers walked along arm-in-arm to show the others that the war was truly over.

"Pastor, you remember Scott Radley, a close friend of my brother," Ed said.

"Sure, hello, Scott," Pastor said.

"Well, Pastor Woodway, this here is Sergeant Tse Tung Lo, Corporal Chin Le and Captain Chou Lin, they used to attend an underground church in Beijing." After hugging each man in a brotherly embrace, Pastor noticed the troubled expression on Larry O' Brian's face. "What's wrong?"

"Oh nothing really, Pastor. It's…Well, I feel like I've walked into a Star Wars movie or Lord of the Rings, where the special effects people have gone crazy."

"This is a new day for a new world, Larry," Pastor said with a smile.

Joey came running up and asked, "Where did all those riders go?" Joey felt arms around him and turned to find his wife snuggled up against him and his kids wrapped around his knees.

"Probably still riding, until the earth is all reclaimed and man is set free from Satan's yoke." Pastor stopped and looked Point Man over, "Lawrence, you've lost over 100 pounds. And your tattoos, they're all gone too."

"Lawrence?" Ed asked. "This big lug's name is Lawrence?"

"All right, knock it off you clowns. Lawrence Joseph Coon is the name." He spoke to Pastor, "Weight's gone and all my ink work gone too…I feel like the guy I was before Somalia." Lawrence pulled his T-shirt up to expose a naked chest, which got everyone laughing.

"Pastor, look!" Ed shouted and pointed to a large group of people who appeared suddenly in the midst of everyone. Hundreds, then thousands and then tens of thousands of white robed individuals suddenly appeared, to stand amongst a stunned and silent crowd of thousands. Within moments, at least a million people were standing together across the post's parade grounds and main post area.

From off to the side, a young boy charged forward when he recognized one of the men and jumped in to his waiting arms to yell, "Dad!" All at once, others began to recognize their loved ones among those wearing the bright white robes of the Heavenly Host.

"Father!" A startled young woman shouted and ran forward.

"Mom!" A teenage boy yelled and ran into loving arms.

"Jerry, is that really you?" A dumbfound wife asked.

"Oh, darling I've missed you so." A wife said to her soldier, killed in Afghanistan.

Families rushed forward to embrace lost relatives and friends, creating a massive reunion in the streets of Fort Greeley and surrounding countryside. Ed even heard several of his former enemy shouting out as their lost family members appeared before them. With tears of joy flowing freely, Ed wrapped his arms around Kira and hugged her tightly against his chest.

It wasn't long before crowds burst out to where people stood on the very ground the fighting had occurred only so recently. Then from the crowd, Ed heard his name called out and looked up to see Scott standing with Becky Sawyer on his shoulders, as they moved through the crowd. With Kira in tow, Ed cut through the celebrating masses until he spotted Kathy Sawyer hurling herself into the arms of a tall man wearing one of those illuminating white robes. With only the man's height and black hair to identify him, that and Kathy's arms wrapped around his shoulders, Ed nearly dragged his wife behind him, while he gently but enthusiastically tried to force his way through the next thirty feet or so.

Finally reaching the couple, Ed asked in a whisper of a voice, "Brad?" Ed was feeling a lot of hesitation mixed in with a good measure of anticipation. It was only through the grace of God that he and so many others like him could control the amount of emotion surging through them.

With his wife hanging on, the man turned around and smiled, "Welcome home, littler brother."

"How…Oh, I know its God, but how…" Ed didn't know how to phrase his question, one a lot of people had this day.

"I know what you want to know, Ed, and how limited I am in what I can tell you all. But I can say that I am here and only here for a brief moment of time, for I and these others must return from whence we came.

"I believe God allowed us to be here to show further proof of His promises to His people." Brad then looked to his daughter, "We are not angels, honey, for those big fellows look quite a bit different than we do and they carry upon themselves some different hefty duties. Hard to explain…But it was us who were chosen to make this ride with them and our Lord, and I can't even try to explain how that felt."

Brad touched the shoulder of his wife and pulled her close, "No, in a moment, maybe a day, I do not know. Only the Lord knows when we will return to our reward. But, we will be waiting for you to join us."

Kathy Sawyer wrapped her arms around her husband, grateful to a loving God for this chance, even a brief one and having the knowledge and faith in what her husband said to be the truth. This lovely earth was still not the beautiful Heaven that awaited each and every one of them. They would all remember how the Lord had split the mighty sun in two to form a golden highway bridge to the earth and send His Host to combat the true enemy.

"Can you tell us about heaven, Brad?" Scott asked.

I could, but you might want to hear it from that young lady standing over there, the one looking at you," Brad replied.

Scott looked over to where Brad was pointing and spotted her. His mouth dropped open when he saw her standing there in her white robe, this beautiful Afro-American princess from his past and he ran to her with open arms.

"Well, that will keep him busy for a while," Brad said with a big grin.

"So okay, big brother…what's Heaven like?"

"Now that, little brother may take some time…."

As the people all over the earth rejoiced, overhead in the heavens millions of angelic voices praised the Lamb of God and sang, "Hallelujah! For our Lord God reigns forever more!"

Yes, I am coming soon." Revelations 22:20 NIV

THE END

Thank you for reading A Coming Storm.
If you enjoyed this book, please consider posting a review.

ABOUT THE AUTHOR

William Casselman was raised in Southern California and he enlisted in the U.S. Air Force in 1971 to become a Law Enforcement Specialist/Military Working Dog Handler. He served the next 10 years in the military and met his lovely wife, Mona Sue, at Eielson AFB, Alaska.

A Vietnam veteran, he left the service to become a police officer in Dillingham, Alaska and spent the next twenty years in Alaskan police work. From patrolman to investigator, he has worked with four police departments and became Public Safety Director for the City of Whittier during the tragic Exxon Oil Spill of Prince William Sound in 1989.

William, a 32-year Christian, retired as Senior Investigator for the State of Alaska gaming program. With 35 years in Alaska, 6 children and 13 grandchildren, William and Mona Sue now live in rural Alaska.

Other Titles from
ALASKA DREAMS PUBLISHING

Ghost Cave Mountain
Inside the Circle
The Silver Horn of Robin Hood
Alaskan Troll Eggs
Through My Eyes
The Professional Ghost Investigator
The Adventures of Jason and Bo

To be notified of the upcoming release of the Sequel & the Prequel to A Coming Storm, please visit the ADP website and sign up for our mailing list at:

www.alaskadp.com

www.ingramcontent.com/pod-product-compliance
Lightning Source LLC
Chambersburg PA
CBHW051929020726
47501CB00001B/46